D0015916

LADY JOKER

LADY JOKER

VOLUME ONE

KAORU TAKAMURA

TRANSLATED FROM THE JAPANESE BY
MARIE IIDA AND ALLISON MARKIN POWELL

SOHO
CRIME

First English translation published in 2021 by
Soho Press, Inc.
227 W 17th Street
New York, NY 10011

Library of Congress Cataloging-in-Publication Data

Names: Takamura, Kaoru, author.
Powell, Allison Markin, translator. | Iida, Marie, translator.
Title: Lady Joker / Kaoru Takamura ; translated from the Japanese by
Marie Iida and Allison Markin Powell. Other titles: Redi joka. English
Description: New York : Soho Crime, 2021.
Identifiers: LCCN 2020032998

ISBN 978-1-61695-701-8
eISBN 978-1-61695-702-5

Classification: LCC PL862.A42295 R4313 2021 | DDC 895.63/5—dc23
LC record available at https://lccn.loc.gov/2020032998

Interior design by Janine Agro, Soho Press, Inc.

Printed in the United States of America

10 9 8 7 6 5 4 3 2 1

LADY JOKER

岡村清二　**Seiji Okamura**
Former employee of Hinode Beer

物井清三　**Seizo Monoi**
Pharmacy owner; Seiji Okamura's younger brother

半田修平　**Shuhei Handa**
*Police Sergeant working in Criminal Investigation,
Violent Crime Unit at Shinagawa and later
Kamata Police Department; Monoi's friend and
fellow horseracing fan*

高克己　**Katsumi Koh**
*Credit union employee; Monoi's friend and fellow
horseracing fan*

布川淳一　**Jun'ichi Nunokawa**
*Truck driver; Monoi's friend and fellow
horseracing fan*

松戸陽吉　**Yokichi Matsudo**
*AKA Yo-chan; lathe operator; Monoi's friend and
fellow horseracing fan*

レディ　**Lady**
Jun'ichi Nunokawa's daughter

城山恭介　**Kyosuke Shiroyama**
President and CEO of Hinode Beer

倉田誠吾　**Seigo Kurata**
*General Manager of Beer Division and Vice
President of Hinode Beer*

久保晴久 Haruhisa Kubo

Metro desk reporter for Toho News, Tokyo bureau,
in charge of Tokyo Metropolitan Police Department
(MPD)'s First Investigation Division

根来史彰 Fumiaki Negoro

Metro desk reserve chief at large for Toho News, Tokyo bureau

菅野哲夫 Tetsuo Sugano

Metro desk chief for Toho News, Tokyo bureau,
in charge of MPD

神埼秀嗣 Hidetsugu Kanzaki

Head of MPD's First Investigation Division

平瀬悟 Satoru Hirase

MPD, First Investigation Division. First Special
Investigation Team, Second Unit. Assistant Police Inspector.

合田雄一郎 Yuichiro Goda

MPD, First Investigation Division. Third Violent Crime
Investigation Team, Seventh Unit. Later joins Criminal
Investigation Division, Violent Crime Unit at Omori
Police Department. Assistant Police Inspector.

安西憲明 Noriaki Anzai

Omori Police Department, Criminal Investigation
Division, White Collar Crime Unit.
Assistant Police Inspector.

加納祐介 Yusuke Kano

Public prosecutor in the special investigative department
of Tokyo District Public Prosecutor's Office;
Yuichiro Goda's former brother-in-law

MEETING MINUTES (ADDENDUM)

- Regarding the item of this past June 10th, in which an employee from general affairs, who opened and read a letter addressed to our company at the Kanagawa factory determined that the letter, being incomprehensible in its argument and unclear in its purpose, contains baseless accounts that affect the honor of our company, and as such at the meeting of the board of directors it was considered how said letter should be handled, and a conclusion was reached that it required no special response.
- Regarding the "Communist Party member" referenced in the letter, Director of General Affairs Kuwata reported that, after consulting with the Shinagawa Police Department as a precautionary measure, he received a response that no such individual had been found.
- Kuwata will approve the disposal of the letter.

August 1, 1947

Recorded in meeting room of Shinagawa temporary office, Tokyo main office

(Recorded by Hamada)

Hinode Beer Company, Kanagawa Factory,
To Whom It May Concern:

I, Seiji Okamura, am one of the forty employees who resigned from the Kanagawa factory of Hinode at the end of this past February. Today, as I am currently confined to my sickbed and can hardly sit up or stand, and with ever so many things on my mind, I have decided to write this letter.

First, what must be made clear is the true intention and the trajectory of how a person who has already left the company has come to address you in this manner.

Recently, I heard from a certain individual to the effect that the Kanagawa branch of the Hinode labor union encouraged my resignation on the grounds of my medical ailment and need for rest only as a pretense when in fact they had been instructed to do so by the police. The branch was apparently advised that, "Since on last December 15th Okamura was seen with a former colleague somewhere in the Shiba district of Tokyo, such a subversive element should be made to resign quickly." The person who conveyed this information to me was a man who was hospitalized in the surgical ward for appendicitis, a self-proclaimed Communist Party member by the name of Eiji Kono, but I do not know whether this is true or not.

Seeing that I am indeed ill at the present moment, I realize that even if such an event did not take place, the day of my resignation would have come sooner or later. Thus, whereas the "issue of last December 15th" can no longer have any effect whatsoever on my life, on the other hand when I think about the identity of my aforementioned "former colleague," I am overcome with deep confusion and trepidation. My "former colleague," that is to say Katsuichi Noguchi, himself resigned from the Kanagawa factory in 1942, but in the case of Noguchi, I know that his resignation took place with an unspeakable amount of disappointment and indignation, and that various circumstances transpired before and after.

The reason I string together such abstract words is that, although

I do not claim to wholly understand what is in Noguchi's heart, today it occurred to me that in certain ways he and I share a great deal in common. First, we are both human beings; second, we are not political animals; and third, we are absolutely destitute. I write this because it is my earnest wish to tell you. It is not because Noguchi told me to do so. I write simply so that this poor soul, who still cannot fathom why he was born into this world, may end his life in peace in the coming days.

Here, I will briefly describe where a person such as I was born, how I was raised, and how I find myself where I am. Memories of my home have recently been welling up inside me as if to stir my entire being, but in contrast to my feelings, the lackluster words that surface make me sound rather detached. Perhaps my sense of reason bottles them up to keep me from losing my mind.

I was born in 1915 in the village of Herai in Aomori prefecture. My family home was in the Tamodai district of that same village. In addition to working as tenant farmers on about an acre of land, my family kept a broodmare offered on loan by the landowner. Since it was difficult to feed a family of eight by these means alone, my parents also assisted charcoal burners, though they were not part of the district's Kita-Kawame union of charcoal burners. The reason for this was that in my family there was no money to purchase lumber for burning coal nor the luxury to hire men to help with logging.

As is well known, the Tohoku region suffers from poor harvests once every three years or so, but the years 1931, 1934, and 1935 were especially hard hit with severe, continuous famine. Out of the four children in my family my elder brother did not attend school and, being the second eldest son, before I reached school age I was adopted by the family who operated Okamura Merchants Wholesale Seafood in Hachinohe, while my younger sister, at fourteen and not even halfway through her studies at Kawadai Secondary School, was employed at the Fuji Spinning Mill in Kawasaki. And my younger brother, who had a minor disability in his left eye, became an apprentice at the Kanemoto Foundry in Hachinohe when he was twelve.

The truth was, since my birth family never owned any paddy fields in the first place, I doubt our situation would have been very different whether there was a famine or not.

Furthermore, my older brother was drafted in 1937. He was assigned to the 108th Division and was killed in the Shanxi province of China in May of 1939. When his draft papers had arrived, my birth family was impoverished because of the stillbirth of a colt for the second year in a row, but I heard that before leaving for war, my brother asked them not to part with the mare until his return. I can only narrate these things through hearsay, of course, since by that time I belonged to a different family.

Although I have always been scrawny in stature and was never a very active child, in the Okamura family I was cherished as their heir. However, life does not work out so easily. After the sudden passing of my adoptive mother, Ikuko Okamura, in 1929, my adoptive father, Yaichiro, remarried and immediately had a son, and there was no longer a place for me. Nevertheless, thanks to this turn of events I was given permission to focus on my education, which I liked very much. After graduating from Hachinohe Middle School and Daini High School, I enrolled in the department of science at Tohoku Imperial University, and during the time I was living in Sendai, the destitution of my birth home was already a distant memory.

As I write this, I realize it may seem as if my life to this point had been rather blessed, but in two ways, this was not the case. First, my body always remembered poverty—the life of a prosperous merchant family never sunk in physically. Second, no matter whether I was in the village of Herai or the town of Hachinohe, to my eyes it all appeared as a frigid scene where the cold wind from the Pacific blew ceaselessly. When I returned to Hachinohe in 1942 after being called to war, activity was bustling all around. The people going to work on the construction of the Takadate airfield marched in line like ants along the bridge over Mabechi River, while on the embankment the factories of Nitto Chemical and Nihon Mineral belched out black smoke day and night, and the sounds of hammering echoed from the dockyards of Samé harbor and the Minato River as ships were hastily built. But neither this Hachinohe nor the briny, idyllic version from the past belonged to me in the first place. Memories of the village may have been stripped away from me once before, but now it is nothing but the gut-wrenching smells and sounds of my family home that return to me. Even just now, as I write this, the smell of the mare's ass has risen in my throat. It is the smell of dung and urine mixed into straw on the earthen floor.

I should add that where I come from, humans and horses slept under the same roof. There were no tatami mats—we usually spread straw or woven mats over the dirt floor. A home like this was called a rag house.

By the way, Herai is a village where countless streams ebb and flow, originating in the mountains of Towada and carving the shape of the river, so it is not as if there are no paddy fields there. The gently sloping mountain terrain where the outline of Mount Hakkoda is visible on clear days is rich with green pastures, and since the late nineteenth century, the vast meadows of an army horse ranch have stretched over the entire forest region of Okuromori. It seems that even my birth family, in my grandfather's time, managed to put up several horses that were procured for the military in the auction held in Gonohe. Not only was the area known as a breeding ground for horses but there was a union of dairy farmers as well and, if my memory serves me right, in the late 1920s the union operated its own milk processing plant. Moreover, as the foremost producer of charcoal in all of Aomori prefecture, there was a designated cargo platform at Hon-Hachinohe Station, and beside it stood a continuous line of charcoal storage facilities. Even now, sometimes in my dreams I hear the sound of freight cars transporting sacks of charcoal, and it awakens me with a chill.

I am sensitive to sounds and smells. My doctor says I am suffering a nervous breakdown, but how can I ever escape from the sounds and smells of my birthplace? When I inhale, the various odors sequestered in that dirt floor cling to the hairs in my nostrils the way the cold wind from the Pacific coils around the gritty straw mats, and when I hold my breath, they seep in through every pore of my body. Every smell whirls inside my body—each of them whistling, cracking, and roaring—before settling into my empty stomach and finally growing quiet.

I've spent a thousand nights like that, the hail or sleet just outside the wooden walls battered by the wind, humans and horses alike listening with shallow breath, father and mother weaving the charcoal sacks in silence, children pretending to be soldiers on the paths between rice paddies where day after day the raw grassy smell of the rice that failed to ripen was stifling, the aging mare's head bent low in a corner of the earthen-floored room, grandfather and grandmother bowing their sooty faces as they stared at the glowing embers tapering off in the hearth. This is the life of horses and cattle with no notion of the future.

I am simply trying to accurately describe the sounds and smells that make my body tremble, but no matter how many times I repeat these words, I am always defeated in the face of that futile and unchanging past. I battle with absolute silence and barren time, as immovable as the mountains to the south.

Let us jump to the present. The main point of this letter is that my "former colleague" Katsuichi Noguchi and I are both human beings. How Noguchi and I are alike does not need to be demonstrated here, but given the fact that both of us were employees of Hinode, perhaps first it would be best to write about what the Kanagawa factory meant to me. Doing so will naturally relate how the "issue of last December 15th" fits into this story.

These days I suppose I am, from head to toe, what people call a 'laborer.' Although I will be the first to admit this, all my life I have been ignorant of worldly affairs, narrow-minded, and dedicated exclusively to my studies and research. During the war I was called an anti-patriot who lacked loyalty and devotion to the country, and when I was conscripted they told me, "Second-class soldiers should act as bullet shields." Like many of my countrymen in the South Seas I tasted unimaginable trials and tribulations, and even though I managed to survive and return to my country, I was not all that interested in the establishment of basic civil liberties within a democracy. When suffering great need in my daily life, I was the type to think, Oh, as long as I can earn enough to eat, everything will be fine.

It was for this reason that I only looked on from the sidelines at the various labor disputes that have occurred since last year, and even during the past general strike of February 1st, I ultimately failed to take my place as one of the six million laborers in the country. What I want to emphasize here first is that I was an ordinary citizen with no political beliefs or societal opinions whatsoever, and because of this, perhaps I was only ignorant of the state of oppression that I should have been fighting against while all along I could have been carrying water for the reactionaries. However, the remorse of anyone who falls into this latter group is irrelevant to someone like Katsuichi Noguchi.

Of course, I know very well that unlike other companies, Hinode Beer has generally valued its employees since even before the war, and that not only the laboratory but also the manufacturing floor and employee cafeteria have always had a bright and liberated atmosphere. When my former professor Kenjiro Yonezawa at Tohoku Imperial University referred me to job opportunities at the navy fuel plant, the board of health at the home ministry, the army medical academy, Nippon Chisso nitrogen fertilizer company, Godo Spirits, and Hinode Beer, among others, the reason why I decided on Hinode without much hesitation is because I had a good first impression of the personnel department at the main office as well as the manufacturing department, I found the equipment in the fermentation laboratory impressive, and with flexible work hours, I thought it was a suitable place to spend my entire career. Of course, when I joined the company in 1937, beer brewing had already been designated as one of the country's most valued industries, so I had some awareness of the responsibility that I would be taking on.

I hardly need to explain that during the five years from the time I joined the company to when I was drafted and went off to the front, all industries in Japan were forced to carry on and work especially hard in the wartime effort. At the brewery, production hit its peak about two years after I joined the company, and then we shifted to cutting back production as per regulation. Yet even as the number of employees dwindled due to compulsory recruitment and conscription, the fact that, in addition to maintaining the working order on the home front, the company upheld its standard of producing the most delicious beer possible, was a source of great happiness to those of us who remained. Since raw materials were controlled, in reality we could not hope to produce the quality we wanted, but every time I saw people enjoying rationed Hinode beer in beer halls and restaurants around town, I felt glad that I had decided to work for Hinode Beer. Hinode was the kind of company that inspired employees to feel this way.

I went to the front in 1942 so I have no knowledge of further hardships in Japan after that. I did not know that the Hinode trademark disappeared from our products once they became controlled goods, or about the air raid at the Kanagawa factory. Perhaps I was among the lucky ones, in that while stationed on an island in the South Seas, from time to time I was able to distract myself with daydreams of the boiling iron pot or the fermented beer storage tank at the Kanagawa factory, hoping only to return home even a day sooner.

When I was discharged at Yokohama port in November of 1945, I could hardly believe my own eyes at the sight of the burnt-out city. The first thing I did was head straight for the factory. The fact was I had no other place to go, being a bachelor with no relatives in the Kantō region. I cannot aptly describe how I felt as the familiar factory upon the hilltop of Hodogaya came into view. I don't know if in that moment my body finally accepted that the last three years at the front had been hell or if my mind could hardly keep up with the sensation of being alive, but more than relief, I think what I felt was a type of despondency, as if my body were breaking into pieces and I was on the verge of collapsing.

Reading this, no doubt you would feel compelled to point out that

I had only been an employee of Hinode for a mere five years, but it is no wonder that a young man returning from that war felt as though Hinode were his only refuge in this country. A family or hometown might provide that kind of sanctuary, but an adopted son like me had nothing. No, I can declare that—not only for myself but for every employee who left Hinode to go to war—our former factory was our only refuge in those days. That is the nature of a company. It would have been the same for Katsuichi Noguchi had he not quit working there. That would have been true even as a former employee who had only been at the factory for two years.

Looking up at the hilltop of Hodogaya, I had tears in my eyes. As I got closer, I saw that the factory I had imagined remained standing was, in fact, not; the roof of the main building had burned and fallen down, most of the facilities had been destroyed, the warehouse and the laboratory building had been reduced to a mountain of rubble, there was no trace of the employee apartments at all, and only part of the cafeteria had been spared. Nevertheless, instead of despairing I could not help but put my hands together in a show of gratitude toward the factory. Please know that this is how happy I was. A notebook had been placed on a desk at the entrance of what remained of the cafeteria, along with a sign instructing demobilized soldiers to write down the date, their name, and contact information, and to wait for word. There were about a hundred names listed already, and among them I found a few colleagues I knew. I believe there was also information about temporary allowances for demobilized soldiers, distribution of socks, cotton cloth, light bulbs, and such for employees, free medical treatment and welfare counseling, and missing persons notices. In that moment, standing before that desk, I know I could not have been the only one whose legs trembled with the realization that I had been welcomed back by my family, and that I had finally returned home.

For a while after that, a third of the factory site was transformed into farmland, and employees whose houses had burned down lived in barracks that they had built there. Even under such circumstances, the company swiftly announced plans to rebuild the factory and, while nothing was yet in production, they distributed a base salary despite repeated delays, so one hardly needs to make comparisons with other companies to say that the employees of Hinode were unmistakably blessed. Of course, considering the absurd inflation of recent years I would be lying if I said I never wondered how one could live on a mere two or three hundred yen, but if I take a moment to calmly consider how the beer industry was also responsible for the livelihood of distributors and general retail shops all over the country, I know I am being ungrateful for this extravagance.

In order to respond to the company's endeavors, the employees spared no efforts themselves. Hoping to resume operations as soon as possible, the maintenance engineers conducted emergency repairs on broken equipment while the sales staff visited distributors every day, and I did my small part by borrowing some preserved yeast from the Sendai factory and working to cultivate it. Looking back, I think it was an extraordinary feat how we managed to restore part of the production line at the temporary factory as early as the spring of 1946. Doesn't the fact that, even though it was only a year ago, I cannot remember the details of what I ate, wore, or thought about during those entire six months of rebuilding suggest that I worked so hard as if I had been bewitched? Naturally, had I not labored so hard, there would have been nothing to fill this gaping emptiness that I appeared to suffer from and, seized by a sense of lethargy and helplessness that made even walking appear tiresome, I would have probably gone insane or died.

As fate would have it, soon after the resumption of production in May, all four factories of Kanagawa, Kyoto, Sendai, and Okayama joined together to form the Hinode Labor Union. The inaugural gathering of labor and management, with even the executives from company headquarters in attendance along with the managers of each factory, took place in a conciliatory mood from start to finish. Seen from the perspective of employees of other companies who could only declare a strike as a societal weapon of laborers against managers who executed one-sided layoffs—and though employee cutbacks at places like Japanese National Railways were excessive—one could argue that the brewery business, long considered an industry for national policy used to collect liquor taxes and operating more or less as an oligopoly or monopoly, had little to worry about. But I am not interested in having such a debate here.

When it comes down to it, the question is: Even though unions were formed in other companies within the same industry at around the same time, why did none of them, Hinode included, incite an actual conflict until that fateful day of February 1st? As far as I can tell, it wasn't so much that there was no need for conflict but that those unions were organized as a token effort by the company itself, in order to present the appearance of democratic management style as instructed by the Supreme Commander of the Allied Powers at General Headquarters. And as for the employees, the mentality of "No Hinode, No Employees" had been fully ingrained into them as well. Perhaps this deserves to be called a new type of industrial patriotic association.

Now, we are getting a little closer to the heart of the matter. While casting a sidelong glance at the deluge of labor disputes arising in the streets, the Kanawaga factory had been bustling with activity since the partial resumption of operations last spring. However, it only appeared this way to those working at the site, myself included. In reality, as long as beer remained under the Price Control Ordinance and with no prospect of a quick recovery of a demand in sales, even a child could figure out the quantity we could actually produce. Looking at the numbers for output that were released every month, it was clear that there would soon be a surplus of equipment and manpower. However, at the same time, all of us working on site had thought that everything would be fine as long as we could make it through the low-demand season of October through March of the following year, and we had heard that last September this sentiment had been echoed by the company and the union. However, as you very well know, once November arrived, the provisional solicitation for voluntary resignation began suddenly. It is laughable that rather than a firing or restructuring they chose to call it a "Recommendation for Resignation."

There is no use debating whether the only two valid choices for the company were either to allow excess labor costs to bankrupt the company, leaving all 270 members of the Kanagawa factory out in the cold, or to use cutbacks to save the remaining employees. As an employee, I can only trust that, given current management, the company and the union came to an agreement after undergoing serious discussions. That is to say further, this has always been the tradition of Hinode, a company that has been in business for fifty years. At Hinode, a labor dispute is unthinkable.

Implementation of the "Recommendations for Resignation" was led by the union, and private interviews with each employee took place as needed. As is well-known, by the end of this past February, a total of forty members silently left the factory with money in hand, each of them citing a family issue, an illness, or a vague reason for not being able to stay. Some voiced anger or resentment but since there were rumors of a second and third round of cutbacks soon, I believe the majority of employees, if they were to meet a dead-end anyway, thought that it would be better to give up while conditions were still favorable. As for me, in addition to not having much strength after contracting malaria overseas, there was also the diagnosis of a nervous breakdown from my doctor, so I decided not to cause any nuisance. However, until this day I had no idea that while such reasonable discharges were taking place, there were a number of men who were released without receiving equal treatment, despite being Hinode employees.

According to the self-proclaimed Communist member I mentioned above, last October three employees at the Kyoto factory, in the face of Hinode's policy against labor unions, instigated a rally where they demanded participation with the unified dispute that was being led by the All Japan Congress of Industrial Unions, and called for the abolishment of the Price Control Ordinance on perishable food items. Citing a breach of their employee agreement, the company promptly fired the three men at the end of the year. I suspect the reason I do not remember hearing about any sort of dispute in Kyoto back then is because those three men's actions were either too subtle to be noticed or because they ended in failure. Nevertheless, why did such firings take place, why did none of the other employees know about it, and why didn't the labor union cause even a stir?

Whenever I reflect on this, I look at my hands and wonder anew what exactly the pride and solidarity of the Hinode employees had meant. "No Hinode, No Employees"—when it comes down to it, did that mentality mean that we must enjoy spinning around as cogs in the company wheel, ignore minor differences of opinion to dream of prosperity under the aegis of the company, and forget about our individual poverty? This must be so because, indisputably, each and every Japanese is as poor as ever. Considering this, I cannot help but remember that man—Katsuichi Noguchi.

If you'll allow me to explain a little, it is not as if Noguchi and I were very close while we worked at the factory. What I do remember is that Noguchi, on the day he started working as a mechanic in the Kanagawa factory's vehicle division in the spring of 1940, had a slightly mischievous sparkle in his eyes, as if he had a dagger concealed in his pocket. But when I remarked to an acquaintance in his division, "That's quite a guy there," he replied in a hushed voice, "Better watch what you say. You'll be accused of discrimination." Being born and raised in northeast Japan, this was the first time I had ever met someone from a buraku village, one of the segregated areas where members of feudal outcast communities still lived.

Since the garage of the vehicle division was located in the rear of the laboratory building where I worked, I saw Noguchi quite often. Noguchi would always cook potatoes in the ashes of the incinerator that was in the back there, and when I told him it was dangerous because there were chemicals mixed in, he just laughed softly and said, "It'll disinfect my stomach and do me some good." He wouldn't listen to anything I said—he was quite stubborn and hard to deal with—but he was a kind man.

Although Noguchi did not talk much about himself, I heard from other people that he was born on the outskirts of Saitama prefecture and he was the only one in his village to graduate from secondary school. He then moved to Tokyo where, while working as an apprentice at an ironworks in the Arakawa district, he met the former factory manager Yukio Sasahara, who asked him if he would join Hinode. But I also heard that behind this arrangement was Hinode's plan to acquire a site for construction of their new factory near the village where Noguchi was born, and his employment was a ploy to smooth over their relationship with local tenant farmers who would soon lose their farmland. Hinode had also promised that once the factory was completed on the new site they would hire a few men from the same village, and Noguchi and three other men were sent off to each Hinode factory in advance of this negotiation.

Incidentally, I know that the plan to purchase said site was postponed around 1941, but according to the same self-proclaimed Communist member I mentioned, Hinode withdrew the plan altogether in 1943, and have now already decided on the purchase of a different parcel of land. Moreover, the three men who started working at the company in 1940 with Noguchi were the same three men who were fired from the Kyoto factory for instigating a conflict.

Then, in the spring of 1942, the former factory manager Sasahara suddenly left the factory for personal reasons, but in the afternoon of the day his departure was announced, the usually reticent Noguchi had a word or two to say about it. "My employment has become a problem for the company," he implied. Five days later, he wandered into my laboratory building and told me that he had submitted a letter of resignation because he was returning home, and that he had already sent his belongings by train. His expression was as obstinate as ever, but just when I thought I saw a hint of torment in his eyes, he said, "What I wouldn't give for a glass of Hinode beer. Who knows when I'll have a chance to drink it again," and laughed softly again.

I took him to the factory, poured some from the storage tank and gave it to him. He drank it down happily and thanked me, and then he left. It was quite a few days later that I learned that he had received his draft papers the day before.

Why did Noguchi submit his resignation before going off to war? I'm sure there are circumstances that I don't know about, but I can only imagine Noguchi had reached the decision for his own reasons and after much agonizing, and that despite everything, his strong attachment to Hinode made him crave one last glass of Hinode beer. For the briefest of moments, Noguchi—like me and many others—had dreamt of prosperity in a company called Hinode. Ah, the taste of Hinode beer that we were treated to at our farewell party is coming back to me now.

Now, let me address the issue of "last December 15th." That day, I was visiting a hospital in Tokyo. When I got off the train at Hamamatsucho Station, I had just thought to myself, I've seen that man's face somewhere before, and the man called out my name. It was Katsuichi Noguchi. I asked him what he was doing here, and he responded that he had hurried to Tokyo because there were important meetings taking place in the city, starting that day.

It had been four and a half years since I had last seen Noguchi, and though he was in perfectly good health, he looked quite pale. When the times change as drastically as they have, even the demeanor and expression of the people also change, and it seems as if our voice as the Japanese people has grown louder, but Noguchi was much the same as before. He sat on the bench, quiet and still like a rock. No, perhaps it would be more accurate to say that he appeared a little lost or behind the times—like a soldier who had just returned from war—with his cheeks faintly flushed, he was half excited and half stunned.

He told me he had indeed returned to Japan in February and was now working in the mining industry in Hokkaido for Mitsubishi Bibai after answering a call for workers in his prefecture.

"Tokyo's pretty cold too, isn't it? These days in the coal mines they give you plenty to eat, if nothing else, so I ought to have energy, but

I'm afraid my mind's not all there. There is a national convention so my friends put up the money and took care of the travel expenses and whatnot so I was able to make it here as a branch representative."

He laughed a little. It goes without saying that the national convention he spoke of was the second convention of the National Committee for Buraku Liberation, but what I wish to tell you here is not the story of the convention but that of Noguchi. It is not about basic human rights or democracy or anything like that—this is the story of what it means to be alive.

On that bench on the platform, with the collar of his overcoat turned up and his shoulders hunched up like a child, Noguchi began to speak slowly in a soft voice, a faint smile on his lips.

"I live in a vile time in history. I was struck by this thought when I received my draft papers and I realized I would rather run away. My parents and siblings, they said if I didn't go to war like everyone else, they would lose face in the village. But when I told them I couldn't do it, that I would do anything else for them but I could never become a soldier of the Imperial Army, in the end my mother said she would call the military police, my father said he would sacrifice his own life to beg forgiveness from the people of his village, and my extended family had the audacity to show up at our house yelling and threatening me with bamboo spears. When I saw all that, I asked myself how much more vile we could possibly be. The only reason people say you are less than human for not being willing to shoulder a gun for the emperor is because they are scared of being ostracized by the entire village, of being treated even more horribly than before. So everyone's howling like scared dogs and preying on one another. It's vile that the memory of starvation is so ingrained into our daily lives, which consist only of working, eating, and sleeping. It's vile that we can't be rational. In that sense I think the entire country of Japan is vile. Having said that, if I had run away my parents and siblings would have been the ones to be ostracized and left to starve to death, so I eventually went to war, but there's nothing more pathetic than the poor going off to invade a poorer country. I should have known this better than anyone else, but they told me I'd be killed if I didn't kill first, so I became a killing machine—I can hardly stand being human any more. You might object to me saying this, Okamura, but I think those of us who survived to see the end of the war have been chosen by heaven to live on carrying the burden of these vile sins.

Although I live in a vile time in history, I also feel as if I am seeing the faint light of the dawn of a new generation. To tell you the truth, I cannot contain this hope welling up inside of me. It is a hazy glow, but I've never felt like this before. If you believe that a new era is something you create yourself rather than something you wait for, then we can make short work of that damn prime minister of ours, Shigeru Yoshida. The top officials of the liberation committee talk about all kinds of things, but more than a democratic revolution or anything like that, just being alive here and now makes me itch with happiness . . . or is it fear? I am happy that I can talk like this with you, Okamura. Even if it is only my imagination, I feel so refreshed—as if the dirt that is embedded in my body will be washed away. The way I see it, if a rice plant that has been curled and twisted by the cold for hundreds of years can start growing again, then I think that time is now. Personally, I would rather be a stalk of wheat that stands upright when it ripens rather than rice that bows its head."

Noguchi had faltered now and then as he spoke. Having finished, he eventually joined an acquaintance he had been waiting for and left. But he left me with these parting words: "Oh, speaking of which, that Hinode beer sure was delicious. That amber color itself is enchanting, and that popping sound of the carbonation is like music. I believe that beautiful, delicious, and pleasing things save us from vileness. That's what I learned from the beer. Too bad I didn't learn it from the company, Hinode."

Whatever Noguchi said, I don't doubt he was one of the employees who shared that brief dream at Hinode.

So, has the "the faint light of the dawn of a new generation" of which Noguchi spoke really arrived? Is it that I am blind to it, or have I alone been left behind, standing still? Noguchi spoke of a new generation—his cheeks red, his body aquiver—but how on earth had he attained such vitality? While I remain stunned with this vague emptiness within me, where had he gained the strength to shoulder this vile history and to set out on his own, brimming with such joy for life?

Or, perhaps the "the faint light of the dawn of a new generation" is nothing but a momentary delusion of his, and he has already awoken from it by now. Or did he simply speak of his hope for his own sake? I do not know which is the case.

But I do know that Katsuichi Noguchi is Japanese, just like the middle-aged lady cleaning my hospital room right now, the children causing a racket out in the hallway, and the woman who looks like a hostess walking by below my window just now—and myself in this hospital. We are all Japanese just the same, ants silently carrying on our daily lives, our individual progress making up the vision of this country. In such a country there is a man who sees "a ray of light coming through," a man who is still complaining long after he has left his company, the ghost of a former politician of the Imperial Rule turned democrat, another democrat who touts revolution while busying himself with internal conflicts, and if you look down below there are black-marketeers and thieves possessed by demons; the sharp-eyed unemployed men and street urchins, strident laborers, entrepreneurs hoarding vast amounts of raw materials, or perhaps in the country there are farmers stockpiling rice and potatoes, land owners listening for the sound of their financial ruin approaching, and impoverished peasants who never had anything to lose—the disparate lives of all these ants came together to form this vision of Japan, a vision that is bustling on one hand and yet somehow despairing and more chaotic than before.

Not long from now, there will come a day when Japanese people will enjoy a glass of beer like before, but when that day comes where will I be and what will I see, what will have happened to those black and broken fingernails of Katsuichi Noguchi, what will the village of Herai look like? In my state, I am incapable of envisioning a single one of these things. When that time comes, what will I be thinking as I gaze at the logo of Hinode Lager Beer, and what would those forty former employees who left the company this past February think, and what would Katsuichi Noguchi and those three men from the buraku village fired from the Kyoto factory think? Only G-d knows.

June 1947
Seiji Okamura

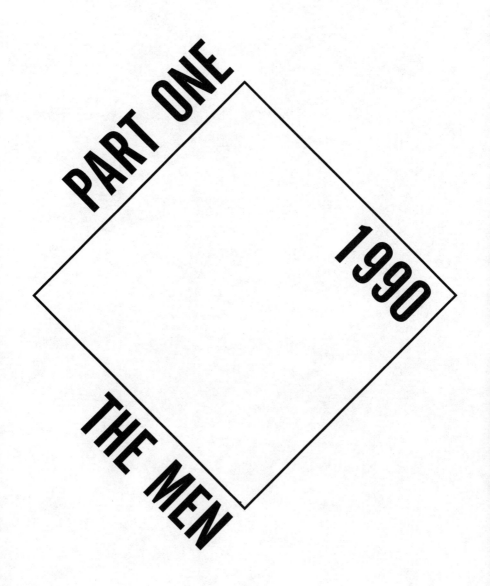

PART ONE

1990

THE MEN

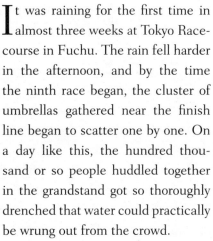

物井清三

SEIZO MONOI

1

It was raining for the first time in almost three weeks at Tokyo Racecourse in Fuchu. The rain fell harder in the afternoon, and by the time the ninth race began, the cluster of umbrellas gathered near the finish line began to scatter one by one. On a day like this, the hundred thousand or so people huddled together in the grandstand got so thoroughly drenched that water could practically be wrung out from the crowd.

Rising above the low hum that filled the second level of the grandstands, a heavy groaning sounded from time to time, like air seeping out of a broken exhaust pipe. A girl sitting on a bench, contorting her upper body and twisting her neck about while shaking from side to side, was gasping out her breath, forming an indistinct word composed only of vowels: "Aaaa, ooo." It was the girl's way of saying "Start."

Sitting on the girl's right side, the man accompanying her looked up. He blinked his heavy eyelids and muttered, "Be quiet," but the girl, contorting her mouth and shaking her head up and down vigorously to express the joy of having had her feelings understood, let out a hoarse scream.

A single strand of rope was

wrapped around the girl's waist, and it was tied to the bench. The girl was well over twelve years old, but because her neck and upper body were unstable, she had to be tied to the bench to prevent her from falling over. That day the girl also gave off a sour smell of blood, and every time she moved the stench permeated the air around her. The man accompanying the girl sat next to her, seemingly unaware of this, as she continued to wobble her neck and groan, until he lowered his head to doze off again.

Say, where did I leave my umbrella? Seizo Monoi suddenly wondered and, taking his eyes off his newspaper, looked at his feet beneath the bench. Without adjusting his reading glasses, he scanned the blurry concrete floor before picking up his black umbrella, which was being trampled by the canvas shoes of the girl sitting next to him. A wet and withered piece of newspaper was stuck to the cloth of the umbrella. His eyes caught the words "Superior Quality, 100 Years in the Making. Hinode Lager" in an ad printed on the page before he shook it off.

Beside him, the girl had begun stamping her feet again and wringing from her throat her version of the word, "Start, start!" It was the beginning of the ninth race, a six-furlong race for three-year-old colts and fillies. As Monoi raised his head to witness the start of the race he had not bet on, he wondered if the smell of blood wafting from the girl was only in his imagination. He unconsciously turned his neck so that the right half of his face was positioned toward the racecourse. He had suffered an accident as a child that had cost him most of the vision in his left eye when he came of age and now, in his late sixties, that side had gone completely dark.

The overcast weather darkened the racecourse, and the horses that took off from across the infield looked as if they were swimming into a stormy sea with jockeys in tow. In November the turf track still bore shades of green, but perhaps from the color of the rain or the sky, the entire course was dulled to an inky darkness, and the dirt track to the inside of the one on which the horses now ran looked like a black sash, frothy with mud. A live feed of the ground's surface was displayed on the jumbotron located directly across from the grand-stand.

Monoi was looking at the dirt track because the next race—the tenth, and the one he planned to bet on—would be run on this course. As was always the case, imagining the weight of the horses' hooves, he was consumed by an inexplicable restlessness that made his insides leap. After all this time, the sight of the horses—kicking off dirt as their rumps were whipped and veins stood out on their throats—still filled Monoi with wonder. The horses, he thought to himself, couldn't contain the latent excitement that rose within them as they felt the menace and the relentlessness of the earth and the weight of every step of their four legs. They must have been born to feel this way—no animal on earth would run just for being struck by the crop.

The 1,400-meter race on the turf track went on while Monoi was pondering this, and just as the pacemaker and the stalker neared the finish line side by side like conjoined dumplings, the favorite, Inter Mirage, came storming from the rear, causing the crowd in the stands to roar for a moment. However, as the frontrunner shot to the finish line, the clamor dissipated into a sigh that was soon engulfed by the sound of the rain thundering down on the roof.

Monoi folded the newspaper with the tenth race's details in his lap and, looking up at the electronic scoreboard, which was visible from the second-floor seats, checked the ninth race's placings out of amusement. Ever Smile, a horse he had seen win in his debut on the 14th last month, had placed fourth today, two and a half lengths back. Thinking that was probably as good as he could do, Monoi murmured to himself that Ever Smile was still a three-year-old colt after all. The horse wasn't a particular favorite of his, but the day after the race last month was when his grandchild—his daughter's son, who was about to turn twenty-two—had been killed in an accident on the Shuto Expressway, so it surfaced in his mind briefly. That same moment, large drops of rain started to pelt down on the racecourse again, dis-tracting Monoi. An ever-widening pool of water had formed on the surface of the dirt track, visible beyond. The next race would be like running through a muddy rice paddy.

It would be impossible to decide on a horse for the tenth race without seeing the ones entered, up close in the paddock. The horses gathering now were used to a dirt track, but not a single one of them had a record of performing well in sloppy conditions like today. None of the horses had a marked difference in weight either. If it were to be a race among horses of similar standing and appearance, all the more reason why it would not do to pick one without seeing the nature of the horse just before the start. He reached this conclusion easily, but the truth of the matter was that he couldn't be sure. Only the horses knew the answer.

As soon as Monoi decided to head over to the paddock, however, the stats of the horses competing in the eleventh race flashed across the projection screen in front of the finish line. He had yet to decide if he would bet on the eleventh race, but just in case, he took a minute or so to jot down the weights of the horses in the margin of his newspaper. Then, as he swiveled to his right on the bench, the wobbling head of the girl he had forgotten about there for the moment suddenly swung around and leaned toward him. The girl, slightly squinting up at Monoi, grunted, "Eennhh, eennhh."

Perhaps the girl had said, "Wind." When Monoi turned back to the racecourse, the rain draping over the grass was blowing at a diagonal. It looked as if someone had pulled an ink-black curtain across the ground.

"Oh, you're right. The wind."

Monoi gave a half-hearted response to the girl's words and patted the small head he had grown accustomed to over the last six years. The smell of blood rose again. Monoi thought subconsciously, the scent of a mare's urine.

Propelled by a slight, rootless irritation, Monoi called over the girl's head to the man accompanying her. "Nunokawa-san. Are you going to bet next?"

The man he had called out to raised his head and turned his eyes

toward the newspaper he had hardly glanced at even though he had
been there since morning. He shook his head and responded, "Sixteen hundred in bad conditions? I don't need that."

"Inter Erimo will race. His first since he's been upped in class."

"Erimo's too stiff. You like him, don't you, Monoi? He's not for me
though."

Nunokawa gave Monoi his trademark faint smile and held firm.
He was a man who only bet on the main race and safely chose the first
or second favorite, so he never won big but never lost a lot of money
either. He demonstrated no partiality toward a particular horse, and
anyway, he barely even looked at the newspaper racing columns. He
came with his daughter to the same second-floor seats in front of
the finish line every Sunday not so much for his own enjoyment but
because his daughter liked horses. Once he had installed his charge
in her seat, he usually nodded off or stared blankly at nothing.

Nunokawa was still a young man. He could not have been much
past thirty, a fact that was obvious from the incomparable luster
of his skin. When Monoi first met him six years ago, the sight of
this tall figure—easily over six feet—slouching on the bench had
instantly reminded Monoi, despite his rather paltry knowledge of art,
of a Rodin sculpture. When Nunokawa told him he had served as a
member of the First Airborne Brigade of the Self-Defense Force stationed at Narashino, Monoi thought it was no wonder, with such an
impressive stature. Nunokawa had a melancholy look in his eyes, but
Monoi made the clichéd assumption that being the parent of a disabled child must be quite difficult at such a young age. Nevertheless,
Nunokawa's crude and awkward manner of speaking and the honesty
in his expression, which clouded over with frustration now and then,
made Monoi feel a sense of affinity with and fondness for him. As
far as affinity went, however, aside from the fact that Monoi himself had a disability in one eye and was also taciturn and awkward, they
had nothing specific in common. Because having a disabled daughter
required a good deal of money, for several years now Nunokawa had
worked as a truck driver for a large transportation company. He spent

six days a week going back and forth relentlessly between Tokyo and Kansai in a ten-ton truck.

"Erimo will run on the dirt track." Monoi said this almost to himself as he got up from the bench to walk to the paddock. Once he walked down the stairs and reached the lines in front of the pari-mutuel betting windows on the first floor, he realized that he had once again forgotten the umbrella he had just retrieved, but it wasn't enough to detain him. His forgetfulness progressed every day like a painless gum disease; until the day his teeth fell out, there was time enough to rot.

Just in front of the paddock, there was a man seated by a pillar in an alleyway where drifting trash had collected. The sight of him caused Monoi to pause in his tracks. The man, in his mid-twenties, sat cross-legged with his young body bent awkwardly forward, his face buried in the newspaper that he held open with both hands. Monoi always encountered him in this same exact spot, and every time the man was intently studying his newspaper in a similar posture.

"Yo-chan."

Monoi called to the young man, who acknowledged him by briefly raising his eyes from the newspaper before dropping his gaze again.

The man's name was Yokichi Matsudo, but everyone called him Yo-chan. He worked at the local factory in the neighborhood where Monoi lived. On the day of the funeral for Monoi's grandson—who knows how he'd heard about it—Yo-chan brought over a condolence offering of three thousand yen tucked into a business envelope. When it came to horseracing, he was a Sunday regular like Nunokawa, but Yo-chan always bought up three or four of the Saturday horseracing papers as well as the evening newspaper, and would spend the whole night grappling with the racing columns in his cramped apartment. Right up to the start of the races, he would still be staring intently at the newspaper, which he held ten centimeters before his face, trying to predict their outcomes, until he could no longer tell what was what and a blue vein stood out on his temple. It was always the same routine with Yo-chan.

Monoi spoke gingerly to the lowered head. "You betting next?"

"Only on the eleventh race today. Got no money."

"Which one?"

"Diana—maybe. I'm not sure." Yo-chan nervously folded his newspapers with his dirty black fingernails and, tucking a worn-down red pencil into the pages, said to himself, "It's gotta be Diana," and further mumbled, "Will three come first, or will it be four . . ."

Suddenly, a man who had been sitting shoulder to shoulder with Yo-chan got up and began to walk away. He was around thirty or so, with an unremarkable appearance from the neck up, but then Monoi couldn't help noticing the flashy vertical striped jacket he wore over a purple shirt, and his white loafers with the heels crushed down. Yo-chan's gaze was also drawn to the man and he responded, "An acquaintance."

"Who is he?" Monoi asked.

"A guy from the credit union who comes to the factory."

"Huh."

"He's a Zainichi Korean. Always pissed off on Sundays."

As Yo-chan said this he flashed his teeth a little, his shoulders shaking as he laughed without a sound.

In that moment Monoi failed to make out Yo-chan's spurt of words, but he assumed it was because of his bad hearing and didn't bother asking him to repeat what he had said. After all, Yo-chan was as young as Monoi's grandson, and everything about him—from his outlook on things to the way he used his chopsticks—only caused Monoi to feel ill at ease. It had been the same with his grandson who died on the 15th. In any case, the way Monoi saw it, the man walking away seemed to belong to that particular vein of shady underworld connections, though he had no clue as to why he had gotten such an impression.

"Diana might be a win," Monoi said, bringing the conversation back around.

"Middle odds at best. Not a dark horse," Yo-chan corrected him soberly, though his face was already buried again in his newspaper.

Monoi spoke to his profile. "Come by my house tomorrow. We'll go out for sushi." With that, he walked away.

Monoi had lingered long enough talking with Yo-chan that there was already a battery of umbrellas around the paddock. He stepped into the rain and peered at the paddock through a gap in the crowd, but after realizing that he couldn't see, he gave up and decided to watch the horses on the various monitors that were around the betting windows. In just a short time he was drenched, so he returned to the shelter of the building and stood beneath a monitor in the crowded passageway. The screen only showed one horse at a time; here was horse number four, a jockey astride him. He was a six-year-old stretch runner who had always run in the nine-million-yen class but, as if himself aware that he had been losing his edge lately in the homestretch, he walked with a heavy, drooping gait. Then came horse number five. He had a lucid expression, seeming fully matured at four years old, and he pulled against his reins and bared his teeth as if he wanted to say something. Next came horse number six.

The rain had not let up. One could practically make out every single raindrop that fell on the horses. Since their bodies were covered entirely by hair, getting wet meant their own body weight would be more of a burden. Infected by the languid mood of the horses, Monoi's focus started to drift away from the race.

I could use a pick-me-up, he thought to himself. At times like this, it was best to simply let go and sink five thousand yen or so in a single race on the horse he had initially chosen, and if he happened to win it would be all good. If not, all he could do was apply himself better in the next race. Monoi never had much attachment to the bets he made, and perhaps that was why both his interest and his money had lasted for more than thirty years. "Erimo is next," he said to himself, and though he had not intended to, he moved through the crowded passageway to see the horses warm up on the main track. A throng of men, unable to go out onto the field by the main track due to the rain, had already gathered by the exit from the grandstand, and Monoi could barely get a clear view by craning his neck. There, he waited for the horses moving in from the paddocks to line up, and from a distance he stared at the almost otherworldly movements of the horses' legs for more than ten minutes. He turned to the clock as he thought to himself that it all came down to potential.

Only fifteen minutes left until the start of the race. He had a few bets he had been tasked with by an acquaintance, so he hurried to the ticket windows. There was no sign of Yo-chan at the foot of the pillar where Monoi had seen him before—where had he gone off to? Gathered in front of the betting windows all he could see was a long line of heads jostling each other. As he stood there being pushed and shoving back over the course of ten minutes, habit induced his excitement and made him think, "Yes, Erimo it is." When he reached the window, he slammed down five thousand-yen bills and heard himself shout, "Number two to win!" He grabbed the ticket that appeared and quickly pushed forward three more thousand-yen bills and barked, "One-two. One-five. Two-five!" These were for his friend. As he came back out to the passageway with the tickets in hand, the bell signaling the two-minute cutoff before the start rang above his head, followed by the reverberating sound as the chain of ticket windows closed.

On his way to the second floor of the grandstand and with the fanfare as the horses entered the starting gate ringing in his ears, Monoi ran into Nunokawa, who was clutching his daughter under the arm with one hand while carrying a folding wheelchair in the other as he ran down the steps.

"She messed her pants," Nunokawa mumbled and gestured with his chin at the girl.

When Monoi's eyes fell upon the girl, he saw that a stain had spread over the crotch of her blue pants. Aha, he thought to himself, troubled by the sudden image of a mare's ass that came to mind again.

"First time?" he asked.

"I think so . . . No, I don't know."

"What is your wife doing today?"

"Shopping. I think she's probably home by now."

The two men awkwardly lowered their voices beside the girl, who groaned, "Ah, ah, ahh," as if to say something, throwing her arms and legs around, her neck wobbling. She was in a foul mood. Nunokawa looked down at her blankly as if his mind had gone off far away, then in the next moment, a blue vein at his temple quivered as his expression registered extreme irritation. However, each expression was gone almost as soon as it appeared.

"She's a lady now," he let out roughly.

If she had gotten her period, the girl had indeed become a lady, starting today. Thinking that was one way to look at it, Monoi muttered in agreement but could not find the right words.

"I could place you a bet for the eleventh race," Monoi finally said.

Without a moment's hesitation, Nunokawa replied, "Ten thousand yen for Lady-something-or-other to win."

Monoi again puzzled over how he should respond. "There are two horses with the name Lady."

"Then five thousand yen each."

"Better make it a place bet."

"That's none of your concern."

With the hand that was holding his daughter, Nunokawa struggled to fish out a ten-thousand-yen bill from his wallet and hand it over. Then, for the first time in the six years that Monoi had known him, he left without a parting word. Flanked by his daughter in one arm and the wheelchair under the other, he disappeared into the crowd of people in the passageway.

Monoi, on the other hand, ran up the stairs and wedged himself into the crowd of people that was now packed as far back as the passageway. He craned his neck, turning the right half of his face toward the track. The tenth race had taken off from the south side, the eight horses dancing into the sea of rain.

The black sash of the dirt track stretched out before them. The horizontal line of horses edged back and forth as if cutting into a sand dune and, in the blink of an eye, they approached the third turn, the competition still neck and neck. Far beyond the mist, the colorful helmets of the jockeys blurred into one another and wavered. In the second block, Erimo's black cap appeared to have started a little behind. The horses were now breaking into three groups as they ran past the screen in front of the finish line. The rumble of hooves on the ground grew closer. Erimo was still in last place.

With two horses taking the lead, the remaining six rounded into the fourth turn, only a nose or a neck between them, and entered into the five-hundred-meter homestretch. The cheers that erupted from within the grandstand swelled into giant waves. The eight horses were now edging back and forth in a frenzy as Inter Erimo came surging up on the far outside. Erimo was quickly gaining. Will he pull it out? Will he? Monoi wondered as his own neck stretched forward. He watched as Kita Sunline at the top broke away, followed by Saint Squeeze half a length back, and then Erimo, another half-length behind. The cheers and roars of a hundred thousand or so people spilled over, the losing tickets scattered at once into the air, and the tenth race was over.

The quinella bet was set at 1-5. One of the tickets Monoi had purchased for a friend had won, but looking at the odds, the winnings would be just enough for a cup of coffee. Erimo had not been able to take the lead but, judging from this demonstration of the power of his hind legs, Monoi figured it would be more than worthwhile to continue betting on him. He also wondered why this time, as Erimo charged forward, the exclamation that ordinarily sprang from his lips had not risen up; he assumed his grandson's death still cast a pall over his mood. Engulfed by the crowd of people for the first time in three weeks, neither his body nor his mind felt back to normal yet.

Monoi gave up on running out to the paddocks as they pre-pared for the eleventh race and instead lit up a cigarette in the grandstand, where people were already quickly dwindling. The front-row bench where Nunokawa and his daughter had been sitting was completely empty now. On top of it was the solitary umbrella he had forgotten, and the pages of a discarded newspaper were littered everywhere as the rain beat down upon them. Picking up the umbrella, he saw that a losing ticket was stuck to its fabric. As he swatted it away with his hand, suddenly the phrase "Superior Quality, 100 Years in the Making. Hinode Lager" flitted through his mind.

Now, where have I seen those words? he wondered, but could not remember. *Superior Quality, 100 Years in the Making. Hinode Lager.* A television commercial, a Viennese waltz playing over the backdrop of a photograph of an old beer hall from the Meiji or Taisho era, the tagline appearing in gold letters. The version that aired during the height of summer displayed fireworks over the Sumida River with the words *Summer in Japan. Hinode Lager.*

Ever since his grandson's funeral, he felt as if a small object had lodged itself in the blood vessels of his already forgetful brain, and one thing or another would cause it to rumble around in there—he knew now this must be why. Right before the accident, his grandson Takayuki had finished a second round of interviews with Hinode, and had only to wait to receive his employment offer for the following spring. Monoi had heard about it from his daughter and son-in-law at the funeral.

He had married away his only daughter, or rather, she had run off on her own to be with a young dentist in Setagaya, and aside from coming to show him their infant son just after he was born, the couple never stepped foot in her parental home. The few times Monoi saw his grandchild were when he had taken him to Ueno Zoo or Toshima Amusement Park when the boy was young, and after that he sent off a congratulatory gift whenever his daughter called to report that he had gotten into Keio Preschool, then Azabu Middle School, then Tokyo University, and so on. He had figured it was about time for his grandson to graduate from university, but what would happen after that was beyond the scope of Monoi's concern. Even when he had heard about Hinode Beer, the only vague image he had was of a "large company" that had been around for a while, and Monoi himself rarely drank beer.

Right, it was Hinode. He reminded himself that if Takayuki were still alive, he would start working for Hinode next spring. But when he tried to recall the face of a grandson whose voice he had barely heard in years, his mind came up blank. Monoi had another relative who'd also worked for Hinode before the war, but he had been adopted by another family before Monoi was born.

Nevertheless, the death of someone younger than oneself was a sad thing. When he thought about it, ever since his grandson died, his nerves had bothered him and he couldn't relax; he constantly found himself dwelling on his past or pondering the remaining years of his life—which at this point barely merited much worry—and often before he even realized it, he found himself lost in abstraction. Five years ago when his wife had passed away, it wasn't like this at all. Maybe because he himself was five years younger then . . .

After finishing his cigarette, Monoi went off to place his friend's bet for the eleventh race, and again lost himself for a moment as he was swallowed in the crowd around the betting windows. Resigned to being out of sorts that day, he decided not to make his own bet, but once he had the other person's ticket in hand, he rushed back to the stands to watch the fourteen fillies as they warmed up for the eleventh race. In these thirty or so years, he had never gone home without sitting through the main race. That habit was the only thing creating the rhythm in his gut. Glaring at the racing column, his eyes drifted to the four-legged creatures as they went back and forth at their respective paces on the main course. How about Ayano Roman, fresh off a break? Sweet Diana, the one Yo-chan had bet on, looked good as she sprinted for about two hundred meters and then shook herself off. She might run a good one. As for the two "Ladies"—the first time Nunokawa had ever placed a reckless bet—Monoi saw one ran with her chin up but he lost track of the other one.

Figuring it must be about time for the horses to enter the starting gate, Monoi was surveying the south side of the track when another acquaintance appeared and uttered a brisk "Hello." The man had a can of oolong tea in one hand as he crouched down in the aisle beside the already fully occupied benches. It was none other than Handa, the person who had asked Monoi to place a bet for him.

Handa was a detective at the precinct in Shinagawa or somewhere like that. Since his work schedule was irregular, these days he rarely showed up at the racecourse. Instead, he would come to Monoi's drugstore late at night to purchase an energy drink, and while there he would also ask Monoi to place his bets. Monoi had no idea where the man lived, although he had known the guy for a good six or seven years now, just like Nunokawa.

"Thought you were on duty," Monoi said.

Handa craned his neck to see the last of the horses warming up as he replied, still brusque, "I was in the neighborhood." In business shoes and a duster coat, he looked clearly out of place in the stands on a Sunday, but Handa seemed to pay this no mind. Perhaps he had a made a big arrest or something at his job; his broad shoulders seem to be dancing a little. Like Nunokawa, Handa was also still a young man.

Monoi handed the tall man the single winning 1-5 ticket from the tenth race, and the three quinella bets for the eleventh race that was about to start. Handa said, "Thanks," as he stuck out his hand to receive them, his eyes continuously scanning the racecourse now hazy with rain. It just now occurred to Monoi that Handa was also betting on Sweet Diana.

"How are they? That guy and his kid . . ."

As if he had suddenly remembered them, Handa gestured with his chin to the front-row bench where Nunokawa and his daughter had been sitting until about half an hour ago.

"The ex-army guy and his daughter? She became a lady today. They went home a while ago."

"What do you mean by lady?"

"She got her first period."

"Huh."

The matter did not quite seem to register in the detective's mind, as Handa nodded vacantly and took a sip from the oolong tea in his hand. The can bore Hinode's trademark seal of a golden Chinese phoenix. Then, after tossing aside the can, Handa stared straight at the racecourse and nothing else.

The horses began to assemble at the starting gate on the south side across from the stands. Monoi craned his neck, gathering the collar of his jacket closer. The rain was relentless, blowing every which way in the wind that strengthened then slackened in turn, creating a leaden maelstrom over the large expanse of the racecourse.

While they waited the few seconds for the gate to open, the wind and rain blew the tickets littering the stands into the air until the white specks obscured the sky. Monoi stretched his neck even farther and looked out into the distance. For an instant, the pale green of the turf track morphed into grassland hazy with large flakes of snow, the tracks of the Hachinohe railway of his birthplace laid across it, a freight train carrying charcoal and lumber running over the tracks and leaving a rumbling sound in its wake. On either side of the railway tracks the grassland stretched out as far as the eye could see, and beyond it to the east was a black shoreline the color of iron sand—once the train disappeared from sight nothing was left but puffy flakes of snow. In the hazy port beyond the tracks, there was dust and soot rising from the tin roof of the foundry. The shipyard and the ironworks. The main roof of the fish market. The squid fishing boats. And farther offshore the freight vessels en route to Dalian. As he squinted, the snowscape from a half century earlier transformed once again to the turf track, and the fourteen horses were dashing into the spray of water.

"Here they come, here they come!"

Slapping Monoi's knee, Handa leaped to his feet. A horse was driving in from the very back of the pack as they rounded into the fourth turn. Was that Ayano Roman? Monoi also rose from his seat. Sweet Diana was pulling away. Ayano Roman gave chase.

"Go—!"

Handa began to shout. A sound also escaped from Monoi's lips. In that moment, both Monoi and Handa were one with the horde of a hundred thousand filling the stands.

秦野浩之

HIROYUKI HATANO

2

Hiroyuki Hatano strained his ears. The phone was ringing. Sounds that he wouldn't have noticed before while he was working now registered in his hearing often. The pitter-patter of a child's feet in the waiting room. Then the sound of a man coughing.

Hatano was preparing a lower molar for a root canal procedure, trying to gain access into each curved canal of the molar's roots. The sensation of the reamer blade striking the canal walls made his fingers jittery. Is that where it's getting caught? He swapped the instrument for a K-type file—one with a differently shaped blade—inserted it into the canal and, using the superfine tip, began to file the canal into the proper shape. As he shaved away the dental pulp, the file began to glide smoothly up and down, all the way to the apex.

The phone rang again. The receptionist answered immediately, but the ringing was replaced by the sound of her low murmuring. Last month, he had taken a weeklong break after the sudden death of his son, who had been about to turn twenty-two. Although it had already been two weeks since Hatano reopened his office, there had been a backlog of over five hundred patients, and the phone still rang all day long with people calling to reschedule their appointments.

Holding the small file between his thumb and index finger, he pushed the blade further as he moved it up and down. Just as his fingertip sensed that he was only one or two tenths of a millimeter away from the apex, a dry snap sounded at the end of the file he held in his hand. The patient, her mouth held open, yelped.

Had he broken the file, or inadvertently pushed the sealer beyond the apex? Hatano knew the answer. In the next moment, he automatically picked up the X-ray photo and held it up to the halogen lamp above his head, but this was all a pose, just a diversion from his momentary confusion. Before the procedure, he had meticulously examined where and at what millimeter he would drill a hole, measured the rubber stoppers on the cutting instruments, and confirmed the position of the canals.

"Owww . . ." The grimacing female patient let out a cloying complaint.

"Hang on a little longer." Hatano responded in a brisk tone that was neither harsh nor kind, and prompted the patient to open her mouth again. Hatano would be forty-seven, but just as his body, sculpted into shape by more than twenty years of tennis, had not changed over the years, his manner toward patients remained exactly the same as the day he opened his dental practice. The impression he gave could be described as a gentle coldness and, peering from above the mask that covered half his face, his eyes hardly even paused on the patient's face as his gaze darted back and forth between the patient's chart and oral cavity. And the face that looked out from his mask showed no trace of a man who had recently lost his only son.

Hatano looked closely into the patient's mouth. In the chamber of the molar from which he needed to remove the pulp, he had prepared a proper access with his dental drill. With twenty years of experience in dentistry, he had confidence in his drilling skills, and in fact, the problem was not with the size or shape of the opening. Perhaps the opening had offset the angle necessary for his reamer to find the proper glide path through the root canal, or he had made a simple mistake when calculating the working length. As he thought about this, his eyes fell on the instrument tray by his hand, and the No. 30 file he had just been using. The rubber stopper, which he thought he had placed firmly at a right angle when he first adjusted the working length, was now slanted diagonally.

In that instant—before he could even register his own shock at the sight—Hatano averted his eyes. He thought someone else might have seen him, but the female assistant working across from him was looking away, still holding the suction in the patient's mouth. His other assistant, taking a break from sterilizing instruments, was busy grooming her nails. Hatano threw the file with the crooked rubber stopper into the sharps container and picked up a new one.

All he had to do was pass through the opening in the canal again. If he overfilled the canal, or pushed sealer beyond the apex, she might be in pain for a while, but as long as it did not cause any inflammation, there was nothing to do but leave it alone. If he had perforated the canal wall, he would have to repair this before he restored the tooth. Pondering what had happened with the self-reproach that always bubbled up inside him at a time like this, Hatano resumed filing and refocused his attention on the sensation at his fingertips.

An infant was crying in the waiting room. The man coughed again. The phone rang.

Once he had finally passed the No. 30 file through the opening, he stepped up to the next sized file, No. 40, and had just begun enlarging the root canal when the receptionist popped her head in from the other side of the partition. She looked as she often did when she was unhappy about something. "Telephone."

"Who is it?"

"Someone named Nishimura."

"Ask for the number, please."

"He said he'll wait."

"Never mind. Just ask for his number."

The receptionist retreated. Hatano exchanged the file for the reamer and began removing the pulp. Each time he pulled out the reamer, he wiped the dark red tissue that clung to the blade onto a piece of gauze.

Even now, despite the precise, mechanical movement of his fingers, Hatano noticed that he was a bit distracted by the immovable fog that had filled the space just behind his brow since the death of his son. The fog had formed into an indeterminate mass, so that he could no longer distinguish his despair from his doubts, and he felt as though only a tiny tremor could make it explode. And who is this Nishimura, anyway?

He finished cleaning and sterilizing the root canals, irrigating them with sodium hypochlorite. He called to his assistant to prepare the sealer, and inserted the gutta-percha into the canal before the temporary filling. Then he asked his assistant for the sealer but it did not arrive immediately. I told you to prepare it, he thought. Hatano put out his hand and waited three seconds. He took the ZOE cement that appeared on a glass slab, filled the pulp chamber with it, pushed it down, and, with the same hand, turned off the halogen lamp.

"We'll see how it goes for a while. It's just a temporary filling, so be careful when you chew. If you feel pain, give us a call." As he spoke these words to the patient, Hatano was already washing his hands at the sink. The only thing on his mind was the two minutes he had lost because he had to redo the root canal preparation. He wiped his hands, and even while he was filling out the patient's chart, he locked eyes with the receptionist who had popped in her head again through the partition.

"Doctor, telephone."

"Switch it over."

In the mere twenty seconds it took him to finish what he was writing on the patient's chart and stand up, his next patient was already seated in the examination chair. With a quick glance at the fully occupied waiting room on the other side of the partition, Hatano retreated to his small break room and closed the door.

"Dr. Hatano?" A man's voice addressed him through the receiver. "My name is Nishimura."

"Nishimura who?"

"I'm with the BLL."

What caught Hatano's attention was not the abbreviation for the Buraku Liberation League but the slight weariness with which the man said, "I'm with . . ." His voice carried the tone of a relatively seasoned yakuza. But then Hatano immediately second-guessed himself. In downtown Kobe, where he'd lived until he was four years old, the officers at the police box near the house where he was born used to speak with the same languid inflection.

"What is this about?"

"The other day, a letter arrived at the human resources department of Hinode Beer. It listed the Tokyo chapter of the BLL as the sender, but apparently no one at that chapter has any knowledge or record of it."

As Hatano listened, he pondered idly: Who is this, where did he get this information from, and what is he trying to threaten me with? While he understood what the caller was implying, since the sudden death of his son, everything around him had lost the sense of reality, so that it felt as if he was listening to a distant voice on the radio. Indeed, only a few days ago, he himself had sent a letter to Hinode Beer claiming to be from the Buraku Liberation League, but he could no longer even recall the experience of writing such a letter.

"What do you want?"

"Doctor. You know there are such things as defamation and obstruction of business?"

"Please tell me what this is about."

"We at the Tokyo chapter have also previously made demands on Hinode to improve their business practices, so we are fully aware what kind of company they are. But you, doctor, are a stranger to us. We don't owe you anything that would account for you using our name without permission. How about we talk this over in person?"

"If that's the case, I will state my apology in writing."

"Don't get me wrong, doctor. We just want to be useful to you. Consider it solidarity among comrades burdened with the same suffering."

"You won't raise your voice. You won't put up libelous ads or distribute leaflets. If you can promise me these two things we can meet. I have patients to see so please come to my home at nine tonight."

"Then we'll see you later."

After setting down the receiver, Hatano muttered to himself, "To hell with the BLL," without even realizing that the words had spilled out of him. At the same time, he shivered with a dull pain that spread through his whole body. Hatano then promptly banished from his consciousness this physical reaction to the phone call. Out of habit, he checked his reflection in the mirror to make sure there were no traces of medicine or bloodstains on his white coat before adjusting his collar.

I guess that's what you call forgery, he thought. He had sent a query to Hinode Beer using the name of an organization with which he had absolutely no connection, so he had gotten what he deserved. Paying some amount in damages would be inevitable. Standing before the mirror, making these matter-of-fact decisions, Hatano's consciousness drifted in a world that had lost all color, as it had these last three weeks, and soon the only thing he could be sure of was the unfamiliar, fuzzy sensation of the fog settled behind his brow.

The actual time Hatano had spent taking the call amounted to no more than two minutes or so. Returning to the examination room, he automatically washed his hands, and without so much as a glance at the patient's face, he apologized for the wait and quickly scanned the patient's chart. The letters "fist" were scrawled across the page. Cleansing a fistula from an infected root canal. The second time today, he thought.

"How's the pain?" he asked the patient as he peered into the oral cavity and began to remove the temporary filling. The phone call was no longer on his mind. Instead, the image of his son's head as he was laid out in the hospital's morgue was stuck behind his eyes and refused to move. Except that it was not so much a head as a mass of crumpled flesh.

THE LAST PATIENT LEFT A little after eight in the evening, and Hatano locked up the office himself and returned to his fifth-floor apartment in the same building. The day after the funeral, his wife had fled to their vacation home in Oiso. Although she returned every now and then for a change of clothes, she left things in disarray like a bandit, taking only what she needed at the time. The apartment, now occupied by a single man, was hopelessly messy. In the pitch dark, Hatano first stepped on a mountain of newspaper, then on what felt like a cushion, until his hands fumbled around in the darkness and he finally managed to turn on a lamp. Next he washed his hands out of habit, without even glancing at his face in the bathroom mirror. He then returned to the living room and, once he had settled down on the sofa with a bottle of whisky and a glass in hand, there was nothing but the long night ahead.

Just as it had been for the last three weeks, the only thing fixed behind his brow was the image of his son's face, expanding and shrinking in turns, like an abscess building up the pressure in his blood vessels. The expression on his son's face grew stranger to him with each passing day—rather than on the verge of saying something, the face merely stared at him. Hatano gazed back, occasionally wondering just whose face this was, and though he tried to jog back his memory to when the face was still familiar to him, he always failed. This pattern had repeated itself ever since the day of the accident.

Three weeks ago, on October 15th, the phone call had come from the police after eleven o'clock at night. Through a clamor of voices on the other end of the line, a voice informed him that his son had been involved in a car accident, and before Hatano could even take a breath, the words that he had suffered a cardiac arrest followed. Hatano and his wife rushed to the Saiseikai Central Hospital in Mita, where a member of the ambulance crew told them that their son had died instantly, along with a whispered warning: "It's best that your wife does not see the body." His son had crashed into a wall near the Hamazakibashi junction of the Shuto Expressway's Haneda Route at a speed of 100 kilometers per hour. The car was totaled; his son's head had smashed through the front windshield and was mangled to the point where it looked like nothing more than a mound of dark red meat—were it not for the black hair he would not have recognized it as a human head. Under such circumstances, it was impossible for Hatano, as a parent, to comprehend that this was his son, Takayuki.

And as a parent, his first question was what his son was doing speeding along the Haneda Route at 100 kilometers per hour so late at night. Hatano had bought a Volkswagen Golf for him three years ago on the condition that he would take it back if his son was ever caught speeding. Takayuki enjoyed driving it, but he wasn't enough of a car lover to go for long drives every weekend. At the time of his death, his son had been spending his nights at the laboratory at the pharmaceutical department of his university, preparing his graduate thesis, so the Volkswagen had remained in the parking lot of their apartment building since before the summer, and even during the few times Takayuki had returned home for his recruitment exams with Hinode Beer, he had only turned on its engine to let it run.

The last time Hatano saw his son was Thursday, October 4th, more than a week before the accident, the day his son came home for his first interview with Hinode. His son had been his usual self, and that night as they sat around the dinner table as a family, when Hatano asked how the interview had gone, his son sounded fairly confident as he said something to the effect of, "Companies have a lot more vitality than universities." He spoke enthusiastically of how, once he was hired, he would continue his research on immunization at the lab in Hinode's pharmaceutical business department, which had seen significant growth recently. Through the eyes of a parent, from his studies to his sound health to his good looks, Takayuki was above average in all respects, but since he had not known much hardship in life, Hatano felt it would be better for him to stay in graduate school than go to work for a major corporation, but that wasn't enough reason to dare to refute the wishes of his grown son. He also figured that his son must have his own reasons for wanting to apply exclusively to Hinode Beer, so he had let the question pass without pressing it further.

Then, Hatano himself left for a business trip from the eighth to the tenth, a dental surgery conference in Kyoto. According to his wife, his son had his second interview with Hinode Beer on the tenth, and after returning home briefly, he told his mother he had to go back to the lab to work on an experiment and left.

His wife would later say that there wasn't anything different about their son at the time, but on the sixteenth—the day of the wake—Hatano heard a story he would never have imagined from another student in his son's pharmaceutical chemistry seminar. It was revealed to him that on the evening of the tenth, his son, who was supposed to have returned to the lab, called there to say he was sick, and that he had been absent from the seminar since the eleventh. Hatano felt utterly bewildered, as if, in addition to the accident on the Shuto Expressway, he had glimpsed another side of his son. And after the funeral on the seventeenth, he found, among the mail that had not been opened since the day of the accident, a letter from Hinode Beer.

The envelope, postmarked on Saturday the thirteenth and delivered on Monday the fifteenth, was strangely thin. Inside, there was a single sheet of stationery that read, "We regret to inform you that we have rejected your application," and so on. For a University of Tokyo student with a glowing letter of recommendation from his seminar professor, impeccable grades, no trace of ideological bias— on the science track no less—normally a rejection would have been unthinkable. The next day Hatano went to see the professor who had written the recommendation; he too seemed mystified, and told Hatano that on Friday the twelfth he received a courtesy call from Hinode informing him about the rejection. According to them, his son had scored nearly perfectly on his written exam, and although his first interview had gone smoothly, in the middle of his second interview he had apparently told them he did not feel well and had left, never to return.

Well then, had his son truly fallen ill? Was it true that he left the interview? Assuming his son had lied, there must have been a reason why he needed to make up an excuse to get out of the interview, but what the hell could that have been? Was his son at fault, or did the blame fall on Hinode? As a parent Hatano considered many different possibilities, but common sense forced him to conclude that the fault lay with his son. In between Takayuki's first interview on October 4th and his second interview October 10th, therefore, something drastic must have happened to his son.

Hatano called every student in his son's seminar, checked the phone records at home, looked at the passbook for the bank account where he deposited and his son withdrew his allowance, and searched everywhere in his son's desk and closet, poring over his letters, notebooks, and belongings. As for his son's expenditures, in June he purchased a fishing reel for his sea fishing trip, in July he spent five thousand yen for a party given by his lab, and in August and September there was a receipt for eight thousand yen for photocopying, and another receipt for twenty-six thousand yen for some books he had purchased. Until October 10th, there was no record of him missing his lab or seminar. His letters consisted only of a few greeting cards from a former high school classmate who was a particularly good correspondent. His notebooks were filled with lecture notes, with nary a doodle. Just in case, he also checked the communication record on his son's PC, but aside from accessing his lab's computer, there were no other addresses.

So then, what else is left? Hatano considered the possibility of a girlfriend. Although he had never mentioned it to his parents, his son's seminar friend informed him that his son seemed to have dated a few female students during his first two years, while he was at the College of Arts and Sciences on the Komaba Campus, and had continued seeing one of them until the summer of this year. But for a science student who spent his nights at the lab, there were limits to having a relationship, and considering his son's personality, it was hard to imagine that his involvement with someone would have affected such an important business interview. In any case, could this female student he was only seeing until this summer really have been considered his girlfriend? Hatano scrutinized the register of funeral attendees, but none of the female names seemed to be likely prospects.

And so he ruled out each and every possibility in the twenty-two-year-old university student's small circle—including family, university, friends, fishing buddies, and so on—Hatano's suspicion deepening all the while that there was something else going on in his son's life. The only thing left was Hinode Beer. For whatever reason, his son had actively sought to join this company, and yet decided to leave in the middle of his second interview. Perhaps then he felt like he couldn't even show his face at the lab, considering that his professor had written a recommendation for him.

The name of the company at the source of all this was branded on Hatano's brain, he couldn't get it out of his mind. Even so, what sort of problem could there be? Hinode was a trillion-yen business that ranked among the twenty most profitable firms in Japan. During their corporate recruiting process, was it really possible that the company had made the kind of blunder that would force an applicant to abandon the process mid-interview?

And then suddenly, a voice had arisen from deep within his gut that told him: yes. If he was trying to imagine the company's point of view, there was just one issue to consider.

Until the age of four, Hatano's permanent address had been in a district within the city of Kobe that included a number of segregated buraku communities, and that was where his father had been born. He knew that such matters no longer caused a stir in Japan, and he knew full well how unlikely it would be for a company to look up the lineage of an applicant's parents during the screening process for new employees, but once he had latched onto this thought, Hatano's mind began to circle around it. This world to which he had had no connection for more than forty years now had not come looking for him, but rather, he had called it forth on his own. With no sense of reality, he started to follow the scent of his memory, and without feeling any actual pain, he begin to think: discrimination. Though it was nothing more than a linguistic concept without substance, he continued to cradle it in his arms until it gradually grew warm and began to give off an odor, and the odor further expanded the concept, until an even stronger smell of something rotten began to rise.

It was at this time that Hatano wrote his first letter to Hinode Beer. Suddenly, almost as soon as he had picked up his fountain pen, he began to write as if on auto pilot: I have an issue with the way that my son, Takayuki Hatano, was evaluated during your screening process for new employees, and as a bereaved parent, I am deeply anguished.

Ten days later, a businesslike reply arrived from Hinode's human resources department, stating that the screening process had been impartially conducted, and even then the thinness of the single-page typewritten letter had provoked a strong reaction in Hatano. The stink of discrimination became even more pungent, and as it continued to intensify, he immediately sent out a second letter. This time, instead of his own name he assumed the name of the Tokyo chapter of the Buraku Liberation League, typing out the words on different stationery. He did not think much about his language. And then, on November 2nd he dropped off the letter at the Shinagawa post office . . .

No, hold on. He had sent the letter on the second. It would have arrived at Hinode on the third. But the third was a holiday so the offices were closed. The fourth was a Sunday. So then, the day the person in charge of mail in the human resources department opened the letter would have been Monday the fifth—which was today. This afternoon's call from that Nishimura would mean that Hinode had opened the letter this morning, then immediately judged its content and contacted the BLL. That was a startlingly swift response from the company. The rotting stench emanating from Hinode Beer was stronger than ever. It was like a tooth secretly decaying beneath the white resin with which it had been beautifully restored. Like the anaerobic bacteria decomposing the pulp, melting it into putrid, dark red mash—what else could this be other than the rot hiding deep within the trillion-yen corporation?

Hatano allowed the involuntary twitching of his facial muscle to work his mouth into a sneer. He continued to drink for a while longer, until nine o'clock came around. The doorbell rang and, getting up from the sofa and slowly making his way to the front hall, he opened the door. He saw the faces of two men.

"I'm Nishimura. I called earlier."

The dark-skinned man who introduced himself in the doorway looked to be about fifty years old. On the right side of his jaw, punctuating a smooth, expressionless face with otherwise unmemorable features, was a mole about ten millimeters in diameter. That mole was what Hatano saw first, and more than anything else about the man's appearance, it left a lasting impression. The second man was about forty with an unimpressive countenance and somber eyes. They both wore plain off-the-rack suits, gave off a strong smell of hair product, and beneath the too-short hem of their slacks, casually showed off their expensive Armani and Gucci shoes. Hatano, however, was of no mind to judge what this hodge-podge signified.

"We won't take too much of your time."

As the man who called himself Nishimura spoke, Hatano stared at his face with its peculiar lack of emotion, his eyes scarcely moving as he spoke, and wondered what type of man he was—he really had no idea. The two men sat down on the sofa without so much as a glance at the disorderly apartment, each of them placing their respective business cards on the table and sliding them toward Hatano with a single finger. Both bore the title, "Buraku Liberation League, Tokyo Chapter, Executive Committee."

"What line of work are you in?" Hatano asked.

Relaxing only his mouth, Nishimura responded, "Shrewd eye. I should have known you'd ask, doctor," and presented another card. It read, "Look, Inc., Managing Director."

"What kind of company is this?"

"Manufacture and wholesale of women's shoes. Since you were born in Kobe, doctor, you probably know it. We are based there."

Hatano looked at the delicate fingertips of Nishimura's hand, which he had placed on his knee. Recalling from his youth seeing the hands of the people working in Kobe's small factories, and then thinking of the Armani shoes Nishimura had just taken off on the concrete floor of his entryway, he thought, No way. Nishimura may or may not have been a shoemaker, but Hatano nevertheless recognized the feeling that was slowly being restored within his own skin. At the same time he was aware of the sort of tediousness exhibited by self-proclaimed activists whose motivation had been reduced over time to a fixation on being descendants of a segregated buraku community. Even as he tried to decipher all this, Hatano's interest in Nishimura's identity had already waned.

"What do you want?"

"First, regarding the recent loss of your son, no doubt you are quite disheartened. I want you to know that we fully understand that."

"I'd like you to get to the point quickly. If I've caused you trouble, I'll pay what I need to pay."

Nishimura paused briefly before continuing. "Even wearing a lion's pelt, a fox is still a fox," he said. "By the way, doctor, your mother seems to be doing well."

"If you have something to say, make it quick."

"I hear these days hospitals with fewer than a hundred beds are all having trouble managing, but privately run clinics, on the other hand, are going strong as long as they have the trust of the local community. Business also seems to be flourishing at your mother's practice in Kamakura."

"This doesn't involve my mother. Please tell me what you want."

"Why don't we start by you taking off that lion's pelt? Doctor, you shouldn't forget the circumstances under which you and your mother left Kobe in 1947. Not that I'm suggesting you engage in class warfare."

The man's implication was clear. During the war, Hatano's mother, a doctor and the second daughter of a wealthy physician's family in Kamakura, had taken a post as at the central municipal hospital in the faraway city of Kobe, where she fell in love with a patient. The awkwardness of this talk of the distant past tumbling unexpectedly from the mouth of a stranger had the converse effect of numbing Hatano's surprise.

The man with whom his mother had become infatuated—Hatano's father—had been temporarily conscripted to work in the Kobe steel mill, and though he was handsome enough to call to mind a Japanese Rudolph Valentino, because it was wartime and because he came from a district where there were many segregated buraku communities, Hatano was born out of wedlock. After the war, Hatano's parents were finally legally married, but his father had become caught up in the swell of the rising democratic movement and transformed into a passionate buraku liberation activist. Meanwhile his mother, a young lady brought up in comfort, was held up as a poster child for the adage that there was no sin greater than ignorance. Dragged day after day to liberation committee gatherings and drowning in leaflets, it wasn't long before she called it quits. Ultimately, the marriage did not last five years, and with a suitcase in one hand and her small son in the other, his mother fled back home to Kamakura on a jam-packed Tokaido Line night train. Hatano could still faintly recall the crowded cars of that slow-moving train.

"I don't remember anything about Kobe," Hatano responded simply.

"Even if you have forgotten, doctor, people like to poke around for all sorts of old wounds. I'm sure this business with Hinode comes down to just that as well. It's too bad for you, doctor, but that's the way of the world."

From his breast pocket, Nishimura took out a sheaf of paper and gently waved it at Hatano. The bundle was slightly smaller than letter-paper size and looked to be about twenty or thirty pages thick, but for the time being it remained in the man's hand and was not presented to Hatano.

"Your wife's maiden name was Okamura, wasn't it? Do you have a relationship with her family?"

"Barely."

"Does the name Seiji Okamura sound familiar?"

"No."

"He would have been your wife's uncle."

"My wife's maiden name is Monoi."

"Seiji Monoi was adopted and became Okamura. I'm sure you've heard the name Okamura at least."

"No. I hardly see anyone from the Monoi side of the family."

"I guess this is what they call an amazing coincidence, because it turns out that Seiji Okamura also used to work for Hinode's research lab. He was a graduate of Tohoku Imperial University and seems to have been quite accomplished. He started working for Hinode in 1937 and left in 1947, but the letter he wrote to Hinode just after he resigned from the company still exists. This is it, right here."

"Why would you have a letter addressed to Hinode?"

"As for its source, well, let's just say Hinode lost track of it forty-three years ago. Now, what's crucial about the contents . . ." Nishimura said and slowly waved the sheaf of paper in his hand. "How can I put this? Okamura himself may not have had an ulterior motive, but from the company's perspective, the nature of this letter is not something they can simply ignore. Depending on how you read it, it can be interpreted as libel or blackmail."

Who was this relative of his wife he had never heard of? This stranger who worked for Hinode half a century ago and sent them a threatening letter? Deep within Hatano's mind, now loosened and relaxed from the whisky, new and unaccustomed thoughts began to percolate.

"In the letter Okamura-san refers to four of his colleagues at the company. All four of them were from a segregated buraku community.

One of them left the company of his own accord while the other three were wrongfully terminated, but the liberation committee at the time had researched the case and there's a record of them submitting a claim to Hinode—so what Okamura-san writes is true. Anyhow, Hinode, learning from the experience of being justly suspected of wrongdoing, henceforth became especially sensitive to problems of this nature."

Hatano stared absent-mindedly at the man's lips as they continued to move. With each passing moment, his words seemed to lose their meaning and disintegrate, as Hatano felt his memories of the buraku village—memories that had been brewing in his own head for the past five days—gradually becoming meaningless as well. At the end of the long and dark tunnel of prejudice in which the history of this country was created, people still used the barriers that remained in some places as an excuse—but what did they really want? If the barriers were taken away, these same people were likely to denounce the widespread ignorance and indifference outside the tunnel, then proceed to erect a new barrier so that they could stubbornly cling to defending their reason for existence. Equality and prejudice—wasn't the role of each of them, complementing the other, simply to guarantee this small sector of humanity their raison d'être? On the other hand, his twenty-two-year-old son had no connection to any such conversation about equality or discrimination, nor did he play any part in the world that they were discussing . . .

Hatano poured more whisky into his glass and continued to gulp it down. It seemed to him that Nishimura's languid drawl shouldn't be considered critical or threatening. It sounded more and more like static noise that had nothing to do with himself or his son, and it was only the alcohol that gave him the strength—barely—to keep listening.

Meanwhile, Nishimura continued to run his mouth. "By the way, Hinode has another delicate external matter pending. Have you read today's Nikkei?"

Nishimura's companion took out two photocopied pages from the breast pocket of his suit and placed them on the table. Both of them were non-boldface newspaper articles from below the fold in the business and financial columns. One read, "Chunichi Mutual Savings Seeks Bank for Settlement Approval," while the other was titled, "Ogura Transport Announces Management Changes."

"I'm sure you've at least heard the name Ogura Transport. They are a major player in land transportation. Chunichi Mutual Savings is the Ogura Group's leading bank. These two articles are related. You know the old proverb, 'When the wind blows, the coopers prosper'? One event can have an unexpected effect on another. What's more, Hinode is also connected . . ."

Hatano glanced over the articles to stave off his lassitude. During an inspection by the Bank of Japan, several obscure points were discovered in the management of Chunichi Mutual Savings Bank. Of their ¥850-billion loan balance, ¥280 billion had insufficient security. They were suspected of dispersing loans to avoid hitting the maximum allowable real estate loans and broker loans, and the investigation by the Ministry of Finance was ongoing, the article said. Meanwhile, Ogura Transport suffered a ¥50-billion stock loss and, seeing as they would likely be in the red this quarter, current management would take responsibility and step down. Having reading as much, Hatano tossed back the copies.

"First, Chunichi Mutual Savings Bank. They've got a hefty trillion yen in total deposits. According to our sources, we know that half of their total loans, meaning five hundred billion, is irrecoverable, but their biggest problem is that the few city banks that are their biggest shareholders are standing ready to take over their hundred branches. First thing next year, they will announce their absorption and merger. After all, the major city banks and the finance ministry have been plotting together to make sure this will happen."

"What does this have to do with me?"

"Now, just listen. As for Ogura Transport, the stock blunder that's mentioned in the article is just a front. In reality, a certain group of corporate raiders has bought up the majority of Ogura stock on the market, and now they are demanding that Ogura and its main bank, Chunichi Mutual Savings Bank, buy back the stocks they've snapped up. In short, the corporate raiders have something on both Ogura and Chunichi that makes them unable to refuse the demand. For example, there's a twelve-billion-yen loan that Chunichi has made to Ogura Development, a subsidiary of Ogura, in the guise of a land purchase. From what we've heard, three billion of that has disappeared into politico pockets. In any case, the story is that the nonbank that has funded the group of corporate raiders that's driving Ogura into a corner is said to be affiliated with a certain major player in those city banks that have tried to take over Chunichi."

"I'd like you to get to the point."

"This is the point. Early next year that certain city bank that will have absorbed Chunichi will set out to save Ogura. At that time, Hinode Distribution, currently a designated shareholder in Ogura, will also send their members to Ogura's board of directors. This is the scenario that's been planned out. Hinode Distribution is of course Hinode's subsidiary. And that same city bank is Hinode's main bank. What do you think? That's corporate society for you."

"I'm just a dentist."

"To speak plainly, if anyone were to make a peep about the situation with Ogura, it would immediately trigger a secret investigation by law enforcement. That's what this is all about. There is already a talk that a journalist based in Osaka is sniffing around. Bringing charges of financial crime is tough as it is, and with politicians involved, who knows what will happen next. Oh, and by the way, that journalist also makes an appearance in this letter too. I mentioned before—he's one of the three who had been wrongfully terminated by Hinode long ago. Though the letter doesn't mention him by name."

"I don't see how this nonsense relates to myself or my son."

"You call this nonsense? Of course, Hinode's current management has abandoned their preferential treatment of particular universities, and they've been actively hiring foreigners and people with disabilities, so I'm sure outwardly they seem like an enlightened, liberal company. However, that's different from the problem with your son. Just when they are getting nervous about the whole Ogura issue, to receive a letter like this is . . ."

Nishimura waved the thick bundle of paper even more energetically before Hatano's eyes. But it was still a letter written by a complete stranger whose name he had never heard of, and the talk of some transportation company and this bank seemed even more remote.

"I told you, I don't know any man named Okamura."

"Tell that to Seiji Okamura. Believe me, there's no human resources manager who wouldn't be troubled by a letter like this."

"Did Hinode's representative say something about this letter to my son?"

"The answer to that question is this: however Hinode dealt with your son, so long as this letter is addressed to Hinode—never mind that it's from forty-three years ago—Hinode can't just say they don't know anything about it. You get what I'm saying?"

"I don't."

Hatano shook his head, and for the first time Nishimura contorted his mouth a little into a faint smirk, but his eyes still did not move. "A well-bred man like you, doctor, doesn't stand a chance against a corporation, no matter how you try. Before sending two half-hearted letters to Hinode, I might have suggested you hire a lawyer."

"Where did you see the first letter?"

"I can't tell you that."

"Did someone from Hinode call you about the second letter?"

"Well, you're free to presume whatever you like. In any case, a business has the right to defend itself. At a time like this they would never think of hiring the relative of a man like Seiji Okamura—no matter how distantly related. Even if it's a one-in-a-million chance, your son could be Seiji Okamura's heir. The company would never take on such a risk. As you will understand when you read this letter, Okamura-san clearly criticizes a company called Hinode. Even if it is by coincidence, he also refers to the journalist who is poking around Ogura Transport, a company at the center of this whole mess. That's it right there—you're out."

"Are you a Hinode spy?"

"Why would you say that? I'm only taking the time to tell you all this so that you don't misdirect your anger. Besides, there'll be trouble if you go on using the BLL's name."

"If there is a right direction, I'd like you to tell me."

"As I said before, whatever the reason your son decided to leave in the middle of his second interview with Hinode, Hinode has a lot of stories they would rather not have dug up. That's where this letter comes in."

Nishimura placed the sheaf of paper on the table for the first time and pushed it toward Hatano.

"It's a copy, but it's yours to keep. At this time Hinode would no doubt react sensitively to a letter of this nature. I suggest you do as you please. But, I ask you to keep the source of this letter confidential." The words were barely out of his mouth before Nishimura and his silent companion stood up from the sofa.

"How much?"

At Hatano's question, Nishimura's eyes flickered like a dark blade, as if he had been waiting for just this moment.

"I could have you write us a check for ten or twenty million yen right here, you know? But I'm afraid we're not in the business of taking money from amateurs. More importantly, you're a rich man, doctor, so I'm sure you play around a bit with stocks. If you own any Hinode stock, I suggest you sell it in the near future. I promise you this: Hinode stock will plummet very soon."

As Nishimura said these last words, the look of a seasoned yakuza flashed across his face, and then he left with his associate.

FOR A LONG TIME, HATANO stared at the thick bundle of paper on the table. The photocopy itself was new, but it looked as if the original document had been repeatedly duplicated using a blueprint process, and perhaps because the original letter was written in pencil, the letters were blurry and rubbed away so that he had to hold it up close in order to decipher them. At the top, the letter read: *Hinode Beer Company, Kanagawa Factory. To Whom It May Concern.*

With grim determination, Hatano began flipping through the pages. One, two, ten, twenty, thirty-one pages of stationery covered with thin, meticulous characters. On the thirty-first and last page was the date, June 1947, and the signature of Seiji Okamura.

Seiji Okamura. After ruminating on the name he had never even heard before, Hatano put down the letter for the time being and grabbed the telephone receiver. He dialed the number of their vacation house in Oiso, and after about a dozen rings, he heard his wife's curt "Yes?" as if she already knew the only person it could be on the other end of the line.

"Do you know a man named Seiji Okamura?"

"Who?"

"Seiji Okamura. He's one of your father's brothers."

"My father's last name is Monoi. Don't be stupid."

He was unaffected by the abrupt phone conversation. After setting the receiver down, Hatano brought out a dictionary from his study and began to handle each page of the letter again as he would a stack of patient charts. He looked up the reading of each arcane character he was unsure about in the dictionary and meticulously noted the proper reading in the margin.

The author of the letter began with the words, "I, Seiji Okamura . . ." and first explained how someone who had left the company came to write a letter to that very company. There was mention of a man named Noguchi who had also left Hinode for some reason before the war, and of how Okamura's relationship with this Noguchi caused him to fall under the scrutiny of the police and the company—allusions that made Hatano, the son of a liberation committee activist, perk up with recognition.

Okamura proceeded to talk about his birthplace, revealing the geographical features of a village that was apparently near Hachinohe in Aomori prefecture, the lifestyle during the early Showa era in the 1920s, his family structure, and the whereabouts of his brothers and sisters. According to the letter, Okamura was the second oldest of four siblings, and he had one older brother and a younger sister and brother. The eldest son died in the war, so his younger brother—the one with the disability in his left eye who became an apprentice at the foundry in Hachinohe at the age of twelve—must be Hatano's wife's father, Seizo Monoi. As he continued to read, Hatano tried to picture the man's face. Hatano had seen him three weeks ago at his son's funeral, but his mind had been far away at the time, so between that and the fact that he had had very little contact with him previously, Monoi's face was blurred in his mind, his features indistinct.

According to the letter, Okamura was adopted into a wealthy merchant family, and after graduating from Tohoku Imperial University without any difficulty, he joined the research lab of Hinode's Kanagawa factory, was conscripted to the front just like everyone else, and later demobilized and sent home. In his life immediately after the war, Okamura diffidently and somewhat feebly called himself a "laborer." Hatano did not know what it felt like to identify as such, but he could at least understand that at the time the letter was written, the position of a "laborer" was in direct confrontation with that of a capitalist. Then again, Okamura seemed more like a forerunner of the era of union-management cooperation that began in the early 1960s, more than a dozen years after the letter was written, one who should have been welcomed by those company men, and so he was quite different from the "laborers" that Hatano remembered. Hatano could faintly recall the general strike of February 1, 1947, but in his memory his father appeared with a white headband around his head, going off to liberation committee meetings and canvassing door-to-door day after day, shouting and yelling in a way that made him seem like a stranger.

Meanwhile, Okamura had written with startling naïveté about his interaction with this man Noguchi from a segregated buraku community whom he had met at the Kanagawa factory before the war. Okamura seemed at that point to have finally learned about the existence of discrimination for the first time, yet he still languished in the realm of confusion—even the part where he questioned how Hinode's Kyoto factory wrongfully terminated those other three employees from the segregated buraku community was far from what could be called criticism against the company. If anything, until the very end, Okamura seemed to consider Noguchi and the others "Hinode employees" just like himself, even going on about how moved he was by the brilliant life force of Noguchi, whom he encountered again in Tokyo in late 1946. His perspective, which seemed to empathize deeply with the human condition, could not be more different than that of an activist.

No, it was utterly different . . . Hatano murmured to himself. The same day in late 1946, when Okamura said he had run into Noguchi at Hamamatsucho train station in Tokyo, Hatano's father would have also gone there to attend the liberation committee's national convention, which was held nearby in Shiba. For the first time in his life Hatano tried earnestly to picture that distant day. By then, his father bore no trace of the handsome young man his mother had fallen for so passionately. In the eyes of the triumphant man who walked along the platform of Hamamatsucho Station—nostrils flaring, his flushed face now almost indistinguishable from the other activists who had also absorbed the lessons of socialist textbooks—the sight of a man like Okamura, his head hanging down and deep in self-reflection, would not have even registered. The same would have gone for that guy Noguchi—Okamura would not even recognize him once they had parted ways and Noguchi went to join the convention, donning the look of an activist. No, Seiji Okamura was unlike any of his contemporaries.

When it came down to it, this Okamura was but one of the many former employees who, though one day they were encouraged to resign and indeed left Hinode, still couldn't cut their ties to the company. What's more, the poverty of his family, the company, the war, his illness—all of it was simply reduced to his personal experience, not once did he try to place himself in the context of society or history. For this reason, the writer himself could only barely make out the miserable workings of his life that were apparent to the reader of the letter. And, in contrast to the hundred million Japanese people of his generation who frantically struggled to survive each day, he was nothing but a pallid, highbrow man who had been left behind by the changing times. When Hatano sketched this vague portrait of the author of the letter in his mind, he was shocked to realize that his own perspective fell on the side of the activists like his father and Noguchi. This was something he never would have imagined. It stood to reason that the blood of those born in the segregated buraku communities and socialists coursed through his veins, while the blood of this aimless Okamura flowed through his wife's. What a joke!

But wait. Didn't this also mean that this Okamura's blood ran through his dead son's veins too? Faced with a glimpse of discrimination for the first time in his life, had Takayuki been simply confounded, lacking any opinion about society whatsoever? And then, swept up by external forces, did he lose his way, his solitary thoughts languishing in confusion, until he sped off in his car and crashed to his death?

No, hold on. Perhaps Hatano himself was the one who resembled this pathetic invalid Seiji Okamura. Despite the location of his birth in Kobe, he himself held no such historical or societal opinions, and even after losing his son, when he first recognized all this to be "discrimination," he had kept his distance, and then the ineptitude with which he had sent those libelous letters, not even knowing his own intentions—were his actions not exactly like Okamura's . . . ?

Hatano set down the sheaf of pages and turned it over. Starting afresh, he emptied his mind and, one by one, reexamined each new piece of information that had come his way during these past few hours.

First, there was the fact that a letter addressed to Hinode from forty-three years ago, which had been copied repeatedly, still remained in the hands of a stranger. The existence of this version of the letter, which the company never would have released, could only indicate either sinister intent or criminal behavior.

Next was the question of whether or not this issue with Noguchi and the three wrongfully terminated employees in the letter still held any significance. If Nishimura, who claimed to be associated with the BLL, was right and Hinode still considered one of those three men to be persona non grata, that would mean that the contents of the letter were still very relevant.

Furthermore, had Hinode truly hesitated to hire Hatano's son because of this letter? Nishimura had implicitly advised him to use this letter from the past to blackmail Hinode, but what Hinode had actually done to his son had yet to be established.

And finally, where and from whom did Nishimura hear about the two letters Hatano had sent to Hinode, or the fact that his son left in the middle of his second interview? Nishimura's business card said he was an executive of the Tokyo chapter of the BLL, but he had not made a single claim for the BLL itself. He wasn't that kind of associate. There was no shortage of people out there who claimed to be a part of an organization for social integration or working to end discrimination against burakumin—the caste of descendants of segregated communities—but that wasn't it, either. Just who was he? Where did he come from, and what had he come here for?

Hatano mulled this over for about five minutes, but ultimately failed to reach any conclusion. After all, for Hatano, whose world consisted only of universities, academic conferences, dental societies, and tennis, five minutes was enough to ponder one thing or another, and once he was at an impasse there was nothing else to do. His apathy resurgent, Hatano glanced once again at the bundle of paper and now wondered what could have happened to Seiji Okamura, a man whose blood may have coursed through Takayuki's veins.

Hatano suddenly sprang up from his seat and went to look for the phone book. He searched for a telephone number he himself had never once called in the past twenty-some years. It wasn't until he had already picked up the phone and dialed that he glanced at the clock. It was three minutes before midnight. As he wondered if it was too late to be calling, the phone had already started ringing, and someone answered right away.

"Yes, this is Monoi." A raspy voice. In the background, there was the sound of the television.

"I'm sorry to call you so late. This is Hatano." Once he identified himself, the voice on the other end of the line responded with a note of surprise.

There was a momentary pause, as if they each needed to picture the face of the other. Even though they were in-laws, prior to the funeral they were barely acquainted with one another. Then Seizo Monoi asked, "Have things settled down for you?"

"Ah, yes, thank you. I'm surprised you are awake at this hour."

"Yes. Well, when you get older, you drift off while watching TV . . ."

"I'm sorry for the rude question so late at night, but is Seiji Okamura your older brother?"

"If you mean Seiji Okamura of Okamura Merchants in Hachinohe, then yes."

It was Hatano's turn to be at a loss for words. "The dental association had a social gathering, and a couple of older doctors there were talking about being in the military during the war. One of them mentioned an army buddy by the name of Seiji Okamura, and I thought he may have been a member of the family on your side . . ."

"I see. And what about Okamura?"

"When I asked my wife, she said she didn't know him."

"Oh, yes. I have never spoken about him to my daughter. Another family adopted him before I was born, and I myself barely know anything about him. I met him a few times in Hachinohe, but that was over fifty years ago."

"Is that right? This older doctor was wondering how Okamura might be doing these days."

"My older sister and her husband who take care of the family home in Herai told me he passed away. I think it must be have been in 1952 or '53."

"Oh . . . Well, I guess when you lose your son, you start to wonder about family, even distant relatives. By the way, do you still go to the racetrack?"

"Uh, yes. I'm ashamed to admit it, but when I'm watching the horses, I can forget about the bad stuff."

"If there's ever a time, I would like it if you could teach me how to place a bet. Well, I'm sorry to have bothered you so late. Please take care of yourself."

"Yes. Same to you."

After the perfunctory conversation ended and he'd hung up the phone, Hatano was struck with a strange and fleeting sensation. Born from the same womb as Seiji Okamura, and with his voice appropriately hushed for the late hour, Seizo Monoi sounded the way Hatano imagined Okamura himself would sound.

Holding the thirty-one-page letter bundle in his hand, Hatano left the living room and went into the room his son had occupied until the beginning of summer. The eight-mat space was organized to the point of starkness. There were only drably colored textbooks and a few fishing magazines on the bookshelf. There were no pictures of celebrities on the walls, and when Hatano had gone through the closet a few days ago, he had not found even a single provocative magazine. It was a room of a twenty-two-year-old honor student—too serious, too carefree, too inexperienced—and yet he had hidden away something he could not even tell his parents.

Hatano sat down at his son's desk in front of his PC, opened the drawer, and pulled out a Walkman and a brand-new cassette tape still sealed in plastic. He checked the device, which he had used at dental meetings but not anytime recently, to make sure that the power still worked and that the tape was feeding properly. Then he laid the letter bundle on the desk, folded the corner of each page so that they would be easy to turn, and fanned them out in a row. Listening for noise outside the curtained window, he realized that it was past the hour of the last train on the Odakyu line that ran 300 meters south of his home, and that the clamor of the streets around the train station had long dissipated. From time to time he heard sounds of the exhaust from cars on Seijo Street, but he figured that they were not loud enough for the Walkman's small microphone to pick up.

Hatano then looked at the first page of the letter.

Hinode Beer Company, Kanagawa Factory. To Whom It May Concern.

Should he say something before the opening line? He hesitated a moment but, thinking that he owed them no explanation whatsoever, he made up his mind. Hatano hit the record button on the Walkman and, pausing for two seconds, began to read the letter aloud: "Hinode Beer Company, Kanagawa Factory. To whom it may concern." No, he didn't just read it; he narrated it on behalf of Seiji Okamura.

"I, Seiji Okamura, am one of the forty employees who have resigned from the Kanagawa factory of Hinode at the end of this past February. Today, as I am currently confined to my sickbed and can hardly sit up or stand . . ."

He figured Okamura had been a man of few words who faltered in his speech. In trying to resurrect such a man forty-three years later, Hatano took on a slightly hesitant tone and spoke quite slowly.

". . . My 'former colleague,' that is to say Katsuichi Noguchi, himself resigned from the Kanagawa factory in 1942, but in the case of Noguchi, I know that his resignation took place with an unspeakable amount of disappointment and indignation, and that various circumstances transpired before and after . . ."

Hatano read straight through to the end without any inflection, as if he were chanting a sutra, and once he had practically filled both sides of the sixty-minute tape, he signed off with the date and name. He inserted the tape into one manila envelope, sealed it, then inserted the package into another manila envelope before sealing that one and affixing enough stamps. He typed up and printed out a label with the address of the human resources department at Hinode's main office in Kita-Shinagawa, leaving his name and return address blank.

After finishing these tasks, he threw the thirty-one pages into the trash. He then returned to the sofa, put on the CD of the singer Yuming that his son had left behind, and drank until three in the morning.

Early the next morning—the sixth—Hatano woke after sleeping for about three hours, took the envelope and drove his Mercedes-Benz to the Shinagawa post office in Higashi-Oi, where he deposited it into the same mailbox as before. Afterward, he opened his clinic at half past eight and started seeing patients by nine, as usual. By the time noon rolled around he already felt like the tape recording was the work of someone else—not him—and before he knew it, all that remained in the back of his mind was—the same as yesterday—the image of his son's head, covered with blood.

KYOSUKE SHIROYAMA

城山恭介

3

It took less than twenty minutes to drive directly from his house in Sanno to Hinode's main office in Kita-Shinagawa, but since his days as managing director, Kyosuke Shiroyama would instruct his driver to take twice as long by meandering along a different route every morning. One reason for this was to secure the time to scan through the sections of the newspaper he had not finished reading at home; another was to observe the backstreets he did not normally pass by, the secluded stores, the signage and billboards, the flow of commuters.

It had been thirty-one years since he joined Hinode Beer. Even now that he had assumed the position of president and CEO in June, he retained basically the same perseverance he had attained by spending two thirds of that time in the front line of the sales division. No, in terms of both ability and character, Shiroyama knew there was simply no way for him to change.

Unlike other alcoholic beverages, beer acutely reflected the sensibility of the times and the quotidian emotions of the people. Thus, copious research was always conducted before the release of each new product, but Shiroyama occasionally felt caught between his salesman's desire to maintain his intuition about the accuracy of such research even now that he had reached the top and the awareness that he was no longer in a position to share his personal hunches about a single product. Now that keeping an eye on current figures as well as the status of the entire company was his job, this incapacity to shed the perspective of front-end sales had, in effect, ultimately turned Shiroyama into a prudent manager who carefully considered the opinions of others and actually in some ways made him more agreeable.

He had never told anyone about his morning prowls—not the other executives, much less the general employees—out of concern that it might put unnecessary pressure on them. As usual on that Monday morning, November 12th, Shiroyama spent about ten minutes scanning the Nikkei's personnel column, then as the company car drifted around the Yashio Park Town residential complex, he gazed out at the morning scene and, opening the window a little, breathed in the salty air. With fifteen minutes still to spare, his driver offered to take him through the neighborhood of James's Slope, to which Shiroyama agreed, and as the car turned toward the waterfront and carried him along, his eyes continued to scan the scenery outside. In a rapidly changing city like Tokyo, less than a couple of weeks went by before a new store or new billboards popped up here or there.

Still, this whole time Shiroyama's mind was never at rest. He lined up the affairs of the day in his mind, confirming what was urgent, worrying about the year-end account figures that would arrive in the middle of the winter sales campaign, deliberating over the next term index that had already arrived, reminding himself about the mid-to-long-term agenda items he would need to act on soon, and mulling over the angles and the sequence of the groundwork he would have to lay to reach a consensus at the next board meeting. On that day, his mind was predominantly occupied—for the time being—by the November forecast for next month's figures as well as the numbers from October's monthly interim financial statement, followed by other sundry concerns that asserted themselves one after another.

Hinode Supreme, a new product that had gone on sale in the spring, had already proved to be a big hit, clearing its first-year goal of thirty million cases by October, so Shiroyama felt somewhat at ease, but his concerns still seemed myriad. The gross domestic demand for beer had been on the rise these past few years, but the gradual decline of Hinode Lager, which had dominated the market for a quarter of a century, had now become the trend of the times. Last year, Hinode experienced a historical nadir when its share dipped below fifty percent, and management had been overhauled. And so, compelled by an onslaught of new products developed by their competitors, for the past two years Hinode had been reconsidering its product range, which relied too heavily on the lager, and had shifted toward a more diversified strategy. But the result of Hinode's relinquishing its fortitude as the stalwart of the industry was that ultimately every company was dragged into a grueling, never-ending competition that forced all of them to increase their advertising budgets and to overproduce new products to maintain their market share. The situation was unlikely to change anytime soon.

The massive process industry that was the beer business operated on razor-thin profit margins to begin with, and they faced heavy competition abroad due to high liquor taxes. All of them had attempted to diversify but even for Hinode, whose pharmaceutical business was doing well, beer still exceeded 96 percent of their overall sales, thus things were not so simple. Moreover, at a time when external pressure to censure conglomerations of keiretsu-affiliated groups was sure to grow stronger on the heels of the Japan-US Structural Impediments Initiative, it was obvious that the company could no longer continue to skirt the issue by importing foreign brands and making licensing deals. Therefore, showing progress on their strategy to form a new business alliance with an overseas manufacturer—the company's one and only offensive—was Shiroyama's biggest responsibility during his term in office.

As a matter of fact, the world's largest beer manufacturer, Limelight, with whom Hinode had held an exclusive distribution agreement for the last ten years, was privately consulting with them about their interest in establishing a joint venture. This was a complicated issue, and if they did not meticulously deliberate the terms, the company ran the risk of coming under fire from the Fair Trade Commission— which despised Hinode's oligopolization of the market—and would force them to swallow unfavorable conditions. Even if they formed the joint venture, there was still the fear that domestic products would be upstaged in the future, pinned down as they were by the high liquor tax. And, considering the long-term effects, it might very well hasten their self-destruction to release their nationwide network of six hundred distributors from their contracts. Yet if they were to backpedal even the slightest and this opportunity went elsewhere, everything would be lost. Limelight's move was top-secret, so he would have to keep a close watch on Japan Fair Trade Commission's activities and figure out the right time to start laying the groundwork with the National Tax Agency.

Meanwhile, among their domestic concerns was the issue of a new Nagoya factory. They were accelerating construction because of a desperate need to raise their beer-canning rate, but due to sudden increases in land value, the site acquisition wasn't progressing very smoothly. Then there were the liquor discount stores, who would undoubtedly gain strength from the easement associated with last year's partial revision of how applications for liquor licenses would be handled. This issue would lead to the destruction of every company's network of distributors that had been established during beer's hundred-year history, so realigning their sales channels was an urgent matter.

On the logistics side, he had to figure out what to do about the relationship between Hinode Distribution and the Ogura Group. Personally, he wanted to reassure himself of the bank's intentions regarding their purchase of additional Ogura stock, but what would be the consensus of the board?

"Are we about ready, sir?" asked his driver, always punctual.

"Yes, go ahead," Shiroyama replied.

The driver promptly brought the car over to the front of their main office on the south side of Yatsuyama-dori Avenue in Kita-Shinagawa. The company's new building, completed three years ago, consisted of forty floors paneled entirely in solid granite, which an architecture magazine wrote off as a nouveau-riche knock-off of 1920s New York. The first and second floors housed the Hinode Opera Hall with its world-class acoustics, and on the top floor was the Hinode Sky Beer Restaurant, managed directly by the company's dining division. The remaining thirty-seven floors were occupied by all of the various corporate divisions and twelve of their affiliated companies.

At a quarter past eight, Shiroyama walked through its entrance alone. When he became president he had scrapped the practice of the executive secretary greeting him at the door, so he also carried his own briefcase. He believed that the elimination of wasteful time and expenses must begin at the top, and the matter was considered by and agreed upon by the board. He had also decided that all eight thousand employees of their fifteen regional divisions, forty branch offices, and twelve factories in the nation should be referred to at the company with just the polite suffix "san" after their names, rather than using job titles to refer to superiors. This wasn't to put on airs. Rather, it was implemented to motivate and streamline their organization, but Shiroyama knew that some of the board members viewed it as an aggressive step toward the implementation of a Shiroyama system. It was necessary for him to pretend not to hear talk such as this—otherwise nothing would get done.

From the time he entered the lobby and headed to the elevator banks until he reached the president's executive suite on the thirtieth floor, Shiroyama repeated a mechanical "good morning" about a dozen times whenever he encountered an employee. Since way back, no matter his position at the company, people had always said that his appearance seemed to represent the average Hinode employee, and even now that his hair had grayed, that had not changed and he still did not stand out at all. More than a few times during his stint as managing director, he would walk around the office and hear an employee who passed by murmuring to someone else, "Who's that?"

And when he'd worked in sales as a young man, he had had trouble getting clients to remember his face.

But now that he had become the "face" of Hinode, he had stopped hearing whispers, although at the Japan Business Federation or the Chamber of Commerce and Industry, this was basically the status quo. What it came down to was that they had entered an era in which, by working hard, an anonymous sales machine could rise to the top of management before anyone noticed. As a CEO, Kyosuke Shiroyama was in the vanguard of his generation—men born in the second decade of the Showa era, who were not baptized by the romanticism of the preceding Taisho era. He wasn't cut from the same cloth as those corporate men who adorned the covers of business magazines, nor was he a model of management philosophy. He simply bore the responsibility to protect the profits of all of Hinode's shareholders and employees. Shiroyama acknowledged that he was a management machine that, though lacking a recognizable face, ran the company with sound business acumen and reasonable leadership ability. In truth, he knew would never be anything beyond that.

As he entered the executive suite, Shiroyama said another "good morning" to his secretary, who had risen from her desk in the anteroom. Then, he finally opened the door to his own office in the back.

The secretary, following immediately after him, asked, "May I confirm today's schedule?" She waited until Shiroyama had placed his briefcase on the desk and sat down before presenting an enumerated list to him. Her name was Takako Nozaki; she had been working in this same office for over twenty years. She was a woman who seemed to know instinctively the most efficient way to do things, so Shiroyama rarely made any demands of her. One would not call her beautiful, but there was something comforting about her low, calm voice.

"Will you attend the breakfast meeting at 9? The car will pick you up for the Japan-US Businessmen's Conference at 9:45. Please don't be late. Will you look at the report now?"

"In the car."

"Then I'll gather the documents and wait for you by the entrance. Also, the interview with Asahi Shimbun at 2:30 will be twenty minutes, including a photo session. The questionnaire is . . ."

Ms. Nozaki showed him another sheet of paper with an itemized list of questions, but she knew they would never stick in Shiroyama's mind at such a short notice. "I'll look over them myself beforehand," she added diligently.

"There won't be your usual rounds within the company at 3 today. The task force for the construction of the new Nagoya factory will give a briefing at the business development division, so please attend that instead. The board members who will also be in attendance are listed. Then at 4:15, the honorable Sakata-san from the Liberal Democratic Party will be calling, so please don't forget."

On the schedule, prepared with a word processor, were the words, "Thank-you call from S." The call was in regard to a fundraising ticket.

"Yes. I understand," Shiroyama responded.

"Then, at five there's the ceremony for the Hinode Cultural Awards."

With that, she placed a slim pamphlet in front of him. The award was a project of the Hinode Cultural Foundation, established ten years ago, with both art and music categories. Feeling embarrassed that he had forgotten all about it, Shiroyama replied simply, "Yes."

"The list of recipients and their work is in the pamphlet."

"I'll take a look at it in the car."

"I'll have the car ready for you at the entrance by 4:30. Then, you will be returning at 7 . . ."

And that was that—the confirmation of his schedule first thing in the morning took three minutes. Another three minutes to go over publicity events and advertising, as well as crucial matters regarding business at the different branches and factories.

Last came the reports from the beer, pharmaceutical, and business development divisions, which arrived every Monday; the stack of October's monthly interim financial statements; and clippings from trade publications such as food industry newspapers, all compiled into a folder. After placing them on his desk, Ms. Nozaki then delivered a carafe of water and a glass and promptly disappeared by eight-thirty.

Shiroyama looked at his watch. He had less than half an hour until nine, the official start of business. The accumulation of these half hours every morning was a small point of pride for Shiroyama. He laid out all four sets of documents on his desk, including the reports and the interim financial statements, and began scanning through all of them at once. When it came to numbers, his instincts were useless unless he looked at them everyday. He had no intention of criticizing the details of the accounting; he never said anything about numbers during management meetings, but taking a broad view of the numbers aided him with various decisions, including whether the company was proceeding properly day-to-day, and whether there were any unusual changes in its progress.

But first, last week's results for Hinode Supreme: 520,000 cases. The report noted that, looking ahead to increased demand forecast over Christmas, there was the potential to restore the weekly sales pace of 700,000 cases. Based on the rate of orders to the end of the term, the cumulative forecast was set at upwards of thirty-five million cases. This would ensure them their next-term goal of seventy million cases. However, if the lager—which dominated with 80 percent of their product range—were to fall short of the previous term's cumulative total, this term's year-over-year sales could be on the brink of a deficit.

Next, he quickly skimmed the results of each branch, as well as the production rates and inventory numbers for each factory.

Then it was on to product trends of rival companies. The business development division had done an analysis on the strength of "Winter Dry," which Mainichi Beer—the number two company in the industry—had launched that month as part of their winter strategy. "In terms of product development, what merits special mention is the shift in perspective. As for sales, note their targeted promotion to bars and restaurants, their focused campaign in the greater Kantō region, an increase of rebates, and so on." There were no comments on Winter Dry's reduced alcohol content. Shiroyama made a mental note of this, and his eyes flew to the reports from their product development division. Come to think of it, what happened to their next-term plan to stay ahead of the health craze by making a lower alcohol content the focus of their development concept?

Just as he started to turn the page, he suddenly heard Ms. Nozaki's voice through the intercom on his desk.

"Vice President Shirai and Human Resources Manager Tsuka-moto are here to see you."

Shiroyama looked at his watch. Eight thirty-five.

"Send them in," he answered into the intercom, wondering what they could possibly want now since they were about to see him at the breakfast meeting. The door opened just as he had stacked the documents he had spread on his desk and closed the folder.

"Sorry to bother you so early." The man who said this as he entered was Vice President Sei'ichi Shirai, whose tone was as bland and curt as always. Following behind him was the human resources manager who, in marked contrast, spoke with shoulders hunched somberly and bowed deeply as he said, "I'm afraid we have a situation that might cause you some concern."

Internal strife? Shiroyama wondered how long this would take as he offered them a seat. After all they only had twenty-five minutes to spare.

"So, what is it?" Shiroyama had cut to the chase, just as Shirai replied bluntly, "We received an anonymous, well, tape, instead of a letter."

According to Tsukamoto, who explained the situation, during the selection process for new employees in October, there had been a University of Tokyo graduate who left in the middle of his second interview, saying he felt unwell. He was rejected after apparently going home and failing to return, and subsequently on two separate occasions the human resources department received a letter from the student's father who raised doubts about their selection process. The father was a dentist with a private practice in Setagaya, and he was from a segregated buraku community in Hyogo prefecture. The father was convinced that there was some kind of discrimination in Hinode's screening process. Although the human resources department had responded to his first letter, the second time he had used the name of the BLL, and so they had left it alone, after which they received this cryptic cassette tape.

The truth was, it took Shiroyama about three seconds to decipher the abbreviation BLL. It took him another minute to understand the point of the story, after which he suspected there must be some kind of mistake. Even if it were true, he settled upon mild wonderment as to why such a matter had made it all the way up to him.

"Here is a transcript of the tape."

On the first page of the stack of A4-size paper that Tsukamoto presented him were the words: *Hinode Beer Company, Kanagawa Factory, To Whom It May Concern*. Shiroyama distractedly leafed through the twenty or thirty pages and was shocked to find the date June 1947 on the last page. He quickly turned back to the first page and began scanning through the document.

"We had the Kanagawa factory look into it, and the Seiji Okamura who appears here did in fact leave Hinode in 1947," Tsukamoto continued. Meanwhile, Shiroayama's eyes quickly singled out various words from the contents of the pages. Place names from the Tohoku region such as "Hachinohe" and "Herai." Phrases such as, "someone from a buraku village," "labor union," "conflict," "General Strike of February 1st," and "discharged." And finally, "The second convention of the National Committee for Buraku Liberation." Ah, right, that's what they used to call themselves, he recalled, but that was the extent of it. He reread the last lines of the transcript of the tape, the whole of which amounted to many pages, but he still could not fathom the intention of the sender.

"Is this all?"

"Yes. Whatever his objective may be, it seems to involve our employment screening process, and since the problem also concerns the reputation of the company, we thought that this decision goes beyond the discretion of the human resources department, including whether to report it to the police or to ignore it. That's why we are informing you," Tsukamoto said as he rubbed his hands idly.

"Do we have the original letter that this Okamura sent to the Kanagawa factory?"

"The factory has no way of looking up something from all the way back in 1947, so whether or not such a letter actually existed . . ."

"The father of this student in question, you said he used the name of the BLL in his second letter? Does the sender of the tape identify himself?"

"No. But the labels and postmarks are the same, and according to our investigation, this Seiji Okamura turns out to be a distant relative of the student."

"Aha . . ." Shiroyama uttered ambiguously, but what was beginning to concern him more were the company's internal issues that tended to reveal themselves in situations like this. In the first place, what was the general affairs division doing about it, since they were normally expected to handle this type of problem? Moreover, whether this was a general affairs or a human resources issue, Shirai was not the executive in charge. Shiroyama glanced at Shirai as this thought crossed his mind, but Shirai wore an innocuous expression, as if everything had been obvious to him from the beginning.

"I understand the situation," Shiroyama said again to Tsukamoto. "I will let you know what I decide later. Please see to it in your department that word doesn't get out about the tape."

"I will do so."

With a look that seemed to bemoan what an unlucky day this was, Tsukamoto stood up from his seat and bowed as he left the room. When Shiroyama had joined the company in 1959, Tsukamoto had already been occupying a desk in what was then called the personnel division for quite some time. They hardly had any contact until Tsukamoto became head of the division, but he had settled in at the company—Tsukamoto was a dyed-in-the-wool pencil pusher—and was now a diligent support pillar in the corporate structure. Though the lackluster of this man presented itself as a minor concern for Shiroyama.

On the one hand, Sei'ichi Shirai was an executive both in name and in practice—here was a man who had transformed the company by putting an end to the lockstep and conservative tradition of Hinode's executive team. His appearance was just as unremarkable as that of Shiroyama, but of the thirty-five board members, Shirai's keen foresight and ability to get things done was second to none. Ten years ago, when Hinode still had a 60-percent market share, Shirai was already criticizing the beer business's inefficiency and lack of viability, and its difficulties competing against foreign products. Since then, he had created a diversified, long-term plan that anticipated the future, and as a result of his laying the groundwork for the improvement of Hinode's stronghold, he now played an integral role on Hinode's executive team as EVP and head of business development. Shirai's approach—neither a simple pursuit of profit nor a prosaic philosophy—evaluated corporate activities as a holistic system on a macro level, and in a way, this is what made him a prime example of the management machine. But Shirai possessed something Shiroyama fundamentally lacked, even if they were part of the same management machine, and if Shiroyama were honest with himself, this was a constant source of anxiety. Shirai had spent considerable time living abroad in the US and Europe, and his true worth was his will and the assertiveness with which he made that will known.

Such thoughts now flickered in Shiroyama's mind as his eyes drifted over the cityscape seen from the large windows on either side of his desk. The commanding view from the thirtieth floor undulated outward, as if the random unevenness of the buildings below had been leveled, and for an instant the wriggling cars and people looked like products rolling along an automated factory line. There were times when Shiroyama looked down from the window and wondered if his was the same general perspective as all CEOs, but no doubt in Shirai's eyes, from this height the scene appeared to him as a line that should function at the highest efficiency in every respect. What stretched out before him was a system—it was neither human nor thing.

On the other hand, Shiroyama moved of his own accord, his body feeling lighter or heavier from day to day, still carrying a sense of having sold goods with his own hands for more than twenty years, and perhaps it was because of this—if he were to let his feelings be known—that his and Shirai's sensibilities were somewhat incompatible.

Incidentally, there was another EVP at Hinode, Seigo Kurata, who had taken over the beer division after Shiroyama had been promoted. In contrast to Shirai, who continued to push for diversification, Kurata sustained the reality that beer still topped 96 percent of their overall sales. It was clear as day that Shirai was only able to wield his talents because there were men like Kurata who sold beer to the tune of 1.2 trillion, and now that under the current executive structure both Shirai and Kurata had become EVPs, the truth was that the difference in their approaches to corporate strategy divided the board into Shirai and Kurata factions even more than before.

What this difference came down to was whether to focus on a long-range outlook or the concerns of the moment. This disparity was brought to a head two years ago when, confronted by declining sales of their lager, a decision was forced regarding whether or not to proceed with a diversified product strategy. If they were to incite a competition, randomly releasing new products several times a year to counter other brands' offensives, it would lead to a significant increase in costs to reorder production lines, as well as increased costs for product and sales management, and expanded advertising and promotional fees and so on—all of which would mire them down, essentially putting a noose around their own neck. It was a decision that could weaken the entire beer industry, so Shirai insisted that he could not agree to an excessive diversification of products, but at the core of his logic was an assessment of the managerial efficiency of Hinode's entire system, which already carried twelve factories.

Meanwhile, on the beer division's side, Shiroyama and Kurata ensured that if it came to that, Hinode, with its basic and fundamental strength, would be last one standing, an assertion driven by pride in the Hinode brand and the current hard-and-fast numbers. It was a futile clash—each side was correct in their own way but only about their own argument—and ultimately, on the judgment of the current chairman, they agreed to a fair enough compromise—they would issue new products when they needed to, and when they didn't need to they wouldn't.

Shortly thereafter, a longer-than-anticipated decline in lager sales precipitated Shiroyama's promotion from head of the beer division to president, on the consensus of the board who had no choice but to strengthen the beer business, however the fact of the matter was that the need for diversification was more urgent than ever. Shiroyama and Kurata's beer lines, which had been the backbone of Hinode for so many years, were now the last stand and, more than anyone, Shiroyama was aware of the drastic reform that the division required. He had yet to acknowledge it publicly, though. In these board meetings where various emotionally-charged conflicts, factional manuevering, and backroom deals were the norm, it was important to bide one's time for the right moment to say anything.

Obviously the real reason Shirai had appeared during the busiest time in Shiroyama's morning was because he intended to make a deal with him, one that presumably had to do with controlling some kind of move by Kurata. But Shiroyama made a point to devote enough time to ascertain Shirai's motive for showing up like this, especially since Shiroyama's sentiments were so clearly aligned with Kurata's.

The human resources manager Tsukamoto had left after delivering his somewhat absurd story, and now Shirai leaned forward slightly, as if to signal that he was about to begin the real topic of conversation. Here it comes, Shiroyama thought, and glanced at the clock. Eight forty-three.

Shiroyama thought back over Tsukamoto's explanation, recalling that there were certain problematic details. "I have two questions if you don't mind," he said, beating Shirai to it. "First, how did you become involved in a matter that you are not in charge of?"

"Oh, that. Tsukamoto had been looking rather pale in the face these past few days, so I just happened to ask him what was the matter. Not surprisingly he was loath to admit that they'd received an anonymous letter and a tape over trouble with the screening process for new employees," Shirai responded without any defensiveness. "By the way, Tsukamoto forgot to mention something important. This student, Hatano, he was killed in a car accident on the fifteenth last month. They say he was speeding, but it's not unthinkable that his father may have lost all sense because of it."

In the moment Shiroyama took to find the words to respond, Shirai added, "It's an unfortunate story, sure, but since it was a car accident, I have to say that it's of no concern to our company."

"Can I trust nothing took place that would make the other party suspicious of us?"

"I myself was at the second interview, so I can guarantee you that."

"But I would think rejecting a University of Tokyo student who made it as far as a second interview is out of the ordinary, no matter the reason."

"You're absolutely right. Since Hatano left in the middle of his interview on the tenth because he felt sick, the next day the screening committee did in fact get into a minor debate about how to handle his case. Ultimately, we decided that in order to reject a student who came with a recommendation, we would need to meet with him again in person, so on the eleventh I instructed human resources to contact him—"

"And?"

"When I asked Tsukamoto about it earlier, they had contacted neither his home nor his university. He said they only contacted the university on the twelfth to let them know his application had been rejected. When I pressed Tsukamoto about what exactly happened, he said that Kurata had apparently instructed human resources not to bother any more with this student. Then I asked Kurata about it—"

Shirai paused to take a breath. Then he came out with it slowly. "This whole thing traces back to a problem with Sugihara's daughter."

"You mean Takeo Sugihara?"

"Yes."

This past June, in a staff reshuffling, Takeo Sughihara had been appointed deputy general manager of the beer division and a board member. Twenty-five years ago, Sugihara had married Shiroyama's younger sister, so their daughter was his niece. Naturally, Sugihara fell into line with Shiroyama and Kurata.

Unable to immediately grasp the situation, it took a moment for Shiroyama's shock to form. Shirai continued in a clerical tone, ignoring Shiroyama's confusion. Shirai was like a blowfish, Shiroyama had often thought. Shirai the blowfish never suffered from autotoxemia, always saying the reasonable thing in a coherent manner, but now and then the people around him would fall victim to his poison.

"Shiroyama-san. I will only speak of the facts here. Your niece had been dating Hatano at University of Tokyo, and apparently she told her father that she wanted to marry him after graduation. When a parent hears such a thing from his daughter, well, he's going to look into the young man's background, isn't he? The result was, there was an issue with the father's family register, so Sugihara told his daughter he wouldn't allow it—this is the story that Kurata forced out of Sugihara the other day."

Hearing this much, Shiroyama finally felt his heart quickening, but the reality of the situation still had not hit home. During the past thirty-one years, his work or the mention of it had never carried over into his personal life—not even once—and his mind now experienced a dull confusion for the first time.

He had seen his younger sister over the summer during the Obon holiday, the festival of the dead, but the last time he saw his niece's face had probably been at New Year's. His niece had worn a kimono, which had been made specially for her coming-of-age ceremony, and his sense of admiration that she had grown into quite a young lady quickly dissipated when she put out her hands and, with an obsequious bow of her head, asked, "Uncle, my New Year's money?" It did not matter that she was a University of Tokyo student—in Shiroyama's eyes, she was still just a girl. Speaking of which, at the beginning of fall, hadn't Sugihara himself mentioned that she would either go on to graduate school or study abroad? As he vaguely recalled these things, Shiroyama calmly examined each facet of the story, one by one.

When did Sugihara speak to his daughter about her boyfriend? And at that time, did he say anything to her about Hatano's buraku connections? Did she then tell this young man—Hatano—about it? And if so, when? Until these things became clear, the cause and effect of Hatano's leaving during the second interview on October tenth remained uncertain.

Shirai continued, ignoring Shiroyama's prolonged silence. "Shiroyama-san. Whatever the reason Hatano decided to leave before the completion of his second interview, I think it's best for Hinode not to get involved. There was no blunder on the company's part, at least not in terms of the screening process, so there is no need to say more about it."

"I'd like to know—was Sugihara at the second interview or not?"

"He was not. If Sugihara and the student in question had come face to face at the interview, it would have complicated matters, but since they did not—no matter what transpired personally—we should deem this occurrence as unrelated to the company."

"Then why did Kurata go to the trouble of instructing human resources to quash things?"

"That has to do with an extortionist," Shirai answered simply.

This cleared away one of Shiroyama's suspicions, and the pieces fell into place.

"You mean the story was leaked . . ."

"It seems that way. Since Hatano disappeared from the site of the interview, human resources had a lot to handle that day and was distracted."

"What have been the extortionist's exact moves?"

"On the night of the second interview, Kurata received a strange call at home from someone who wouldn't give his name. The caller mentioned the name of a certain individual, and that this person has a connection with Seiji Okamura, who is a distant relative of Hatano."

Shiroyama looked down at the name "Seiji Okamura" on the first page of the transcript of the anonymous tape.

"And who is this individual?"

"Yoshinori Toda. The tape does not mention him by name, but it refers to him. He's the man who was fired from our Kyoto factory in 1946 for inciting a dispute. I've looked him up—he now works as a freelance writer, and he's been digging around about Chunichi Mutual Savings Bank."

In his mind, Shiroyama was able to make some sense of the story. Someone who had heard about Hatano's second interview deduced that the incident was relatively unusual, quickly fished around the student's family history, somehow found the name Seiji Okamura among his relatives and, while he was at it, uncovered Okamura's erstwhile connection to this writer Toda, which he determined could be of use.

"In any case, I assume Kurata warned human resources against saying anything sheerly to avoid trouble, but in the interest of maintaining consistency, what he did was not very good," said Shirai, arriving at his first conclusion. Shirai's method was to stick pins, one by one, into those surrounding him, as a means of securing his own logically coherent path. Just now, he had stabbed a pin into Kurata's wings over his handling of the matter within human resources, and Shiroyama wondered if by bringing up the story of Sugihara and his daughter, who were his relations, Shirai had meant to pin his own wings as well.

The blowfish himself might have had no such intention, and now he lightly scratched his head of abundant gray hair, then with the same hand tapped Shiroyama's desk as he sat upright in his chair. There were many employees who, whenever Shirai adjusted his position like this, felt compelled to straighten their own posture.

"You know, Shiroyama-san, even supposing this tape was just a prank, if someone is pulling the strings behind the scenes, I feel this problem needs a bit of attention."

What Shirai was trying to say now was probably similar to what Shiroyama had been thinking as he listened to Tsukamoto's version of the story. Shiroyama sensed this was not a conversation he should ignore, so he prudently kept his personal feelings to himself for the time being.

He looked at the clock. Eight-fifty.

"Please go on," Shiroyama succinctly encouraged him.

"The Okada Association is behind this," Shirai said. Just as Shiroyama had expected.

Known as an enterprise composed of corporate extortionists, corporate raiders, loan sharks, and financial brokers, among others, the entity known as the Okada Association was in fact the corporate underling of a large crime syndicate known as the Seiwakai, or so Shiroyama had heard from top officials at the Tokyo Metropolitan Police Department. Ultranationalist bigwigs guarded access to Seiwakai, granting entrée to various politicians, followed by a trail of government agencies and financial capital from commercial banks and securities. Among Hinode's board members and the representative from general affairs whose job it was to deal with such corporate extortionists, they were referred to simply as "Okada."

Confidentially Shiroyama had been informed that both Ogura Transport, a company affiliated with Hinode, and Chunichi Mutual Savings, its main creditor, were currently facing loan problems, and that Okada was secretly and intricately entangled in the situation. He immediately understood that this situation must be connected to that one.

Hinode was not directly involved in the matter with Ogura and Chunichi, but as long as Okada was involved, it was hard to deny an indirect connection. Moreover, since this was by nature a world in which people got away with offering their right hand to shake while making threats with their left, it wouldn't be out of the question for

Okada to use Hinode's years of loyalty against them and launch a new attack. Shirai's remark—The Okada Association is behind this—implied all of these circumstances. Nevertheless, Kurata was the one who had managed the company's relationship with Okada for years, and Shirai still had no business offering his opinion on the situation.

"So, what kind of moves have they made?"

"Neither Chunichi nor Ogura will be able to avoid an investigation at some point. Having anticipated this, Okada has probably started taking precautions."

Sure, but just how accurate is this story? Shiroyama wondered as he nodded cautiously.

"It means Okada is also getting nervous. It's a good time to strike," Shirai pressed on, his speech now progressing to the pet theory he had been hinting at for quite some time. "I've made the same suggestion to Chairman Suzuki, but we should wait and see how the situation may change before intervening in the management of Ogura Transport. If we were to pursue things now, the public would say Hinode has bought up stolen goods. That would give Okada even more leverage against us."

"Yes."

"Our main issue is Limelight. As the executive in charge, I'm most fearful of the JFTC exploiting our weakness. They might leak the story of our joint venture with Limelight to put pressure on us. Then again, Okada might also leak it. You can't deny that we are walking through a minefield right now."

"Right."

"And I know you have no objection to the assessment that Okada is a malignant tumor for Hinode. There is a right time for settling accounts. Luckily for us, this time Okada has exposed its tail in a completely unrelated matter. Now, about this tape with the reading out of Okamura's letter—wouldn't it be fine to notify the police about how the tape was sent to us by the student's father, at least?"

"What?"

"I'd like to figure out a way to file a claim with the police, without naming that dentist Hiroyuki Hatano as the sender of the tape. I also want to include the second letter where he assumed the BLL's name."

"—Perhaps you're right."

Shiroyama looked at the clock. The minute hand read five to nine. Time was up.

"I understand what you're saying. I'll talk it over with Kurata."

"Please let me know your decision as soon as possible. It's already been five days since we received the tape."

"Indeed. Personally, I can't help but feel we did wrong by that student Hatano, so I'm reluctant to involve a grieving father in a police matter in addition to all that's happened. At this point, it's not as if we've suffered any actual damage."

"Once we do suffer damage, it'll be too late. To be honest, I have a bad feeling about this," Shirai said as he stood up.

"What do you mean?"

"There is no such thing as a premonition without a cause. Just like there can be no revelation for those of us who don't pray."

Every so often, Shirai made reference to the fact that Shiroyama was a Christian and he himself non-religious, but each time he did so he looked like a young man weary of debating conceptual matters. There was no time, however, to respond to his remark. Shiroyama also rose from his seat. Outside the thirtieth-floor window, the morning cityscape emanated a faint glow as it basked in the thin sunlight of late autumn.

"By the way, which board members know about the tape?"

"You, me, and Kurata," Shirai replied. The executives in charge of general affairs and human resources, who ought to have been informed in cases like this, were kept out of the loop. Well, well, Shiroyama thought. Shirai had also stabbed a pin through Tsukamoto from human resources.

AS A SALES MACHINE, SHIROYAMA'S sole mission had been to sell as many cases of product as possible, and throughout those years of experience he himself had witnessed his fair share of the ins and outs of corporate activities, but it wasn't until he was promoted that he became acutely aware of the tumor that was stealthily attached to such ordinary occurrences. A beer company couldn't get by just making and selling beer. Not that Hinode was special—it was the same with any other corporation.

After revisions to the Commercial Code in 1982, there were generally two roads that corporations could take. One way was to sever all ties to corporate extortionists; the other was to maintain a relationship by subtly changing its form, and like so many other corporations, Hinode opted for the latter. The reason went far beyond the simple need to avoid trouble; the choice was made in the face of a reality that, even before the Commercial Code, corporations alone could not change the systematic customs of this country.

In Hinode's case, however, the various expenditures to the Okada Association far exceeded an amount that could be approved by the manager of general affairs, and it was a dubious honor that the responsibility of dealing with Okada had been tacitly entrusted to Kurata. The fact was that, after all these years, nobody on the board could determine the limits of reasonable conduct—or just what that meant, anyway. Under such circumstances, when Shirai took his position as a board member six years ago, he asserted the need to settle their accounts as soon as possible, a hair-raising prospect for all the other members. At the time, Kurata had scoffed at the notion, indignation draining the color from his face. "I'd appreciate if you wouldn't so easily insinuate yourself into a matter I've been taking responsibility for," he had retorted.

The context for the argument's turning so emotional was the corporate culture that supported such deep personal connections to political and business circles and ultranationalist groups, connections that had carried over from the zaibatsu era. Since a beer business couldn't exist without distribution, in addition to its network of ten affiliated land transportation companies, Hinode controlled extensive real estate throughout the country. One might say that here was where the problem stemmed from, but every root was entwined with all of Japan's economic activities and financial capital. Kurata could not be faulted for recognizing that it was not so simple as one corporation upholding a naïve sense of social justice on its own. Justice for a corporation was its ability to reap a profit.

And yet, Shirai was also correct that there was no long-term gain in Hinode's continued entanglements with these subterranean roots. Shirai was not simply urging them to settle accounts. His argument was that they needed to make careful preparations and the necessary calculations in order to sever all ties. Shiroyama was well aware that over the last six years Shirai had been looking for an opportunity at every turn to lay the groundwork at board meetings to build consensus for his strategy.

Shiroyama also knew that the tide was about to turn. The economic boom would eventually end. Real estate and stock prices would readjust accordingly. If he were to predict what would succeed this gilded era of mass consumption, it would be, in a nutshell, "petit-bourgeois fastidiousness." The mentality of citizens that could be summed up in such key words as thriftiness, downsizing, simplicity, and individualism would drive them to abandon material wealth in favor of emotional fulfillment, and to insist upon "fastidiousness" in society. In such a demanding era, the character of the political world, not just banks and corporations, would be challenged to follow suit. The age in which corporations would be scrutinized about their social responsibility and morals before their pursuit of profit was just around the corner.

If he were to examine his own company this way, Hinode's management practices, which boasted an equity ratio of 47 percent, were clearly sound, but the reality was that Hinode's overwhelming superiority did not align with an image of "fastidiousness." From their ties to the National Tax Agency on down through various regulatory agencies, to their corporate keiretsu alliances throughout sales and distribution, and their designated shareholders comprised of major banks and insurance companies—every one of these factors would be considered out of step with everyday people's lifestyle. And if their connection to a shadowy realm such as Okada became public, Hinode's hundred-year-old brand image would collapse.

It was true that something had to be done about Okada. And just like that, Shiroyama had added another item of concern to his list—and it was still so early. But by the time he entered one of the executive conference rooms with Shirai, he wore an expression appropriate for the start of the day, presenting himself to the staff assembled there and repeating more morning greetings.

The executive breakfast meeting that took place the second Monday of every month had been a tradition at Hinode for more than twenty years. Those invited included the twenty executives at the main office as well as the presidents and vice presidents of each subsidiary company, but since they each had their own various affairs to tend to, attendance generally amounted to around twenty people. Since everyone sat down in the order they arrived, seatmates changed every time, so that they spoke with different people about different topics. Thus, while they ate their three-thousand-yen bento boxes delivered from Matsukado, they exchanged only generic news and information; there was a tacit agreement that serious subjects would not be discussed.

When Shiroyama took a seat, he found himself for the first time in quite a while next to the president of Hinode Beverage, who had already dangled the new health drink commercial that had gone on air last week as a conversation starter. "That monster that goes dancing by, it's pretty weird, no?" "The monster's supposed to be from Saturn." "Oh, really?" "Now I get it, that's why it's wearing a skirt." "Oh, that's a skirt?" And so the mindless chatter around him continued.

"Say, Shiroyama-san. That commercial for Lemon Sour, it's weird, right?" President Ishizuka of Hinode Beverage suddenly addressed him, to which Shiroyama replied vaguely, "Oh, sure." Meanwhile, a scan of the room confirmed that Takeo Sugihara was not present. Since Sugihara regularly attended this meeting, Shiroyama wondered if his absence today might mean that Kurata, his superior, had spoken to him about the issue with his daughter.

"Well, that ad is now a hit. It seems that young people today appreciate a fresh kind of 'weirdness.' That's what the guys from Mainichi Advertising tell me," President Ishizuka continued.

It was Seigo Kurata who responded, "If that's the case, our '100 Years in the Making' spot with its gold letters and Viennese waltz might be too orthodox. And that one's also by Mainichi Advertising."

Kurata was a big man—the exact opposite of Shiroyama and Shirai—and his taciturnity, in inverse proportion to his physicality, also made him stand out among the board members. His face was even less remarkable than Shiroyama's and Shirai's, yet he gave the impression that only actual results mattered, which had earned him the nickname "the whiz" within the corporate world, and no one would deny that his savvy was the backbone of the beer division. To wit, in the caricatures that appeared in last month's in-house newsletter, this silent torpedo of a man was rendered as an ox with a nondescript face, while Shiroyama was depicted as a penguin and Shirai as a woodpecker.

Even now, after taking the position of vice president, Kurata never took his eyes off the various numbers coming in from their branch offices and stores and, with every inch of the company's sales network in mind, he read the weekly stats and compared these figures with the marketing analysis reports. He would observe any variations silently for the first month, and if they continued for a second month then he would call the branch office or stores directly himself; in the mornings Kurata's phone line was generally busy. He was never in the office in the afternoons—almost every day of the week he was off visiting a branch company or a factory or a distributor. Back when he was still deputy sales manager, one of the executives had remarked, "Kurata is a torpedo." What he had meant was that one could not see Kurata's face because it was always submerged beneath the numbers.

And for the past ten years, Kurata had neatly tucked away his relationship with the likes of the Okada Association somewhere within his businesslike persona. Owing to the incompetence of the director of general affairs and the executive in charge at the time—who knows what the actual details were—apparently one of the EVPs had simply asked Kurata to take care of the problem. It was a while before Shiroyama, his superior, even learned that Kurata was handling it, and when he asked him about it, Kurata maintained his tight-lipped nature. Before Shirai started poking around about it six years ago, it was considered taboo to mention Okada at board meetings, and whatever weariness or frustration Kurata may have felt in shouldering such a taboo on his own could only be glimpsed in his slight stoop.

The conversation around the table had not let up, and with Kurata's comments added to the mix, Hinode Lager's 100 Years in the Making commercial became fodder for all. "It's true that Hinode Lager can come off as orthodox, but that Viennese waltz spot actually flips our brand image on its head and pushes it to the edge. Does everybody see that?" asked an executive in charge of advertising. Someone then replied, "You're right. That commercial is an elegant spoof," while another added, "We ought to try selling beer by embracing the weird," which was followed by laughter.

Ishizuka continued, "I met with the managing director of Dentsu the other day. He heartily endorsed the new commercial. He said Hinode's sense for advertising is really cutting edge." Shiroyama agreed with this. Once Hinode stopped depending on the overwhelming dominance of the lager—and in order to strip away their imposing and traditional image in accordance with their diversification policy—their entire advertising strategy had been entrusted to their young employees. This was already starting to show results. After all, they were the ones who had turned Shiroyama into a penguin and Shirai into a woodpecker.

"That's great to hear," Shiroyama said, and a chorus of agreement and series of nods followed. Then someone else offered, "I hear the cultural awards this year were a great success," and the conversation flowed into another direction.

"Where's Sugihara?" Shiroyama asked Kurata, trying to be nonchalant.

"A business trip to the Osaka branch," Kurata responded tersely, leaving it at that for the time being. Just then another executive quipped, "Speaking of which, I hear the Supreme is doing well in Osaka," which was followed by "Not surprisingly, in the Kansai region they seem to prefer a higher alcohol content," and then, "Even if we reduced the alcohol content for the Tokyo market, I think it would take a few years for the Kansai region to follow suit." Finally, it was Kurata who said, "We need to start thinking about region-specific products."

"By the way, Shiroyama-san. I hear there'll be a CIA spy at today's Japan-US Businessmen's Conference," another executive piped up.

"Surely they're not getting money from some corporation," Shiroyama shrugged it off with a bitter smile.

Shirai interjected, "We'll just have to let the auto industry be their target for a while." However, everyone was aware that the delicate, behind-the-scenes negotiations with Limelight were about to begin, and so the topic was swiftly dropped.

Just like that, his first-item-of-the-day breakfast meeting was finished in a quick half hour, and Shiroyama got up from his seat, leaving half of the Matsukado bento box that he usually polished off. Reminding himself that Ms. Nozaki would be waiting for him with his briefcase at the front entrance at nine-forty, he hesitated a moment as he left the conference room, overcome with unease that he had forgotten to do something.

Then, perhaps waiting for just such an opportunity, Seigo Kurata began casually walking alongside him. "The matter with the student Hatano and his father," he said. "Did Shirai tell you about it?"

Shiroyama nodded.

Since he and Kurata had worked in the beer division together for a quarter of a century, selling beer side by side, they were in lockstep with each other, both literally and figuratively. Kurata may have been known as a torpedo, but there was great range to his quiet breathing, and he often silenced himself to contain his rising emotions—all this Shiroyama felt he understood. After they both became executives, they had consciously started to distance themselves from each other, but in the time it took to cover the dozen steps to the elevator hall, they managed a brief exchange.

"There's no need to be concerned about the issue with Sugihara and your niece. Sugihara's investigation into Hatano's background had nothing to do with the company."

Kurata's voice was low and people thought of him as deadpan, but Shiroyama's ears picked up each and every emotion lurking beneath the surface as clear as a bell. He was conscious that Kurata was extremely irritated, though at what his irritation was directed he would never know.

"And besides, Okada hasn't fully grasped the story either. Besides sniffing out the trouble with the second interview, all they've managed to do is look up Hatano's family and dig up material they can use from that letter sent by a distant relation they somehow happened to get their hands on."

"Was it that journalist?"

"Yes. And by the way, I'll make sure Okada's exposed tail gets a little thrashing this time."

For an instant, Shiroyama thought he had misheard him. It wasn't that Kurata had said the same thing as Shirai. Using his own methods, Kurata was making every effort to contact Okada, find out whatever information Okada had on hand and, once he had determined their motive, he intended to launch an attack. Even in a world where shaking hands with the right hand while doing battle with the left was common, for Kurata—who had dedicated himself to maintaining their relationship with Okada—to say such a thing had serious implications, which went beyond Shirai's argument.

"Is the situation with Ogura and Chunichi that serious?"

"There's word going around that S. might get caught up in the mix."

S.—suddenly Shiroyama pictured the face of Sakata, the representative who was scheduled to give him a thank-you call that afternoon about the fundraising ticket, but he could not imagine the circumstances in which the most influential figure in the ruling party would be swept up in an investigation. Yes, Shiroyama dimly recalled having been warned that attention must be paid to the flow of money related to the land purchased by Ogura Development, Ogura's affiliated company, as it could lead to a bribery scandal, but it was difficult for a corporate man like himself to grasp all this. If such a possibility really did exist, then it was all the more urgent that they settle accounts with Okada, lest it land Hinode in real trouble. Though it rattled him a little, his annoyance about this and the necessary steps against Okada were still both so vague in his mind that they didn't seem relevant to today or even tomorrow.

"It means we've arrived at the moment when Shirai's arguments make sense," Kurata murmured softly, his words cast down at his own feet. Shiroyama could not make out the tone of his voice as it reached his ears. Kurata continued, touching upon the specific measures he would take. "I'll have general affairs file an official claim with the police. And I'll make sure that we don't refer to either Okada or the dentist."

Kurata was saying the same thing as Shirai, but without elaborating on how he had reached such a conclusion, which, at this late stage, irritated Shiroyama. "Kurata-san. This issue must eventually be brought before the entire board. When you feel it's necessary for everyone to be made aware of what has happened, I urge you to report it immediately."

"When the time is right, I will. For now, we need to take care of accounting." Kurata finally looked up as he said this. The sunlight streaming through the windows of the elevator hall shone on his face. Shiroyama considered that the same view from the thirtieth floor must appear differently to Kurata than it did to him and to Shirai.

"Make sure we at least clear last year's figures," Shiroyama said.

Kurata immediately responded, "Just point one percent more. That's two hundred seventy thousand cases."

"If only the lager's numbers would rise."

"I'm also dissatisfied with the numbers from the past two weeks. I'll have all the branches reset their target numbers for next month, and I'll drive them to hit two hundred seventy thousand cases no matter what. You'll see."

As he said this, Kurata's face gleamed with a vexing confidence.

SHIROYAMA'S DAY WAS NOT PARTICULARLY busy. By the time he returned to the office after the Hinode Cultural Awards at the Hotel Okura—having put in a brief appearance at the reception—it was just after seven-thirty. He sent Ms. Nozaki home, thanking her for her efforts, and once he was alone, he sorted through the telephone messages and memos that were arranged on his desk along with his mail, and then spread out the business reports and interim financial statements that he had not gone over that morning.

By the time he started writing in the daily log that he kept, it was eight-thirty.

8:35 A.M.: *Visit from Shirai and Tsukamoto. Confirm any issues with chain of communication within human resources.* Shiroyama's hand halted after he had written these words on the first line. It was the end of the day, so he allowed himself to draw out the personal incident that had been bothering him since the morning and think it over, then reached for the phone.

The phone rang four times before he heard a young woman's voice say, "Sugihara residence."

"Yoshiko?"

"Oh, Uncle. Are you still at work?"

"Yes. It's been a while. How are you doing?"

"My thesis isn't coming along very well," she replied. Usually his niece was much more effusive: I'm great! When are you taking me out to eat, Uncle?

"Is your father home?"

"Yes. I'll go get him."

"Before you do, I'd like to ask you about Takayuki Hatano. I'm sorry to hear that he died in a car accident. Did you know he had applied for a job here?"

"No." The girl replied after a brief pause, and her voice shook with genuine distress.

"Hatano had his second interview with the company on the tenth of last month. When was the last time you saw him?"

Now she waited for an extra moment before responding, "October ninth."

"I'm sorry to be so intrusive, but where did you see him?"

"At the university." His niece's voice had sunk lower and, on the verge of tears, she said, "I'm going to switch to the phone in my room, could you hang on?" She put the phone on hold, and as Shiroyama waited, part of him began to regret making the call.

He heard his niece's voice return. "Did I cause some kind of trouble for the company?"

"No, this isn't about that. So on the ninth, what did you and Hatano talk about?"

"I told him I'm leaving home and I wanted him to come live with me—"

"And why would you do such a thing?"

"Because Mother and Father are stupid."

"You have to be more clear. Explain it to me."

"I had kept our relationship a secret, and when I finally told my parents over summer break, Father hired a detective agency to investigate Hatano's family, and he told me to forget about marrying him because his father was from a segregated buraku community. And I figured I don't need parents who would say such stupid things in this day and age. So I took my savings and looked for an apartment. When I saw him on the ninth . . . I had no idea he was applying for a job at Hinode. He told me he was going to graduate school—"

"When you saw him on the ninth, what did you two talk about?"

"He was shocked when I told him I was leaving home . . . He asked me why things had come to this so suddenly, and I had no idea how to explain it to him and—"

According to his niece, on October ninth, in the course of describing to Hatano the details about what had happened, she

ultimately brought up the issue with the segregated community. Shiroyama had to stop himself from shouting at her—he was at a loss
for words. His niece had meant no harm, but she had been quite
thoughtless. He wondered how his sister and Sugihara could possibly
have raised their daughter to be this way.

Since Shiroyama remained silent, his niece asked again in a tearful
voice, "Did I cause problems for the company?"

"This isn't about the company. It's about you and Hatano. You
should have thought a bit more about his feelings. Do you understand? Your parents may be stupid, but you behaved inconsiderately
yourself."

As he listened to his niece's weeping over the phone, he kept
asking himself, What is the point of saying all these things now?
What good does it do to act rationally now? How am I going to deal
with this situation? These questions shook him to his core.

"And did you attend Hatano's funeral?"

"How could I? His parents have no idea who I am. There's no way
for me to apologize!"

"Yoshiko. Listen to me. Hatano's car accident is not your fault.
You didn't kill him. Do you understand? With that said, you must
now think about his grieving parents first, and there's something you
must do. So must your parents. This is not a problem that you can
figure out and resolve on your own. I will talk to your father for you,
so please put him on."

While he waited on hold again, he pondered what his niece, Sugihara, and his sister could have possibly been thinking over the past
month. Shiroyama thought about how for quite some time he and his
wife had been living a monotonous and peaceful life after sending a
boy and a girl of their own into the world without much trouble—
no, actually what he felt now was displeasure toward his relatives
coupled with anger about the dishonor that would reflect back on
him. This fact itself was already the source of an uneasiness he had
never grappled with before. In particular, he was nothing if not livid
when he thought about Takeo Sugihara's absence at this morning's

breakfast meeting and his almost certain lack of focus on his work; and as a fellow salaryman who knew there had to be a better way to have handled things, his fury only mounted when he considered such incredibly careless behavior from Sugihara, a man who had followed a steady and sure career track.

A despondent voice came on the line. "Yes. Sugihara speaking."

"I heard all the details from Yoshiko regarding this student Hatano. Make some time tomorrow and go with her to pay your respects to the deceased."

"About that, Kurata said—"

"This doesn't concern the company. It concerns our family. It concerns your own integrity."

"I wanted to go see them. But Kurata must have his own reasons too! He told me to pretend I had nothing to do with it—what was I supposed to do?"

"I don't care about the company. This is a family problem. I'll take responsibility for the company—I'm well aware of Kurata's thought process. I will speak to him myself, and you do what you must do as head of the family. Hatano's father is a dentist, so best to visit him during his midday break, or after he's finished seeing patients. Understood?"

Sugihara hesitated briefly before he asked, "Is this about the Okada Association?"

Shiroyama was forced to reiterate, "That has nothing to do with your family's problem." Though as he spoke these words, he felt disgusted with himself and wondered what right he had to stick his nose in someone else's family business. This was not Sugihara's family problem at all—it was indeed the company's problem. Sugihara, bemoaning what he could have possibly done differently, felt real anguish, yet the words out of Shiroyama's mouth were so haughty and stereotypical that he himself shuddered.

"You are a father before you are a company man! No need to mention how you investigated his background—it could lead to more misunderstanding—but I'd like you to consider the feelings of these grieving parents, and to treat them with as much respect and courtesy as possible. I ask you as your brother-in-law."

Shiroyama recoiled from his own mean logic, but a part of him coolly observed such reasoning and assessed, So this is the kind of man I am. He had advised against mentioning the segregated community because that's what he would have done himself, but this calculation was based upon the company's need to avoid falling victim to Okada's dirty tricks and people's suspicions. No doubt Sugihara saw through these contradictory arguments.

"I'll go see the boy's parents tomorrow. I'm sure it will help to alleviate my own distress, and that of my daughter and wife too," Sugihara said with all the sarcasm he could muster, and hung up the phone.

As Shiroyama replaced the receiver, he gazed at the night view that stretched out beyond his desk. The cityscape that this morning had resembled an orderly factory line was now a vast sea of lights.

In a momentary daze, Shiroyama had the sense that he now faced an unexpected uncertainty. What plagued him was an inchoate anxiety—an instinct to avoid the fact that his own relative's brief and careless remark had, however indirectly, precipitated the death of a student and shaken, if only slightly, the state of a corporation. When he found out what his niece had said to Hatano, in that instant Shiroyama's mind had intrinsically rejected that reality. And even had it not, he would still have avoided working out the exact thoughts that were running through his head now. What he ended up with was the singular, indeterminate emotion that was the uncertainty of life itself.

On the other hand, Shiroyama wondered if there was an appropriate end to this complex situation that his niece's single remark had triggered. Would time sort everything out? Would it eventually be lost amid life's miscellaneous affairs? Would the feelings of the parents who had lost their only son—and those of Sugihara, his wife, and his daughter—be allayed so easily? And so on, he reflected. However, it did not take long for him to realize that such contemplation was an act without an end.

His thoughts having returned to the uncertainty of life, Shiroyama put away these emotions for the time being. He then picked up the phone again and dialed the office of the general manager of the beer division.

"This is Shiroyama. Could you give me three minutes? I'll head over right now."

"I can come to you," Kurata said.

"No. I'm on my way."

Shiroyama fixed the necktie that he had loosened, and left his office. He took the elevator one flight down to the twenty-ninth floor to find Kurata standing in the elevator hall. Shiroyama appreciated that he had hurried to meet him, but Kurata's appearance—his necktie loose, complexion pallid, and his shirt sleeves rolled up—made for a dreadful sight, obviously indicating that until this moment he had been buried in reports at his desk. Unbeknownst to most employees, though, this was Kurata's default nighttime look.

As usual, Kurata immediately took in Shiroyama's expression and asked, "Should we go to my office? I've got our competitor's newest product perfectly chilled." He kept his own mien scrupulously calm.

"No, no. This is no time to be drinking," Shiroyama responded absently, feeling obsequious as he became aware, after all this time, of his obligation to his employees—Kurata included—and the company. "Kurata-san. Given the situation, I must tell you this. In regard to that student Hatano, I've just questioned my niece about him and she told me that on the day before the interview, she told him about the issue with his father's birthplace. I don't even know how to apologize—"

"No. As it stands, this has nothing to do with your niece. It's my fault for giving Okada an opportunity to take advantage."

"No. This is also a problem for Sugihara's family, so I've asked him to pay his respects—as a father—to the boy's parents. I ask for your understanding about this. Please." Shiroyama bowed, and Kurata waved off this gesture with his hand.

"I understand. But please allow me to handle the matters of the letter under a false name and the tape. I'd like to be able to prove at least one incidence of Okada's involvement. Once the police have identified the suspect and how they acquired Okamura's letter, we'll withdraw our claim."

"I understand. That's all I wanted to say. I'm sorry to bother you so late."

"It's no problem. Thank you for coming down here."

It happened just then, as Kurata reached over and pushed the elevator call button for Shiroyama. In the brief moment when Kurata extended his arm, a pungent smell wafted from his body. Shiroyama's nose wriggled unconsciously, but by the time he had realized it was the smell of whisky, the elevator doors had already opened.

Shiroyama stepped into the elevator and stared back at Kurata, who stood outside the door and bowed once. He searched for the right words, but the door proceeded to close, and Kurata disappeared from sight.

半田修平
SHUHEI HANDA
4

Shuhei Handa got off the train at Shimbamba Station and thought to himself, I must've stepped on something. Skipping the hassle of removing his shoe to check what it might be, he kept walking to Shinagawa Police Department and had run up only a few stairs when a grinding pain finally shot through his right big toe. Handa moved aside to the wall, took off his right shoe, and flipped it over.

A shard of glass had pierced the worn-down rubber sole of his shoe. Handa stared at it for two seconds—his first thought was that it would cost him ten thousand yen to buy a new pair of shoes. Then he saw the bloodstain at the toe of his sock and smirked. *Plus another five hundred.* He gave himself a little self-diagnosis: *desperation has made me quite generous lately.* He seriously considered taking this opportunity to buy himself a pair from Gucci or Bally as, still standing on one foot, he tried to dislodge the deeply embedded glass with his fingertip.

While he stood there, he heard light footsteps coming up the stairs and a voice say, "Excuse me," in passing. Handa lifted only his gaze and saw stark white sneakers on a man's feet running up the stairs.

It was the young assistant police inspector assigned to Investigation Headquarters from Tokyo Metropolitan Police Department. His name was Goda or something like that. In contrast with his unobtrusive suit and trench coat, the man's obviously lightweight and comfortable-looking white sneakers were so bright they made Handa blink. He was at a momentary loss—loafers from Gucci or Bally suddenly paled in comparison. Did wearing sneakers with a suit mean that the guy was simply tasteless, or that he had tremendous self-confidence? I don't like it either way, Handa thought as a shiver ran down his spine.

Tossing aside the glass shard he had finally managed to remove and putting back on his shoe, Handa stood on both feet again. The action caused him to look up, and he realized that the sneaker guy who had just run up the stairs was standing on the second-floor landing, looking down at him. As if momentarily lost in a void, the man's colorless eyes focused above Handa's head for a second or so, rebuffing Handa's scrutiny. Then, just as abruptly as he had stopped to linger, the man disappeared.

The incident was fleeting, and Handa ascended the rest of the stairs, unable to make sense of it. In such slivers of time when the rhythm of his day was disrupted, Handa always liked to indulge in a certain daydream. Were he not to, the sliver would rupture into a deep fissure, which could transform into a torrent of anger that might destroy him. To keep this from happening, he had subconsciously equipped himself with this self-defense mechanism, a reverie that always involved him catching the Investigation top brass off guard by beating them to the punch.

In the dream, he raises his hand slowly at an investigation meeting. Confronting the wannabe-bureaucrat showoffs from MPD with definitive evidence, he says, "The prime suspect is So-and-So." Just as the room is thrown into tumult, the top brass start whispering among themselves in a state of confusion. He'd probably piss himself from such pleasure, such giddy satisfaction that particular moment would give him.

He shuddered at the mere thought, it was so dark and obscure, but Handa convinced himself of this final twist in his horrible diversion by telling himself that every last one of the forty thousand cops at the MPD lived in a constant state of gloom, always on the verge of dying in a fit of indignation.

Handa played out such innocuous daydreams several times a day, but now, as he briefly gave himself over to his habitual fantasy, a dull agitation began to whirl inside his head. The sensation felt exactly like a washing machine full of dirty laundry, lumbering through a cycle with its heavy load. Yet for the past two weeks or so, since the start of the month, his daydream no longer seemed so groundless. He had been trailing a number of possible suspects on his own, without permission from Investigation Headquarters. He had no physical evidence yet, but if even one of his hunches proved correct, the day when he might pull the rug out from under those MPD bastards was not just a distant dream.

Handa pondered this as, at ten minutes to eight, he reached the door of the meeting room located on the second floor of headquarters, but before he could open it, a colleague from the Criminal Investigation Division came up behind him and said, "Chief wants you upstairs."

It didn't amount to a foreboding, but Handa felt his irritability mounting. The wound from the shard of glass in his right foot suddenly began to throb. On his way up the stairs to the third floor, he removed his shoe again and looked at his right big toe. He touched it and confirmed that his black sock was slick with blood. As he was fumbling along, a certain thought slowly occurred to him, flickering behind his brow. Right, must be about my extracurricular investigations. But then immediately, instead of the panic of being driven to the edge of a cliff, the usual daydream came surging in as if to compensate.

Today marked the hundredth day since, at the height of summer, the corpse of a man with his head beaten in had been found in the bushes of a park behind a school in Higashi-Shinagawa. The victim was a senile seventy-six-year-old who liked to wander, a resident of a special care nursing home located just inside Minami-Shinagawa, about one kilometer from the crime scene. Around ten in the morning on August tenth, children who had come to play in the park found his corpse. After receiving the call, Handa—as an officer in CID—had run to the scene from the Shinagawa Police Department, which was not far away. The body had already been there for about half a day in the August heat, and showed significant livor mortis.

The neighborhood around the crime scene was dense with businesses and long-standing residences, creating a labyrinth of one-way alleys. The streets were practically deserted at night so there were no eyewitnesses; they were unable to recover any helpful footprints from the pavement where the corpse was found, nor a weapon. There were no signs of struggle on the victim's clothing, and no articles left at the scene that might belong to the perpetrator.

On the victim's head there was a laceration above the right auricle, which appeared to have been made by a blunt weapon with a relatively large surface of impact. Since there was no evidence of a struggle, at first it was suspected that the crime had been committed by an acquaintance, but when Handa saw the crime scene, his immediate thought was, *Practice swing with a baseball bat or a golf club.* Handa did not play golf, but to relieve stress he often went to a park in his neighborhood to swing a bat or a bamboo sword. He always made sure there was nobody around him before he started swinging, but once in a while a child would dart out from nowhere and give him a scare. Perhaps his hunch sprang from this habit.

From the results of a detailed analysis of the crime scene, it was known that, based on bloodstains and bits of skin and clothing fibers recovered from the pavement, the victim had been struck in the head, then—with both hands holding his right auricle—he had been thrust down diagonally, falling on his side, after which he was dragged for about one meter and laid down in the bushes. The temporal bone where he had apparently been struck with a heavy blunt weapon suffered a depressed fracture, and from the cut on his scalp, they recovered a piece of film coated with traces of carbon resin. Judging from the victim's height and angle of the active surface of the fracture, the presumed weapon was either a driver or 2- or 3-wood golf club with a heavy carbon head that had been swung diagonally from below—and based on the paint chip, it could even be narrowed down to two or three brands. Handa's intuition had been correct.

The investigation began during the hottest part of summer, and Handa too had been dispatched from his precinct to Investigation Headquarters; for days he had canvassed the immediate vicinity of the crime scene on foot. An investigation could not move forward unless it could be backed up with the goods.

Early on in the initial investigation, he learned that the victim had no debt or savings to his name, and given his age, it was unlikely a crime of passion, so the investigation could reasonably be narrowed down to two possibilities: a grudge attack or a random crime. The victim's wanderings were just that—they had no fixed course—and although the nursing home had filed a missing person report on the ninth, the day before the crime, it was unclear even when he had disappeared from the facility. A few witnesses had been in the vicinity of the building, but the time and location of these sightings were all different, and when pieced together, one could only surmise that the victim had been roaming about a five-hundred-meter radius of the facility until early evening.

What was more, the victim's social circle was particularly limited; he had no friends at the nursing home and was not in correspondence with anyone outside of it. No one in either of his two sons' families had visited the home for years. The family members had no motive, and their whereabouts before and after the estimated time on the day of the crime had all been confirmed. Under these circumstances, it seemed unrealistic to imagine the profile of a suspect who held such a hardened grudge against the victim that they had attacked him and bashed in his skull with a golf club.

On the other hand, following the theory that someone happened to be taking a practice swing in the park with a driver, the first step was to determine whether someone may have been near the crime scene with an object of appropriate length, or whether there was someone who regularly practiced swinging in the park. This process had to begin along the road that led to the crime scene, gradually expanding outward and checking off the thousands of businesses and residences one by one.

Reports had started to filter in little by little during the investigation meetings that took place each morning and evening. However, hardly any strayed from a variant of: "So-and-so keeps a driver in his locker at the office. On the day of the crime he was at work." Everyone kept any further information to themselves so that nothing seemed clear, no matter how many of these reports came in. As a result, it was impossible for the lowest-ranking investigators to gain any perspective on where to focus their search. There was no evidence to be found in the area where Handa's team had been assigned—not even anything worth hiding—and as the autumn equinox came and went, that was still the case. To be sure, the area within a two-kilometer radius of the crime scene had been divided into six sections, and the eastern section assigned to Handa's team consisted largely of landfill in Higashi-Shinagawa with Shibaura canal in between, as well as the southern half of the Shinagawa wharf on the opposite shore.

On the wharf, there was only a container terminal, a thermal power plant, and oil storage tanks. The landfill in Higashi-Shinagawa, on the other hand, was occupied by three warehouse companies, the storage facility of a trading company, two buildings that housed, respectively, the Toyo Suisan seafood corporation and the fishing industry union, three municipal housing complexes, and finally, a facility under construction, a vacant lot, and the Tennozu baseball field. Handa spent all day long wandering back and forth along roads where only trucks passed, peering into trash cans, writing down the license plate number of every car that occasionally drove by, learning the faces of all the residents of the housing complexes—he even tracked down about a dozen of them who practiced their golf swings—but that was it. And yet, every morning and evening at the investigation meetings, his nature as a detective made him listen keenly in spite of himself, hoping that something good might turn up.

It was early October when Handa decided to stray from the landfill industrial zone. One Sunday, in the empty lot in front of the housing complex within his designated area, Handa came across a resident, with whom he had a nodding acquaintance, happily swinging a driver. "That must be brand new. How nice," Handa said, and as he soon grew bored of listening to the guy's long-winded explanation of the firmness of the shaft and the angle of the loft and whatnot, an idea suddenly flashed in his mind: a pawnshop. The suspect would have gotten rid of the golf club once it had been used as a weapon, but a driver was expensive to begin with, and if the thing had cost him a hundred thousand yen, all the more likely that he would dispose of it not in the garbage but at a pawnshop.

Handa spurred his partner, a police sergeant named Kimura, to join him and, starting from their base in Shinagawa, together they began checking out pawnshops. Handa had no particular expectations; he simply figured it was better than napping on the baseball field. Detectives often went around to pawnshops in search of stolen goods, so he had his fair share of contacts. It started out mostly as a way to kill time, but in mid-October, he almost ran into two detectives from MPD at a pawnshop within the Meguro precinct where he used to work and, after learning that this in fact where they were focusing their efforts, he grew even more fired up about his rogue mission. He reconsidered every person they had identified so far as owning golf clubs, he paid closer attention on his pawnshop visits, and he decided to select a number of people who either worked at one of the businesses or lived in housing near the crime scene and began to trail them.

Then the following month, he narrowed down his targets even further and shadowed them for two weeks. One was a man who lived in Fuchu and used to go to the driving range every Saturday but around summertime had stopped all of a sudden. One man was a resident of

Higashi-Shinagawa Public Housing No. 4 who had quit his job some time after the crime and now worked for a different company. Yet another was a self-employed businessman who replaced his full set of golf clubs shortly after the crime. The names of each of these men were now written in Handa's pocket notebook.

And today was Saturday, November 17th. They found out that I've gone off course, Handa thought to himself again vacantly. He had no memory of whether he had considered the consequences when he decided to go rogue, knowing all along that he would eventually get caught. Most likely he hadn't thought about anything at all.

The fact that he had been discovered at this point in time clearly meant that somebody had ratted him out, but he had not even processed this yet. There was someone out there who had pulled the rug out from under him before he could outwit anyone. He had been done in. Before a bud could even sprout, his seed had been plucked and trampled underfoot. He had been defeated. He kept all such thoughts at bay—for were he to acknowledge them, he would shatter into a million pieces.

Since the workday had not begun, there were only a handful of people from the white-collar crime and burglary units in CID, and another few from records and forensics. If you were to take away everything colorful in a public school teacher's lounge—the plastic desktop files and flower vases—and instead run it through a mousy filter and pipe in a hushed and chilled silence, you would be left with the CI office of the precinct police department.

Handa had grown up in company housing for an ironworks in Kamaishi, and when he graduated from university in Tokyo, he did not care where he worked as long as the place saw daylight. He applied to several private companies, but when he learned that all the available positions were technical and would have him working in a factory, he figured he would be better off in the police force so he became an officer. After he signed on, though, he realized that only MPD headquarters in Sakuradamon enjoyed a certain bland brightness, while the other bureaus were so bleak and damp that mushrooms could grow.

A superintendent named Miyoshi sat at the chief's desk in front of a window with the blinds drawn even though it was morning. Standing next to him was an inspector acting as deputy chief; both had a glassy, dreary look, their eyes like the tightly closed shells of dead clams. When Handa came in, the deputy chief motioned to him like a customer in a restaurant calling over a waiter, and Handa obediently walked over and stood before the desk.

"Starting today, you no longer report to the second-floor Investigation headquarters," said the deputy chief. "You know why, don't you?"

Handa thought about this as best he could, and for the time being, decided to go with, "No, I don't."

The dead clam thundered, "You idiot!" His bellow reverberated off the steel desks and lockers, rushing over the heads of his colleagues who were holding their breath and pretending not to notice, and bounced up against Handa's back.

"I know where and what you've been up to these past six weeks." This time Miyoshi spoke. "Would you argue that you've haven't infringed on someone else's turf, while neglecting your own duties?"

The deputy chief started shouting again, spraying spittle. "This deviancy is inexcusable!"

It wasn't that he couldn't explain himself; rather, in the police force, the very act of explaining was unacceptable. Handa knew on a gut level that the police way was to agree with the higher-ups when they told you something was black, and then to agree again when they told you it was white. Each time he uttered such token "yeses" he lost another shred of dignity. Of course he was pretty used to this by now, but lately Handa had the feeling that a new and unfamiliar identity was forming within him.

Handa succeeded in controlling his immediate fury by passively observing this other self, head hung low as a shower of reprimands rained down.

"Don't do it again," Superintendent Miyoshi said tersely.

"Yes, sir. I'm sorry," said Handa, bowing once.

"From today on, you'll be in charge of a different case, under the command of Inspector Takahashi."

"Yes, sir."

"That'll be all."

Handa bowed once more. Superintendent Miyoshi stood up and left the room to attend the investigation meeting. Handa watched him go, picturing the word "subservient" on his back, dangling like a worn-out doormat. Miyoshi was nothing more than a figurehead at these meetings, sitting with the department chief in the top-brass seats in front of the blackboard, keeping quiet and sitting still before the head of the first unit of Violent Crime who had deigned to be there from MPD.

As soon as Miyoshi was gone, Inspector Takahashi from the White Collar Crime Unit, to whom Handa was reporting as of today, called out to him.

"Handa. Wait for me downstairs. I'll be right there."

"What's the case, sir?"

"Defamation and obstruction of business."

The charges didn't register with him. All Handa could think as he bowed and left the room was, *So that's it for me as a violent-crime detective.*

But once he was out in the hallway, his innate obstinacy kicked in, and he couldn't stop wondering why he had strayed from his assigned territory. When the pawnshop idea occurred to him that day, it had merely been the stimulus. He knew that for a long time now, something inside him was ready to burst.

Shortly after the start of the investigation, headquarters had presumed that the suspect had walked into and out of the park where the crime had taken place. This was because there was nowhere to park a car in the surrounding alleys. If the suspect either lived or worked near the scene, there was a certain distance he could have walked. Say that distance could be covered in at most five minutes, and there were a limited number of residences and businesses within the designated area. At the very least, that line of thinking made it clear early on that there would be no suspicious persons in the eastern section assigned to Handa. Even just hypothetically, it was not impossible that the suspect might have occasionally gone to the large park on the landfill to take practice swings, but what it came down to was that the entire district to the east of the crime scene, including the landfill, had always been outside the scope of the investigation, and Handa's team, assigned to investigate that very area, had been ignored from the onset.

His team never had anything to report at the morning and evening meetings, and as soon as Handa started to speak, "We, uh—" the head of the seventh unit from MPD who led the meeting would often interrupt with, "Next," and move on. Another time, Handa had run into a sergeant from the same seventh unit at the entrance to the police department, and who knew what the guy was thinking as he muttered in disgust, "You guys get an afternoon nap, don't you?" The truth was, Handa had just inadvertently let out a yawn.

It was all because of those futile weeks. Handa concluded as much for now, but there was no guarantee that those fruitless days would not lead to still more fruitless years. More than any immediate remorse, Handa was conscious of the muck that was spreading around his feet and seized by a sense of powerlessness—that by just standing there he would sink even further. This is worse than usual, he thought. Even the usual daydream that would come to him at a time like this seemed dead and gone.

Just as Handa had started to descend the stairs, he saw the investigators who had come out from the meeting room on the second-floor landing. As usual, the meeting must have ended in a matter of minutes. The investigators were just about to disperse down the stairs, paired off to their respective assigned districts. Among them, Handa saw his colleague Kimura, who had been his partner up until yesterday.

Taking care not to run into the group, Handa stopped partway down the stairs and waited for them to leave. Standing there, he caught sight of one of the men about to descend from the landing below, and Handa knew it was fate that he could also see the white sneakers on the man's feet.

He felt as though something had suddenly bubbled up inside him with a force that he himself could not contain—Handa stormed down the stairs, running a few steps past the second-floor landing, and reached out a hand. He grabbed the shoulder of the assistant Police Inspector Goda or whatever his name was, shouting, "Hey!" as the man turned around.

"Hey, you. You were looking at me before. What was that about? Why were you staring at me?"

The assistant police inspector, who looked to be around thirty or so, set his narrow, reptilian eyes, which brimmed with iciness, on Handa's face. Then, as if the words being spoken to him had finally reached his ears, he brushed aside Handa's hand and said simply, "I heard a sound."

The shard of glass that had pierced his shoe. The tiny sound it had made as he threw it away. This was just the sort of inexplicable discrepancy that Handa found bewildering, and it made him dizzy, as if he had been struck twice just to drive home the point. He now lost the conviction that this assistant police inspector had actually been looking at him, yet without knowing what he was doing, he was swept along by physiological excitement that was amplified in the blink of an eye.

"So what? Why were you looking at me?"

His arm and cry shot out before he was even aware. Handa grabbed the assistant police inspector, only to be pulled off by his fellow officers, one of whom snapped "idiot" while shoving him aside. The inspector himself, who had barely furrowed his brow, turned swiftly on his heel and descended the stairs.

In the span of a few seconds as Handa watched him leave, he was unable to even remember just what had set him off; he was only aware of the heavy muck around his feet dragging him down further. *I'm the only one mired in this crap.*

The only sound in the now-empty stairway hall was his own

labored breathing. His toes felt slippery inside the blood-soaked sock in his shoe. Just as Handa went to remove his shoe once again, Inspector Takahashi came down the stairs, briefcase in hand, and so he lowered his foot.

"Hey, so we're going to the main office of the BLL's Tokyo chapter now, and then to a dentist's in Seijo. Here is the letter outlining the charges. Hinode Beer is the accuser. The accused is unspecified."

The inspector's businesslike tone inevitably pulled Handa back to his duties, and he accepted the three-page document thrust at him. Scanning it quickly, he learned that Hinode Beer had recently received a letter written under an assumed name and a cassette tape from an unidentified sender, and was requesting that the sender be appropriately punished for undermining their credibility and obstructing their business. As he singled out the words, "Buraku Liberation League, Tokyo Chapter," Handa felt the muck around his feet steadily pulling him down further. He felt the world around him darken, as if he alone were under a sky so dark that made it hard to believe it was morning for everyone else.

"A segregated buraku community?"

"Oh, what we're dealing with is a pseudo anti-discrimination association. Hey, let's get a cup of coffee before we head out. I'll show you the transcript of the tape."

"The dentist is the pseudo anti-discrimination association?"

"The dentist appears to be the sender of the tape. The department chief ordered us to see if he will consent to an interview, to hear his side of the story."

Without any of this making sense to him, Handa replied, "Understood." He exited the police department, following behind Takahashi, who wore the mien of a judicial scrivener in a country village or a notary public office's administrator. It was quarter past eight in the morning.

ANOTHER PERSONALITY EXISTED WITHIN HANDA, a personality that had been trained and disciplined in the police force. This character hissed persistently in his ear, *They won't get away with this. Just watch.*

Handa spent half his day listening to this voice, testing his patience, as if he were staring fixedly at a fishing bobber on the surface of a pond that didn't move an inch.

The truth was, when he had been given the transcription of the letter from the tape to look over that morning at the coffee shop, he only registered the shapes of the letters on the pages, and then at the BLL's office, nothing lingered in his ears other than the obviously annoyed tone of the full-time staffer who came out to meet with them. To begin with, despite the fact that a complete stranger had sent, in the form of a tape recording, a letter addressed to Hinode's Kanagawa factory originally written back in 1947, the company did not even acknowledge in the content of their official complaint that this very letter may have been lost or stolen. On the other hand, it was unlikely that the accused stood to gain anything by sending an incoherent letter or a tape to Hinode. As far as Handa was concerned, this must simply be a case in which both sides were making claims against a mistaken opponent.

Apparently, Hinode had received another letter that the dentist had sent—one with a signature—and after filing their complaint, the police department had verified the fingerprints on the signed letter, the letter sent under an assumed name, and the tape—all of which Hinode submitted voluntarily—and since they matched up, all three items were determined to be the work of the dentist. But Handa, who only ever handled violent crimes and robbery, could not fathom why, even at the discretion of both parties, they had to deal with such a trifling case where the motive remained unclear.

Wondering if his own sensors were haywire or if the world had gone insane, at one in the afternoon Handa found himself with Inspector Takahashi in the residential neighborhood of Seijo. Standing in front of a luxury apartment building near the Seijo Gakuen School playing fields and looking up at the structure with its bijou roof terrace that would have made cat burglars drool, the only thought that surfaced in Handa's mind was, *'Bout a hundred million yen.*

The dental office was located among two or three boutiques that jutted out from the ground floor of the building, and there was nothing particularly eye-catching about its unexpectedly old-fashioned and plain nameplate that read, "Hatano Dental Clinic," or the glass door of its entrance. Eyeing the sign on the door—AFTERNOON APPOINT-MENTS FROM 2 P.M.—Takahashi made a call from a nearby pay phone and announced that the dentist would meet them at home before they ascended the elevator to the residences on the fifth floor.

When Handa saw the man named Hatano, his first impression was, to put it simply, a butterfly in a specimen box. The outward appearance was perfect, yet it was nothing more than a still life that would shatter at the slightest touch. Truth was, the man's appearance—combining the nonchalance of an unsullied, sheltered son of a good family who had grown straight into middle-age, the coldness of a man who seemed to be made up of only a high IQ, and a melancholy that betrayed hints of a rather complicated thought process—was hushed over, and there was an emptiness to him that seemed to stem from more than just the fact that he had lost a son. And there was a slightly unusual twitchiness to the way his eyes moved.

Nevertheless, it was clear that his life had disintegrated, his vast, luxurious living room strewn about with discarded clothes and per-meated by the mustiness of a space long deprived of fresh air and the sour stench of alcohol. Hatano sat down on a sofa at the center of this room, and the first words out of his mouth were, "It was my mistake."

According to the account that began to spill forth from Hatano, he had been wrong to suspect that there had been any kind of dis-criminatory action by Hinode Beer against his son, who had taken the company's recruitment exam, and the fact of the matter was that his son had become mentally and physically unstable from the shock of the opposition from the parents of a school friend he had been dating, saying it was too soon for them to marry. Hatano spoke in a clear and coherent manner, as if he was talking about someone else, and there was no detectable amplitude in his emotions whatsoever.

"Then, are you saying that you've calmed down now that the parents of your son's girlfriend came to pay their respects?" Inspector Takahashi prodded, but Hatano made no response.

Takahashi went on to explain that Hinode had filed a complaint on the basis of defamation and obstruction of business, and that, formally, participation in this investigation was voluntary, so Hatano did not have to talk about anything he did not wish to. The expression on Hatano's face, though, made it hard to tell whether he was even listening.

The inspector assumed a businesslike manner toward the dentist and began to ask the necessary questions. First, regarding the contents of the tape, did he or did he not make a tape recording of a letter addressed to Hinode's Kanagawa factory from a man named Seiji Okamura in 1947? The letter had no rightful business being in Hatano's possession, so how did he obtain it?

Hatano told them that he received the letter from two men who had paid him a visit on the night of November 5th. One of them identified himself as so-and-so Nishimura, an executive committee member of the Tokyo chapter of the BLL, but since he had thrown away his business card, he could not remember his name precisely.

"Could you describe the features of this Nishimura?"

"He was about a hundred and sixty-five centimeters tall. Medium build. Around fifty years old. Dark complexion. He had thin fingers. A mole about ten millimeters in diameter on his right jaw."

Hatano listed the characteristics robotically, and Takahashi recorded them in his notebook.

"And, what did Nishimura want?"

"I had used the BLL name in my second letter, so he came to ask me about that. As for the issue of my son's being rejected during Hinode's screening process for new employees, Nishimura said something about how Hinode had their own reasons and then, suggesting that it could be useful, he left behind a copy of the letter."

"Did he mention specifically what Hinode's reasons might be?"

"He said something about the financial situation of a company called Ogura Transport and its main bank. I told him I didn't understand."

"Was that bank by any chance Chunichi Mutual Savings?"

"I think so, yes."

"What specifically did he say about it?

"Something about bad loans and bypass loans. I don't remember exactly."

"How did Nishimura say those issues are related to Hinode's screening process for new employees?"

"Seiji Okamura refers to a person in his letter, someone who happens to be investigating the problems with Ogura Transport. He was apparently one of three men from a segregated buraku community who were fired from Hinode's Kyoto factory in 1946."

Takahashi's hand continued to move rapidly across his notebook pages. Handa sat idly next to him.

"By the way, doctor, did you believe all along that the person you were speaking with was from the BLL?"

"No."

"Then, what did you make of this person who assumed a false identity and talked to you about the economy?"

"I don't know."

"Some guy whom you've never met pretended he was from the BLL and brought up a story about your son out of the blue, right? Didn't you think that was suspicious?"

"No, not really. When it comes to buraku and discrimination, whether it's fact or fiction, it's not uncommon for the conversation to take off on its own in ways you wouldn't expect."

"By the way, did Nishimura say anything about the source of the letter?"

"No. I asked but he didn't respond."

"Did Nishimura demand money for the letter?"

"No."

"Do you still have the letter?"

"After I recorded the tape, on the morning of the sixth, I threw it in the trash."

After this exchange, Takahashi's inquiry turned to Hatano's intention in sending the tape to Hinode. Hatano replied that, as he pored over the letter written by this man Seiji Okamura some forty-three years ago, he developed a certain sympathy toward the man, and he felt compelled to say something to Hinode on Okamura's behalf. There was no specific reason involving his son, and the story that he was motivated by nothing other than his vague aversion toward the corporation Hinode seemed at once plausible and implausible.

"How do you feel about sending the tape now?"

"I think it was pointless."

"Do you regret it?"

"I wouldn't do it again. Even if Hinode were at fault about my son, I have no interest in questioning them any further."

The conversation proceeded swiftly, without any hitches, to reach a conclusion, and Takahashi slapped his knee lightly.

"Well then. We would like for you to issue a voluntary written statement based on what you just said, so would you come to the Shinagawa Police Department tomorrow? From there, we will confirm with Hinode whether they intend to withdraw the charges."

"I will take responsibility for what I've done."

"No, no. There's no need for that. Following procedure, we will issue a statement, but since your cooperation is voluntary, the signature and seal are up to you. More importantly, I feel it's best that you maintain a record of the details about this Nishimura person visiting you."

Sitting next to the inspector, for a fleeting moment Handa wondered why he would suggest this, but Hatano himself did not inquire further, he simply replied, "I'll come by tomorrow."

Takahashi acknowledged him and stood up, so Handa followed. Hatano gave no other response, and since he made no move to show them out, the two took leave on their own, but as they opened the front door, they ran into a woman standing just outside. The woman asked them who they were in a sharp voice.

Handa fumbled for a reply while Takahashi succinctly responded and followed up with a question. "We're from the Shinagawa Police Department. Are you Dr. Hatano's wife?"

"What's wrong?" the woman asked, rooted to the spot. "Did my husband do something?"

"No, no. We just came to ask him a few questions. No need to worry."

Takahashi had barely finished speaking when the woman rushed past them, with such force it seemed she might crash into the front door, before disappearing inside.

On the elevator ride down, Takahashi muttered, as if just now remembering it, "Her suit was Valentino, seven hundred thousand yen. Her Hermès Kelly bag, eight hundred thousand."

The surface of Handa's mind tried to recall the appearance of the woman they had just encountered, but his only impression was that of a woman in her forties, with a garish visage that showed no signs of aging, sporting what seemed like a freshly-set coiffure. He did notice that she was put together in a chic black ensemble from head to toe, but the labels were beyond his ken.

"By the way, does this case really require a written statement?" Handa inquired.

Takahashi immediately replied, "You don't know who Shin'ichi Nishimura is?"

"You know him by name?"

"Of course I do. There's only one Nishimura with a centimeter-wide mole on his chin. He's a second-generation Zainichi Korean, and his real name is Hoyeol Kim. He's been on the list of corporate extortionists for ten years."

So here was the target of the White Collar Crime Unit. The knowledge finally generated a small ripple on the pond within Handa's head, but not one big enough to cause his bobber to move. He merely responded, "I'm sorry I wasn't aware."

Takahashi looked suddenly irked, as if he hadn't realized he was working with someone so stupid, and he started walking ahead. Handa followed him sluggishly.

"Where are we going now?"

"To a loan shark's. We need more info on Nishimura. Listen. This Nishimura has nothing whatsoever to do with the BLL. Nor is he associated with Hinode. But this man used the BLL's name to get to a dentist he had never met before, and for no charge he handed over an internal document from Hinode that who knows where he got. If this doesn't smell fishy, I don't know what does."

"I see."

So this is my life from here on, Handa thought.

The moment he looked up at the leaden sky above the residential street, out of a years-long habit, a second daydream slipped through Handa's mind. It was another simple fantasy, in which one day out of the blue he slams down an envelope with the words Letter of Resignation onto his boss's desk. But the image soon faded feebly, without giving him much pleasure. At this point there was not a single circumstance that would make Handa's resignation matter to anyone. There was no reason for his boss, the police department, or MPD to be surprised, or for any of them to turn blue in the face trying to convince him to retract his decision. It was not as if anyone would fear or regret his resignation.

Handa accompanied Inspector Takahashi until dark as he made the rounds to several loan sharks in Shinjuku as well as the offices of a few financial brokers, after which they returned to the department, where Takahashi outlined Shin'ichi Nishimura's profile and modus operandi, then he ordered Handa to review each of the briefing points for the interview with Hiroyuki Hatano, set to take place tomorrow, the 18th. Nishimura currently worked as an errand man for several corporate underlings of a large crime syndicate called the Seiwakai. Among those in Seiwakai's employ was an influential underground financial group known as Okada Association, and the issue was whether Nishimura was somehow connected to this Okada group, and so on. Handa finally understood that, quite simply, for Investigation unit two, who handled financial incidents, Hinode's complaint letter was nothing but a fortuitous excuse.

When he finally left the department just before nine that night, he saw that the light in the second-floor window where homicide was located still shone brightly, but the indignation it roused was somewhat dulled. Diagonally ahead on his way to Shimbamba Station, the glimmering office buildings of Hinode Beer and Sony rose into the night sky above Kita-Shinagawa. Like stars fallen to earth, their beauty never ceased to amaze him.

Handa gazed up at the cluster of gleaming high-rises. Although he knew that each one was populated by workers who wore out their shoes trying to make an extra yen, he still felt nothing in common with them and, faced with another wave of alienation, he looked away.

On his walk to the station, that other self—like a devil on Handa's shoulder—blustered, *Just watch, I'll quit soon enough.* Chastened, Handa wondered, *How many years have I been saying that?* The reality was that he had no choice but to go on working tomorrow and the next day, gaining back his self-respect and confidence only in his dreams. No matter how fed up he claimed to be, the thought of getting a new job at a security company where he'd end up directing traffic at some construction site practically made him want to die from anger.

Handa got on the still crowded train, stood in silence gripping the strap, and got off at Kojiya Station. Weaving through the tiny shopping district around the station where only the neon signs of the pachinko parlor blinked away, he came out on Kanpachi-dori Avenue and headed in the direction of Haneda Airport. He had not walked more than a minute or so when the road lined with only businesses and old machiya houses began to feel deserted, and there were no more lights beckoning passersby. Commuters rushed home as if chased by the sea breeze, briskly disappearing down back streets, and at the corner before a small rail crossing, Handa too slipped into an alley in the neighborhood of Haginaka.

He lived in tower two of the Daini Haginaka Apartments on the west side of Haginaka Park, and though he arrived there soon enough, Handa stood in the alley and hesitated for a few seconds. The lights were on in the top-floor window of the five-story building. Inside, his wife, who usually came home around nine, would be doing laundry and tearing open the packages of prepared food she brought home as a late supper for herself and her husband from the Ito-Yokado supermarket where she worked. Sashimi and simmered greens. Braised burdock root with carrots. Since he made it a rule not to drink at home, there was not a single can of beer in the refrigerator. Standing there, all Handa could think about was a beer, so he decided to keep going past his building.

Intending to make a detour until ten or so—another thirty or forty minutes—Handa went along the alley that continued toward Haneda Airport. Within minutes he arrived at Sangyo Road, beyond which was the district called Haneda. During the day choked with exhaust from cars heading to the airport, and at night untouched by the lights from the neighboring airport, the neighborhood was pierced by the overpass of the Shuto Expressway running above the densely packed rooftops of machiya houses that modestly overlapped one another. There was a small shopping district along the other side of the road under the overpass. In the evening most of the stores were closed, but there were still a few lights on here and there—a soba eatery, a cheap Chinese restaurant, a liquor shop.

First Handa bought a can of beer from a vending machine at the liquor shop by the overpass. He pulled the tab open right there, and sipped a mouthful of freezing cold beer. The pharmacy kitty-corner to where he stood was still open. Without any neon, the signage of the store was obscured by the nighttime shadows, but there, on the glass door where the curtains were pulled shut and illuminated from inside, was the name Monoi Pharmacy.

As Handa gulped down another mouthful of beer by the side of the road, the glass door of the pharmacy opened and a man came out. Handa recognized his horseracing buddy, the ex-army man, who that night had a ten-centimeter-wide bandage wrapped around his head. He also noticed Handa, and he paused wearily to mutter, in place of a greeting, "Look at this mess."

"Were you in an accident?" Handa asked.

"Yesterday. On the Tomei Expressway," Jun'ichi Nunokawa answered. "The fucking ten-ton trailer in front of me suddenly swerved out of its lane. The minute I hit my brakes, a ten-car pileup. My truck is a fucking wreck."

"You're lucky it wasn't any worse."

Jun'ichi Nunokawa paused for two seconds after Handa said this, then spat toward the ground at his feet, "I missed out on dying."

Missed out on dying? I see—the parent of a disabled child thinks about things like this. Handa tried to imagine, but he could neither empathize nor did he feel compelled to ask any further about it.

"Betting on the horses?"

"Yeah."

"Well, then. Gotta be going."

Neither of them asked if the other was going to Fuchu on Sunday, tomorrow. Handa was in no mood to talk, and Nunokawa didn't seem like he was either. Nunokawa got into a minivan parked on the side of the road. Handa had not noticed until then, but within the vehicle's dark interior two arms were swimming in the air without making a sound. Nunokawa's daughter was flopped over on the flatbed, thrashing around. As soon as the engine started, the minivan in the hands of a professional driver glided away like a speed demon, and disappeared along Sangyo Road.

With his can of beer in one hand, Handa rang the bell in front of the pharmacy, opened the glass door, and stuck his head inside. The display shelf of discounted detergent and toilet paper that was placed outside during the day had been brought inside for the night, and it made the tiny store so cramped it was difficult even to step inside. The owner, Monoi, parted the curtain at the back of the store and popped his head through. As soon as he saw it was Handa, he came out, saying, "You're early tonight," and pushed the shelf out of the way for him. "There. Come in."

Although Handa knew that Monoi had lost his grandson last month, the man was impassive and taciturn to begin with, and to the outward eye Handa could not detect anything to suggest he was terribly despondent. His aspect had always been quiet and plain, but since he did not wear his sunglasses at night, his milky, immobile left eye made him look a little peculiar.

An old lady pharmacist tended the store during the day, so as befitting a retired old man, Monoi puttered around the neighborhood, playing shogi at "Elder Haven" and shopping at the supermarket, then coming home in the evening to fix something for himself to eat and to mind the store as he watched TV, before closing up around eleven and going to bed. Sunday was for horseracing. Over the past six or so years of frequenting the pharmacy, Handa had pieced together the way that Monoi whiled away his day. Sometimes when he stopped by the store, Handa would smell something burning on the stove.

"Nunokawa was just here. He has a head wound from an accident," Monoi started to say.

"I saw him outside," Handa replied. "He seemed pretty stressed."

"It's quite a lot of trouble. He has to submit a written explanation to the company, and the police called him in."

"I see."

"If it'll mean a few days off, an accident isn't the worst thing. That's what I tried telling him."

During this short exchange, Monoi had put on his reading glasses, taken out last Sunday the 11th's two winning tickets from the drawer of the register, and with a "Here you are," carefully placed them on the counter. Handa thanked him and took the tickets. The two races he had asked Monoi to bet on had both won. He did not bother asking what the dividends were, it just meant that enough cash for a drink was back in his pocket.

Handa took a swig from his can of beer.

"What about tomorrow's race?" Monoi asked.

"I didn't even have time to buy the paper."

"I have it. You wanna see?"

"No. I'll pass for tomorrow."

Just when he took another swig of beer, a woman walked past on the other side of the curtain behind Monoi, causing Handa to pause for a moment with his can in midair. A black suit and the contour of calves in stockings. From the neck up she was hidden by the curtain. That suit, Handa thought, it was the Valentino he had seen earlier at that dentist's home. Noticing Handa's gaze, Monoi himself turned around and mumbled, "My daughter's home for a bit."

What are the odds? Handa almost said out loud. Of all the people . . . the grandson who had died was the son of that dentist and Monoi's daughter. But he was struck speechless for only a moment. He could not refer to a case that was still under investigation, of course, and Handa found such a coincidence encountered at the end of the day as cheap as a TV drama, which made him feel alienated all over again. He gave a noncommittal response, "Oh, really?" and finished the rest of his beer. The wind seemed stronger outside, as the glass door facing the street rattled noisily.

"I'll buy the paper for you before next week's Japan Cup," Monoi said.

"I wonder if Oguri Cap will run."

"I hope so. If he does, I'll bet on Oguri."

"Are you going tomorrow, Monoi?"

"I've got nothing else to do."

"Well, sorry to leave you with this but—"

Handa placed the empty can on the counter, said goodnight, and left the store. He heard Monoi pushing the shelf back on the other side of the glass door.

Handa purchased another can of beer at the liquor shop's vending machine. In front of the intersection on Sangyo Road, he pulled the tab open and took a sip. Crossing the intersection and walking straight down the alley would bring him to his apartment in Haginaka, but his feet would not move and he remained drinking by the side of the road. Before him was the factory wall of Yamamoto Rolling Stock Manufacturing. All along the deserted industrial road were corrugated-metal and concrete fences, a succession of street lamps.

Back then, just what was I hoping for? Handa wondered. To sit at a desk where the sun shone brightly. To make a fairly stable living and lead a respectable life—wasn't that all? He had become a policeman with a single, pathetically ordinary desire—and what now?

He threw his empty can into the road, where it was swiftly crushed beneath the tires of an oncoming truck with nary a sound. Ah, that's me, right there. As soon as the thought crossed his mind, that other self grumbled, I'll show them soon enough, just wait.

物井清三
SEIZO MONOI
5

Seizo Monoi stared at the trademark seal of Hinode Supreme on the empty beer can that Handa had left behind. Crushing it with his hand and tossing it into the wastebasket, he passed through the curtain and returned to the living room of his home.

His daughter Mitsuko had clearly been waiting to launch into him. "All you care about is horseracing!" she shouted. Her tone was sharp—as if each consonant was catching on a hook—and it made Monoi's ears buzz. Just like her late mother, his daughter had always been strong-minded, but at least when she was a girl, she had not spoken to him like this, he thought to himself.

She was probably just irritated because their conversation had been interrupted by a string of customers. This whole time, at least half an hour, Mitsuko had remained standing, her back to a pillar, claiming that her skirt would crease if she sat on the tatami floor. Her mother Yoshie had also been a rather stylish woman who cut a fine figure for someone born in the early twentieth century, but standing before him now, Mitsuko could not have seemed like more of a stranger to him. When he thought about it, the only time he'd held her in his arms was when she was in preschool. By the time she started elementary school she had already matured into a precocious, miniature version of Yoshie; as a teenager she was practically Yoshie's twin; and by the time she enrolled at the women's college she'd attended, she existed in a completely separate world that Monoi could no longer reach. When she was a college student and he had cautioned her about wearing flashy clothes when out with her male friends, she rebuffed him by saying, "Don't be jealous," while his wife remarked, "Mitsuko has high ambitions. Unlike you."

Monoi was indeed perplexed by the way his manner of thinking and living seemed unfit for the modern era and, shrinking away, his sidelined existence became that of a nonentity who did no more than watch the two striving women in his life. His daughter joined a large insurance company straight out of college, and not even a year had gone by when she announced that she was getting married. Since she had said her fiancé was a dentist, Monoi had intended to arrange a proper wedding, only to be informed that she planned to enter her name in her fiancé's family register and move into his apartment as soon as the next day. He eventually invited her fiancé's family for a formal gathering at a hotel in the city, and the whole matter was put to rest after that.

No doubt a dentist made an incredibly good living. Monoi gathered as much from his occasional encounters with his daughter. She would frequent places like the spa and the gym to refine her figure, have her hair done at the beauty salon every three days, and even when just dropping by her father's home, she would wear haute couture suits that cost a million yen. Normally, were she not in mourning, she would be further decked out in diamond jewelry the size of tiger beans. Before his grandson's demise, she'd rarely ever stopped by anyway, but since the funeral, whenever she appeared in these ensembles on some errand, Monoi had trouble knowing where to look, and he simply cast his gaze downward in discomfort.

If her so-called high ambitions were ultimately to lead a life of affluence and to adorn herself in luxury, there was no question her father never could have provided that for her. Being forced to look upon such wealth, which she paraded in front of him as if out of spite, Monoi couldn't help but feel that his entire life was being denied.

In 1947, Monoi had come out to Tokyo after being released by the foundry in Hachinohe in Tohoku. For a year and a half he had pulled a junkman's cart around Ueno, until he managed to get a job as a lathe operator at a small factory in Nishi-Kojiya in the Ota district, where he slept in a corner of the factory floor. One thing led to another and he ended up marrying Yoshie, who had a four-year-old child in tow, and amid her incessant complaining that they had no money, he made it to age sixty, frugally shaving away steel day after day in the factory. To send his daughter to college on a machinist's pay required rather considerable effort, so he worked overtime every night and got by with a meager allowance for himself, just enough for a pack of Peace cigarettes each day and two or three hundred-yen horseracing tickets every Sunday. Back then he used to seriously consider how his death would at least generate some life-insurance money. When he was fifty he sold off their house in Nishi-Rokugo and spent all his savings to buy a pharmacy that had been run by a distant relative of Yoshie's, but the pharmacy turned out to be a shell that had been used as collateral on a loan—they had basically been swindled. Unable to complain about a relative, though, he now worked desperately to pay off the loan. He wondered how all these things appeared in his daughter's eyes.

It was not something he was ever conscious of now, but Mitsuko was Yoshie's daughter from a previous marriage, so she and Monoi were not related by blood. When he and Yoshie got married, he was too busy making ends meet to have a child, but by the time he could afford to have one Yoshie was already past forty-five, and the doctor said she could no longer give birth.

He wouldn't dare say he was good at living, but he did harbor a mild affection for the life that resulted from his working the way he had. Though if it were to be compared with the good fortune and resourcefulness of others, Monoi had no words to defend it—his modest confidence and pride would all but disappear. Even as he contemplated that Mitsuko must be on edge, having just lost her son, Monoi cast his gaze down out of longtime habit, and could not bring himself to look his daughter in the face. To grow old was to lose patience.

And so Monoi crept back into the warmth of the kotatsu, sitting at the low table with its inbuilt heater, his back hunched as he sipped from his mug of tea, which had turned cold.

"Are you listening?!" Mitsuko's shrill voice hailed down upon his head.

"I'm listening," Monoi mumbled, moving only his lips.

Mitsuko had arrived unexpectedly half an hour ago, and abruptly launched into the story of how the police had been to see her husband, Hatano. Unable to accept that their son, Takayuki, had been rejected by Hinode Beer, Hatano had apparently sent a few accusatory letters to Hinode. As a result, Hinode filed a complaint against him with the police, and it was on the verge of becoming a criminal case.

Whatever had happened, sending harassing letters to a company was so far out of the ordinary that if Hatano, who had always seemed so conscientious, had actually done such a thing, Monoi figured he must have had a compelling reason. But as he listened further, Monoi understood there was much more to this complicated story. His grandson had had a girlfriend whom he intended to marry, but the engagement was suddenly broken off because her parents objected. Could the shock from this have caused Takayuki to have an accident? His girlfriend's parents were not explicit, but wasn't it likely that the reason for their objection was where Hatano's birthplace was registered? Mitsuko relayed all this. Then the conversation took a sudden leap. "It's because you were so irresponsible, Dad," she reproached.

"I've thought about it long and hard over this last month. Everything is definitely Hatano's fault. It's a crime of conscience that he hid his birthplace. His wife and his son were completely in the dark, and the reason why suddenly one day we're faced with this is because Hatano never gave us the explanation he owed us. But go back even further—when a daughter says she's going to marry someone, every parent knows to check out the other family. But you didn't do anything."

"What's the big deal about his birthplace . . . ?"

"What's the big deal?! It's common sense!"

"But didn't you marry Hatano because you loved him . . . ?"

"That's why I'm saying you're an irresponsible father! No matter who he is, if your daughter tells you that she's going to marry a man, it's the parent's obligation to investigate his family!"

"There's no such obligation in this world."

"Maybe not in the countryside of Tohoku, but in Tokyo there is! You're right—I was stupid. A handsome and rich dentist, whose mother's side of the family were physicians in Kamakura. He had a bevy of girlfriends from top universities, so why did Hatano marry someone like me? It was stupid of me not to figure it out. Do you know how humiliated I am right now, Dad?"

Switch the man's and woman's positions, and he had heard the same argument more than enough times from Yoshie, Monoi thought to himself. The proud graduate of a girl's high school, Yoshie had bid farewell to her first husband, an editor for a literary magazine who had studied literature at Waseda University, sending him off to the front less than six months after they were married. And with a mere postcard notifying her of his death in the war, the newlywed bride became a widow, the newborn Mitsuko in her arms. As she'd told Monoi every chance she got, the reason she had decided to marry him when they met, while she was working as a waitress in Shinjuku toward the end of the war, was because she was burdened with a young daughter and had no hope of marrying anyone decent. In a better world, who would take a half-blind, small-town factory worker as a husband by choice? she used to say.

"Do you know how humiliated I am, Dad? I worked hard to raise Takayuki. And he grew up to be such a wonderful boy, much better than I deserve. And now this happens, before his time—all because of his father's birthplace!"

"Now, hold on a minute . . ."

"I don't want to make a stupid fuss over a birthplace either! But it's because I didn't know that I couldn't explain anything to Takayuki. If I had been able to educate and prepare him properly, no matter what the girl's parents might have said, he would have handled it in a more appropriate way. It's Hatano's fault for hiding it. And it's your fault for not stopping me from marrying a man who hid where he was from!"

Mitsuko started to wail, her voice quavering. Monoi could not avoid looking at her in this state. Even Monoi could see that Mitsuko was suffering in her own way, and with no one else to talk to, she had no choice but to take out her indignation on her father. It made no difference how many millions of yen her outfit cost, the person standing with her back to the pillar crying was, after all, his daughter.

"Why don't you sit down—" Monoi started to say, but Mitsuko suddenly exclaimed, "Dad!" Her tone was even more fierce. "Don't you get it? I've been deceived!"

"You've been husband and wife for more than twenty years, why start accusing him of deceiving you? There's nothing you can do but work together as a couple and—"

"If I could do that, I wouldn't be here! Hatano is crazy! I swear he's lost it, his eyes look weird!"

Why does Mitsuko have to speak in such an ear-splitting tone? I'm her father, but even I've had enough, Monoi thought. Then he vaguely remembered hearing Hatano's voice when he had called out of the blue late one night early that month. He had sounded distracted, having lost his son, but there had been nothing strange that could be detected from the tenor of his voice.

Mitsuko's voice pitched even higher. "Hatano told me he's going to the Shinagawa Police Department tomorrow. They'll take a statement from him, and who knows what will happen after that, but his reputation is over, you know. And yet that man, he has no reaction whatsoever. His eyes look weird. I'm telling you—Takayuki meant more to him than I ever did!"

"I don't think you need to worry much about the police—"

"What are you talking about?! Who on earth wants to go to a dentist who gets called in by the police? Rumors spread fast!"

"Nothing's official yet—"

"Don't act like this isn't your problem. This issue involves you too, Dad!"

An issue that involved him. It took some time for him to ruminate on what this meant. He knew that he wasn't entirely uninvolved, but he thought that its effect on him was so small as to be negligible.

Atop a chest of drawers, within an old picture frame, a faded family portrait looked out at them. In 1949, he had rented a small, six-mat apartment near the factory and set up house with Yoshie—the photo was taken to commemorate this event. Mitsuko was four and as cute as ever, and in the picture her new father was holding her hand. The twenty-four-year-old man, who had acquired a beautiful wife and daughter in one fell swoop, looked like a typical country bumpkin, wearing a nervous expression and puffing out his chest. Monoi had framed the photo, and for the past forty-one years, it had been like an ethereal presence in the living room. He had no idea how the two women in his life felt about it, but Monoi himself knew that he had looked to this photograph at various points throughout his life, and now he gazed at it again from the kotatsu.

If he were a man with ten times the guts and that much less patience, he might have murdered his wife and daughter and killed himself along with them. Monoi used to think about this when he looked at the photo, and the thought alone was enough for him just to keep working. In the period just after the war, his marriage to Yoshie was among countless half-hearted marriages between many men and women with no choice but to shack up under the same roof in order to survive. But even still, if they only had money, no doubt they each could have been more at peace. What Monoi regretted was that, for the simple lack of money, he had lived a life untouched by quiet spiritual satisfaction.

Looking back, he had always been haunted by the anxieties of daily life that were naturally ingrained in him, and whenever money became tight, that anxiety transformed into a sharp needle of fear that attacked him. Since he arrived in Tokyo, where it was all he could do to survive, the society around him continued to change at an astonishing speed, and with his meager income that never seemed to rise, he had the constant feeling that he was gradually being left behind. There was no solace at home, with Yoshie calling him worthless every time she opened her mouth, so he had never had the experience of feeling completely at ease. As he grew older, the raw emotions of anxiety and restlessness rusted away, but it wasn't as if this set his mind at peace. In the five years since Yoshie's death, his life had ostensibly grown quiet, with no ups and downs, but he felt that the balance between the positives and negatives over his sixty-five years had been too absurd to call what he had now fulfillment.

Monoi found himself unable to worry as he used to about his daughter, who had led a separate life for a long time already. Now, it was all too clear that he preferred to devote the remainder of his own life to himself, rather than to his daughter.

With no way of knowing what her old father was thinking, Mitsuko continued to speak in her shrill voice.

"I'm so humiliated. That man—he thinks that since he married me begrudgingly, as long as he keeps me in luxury, his duty is done. Not once did he ever approve of a social climber like me. I knew it all too well, but once Takayuki was born, I couldn't leave. I've endured it all this time—twenty-three years!"

"What's the point of telling me this now, after all these years?"

"Of course you'd say that. You've never been one to take responsibility for anything," Mitsuko said as she blew her nose into a handkerchief and ran her hand through her coiffed hair. "I'm divorcing him," she said, her tone suddenly changing. "I'm sure for twenty-three years, our marriage has also been quite a disappointment for Hatano."

"But what will you live on if you divorce him—"

"I'll make sure Hatano gives me half of everything. Besides, our vacation home in Oiso is under my name, so I can sell that off and do what I want. I won't be a burden to anyone."

"Don't say such a thing—"

Just then, the store's bell jingled again.

"There you go. Another one of your horseracing friends," Mitsuko spat out the words, and grabbed the handbag at her feet. "I'm going on a trip for the next two or three days. If the police ask anything, tell them I'm not here."

"Mitsuko, wait—"

Monoi crawled out of the kotatsu and tried to chase after her, but before he could Mitusko had stormed out through the back door, slamming it behind her with a force that could have broken the wooden door.

"Monoi-san." The voice that called out from the store did not belong to a horseracing buddy but to a neighbor. When Monoi poked his head into the pharmacy, the owner of a dairy shop down the block called to him across the display shelf of detergent. "Sorry to bother you so late. My grandson's complaining of a toothache."

"A cavity? Is it swollen?" Despite Monoi's weariness, his response tumbled out by rote. No matter what happened, he thought, this was the only voice he was equipped with—and his only way of speaking with it.

"I think it's a cavity, but he won't stop crying."

"Do you have some cotton balls at home? I'll give you some ointment, so try putting that on it. If that doesn't work, it means it's infected. You'll have to take him to the dentist."

Monoi gave him the ointment, and the shop owner thanked him as he paid and left. "Take care," Monoi said as he saw him out. As he closed the glass door, which was still rattling in the wind, he detected a trace of Mitsuko's perfume in the air of the cramped store. And her cutting voice seemed to still echo around him.

If he'd had the means, he would have chosen to be alone a long time ago, Monoi tried to tell himself in vain. As he did so, one by one, a number of bitter disappointments that he hated to even think of began to flutter through his mind yet again. There was the time when he had to buy a long-sleeved kimono for Mitsuko's coming-of-age ceremony. It just so happened that was the year the factory had a slump and there were no bonuses to hand out, so he had gone from credit union to credit union in a mad rush, but after he had finally scrambled together the hundred-thousand yen to pay for a kimono and obi sash—it was such a cheap garment, even Monoi could see that it wasn't pretty—in the end his daughter had worn a Western-style dress to the ceremony. That kimono was eventually sold off to a pawnshop, without Mitsuko ever even slipping her arm through its sleeves. He could still recall the yellow butterfly pattern of that kimono.

There were other things too. When Mitsuko was in elementary school, the day of her field trip Yoshie happened to be in bed with a cold so Monoi, straight from a night shift, struggled to prepare a bento for her lunch, but when his daughter left for school, the bento he had worked so hard to make was still sitting on the dining table. At the time, Monoi tried frantically to figure out why, finally realizing that the cloth in which he had wrapped the bento box reeked of machine oil—he could only laugh to himself.

Thinking about it as he shoved the display shelf aside to close the store, he realized no one had ever told him about Parent's Day at school, and Monoi couldn't remember ever attending one. For a sixty-five-year-old man, digging up memories of the past was pointless—a waste of the time he had left. But it may have been old age that stirred up memories of this, that, and the other, and he just needed to make an effort to shake them off. Why should he worry what Hatano and Mitsuko were thinking or what they were going to do about their marriage?

Monoi went outside the store and started to lower the shutters. As he did so, a car came from the direction of Sangyo Road, and no sooner had it stopped in front of the pharmacy than a hoarse voice called out from the driver's seat window, "Monoi, big brother!"

It was indeed a night that seemed to bring out all sorts, one after another. The man, big as a tank, got out of a Mercedes-Benz and shouted cheerfully, "It's too early for bedtime." He was the son of the owner of the Kanemoto Foundry in Hachinohe, where Monoi worked half a century ago. The snot-nosed kid who used to tag along after him and call him "big brother" had come to Tokyo thirty years earlier after languishing for some time because of his family's bankruptcy. Now, he managed a respectable mid-sized business, his own ironworks near Ichihara in Chiba, and from time to time he paid a friendly visit to Monoi.

Yoshiya Kanemoto was usually liquored up whenever he came to see Monoi. A smile now broke across his gleaming, bright-red face as he casually pushed a fancy box of expensive foreign liquor toward Monoi.

"Jus' got back from Manila yesterday. I planned to stop by earlier, but hell, I got to drinking," he said, laughing.

"Bet you had fun getting into trouble over there, eh?"

"Aw, don't say that. I have clients to entertain. It's all right."

Monoi glanced at the two men sitting in the back seat of the Mercedes. They may have been associates from the metal industry, though he had known for a time that Kanemoto had ties to corporate underlings of a particular vein, and Monoi offered a few words of warning again that night. "It's not all right."

In the dialect of their hometown, Kanemoto reassured him that there was nothing to worry about, simply feigning ignorance. The sight of this fifty-year-old man, who bore no trace of the shy child from long ago, made Monoi feel more bewildered now than anything else.

"Well, I'll come by again. Don't catch a cold, big brother."

With that, Kanemoto cheerily got back in his car and turned back the way he'd come. From the window of the retreating car, an unfamiliar man of that particular vein—without a doubt from the shady underworld—glanced at Monoi. His face was somber, with a large mole on his jaw.

Monoi considered the gift of foreign liquor in his hands for a moment, and then placed the box in the basket of his bicycle. Although his plans had been thrown off by his daughter's coming by, he finally had time to set out on a visit he had been meaning to make all evening.

The person he wanted to see was one of his horseracing buddies who lived in the service apartment of a small factory in Higashi-Kojiya, about a ten-minute bicycle ride from the pharmacy. Typically he would drop by the pharmacy every so often, but he hadn't recently, and last Sunday he hadn't been at the Tokyo Racecourse in Fuchu, so Monoi hadn't seen him for two weeks—since the fourth of this month. The guy barely had any friends or acquaintances, so assuming he was still alive and kicking, about this time of night he would have his head buried in horseracing newspapers in preparation for tomorrow's races.

Monoi lowered the rest of the shutters, locked up, and with his short work coat still on, he got on his bike and began pedaling toward Sangyo Road.

He rode slowly on the deserted sidewalk and, after passing over two pedestrian bridges, he turned east into a backstreet just beyond the Minami-Kojiya bus stop. When Monoi had first arrived in 1948, the row of telephone poles that lined the dusty Sangyo Road had extended far into the distance. The barracks of small factories, reverberating with the bustling sounds of lathes and grinders, had stood amidst the wooden-fenced traditional minka houses and the vacant lots and fields where the sea breeze wafted through. Not long after, large factory buildings rose up along the Tama and Ebi-tori Rivers, while further inland, the factories grew gradually smaller in scale and closer together, forming a maze-like district where a penny-candy shop stood next to an ironworks. During the period of rapid economic growth after the war, buildings for small businesses replaced the barracks, cheaply-made ready-built homes took over where the minka houses had been, and condominiums filled in the vacant lots, but the scent of the air that filled Monoi's nostrils had barely changed. At night, when the exhaust and dust had dissipated, the smell that seemed to seep from the roads and the walls of these buildings was still that of oil and rust.

Thanks to the recent economic boom, the windows were still lit in the relatively larger factory buildings on this block in Higashi-Kojiya. From the smaller factories, light that escaped from under doors facing the alleyways and the sound of machine tools indicated where work was still going on. Down one of the backstreets, Monoi looked up at one of the second-floor windows of a two-story stucco apartment building and, checking that it was dark, he parked his bicycle in front of the factory next door. A faint light filtered out from under the sliding door that read Ota Manufacturing, but there was no sound of machines.

"Are you there?" Monoi called as he opened the sliding door, and from the back of the workshop, Yokichi Matsudo, "Yo-chan" as he was called, turned to face him.

Among the eight thousand small factories in the Ota district, Ota Manufacturing was mid-size, employing ten workers to make high-precision dies for plastic products. Within the less than thirty-five hundred square feet of the long, narrow building, there were two late-model NC lathes, two copy lathes, two universal milling machines, one vertical milling machine, two drill presses, and one slotter, used to carve out molds for all sorts of plastic products—from space rocket parts to children's toys—out of black steel charge, accurate to one thousandth of a millimeter. In Monoi's time, they had been armed with a single lathe or a milling machine set up with an indexing head, but had tackled everything from milling cams for automobiles to machining grooves in shafts to gear cutting. But the production efficiency and range of products handled had changed entirely. For instance, when Monoi saw the die in progress that was set by the front entrance, he had no idea what kind of mold it was.

The workshop was dim, and Yo-chan sat beneath a single naked bulb that illuminated the work desk in the back. On the cluttered desk, he had lined up a colorful array of canned soft drinks amid the horseracing newspapers.

"Cold out tonight!" Monoi called to him, and this time Yo-chan turned only his face to him, dropping his eyes to his own hands without a word. He held a micrometer in his right hand, in his left, a piece of soldering wire.

After measuring the diameter of the solder with the micrometer, Yo-chan reached his right hand toward the tool drawer on top of the desk and started looking for a drill bit for the drill press. Monoi momentarily wondered what he was up to. His eye caught sight of Yo-chan's left hand as he placed the solder on the desk. His thickly bandaged index and middle fingers were too short. There was nothing beyond the first joints. In shock, Monoi grabbed Yo-chan's left hand, and with no change in expression, Yo-chan said simply, "An accident."

"When?"

"The eighth."

"Was it the lathe?"

"Uh-uh. A coworker was carrying a die. The guy's hand slipped, and it dropped right on my hand." As Yo-chan said this, he gestured lightly with his chin at a shelf in the front where some kind of die big enough to fill a grown man's arms sat. *That thing fell on your fingers?* Monoi thought, speechless.

"I got an X-ray right away at the hospital. The bones were crushed. Before they could operate, the fingers got all swollen and turned purple," Yo-chan said matter-of-factly.

"Can you move your fingers?"

"More or less."

"What about the guy who dropped the die?"

"He quit."

"You didn't report it to the police?"

"I'll get workers' comp. As long as I have three fingers left, I can work."

Yo-chan was a man who only ever spoke this way. His instincts and emotions were sunk deep below the skin, never surfacing in any perceptible form. His features had barely changed since he started working in this factory after graduating high school seven years ago.

His face was pale from spending all day long inside the factory where the sun never shone, but even still, the flesh was gone below his cheekbones, sharpening them even further, and his jawline was as slender as a teenager's. Now that face looked all the more vulnerable in the murky light.

"Did your boss by any chance tell you to keep the accident under wraps?" Monoi tried asking again.

"I was the one who told him to forget about it," Yo-chan said, not even lifting his face.

"Why?"

"Because whatever." Yo-chan rummaged through the drill bits arranged by size inside the tool drawer and then asked, "Do you see a one point four?"

"A regular cutter?" Monoi asked. Shifting his reading glasses, he reached into the drawer, found the small plastic case that held the 1.4-millimeter bits, and handed it to him. Yo-chan took out a twist drill bit that was as fine as a sewing needle from the case, spun his seat around, and set it into the spindle of the hand-feed drill press behind him. Then, he grabbed one of the aluminum juice cans that were lined up on the desk, turned it upside down, and placed it on the drill press's round worktable.

"What are you doing boring a hole in the bottom of a juice can?" Monoi asked, to which there was no immediate response. Yo-chan used the hand-feed to place the tip of the drill on the bottom of the can and pulled down the handle. A fine powder of aluminum scattered about, and within a second a hole appeared from which orange juice dribbled out.

Yo-chan moved the can with the hole to the work desk, and wiped away the spilled juice with a dark towel. He set that aside, and then began to file the end of the soldering wire. As he watched, Monoi figured out for himself that Yo-chan was trying to insert the end of the sharpened solder into the hole he had just made in order to seal it back up.

"I had been reading tomorrow's racing column, but my fingers hurt and I couldn't sit still," Yo-chan murmured as he continued to sharpen the soldering wire. "And there's something that pisses me off, too."

"What's that?"

"The ends of my fingers they cut off at the hospital—I thought they were going to give them to me after the surgery, but they just threw them away. Those were part of me, and when I think about how they threw them out in the garbage, it's unbearable."

And if they had given him the severed fingers, what would he have done with them? Monoi wondered. "I guess so," he mumbled, but he had no idea of the private despair Yo-chan might be feeling about losing his fingers because of someone else's mistake.

Monoi took two glasses from the sink in a corner of the workshop and placed them on the work desk. He opened the gift box of foreign liquor, took out an ornate bottle that seemed like Scotch, and poured a little into each glass. While he did this, Yo-chan furrowed his brows as he held the end of the soldering wire with pliers and tried to jab it into the hole in the juice can.

"The hole is too small," Monoi told him. "How thick is the solder?"

"One point six."

"Then the hole must be one point five," Monoi looked for the case of 1.5-millimeter drill bits in the tool drawer and placed it by Yo-chan's hand. As he did so, Yo-chan took a swig of the whisky that Monoi had poured and whispered, "Ah, that's good," grinning for the first time.

For Monoi, though, whisky neat was too strong, and as soon as it touched his lips his face screwed up involuntarily. Yo-chan must have noticed, because he got up from his seat and brought over a cup of water from the sink without a word. He also produced a space heater from somewhere and placed it at Monoi's feet. Monoi added some water to the whisky and paused to catch his breath. The space heater warmed his feet too.

Meanwhile, Yo-chan enlarged the hole in the can with the 1.5-millimeter drill bit and once again began pushing the end of the solder into it. This time the solder went in smoothly and, after wiping the plug he had made with the solder again with the towel, he smeared instant adhesive all around it. Then he snipped off the remainder of the solder with a pair of scissors, filed down the head, and after he had sandpapered it some more, he held up the bottom of the can for Monoi to see.

"Well?"

"Let's see," Monoi said. If the slight unevenness on the surface could be mended with a thin layer of putty and then coated with paint the same color as the aluminum can, it could be finished to a degree that would make the hole imperceptible to a layman's eyes—that was Monoi's opinion. No, if the objective was to fill in the hole that he made, instead of using a drill press that carved the hole cleanly, it would be better to pierce the can with a scriber or something to give a slight breadth to the edge of the hole, which would expand the joint area of the solder that was supposed to act as a plug. *If it were up to me, that's what I would do,* Monoi thought.

"What are you going to do with that?" Monoi asked.

"I'll put sand or something in the can of juice and make the nurses at the hospital drink it. As payback for throwing away my fingers."

"You should present it to them with a decorative noshi gift tag that says, 'Give me back my fingers,'" Monoi chimed in, and Yo-chan laughed a little, perhaps feeling better, and left it at that.

"More importantly, your fingers. Do they still hurt?"

"A little."

Yo-chan set down the aluminum can, and pulled toward him the horseracing newspaper that had been left open. As he did so, some kind of thin booklet slipped out from beneath the newspapers. He picked it up—it was a color-printed pamphlet that said PC-98 Series.

"You buying a PC?"

"If there's a cheap one. We're entering the era when horseracing odds will all be computerized. That's what Koh says."

"Koh?"

"Katsumi Koh. The one from the credit union."

"Oh, the one with the flashy suit . . ."

"He usually looks normal. Though not so normal inside his head."

"Oh, yeah?"

"If he could, he says, he'd be someone different every day. A salaryman on Monday, a business owner on Tuesday, a gangster on Wednesday, a regular Japanese on Thursday, and a Zainichi Korean on Friday."

Yo-chan relayed this without much interest, lazily resting both elbows on the newspaper as he hung his head. Monoi, for his part, had no hypothesis to offer about this credit union fellow. Despite the flashy attire of the man he had seen earlier this month at Fuchu, Monoi's general impression had been based on how the guy carried himself and the look in his eyes—there was nothing specific to say about it, except that the guy seemed to belong to that particular vein of the shadowy underworld.

"You guys talk often?" Monoi asked.

Yo-chan, his nose still buried in his newspaper, answered, "Sometimes." The columns for races ten and eleven tomorrow, the 18th, were already scrawled over with red pencil. Race eleven was a 2,500-meter GII handicap turf race. Yo-chan had drawn two circles around Foro Romano, a fifty-two-kilogram lightweight.

"You always hope for a lucky break, Yo-chan."

"His workout times are good. I want this one to make the pace and hold the lead."

"I think Romano will tire out a bit. The favorite Genève Symboli will break away, and it'll come down to who goes after him . . ."

"You betting on Symboli, Monoi-san?"

"I'm going all-or-nothing on Saint Bid. He did well in the Tenno Sho."

"Yeah, I have a feeling he'll finish fast . . ." Yo-chan's red pencil traced the circle already drawn around Saint Bid, and he went on muttering to himself. "For the second half of the race, it'll come down to whether he can keep up with the horses in sixth, seventh, and eighth place . . ."

It was already near midnight, and Monoi's eyelids had started to feel heavy as he listened to Yo-chan's mumbling fade in and out. The late night hours always went like this, his companion a young man with enough stamina to go until morning once he got started on the horse columns. Anyway Monoi knew that if he were to go to bed at this hour, he would still awaken before dawn, get up to use the toilet and then, unable to fall back asleep, he would instead be yawning until noon the next day. Since he was up now, it was better for his health to stay up a little longer, and sleep soundly until morning.

The late autumn sea breeze that blew across the tin roof of the factory made a sharp, high-pitched sound. To Monoi's ears, that sound carried with it the exact color and shape of the whitecaps in the vast ocean that lay beyond Haneda Airport. Meanwhile, beneath his lowered eyelids, the nichrome wire glowing red inside the space heater at his feet transformed into a single flame that grew bigger and bigger, and just as he thought it had turned into a blaze of coke burning in a furnace, Monoi found himself fumbling, half asleep, through images of the foundry in his hometown from fifty years ago.

This factory melted down pig iron, scrap steel, and casting scraps in a cupola furnace, casting these into molds to make engine parts and cable drums for fishing boats.

The structure was about 10,000 feet square, its walls and roof made of corrugated metal, with the ground left as sandy soil. The roof rose higher above where the cupola was installed, and there was a gap to let the heat out, from which soot and dust mingled with sparks escaped along with a foul odor. When rain and snow fell through the gap in the roof, it would land on the two five-ton cupolas inside and cause steam to pop and hiss while the ventilator groaned. Beneath all this, the outdated cupolas shuddered as they blazed on, always sounding as if they were about to burst apart.

His job as a twelve-year-old apprentice factory hand had included carting in a fresh supply of coke split that was used to adjust the burn rate of the furnace. By the time he was fourteen, he had been appointed the task of shoveling the coke as instructed into the charging door of the furnace, and by sixteen, he had learned to check the heat level on his own by sight. Stoking the cupola was a battle against time, and if there was even slightly too much or too little blast air, the coke bed would burn too hot or result in incomplete combustion. If the coke and the charge were not packed in just right, it lowered the thermal efficiency and the temperature of the molten metal would drop. Whether the furnace was burning properly could not be detected until the melted iron started to drip down. Then, giving off a pale yellow light, the fifteen-hundred-degree molten metal would flow down the tap hole, and the more experienced workers collected it in ladles and poured it into one after another of the molds lined up on the bare ground.

The castings were heavy, as were the castings alloyed with silica sand and the scrap steel used as metal charge. The factory workers all had muscular upper bodies, and the skin of their palms was darker and thicker than a charcoal burner's.

By the time Monoi became an apprentice in 1937, the port of Hachinohe, where the foundry was located, was already crowded with the large roofs of the municipal fish markets and refrigeration plants, and behind the hundreds of fishing boats lined along the quay were the shipyards and the ironworks and the foundries—all day long, the alleyways clamored with the sound of hammers from the shipyards and sparks from the lathes, horse-drawn wagons carrying fish and the cries of the migrant fishermen coming and going. On mornings when tuna were hauled ashore, he was awakened by the frenzied atmosphere of the auction, and if there was a good catch of sardine or saury, then he would be woken up by the splintered cries of black-tailed gulls flocking around the minnows. Soon after, when the three-thousand-ton quay that stretched out like a desert was erected right next to the fishing port, the large cargo ships laden with ore and grain as they approached the quay were visible from the foundry windows that were always left open, and along with the shouts of the longshoremen, the smoke and steam spouting from the freight trains as they came in on the service tracks beside the quay reached all the way to the workshop.

The charging door of the cupola was set as high as the roof of a two-story building, so that when he was up on the ladder, from time to time through the window he could just make out over the rooftop of a warehouse the tips of the small flags sending off the procession of conscripted soldiers as they marched along the roadway behind the factory. Then, passing outside the window every day around noon was the cart of the junkman who made the rounds of the foundries gathering scrap iron, and the man would always call out sleepily, "Hey there! Hey there!" In the early evenings, a peddler woman appeared at the back door, and the foundry owner's wife would buy whale meat or dried herring from her. On days when the woman did not come by, their dinner would be cold radish or cabbage soup with sardines.

Work at the foundry ended around sundown, but after that, there was still the daily maintenance of the cupola to attend to. By then, the hustle and bustle of the day had subsided and the pitch-dark port became a refuge for the sea breeze, the lights of the Dalian-bound cargo ships anchored offshore began to sway like lanterns in the streets at night, and the vortex of the wind soon came surging all the way up to the foundry, rattling the tin roof. As he scraped off the oxide residue that clung to the firebricks inside the cupola, the silence of the night penetrated deep into the core of his mind until he would finally look up and see fluffy snowflakes falling down through the gap in the roof, falling on the tracks of the Hachinohe Line that ran just behind the foundry, falling on the bus route—the same snow that was falling on the mountain village an hour's bus ride from the foundry. In the summer, what fell through the gap in the roof were moths and beetles.

Hachinohe in summer, from the meadows in the town center to the fields that spread out toward the mountains along the bus route, burst into a stifling, uniform green. On the morning when he returned to the village for the Obon holiday, he would take out his only good clothes—a white shirt and pants and a pair of socks—don a straw hat atop his freshly shorn head and, carrying the cloth-wrapped parcel of dried squid and fish that the missus had prepared for him, he set off from the foundry.

Perhaps it was the summer of 1941 when, on the bus ride back home, Monoi saw Komako, the mare that his family in the village had reared on loan, being led away by a horse dealer. The landowner had finally decided to abandon Komako, who was too old to foal. Komako had come to the family the year Monoi was born, and he and the mare had lived under the same roof ever since. In 1937, when his eldest brother, Sei'ichi, was conscripted, he had begged the family to keep the mare until he returned home, but since that time the mare had had stillbirths and difficult labors. From the window of the bus as Monoi watched the mare being taken away, he was suddenly overwhelmed by an emotion that made his entire body tremble, as if quivering from hunger pangs, and he had stared, wide-eyed. A mare that could not give birth could only be taken to the slaughter, and he futilely thought anew how neither the person who would turn Komako into meat and eat her nor the person who would get money from selling her was a tenant farmer like his family. Watching Komako, drooping her thoughtful head and swinging it gently from side to side as she was led through the lush green fields along the bus route, made him suddenly wonder whether there was any future for him at all. Long after that, Monoi would recall this question time and again.

During the war, the foundry became a designated factory of the Japan Industrial Patriotic Association and they made the bodies of hand grenades, but the real enemy was his own body, wasted away by malnutrition. Burdened with a listlessness that made him feel as if he were carrying sandbags on his back, he paid no attention to the state of the war. But charge material and fuel became harder to come by, and before he knew it, the large fishing boats were mobilized into a transport convoy and disappeared. The auction at the fish market was discontinued under regulation, and the number of cargo ships entering the three-thousand-ton quay grew fewer by the day, replaced in the port by long lines of female students on their way to and from work on the construction of a gun battery on Kabushima.

In the spring of 1945, all the men who remained in the

neighborhood disappeared as they were organized into the combined brigade of the Hachinohe defense, and the only ones left at the foundry were the owner Kanemoto and Monoi, with his impaired eye. The cupola was rusted, and the shelves for work in progress and the raw material storage area were empty. Day after day went by with only air-raid drills and volunteer construction work to keep them busy and it may have been, in a sense, an oddly peaceful time during which there was no need to look for meaning in life. In August, at the height of summer, the pumpkins that Monoi had grown in a field near the foundry were ten centimeters in diameter, and the spider lilies that poked out here and there among them were bright red. Yet again that year, the rice in the nearby paddies did not bear fruit.

He was twenty when the war came to an end, the world Monoi saw around him made him think of a castle that had collapsed overnight, a swarm of ants scattering from the wreckage. Resourceful worker ants—those who had used their wits and fattened themselves up before the ruin—were no longer around. Meanwhile, for the less resourceful forager ants, there was still only the endless cycle of each day's desperate struggle to acquire enough food.

In reality, even six months or a year after the end of the war, goods such as pig iron and scrap steel never appeared on the market, and the foundry remained at a standstill. The owner Kanemoto had not been clever enough to squirrel away goods during the war, so they had no reserves with which to survive off the black market. The demobilized factory workers left one by one, and by the summer of 1946, the owner and Monoi were again the only two left, and all that remained of the foundry were a bucket full of burnt coke dregs and a small heap of casting scraps from hot-water spouts and the like. While the owner went out looking for work and materials, Monoi tended the vegetable garden with the missus, and he managed to find work as a day laborer at the port, so there was just enough to feed himself and the Kanemoto family, but his hope that it would all turn around soon diminished by the day. In its place, a feeling began to take hold that nothing more could be done, neither about himself nor the factory.

And then, in late autumn 1947, the foundry owner called him into his office, where he took out a large bottle of beer from the safe, set it on his desk, and said, "This mighta gone bad, but have a drink?" It wasn't a regulation bottle or rationed goods—it was a real Hinode beer with its trademark seal of a golden Chinese phoenix taking flight. He must have stashed it somehow before the wartime beer distribution became controlled. He did as he was told, taking a sip from the glass of that old beer, and then the owner asked Monoi to resign because he wanted to close out the factory. It was as if his ten years of loyal service had just evaporated with the froth of beer, but there was no one to blame—Monoi knew full well that it was simply the way of the times. Just as he knew that no good would come of reproaching him, Monoi did nothing other than hang his head.

But that night, Monoi had an unexpected, once-in-a-lifetime experience. In the middle of the night, before he even realized what he was doing, he had somehow managed to pull the fuel oil out of the cupola's ventilator and carry it in a bucket to the main house, gripping an iron poker in his other hand. At that moment, as chance would have it, his stomach started to hurt—a bout of diarrhea from the old beer—forcing him to run to the toilet where he finally came to his senses. Had he not ended up in the toilet, he had been about to beat to death all four members of the Kanemoto family and set the factory on fire.

Monoi shuddered at this violence that had come from out of nowhere, and he was left speechless. He had always thought of himself as mild-mannered, but the realization that within him resided a fiend who could do something so unpredictable was so startling that it upended his entire twenty-two years, and for the time being at least, the extreme poverty and enduring hunger of yesterday vanished. Still shivering, he wept and told himself over and over again that he was a horrible man and—with great remorse for his parents—regretted that he had ever been born.

Monoi convinced himself that this had been the first and last time such a thing would happen, that he would never do it again, but once his fit of passion had subsided, the profound lethargy that followed felt all the more intense. And in that moment, as he gazed out at the brightening sky through the small window in the toilet, for the first time ever he considered his own life, and he wondered if he was no better than a horse or an ox. In that moment he also reflected upon the hopelessness and destitution that had seeped into every aspect of his life, from his beginnings on the sooty earthen floor of his village home all the way to the present.

Early that morning, when he left the factory with his belongings wrapped in a single cloth, the youngest son of the Kanemoto family, Yoshiya, came running after him calling, "Big brother! Big brother!" but Monoi did not respond. That day, the tracks of the Hachinohe Line that ran along the coast and the bus route beside it were lightly dusted with snow, and the grass was still lush and green. As Monoi walked, he pictured himself as Komako as she was led away along the village bus route, and he continued to ask himself whether he had any future.

Right, so that was Hinode Beer . . .

His stomach fluttered at the resurrection of this taste from the distant past, and Monoi came back to himself. He pushed away the newspapers that were crumpled beneath his elbow, and took another sip of lukewarm whisky.

It had been a long time since he'd last recalled the fiend he had become just that once, forty-three years ago, and even after all this time he shuddered anew with repulsion, and he took another sip of his whisky.

Yo-chan's head still hovered twenty centimeters above the newspapers, but he was no longer looking at the racing column. Seeming to stare through the five uneven fingers of his left hand that lay atop the papers, his gaze appeared neither blank nor focused. Yo-chan would at times become lost in a trance like this, but his face looked so colorless and transparent that there was something ghastly in his utter lack of expression.

"Yo-chan, what happened?" Monoi asked gently.

"I . . . I set a fire this morning." Yo-chan spoke in a voice as mono-tone as ever.

"Where?"

"The house of the guy who dropped the die on my hand."

"You set his house on fire?"

"I had planned to call him outside and punch him. But then that seemed like too much work." As Yo-chan went on mumbling, he stared at his left hand that he held out before his eyes, which remained as colorless as before.

"A human body . . . They throw away the fingers they chop off in the garbage, right? And when you die they'll burn you all up in a gas furnace. So it's not even worth a punch," Yo-chan said to himself.

"What do you mean by worth?"

"Like a hundred or a thousand yen. Everything has a price."

"If that's true, there's no worth to a human mind, either."

Monoi thought Yo-chan hadn't been listening—after Monoi's response, Yo-chan's head had again hovered above the newspaper—but after a while he mumbled, "I wish I could scrape out the contents of my mind, and instead fill it with sand or something. With smooth, pure-white sand . . ."

Yo-chan had grown up in an institution, and it had been seven years since he graduated vocational high school and started working. Even though he earned more now than salarymen his age, he wished to fill his mind with sand—Monoi could not understand just what exactly this guy was thinking. Perhaps this was what the young people meant by "snapped," but even so there was something exceptionally cold, unfeeling, and dangerous about the way Yo-chan had snapped.

Come to think of it, even though they were about the same age, he doubted that his grandson Takayuki—blessed with everything from a wealthy home and loving parents to a promising future—would ever have thought of filling his own head with sand, no matter what. As he pondered this, he looked over again at Yo-chan's small head bent over the newspaper.

"So that house, how much did it burn?"

"Just under the eaves at the front door."

"You sure?"

"Yes."

"Well, in any case, don't you dare do it again."

Monoi lightly patted the silent young man's shoulder, and got up from the stool. Although Yo-chan had set fire to someone's house, his act seemed considerably different in substance and meaning from Monoi's own eruption forty-three years ago, and he could only admonish him not to do it again.

He made his way back on his bicycle, with nothing but the cold wind left on Sangyo Road, and though his body was now awake, reminiscences of the wind and snow and the sound of the grass in his hometown were still bursting forth, little by little, from somewhere within him. Three days after leaving the foundry in Hachinohe, Monoi had packed the 1.8 liters of rice that his parents had scrambled together in his bag and boarded an Ueno-bound train at Aomori Station. Monoi remembered being crammed inside the train overflowing with passengers carrying black market rice and potatoes, and though he had felt desperate and anxious, he was at the same time steeped in a buoyant sense of freedom. It was similar to the feeling he had experienced on the day he left home for the first time at the age of twelve to become an apprentice in Hachinohe, accompanied by his father and rocked about in the bus. It made no difference to him whether it was a bus or a train, as long as the road led him somewhere far away, whatever might lie beyond.

But it had been forty-three years since that day. He had eaten thousands of cups of rice and shit them out just as many times, but where the hell had he escaped to? Whenever he would think about it, the more than half a century's worth of time always collapsed into a hollow, and the wind swept through his entire body. The quiet conclusion that he had not escaped anywhere had occurred to Monoi a while ago, but now that he had reached a point in his life when there was no longer time to start anew, the void in which he found himself was quite possibly even deeper than the one in his hometown.

Any liquid, no matter how complex, would surely break apart if it continued to spin in an endless centrifuge for over half a century. And the components that were now scattered about included the earthen floor of the house in which he was raised in the village of Herai, the millet fields, smoke from the burning charcoal, the deeply lined faces of his mother and father, Komako's drooped head, dried radish, all sorts of images of the foundry in Hachinohe, the chill of the Pacific wind and the green smell of grass that clung to each of these memories, and finally his own solitary body in which all of these resided. Aware of the unbearable weight of still not knowing if he had a future, Monoi arrived at the Haneda intersection where he turned into the shopping district.

It happened that moment. A motorcycle was parked in front of the pharmacy, and a patrol officer he recognized from the nearby police box turned to face him.

"Oh, Monoi-san," the officer said, raising his hand in greeting. "I just got a call from the Seijo Police Department. Is Mitsuko Hatano your daughter? Can you get in touch with her? If not, would you mind coming with me?"

"What about my daughter?"

"No, it's her husband."

"Hiroyuki Hatano?"

"He jumped into the tracks of the Odakyu Line. They say he died instantly."

Monoi, suddenly unable to recall the face that went with the name, responded, "I see." Then he said, "Thank you for your trouble," and bowed his head. Perhaps sensing something peculiar about his reaction, the officer looked at him dubiously, seemingly taken aback. He told Monoi the name of the hospital, and left it to Monoi to contact his daughter.

"Well, then . . . Thank you," the officer said and straddled his motorcycle.

After the officer had driven away down the alley, the trademark seal of Hinode Beer shone from the vending machine of the liquor shop kitty-corner to him. It felt all the more bizarre that the same seal of a golden Chinese phoenix that he had seen forty-three years ago in the foundry in Hachinohe should be there now. *I never had a future. I didn't escape anywhere after all.*

PART TWO

1994

THE NIGHT BEFORE

物井清三

SEIZO MONOI

1

Sunday morning, Monoi retrieved the newspaper and saw the headline on the front page, CRIMINAL INVESTIGATION OF OGURA GROUP IMMINENt. He scanned the article and set down the paper, and just as he had found the scallions and deep-fried tofu in the refrigerator and started the miso soup, a call came in from Shuhei Handa, who asked, "Did you read the article about Ogura?"

This was the third investigation into Ogura. This time, the investigation centered on Kimihiro Arai, a representative of Takemitsu, a group of corporate raiders that had bought up shares of Ogura Transport between 1986 and 1989. Arai was suspected of extortion for demanding that Ogura buy back his shares shortly after he had become a board member at Ogura Transport in early 1990. Arai had already been arrested and charged two years earlier in a separate suspected extortion case against Ogura.

According to the article, the decision by the District Public Prosecutor's Office to move forward with a third investigation was prompted by the fact that, when the situation first came to light in 1991, charges had not been filed against Ogura's management, who were suspected of aggravated breach of trust for agreeing to the buyback of Takemit-su's shares, and now that the statute of limitations on said case had expired, an inquiry into defendant Arai had been deemed essential for identifying the flow of money behind Ogura's series of suspicious activities. The article further stated that this latest investigation into Ogura would be carried out amid the stalled investigation of the so-called "S. Memo" scandal, which dated back to 1990, when Ogura's main bank, the former Chunichi Mutual Savings Bank (absorbed and merged into Toei Bank in 1991), had fallen into financial difficulties and an influential politician from the Liberal Democratic Party had apparently promised to support its plan for rehabilitation. Three bil-lion of a twelve-billion-yen loan that the former Chunichi Mutual Savings group had made to Ogura Development in 1990, in the guise of a land purchase and development of a golf course, was suspected of being in violation of the investment law, and the latest investigation would inevitably have an impact on the outcome of the trial of two suspects arrested and indicted in this case—the former Executive Managing Director Koichi Yasuda and former Company Auditor Tatsuo Sakagami, both of Chunichi Mutual.

"I glanced at it, but—" Monoi said.

"What an useless article," Handa finished for him.

Ordinarily the Ogura-Chunichi Mutual Savings scandal would have had nothing to do with either Monoi or Handa, but the reason they were forced to pay attention to it had to do with Hiroyuki Hatano.

When Hiroyuki Hatano committed suicide back in November 1990, Monoi had been called in by the police, and was suddenly questioned about his relation to Seiji Okamura—what kind of person Okamura was, when was the last time Monoi had seen him, whether he knew about the letter Okamura had written to Hinode Beer back in 1947, and so on—leaving him utterly bewildered. That was when Monoi learned that Hiroyuki Hatano had somehow acquired this old letter of Seiji Okamura's, recorded the letter onto a tape, and sent it to Hinode. At his age, Monoi had assumed he would never again experience such a change of heart, but this document written by his elder brother Seiji Okamura, whose face at that point he could not even remember, caused a small waver in his chest, and since then, having tucked away his memory of the transcript of the letter that the police had shown him in a corner of his mind, he had often found himself sitting before the family altar in his home, at a loss for what to do.

Then, at the Buddhist memorial service held forty-nine days after Hatano's death, Monoi found out that Handa was handling the investigation into the letters and the tape that Hatano had sent to Hinode Beer. Handa told him that Seiji Okamura's letter had been given to Hatano by a corporate extortionist, but when it came to the crucial points such as the circumstances of how the extortionist came to be in possession of the letter sent to Hinode Beer over forty years ago, and why he had given it to Hatano, these were not yet clear to him.

Furthermore, Handa explained that when the extortionist had given the letter in question to Hatano—a dentist whom he had never met before—he had apparently referred to the financial difficulties of Chunichi Mutual Savings Bank and Ogura Transport. This was the point from which Monoi's interest in the sequence of the Ogura-Chunichi Mutual Savings scandal originated.

At the same time, it seemed that Handa had been chewed out pretty well by his superiors after Hatano had killed himself the same day they had questioned him about Hinode Beer's complaint letter. Handa might have been driven more by his own dissatisfaction about the case rather than a particular interest in the substance of the scandal. This was probably also why he had spoken to Monoi in such detail about the investigation, which he normally would have kept entirely confidential.

These being the circumstances, the two of them had kept an especially close eye on articles that appeared in the newspaper, but the mysterious connections between the Ogura-Chunichi Mutual Savings scandal, the dentist, the extortionist who had made contact with the dentist, Seiji Okamura, and finally Hinode Beer remained as indistinct as ever, and frankly Monoi was starting to lose interest.

Handa was a different story, though. As he himself would say, he had always had a tenacious personality, and despite having dismissed the article as useless, now he asked, "I bet that dude from the credit union knows all about this kind of money circulating underground. Do you think he'll be at Fuchu today?"

"It's the Tenno Sho. Of course he'll be there."

"I'll be there today too. The Emperor's Cup will go to either Biwa Hayahide or to Narita Taishin, right?"

Since Hatano's suicide, Handa had seemed somewhat lackluster about his work. Last year, he had transferred to the Kamata Police Department, and even though he said things had picked up a little again, if he was sneaking out of work to go to Fuchu, then he must not be so busy after all.

Then, as if he had just remembered, Handa changed the subject. "By the way, what did the private detective say?"

"They found an old man who fits the description at a nursing home in Akigawa, but I'm sure it's the wrong person again," Monoi replied.

Last year during the Obon holiday—the festival of the dead—when he went to visit his family graves in Hachinohe, Monoi had decided to seek out Seiji Okamura's grave as well. When he'd inquired with Okamura Merchants about its location, they told him that the last contact they'd had with Seiji was a postcard sent from Tokyo around 1953. Since his long-lost brother's family register was still listed in Hachinohe, Monoi decided he would spend some time looking for Seiji. This was how, after New Year's, he came to hire a private detective agency, but after three months there had been no solid leads, and he no longer expected much.

"I hope they find him," Handa said.

"Thanks."

"Well, see you at Fuchu." With that, Handa hung up the phone.

Just then, the bell in the pharmacy rang, and when Monoi stepped outside he found Yoshiya Kanemoto, in golf attire, standing by his parked Mercedes.

"Big brother, have some of this ginseng. It'll perk you right up," he said and thrust a paper bag at Monoi. It was obvious he had been gambling in South Korea again.

"I'm well enough, but thanks anyway," Monoi said, taking the bag. Inside the Mercedes was another man going to play golf with him, and he nodded perfunctorily at Monoi. He knew the faces of a few of the yakuza whom Yoshiya ran around with; today it was the always-somber man with the mole.

After Yoshiya went off to play golf, Monoi was finally able to have his breakfast of miso soup and fish simmered in sweet soy sauce. He then did a bit of tidying out in front of the pharmacy, which was closed for the day, and left the house before nine, slightly earlier than usual.

THAT DAY—APRIL 24TH—MARKED the second day since the horserac-ing venue had moved from Nakayama to Fuchu. For the first time in a while, a number of Monoi's friends turned out, and before it was even noon, the usual faces had gathered in a corner on the second-floor of the grandstand facing the track. The crowd was bigger than usual, since the Spring Tenno Sho was taking place at the Hanshin Racecourse, but most of the people were looking at the horseracing newspapers in their hands rather than at the early races happening before their eyes, and the cheers rising from the grandstand after each race that morning were still muted.

Upon arrival, Handa, true to his word, grabbed Katsumi Koh—"the dude from the credit union"—who was already there and, thrusting the morning paper at him, said, "Explain this to me, will ya?"

Koh glanced sidelong at the front page and replied derisively, "It means the investigation has finally hit a wall. Who would be stupid enough to leave any trace of a bribe to a politician?"

"I want you to tell me about the 'alchemy' behind all that, the tricks those guys use to make the big money."

When Handa pressed him, Koh offered only a teaser, "First thing you need is capital," and refused to divulge anything further. Mean-while, Nunokawa's Lady exclaimed, "Uuu, eer!"

Nunokawa's daughter was as energetic as ever, twisting her upper body, swiveling her head round and round, and issuing cries from her throat. Reaching over from her right, Nunokawa shoved a hunk of cream bun into her mouth, but the girl spat it out, along with plenty of drool, and it fell onto her lap. Breadcrumbs were littered around her feet.

"There, she doesn't want any more." From the girl's left side, Monoi grabbed the package of pastry and a towel from Nunokawa. As Monoi wiped the girl's mouth with the towel, she shrieked, "Uuu, eer" again and happily bounced atop the bench, kicking his shin. Now sixteen, the girl had put on some weight, and despite her short stature she was too heavy for her mother to deal with during her weekend visits home from the special care facility, so the job of tending to all her personal needs now fell to her father. Thanks to this, Nunokawa—sturdy as he was—seemed to be having trouble sleeping due to back pain. Not that he complained much about it, but his virile stature did appear slightly diminished. Taking the opportunity to foist his daughter on someone else for a few minutes, Nunokawa yawned over the newspaper spread open in front of him.

"Uuu, eer!" The girl cheered at the top of her lungs again.

"Hurdle? Yes, that's right. The steeplechase is next. Who do you think will win?" When Monoi asked the girl this, she contorted her neck and jutted her forehead toward the racecourse, indicating a horse. The horse warming up before the finish line wore a saddle-cloth with the number six, and when he checked the newspaper he saw that it was High Beam, the most popular horse. Amused, Monoi turned to face his three friends in the seats behind him.

"Hey. Lady says number six will win next. Someone bet on it."

"Quinella on six-eleven. I'm feeling pretty good today." This from Yo-chan, but alas, he was talking about the Tenno Sho.

From beside Yo-chan, with his head buried in the newspaper and gripping a red pencil, Koh spoke up, "Monoi-san, quinella bet on six-eleven, bracket quinella on six-eight. You can bet all your money today, you can't lose."

"The capital will come from Koh's credit union. A loan without collateral, no less," Handa cut in from beside him.

Koh curled his lip a little and snickered. There was something peculiar about his snicker.

Katsumi Koh had joined their group in early spring three years ago, shortly after the soaring stock and land prices finally began to correct. Everything was immediately colored by the economic recession, and as if even financial institutions—and their employees—were suddenly at leisure, Koh began to show up at the races every Sunday, sitting with Yo-chan at the foot of the pillar by the first-floor betting windows. The reason Koh got along with Yo-chan was simple—"The guy doesn't talk about money," he said.

According to what Koh had told them, he had graduated from Keio University in accordance with his parents' wishes; then a friend of the family had invited him to work at the credit union, where he devoted himself entirely to the loan business—for ten years he never returned home before midnight. At the beginning of 1990, when he had had the highest sales performance in his branch, he had coughed up blood from a gastric ulcer and was hospitalized. After two months of convalescence, he had returned to work, only to learn he had lost his spot. Apparently that's the way it goes in finance. He was reassigned to deposit affairs, and now that his days consisted of collecting small monthly deposits of ten or twenty thousand yen from general, non-member customers, Koh said, his life had gotten easier. In truth, he had the face of an exceptionally ordinary company employee.

On the other hand, Koh's attire—which Handa liked to describe as "host club or hot-spring-spa after-dinner show"—was anything but ordinary. Today he was wearing a double-breasted Italian suit and an eye-popping lime-green necktie. This façade seemed, in part, an effort not to be made fun of as "too straight" by the employees of his family's business, which operated a wide array of pachinko parlors and amusement arcades, or by the various organized crime underlings he came in contact with, but even so, Monoi still detected a shadow of that particular vein about him, and his first impression that he belonged to that dark underworld remained unchanged.

Nevertheless, this did not take into account Koh's undoubtedly complex psychology. He felt an emotional distance toward all Japanese people, yet at the same time, he himself said that when it came to other Zainichi he was "at odds with everything from their values to their speech." Handa, the detective, and Nunokawa, the ex-army man, treated Koh as different simply because he was a Zainichi.

"If you say so, Handa-san, I'll loan you a million if you promise to give me back thirty percent of your winnings," Koh said from behind Monoi.

"You better look for another victim," Handa spat out. Koh snickered again. Yo-chan was still glaring at his newspaper, the headphones from a portable radio in his ears. Nunokawa, stifling one of his many yawns of the day, stole a glance at the group of young women occupying the space about three seats away from them, a single furrow appearing between his brows. In the last two or three years, it seemed that horseracing had even become wholesome entertainment for young people, as the number of teenage girls and student-types had increased considerably. Lady had been attending the races for ten years already, and she now watched gaily, rocking the bench beneath her.

Below them, the 3,100-meter steeplechase had started on the dirt track. Each man—Monoi and his friends—raised his head slightly, watching the horses as they ran on the dirt track beneath the overcast sky. Seen from afar, the movements of the horse and jockey that leaped to the front looked awkwardly mechanical, like a crankshaft going round and round. When one of the jockeys took a spill halfway through the far turn of the first lap, Nunokawa's daughter, who hated to see anyone falling from a horse, let out a full-throated scream.

After sweeping past the grandstand, the pack of horses slowed the pace for the backstretch of the second lap. The horse wearing the number six, High Beam, started to inch forward about midway through the straightaway. "There he goes," Monoi said and patted the girl's back, and the girl whirled her neck in broad circles and tried to say something. At the final obstacle before the fourth turn, a couple more jockeys fell in succession, and with two more horses out of the race, the final surge of ten horses in the homestretch ended with High Beam breaking out to the finish line.

"Look at that, number six won," Monoi said to Lady, but the girl, having seen the falls right before her eyes, was lolling her head downward as she began to sob, which made Nunokawa growl, "Cut it out!"

Behind them, persistent as ever, Handa continued to pester Koh. "How can tens of billions of yen be moved around so easily in the first place? Explain this to me."

Monoi strained his ears a little to listen in on them now.

"You can't make money without circulating it. Every time money moves, someone benefits. That's why it goes around," Koh said.

"Then in the case of Chunichi Mutual Savings, who circulated the money and how, and who benefited from it?"

"They all circulated it together, and each of them benefited. Listen. Those guys, first they looked for a flash point to take advantage of. Chunichi Mutual Savings was a triple whammy: management in trouble; an accounting fraud; infighting between management and the founding clan who were their top shareholders. Next, they created a fixed-race scenario. Then they recruited those who wanted in on it. They had their plan. All they had to do was execute it."

"You mean how one day out of the blue the founding clan sold their stock holdings to a third party?"

Right, that's what had happened. Monoi himself briefly contemplated the course of events that had been reported in the media. Using Zenzo Tamaru, a businessman with political ties, as their middleman, the founding clan of Chunichi Mutual Savings had sold off their stock holdings to a third party, and it was speculated that the management of Chunichi Mutual Savings, finding themselves cornered into this third-party takeover, had been promised support by the influential politician from the Liberal Democratic Party known only as "S."

In addition, there was talk that "S." had received money in return for his aid, and that the murky twelve-billion-yen loan Chunichi Mutual Savings had made to Ogura Development for the land purchase and development costs for a golf course was used as a slush fund. The charges against the two executives of Chunichi Mutual Savings who had already been arrested were related to this loan. Incidentally, according to the newspapers, the three billion from the twelve-billion-yen loan that was suspected of being in violation of investment law had been loaned to Ogura Development through a keiretsu-affiliated nonbank. This matter had been exposed due to a lack of registered documentation when the broker loan and the revolving mortgage were established. The land Ogura had originally purchased for the golf course was a mountain forest worth only about one billion yen, and of course no golf course was ever constructed. And S. had not given any support to Chunichi Mutual Savings either.

Ultimately, the current of money did flow to its predetermined destination. After a while Kihachi Takemura, the third party to whom the stock holdings were transferred from the founding clan, sold off the shares to Toei Bank, and eventually in 1991, Chunichi Mutual Savings was absorbed into Toei Bank. As Koh had said, it was clear that things had unfolded according to a plotline someone had planned out, meaning that the founding clan of Chunichi Mutual Savings; Kihachi Takemura, who received the stock transfer; Toei Bank; the businessman with political influence, Zenzo Tamaru; and the unknown politician had all worked together to circulate the money.

"If that's true, where did the loan to Kihachi Takemura for the funds to buy the founders' stock holdings come from in the first place?" Handa pressed on.

"Takemura? He's an old ally of Zenzo Tamaru, so with one call to action from the Okada Association, a loan is no big deal. I'm sure they gave it to him without even any collateral."

"So the connection between the founders, Takemura, Toei, and the politicos is Zenzo Tamaru? He's the one who plotted the scenario?"

"A detective shouldn't even mention the name Tamaru," Koh retorted, but Handa was unfazed, and continued to pepper him with amateurish questions.

"Then the corporate raiders, Takemitsu, buying out Ogura Transport's stocks was also part of the scenario?"

"I'm sure that was different from the main narrative, but in any case, they're all connected somehow and they're all floating each other at the right time. Buying out thirty-four-million yen worth of Ogura Transport stocks is no small thing, you know. If the average share price from '88 to '89 was twelve hundred yen, that comes out to over forty billion yen. And Toshin Finance, who loaned Takemitsu's Kimihiro Arai this amount of money, was a subsidiary of Toei Bank."

"Forty billion . . ."

"That's the capital. First, Arai drove up the stock to its highest value of nearly nineteen hundred yen through speculation. Then, in exchange for selling the stocks he had bought up, he demanded that Ogura Transport and its main bank Chunichi Mutual Savings buy back the stocks at a relatively cheaper price. The newspapers reported it as sixty-one point two billion, so working backward, that comes out to about eighteen hundred yen per share. A return of twenty billion on forty billion capital—that's the work of the likes of Takemitsu."

"It sounds like Takemitsu's Arai railroaded them into giving in to his demand, but I guess neither Ogura nor Chunichi could do anything because he had the dirt on them."

"What dirt? Whether it's Ogura or Chunichi Mutual Savings, they tried their hand in the underworld, and when the time was right, they sucked out as much honey as they could. Same for Tamaru. And Takemitsu, too. Talk about dirt—they all had something on each other. It was a give-and-take so that no one would have to suffer a huge loss, they saved face for one another. At the same time, those guys are playing a serious game of who traps whom first."

"In their world, extortion is considered a serious game, huh?"

"If you're talking about Arai, all it shows is that he failed to do enough behind-the-scenes maneuvering. Right about now, I'm sure Tamaru—through a lawyer—is getting hold of Arai in jail and demanding that he take care of the mess he's made."

After a short pause, Handa grumbled, "Well, you sure know a lot about this."

Without letting on how he took this summation, Koh replied in a drawl, "I grew up breathing that kind of air."

Perhaps Handa couldn't find the right words to respond, or maybe he had lost interest, but instead of a reply, he slapped the back of the bench with his newspaper and their conversation ended there.

Down on the racecourse, the horses in the sixth race had finished their presentation in the paddock, and could already be seen warming up. It was now past noon, and though just a little while ago the girl had not wanted any more to eat now she said she was hungry again, so Monoi delivered a piece of the cream bun to her mouth. Nunokawa, still staring out at the tracks with sleepy eyes, did not even look at his daughter. Instead it was Yo-chan who, as usual, had gone to buy some milk for the girl. Inexplicably, Yo-chan took surprisingly good care of her.

As Monoi's gaze alternated between the four-year-old horses with their carefree limbs moving beneath the tranquil, overcast spring sky and the drooling mouth of the girl, his mind wandered back to Ogura and the former Chunichi Mutual Savings, and he pondered just who, if any, of those involved had taken a loss. Even though they had basically been swallowed up, it wasn't as if the individual employees at either the former Chunichi or Ogura had incurred any debt, nor had they lost their jobs. Even for the two former Chunichi executives—it was more like they had drawn the short end of the stick—neither they nor their families were going to end up on the street. When money circulated, it meant that debt had to circulate somewhere as well, but still, the amount they were dealing with was so large, it seemed unthinkable that just one person would have to pay the price in the end. When Monoi finally realized that not one of them had ended up losing his shirt, he felt dispirited.

In that moment, as he suddenly remembered the image of the mare

Komako that had been sold off half a century ago, a certain thought went through his mind. It was as Koh had said, one couldn't make money without circulating it, but the money circulated by those who had already made their fortunes—where did it come from in the first place? From the hands of Monoi's father and mother as they carried sacks of charcoal in his village, from his own hands that kept the cupola burning, from the hands of his older sister who worked as a factory girl, from the hands of Seiji Okamura as he made the beer—wasn't the money born of these hands? And yet, into these hands came only barely enough money to eat, while the rest became someone else's wealth. Not only that, but just as Komako, the last resource of an impoverished family, had been taken away by the landowner, and just as the bucket of casting scraps left behind in the vacant Kanemoto Foundry had been carried off by the debt collector, there was no doubt that a fortune had been amassed from every last drop wrung from the have-nots and the guileless. Indeed, Monoi knew it was too late to realize this now, but as it revived the dormant sense of stagnation that had saturated his entire life, he felt all the more dispirited.

Half a century after the war, he compared the sense of entrapment of this one little ant that had failed to escape to how he had felt just after the war ended, that sense of shivering in total darkness. The very space and time in which he existed were contracting with each moment, as if that time and space were running out, a feeling akin to impatience. The mild yet puzzling bouts of frustration he experienced daily, the way he became lost in thought like this, and the abstraction he unconsciously fell into as he pondered these many things—all of it made him feel jittery, a sort of relentless torment.

Monoi wiped Lady's mouth with the towel—she was drooling and smacking her lips as she ate the cream bun. His hand reached out to her automatically, but to be honest, at the same time he could not help feeling repulsed by the sight of her shirt collar covered in drool and breadcrumbs. Next to her, Nunokawa, silent and still, kept his eyes on the racecourse, while behind him Koh took the conversation in a completely different direction.

"Can't you move some money into fixed deposits this month? A hundred thousand yen would do," he said to Handa, trying to get a modest deal out of him.

Beside them, Yo-chan held out a carton of fruit-flavored milk he had just come back with, saying, "Here you go."

Monoi helped the girl drink the milk through a straw, which she clenched with her teeth as she squealed with delight. At home, she was never given anything sweet since fixing cavities was such an ordeal, so the only-on-Sunday cream bun and fruit-flavored milk were her favorite treats.

Nunokawa, finally looking more like himself again, lifted his head. Just as he seemed to cast a glance at his daughter, his gaze passed over her head and settled on the three men sitting behind them.

"Hey, Koh-san. Where would you say the real money is in this country?" Nunokawa suddenly asked.

"City banks, major securities companies, life insurance companies, a sector of the large corporations, religious organizations. Why do you ask?"

"As I drive all day along the Tomei Expressway between Tokyo and Nagoya, I like to kill time wondering which one I'd take down, if I could. Like you said, all you need to look for is a flash point, right?" Nunokawa had turned to face forward again, and he muttered as if he was talking to himself.

"If that's the case, then it's manufacturers you want," Koh responded without missing a beat.

"Why manufacturers?" It was Handa who asked this.

"Companies that make things understand the value of money. Manufacturing begins with calculating the cost of a single rivet or screw. Once the product has been created, they have to sell them one by one for a specific price. With a gross profit of two or three percent—it's backbreaking work."

"So?"

"Because they understand the importance of money, they suffer the most when it is milked out of them."

"That would be heartless," Handa said, laughing.

As he listened to the idle chatter, it occurred to Monoi that he himself held various deep-seated grudges against manufacturers in general. The foundry in Hachinohe where he had become an apprentice at the age of twelve; Hinode Beer, where Seiji Okamura had worked half a century ago, the same company his grandson had recently tried to join; and the factory in Nishi-Kojiya that was once his workplace for a quarter-century. The reason these grudges still smoldered deep within his gut was unclear to him—it wasn't as if he had particularly strong feelings about each company, yet certainly the hue of his own life spent observing these various entities in their respective heydays had been somber, devoid of color.

Behind him, Yo-chan mumbled, "What would you do if you got their money?" and then fell silent again.

"Manufacturers, huh?" Handa said to himself, and he too fell silent. The fanfare as the horses entered the starting gate sounded, and Lady let out a joyous scream from atop the bench.

The four-year-old colts and fillies started off the 1,400-meter race on the backstretch of the turf track. For the fewer than ninety seconds he observed the race, wondering which one would pull out ahead, Monoi's mind was blank.

The horses' legs stood out in bright relief as they ran on the spring turf. As the front line of the pack's progression shifted forward and backward freely, the eleven horses rounded the far turn, advancing and retreating by a nose. Two front runners had slipped ahead. Another horse closed in on them from the outside. And in that flash of a moment, when Monoi narrowed his eyes and wondered if this horse would overtake them, he thought he saw the horse's legs stumble, then the jockey was suspended in the air before careening sideways. The streak of the jockey's green helmet. The number seven on the saddlecloth of the horse that had lost its rider.

A cry issued from the girl's throat, and her head and arms began to whirl violently. The movement of the spectators' rising from their seats in the grandstand formed a tsunami. The crowd roared as the pack of horses crossed the finish line, then stirred and shook with excitement as the stretcher was rushed out.

Monoi checked the racing column in his newspaper and confirmed the name of number seven's jockey—Shibata. He was from Aomori, the same prefecture as Monoi's hometown, and he had been riding horses for as long as Monoi had been attending the races, more than twenty years. He was not a flamboyant rider, but Monoi was rather fond of the way he drove his horse, a style that conveyed his grit and passion. The jockey was always careful at the start of the race, but he had misjudged it today and Monoi felt regret as he watched Shibata being carried away on the stretcher.

The buzz in the grandstand refused to settle down, and Koh said, as if just now thinking of it, "If we're talking about a manufacturer, go for something big. Toyota, Nippon Steel, Mitsubishi Heavy Industries . . ." He continued to list names.

"I'd pick Sony or Hinode," said Handa. "Back when I was at the Shinagawa Police Department, I would always stare out at their buildings from Shimbamba Station. At night, they looked like fortresses of light."

Now that Handa mentioned it, Monoi recalled having seen the nightscape of those two companies' headquarters. He gave the rest of the fruit-flavored milk to the girl, who was still fretting beside him. The milk was already turning lukewarm, and the girl had crumpled down the end of the straw with her teeth. In spite of this, one sip of the sweet milk calmed her down a little, and she spat out a word that meant "yum."

Not long after this, Nunokawa thrust out a ten-thousand-yen bill. "Mind if I go take a quick nap? Watch Lady for me. I'll be back by two." Without waiting for an answer, he stood up and walked away— he practically fled. Monoi and the three men behind him watched Nunokawa go. None of them uttered a word, they just looked at one another.

In that moment, as Monoi watched the retreating figure of Nunokawa, who must have felt a spasmodic need to get away from his daughter even for a little while, he sensed in him a bottomless gloom, but as an outsider Monoi had no right to say anything about it. Shifting his thoughts, he turned to Yo-chan behind him and asked, "Isn't there a wheelchair-accessible bathroom here?"

"I'll go look for one," Yo-chan replied and nimbly got up from his seat.

Yo-chan returned after about five minutes to announce that he had found a bathroom, and he added, "I just heard on the radio. The managing director of Toei Bank, Yamashita or something, apparently he was shot and killed in front of his home."

This time, it was Handa's turn to rise immediately from the bench. Saying there might be an emergency deployment, Handa too disappeared.

城山恭介

KYOSUKE SHIROYAMA

2

From the regular tee of the 184-yard par-three seventh hole, his shot barely missed the pond in front of the green, and he tensed up for a moment. Right after seeing the ball fly off, he realized to his dismay that he had sliced it, but he put off dissecting why he had done so and, telling the string of players behind him with a sheepish grin, "I'll see you up there," Kyosuke Shiroyama quickly moved on, chasing after his ball.

Hinode's Kantō regional competition took place every spring and fall at the Matsuo Golf Club in Chiba and was renowned for its huge turnout. Each time, fifty representatives from among all the distributors in the Kantō area were selected fairly, in a rotating order, from the main offices, branch offices, and sales offices, regardless of their size. From Hinode, in addition to the chairman, the president, two vice-presidents, four board members, and the sales manager and deputy manager of the beer division's main office, sales managers and representatives from their five regional offices and two branch offices in the Kantō area were also invited, totaling twenty-four members. From Hinode's subsidiaries and affiliated companies, another ten representatives were selected, again in fair turn. It was a successful event with eighty-four in attendance, all told.

Similar regional golf competitions occurred in conjunction throughout Japan in Hokkaido, Tohoku, Hokuriku, Chubu, Kinki, Chugoku, Shikoku, and Kyushu, and for the past twenty years, this traditional event had been a proud display both within and outside the company of the solidity of Hinode's unique network of production, distribution, and sales. However, now that same network also seemed to symbolize a lumbering Gulliver, and Shiroyama knew that he would like to put an end to the event within the next few years, but in the same way that sundry unresolved items accumulated into a mountain, overturning tradition was always a Herculean task.

The members were divided into In and Out groups, and that day Shiroyama was on the ninth "In" team—his teammates included the president of Tomioka, a major distributor; the president of another major distributor, Iida Shokai; and the president of Sato Transport, an affiliated company.

The competition had started at nine in the morning, and by the time Shiroyama—the fourth player on team nine—had landed his ball on the seventh-hole green, it was past noon. He had nailed his approach shot from the edge of the pond, and the ball had landed two meters in front of the pin, so he thought he could make par. The cup was on a gently rising slope. The president of Sato Transport, who had holed out before him, called out, "Take your time."

Although Shiroyama's golf game spanned thirty years, he did not put in much effort, sometimes managing to break a hundred— sometimes not—and he did not have much enthusiasm for it, either. He set his aim squarely on the putting line and putted the ball as usual, and when the ball luckily reached the cup, light applause rose from across the green.

Shiroyama hurried off the green and, swapping his club for a 3-wood for the next hole, began walking with the other three members on his team. "I hope it doesn't rain," the president of Sato Transport said, looking up at the overcast sky.

"It should hold up," Shiroayama replied.

The two distributors were engaged in their own conversation: "Instead of a price hike, there's a better chance for a price slump," to which the other replied, "We'll see what kind of prices the major supermarkets will set."

They were discussing the outcome of retail prices of alcoholic beverages, which were set for a simultaneous increase on May 1st. The manufacturer's current suggested retail price of 220 yen for a 350-milliliter can would be raised to 225 yen, but the major supermarkets were strategizing instead to engage in a price war by extending their discount rate even further. There were reports that, depending on the supermarket, the price would be set from as low as 193 yen. Several years ago, the nationwide price of beer had started to collapse in discount liquor stores, but until now supermarkets had held their discounts to a few yen per can. But this time, it appeared certain that a large-scale price reduction of a minimum of ten yen ranging up to twenty yen was about to happen. Although he could hear the two men's conversation, there was no way for Shiroyama to respond to it offhandedly, so he chose to ignore it and instead turned his gaze to the beautiful undulating green before him.

Shiroyama was fond of the Matsuo golf course, with its thick groves of Japanese cedars and the fairways that seemed to ripple out from beneath them, each of which were always serenely quiet. No matter where he was on the course, he could look upward and see only the cedar trees rising to the sky above. As he made his way around each of the eighteen holes, he drove the ball into the air from this deep green expanse devoid of anything superfluous. The ball then dropped back down onto the green carpet, and he launched it up again. Prizing the tranquility of these hours, Shiroyama still came here to chase the ball around, but in his four years at the top of a company that sold a trillion and three hundred billion yen worth of beer, the truth was that there had barely been a moment to take a deep breath amidst this sea of green.

During Shiroyama's thirty-five years of service to the beer industry, things had never been as severe on so many different fronts as they were now. Due in part to last year's cool summer, the year-over-year aggregate demand for beer had fallen into the negative for the first time in nine years, and last year's decrease in demand was further confirmation of a declining trend in average spending per customer in the midst of three years of stagnation resulting from the collapse of the bubble economy, as well as of signs that alcohol consumption itself was leveling off.

Meanwhile, if he considered the arena of production, distribution, and sales of alcoholic beverages, first of all, the diversification of sales channels of alcoholic beverages had accelerated considerably as a result of partial revisions in 1989 and 1993 of the guidelines for obtaining a liquor license, and deregulation under the Large-Scale Retail Store Act. The market expansion of discount liquor stores gained even more traction, and now that conditions were increasingly favorable for convenience stores and major supermarkets to venture further into the alcoholic beverage business, the competition within various channels to drive prices down had turned fierce—this was directly connected with the all-around decrease in sales at liquor stores in general—and the entire keiretsu-based conglomerate structure of primary wholesalers, secondary wholesalers, and chain liquor stores that the beer industry had established over its hundred-year history was at this moment in time shaking from its very foundation.

There was a sector of liquor stores that had adopted the strategy of franchising or converting into convenience stores in order to survive, but small-scale retail stops that couldn't afford such options were no longer able to keep business going. The wholesalers, in turn, were also suffering from an undeniable drop in sales due to the undercutting on unit price and the slump in consumption. For liquor stores and wholesalers both, even if they were to streamline their businesses to counter the narrowing profit margin, the current keiretsu system was nothing but an impediment to cost-trimming strategies, such as bulk purchasing and refining the product line with strong sellers, and it only exacerbated the management inefficiency. On the other hand, within the wholesale industry where family-run businesses were common, measures to strengthen management infrastructure and improve their competitive edge, such as mergers among small to mid-size wholesalers or absorption by larger wholesalers, were not the kind of thing that could happen overnight.

Separately, instead of focusing on domestic beers, with their high liquor tax that never turned a profit no matter how many units they sold, convenience stores and large supermarkets were beginning to engage in direct sales by partnering with foreign beer manufacturers to develop their own in-house brands or forming exclusive distributor agreements. As of May 1st, a 350-milliliter can of domestic beer would cost 225 yen. Meanwhile, an imported brand sold directly by a certain convenience store cost 180 yen. Such direct transactions between major mass retailers and foreign manufacturers had resulted in beer price-busting and diversification of sales channels. Moreover, foreign products that benefited overwhelmingly from tax rates and raw material costs had been streaming into the country. What these situations suggested—as far as domestic beer manufacturers were concerned—was a future for the beer industry that promised to chip away at Japan's hundred-year-old sales and distribution system and ensured a decline in sales for Hinode, the company that had dominated such a system.

Every manufacturer nowadays was being forced into reforming their business structurally, but complex problems—such as reassessing the distributor network, including the rebate system; restructuring wholesalers; restructuring and cutbacks with small-scale liquor stores; reevaluating the immense publicity and advertising costs shouldered by the manufacturers, as well as the labor costs of maintaining their regional sales network; and restructuring the land transportation industry in order to streamline distribution channels, for both manufacturers and for distribution and sales at every level— these could all only be realized five or even ten years from now.

Nevertheless, the fact was that, in just a week, when the shelves of liquor shops and vending machines were lined with 225-yen cans of beer, at the same time discount stores, convenience stores, and major supermarkets would be stocked with imported beers and their own label beers for less than two hundred yen. The price difference for a case of twenty-four beers could amount to nearly a thousand yen. For Hinode this meant that, a week from now, the brunt of this impact would be felt by the six hundred dealerships and the 130,000 general liquor stores around the nation. Over the last half year, Shiroyama himself had taken the lead, wearing out his shoes visiting clients—to the point that, even now just standing on the grass, his feet hurt a little.

"The long-range forecast predicted that this summer will be extremely hot," the president of Sato Transport called out to the two men from the distributors.

"Yes. Things being what they are, all we can do is pray for good weather," the president of Iida Shokai replied.

"I don't know what we'll do if there's no hot weather to drive up business," the president of Tomioka followed up.

Since the kickoff to the spring sales season had not gone so well for any of them, Shiroyama agreed that they must count on the weather. Their competitors doled out new products again this spring, but Hinode had not. While sales of the lager and Supreme were still steady, they had decided to prioritize a large-scale reform of their domestic product line and the reorganization of delivery terminals in order to simplify their distribution system, but current sales figures were still forefront in his mind.

As they emerged from the grove of cedar trees, team number three was waiting to tee off at the par-four eighth-hole. Shiroyama saw that the man gripping the long-iron was Sei'ichi Shirai, and he appeared to be having trouble addressing the ball. The eighth hole was a dogleg with a narrow fairway shaped like the hollow curve of a suribachi bowl, which made the tee shot crucial, but Shiroyama could see right away that Shirai was restless and taking far more time than usual.

Shirai's golf game was similar to Shiroyama's but the way he played could not have been more different. Shirai had always been the type to first envision a conquest that was a level above his own skill, and then seek out various methods for achieving it. While Shiroyama paid more attention to his overall score, Shirai would go after a difficult course and be happy as long as he parred just one hole, even if he triple-bogeyed the other seventeen. Shirai's approach to golf seemed somehow to correlate with the way he worked and his management philosophy—though there was quite a gap between his ideal and reality—and at times his pursuit of a strange shot made it hard to tell if he were calm or just moody, so it was interesting to watch him.

Shirai finally pulled into his backswing and followed through relatively cleanly, sending the ball flying. Shiroyama couldn't see where it landed, but since light applause rose immediately from the crowd, he presumed the ball was in a good position.

Shirai maintained a breezy countenance in front of all their distributors, but the truth was that he was incredibly busy, approaching the conclusion of four years of ongoing negotiations for Hinode's joint venture with Limelight—an event that would determine the course of their entire industry. Playing golf today must have really pushed him to the limit physically, but in order to divert the attention of the newspaper reporters and industry insiders, who were paying close attention to how the terms of the negotiations would pan out, and to evade the doubts and suspicions of rival companies, it was absolutely crucial for him to attend the competition as usual, looking as if nothing was amiss.

Waiting for his turn to tee off, Shiroyama made small talk with those standing around him, as once again he pondered questions about the joint venture he would have to make a final decision upon in a few days' time.

In the fall of 1990, when Limelight revealed their intention to dissolve Hinode's exclusive distribution agreement and to establish a new joint corporation with them, Hinode had been genuinely dismayed to realize that Limelight's objective was a full-scale entry into the Japanese market. The terms of the joint venture that Limelight presented would have limited Hinode's investment to 10 percent, with Limelight controlling all agency and management rights, and with regard to sales routes—the most crucial issue—Limelight would be free to select them as they saw fit, without being restricted to Hinode's network of keiretsu distributors. Moreover, the period of the joint venture was for ten years. In sum, the joint corporation that Limelight proposed would, rather than fitting into Hinode's network of affiliated companies, operate as a completely independent competitor that would dominate a corner of the Japanese market, and it was merely a formality of borrowing the name of a domestic manufacturer to get around the restriction on obtaining a license to sell alcoholic beverages.

Shiroyama and all the other executives were appalled at this, and during the first year of negotiations, the option to dissolve their existing relationship with Limelight was also on the table. Now that the past ten years of Hinode's business expansion efforts were finally bearing fruit, Limelight's products had reached domestic sales of seven million cases per year with a market share of 1.3 percent, and while dropping those figures would be, for the time being, a considerable loss for Hinode, the long-term damage incurred, were they to accept the terms Limelight insisted upon to establish a joint corporation, would be incomparable. Opinion was divided among Hinode's board members—either force Limelight to change the terms of the joint venture, or lose the 1.3-percent share by dissolving their relationship.

Nonetheless, last fall, after three years of negotiations, the tenacious bargaining led by board member Shirai had yielded results—Hinode's investment ratio was now forty-nine percent, and while management rights had been ceded to Limelight, the condition was that their sales routes would be restricted to Hinode's network of keiretsu distributors—and they had hammered out an agreement in mid-October. Afterward, both parties began drafting a prospectus to submit to the Japan Fair Trade Commission as soon as possible, but at the last minute, the JFTC had suddenly intervened. Limelight concluded that the winds were in their favor, what with the progress of the Japan-US Structural Impediments Initiative, the advent of a coalition government that had pledged deregulation and to open up markets at home and abroad, and the subsequent stricter enforcement of the Antitrust Act. Thus, they had cannily scrapped their agreement with Hinode and run to the JFTC.

The JFTC deemed the domination of Japan's domestic beer industry by four major companies an oligopoly and saw the extensive licensing system of production, distribution, and sales in the interest of liquor-tax collection as an impediment to full and open competition and a breach of the Antitrust Act, and had always been looking for the right opportunity to strike. Now, Limelight tried to put the screws to the JFTC to form a joint venture with Hinode under their original terms, but upon receiving this proposal, the JFTC's leadership proved to be more obstinate than ever before. According to the JFTC, the dissolution of the domestic oligopoly and the opening of proper free-market competition were not the only prospects if Hinode were to establish a new joint corporation in accordance with Limelight's plan. The JFTC even made the veiled threat that if a domestic manufacturer did not agree to such a joint venture, then beer, along with automotive parts, flat glass, and telecommunications, could all potentially become the target of Japan-US trade negotiations.

The JFTC took such a strong stance because, to put it simply, if one of Japan's manufacturers did not take on Limelight's aggressive demands, they would find themselves in a situation where they were unable to respond to requests from home or abroad and that Hinode was the only manufacturer with enough basic and fundamental strength to do so. Meanwhile, the National Tax Agency, who ordinarily should have protected the domestic manufacturer in order to secure the liquor tax, proved itself to be consistently weak-kneed, in part due to the chaotic political situation, and failed to demonstrate any leadership. However, considering the current trends, this problem would have occurred sooner or later, so ultimately one could say that Limelight had shrewdly taken the pulse of the times and come out victorious, while Hinode had gone on the defensive and lost.

In any case, fearing the remote chance that Limelight would join forces with a convenience store that sold seventy billion yen worth of beer annually, Hinode had, since January this year, returned to the negotiating table and, hoping to extract even a small concession from Limelight, Shirai had been hard at work right up to the day before yesterday. Even if they were to accept their conditions as they were, it might not have a significant impact on the basis of Hinode's management itself, but in the future it would wreak incalculable havoc on the entire beer industry, Hinode included. Once they set a precedent, other huge foreign manufacturers might launch similar successive offensives. If that were to happen, as of now the domestic industry had no countermeasures.

Over the last three months, many of those on the board of directors could not help but express resistance to an industry giant like Hinode willingly choosing a path that would ultimately lead to their network of distributors being devoured by a foreign manufacturer. And yet, no one would come out and say that there was any way they could refuse the joint venture. Shirai himself, from the start, had been of the opinion that if this road was indeed inevitable, it was in their best interest to prepare for it now, and Shiroyama too, after thinking it over countless times himself, was verging on the decision to accept their demands.

As for Hinode, they would be able to add Limelight's share to their overall sales for the duration of their ten-year joint venture, but if by that time, when Limelight had been set up independently and the era of full-scale free competition would begin, they still did not have a structure in place at least to cover their loss in shares of the beer market, there would be no future for Hinode anyway. What was more, if Limelight's raid into the market were to bestir the wholesalers and liquor stores themselves to finally accelerate the streamlining process that had languished for so long, then in the long run that could even be seen as a benefit.

The rest depended on how they would accede to Limelight's demands. If they were to swallow them whole, they would lose face in front of their competitors and every one of their distributors. Late last night, Shiroyama had instructed Shirai to present one final condition to Limelight. Namely that, during the first three years of the joint venture, Limelight must maintain the same suggested retail price as domestic manufacturers. For now, they would push for this one concession, and wait to see what would be their move. On Monday—tomorrow—Shirai was expected to return to the negotiating table with Limelight.

Presumably, this would bring the four-year-long joint-venture issue with Limelight to a conclusion. On Wednesday the 27th, they would summon the board of directors to present their final decision, and on the 28th they would convey the terms of their resolution to the JFTC and Limelight, and once the various procedures had been squared away, they would announce the joint venture by mid-May. However, as far as their business was concerned, before that could happen, they needed to explain the situation and build a consensus first among their designated shareholders, as well as their major distributors and competitors. The joint venture with a behemoth like Limelight—a corporation that held a 10-percent share in the global beer market and whose scale of production was one-and-a-half times that of all four major Japanese companies put together—no matter what form it took, it was sure to send shock waves in all directions.

The consensus-building was scheduled for the week beginning Monday, May 9th, after the Golden Week holiday ended. As Shiroyama made these calculations in his head, the queue in front of him to tee off grew shorter by the minute, while a new line had formed behind him.

A bird's call above his head reached his ears, and when he looked up the slightly overcast sky showed faint streaks of sunlight. Shiroyama breathed in the air, thick with the scent of new buds on the trees and, just as he had begun to contemplate the aim of his impending shot, the president of Sato Transport said casually, "About this morning's paper . . ."

Shiroyama, detecting the gloom in his voice, nodded lightly and replied, "I know."

Within Hinode, this morning's article on the criminal investigation of the Ogura Group was generally received without much surprise, but Shiroyama imagined that it must have been a source of recurring concern for their affiliated transportation companies. The management situation of every one of those companies was more or less the same as Ogura, and during the bubble years many of them, in order to offset the low profitability of their land transportation division, had dabbled in speculative assets and invested in real estate for diversification. Sato Transport was one such company. Since the year before last, Hinode had been sending their executives to Sato Transport and, as part of Hinode's efforts to restructure their distribution division, they had leased a section of the truck terminals and service routes that Sato Transport held in Saitama and Chiba, with an eye toward strengthening the company's management base. With Ogura, three years ago, before their scandal became public, Hinode had shelved plans to join their management, and because of this people said they had played it well.

In reality, although the plan to join their management had been shelved, Hinode's business partnership with Ogura had progressed steadily, and plans to improve their distribution network were still on track. The criminal investigation of Ogura alone would not destroy the company, and there were no other factors that would cast doubt upon Ogura, whose management team had already been fully overhauled and renewed. In that sense, Hinode had reaped well indeed.

"I do feel bad for Ogura. They had to send out apology letters to every single client, and even their drivers had to go around paying courtesy visits," the president of Sato Transport mumbled. Shiroyama responded simply, "You're right," and avoided any further conversation.

A stir arose from the back of the line, which then turned into sighs and murmurs. Shiroyama turned around to see everyone peering at the seventh-hole green across from the grove of cedar trees. Cries of "So close!" and "He almost made it!" rang out.

"Whose shot was that?" Shiroyama called out toward the back.

"Kurata-san. Ten centimeters away from a hole-in-one," someone shouted back.

"Ah, Kurata-san . . . No wonder," another voice mumbled. Indeed, it was not surprising for Kurata to almost make a hole-in-one on a par-three hole. Ever since he was young Kurata had been an avid golfer, and in his days as a salesman, whenever he had any spare time he would head to the links to practice alone. Of course, now that he was an executive vice president he no longer had the time and his score had suffered, but back when he was in his forties he had always been a single-digit player—he was even a zero handicap for a while. Perhaps natural ability and focus were not things that deteriorated with age, and since on his good days he could still easily drive 270 or 280 and certainly sink a three-or four-meter putt, at every competition someone would complain that playing without a handicap was not enough for Kurata.

Shiroyama tried craning his neck a bit to see between the rows of cedars, but he could not catch sight of Kurata. When Shiroyama bumped into him at the club house that morning, Kurata had whispered to him that there was no sign of the Okada Association making any new moves following Ogura's criminal investigation, nor was there a possibility that it would reach S. from the Liberal Democratic Party, yet there had been no sense of relief in his tone. Hearing this report, Shiroyama felt much the same—this was the natural reaction of a person involved who, every time the District Public Prosecutor's Office made a move, had to fear the repercussions of the investigation reaching Hinode and being exposed for violation of the Commercial Code.

Last year, Hinode had finally begun the process of ending their relationship with the Okada Association and, under the guise of purchasing a painting from them, had paid them a billion-yen settlement, and the two parties had signed a document. Even so, Kurata, who had singlehandedly orchestrated the difficult negotiations and brought it to an amicable conclusion, and Shiroyama, who as president had made the final decision, shared a common destiny with Okada should the situation take a turn for the worst. In the first place, the whole process was executed after they had carefully determined that such a possibility was as close to zero as possible, so that Shiroyama did not feel too pressured, but Kurata, having been directly involved in the negotiation, may have reacted to the situation differently. In private, Kurata may very well have been disquieted by the article in this morning's paper reporting the criminal investigation of Ogura, but even then, the fact that he still managed to come close to a hole-in-one was reassuring to Shiroyama, for the time being at least.

"I'll see you a little later," the second player from the preceding eighth team said as he set out from the tee, leaving just two players ahead of Shiroyama. *Now, for this tee shot, I'll aim for the middle of the curve in the dogleg, about 170 yards.* On this eighth hole, he always got caught in the trees flanking the course, so he wanted to make it today. Shiroyama donned his gloves again and, as he was warming up his wrists, he happened to look up across from the tee.

He saw someone running toward him, taking the long way around the tee. By the time Shiroyama had squinted to realize it was Fujii, the Tokyo branch president, Fujii had walked through the cedar grove and approached the back of the queue for the eighth-hole tee. As Shiroyama wondered whom he needed to talk to, Fujii whispered something to an executive named Shibasaki, who in turn took off in a trot toward Kurata at the very end of the line and whispered to him.

Shiroyama's and Kurata's eyes met. Kurata excused himself to those near him and, once he had reached Shiroyama at the front of the line, he said, "Managing Director Yamashita from Toei Bank passed away just a while ago."

He did not whisper the words, so the people around them heard as well, and a stir rose at once. Yamashita's death being what it was, those who did business with Toei must have quickly considered sending telegrams and making condolence calls. Shiroayama, on the other hand, had perceived the flash of some sort of sign in Kurata's grim stare.

He understood that something was amiss, and for the moment

he excused himself from the presidents of the distributors and Sato Transport. Kurata and Fujii followed him. Once they reached the cedar grove, Kurata came up beside him and said quietly, "Apparently someone shot him in front of his home in Den-en-chofu."

Shot him? Shiroyama wanted to ask, but he found himself speechless.

"I've had general affairs confirm with the police a number of times—there's no mistake. I've got the director of general affairs going to the hospital right away."

As Shiroyama listened to Kurata speak in a tone rigid with feigned calmness, he finally regained his own voice. "What about Teradasan?" he asked.

"He's at the main office," Kurata replied.

Terada was the president of Toei, and as the largest shareholder he was also a member of Hinode's board of directors. Shiroyama tried to picture him at the Toei head office just then.

"Which of our executives are still in Tokyo? Call one of them up, and tell him to act as point person with Toei. If possible, tell him to go to the Toei head office first."

"I'll ask Sugihara," Kurata said and immediately took out his personal cell phone.

Shirai, who must have just finished the eighth hole, came running through the grove carrying the wood he was about to use for the next hole. His brows were furrowed with irritation as he asked them, "How should we proceed?"

"How many teams are left of the Ins?" Shiroyama asked.

"Two or three, I think."

"Let's just finish the front nine. After that, let's gather the board members together before lunch . . ."

"Right," Shirai said to himself and walked back the way he came.

Kurata, who had finished his call, asked, "Should I reserve a separate room?"

"Yes, please." Shiroyama turned to Kurata and Fujii and urged them, "Now, let's all get back to the game."

Just then, someone else called his name and stopped Shiroyama in his tracks. It was Chairman Keizo Suzuki, who should have finished the front nine by this time and been on his way back to the club-house, but was now walking briskly through the grove toward him. Sixty-five years of age, Suzuki was slightly out of breath as he whispered the words, "It's the Seiwakai," referring to the crime syndicate.

Shiroyama gave him a vague nod, unable to respond otherwise.

"Please consider security measures for all of our executives immediately. I'm counting on you," Suzuki said.

"Yes," Shiroyama said and nodded again.

"In a situation like this, we must spare no expense."

"I agree."

During his tenure as president, Suzuki himself had been the one with connections to various characters including Tomoharu Okada, head of the Okada Association; Zenzo Tamaru, their advisor; and Taiichi Sakata of the LDP, among other elected representatives. It was true that he had inherited many of these relationships from his predecessors, and he had left it to Kurata to do the actual dirty work, yet there were still a considerable number of murky issues that only Suzuki knew about. Shirai had questioned Suzuki about these, and had then scrupulously formed a majority opinion on the item at the board meeting so that, during the change in management four years ago, Suzuki was somewhat reluctantly relegated to the position of chairman, and held no representative rights.

Like Kurata, Suzuki did not dare divulge the specifics, but there was no doubt that in his dealings with the Okada Association, he had more than once been in contact with the Seiwakai, who controlled them. Shiroyama felt both frustrated and anxious when he saw the dismal and reticent look on Suzuki's face. There was no way to feel at ease about the situation.

It was bound to happen in the end—after the collapse of their longstanding, codependent relationship with the hyenas that survived off the scraps of inter-corporate dealings, those hyenas would start attacking the corporations directly. Until just recently the financial institutions had continued to make loans to just about anyone, but three years ago, they had all at once changed course with the economic recession, and now there were a considerable number of corporations among their beleaguered customers who were entangled with crime syndicates. It was all well and good while the money was flowing, Shiroyama thought calmly, but today's incident demonstrated what happened when the money ran out and fangs were bared—a bank had been forced to pay the price with someone's life.

Hinode's situation was no exception—in fact, one could even say it was more complicated. The money that Hinode funneled to Okada-affiliated extortionists and political organizations via management consultant companies used to amount to about ninety million a year. This was a large amount for one company to expend, but above all, it was a clear violation of the Commercial Code. The year before last, when they had made the decision to settle accounts with Okada, the National Police Agency had continued to press the four major economic organizations for their cooperation in eradicating corporate extortionists and was pursuing an aggressive policy of exposing each corporation that had violated the Commercial Code. Both Hinode and Okada had sensed a crisis, and both parties—having determined that the damage incurred from exposure would be great—tentatively moved forward with the dissolution of their relationship, but in reality what they had was a truce, with both parties refusing to let the other's vulnerability out of their clutches. Okada knew the truth about Hinode's Commercial Code violations, while Hinode possessed information on Okada and their affiliates' expansive interrelations with various organizations and corporations.

Thanks to Kurata's tactics, Hinode was able to break away, but around the same time, Mainichi Beer had been exposed for furnishing profits to a corporate extortionist, which not only coerced them into changing over their management, but also affected their stock price. As a result of these charges, the police were said to have seized a huge trove of documents that revealed the links between crime syndicates and corporations, and this must have been a serious blow to

Okada as well. Because of Mainichi Beer's exposure, the National Tax Agency had audited Hinode as well, but since there were no tracks in their account books and registries, Hinode managed—narrowly— to avoid any further trouble. Now that conditions surrounding the underground economy were becoming more punitive, who knew how long Okada would just sit idly by? Even though they had reached an agreement with Hinode, might they not still demand something else? There was no way to dispel that anxiety.

"The police are damn sloppy . . ." Suzuki's tone, as he spat out these words, quavered a little.

It was true—ever since the law against organized crime took effect in 1991, the police had been pressuring corporations to eradicate the extortionists, but if these were the consequences, they were too much for the corporations to bear. The managing director of a major city bank's being shot and killed in broad daylight—that was far too high a price to pay, and was absolutely unacceptable.

"Akio Yamashita and I were in the same class at law school," Suzuki continued.

"I remember that."

"He was an honest and courteous man. I feel as if I've been shot myself. Terrible—just terrible."

As Shiroyama listened to Suzuki grow emotional, an image of his own wife of many years, Reiko, alone at home in Sanno Ni-chome, flashed through his mind, and he made a mental note to tell her to be extra vigilant about locking up the house from now on. It was rare for him to imagine the faces of his family while he was out working.

Back at the eighth hole, the president of Tomioka—the third player on Shiroyama's ninth team—was already standing at the tee.

"Oh, excuse me. My turn is next," he said to Suzuki and took off with his wood in hand.

Shiroyama returned to the game, but of course he was distracted and ended up with a double bogey for both the eighth and ninth holes. Even Kurata seemed to have bogeyed on the ninth, a par-three.

After they had finished the front nine, the Hinode staff gathered in a separate room, but the executives and employees alike were dumbstruck. Anything related to Okada had always been handled by Suzuki and Kurata behind the scenes, and even though they received summarized reports at board meetings, most of the members thought of it as someone else's concern—even Shiroyama himself felt that way, to some extent. It was understandable then that at the level of branch offices and sales offices, they had an even more uncertain grasp of the situation.

Meanwhile Kurata, with the typically placid, torpedo-like façade he wore in public, offered nothing more than a brief explanation of the situation and instructions regarding their response to each of Toei's clients. It was decided that President Suzuki and Shiroyama would make an appearance at the wake that would likely be held by the deceased's family as soon as that evening.

Shiroyama himself simply announced that tomorrow morning's board meeting would take place an hour earlier than usual, at eight o'clock. In addition to the existing meeting agenda, they would need to discuss new security precautions for executives.

"Well then, please go to lunch. Explain to your distributors as instructed. Thank you."

They adjourned after less than five minutes, and Shiroyama and Suzuki, who had to return to Tokyo, hastily changed their clothes and set out for the ride home in a company car. Shiroyama, feeling the need to bolster his darkening spirits, tried to think about their new product for next spring, a second lager that was currently in the testing phase. He would like to think that sales of the new product would be at least fifty million cases within the first year, especially if they hoped to reinvigorate the sluggish beer business. He preferred to occupy his mind with such things, but with Suzuki there with him, he could hardly afford to do so.

"By the way, last week I saw S. at a party for the LDP," Suzuki started to say, once they were in the car. "He said their coalition government will be crushed sooner or later, so he's counting on me in the event of a general election. I've never heard him speak so bluntly."

"Did he mean to say that a fundraising ticket is not enough?"

"It seemed that way. I have no idea what he must be thinking at a time like this, while rumors are swirling around after the Ogura scandal. If you happen to see him anytime soon, you'd better watch out, too. There'll be trouble if the likes of Tamaru get involved."

"I'll decline anything other than a fundraising ticket."

"If only it were so easy."

"We need to at least make our intentions clear."

Shiroyama felt hollowed out, forced to juxtapose the thought of the second lager—their single beacon of hope—with his feelings of self-reproach and loathing toward the less-than-idealistic corporate culture. But the brazenness that required him to deliberately set aside his true feelings—that was something he had mastered in the last four years.

SEIZO MONOI

物井清三

3

"Monoi-san, shaved ice!" From inside the store, the lady pharmacist called out to him. "Strawberry or melon syrup—which do you want?"

Her loud voice flew past Monoi's head and evaporated in the scorching sunlight as he watered down the sidewalk.

"None for me. You go on ahead," Monoi called back after a moment, then looked down at the morning glories beneath the woven reed shade. In the intense heat of the summer they were having, the flowers were only about three centimeters wide, and though they bloomed early each morning, by the time he opened the store at nine, they were already wilted and drooping. Whenever he saw the morning glories bearing up under the blazing sunshine, their vines creeping limply outward, Monoi could not help but wonder if the plant, not long for this world, was satisfied with its life, and before he knew it he would be muttering to himself before the morning glories.

The lady pharmacist, picking at her hundred-yen shaved ice, popped her head out from the store and remarked, "If you keep staring at those wilty flowers, the bluesbug will get you."

Reasoning that it was best to avoid the heat of the day, she always visited the shopping district before ten in the morning and brought back things like shaved ice and kudzu mochi. She would consume these sweets and then still manage to polish off two servings of somen noodles for lunch.

"Now, you'll get heatstroke if you stand out in the sun like that. Come inside and have some barley tea. I'm going to cook somen noodles for lunch soon."

"I don't need any lunch today. I'll have a little ochazuke before I head over to Akigawa."

"But you just went there yesterday. And in this heat—you sure are odd."

"You'll understand when you get to be my age."

"I'll be sixty soon myself, but who wants to think about what's ahead?" The lady pharmacist spoke with a mouthful of shaved ice, then went back inside. He could hear the television in the living room at the back of the store; a broadcast of the high school baseball tournament was playing. Monoi tipped his bucket over to pour the remaining water onto the asphalt and realized that it was in fact only yesterday when he last went to Akigawa.

Monoi did not have the blues—he just had a lot on his mind. Several matters had presented themselves each of which needed to be addressed, and lacking specific feelings about any of them, he simply divided his day at random, based on his physical strength, so that he could tackle them one by one. Watering the sidewalk repeatedly, tending to the morning glories, lunching on somen noodles, visiting Seiji Okamura at the special care nursing home in Akigawa every other day—all of these followed the same rhythm.

Monoi returned to the living room and sat down before the family Buddhist altar. He rang the small bell, joined his hands in prayer, and then put away the bowl of white rice he had offered that morning. There were so many departed souls—his wife, Yoshie; his grandson, Takayuki; his son-in-law, Hatano; the grandparents and parents from his ancestral village—all of whom had to make do with sharing a single bowl as an offering. But when he thought about it, it was strange that his older brother Seiji Okamura was not among them. A man whom he heard had died forty years ago was still alive, while the ones who should still be alive had passed away.

Pouring barley tea over the same bowl of cold rice he had removed from the altar, he took out some pickled gourd and eggplant and ate a simple lunch while ruminating on the reason he meant to visit the nursing home in Akigawa two days in a row.

Three months had passed since Seiji's existence had been confirmed at the beginning of May, but a few days ago, Monoi had started to think about taking Seiji into his home. There was no way he could nurture familial feelings toward a man with whom he had been accidentally reunited just three months ago, but when he considered that Seiji was, after all, his biological older brother, he felt it was his duty to care for him, and a part of him thought that, by taking care of Seiji, he might be able to spend the rest of his own life in peace. So long as he had time to be irritated by the hopelessness laid bare by the steady advance of old age, there was no question it was better for him to keep moving and do something useful instead, which is to say, it was more for himself than for Seiji. Nevertheless, considering how old they both were made him hesitate, and then he would waver between thinking he ought to do it with what strength he still had left and thinking it was already too late, so it was not something he could act on easily.

As he delayed his decision day after day, the height of summer arrived and Seiji's body was visibly weakened—yesterday he even refused the beer he used to sip through a straw. And he only had a bite of the watermelon Monoi had brought with him. Seiji had basically been bedridden the entire time, so his loss of appetite was not such a concern, but his fragile state yesterday gnawed at Monoi a bit, and as soon as he woke up that morning he felt the need to visit him again.

With Seiji's progressive dementia, was it physically possible to take the man into his home? And even if the conditions were right, would Monoi really go through with it? The decision was Monoi's alone to make—no one was pressuring him—but even as he slurped his ochazuke, he felt that there wasn't much time left.

Monoi packed an overnight bag with a collared summer shirt he had bought on sale in the shopping district, freshly laundered underwear and a towel, among other items. As for himself, he changed into a fresh shirt, put on a hat to shade him from the sun, and, after asking the lady pharmacist to water the morning glories in the evening, he got on the bus bound for Kamata from the stop in front of his store.

SEIJI OKAMURA HAD ENTERED THE nursing home in the suburbs of Akigawa in 1990. He had been seventy-five years old at the time, and the extent of what was discovered during the private detective's investigation was this: from 1950 to 1953 he had worked as a substitute teacher at a private high school in the Suginami district; after quitting for some reason that had to do with the school's circumstances, he had wandered from job to job: a small printing company, a warehouse company, and a food wholesaler, among others. Apparently he had spent the last ten years in the Sumida district, where he had been the live-in super at a company dormitory. The investigation had stalled because after he left his teaching position, Seiji stopped using his real name and did not update his certificate of residence, either—thanks to this, Monoi ended up paying the detective agency close to three hundred thousand yen.

It seemed Seiji had still frequented hospitals; in 1985, the police, called to the scene by a neighbor, detained him at Tokyo Metropolitan Bokuto Hospital, and after returning to his own room at the company dormitory, Seiji had apparently thrown a few hundred books out the window. Afterward, he did stints in Tokyo Metropolitan Matsuzawa Hospital and Tokyo Musashino Hospital, and four years had passed since he finally arrived at the nursing home in Akigawa, through the assistance of the welfare office. Up until the previous year he had been able to go on walks alone, but when Monoi found him this past May, he was practically bedridden, lying in one of the beds in a six-person room. He was a small man and so emaciated that Monoi thought he might be able to pick him up by himself. The hair on his shaven head, which had started to grow out a little, was stark white. Monoi could no longer recall the face of the man he had met several times in Hachinohe long ago, and perhaps it was his wrinkles, or maybe it was his expression, but when he first saw Seiji, it was as though he were looking at a complete stranger.

"Seiji-san. It's Seizo Monoi. Seizo from Herai."

Seiji had replied, nodding repeatedly, "Oh yes, yes. Seizo-san. It's you, Seizo-san." But though his gaze was fixed on Monoi, there was no movement or reaction in his eyes, and Monoi could not tell if he truly recognized him as Seizo Monoi from the village of Herai. The situation was still much the same.

According to the nursing home staff, Seiji's dementia, or perhaps pseudo-dementia, was worsening, and he had mildly impaired aware-ness and progressive paralysis—even though he could manage to state his own name and today's date, he did not seem to know where he was, where he used to be, where he had worked, where he was born, or the names of his family members. No matter what was in his head, the man lying there in his pajamas was so quiet—more like an object than a living being. Aside from the smell of his diapers he hardly had any body odor, and even the indications of his gender and vestiges of the most basic, commonplace human sorrow had long since disappeared. Most of the elderly patients in his room were in a similar state, but the extent to which Seiji had withered was aston-ishing to Monoi—he was so bone-dry and light that seeing him was almost refreshing. *Oh, I don't mind coming here*—it had been that stillness that first made Monoi realize this.

When he visited every other day, Monoi always called out to him, "Seiji-san. It's me, Seizo from Herai." Gradually, Seiji began to reply, "Oh, Seizo-san. Hello there," but that was it. When Monoi lifted a spoon to him he opened his mouth, when he offered beer through a straw he drank it, and when he changed him into a shirt and pants and took him outside in a wheelchair, he calmly complied. When Monoi had hospitalized his wife, Yoshie, he had fed her with a spoon and changed her diapers, but something about his looking after Seiji made him think that he was doing it to make up for not tending to his parents on their deathbeds.

In the time he had been coming to the nursing home, Monoi spoke about a lot of things to Seiji, who never said a word. He talked mostly about his memories of Herai and Hachinohe, but once he got going, the long-buried and sundry details surfaced one after another, their limitlessness surprising even him. The year Monoi became an apprentice at the Kanemoto Foundry, Seiji was already working for Hinode, but that summer he returned home for the Bon festival and he came to visit him at the foundry. Monoi felt no brotherly connection with Seiji, this person dressed in a fine suit who removed his hat at the door of the foundry and bowed to the factory manager, saying politely in greeting, "Thank you for taking care of Seizo." He felt anxious when Seiji then called him over and asked, "How are you? Everything fine with you?" Seiji's face had been kind, but his manner of speaking was always a little stilted, and although they were related by blood, Monoi had had the sense that Seiji, as the older brother, was trying to patch the void between two people who had not grown up together, and the awkwardness they felt at having nothing in common.

At the time, Seiji had given Monoi some pocket money, just a few yen, and left him with a clichéd encouragement: "We use castings for the equipment in the beer factory too. Manufacturing is a respectable job, so you work hard, all right?"

In the Okamura Merchants family, his second wife had given birth to a boy who would be the heir, and this might have been why Seiji did not return to Hachinohe very often. The next time they saw each other was in 1942, when he came home after being drafted. The owner of the Kanemoto Foundry, having heard a rumor of Seiji's conscription, urged Monoi to go see his older brother Okamura before he left for the front. Still in his work clothes, Monoi quickly set out for Hon-Hachinohe Station, but by the time he arrived the scene at the station was teeming with small flags waving the conscripts off, and over the shoulders of the crowd gathered, he saw Seiji standing there, a sash across his chest with a message wishing him enduring fortune in battle. As Monoi stared at his older brother, the smallest and palest of the five or six men being sent to the front, Seiji noticed him and gave him a small smile, so he returned the gesture with a shy grin. That day, after the train had left, in the dispersing crowd he saw the figures of his parents who had come all the way from their village in Herai, but his mother kept her head bowed the entire time as if to avoid notice.

As Monoi told such stories, he could not tell from Seiji's aspect whether he was listening to any of it—his expression did not change much. But one day, Monoi asked him, "Do you know Hinode Beer?" After a few minutes, as if suddenly remembering something, Seiji responded, "Hinode's beer sure was good." In the anonymous taped recording of the letter that Seiji had allegedly written back in 1947, he had repeated, several times, "Hinode's beer sure was good," and just now he had spoken those same words in a reflective tone, as if that very memory had returned to him. And yet, when Monoi followed up with the question, "Do you remember the Kanagawa factory?" there was no further reply.

Every time Monoi visited Seiji, he now brought a can of Hinode beer and let Seiji drink it through a straw. Yesterday, he had not drunk the beer, but when Monoi pulled off the tab and set the can on the table, Seiji had stared at it for a long time. It was a can of Hinode Lager, the label bearing the same golden Chinese phoenix taking flight from half a century ago. Seiji's gaze was fixed on it for so long that Monoi felt compelled to ask, "The Hinode label makes you feel nostalgic, huh?" but after a while Seiji only mumbled, "Hinode's beer sure was good."

Monoi got off the train at Akigawa Station on the Itsukaichi Line and, after buying a can of beer and the soft adzuki bean jelly that Seiji liked at a shop in front of the station, he got on the bus. After they made their way up the Takiyama Highway along the river for about fifteen minutes, the Ryokufuen Care Home appeared beside the rolling hills of Nishi-Tama Cemetery.

From the bus stop it was about a five-minute walk uphill, and by the time Monoi made it to the entrance of the nursing home he was soaked in sweat. As he stood there for a moment mopping his brow, the bright voice of a female staff member called out to him from the pass-through window of the administrative office. "Well, look who's here! I wonder if Okamura-san is up. It's nap time right now." Here, both residents and visitors—as long as they were senior citizens— were addressed as if they were barely in preschool. Monoi never got used to this, but instead of feeling annoyed, the subservient words, "Oh, that's very kind of you, thank you," sprang from his lips and his body bent forward to bow of its own accord. Monoi bowed two or three times toward the window before he changed into a pair of slippers, and headed toward the building where all the bedridden elderlies were housed together.

Sure enough, at two o'clock in the afternoon the majority of the residents were napping, so there was no recreation or entertainment, or staff making rounds. The sultry air from outside meandered in through the screened windows and over the linoleum floor, so clean it was rather bleak, and somewhere wind chimes were ringing. The doors to the rooms had all been left open. Monoi craned his neck to peer into one of them.

Seiji was at the far end of the row of six beds. He was lying face up, his head on a pillow, his eyes wide open, in this spot that, around this time of the afternoon, was always bathed in western sunlight. Before he could even call out his usual greeting of "Seiji-san!" Monoi froze, staring at his face. Time seemed to stop altogether and Monoi dazedly recalled the faces of dead cattle and horses he had seen being carted away along the bus route in his village so long ago.

Seiji's half-open mouth was contorted into a split and twisted shape, his eyes glaring up at the ceiling were rolled back, his taut cheeks were sunken beneath the cheekbones. Seiji Okamura was no longer there—all that remained was a carcass, its expression no different from the corpse of one of those animals. A jumble of memories flickered behind Monoi's eyelids—the sparkling dust rising from the bus route, the smell of the grass, the cicadas' song, and the bulging eyes of the carcasses atop the cart.

Taking a deep breath, Monoi realized that his plan to take Seiji home to spend the rest of his life in peace had been eclipsed, and then the vast, intangible question—*What is the meaning of one's life?*—flashed in his mind. The notion that, in death, human beings and livestock were all the same had also struck him when Yoshie had died. Just before she passed away, Yoshie woke up from her coma and gave a tormented cry, contorting her mouth like Seiji's and widening her eyes in a hideous stare.

Monoi pushed the red emergency call button, and was forced to wait several minutes for someone to finally arrive. The wind chimes continued to ring. None of the elderlies in the room made a sound— one of them slowly waved a fan up and down as he gazed at Monoi and the dead man. The other four residents, lying in their respective beds, did not move a muscle, and one of them emitted a low snore. Then the doctor and a staff member came in, and after going through the motions of checking the patient's pupils and taking his pulse, the doctor said, "Well, it was his time," while the female staff member remarked to no one in particular, "I'm so glad he went peacefully."

Monoi, still staring at the stiffening corpse, found himself in the midst of a whirlpool of indescribable emotions that welled up from who knew where. The sight of the body before him triggered a cascade of images, indistinguishable from one another—the many animal corpses he had seen in his childhood, Komako drooping her head as she was led away by the horse dealer, Yoshie's unsightly death face—and even though he felt no personal grief, it was as if suddenly, with a shrill roar, all the parts of his life were being stirred up and drawn toward that corpse. Amid the cacophony, he heard his own voice whisper, *This is the extent of being human,* and *This will be you tomorrow,* but when the noise eventually subsided, alongside the sense of emptiness that descended upon him, Monoi heard a different voice: *I will avenge you, Seiji-san.*

Monoi unconsciously strained his ears to hear it. He knew it was the voice of the same fiend he had heard that once, half a century ago. This time, it was with a quite different and surprising sense of calm that he listened to this voice and acknowledged it as evil.

"Hinode Beer," Monoi mumbled to himself, and the sound of his own voice snapped him back to the present. Once he emerged from the tunnel of emptiness, the only things that remained in Monoi's mind were the look in Komako's eyes and the idea that Hinode Beer should pay for Seiji's half-century of despair. Monoi felt a slight chagrin as he took another look at the idea that had just occurred to him, but whatever hesitation and doubt ordinarily that would have accompanied it must have already been eliminated by the fiend who had taken hold of him for the first time in fifty years. While the nursing home staff was cleansing Seiji's dead body, Monoi turned over this idea in his head, so that even afterward, he never once felt troubled by the various matters that needed to be settled following the death of a family member.

Monoi called Okamura Merchants in Hachinohe from the pay phone at the nursing home, but the current owner gave an evasive response, obviously annoyed. Back in May, when Monoi had notified him of Seiji's existence, he had sounded much the same, so this was not a surprise. The owner eventually told him, "We can't be there right now, so if you could take care of things, we'll pay the expenses." According to the nursing home staff, the city would foot the bill for a simple cremation that included a wake and sutra chanting, so Monoi asked them to arrange for the temple to give Seiji a short posthumous Buddhist name, just five characters long, and told them that a more elaborate funeral was not required.

By early evening, Seiji had been dressed in white, laid out in a coffin, and placed in the wake room. His grimace had been fixed to resemble a sleeping face and his eyes had been closed, but there was no one besides Monoi to say farewell. The soft adzuki bean jelly and can of beer that Monoi had brought for Seiji were transformed into offerings and had been placed next to the chrysanthemums and incense that the nursing home had supplied. A Buddhist monk came from some temple, bringing with him a memorial tablet of plain wood, upon which was written in ink a generic posthumous Buddhist name: "Seishorenkoji." After the monk had chanted sutras for about fifteen minutes, Monoi handed him one hundred and fifty thousand yen wrapped in paper. He had run out to the bank in front of Akigawa Station to withdraw the money, as a nursing home staff member had whispered to him, "Thirty thousand yen per letter should suffice." When Yoshie died, it had cost him four hundred thousand yen for an eight-letter name, so it was a bargain this time.

It was past seven in the evening by the time these affairs had concluded, so instead of going home to Haneda only to come back the next morning for the cremation, Monoi decided to keep vigil at the nursing home that night. When he called the lady pharmacist, she peppered him with nosy questions—*When did he die? How old was he? What will you wear to the funeral?*—and hounded him that since it was family, for the sake of appearances he should at least close shop during the mourning period, until Monoi finally told her, "Then go ahead and take the day off tomorrow," and quickly hung up the phone, only to realize, *Ah, the morning glories will wither and die.*

Next, he made three more calls. The first one was to Ota Manufacturing in Higashi-Kojiya. Between the recession and the fact that it was almost the Obon holiday, the factory wouldn't have been running, but Yo-chan always lingered there alone until the wee hours, because he said it was cooler than in his apartment. Sure enough, Yo-chan answered the phone. When Monoi asked him what he was doing, he replied simply, "TV."

Monoi explained the reason he was calling. "I'd like to meet with Katsumi Koh. Can you get in touch with him?"

Without even asking what it was about, Yo-chan replied, "I'll give you his cell phone number," and read the number to him.

"So, what are you doing over the Bon holiday?"

"Nothing."

"I'll come by tomorrow night for a little bit, if you don't mind. Do you want anything?" Monoi asked, and Yo-chan immediately replied, "A new brain."

Next, Monoi tried calling the number he had just been given. Around this time in the summer, the only time Monoi would bump into Koh was on the occasional Sunday at a WINS off-track betting site in the city, and so with no idea where he might be or what he might be doing, Monoi heard him answer the phone, "Hello, Kowa Credit Union. This is Koh." His voice was stiff and businesslike, quite different from what it sounded like at the racecourse.

"Sorry to disturb you. This is Monoi from the pharmacy," he said.

"Oh, of course," Koh replied, shifting into his salesman tone. "How can I help you?"

"Koh. That story I heard you talking about back in April at the racecourse in Fuchu. This old man has decided to give it some serious thought."

"What story?"

"The one about milking money out of a big corporation."

With that, Monoi hung up the phone. Then, he made his third call. This was also to a cell phone and he had no way to know the person's whereabouts, but there was a ten-to-one chance he wouldn't be tied up with work. When, as expected, he answered, "Handa speaking," Monoi heard the background noise of a pachinko parlor.

"Seiji Okamura died today. This old man has a lot on his mind, but—here's the question, Handa-san. Do you have any interest in squeezing money out of Hinode Beer?"

Amid the jingling of the pachinko machines Handa shouted back, "What? What did you say?"

"Back in April at Fuchu—you and Katsumi Koh were talking about it. We could do it just like you said. Why don't we shake down Hinode Beer?"

Once Monoi repeated himself, Handa paused before answering and, for several seconds, there was only the noise of the pachinko balls clinking as they fell. Handa finally replied, "You do realize I'm a police detective?"

"Yes, of course."

Monoi replaced the receiver. Despite having just concocted this plan, his first thought had been that—whatever the plan entailed— he was nothing on his own and he would need conspirators to carry it out. As he considered those in his circle, the faces of Koh and Handa were the first to surface in his mind—not because they had been the ones discussing how to extort a company. Monoi had a certain intuition when it came to judging a person's character. Both Koh and Handa, if they were to go through with something, would do it as a crime of conscience. Monoi had intuited this aspect of their characters.

After making the necessary calls with a clerical efficiency that surprised even himself, Monoi returned to the wake room, where he sipped the to-go cup of saké he had bought that evening near the train station and smoked a cigarette. There was no trace of the sudden vicissitudes of emotion that immediately followed his discovery of Seiji's body, and even though he had been ruminating on how to go after Hinode Beer, he showed no sign of any significant change that had occurred within him.

His discovery of Seiji's corpse had dragged Monoi into a dark tunnel, and in reality, emerging from that tunnel and arriving at Hinode Beer was not such a leap for Monoi; rather, it underscored the very uncertainty of life. After all, in this fleeting world where suddenly one day a wealthy dentist jumps in front of a train, or a brilliant scholar who graduated from Tohoku Imperial University dies in a nursing home with no one to bear witness, it was hardly a surprise for a former lathe operator who was about to turn seventy to now, out of the blue, come up with the idea of blackmailing a major corporation.

To avenge Seiji—this most seemingly plausible rationalization had quickly paled, and when he surveyed the scene anew, there was nothing other than that the money was there for the taking. In fact, Monoi couldn't help but think he was destined to bring this about.

However many years ago it was, he had contemplated the way of this world, with those who amassed their fortunes on one side and those whose diligent efforts supplied the capital for such wealth on the other, and yet, here he was, never having experienced any particular kind of awakening. The thought of giving in to the fiend seemed to suit him.

"Now that I think about it, Seiji-san, you were never one to talk about laborers' rights or anything like that, were you? It seems I too lack the mind for such things, but then again I can't resign myself to working like an animal."

Monoi spoke to the coffin this way, and pulled open the lid of another to-go cup of saké.

"Where am I trying to go, I'm not quite sure myself, but no matter where I end up, all I have to worry about is myself. I no longer need the Shinto gods or Buddha. That's what I think, anyhow."

Monoi took off his shoes and settled into the sofa, working on his second cold saké. Now that Seiji had been placed in the coffin, his face as it was had begun to recede, as had the fact that until just half a day ago Monoi had intended to take custody of Seiji—that too had drifted away—and Monoi was once again engulfed by that familiar sense of hopelessness, pulled along by the current of time that turned murkier as it washed over him. And yet, thanks to the fiend enshrined deep within his belly, perhaps he felt a twinge of heat, as if there were a tumor growing inside him.

As he dozed off, leaving a bit of his saké unfinished, Monoi recalled the faces of his grandparents and parents and siblings back in Herai, sifting through them in his mind one by one as if turning the pages of a photo album. Strangely, even though until now he had always thought that everyone in his family—Seiji Okamura included—had the same indistinguishable, quiet mien, when he looked more closely, each face was imbued with its own severity, melancholy, or even a slight hostility, giving the overall impression of petty riffraff.

And as he turned another page in his memory, among the small-jawed, inverted triangular faces peculiar to Monoi's family, there he was—Seizo at about seventeen or eighteen years of age—with his one good eye that shone with a particular slyness. That face appeared in a commemorative photo that had been taken at the foundry in Hachinohe. Monoi stared at it, and realized with a bit of surprise, *Even back then, I can already see a glimpse of the fiend.*

The following morning, Monoi had Seiji cremated at the city crematory and, carrying the urn with his remains and the memorial tablet both wrapped in a cloth, he returned to Haneda shortly past two in the afternoon. On the glass door of the pharmacy, across the notice that the lady pharmacist had posted to announce the store's temporary closing, the words *In Mourning* were written messily and ostentatiously. Before doing anything else, Monoi gave a bucketful of water to the wilted morning glories. Then he went inside, where he set the urn and the tablet atop the altar. He burned some incense, struck the gong, and joined his hands together in prayer. He gazed at the small altar, so crammed that it resembled the corner of the hearth in his birth home in Herai, where the seven members of his family had slept on top of one another.

Since he had only dozed a little the night before, Monoi took a nap for about an hour, after which there was a relentless stream of neighbors who came by, saying, "Who else passed away?" and "Let me pay my respects." Monoi received them in his usual way, offering beers and glasses of cold saké, but with so much on his mind, he hardly listened to the nostalgic reminiscences of the old fogies with nothing better to do.

In the early evening, the owner of a neighborhood eatery came to pay his respects, so Monoi ordered two sets of grilled eel over rice, and by the time he found the right moment to slip away from the pharmacy on his bicycle, it was just after six. The sun had yet to go down. The steel door of Ota Manufacturing had been left open, though there was a CLOSED FOR OBON HOLIDAY notice taped on it. He found Yo-chan hunched over beside the work desk at the far end of the room, apparently sanding something with a file. When Monoi peered down at Yo-chan's hands, he saw that he was beveling the edge of his cutting tool's blade and the corners of a chip breaker. It was detailed handiwork that measured no more than 0.05 millimeters long. Monoi had taught Yo-chan how to do this ten years ago, recommending that he do it whenever he had spare time in order to avoid getting nicks on the tool blades, but back in the day when he had been swamped with work at the factory, the truth was that Monoi rarely kept up with it himself.

"Koh came by around noon," Yo-chan said without even looking up. "He wanted to know what I think about you." His shoulders wobbled a little as he snickered.

"And what did you say?" Monoi asked him, but whether Yo-chan never had any intention of responding or he had already forgotten that he had been the one to start this conversation just now, he just kept silent, moving the whetstone with his oil-covered hands. Even though work had slowed in the recession, Yo-chan was still at the factory at least twelve hours a day, and when he had no jobs to do he sharpened tools and milling cutters one by one, so that the equipment here was almost insufferably shiny.

"Go and wash your hands. Let's eat this eel."

"I'll go buy some beer."

Yo-chan went out and was back in about three minutes, setting three cans of Hinode Supreme and two to-go cups of saké on the work desk. Monoi laid out the bento boxes of grilled eel, still nice and warm, on the desk and the two of them toasted—Monoi with the saké and Yo-chan with the beer—and began to eat. Outside the open door of the factory, the early evening breeze had finally started to cool down.

Monoi still wondered just what Koh had said to Yo-chan, having apparently come sniffing around so soon after receiving his call last night.

"What did you tell Koh about this old man?" Monoi asked him again.

With a mouthful of rice, Yo-chan replied, "I said you're between good and evil."

"You're probably right. Who do you consider a good person then?"

"The lady who cooked the meals at my institution, I guess."

"Oh?"

"After we aged out of the institution, she would send each of us a postcard like clockwork every year, but it seems she passed away last month."

Yo-chan took out a postcard from the pocket of his workpants and showed it to Monoi. The postcard had arrived the day before, judging by its postmark. It was an invitation to a memorial that would be held at the institution, and the woman, whose last name was Kimura, had apparently died at the age of sixty-nine. Monoi didn't know what to think about this good person, a stranger who had died at the same age that he was, and he had even less insight into the mentality of the young man who was faithfully carrying around the postcard.

Returning the postcard, Monoi said, "Actually, my elder brother passed away yesterday. I cremated him just this morning."

Yo-chan's chopsticks stopped moving at this news. He stared at Monoi.

"Don't worry, he was adopted into another family when I was young, I can hardly even remember his face anymore," Monoi quickly added.

After a while, Yo-chan said, "Koh's grandmother has cervical cancer. She only has a few days left, apparently." After another long pause, he murmured as if the thought had suddenly occurred to him, "Nothing but funerals lately."

Now that Yo-chan mentioned it, Monoi agreed that, indeed, this summer had seen many deaths. "Did Koh say anything else?"

"Said he'll come by tonight after work. He wants to discuss something with you."

"Is that so?"

If that was true, Monoi thought, Koh's response came a little too quick for an ordinary employee of a local credit union. On another hand, he had always known that Koh's job with the credit union was only temporary or a cover of some sort, so there was no reason to be surprised. What mattered was which face Koh would expose from behind his cover in response to Monoi's provocation to "squeeze money out of a corporation." Monoi had to know what, if anything, Koh had said to Yo-chan.

Anxious to find out, Monoi said slyly, "Say, what would you do if you had money?"

"I would buy a large burial plot, pay off the fees for permanent use, and build a solid tomb. I don't know who my ancestors are, so I don't have a family gravesite," Yo-chan replied. His expression remained as inscrutable as ever, and Monoi could not tell if he was serious or not.

"All you want is a grave?"

"If you mean something you can buy with money, then yes."

"Maybe I'm too old to understand what you're saying."

"What about you, Monoi-san? What would you do if you had money?"

"I don't know. I already have a grave . . ."

"You can spend all your money on horseracing."

"I suppose so."

While he picked at the grains of rice stuck to the side of the bento box, Yo-chan breezily cut to the heart of the matter as if he were making small talk. "You're taking money from a big corporation, right? I heard from Koh."

"I'm just thinking about it, that's all."

"But why now?"

"There's no deep meaning behind it. It's just that, as an old man, my life happens to have brought me to this."

"I was shocked," Yo-chan said after a brief pause, then turned on the television above the work desk. As the cheap set took its time to grow bright, the sound of the merry voices of talk-show celebrities blared out, one octave higher than normal.

Yo-chan stared at the people convulsing with laughter on the screen, his eyes hardly moving at all, while Monoi shifted his reading glasses as he surveyed the faces, which seemed indistinguishable from one another.

"Is this the comedy duo Downtown?"

"No, Tunnels."

"Same difference."

"Monoi-san. Are you really taking money from a company?"

"I'll decide after I discuss it with Koh."

"Are you quitting horseracing?"

"No. This old man's life won't change at all, I don't think."

"I guess I have no imagination."

Monoi knew that Yo-chan meant that he couldn't understand because he had no imagination. Once he had cleared away the bento boxes and the empty cans, Yo-chan returned to sharpening his cutting tools, leaving the TV on.

Meanwhile, Monoi thought about how, when this idea about a corporation first came to him, he had not given any thought to Yo-chan's existence, and he felt a little dismayed by the many trivial details that had eluded his initial calculation. It was irresponsible of Koh to leak the story to Yo-chan so quickly; Monoi had forgotten that if he were going to do anything, there would be a mountain of issues—including gossip—that he needed to take care of first. Then again, considering that this was not something a good person would undertake in the first place, he decided that the wellbeing of others was beyond his concern.

"Yo-chan. This is my own personal matter."

"I'm not gonna tell anyone." His head was bent over the whetstone. "Anyway, when Koh gets here, okay if I listen?"

"What for?"

"I want in."

"You'll ruin your life."

Yo-chan, pretending not to hear, did not reply. After a while, as if he had suddenly remembered it, he asked what was the proper message to write on the decorative noshi gift tag when sending an offering to the surviving family members for the first Obon holiday after someone's death. Monoi instructed him to write the characters for goku—a sacrifice.

◆ ◆ ◆

WHEN KATSUMI KOH CAME BY it was past nine in the evening. He was clad in a suit and carrying an attaché case, and it was obvious he was on his way home from work. His appearance was entirely different from that of the man they saw at the racecourse, but with his mumbled, "Damn, it's hot," and the way he yanked off his necktie as he walked in, he had assumed the same inscrutable façade of the Koh they knew.

"Monoi-san, when you called yesterday I was in a meeting." After giving this excuse, Koh downed the beer that Yo-chan handed him and, taking out the bag of rice crackers he kept in the drawer of Yo-chan's work desk, he said, "I can't eat much during the summertime," and popped a handful of the rice crackers in his mouth. Watching him, Monoi had the sense that this really was Koh's lifestyle, and since nothing about him suggested he normally went out drinking around Ginza, it seemed to him that Koh wasn't kidding when he said he usually spent his nights fiddling with his computer or reading a book. Tonight, Koh had arrived true to form, with his salaryman face on. Monoi wondered if this meant that Koh had heard his talk of corporate extortion with his businessman's ear.

"I called you out of the blue, it must have been a surprise," Monoi said.

"Not really. Compared to what we money lenders do everyday, shaking down a company is nothing," Koh said bluntly. He looked every bit as nonchalant as his remark indicated.

"Huh. Is that so?"

"As long as you don't give a damn about the morality, it's best to go straight to stealing the money. That way everything will match up for accounting."

Monoi remembered now that he had heard Koh himself say a number of times how, until an incident like a bank run forces them to suspend operations, a financial institution never knows their final income and expenditure. If the borrower of a hundred-million-yen loan were to struggle with their financing and run into problems paying interest, the financial institution would simply give them an additional loan equivalent to the amount of interest owed, thereby increasing the total loan amount. Then finally, if the borrower were to fall behind on their principal payment, the institution would typically resort to seizing collateral property, but now that collateral value had depreciated due to the fall of land prices, instead of settling accounts the institution would switch the loan over to their affiliated non-bank. In this way, over a hundred million yen the loaner-borrower relationship would be diversified or bypassed again and again without anyone chalking it up as a loss and it would continue to circulate until eventually someone took the fall.

A financial institution could not make money unless it loaned money. When times were flush, city banks funded credit unions and others with a few hundred billion yen, and in the case of Kowa Credit Union, where Koh worked, even now 40 percent of their deposits were tied in some way to city banks. In return, credit unions gave loans to corporations that were introduced to them by city banks, so that the city banks that made the original deposit were sure to profit through interest. Meanwhile the credit unions built up their figures by increasing the number of loans made with deposits from the city banks. In this way, from the outside it would seem that the calculations for credits and debits matched up in all the account books, but according to Koh it was only the numbers that matched up.

As Koh talked about all this, he seemed somehow removed from any sense of guilt—rather than seeming negligent, Monoi was once again reminded of Koh's pervasive and utter indifference to society. This indifference coated all of Koh's words like a tasteless and odorless poison, and Monoi suspected that the shadowy aura that Koh exhibited every Sunday also stemmed, in large part, from this cold-blooded indifference.

At any rate, Koh had said flatly that he wasn't surprised by Monoi's plan, but neither was Monoi surprised by his reaction. If Koh were the kind of person who tormented himself over the deceitfulness of financial institutions, Monoi would never have approached him with such an idea.

"Anyway, how's your Kowa Credit Union doing these days?" Monoi asked.

"The city banks are starting to withdraw their deposits."

"Oh?"

"So in order to fill those gaps, we are trying to round up large fixed deposits from the general public. We're now offering four point two percent interest for a year-long fixed deposit of ten million yen or more. Double the interest of the city banks. That's what yesterday's meeting was about, too. Scatter the four point two percent bait, they said."

"Four point two is pretty amazing."

"After adding the acquisition cost to the official discount rate, we just barely make a profit at two point five. If we set the interest above that limit, we only go deeper in the red the more deposits we acquire. But they still want us to do it."

After explaining all this, Koh handed Yo-chan two thousand-yen notes and asked him to go get some more beer, then slipped a Dunhill cigarette in his mouth. Since the first time Monoi met him, Koh's brand of choice had always been Dunhill. His lighter was Cartier. Monoi knew the names of these foreign brands because of the wristwatches and handbags that his daughter Mitsuko wore. At first he had thought the name Cartier sounded like the Japanese for "minor wisdom," which made him tilt his head quizzically, and then when he heard how much they cost he could only sigh. Despite Koh's cloak of indifference, he clearly earned a comfortable salary. Monoi could only surmise—from the side of Koh that he was seeing tonight—that the man's sense of guilt toward his clients and distaste for the kind of work he did were reaching a sort of haphazard accumulation.

"Anyway, about what I said on the phone yesterday . . ." Monoi started.

"I said I wasn't surprised, but I don't know what you expect me to do."

"This isn't really the reason, but yesterday, my elder brother, who was about to turn seventy-nine, died at his nursing home."

Monoi gave an equally concise and ambiguous explanation of his relationship with Seiji Okamura; how Seiji used to work for Hinode Beer; how he was forced to resign during the turbulent postwar years; and how after drifting from job to job, he finally died of dementia. All it amounted to, he said, was the story of a single, unfortunate life—nothing more.

Koh fiddled with the empty beer can on the desk to pass the time while he listened to Monoi, but spoke up as soon as he had finished. "The more determined the corporation, the greater the number of people they cast away, used up and discarded, in order to survive— that's for sure," he said. "That's how they have so much capital saved up," he added. "But Monoi-san, it's not like you're in need of money. Why would you want to extort a corporation?" he asked.

"All I can say is that my sixty-nine years' worth of life has led me to this point," Monoi replied, choosing his words. "The reason I approached you is because I wanted to hear the opinion of someone who is well versed in the financial affairs of a corporation. If you say it's impossible, I'll just have to reconsider."

"When attacked on a matter that concerns their reputation and credibility—unless it's an exorbitant amount—a company will generally pay up. I wouldn't say it's impossible."

"How about Hinode Beer?"

"Hinode, hmm . . ." Koh said, and he stared for a little while at the smoke rising from the cigarette between his fingers. His expression looked as if he were calculating something in his mind. Then, he replied simply, "It's not bad," and tossed another handful of rice crackers into his mouth.

"What do you mean by not bad?" Monoi asked.

"The stock price of food and beverage companies fluctuates comparatively easily. Unlike the machinery or the metal industries, their business is directly connected to the consumer, so a threat packs an extra punch for them."

Monoi tried to listen carefully, though he had a hard time imagining where Koh was coming from, and what he was talking about.

Perhaps this was because day after day in the financial world, Koh was exposed to situations that came perilously close to extortion, or perhaps because, when it concerned his family business, that air he had talked about breathing was shared by those in the shadowy under-world—but in any case, the enigma that was the true Katsumi Koh was peeking out from beneath his veneer of an ordinary salaryman.

And yet, the person who occasionally stopped by the factory, set-ting his rice crackers on the desk alongside a can of beer, teaching Yo-chan how to use a computer, and laughing as they played TV games together—he was also Katsumi Koh. Even now, his eyes seemed far from wicked. In fact, he seemed as defenseless as a child with no ulterior motives, his legs sprawled out lazily, having let his guard down somewhat.

One side was dangerous, the other was harmless. Put both sides together and, when it came down to it, Monoi did not know what kind of man Koh would be. But Monoi's plan to extort money from a corporation itself was so far outside of ordinary—in that sense he and Koh were equally menacing.

"Say, Koh. How would you feel about coming up with a plan that ensures we'll get the money?"

"Drawing up a plan is the same thing as executing it," Koh said, laughing. His expression turned serious once again. "Before we get to that, I'd like to know your true motive, Monoi-san."

A *reasonable request,* Monoi thought. "You may laugh, but this old man just wants to see those who made a fortune suffer. Lately, I've been thinking about this more and more. I was born into a family of tenant farmers in Aomori, and the memories have come flooding back . . ."

Koh, listening quietly, stared straight into Monoi's eyes for the first time that evening. Then he said, "I wouldn't laugh. I'm a Zainichi, after all."

Yo-chan returned, and set out the beer and sake he had brought back on the work desk. He had said he wanted to listen, and he feigned ignorance as he sat at the end of the work desk and returned to the task of sharpening his cutting tool. Koh merely glanced at him without saying anything.

Monoi was in no hurry to force a decision from Koh, so instead he went off on a tangent. "By the way, Koh. What would you like to do if you had money?"

"Me?"

Koh stopped, the new can of beer in his hand frozen in midair, and once again he glanced briefly at Monoi. Up close, Monoi stared back at Koh's single-lidded eyes, the whites showing beneath the iris, and realized that, over these last three and a half years, he had never looked carefully into his face. But there was no distinguishable expression in Koh's eyes as he returned Monoi's gaze, and like the sliding fusuma door to an inner drawing room that opens briefly only to close again immediately, he looked away.

"My family operates the kind of business where money comes rolling in everyday, ten or twenty million yen at a time, you know? I've never had to wonder what I would do if I had money. Why would I, when money is the only thing I've got enough to rot."

"I wouldn't know, I've never experienced anything like that."

"But my folks are different. After the war, they worked twenty hours a day making moonshine and working in the black market until they saved up enough money to start their own business."

"I see . . ."

"For some reason I don't see eye to eye with them, so I've always worked outside the family. I guess I don't really know myself."

Koh stopped speaking abruptly, even though he had been the one to bring his family up—either he wasn't sure how to explain it concisely or he had lost interest in talking about it. Monoi wasn't quite sure what Koh was trying to say, but that night he could feel it in his bones, that ill will he had sensed Koh harbored for his people and that he was unable to distance himself from.

"Actually, my grandma is about to die," Koh said, his tone changing suddenly. He gave a belch that transformed into a big yawn. When he opened his mouth wide, he revealed his beautifully set teeth—a mark of his parents' thorough attention since he was young. Monoi took notice of such a thing because when he himself had been in the prime of his working life, he had not had the means to fuss over such details, and as a result his daughter Mitsuko's teeth were riddled with cavities, for which she had held a deep grudge ever since.

"Yes, so I've heard. Yo-chan told me."

"My grandma is the one who controls the bulk of our real estate. The family business uses it and pays rent, but when my grandma dies, her estate will be divided among six brothers, including my dad. All of his brothers are gunning for the right to control the company, so it's a hell of a situation. True story."

"Huh."

"I'm in the finance world, after all. I can't just cut ties with the family business, but it's not as if I'm in the Chongryon—you know, the General Association of Korean Residents—and I don't have any Zainichi relationships either. So it's getting to be a crucial stage for me too . . . which brings me back to Monoi-san's plan."

After a long detour, the conversation had returned to its starting point. Monoi could not immediately grasp how the "crucial stage" that Koh mentioned tied into squeezing money out of a corporation.

"You mean about my plan to extort money from Hinode Beer?"

"Let's make a deal," Koh said, leaning forward a bit. His gaze was languid, as if he were still feeling the effects of his recent yawn, but the words that came out of his mouth next were far from languid— they were purely business. "If you're serious, Monoi-san, I will take on the responsibility of coming up with a surefire plan to get the money. You will have my full cooperation. In exchange, if it's Hinode Beer you're going after, the surefire plan we take will have an impact on their stock price. How does that sound as a condition?"

"I'm not sure I understand . . ."

"I'd like to help an acquaintance of mine profit from his Hinode stock. In exchange, I will ensure that your plan will succeed. Of course, the stock will be sold through a securities company."

"Are you talking about the underworld?"

"It has to do with speculation. To make a long story short, I have a plan that will protect my parents' company from my relatives."

Despite what Koh said, it was apparent to Monoi that if there was no shady underworld connection at all, Koh would have no need to confirm anything with him in the first place. Monoi would be obliged to consider the pros and cons of adding an extra layer to his initial plan, but for the time being he responded, "All right, I'll think about it."

"Don't repeat what I just said," Koh added tersely, and for a brief moment Monoi thought that he saw a flash in Koh's eyes that did not belong to an ordinary salaryman. Before he could dwell on it Koh was back to his usual self, calling out, "Hey, Yo-chan, let's go to Makuhari next week," to which Yo-chan responded, "Sure," without even raising his eyes from the work desk.

"What's in Makuhari?" Monoi asked.

"An expo of the newest video game software."

Koh wrapped a rubber band around the opening of his rice cracker bag and put it back in the drawer of the work desk. Then, turning toward Monoi again, he said, "You know, in a situation like this, Handa would be useful."

"But he's a cop."

"Precisely. You can't pass up the chance to use a cop when committing a crime. Besides, I know for sure he'll come in on it."

"Why do you think so?"

"A sixth sense. Last week I saw him at WINS, the off-track betting parlor, and he looked like a fresh mackerel that was already rotting from the inside. Like he was itching to do something—I'm sure of it."

As Koh rose from his seat, his jacket and briefcase in his hands, Monoi said, "When it comes to doing anything with this old man, you'll have to go without your underground ties."

After a second, Koh burst out laughing, but as he turned to leave, he resumed the stoop of an exhausted businessman.

Once Koh was gone, Yo-chan actually lifted his head to speak, from his corner of the work desk. "You can say that, Monoi-san, but Koh is a man of the underworld."

"I know that," Monoi responded.

"Trust Koh, or give up on Hinode Beer. It's up to you, Monoi-san. If you do this, I will too. If I go on living like this, I'll die of boredom."

Yo-chan promptly delivered his simple and definitive conclusion, then he pulled a newspaper specializing in horseracing out from under whatever was on the desk, and bent his head low over it.

THE NEXT DAY, SHUHEI HANDA was the one who called Monoi to say he would stop by after work. Handa appeared at the pharmacy a little before 9 in the evening, and as soon as he opened the glass door he started talking. "That guy Nunokawa. This morning, he called the department saying his wife had set her futon on fire, and what should he do . . ."

"What?" Monoi couldn't help but gasp in response.

"I called his local precinct in Tsukiji, and they said a small fire did break out at Nippo Transport's employee dormitory in Kachidoki, but they said it was from smoking in bed. I told Nunokawa to keep his mouth shut. Told him to take her to a hospital instead."

Handa spoke practically nonstop. Pushing aside the display shelf of detergent and toilet paper that had been brought in from outside for the night, he made his way into the store.

"Come on in," Monoi called to him anyhow.

Nunokawa had seemed pretty desperate since around springtime, but given his complicated situation as the parent of a disabled child, there was nothing that Monoi and the others—fellow horseracing fans and nothing more—could do for him. Monoi wondered briefly who would look after Lady if her mother spent time in the hospital, but it was a pointless concern.

"If the firefighters hosed down the house, there must be an awful mess to clean up." Monoi finally found a few words to say.

"I went to help him this afternoon," Handa replied. "Not just the futon—everything from the tatami floors to the furniture is a total loss."

"Well, it was good of you to go to the trouble."

"I was off-duty this afternoon anyway."

As he passed through the store and stepped up into the living room, Handa glanced at the plain wooden memorial tablets and urns arranged on the Buddhist altar, and he lit a stick of incense and joined his hands together. Then, after hearing about how Seiji Okamura had died, he said, "The day before yesterday, I was at a funeral too. You remember Takahashi from the Shinagawa Police Department, right? That detective . . ."

"Oh, that guy . . ."

When Hiroyuki Hatano committed suicide, Monoi had visited the local police department in Seijo where a detective had brought him into a separate room and questioned him insistently about Seiji Okamura's letter. The detective, who came from the Shinagawa Police Department, had asked him at length about Hatano's last phone call to Monoi and his relation to Seiji, and he also asked in detail about Monoi's family, where he had worked after moving from Hachinohe to Tokyo, and his own family circumstances—that had been Takahashi. Monoi remembered him as a man in his fifties with a thoroughly unremarkable appearance, save for the strangely haunting light in his eyes.

According to Handa, in 1992 Takahashi had been transferred from Shinagawa to the Koiwa Department's Police Affairs, and then this spring he had been hospitalized with cancer, and died the day before yesterday. Four years ago, the reason a veteran detective who had exclusively handled white-collar crime had been harassing Monoi about Hatano's case had something to do with a group of extortionists who were suspected of giving Okamura's letter to Hatano, and apparently Takahashi had doggedly pursued this thread afterward as well. But due to internal circumstances on the police force, he had been shunted over to Koiwa, and since then had been relegated to his desk everyday, working on administrative tasks in Police Affairs—so for someone who had still been on active duty, Handa said, his funeral was poorly attended. Handa had occasionally gone to visit Takahashi in the hospital, reasoning that the man had once been his superior, if only for a short time.

"The last time I saw him, a week ago, Takahashi asked me to look up the criminal record of a man named Yoshiya Kanemoto. I thought it was just the delirium of a gravely ill person so I paid no attention, but he said Kanemoto is a golf buddy of the extortionist Shin'ichi Nishimura, and that Kanemoto himself stops by the home of Seizo Monoi about once a month."

"You mean Yoshiya Kanemoto of Kanemoto Foundry?"

"That's right. You know him, don't you, Monoi-san?"

"Yoshiya is the son of the owner of the foundry in Hachinohe where I was an apprentice. I used to look after him. Of course this was over half a century ago."

"What's your relationship with him these days?"

"He was very attached to me when he was young, so he still comes by to bring me things from time to time. Some foreign liquor, or ginseng or some such."

"Takahashi said Shin'ichi Nishimura has been to your house with Kanemoto."

"I don't know anyone named Nishimura."

"The man has a one-centimeter mole on the right side of his chin. Try to remember."

Monoi started to feel a bit foolish as he looked back at Handa, who at some point had assumed the tone and gaze of a detective, but after being prompted, he reluctantly dredged his memory for the face of the man with the mole—the fellow he had occasionally seen in Yoshiya Kanemoto's Mercedes.

"Yes . . . I've seen a man with a mole."

"That's Shin'ichi Nishimura. He's the one who gave Seiji Okamura's letter to Hatano. That's quite a man to know, Monoi-san."

"But I've never even spoken to him."

"I explained it to you four years ago, didn't I? What the police focused on in the dentist's case was how, exactly, Nishimura had gotten hold of Seiji Okamura's letter from forty years ago. You are

Seiji Okamura's younger brother, and on top of that you are associated with Nishimura—no wonder you're marked. That's just how this world works."

Having said as much, Handa finally grabbed the can of beer he must have bought from the vending machine next to the liquor shop across the street and, popping the tab, he took a sip.

Monoi, on the other hand, having been blindsided by such an unexpected story, felt as if he had something caught in his throat. Just last month, Yoshiya Kanemoto had appeared with a cheerful, reddened face and brought him a watermelon; it was hard for him to believe that the police had surveilled even the minute-or-two-long conversation they had standing by his storefront.

"But isn't the case with the tape Hatano sent to Hinode Beer already closed?"

"Yes. Especially now that the crusading investigator has died."

Handa seemed to have found Takahashi's funeral thoroughly infuriating. Without even being prompted, he talked about the service, which had taken place in a small temple in Machida; how neither the deputy chief nor any detectives from the Criminal Investigation Unit offered any words of remembrance about the deceased's work ethic; and how as they were waiting for the hearse to leave, there had been a lively conversation about a burglary case that had nothing at all to do with Takahashi. Handa was one to talk—he barely knew Takahashi himself, so part of his frustration as one of the mourners was no doubt to substitute for his personal indignation.

"A man's life is so trivial. No matter how diligently you work, if you don't rise up in the world, you're left out of the loop even in death. And if you do manage to get ahead, you'll be merrily sent off with empty messages of condolence . . ." Handa flashed a rare, wry smile as he spewed such predictable grievances.

"You might be right. You're better off alone when you die."

"That's why they say it's best to be with an older woman," Handa said, offering an equally rare quip.

"Your wife, she's older than you?"

"By ten years. By the time they turn forty-five, they don't even put on makeup any more."

Handa gratefully ate the pickled eggplant and cucumber that Monoi had set out to accompany his beer, saying, "These taste so much better than the store-bought stuff." Monoi sipped his shochu.

"By the way, are Kanemoto's visits irregular?" Handa resumed his questioning. "Does he show up at night or during the day? Has the pharmacist or your neighbors seen him?"

Monoi told him that Kanemoto visited infrequently, usually late at night after he had been drinking or early Sunday morning on his way to play golf; that when his wife, Yoshie, was still alive, Kanemoto had come into his home two or three times for a drink, but in the last ten years Kanemoto's lifestyle had shifted so that now he only stopped by in his Mercedes; that they barely even had what would be considered a conversation when they saw each other, and that he didn't know whether his neighbors had ever seen them together.

"All right. First, you've got to end things with Kanemoto. It would look unnatural if you cut him off suddenly, so do it gradually."

"I understand about Kanemoto. The old man was being careless."

"I'm only telling this because of what you said to me on the phone the day before yesterday."

Handa said this without any particular gravity, then opened his second can of beer. *Ah, he's already on board*, Monoi thought instinctively, and he felt his mood lifting gently as he topped off his own glass of shochu.

"I don't mean for it to be a joke, it's just an idea," Monoi dove in himself. "This old man has decided to squeeze money out of Hinode Beer. I wouldn't know what to say if you asked for a motive, but I think in life there's such a thing as timing."

"'The devil made me do it' is the only explanation for some crimes, but even then there's always some underlying basis."

"Soon after the war ended, I came close to murdering the owner of the factory where I worked, and his entire family. That's the basis.

I always tried to live my life quietly, for the most part. But growing old is not so peaceful, you know."

"You're the type that gives police the most trouble. Your motive is unclear." Handa laughed in an uncharacteristically light manner.

"But Handa-san, what about you?"

"Me? I have a habit of fantasizing. Whenever something bad happens, I always try to compensate by running through a fantasy in my mind to save myself. I've been doing that for so long and then suddenly, I got your call."

"Did anything specific happen?"

"No. I can only say that things have been piling up for me, too. But I'm positive that when I entered the working world, I came in through the wrong door. The police force as an organization, my career as a police detective—all of it is too honorable for me."

The layers of frustration of working in the police force accumulated over time, and during these last ten years, Monoi figured he had seen that frustration surface a fair number of times in Handa's aspect and manner. Although each individual annoyance was simple, as they piled up they tangled into a complicated, inextricable knot. In Handa's case, that knot was also interwoven with twisted obsessions, pride, and ambition. One thing Monoi did not know, however, was whether a fiend like the one he had nurtured in himself existed within Handa. When the time came to cross the line, what would be the force that would drive this particular man over it? Monoi could only wonder as he peered into Handa's face.

"Yeah, right—this morning, for example, what do you suppose I was doing? There I am, yawning after a night shift, when I get a call from the head of the unit—it's six in the morning, and he's on his way to play golf with the department chief. He left his putter in his locker at the office, and he tells me to bring it to him right away. So I have to carry the putter all the way to Komae, bright and early in the morning."

"Did you?"

"The asshole who called me, his only concern is ingratiating himself with the chief and the top brass at MPD, but the sleazier they are, the more I enjoy standing at attention before them. I was as courteous as I could be to the bastard. 'Yes, boss, here I am with your putter,'" Handa said, laughing as he acted out the gesture of bowing his head low. "First of all, I find it hilarious that they have no idea what I'm thinking."

"Huh."

"What I mean is, I have twice the patience of an ordinary man. That's why there are so many opportunities to indulge in my fantasies."

Ah, now I see. This man copes with reality by exchanging humiliation for masochism and indignation for fantasy, Monoi thought. He reacts to the slightest provocation by society, an organization, or another person, and the pleasure he derives from his masochism and fantasies becomes his daily sustenance—a twisted enough state of being. This was the form taken by the fiend within this particular man. It was quite different from the impulsiveness of the fiend within Monoi, but the important thing was that there was a fiend here as well.

"But my plan to blackmail Hinode Beer is no fantasy, you know."

"The amount of time it will take to carry out the crime is actually quite short. In contrast, the anticipation leading up to and the excitement after the fact will be more than enough. That's why I'll do it."

"Thinking about it doesn't cost a thing."

"The satisfaction I'll get from knowing that no one around me has any idea what I'm up to—I doubt you can imagine, Monoi-san. The pleasure of playing the innocent at my respectable job as a police officer at MPD when in fact I'm a public enemy . . ."

Handa rolled the words around in his mouth as if he were already savoring the fantasy, then washed them down with his beer. Monoi also swallowed his determination—*I've got him now.*

"So, Handa-san, that means you're in?"

"Yes."

"No second thoughts?"

"Nope. By the way, could we ask Nunokawa to join us? While he and I were cleaning up his house after the fire, the bastard kept mumbling to himself. Said he was going to disappear . . ."

"Disappear?"

"Look. It's none of our business, but if he wants to leave his wife and child and disappear, then it wouldn't make much difference for him to pull off something crazy before he does. Nunokawa might even change his mind about it all if he got his hands on some money."

The thought of bringing in Nunokawa, who had Lady to take care of, had never entered Monoi's mind, and he was unsure of how to respond. There might be some truth to the idea that money could change things for him, but he was at a loss for words as he recalled how, just last week at the WINS in Suidobashi, Lady's face had looked as she joyfully wobbled her head. In the end, he skirted the issue by replying, "This old man can't make a decision about such matters."

"No, ultimately it's something that Nunokawa has to decide for himself. That guy, in addition to having been trained in the Self-Defense Forces, he's been deconditioned of thinking for himself. It's about time he gave some thought to his own intentions, for once."

Monoi agreed with each of the things that Handa said as he contemplated Nunokawa's inscrutable profile, so familiar after all their time at the racetrack. Indeed, he had never once witnessed any suggestion of individual will—all the guy ever did was sit patiently in silence. Who would be the one to decide the future and fate of that man and his family?

"I leave Nunokawa up to you, Handa-san."

"I'll talk to him. In terms of usefulness, you won't get a better man. It's not for nothing he was in the army, you know."

Handa had already emptied his second can of beer, so Monoi offered him some shochu. "Just one," Handa said, tilting a glass toward Monoi and politely thanking him before bringing it to his lips.

"By the way, I talked to Koh yesterday," Monoi said.

"How's that dude? If you're aiming for a corporation, you've gotta put his craftiness to use."

"Koh said he would cooperate fully, but it seems like he's thinking about profiting from the manipulation of Hinode's stock price. What do you make of that?"

"That sounds like him," Handa said and laughed softly. "I'm sure he's planning on hooking up with a corporate raider or a securities man he knows. As long as we make it a condition that it be entirely separate from us, he can do as he likes. Hell, at least it makes his motives clear."

"Koh said he would keep it separate, but won't it cause problems if we get entangled with his underworld connections?"

"Quite the opposite, actually. Those guys in the underworld are tight-lipped, so there'd be no need to worry about the plan leaking. What's more, however they decide to manipulate the stocks, you'll never see anything out in the open. That's for sure."

"If you say so, then this old man has no objection."

"But it's impossible for me to forget that Koh's dad is a leader in the Korean Association. My relationship with Koh will be strictly business. I need you to understand that."

"I'm sure that's what Koh expects too. But he mentioned the plan to Yo-chan, and now he wants to be in on it too . . ."

"So it's just the usual racetrack crew?" Handa said with a shrug. "Amazing. It's like the tale of Momotaro and his gang." He laughed again.

"If you want out, now is the time."

"No, it's not bad, as far as teams go. In police lingo, we call the geographical and social connections among potential suspects a 'cross section,' but we have almost none of that. If there is no cross section, then those conducting the investigation will have a hard time tracking the group of suspects."

"That means from now on, we'll have to stop gathering at Fuchu and WINS."

"That's for sure. It's a problem that you and I live near each other, so from now on I won't come by your pharmacy anymore. You and Yo-chan can keep seeing each other as usual, but let's tell Koh to stop going to Yo-chan's factory."

"Anything else?"

"We all have to declare any financial debts we have."

According to Handa, shaking down a corporation could take any-where from a few months to a year including setup time, making it impossible for someone running from debt collectors to keep going. The police would first suspect the crime was financially motivated, and they would start by going through client lists of city financial institutions, especially loan sharks, so if any one of the conspirators was carrying debt, it would be all but impossible to execute the plan.

"Then, at last, we work out the plan," Handa said.

"I want to make sure we pull it off."

"So do I."

Monoi had nothing more to say to Handa. He topped off both of their glasses with shochu and they raised them in a silent toast.

"Speaking of Hinode Beer . . ." Handa said suddenly, as if he had just remembered something. "I think you and Hinode have too many connections—the case with Seiji Okamura's letter, and the case with your grandson. If Hinode is the target, your name will undoubtedly come up on the list of suspects the police will imme-diately identify."

"But this old man can't think of any company other than Hinode Beer. Besides, I will leave the actual groundwork to you young people—I'll be right here watering my morning glories, and I have no so-called cross section with any of you either. I have no motive. Even if the police come to question me, I'll be fine."

"Let me give it some more thought," Handa said. Then he mum-bled, "Speaking of Hinode Beer . . ." again as he glanced at the family portrait on top of the chest of drawers. After a moment he tapped his own knee once and said, "Right. That's it." Handa turned back to face Monoi. "A change of subject, but what was the name of your grandson's girlfriend? The one whose parents rejected her marrying him because of his background?"

"Her name? Let me see, what was it . . ."

"You told me you heard it from your daughter, Monoi-san. She was his classmate at University of Tokyo . . ."

". . . Sugihara. That was it. Yoshiko Sugihara."

"How do you write the characters for Yoshiko?"

"I wouldn't know that."

Handa jotted something in his notebook before putting it back in his pocket.

"What about my grandson's girlfriend?" Monoi asked.

"Oh, just something that Takahashi and I had talked about four years ago. After your grandson passed away, Yoshiko's parents came to pay their respects at Hatano's home, right? We were wondering why they didn't attend the funeral."

"I'm sure they felt guilty."

"I wouldn't be so sure. Besides, even if he was in shock because the marriage was rejected, it's still hard to believe that's the only reason an accomplished university student would flee from an important job interview."

At a certain point Handa's eyes had once again taken on the look of a detective—they called to mind the flickering needle on some kind of sensor.

"Who knows, it could very well be . . . I'll check it out and call you with what I find." With that, Handa peeked at his wristwatch and muttered to himself about how late it was already, then got up from his seat. Making an absent-minded excuse that his wife, who also worked full time, would have dinner waiting for him at home, he left at half past ten.

IT WAS ONLY THREE DAYS later when Monoi received Handa's report. Handa called in the evening from a pay phone somewhere with bustling noise in the background. "Jackpot," he said. "Yoshiko Sugihara's father is Takeo Sugihara. He's the deputy manager of the beer division and a board member of Hinode Beer. Takeo Sugihara's wife, Haruko, is the younger sister of Hinode Beer's president, Kyosuke Shiroyama.

That makes Yoshiko Sugihara the president's niece. Monoi-san, are you listening to me?"

"You mean, when Hatano sent Hinode the letter and the tape, Hinode was desperate not to leak the scandal of Sugihara's family, right?"

"Exactly. Hinode is a go," Handa said. "I don't mean to take advantage of a scandal like this, but this counts as a wound Hinode will be forced to conceal from the public at any cost. Even if we don't say a word, Hinode will go on the defensive to protect it themselves. You can't ask for a better situation than this."

"But what if the police sniffs out the connection between Sugihara's daughter and my grandson?"

"Hinode won't let on a thing about that part of the story. And even if the police do sniff it out, it will only lead their investigation down the wrong path. Do you follow me? As long as they consider it a revenge crime, the only suspects they'll turn up are you and your daughter. Meanwhile, Monoi-san, you'll just be watering your morning glories and napping in front of the TV, and on Sundays you have the racetrack. No matter where they poke into, they'll find nothing."

Even though he was calling from a payphone, Handa chose his words carefully, one by one, apparently paying no mind to the dwindling minutes on his telephone calling card. His tone suggested that, more than explaining it to Monoi, he was trying to convince himself.

As Monoi listened to him on the other end of the phone, once again he allowed the fateful bond he had with this corporation—Hinode—to slowly chafe at him. If it weren't for this Sugihara person—this Hinode board member—neither his grandson, Takayuki, nor Hiroyuki Hatano would be dead. Or if Hinode as a corporation had even a shred of integrity, Hatano would never have sent them a threatening letter or tape.

"So you're saying Hinode is a go?"

"Absolutely. Oh, and also, in the *Toho Weekly* magazine that went on sale yesterday, in their 'Face of Japan' feature, there's a photo of Kyosuke Shiroyama. He's dressed casually—a classy, simple summer sweater and faded chino pants. He's even got on a well-worn pair of white Reebok sneakers—this guy has pretty good style. Looks to me like they took the photo on the grounds of a small shrine. I knew I'd seen that landscape somewhere, so I went to confirm it in person, and it was just as I'd thought. You know those stone steps in front of Omori Station? Tenso Shrine is at the top of those steps."

"Ah, I know it. So the president of Hinode lives in Sanno. Of course, a wealthy residential neighborhood."

"The address is in Sanno Ni-chome. I looked it up and checked it out myself. An impressive home. A huge yard, dense trees offering cool shade, and a glass greenhouse. No dog."

Handa spoke as if he were recalling each item one by one in his mind, then he murmured, "A kidnapping might work," and seemed to snort softly.

As this word—*kidnapping*—echoed in Monoi's ears, another thought—*ransom*—ran through his mind, where the numbing effect of the fiend still prevailed, followed by no moral judgment whatsoever. There was merely the realization that, little by little, their plan was being set into motion.

"Hey, I only just thought of this. Sanno Ni-chome is in the precinct of Omori Police Department—to the north it's Oi, in Shinagawa. To the south it's Kamata. All of that is my turf. The emergency deployment instructions over wireless will be leaked straight to me . . . This could get interesting." Handa let his imagination run wild, then regained an administrative tone. "By the way, I spoke with Nunokawa yesterday. I got a good impression. It's still the Bon holiday, so he said he would call you tomorrow or the day after. Also, that Yoshiko Sugihara we talked about got married in '92—now her name is Itoi. I plan on scoping out the situation."

That was the end of Handa's phone call.

THE TELEPHONE CALL FROM JUN'ICHI Nunokawa came in the following afternoon. He too called from a payphone, and there must have been a playground nearby, because children squealed in the background.

Every year, during the time when the main horseracing tournaments moved to the countryside for July and August, Lady's usual care facility also went on a summer break, so Nunokawa and his wife were kept busy looking after their daughter. When Monoi heard Nunokawa's voice over the phone, it dawned on him that now must be that time.

"Yesterday, I put the girl into a special care facility," Nunokawa said. "This place keeps her there over the weekend. With my wife sick, well, it's more than I can handle on my own."

I see, so Lady isn't at home. Hearing this, Monoi felt a rush of both pity for Lady and relief that Nunokawa had been given a little reprieve. He was at a loss for words. Finally, he replied, "I see."

Nunokawa also took a long pause. Even though he was the one who had made the call, perhaps he had not sorted out what he intended to say, for that the next thing Monoi heard was an abrupt, "Damn, it's hot." Nunokawa's voice, as usual, bore no discernable emotion or inflection, and managed to communicate only one or two of the hundred things he could have said.

"Yes, it sure is."

"By the way, I talked with Handa-san. I want in."

"What's your motive?"

"Do I need one?"

"Not necessarily, but I'm sure you've been thinking about a lot of things, too."

"I just want to come to terms with my life."

"What for?"

"I'm sure you can tell by looking at my life."

"Your life? You're a skillful driver, you earn six, seven hundred thousand yen a month, your wife is sick, and your daughter has a disability. So what? There are countless other lives just like yours."

Monoi worried that Nunokawa might take offense and hang up the phone, but the line was still connected. Instead, he heard a guttural "Ah"—more like a yelp than a sigh—that seemed to have erupted from deep within Nunokawa's body, and then, silence resumed. On the other end of the line, the crack of a baseball hitting a bat followed by children's voices cheering and laughter resounded.

There was no rhyme or reason, it was not about happiness or the lack thereof—just that each person led their own fragile life. Nunokawa had said all along that his daughter would stay in a facility until she turned eighteen, but he had no idea how he would take care of her when she was in her thirties and forties. Even if there were plenty of other parents who took care of children with disabilities, as long as the person in question—Nunokawa himself—said he couldn't do it, perhaps the impossible remained impossible.

Handa had said there was a possibility that Nunokawa might vanish, and Monoi guessed that could be what he meant by "coming to terms with his life." Which was all the more reason Monoi needed to question him further. If he were to join them out of self-destruction, it could cause trouble for all of them.

"Nunokawa-san. Take your wife on a nice trip to a hot spring spa or wherever. We're not going to pull this off today or tomorrow, so there's no rush to give me an answer."

"So long as the joker that I drew isn't going anywhere, my answer's not gonna change."

"By 'joker,' do you mean Lady?"

"Who else would it be? Out of a thousand babies, there are only one or two jokers, and my wife and I, we drew one of them. Is there any other way to say it?"

A child born with a disability, a child who dies after crashing into the wall of the Shuto Expressway at 100 km per hour, Seiji Okamura, who suffered from mental illness, and Monoi himself, transformed into a fiend in his old age—of all the fates that fell down from the heavens, in the eyes of a parent, at least, Monoi could not deny that "joker" was a fitting description.

"Then she's a Lady Joker," Monoi said, and as if a levee had broken, laughter erupted from Nunokawa, which went on for a while, and then he hung up the phone.

As if she had been waiting for his long phone call to be over, the lady pharmacist shouted from the store, "Shall I cut up some watermelon?"

"A slice for the altar, please!" Monoi yelled back.

Before long, she came into the living room with three slices of watermelon on a tray. "Here we are," she said. She sat down on the tatami floor and remarked, "That was a long call."

"When your hearing starts to go, you have to ask them to repeat everything."

"Your hearing's starting to go, Monoi-san?"

"Your voice is loud, so I hear you just fine."

Monoi offered a slice of watermelon for the altar, struck the gong, and joined his hands together. Seiji's urn and memorial tablet had been left as they were—since the wake, there was still no word from Okamura Merchants in Hachinohe. If he didn't hear from them before the equinoctial week, Monoi planned to bury Seiji in his family plot in Herai.

After polishing off the slice of watermelon that the pharmacist had bought on sale in the shopping district, Monoi stood up to water the sidewalk as he did every evening. She had gone out to the storefront before him, and had been chatting idly for nearly five minutes with a housewife from the neighborhood, giggling gaily. The housewife had been their customer for going on ten years. She always purchased the same stomach remedy and multi-symptom cold medicine, and now and then she would buy whatever she had forgotten to pick up at the supermarket—cough drops, bug spray, mosquito coils, talcum powder, cleanser, toilet paper, and so on.

The other patrons of Monoi Pharmacy were more or less the same. Under the management of an owner with no business acumen, the pharmacist did a good job; she recommended brands with high rebates for the customers, wangled beer coupons and gift certificates from the distributors' sales reps and cashed them in at the voucher exchange shop, handing him his share: "Here's your take for the day. Fifty-fifty."

The profits from a small pharmacy on the outskirts of the city were negligible, but even after deducting the pharmacist's pay and various other expenses, Monoi still brought in three million yen a year, give or take, and this combined with his pension was enough for a single man of sixty-nine to go on living comfortably.

The housewife, seeing Monoi come into the store, called out affably, "Oh, hello there. I've been wondering about you since I saw the notice that you were in mourning."

"Yes. When you get to be my age, all you do is send people off," Monoi gave a noncommittal response along with a shy smile, and after lowering his bowed head two or three times like a turtle, he walked outside.

Beneath the woven reed shade, the seedpods at the ends of the shriveled morning glories' stems were beginning to swell. Monoi subconsciously tilted the right side of his face toward them, and stared at the seedpods with his good right eye. Making a note in his mental calendar to remove the seeds in a week or so, he suddenly wondered, when these blue morning glories bloomed next year, where would he be and what would he be thinking? Even if he were to get his hands on a large sum of money, for a man who would be seventy, a life of revelry and luxury was utterly unnecessary, and with the most important thing—a sense of peace in his heart—moving ever further away from him, by this time next year, perhaps he would be an even more wretched fiend than he was now.

Monoi contemplated this and, resolving that at least he would no longer live the life of an animal, he murmured to himself, *That would be good enough for me.*

半田修平

SHUHEI HANDA

4

Soon after the autumn equinox, there was an unusual drop in the incidence of violent crime, and Shuhei Handa took this opportunity to start seeing a dentist he knew near Kamata Station, making the excuse to those around him, "This is the only chance I have to get my teeth fixed." Since his police department was being renovated and he was working out of a temporary office building in Hon-Haneda, his visits to the dentist became a good pretext for him to sneak off further afield. Handa also scrounged time from his comings and goings to make gradual contact with his conspirators.

At the end of September, just as their plan had started to take shape, on his usual way to the dentist Handa met up with Katsumi Koh. Whenever Koh was out making daytime rounds on sales calls, he always appeared in the three-piece ensemble of a modern Japanese banker-man: black briefcase, motorcycle, and helmet. He thought these made him conspicuous, so Koh made sure to leave his bike a little distance away.

When Handa met up with Koh at a coffee shop in a crowded shopping district on the west side of Kamata Station, the conversation bluntly got down to the question of how much money they would take from their target. As he ate his curry rice garnished with bright red pickled relish, Koh replied, "As much as we want." Then he added, "Hinode's got money to burn. They can get it from anywhere."

"You don't say. But how do you know?"

"It's obvious. Look at this." Koh thrust toward Handa the publicly listed company asset securities report that had been tucked inside the weekly magazine he was carrying. It was a slim, orange pamphlet titled *Hinode Beer Company*.

"Take a look at the category 'Cash and Deposits' at the very top of the assets section on the balance sheet."

"163.2 billion yen . . ."

"The number from the previous term is next to it. Compare the two, and you'll see there's about a thirty-billion increase. That means money is going in and out by the tens of billions. That cash-and-deposits category lists the instantaneous number at the end of the term on December thirty-first, which doesn't mean that same exact amount will be sitting in their bank account come January first. For a corporation with as many assets as Hinode, the sums of money they're moving around is on a whole different scale—that much becomes clear just by looking at their financial statements."

"So because they're moving around huge amounts of money, we can take as much as we want?"

"Basically. For instance, below that same category do you see where it says 'Other Current Assets'? It says 'other' because they've thrown various types of accounting in there. Short-term loans and reimbursements, temporary advances for travel and business trip expenses, unpaid bills, down payments, and so on. I can't tell what type of money it is unless I see the actual ledger, but you can bet that there's money caught up in there whose actual purpose is impossible for anyone on the outside to know. The fact that they have seventeen billion yen worth of it there—well, they're in a league of their own."

"You said they can get money from anywhere, but where, for instance, would it come from?"

"That's Hinode's problem."

"But say you were in charge of finance at Hinode, how and from where would you get the money? If word got out to the public and to the police that Hinode had caved to criminal demands and coughed up the money, they'd lose their credibility—so they'd need to raise a slush fund without anyone on the outside being the wiser. Now, how would you do that?"

"It depends on the amount, but if it's a matter of two or three hundred million, I would create a random expense item and charge it as a temporary advance, like the one I just mentioned. As for adjusting the account afterward, I would wait until things calm down and then chalk it up little by little as a deductible expense."

Koh talked as if this were the easiest thing in the world. "Let's see, what else . . ." He drew the pamphlet back toward himself. "A common nest for a slush fund is 'Construction Suspense Account' under fixed assets. Hinode's got fifty billion in there this period. Huge, right? When they construct factories or other buildings, they make deals with contractors so that, for example, they can write up the price they've padded with an extra billion yen as a construction startup fee under this heading, and that'll be the end of story. What else . . ."

Koh let his fingers trail lightly over the balance sheet and, mumbling, "This is good too," paused in the middle of the section on liabilities. "This category called 'Deposits Payable' is also useful. See, a beer company pays taxes based on shipments. To insure against the possibility of a client going bankrupt before they can settle their account, they always take a deposit, and this is the category where they record such deposits. For example, Hinode deals with some sixty subsidiaries and affiliated companies, right? Under the guise of a joint marketing fund, they could make each company contribute fifty million, which comes out to three billion. If each paid a hundred million it would be six billion. That money could then be sorted under this 'Deposits Payable.' On the books, you'd see no problem whatsoever.

Combine all these methods I've just mentioned, and coming up with ten billion or so is a breeze."

As Handa listened, he was once again impressed by the finance man's accounting savvy. Though perhaps he was more impressed with the sloppy accounting of large corporations.

"So, Handa-san. How much do you want to take? We should discuss that first."

"That's a tough question . . . How about two billion to start?"

"That's all?" Koh looked up with dismay.

"Listen, Koh-san. We're talking about a crime. The money we get will be paid in cash or gold. That's the iron rule for not getting caught."

"What century do you think this is?" Koh said, looking dumbfounded again. "Transferring money is no big deal if they use one of their overseas subsidiaries and pay in dollars. Nowadays, everyone dealing in illegal transfers uses that trick."

"No—it's gotta be cash. Think of Monoi-san, and Nunokawa, and Yo-chan. How are they supposed to use dollars deposited in some offshore bank account?"

Hearing this, Koh deferred immediately, as if his practicality had been called into question. "You're right."

"Now, if it's cash, there is a physical limit to how much we can carry. Those things you guys use—duralumin cases. How many stacks of ten million can one of those hold?" Handa asked.

"Twenty-one. You're right, it'll weigh quite a bit."

"Then why don't we say two billion for now?" Handa threw out the same number.

Koh replied, "Sure," but he seemed to have little interest in the actual amount, instead moving on to the next subject. "More importantly, what's the bargaining chip we'll use to make them pay?"

"Bargaining chip? Of course we'll go right for the jugular. We'll take their beer sales hostage."

"That sounds good." A smile flickered over Koh's face for the first time and, without looking up, he continued to spoon up the curry rice he had sloshed around on the plate. "If we can reduce their sales, Hinode won't stand a chance—they'll pony up two billion without any questions. In fact, I'd bet on it," Koh said with his mouth full of rice.

"Lowering beer sales is a piece of cake. Isn't that right, Koh-san?"

"There are vending machines all over Japan where anyone can buy beer. Add a little cyanide and that's it—they're finished."

"Idiot. Who's gonna use poison? I'm still a cop, you know?"

Koh guffawed, with grains of rice shooting out of his mouth. "Well then, doesn't matter if it's salt or sugar—the result will be the same." He pushed aside his messy plate.

"That's disgusting, wipe it off," Handa said and threw a paper napkin at Koh, whose shoulders shook as he laughed, wiping away the bits of rice spilled on the table. "That pretty much suits your needs, right?"

Koh glanced up at him briefly, then immediately looked away as he replied brusquely, "Sure." If their beer were to be contaminated with a foreign substance, Hinode's stock price would plummet without a doubt, and the profit from margin trading would be all but guaranteed. But something in Koh's eyes implied that this—a mere bonus to their main plan—should be something they agreed not to discuss.

Handa ordered two coffees from the waitress and brought the conversation back to its original topic. "Incidentally, with regard to the right moment to strike, you still think spring to summer is the window that'll affect their sales the most?"

"I think so. The sales campaign will heat up in April. Hinode hasn't released any new products this year, so they definitely will next spring. They'll have an enormous budget to launch their advertising strategy, so it's best for us to start when their shipments are in full swing. That should be late March."

"All right. Then we'll start at the end of March. Say, in terms of sales, how much would Hinode have to lose before they gave in?"

"If you mean how much loss they can withstand—even if an entire year's worth of sales evaporated, with all their assets they still wouldn't go under. But for senior management it's a matter of responsibility, so I'm sure they'll crack at a much lower number."

"Well then, first I want you to evaluate Hinode's break-even point."

"It's impossible to calculate accurately with just the numbers listed on the balance sheet. I can give you a rough estimate, though."

"That's fine. Next, you can get your hands on data that shows their average monthly shipping volume, right? From there, figure out where they break even for each month. How much loss would they suffer depending on how much shipping decreases, and at what point would Hinode's management start to panic? I want you to create a simulation for those scenarios."

"No sweat," Koh replied succinctly.

The coffee that was brought over tasted awful as usual, as if it had been boiled down. Handa drank this same coffee practically every other day, paying 350 yen each time and sitting in the same slightly dirty chair. As he sipped the coffee, another self-deprecating thought started to spin inside his mind.

He had made a ritual of drinking every last drop of this incredibly nasty stuff. At some point, this very ritual had created the mentality of a hardened cop who no longer even recognized this coffee as awful. And here he was drinking it again today. *Maybe I don't hate the taste of it after all,* he thought to himself. His thirteen years on the police force, where he had been able to nurture his fantasies over a single cup of coffee per day—maybe they hadn't been so bad. And yet, his masochistic tendency had reached the point where he was now trying to destroy all of that by his own hand, and the truth was that he could no longer control it.

Handa contemplated this calmly. He was like an octopus devouring its own leg. If he allowed himself to demolish his career at the police department—a hotbed for his fantasies and pleasures for so many years—where would he go from there? Most likely, he would just set out again in search of even more terrible coffee. Realizing this, Handa's spirit nearly drained out of him.

The point was, something was still missing. For this octopus to consume its own leg, there had better be a cause worth dying for. Kidnapping or tainting beer with a foreign substance was all well and good, but it wasn't enough. Handa lost himself in this burning question, in the urgent but directionless search for that something.

THE BEST PLACE TO MEET up with Jun'ichi Nunokawa was at the wild bird sanctuary in Yashio, where Nippo Transport's truck terminal was located, after he had finished the Kyoto-Osaka-Kobe route. Every evening, Nunokawa left the terminal before eight and drove the six-hour Keihanshin route, as it was called, to Osaka, where he took an hour break during reshipment before heading back. Then, returning to Tokyo shortly after ten in the morning, he would soon take his minivan back to the company housing in Kachidoki. But if he saw Handa waiting for him in front of the main gate of the wild bird park, Nunokawa would circle halfway around the park to the parking lot on the south side, where he would pick Handa up.

Handa always tried to tailor the conversation to fit within the time it took to drive northward along the waterfront to where Nunokawa lived. It was obvious that the truck driver was exhausted after the Keihanshin round-trip, which was 550 kilometers each way. Nunokawa barely seemed to have the energy to open his mouth, and as if this were his last task before he could get to sleep, he forced his heavy-lidded eyes open and merely listened to Handa. Even when Handa had exclaimed, "We're talking two billion!" Nunokawa had only looked at him drowsily without uttering a word.

When they had seen each other in mid-October, however, Nunokawa had handed Handa the thing he had asked for and said, "Will these do?"

Handa opened the manila envelope and took out three standard-size snapshots and checked their subject matter. "Perfect," he replied

The daughter of Takeo Sugihara, one of the executives at Hinode, was living in a luxury apartment in the hills of Takanawa. Yoshiko was married now and had taken her husband's name, Itoi. Her address was listed in her alumni association's directory; once Handa knew her address he had been able to figure out her husband's name, and after making up a reasonable excuse and inquiring at the precinct's local police box, he had learned that her husband was a physician. Handa had stopped by the address several times, whenever he happened to be nearby, and from what he had observed Yoshiko was now the mother of an infant still in diapers. In the mornings she would leave her apartment with her stroller to go shopping at the Peacock Supermarket at the bottom of Gyoranzaka Hill. Sometimes, she would take the baby to Takanawa Park. On three separate days, Nunokawa had taken snapshots of this same mother and child with a compact camera as he drove a rented van along Gyoranzaka Hill. On one thirty-six-exposure roll of film, Nunokawa had mixed in random other shots whose locations were impossible to identify and taken it to a photo shop far from Minato Ward, where he had had them developed and printed as fast as possible.

The faces of Yoshiko and her child were clearly visible in all three photos, which Nunokawa had taken from the driver's seat of the van. The young mother, doing her morning shopping and pushing her baby in the stroller, had the peaceful visage of one who was never far from affluence, and the baby was plump and healthy—the snapshots conveyed nothing significant aside from these plain facts. Nunokawa did not divulge anything about his own impressions of the fortunate mother and child he had observed with his own eyes, and Handa also refrained from asking anything further.

"By the way, Nunokawa-san. Can you steal a car?"

"Stealing it is easy, but if you want to drive it around, you need a key."

"Yo-chan can cut a key. Once the new year starts, in or out of the city, it doesn't matter where, I want you to mark ten or so vans that are sitting in parking lots collecting dust. The darker the color the better. Once you've found them, give me the makes and models for all of them. I'll give you prototypes for the keys to those models, and I want you to insert them into the keyholes, turn them around a few times, and bring them back to me. Then Yo-chan will cut the teeth of the keys."

"So they get nicks where the teeth should be, right? Got it."

A quick learner who did exactly as he was told and said nothing redundant—Nunokawa was indeed useful. The special skills and athletic ability he had developed in the military seemed wasted in the driver's seat of a truck; it would be a shame not to put them to use now in various ways.

"After you pick the cars, we'll choose which roads. You ever heard of the N system?"

"You mean those things that look like rapid surveillance cameras above major intersections?"

"Yes, exactly. Do you know the intersections and expressway toll booths where those things are found?"

"Yeah."

"I want you to investigate various getaway routes from the Tokyo metropolitan area that avoid them completely. It doesn't matter where—the destination could be Tanzawa, Okuchichibu, Fuji, Okunikko—the deeper into the mountains the better. We don't need a hideout, either, but if there's a place where we can spend two or three nights on the mountain, that would be great."

"Driving during the day or at night?"

"Late at night."

"What season?"

"Next year, late March."

"Better find roads that won't be icy."

Nunokawa replied in a clipped monotone that made it seem as if this were no different from his daily work. Nunokawa had decided to join them of his own volition, but he seemed to still be thinking about splitting, and Handa found his detachment both manageable and disconcerting.

"Hey . . . Why'd you join the military anyway?"

"I saw a recruitment poster on the wall at the post office, and somehow I just applied. If I hadn't joined the military, I'm sure I'd be drying daikon radishes at my parents' farm back home."

"Your whole life—everything happens 'somehow' doesn't it? You somehow joined the army, somehow got married, somehow had a kid, somehow raised her, and before you knew it you found yourself in over your head, and the first time you use your own head the answer you come up with is to split. Am I wrong?"

It didn't matter what he said, Handa knew that Nunokawa barely listened when the conversation turned abstract. Sure enough, Nunokawa only mumbled, "I guess you're right."

"Anyway, enough of this 'somehow,' all right?" Handa persisted, hoping to put some fire into his spirit for once.

"And how's your wife doing?"

"She sleeps, she gets up, sleeps again."

"If you need some help, just say the word. I can do anything."

When Handa said this, Nunokawa moved his head vaguely in response.

As they approached the Shioji-bashi intersection, Handa decided to get out of Nunokawa's minivan. As he disembarked, he reached into his bag and shoved a mamushi snake extract energy drink in Nunokawa's lap. For the first time Nunokawa turned to look at him, smiling faintly with eyes that seemed to yearn to say something.

HANDA STILL HAD THE FEELING that "something" was missing, though. And yet, his physical and psychological engines, which were developing the plan, continued to spin at a nearly steady pace, so that on a Sunday afternoon in the middle of November, Handa found himself at Tokyo Racecourse in Fuchu to catch up with his conspirators.

As the time neared for the final race of the day, the passageway to the betting windows became crowded with people—some leaving, some storming the automatic payout machines, and some just loitering around before making their final bet. Handa sat waiting in his usual spot by the pillar, and soon enough Yo-chan's sneakers appeared out of nowhere. One sneaker kicked the pillar, and then Yo-chan took a seat next to him.

"How much did you lose?" Handa asked.

"Five thousand yen."

"You betting next?"

"No. That's enough for me."

Yo-chan had recently stopped shaving his head and begun to grow out his hair, which made him more and more indistinguishable from the throngs at the racecourse. Though when he planted himself right on the floor by the betting windows and buried his nose into the newspaper spread before him, he was still the same Yo-chan. Nevertheless, he was one of the men who was in on the plan, for reasons known only to himself. The only explanation he gave was "because everyone else is," and there was no point pushing him any further for an answer—like Nunokawa, he had done everything he had been instructed to do well enough, and Handa could find no particular reason to be worried.

Handa placed in Yo-chan's palm the tissue-wrapped item he had brought with him. Unwrapping it, with his fingertips Yo-chan picked up a thin steel sheet about the size of a pinkie and brought it closer to his eyes. A few days ago, Yo-chan had cut the notches and the ridges into both sides of the sheet based on the key to Nunokawa's minivan. Handa had then inserted it into the minivan's keyhole and turned it around a few times so that the steel would be imprinted with nicks from the grooves in the cylinder lock.

"You see the nicks?"

"I do."

"Try cutting the teeth out of them."

"That's easy. All I need's like half an hour," Yo-chan replied and slid the piece of steel into his pocket. For Yo-chan, who shaped metal molds everyday with a margin of error of 0.001 millimeter, cutting a car key should be easy as pie.

"After the key, there's this." Handa grabbed the can of beer he had purchased at a vending machine outside the racecourse and held it upside down, then quickly inserted a pushpin into the bottom of the can. Liquid instantly spouted from the puncture, and Handa held his finger over it.

"When you showed Monoi-san before, it was just a can of juice, right? This is what happens when the liquid is carbonated. Can you plug this hole neatly?"

Yo-chan took the can with the hole that measured no more than a millimeter in diameter and from which foam oozed nonstop. He turned his machinist's eye on it and after examining it for about a minute, he said, "It'd be tough. An aluminum can is only point two millimeters thick, at most. With the pressure from the carbonation, I don't think whatever plugs it will stay put."

"So a can would be difficult."

"I could do it with a bottle. The cap of a beer bottle, I mean," Yo-chan said and tossed the can into the trashcan.

"Fine, let's go with a bottle then. And finally, there's this."

Handa placed a paperback book he had purchased at a bookstore he had happened to pass by in Yo-chan's hands, then got to his feet. Yo-chan looked up and down the spine of the book and—muttering "You're shitting me" to himself—leafed through the pages, no longer paying any attention to Handa. The book had the dubious title, *Horseracing Newspapers: How to Read to Win.*

The weak rays of the late autumn sun had started to fade by the paddock, where the horses set to appear in the last race of the day were being led by the reins. The wind streaming through the horses' manes had turned increasingly cold, and the remaining crowd of onlookers had formed a dark gray mass, hushed and still. Seizo Monoi sat on a bench beneath a cluster of a trees overlooking this view, hunched idly over the horseracing paper on his lap. Handa walked halfway around the paddock to reach the bench and sat down next to him.

"Getting cold," Monoi said to him.

"It's almost December, after all."

Handa slipped one of the snapshots that had been tucked into the notebook in his breast pocket into Monoi's hand. Monoi held the photo fifty centimeters away from his right eye and stared at the image of his late grandson's girlfriend and her newborn child. His only comment was, "She reminds me of Princess Michiko when she was young."

Their features were different, but in terms of their refined, well-bred manner and calm expression, they could be said to resemble each other.

The next thing Handa handed him was a clipping from a magazine. Monoi once again held it in front of his right eye and squinted. The article was from a financial magazine, a short, serialized column called *Managers Up Close*, cut out from this month's issue and featuring Kyosuke Shiroyama, the president of Hinode Beer. Handa had been collecting as many articles on Shiroyama as he could find, but the subject was apparently a simple man both at work and at home, for his name appeared mostly in hard financial articles, making it difficult to deduce anything about his private life. This article, however, was a rare find that offered a glimpse into Shiroyama's personal life.

"Huh. In order to sustain long, hard workdays he takes great care of his health above all . . . After a simple dinner, he enjoys a bit of beer or whisky . . . Attends social events one night a week at most. Makes sure to be in bed by midnight and rises early to do his reading . . ."

"If he's in bed by midnight, that must mean he gets home no later than 11 every night. Of the ten times I've trailed him now, he's returned home roughly around ten each time. In a black Nissan President driven by his chauffeur."

"So you think this is our man?"

"Looks that way."

Handa put the photo and clipping back inside his notebook and added, "So far, so good."

Monoi had no further questions. "I'm sure you all could use some money. One of the old man's time deposits has reached maturity, so split this among everyone as you see fit." Monoi handed Handa a manila envelope he had taken from his jacket pocket.

Handa tucked the package in his own pocket. From the feel of it, he guessed it was around five hundred thousand yen. "The return on it will be eight-hundred-fold, just you wait. For now, I'll use this to pay Nunokawa back for the car rental. Then, little by little, I'll start buying the props we need."

"You and Nunokawa should be careful around your wives. Women have sharp instincts."

"I wouldn't worry about that. Not one of us—Yo-chan and Koh included—are the type to get excited. We sure are a motley crew."

The horses were already leaving the paddock for the racetrack, and the spectators had dispersed as well. The sunlight had waned, deepening the gray scene.

"I myself feel a little excited, to be honest . . . Sure, my life hasn't changed, but little by little I can feel my spirits swelling. Well, I knew all along I'd be bidding farewell to my peaceful life when I decided to do this, so I suppose it's all going as I expected."

Monoi's voice, almost more of an interior monologue, reached Handa like a distant echo, its source buried under a thick layer of dust that had accumulated over sixty-nine years. His profile, as he gazed down at the paddock, appeared leathery, hardened and worn-out from a life that had lasted roughly twice as long as Handa's own.

"By the way, Handa-san. Let's give our group a name," Monoi said. "What do you think of 'Lady Joker'?"

"What is that? English?"

"The other day, Nunokawa called his daughter the joker that he had drawn. That's when it occurred to me. If a joker is something that nobody wants, then what better name to describe the lot of us?"

"So Hinode Beer is the one that draws the joker?"

"That's right. Besides, if it weren't for Lady, we'd never have had the chance to know one another like this."

Hearing Monoi put it that way, Handa felt deeply moved. Recalling the image of Lady, who very recently had been wobbling her head joyfully in the grandstand on Sundays, Handa nodded. "All right. I like it. Lady Joker it is."

AFTER PARTING WITH MONOI, HANDA took the train, transferring from the Keio Line to the JR Line, arriving at Kamata Station a little before six. His wife had the early shift that day at the Ito-Yokado supermarket where she worked, so for the first time in a while they had agreed to meet up at the pachinko parlor in front of the west exit of the station. As he left the station building and stepped into the pedestrian crossing at the traffic circle, a bicycle burst out from the side alley beside the pachinko parlor directly in front of him.

Handa stopped in his tracks, as did the sneakers pedaling the bicycle. The truth was, it was those sneakers more than anything else that caught his eye. He stared at them, then took in the faded jeans, dark sweater, and finally the face that appeared above all these.

The man was also regarding Handa, staring at him in a similar manner, but in the next instant, both sides of his mouth spread wide, like the surface of frozen water cleaving apart, and he flashed his white teeth.

"Handa-san, right?" The quality of the man's voice was as stiff as ever, but unlike the last time Handa had heard it, there was a bracing and clear ring to it. No, it was more of an artificial sound, as if his voice had been carved out with a high-performance lathe.

"Oh, Inspector Goda . . ."

"Just Goda. I haven't seen you since we were on that case in Shinagawa. Which department are you working from now, Handa-san?"

"Kamata."

"I see. I was transferred to Omori in February. We're neighbors."

As he said the word "neighbors," his lips drew a fine arc once more.

Handa remembered him clearly now. He was that assistant police inspector with the Third Violent Crime Investigation Team from MPD. He had been assigned to Special Investigation Headquarters that had been set up in Shinagawa Police Department to handle a murder case. But unlike the icy, reptilian face in Handa's memory, the face of the man in front of him was calm and luminous, projecting a vibrant, otherworldly smile, and his closely shaven head—so bracingly handsome—made him look completely different, like a clone. As if in a trance, Handa continued to stare at him, for the moment disbelieving his own eyes.

Upon closer inspection, Goda appeared to be sitting astride his own bicycle, and the contents of the front basket were a basin with shampoo, a soap dish and other toiletries, and a violin case. When Handa's eyes glanced at the basket, Goda immediately donned a shy smile and said, "It's my day off today, so I went to the batting cages, the public bath, and now I'm on my way to a local gathering."

"That's very health-conscious of you. On my day off I usually go the racetrack or play pachinko—oh, and that Theater Palace over there is great, too. In the middle of the day, it's housewives of all stripes . . ."

Handa laughed, blathering on about things he had had no intention of mentioning, and though he tried to scrutinize the façade of the man before him, his opponent put up an impenetrable defense.

"I'd much rather enjoy a triple-feature of adult films instead of arguing with geezers with athlete's foot at the public bath. Anyway, are you off-duty today too, Handa-san?"

It was as if each word that escaped from Goda's bracingly fresh mouth self-destructed before it reached Handa. Such crude and insubstantial remarks rang hollow, coming from Goda, and if they were meant as jokes, they sailed past Handa's comprehension.

"Goda-san, do you play the violin?"

"I've got a rehearsal right now with an ensemble for a Christmas concert over there at Kamata Church. I only dabbled when I was a child, so I'm way out of my depth," Goda said breezily, then peeked at his wristwatch. "Oh, sorry to take so much of your time. Excuse me, I have to go now," he said, bowing his head slightly. Out of habit, Handa's head also lowered automatically as he responded, "Oh, not at all."

Handa, staring at the receding figure as he peddled away on the sidewalk, remained rooted to the spot for a few long minutes. Time seemed to have stopped as everything he had felt back when they had encountered each other on the staircase at the Shinagawa Police Department—the physiological mass of emotion that had erupted within him, the mood and circumstances surrounding him at the time—came rushing back all at once. Handa stood there bewildered, suddenly forgetting where he was.

With the rush of emotion constricting his throat, Handa asked himself, *Did he say Omori Department?* If Goda had been transferred to a local department from MPD, did that mean he had been promoted? No, the director of CID and the acting deputy chief were both someone else. If he was still an assistant police inspector after being transferred, then the simple fact was that he had been demoted. The hotshot from MPD who had walked with a swagger four years ago had been demoted. Handa experienced the pleasure of this realization only fleetingly, for now he couldn't help but wonder what it was about that face, which had been as sleek as glass. Though this was something that—once again—remained beyond Handa's imagination.

Handa tortured himself endlessly, caught up in the illusion as if he were still standing there on the staircase of the Shinagawa Police Department. *Who was that guy?* Who was he to have materialized out of nowhere, carrying a set of toiletries and a violin case in the basket of his bicycle and saying he was on his way to a rehearsal for a Christmas concert before disappearing before his eyes? The guy who had practically cut him off in the crosswalk—as if to taunt him, as if to suddenly slap him across the face, as if to gloat for a brief moment? When his thoughts reached this point, Handa had completely forgotten what time he was supposed to meet his wife, and instead began running toward Kanpachi, in the direction the guy had disappeared.

Kamata Church was located about three hundred meters past the Kamata Overpass, and then down a side street on the left. Following his vague recollection of where it was, Handa dashed into a narrow alley at the corner of a parking lot and, still running, he found the open gates of the church on his right.

Beyond the front garden stood a simple wooden chapel. To the left of the chapel, there was a single-story wooden shack that appeared to be a meetinghouse—parked in front of it was the bicycle he had seen earlier, and he could hear strains of string instruments coming from within.

Without even thinking about it, Handa approached the building and peered inside through the window. Inside the humble, wood-paneled room illuminated by a single light bulb, eight men and women holding violins and cellos were seated in a semicircle around a music stand, and in one corner he saw Goda's face. Had Goda's story about arguing with geezers with athlete's foot at the public bath been a lie, or was it that this man's world was so extraordinarily different from his own? Goda's right hand and elbow, which controlled his bow, and his left hand, which slid along the neck of the instrument, moved with such mysterious dexterity. And his profile, turned toward the sheet music, was focused so intently on the musical notes that the rest of the world seemed to have completely disappeared for him. His face bore no trace of disappointment at having been transferred to a local police department. No, not only the world of the police force but also the grimy public bath, the geezers with athlete's foot, the detective from another department whom he had run into just a few minutes earlier, the smoke and soot from the nearby factory—all of it had been erased from this face. Handa could only stare, deeply wounded by the sight of a face like this, and in that moment, his ears barely registered any sound. He recognized the music as something-or-other by Mozart, which he had heard from time to time at the coffee shop near his department, but whether the music was performed well or whether the players were in sync didn't even reach his consciousness.

Handa was simply aware of the crucial distance between these two worlds separated by a single pane of glass, and for no reason at all he felt his skin prickle as he stood there stuporously. What he saw here was a spectacular absurdity, or perhaps the design of this world was fundamentally flawed. He considered this, but the truth was before he could give it any thought his knees began to buckle and, as if he were about to tumble into a fissure in the ground split by his own two feet, he walked away, reeling in despondency.

He passed back through the alley, and once he had reached Kanpachi, at last he felt the blood rushing back to his brain, which had started to work again dully. If their plan were to proceed as it now stood, a Special Investigation headquarters would be set up not in

Shinagawa where Hinode Beer was located, but in the Omori Police Department, the precinct that covered the home of Hinode's president in Sanno Ni-chome within its jurisdiction. Handa pondered the fact that if Goda were working in Omori now, it was inevitable that sooner or later they would meet again.

So, I will soon force a bitter medicine down that man's throat. I will see that man turn blue in the face.

Handa thought—*Yes, I've finally found that "something."* He never would have expected that "something"—so much bigger than the fantasies he had nurtured in the police force—to have arisen from a police inspector he had not seen for four years, but such was fate. As the vast haze of hatred and gloom—neither of which still held any meaning for him—suddenly started to coalesce around the man who had crossed his path, Handa tasted a fresh, hitherto unknown emotion. When it was the police force or a corporation, and there was no individual face to witness in agony, he might only attain an abstract sense of self-satisfaction, but now he knew that, more than anything, he would enjoy the sight of someone suffering right before his eyes. It wouldn't be long until, inside the small office of the local police department where he had been demoted, that goody-two-shoes with his clear-eyed face would be sobbing, mired in defeat, frustration, and humiliation.

Upon each brick of the plan of attack that he had been constructing up to now, he applied the flesh and blood of this man named Goda, and feeling the plan beginning to pulse with a vivacity as real as something touching his own skin, Handa became euphoric. *This is it*, he thought. *The reason I will commit this crime is because I yearn for this sensation.*

PART THREE

SPRING 1995

THE INCIDENT

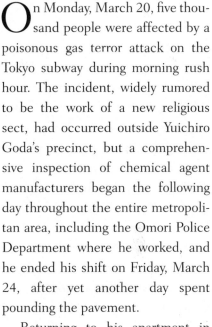

合田雄一郎

YUICHIRO GODA

1

On Monday, March 20, five thousand people were affected by a poisonous gas terror attack on the Tokyo subway during morning rush hour. The incident, widely rumored to be the work of a new religious sect, had occurred outside Yuichiro Goda's precinct, but a comprehensive inspection of chemical agent manufacturers began the following day throughout the entire metropolitan area, including the Omori Police Department where he worked, and he ended his shift on Friday, March 24, after yet another day spent pounding the pavement.

Returning to his apartment in Yashio after nine in the evening, he grabbed his violin and immediately went back out. Playing every day— even when he only had half an hour to spare—had become a minor rhythm in his life over the past year since he had been transferred to the precinct police department. Why it had ended up being the violin rather than, say, jogging or bamboo sword practice remained a mystery, one that he had not even tried to solve. He only knew that what he truly wanted was not so much a routine in his life as time in which to think about nothing at all.

On a bench in Yashio Park near his home, Goda started by practicing his fingering, in accordance with the instruction manual on the Maia Bang method and as he had done thousand of times since he was a child. The part of his brain that was listening to each note was not his auditory cortex but most definitely the part that controlled his reflexes near the cerebellum, and as usual, before long his mind emptied for a brief respite. He was convinced that he didn't do this out of necessity—this fact alone was what mattered—yet he was aware once again of his effort to turn himself into a machine. His own body was much more honest, however, and his fingers were soon too cold to keep moving, forcing him to put down his violin and rub his hands together. If it was this cold here, he thought, up in the mountains the heavy snow of early spring must be falling.

A lone man in a duster coat walked across the park, which had turned desolate after dark. Thinking it could be his old friend Yusuke Kano, Goda briefly followed the figure with his eyes.

Eight years had already passed since Goda divorced Kano's younger sister, Kiyoko, but Kano, who worked as a prosecutor in the Tokyo District Public Prosecutor's Office, was unable to reconcile his own delicate position as Goda's former brother-in-law the way he managed to organize the documents in his office at work everyday. Even now, whenever the mood would strike, he dropped by Goda's apartment in Yashio, which was closer to his office than his government employee housing in Setagaya, and after making small talk and downing one or two cups of whisky, he would lay out a futon to sleep and then leave in the morning. In their university days Kano and Goda had been mountain climbing partners, but now they were both so busy that the mountains felt like a distant part of their lives, and for the last few years this had been the state of their relationship.

The man walking across the park disappeared in the direction of another apartment tower. Goda put away his violin in its case and stood up. It finally dawned on him that Kano had stopped by only the day before yesterday, and he chided himself for being so spaced out.

Goda returned to his housing complex at 9:45 P.M. and started his laundry. He switched on the television, opened the refrigerator, and after taking out a withered bunch of komatsuna greens and an expired packet of tofu and throwing them in the trash, he set a glass on a platform scale and poured 150 grams of whisky into it, then turned off the lights in the kitchen.

The veranda of his tiny apartment faced east, over the elevated Bayshore Route of the Shuto Expressway, and beyond it the Shinagawa switchyard was steeped in expansive darkness. Among the sounds he could hear were the wind blowing across the landfill, cars speeding over the Shuto Expressway, steel doors opening and closing in a hallway somewhere, and the scattered echoes of children's cries.

The television that Kano had given him for his birthday last year came with an antenna and a receiver for satellite TV, but since there was a fee for every channel, he had only subscribed to the sports channel and the BBC. Kano had told him he should at least try to keep up his English whenever he didn't feel like doing anything else, but that wasn't why he watched it—rather, he would give in to boredom and flip it on, listening halfheartedly to the news from overseas that he could care less about, or watching J-league soccer games so he could make small talk at work.

With his whisky in his left hand, Goda sat down on the tatami floor and gazed at the screen for a while and, pulling a few of the books scattered on the writing desk toward him with his right hand, he debated which one he should crack open. The chapter on "Art of Fugue" from the first volume of Glenn Gould's collected writings would be his sleeping aid before bed. He would save *Discourse on Commercial Transactions* for another time. He still could not sing any of the songs in *100 Easy Karaoke Songs*, which he had purchased out of a sense of social obligation. Then, his eyes fell on the March issue of *Nikkei Science*, but when he tried to drag it out the mountain of books came toppling down. He gave up on reading anything and for the moment turned his attention back to the world business report playing on the television, then in the margin of the magazine he jotted down the English word he had just heard, "squabble." He pulled out a dictionary from the collapsed pile of books and checked the definition, and by the time he opened the magazine and started reading an article entitled, "The Birth and Death of V1974—A Nova in the Constellation Cygnus," it was exactly 10:20 P.M.

V1974, which had erupted three years ago, was the only nova in the history of astronomy that could be observed from its onset to completion, and this recording had bolstered significant parts of the theory that novae eruptions occurred in a binary system consisting of two stars of dissimilar masses. While reading about the nuclear fusion that involved otherworldly mass, temperature, and speed, Goda's mind emptied again and he managed to finish off about a third of his glass of whisky.

When he had been transferred to the precinct police department, Goda had considered starting a brand new life—both mentally and physically—but in the end he couldn't afford to actively study for the certification required for a future job. Instead, he bought a new violin with the money he had been saving up for a car and started playing around with the musical instrument he had not touched since his divorce, but even that remained nothing more than hobby that barely took up an hour of his time. At the end of the day, he often fell into an unthinking void, and he would find himself idly gazing at nothing.

Even now, Goda realized that his mind was empty. After grasping around for something, he thought of Kano, whom he had seen only the day before yesterday, but he quickly thought better of it since Kano was always swamped with work and never seemed to have anything urgent to share with him.

Goda tossed aside the copy of *Nikkei Science*, and briefly gazed at the television screen again. There was a story about the management of nuclear power plants stemming from the privatization of electric companies in England. He scribbled the word "grid" on the back of the magazine closest to him, and just as he reached for the dictionary, the phone rang.

Lifting the receiver, out of habit he checked the time—10:55 P.M.

It was the officer on duty in his precinct's Criminal Investigation Division. "About five minutes ago, we got a hundred-ten emergency call about a missing family member." As he listened, Goda switched off the television with the remote control. "We sent an officer from the police box in front of Omori Station and there seems to be something wrong, so could you go check it out?"

"What's my partner doing?"

"There was a burglary in Omori-Minami just a while ago, so he's headed there. I'll give you the address now, are you ready? It's Sanno Ni-chome, number sixteen. Single-family home. The missing person is the husband, his name is Kyosuke Shiroyama. The person who made the hundred-ten call is his son, Mitsuaki Shiroyama."

Goda mechanically wrote down *Ni-16, Shiroyama* on the back of *Nikkei Science*, and scanned the room for his socks. He had cast them off nearby and so he grabbed them and started putting them back on with one hand. *Where is number sixteen in Ni-chome again?* He tried to remember. *Is it on the right at the end of the road past Ito Yokado supermarket?*

Meanwhile, there was another phone ringing on the other end of the line and the officer told Goda, "Hang on." The officer returned after a three-second wait. "MPD control center wants you to scope out the situation and report back. Kyosuke Shiroyama is the president of Hinode Beer."

That's right, he is, Goda mused. He had tracked the names and addresses of VIPs living in his precinct, and the president of Hinode Beer had been among the residents of Sanno Ni-chome.

"Got it. Be there in ten minutes. If you need to contact me just call on the scanner, don't use the wireless. Until you hear back from me, don't say anything to anyone for now. I'll be right there."

Grabbing a flashlight and throwing on a down jacket, Goda ran to the bathroom to rinse with Listerine to get rid of the whisky on his breath. He pushed the bicycle that he kept outside his apartment into the elevator, got off on the first floor, and by the time he started pedaling, it was 10:58 P.M.

Sleet mixed in with wind off the sea as it howled through the streets of the housing complex premises, where a smattering of lights glimmered here and there. *Damn, it's cold,* was Goda's first thought as he pondered whether he should take Ikegami-dori or the Dai-Ichi Keihin highway to Sanno Ni-chome, and it wasn't until then that he finally began to wonder what might have happened. The president of Hinode would have a driver to chauffeur him around, so the fact that the family had reported to the police that he had not come home sounded an alarm. Something must have happened.

IN THE SANNO HILLS, EACH mansion with its lush green estate folded into the next one, protected by labyrinthine streets that all seemed to dead-end in a cul-de-sac. Late at night there were no cars passing by, and the darkness on the roads along the gated walls was total—as Goda pedaled on his bicycle, he felt as if he were swimming in the depths of the ocean. As he approached number sixteen in Ni-chome, he spotted a motorcycle from the police box parked in front of the gate of an estate walled off with Japanese andesine stone. The area was quiet, with no signs of any residents.

Goda stopped his bicycle a short distance away and checked the time. 11:07 P.M.

Next, he quickly scanned the premises from outside. The height of the wall was about 160 centimeters. A thick grove of tall trees surrounded the vast estate, and he could just make out the glass roof of a greenhouse. Beyond it stood an old Western-style home, where light from an incandescent lamp glowed in a second-floor window, as if someone had forgotten to switch it off. A single porch light was lit. He spotted another light on the first floor, obscured by the trees. Looking around, he noticed that the houses on either side and across the street were similar, and the dense trees all around offered little to no visibility.

The gate, which measured around 180 centimeters in both width and height, was made of sturdy cast iron and came equipped with an electronic lock that could only be opened with a passcode. The decorative latticework on the gate wove an elaborate arabesque design, leaving no leeway for a hand or arm to pass through. Beneath the intercom, the neon-bright red seal of SECOM home security was affixed to the gatepost. There was a straight path from the gate to the front door, about ten meters. On either side of the path were deep and shadowy shrubs, as tall as grown men.

Just as Goda was reaching for the intercom, a car turned into the street and stopped on the shoulder. Judging from the age and hurried pace of the young man who got out of the car, Goda knew it must be the son, and he called out, "Are you Mitsuaki Shiroyama-san?"

"Yes," he replied.

"I'm Goda from the Omori Police Department," Goda said, and showed him his badge.

Mitsuaki, who appeared to be almost thirty years old, was dressed in an exceptionally plain sweater and slacks, and his stoic features were devoid of expression.

"Are you the one who called the police? I'd like to speak with you for a minute inside," Goda said in a low voice.

"I'll open the gate." Mitsuaki managed to reply in a measured tone, his shoulders heaving as he breathed, and he lifted the lid of the electronic lock on the gate and entered the four-digit passcode. As he did so, Goda asked him, "Where is your place of residence?"

"I live in the Ministry of Finance's employee dormitory in Higashi-Yukigaya. My mother called to say that my father hasn't come home."

As they stepped inside through the unlocked gate, it closed automatically behind them, reverberating with the dull sound of cast iron colliding. Perhaps alerted by the noise, someone opened the front door, and Goda saw a familiar face peer out—it was Sawaguchi, the senior police officer from the Community Police Affairs Division. Goda gestured to Sawaguchi not to come out, and ushered Mitsuaki quickly through the front door.

Officer Sawaguchi stood on the concrete floor of the dimly lit entry vestibule, and an older woman sat kneeling on the wooden ledge of the raised entranceway floor. Wearing no trace of makeup, she wore a simple cardigan over her slight, petite frame. Mitsuaki, her son, called out to her immediately, "Mom, are you all right?"

"Yes, I'm fine—" the woman replied, with a rather carefree expression. Beside her, the officer spoke into the microphone of his radio, "Inspector Goda has arrived. Over." Cutting through the static, a voice from the control room replied, "Roger."

The woman, who appeared to be Shiroyama's wife, bowed slowly to Goda. "I'm sorry to trouble you so late at night," she said. "My son insisted that we call the police—"

"Forgive me for interrupting, ma'am," Goda said, and he glanced at Officer Sawaguchi.

"I've just been informed of what happened," Officer Sawaguchi said in a low voice, his notepad in hand. "Around 10:30 this evening, a man named Kurata who is a vice president at Hinode called here about a business matter, and she informed him that her husband had not yet returned home. Immediately after, Kurata called back to inform her that, according to the driver, there was no mistake he had departed the office at 9:48 P.M. with President Shiroyama and had dropped him off at his residence at 10:05 P.M. The driver confirmed that he had seen the president go through the gate and walk inside, so it was quite unclear what might have happened. She then called her son, and after hearing the details from her, he made the emergency call at 10:50 P.M. I arrived here three minutes later."

As Goda listened to this report, the long hand on his wristwatch ticked forward again. 11:10 P.M. Since Shiroyama's car arrived at 10:05, sixty-five minutes had already elapsed, Goda noted in his mind.

"Ma'am, please tell me your husband's age, height, weight, and what he was wearing today."

"He's fifty-eight. He's one hundred seventy-three centimeters tall. I think he weighs about sixty-three kilograms, he's a little thin. What he wore today, let's see, a dark navy suit, wool vest, black shoes, and he did not bring his coat with him. I believe his tie had a blue and silver pattern."

Goda wrote this down in his notebook.

"Around 10:05 P.M., did you hear any noise by the gate?"

"No."

"No sound of the car stopping?"

"Perhaps, but when I'm inside the house I can't really hear any noises from outside."

"There has been a string of incidents targeting corporate executives recently, so my father had told my mother not to go out at night. That's why we installed the SECOM service and doubled the locks . . ." Mitsuaki added.

"Does your husband always unlock the gate by himself when he comes in?"

"Yes."

"The SECOM alarm is turned off at that time, correct?"

"That's right. My father always turns on the nighttime alarm system himself when he comes home."

Goda looked at Officer Sawaguchi. "What's the contact number for this Kurata?"

"He's still at the main office, apparently. Here's the direct number to reach him at night. He's called here a number of times already."

Goda looked at the eight-digit number scrawled across the notepad that the officer handed him. "I'd like to borrow your phone," he said to the son. Mitsuaki immediately offered him his cell phone, but Goda declined and reached for the landline that was on one side of the hall stairs.

He dialed the number from Officer Sawaguchi's notepad and someone answered immediately.

"Hello, this is Kurata. Has the president returned home?" Kurata spoke in a hushed whisper, as if he had been holding his breath.

"No, not yet. This is Goda from the Omori Police Department. How would you say the president appeared today?"

"Exactly the same as usual. Tonight was the launch for our new product and it was a great success so he was very pleased. I had just seen him off personally in the underground parking lot a little before 9:50."

He sounded as if he was calmly choosing his words, but the edge in his voice belied his suspicions and fears—the panic he was suppressing showing through. Of course Goda wouldn't expect him to sound upbeat under these circumstances, but he thought that the man sounded particularly gloomy.

"The driver, how long has he been working for the company?" he asked.

"Going on twenty years. He's been driving our executives for a long time."

"Please tell me the name and address of the driver, as well as where to contact him."

"His name is Tatsuo Yamazaki. I don't have his contact information, so I'll get back to you. In any case, please begin your search immediately. You must find the president!"

His composed voice finally gave way to an angry cry. This, Goda thought, sounded much more normal.

"We'll do everything we can, so please listen carefully to what I'm about to tell you. First, please designate a single contact person for the police on your end, and make sure that person will always be able to answer the phone. Next, for the time being please tell all of the executives in the main office, as well as those in management at the branch offices, to be mindful of any phone calls they may receive at home."

"Has the president been kidnapped—?"

"At this point, we don't know anything. It's possible he's been involved in an incident, so stay off your cell phones and car phones, as those could be tapped. Now, the police will be in touch shortly so please have that contact person ready."

Goda hung up first, and then dialed the number of his precinct.

"It's Goda. Get me CID." As he said this to the operator, various images began to whirl around the core of his mind, emitting bright flashes of light: the hushed alley he had seen just a few minutes ago; the wall of Japanese andesine stone; the gate with its electronic lock; the ten-meter path to the front door, with the dense towers of shrubs on either side.

"Yes, CID," answered the officer on duty, whose name was Saka-gami.

"It's Goda. The president hasn't returned. Around 10:05 P.M. he was dropped off at home in his company car, and the driver saw him enter through the front gate, but he's gone missing since. Relay all that to the chief and put a call out to every officer in CID. Tell Konno and Izawa to report directly here. Radios and cell phones are prohibited. Everyone else stand by at the department. All activities should be kept strictly confidential. Next, about contacting MPD . . ."

Goda was aware of Mitsuaki's gaze as he held his breath right beside him, so he lowered his voice even more and held the receiver closer to his mouth. "It's possible he's been abducted, so let the head of the First Investigation Division know that I want to mobilize every relevant department. SIT, Mobile CI Unit, Crime Scene Unit, NTT Task Force—all of them. I'll wait here until MPD arrives. Also, I'd like to keep the landline at Shiroyama's residence open, so no more calls here going forward. All communication should be made via landline to Senior Patrol Officer Sawaguchi at the police box in front of Omori Station. Also, Sakagami-san, do you see a corporate directory lying around on a desk nearby? Check if any other Hinode executives live in this precinct. As for the rest, we'll wait for instructions from MPD. Any questions so far?"

"Hey, wait up!" Goda heard Sakagami yell, then he was on hold for five seconds. "It's the officer on duty from First Investigation Division. He wants to know if you're sure he's missing."

"I'm sure."

Goda hung up the phone, and as Mitsuaki started to say something he turned his back to him and addressed the officer. "Sawaguchi-san, let's step outside for a minute." Officer Sawaguchi turned the switch on the electronic lock on the front door to open it and, letting Goda out first, he wedged an umbrella stand in the doorway to keep it from closing. With the door ajar, they stepped onto the path.

"Can that front gate also be opened from inside with just a switch?"

"Yes. Works the same way as the front door. The wife told me earlier," the officer replied.

"Sawaguchi-san. Many VIPs live around here, so it was my understanding that these parts were considered a priority for police patrol."

As he briefly questioned the officer, Goda pointed his flashlight at the shrubs growing on either side of the path. With their pliable branches, they turned out to be cryptomeria, a kind of Japanese cedar. The trees were planted only 50 centimeters apart and, sprouting from the ground in conical shapes, the dense wall of needles glimmered blue-silver in the beam of the flashlight.

"Yes, that's right. The president of Hinode returns home around 10 every night, so we always patrol the vicinity between 9:45 and 10:15. The president's car always drives right past the police box and straight down the alley as it makes its way here."

"Where were you around 10 tonight?"

"I'm always circling the area, so I'm not sure. But I made sure to drive by so I could see the road in front of here every five or ten minutes."

"You mean you take a different route depending on the day?"

"Yes. I also constantly receive instructions over the radio to go here or there . . ."

This was true. In a precinct containing around 58,000 households, there were eleven police boxes. The average number of households in the area patrolled by one police box was 5,000. If one were to judge based solely on the incidence of burglaries and violent crime, nights in the Sanno neighborhood were peaceful for the most part, but the department-level radio incessantly blared out crimes that were occurring in adjacent areas. If something were to happen in neighboring Omori-Kita, precautionary instructions would come flying to the police box by Omori Station in Sanno Ni-chome, and the patrol routes would shift immediately. Even though there were a lot of high-income taxpayers in this district, with several thousand households to watch over, the emergency calls—a family member is late coming home, the neighbor's dog won't stop barking, an unfamiliar car is parked on the street, and so on—never seemed to end.

"Did you get any calls around 10 tonight?"

"That single-motorcycle accident beneath the overpass in Magome Ni-chome."

"So you were over there then?"

"Yes. It only took about five minutes to deal with, though. Immediately after that, there was a car parked illegally on Ikegami-dori. Then I had to conduct some questioning on another matter . . ."

As he listened to Sawaguchi, something snagged in Goda's mind, but perhaps because he was inspecting the shrubbery at the same time, in that moment he failed to fully process it.

"I'll stop by the police box later, I'd like to see the logbook. Anyway, so you never saw the president's car tonight, correct?"

"That's correct."

"Which means you just so happened to be away from this area around 10."

"That's correct . . ."

Goda suddenly stopped midway along the path. Scattered in the pool of light cast on the paving stone by his feet were several tiny conifer needles. Along with the silver-blue needles, around a millimeter wide and a centimeter long, he identified a few clods of earth that had been trampled over and caked onto the stone. The front gate was about five meters away.

He retrained his flashlight on the shrubs to either side of him and, facing the gate, he saw something in the depths of one on the right side. Kneeling on the paving stone, he stuck his hand all the way into the shrub, down by the roots, and scooped up what turned out to be a piece of paper crushed lightly into a ball around three centimeters in diameter. He uncrumpled it with his white-gloved hands, and as he cast his flashlight upon it, the characters written in ballpoint pen leapt out at him.

Without warning, Goda sneezed, and Officer Sawaguchi let out a short groan. The characters, written meticulously with a ruler and each measuring two centimeters square, conveyed a clear message: WE HAVE YOUR PRESIDENT.

Goda looked beneath the shrub where he had just found the paper and, surveying the dense shroud of trees over the shrubs in the yard, as well as the wall and the front gate, he concluded that there was virtually no chance that it could have been thrown in from outside. Then, he felt another little snag in his consciousness, but his mind failed to process the thought any further.

"All right, you go back to the police box, and please relay by land-line that we've found a note. If they have any messages for us, come here to let me know. Try to make as little noise as possible when coming and going."

Officer Sawaguchi gave a brief assent, and then opened the front gate and rushed off. Goda held his hand against the gate so that it would not make another loud clang as it automatically closed, but the cast iron still shuddered heavily. With the exception of the branches above his head rustling in the cold wind, there was not a single sound coming from the surrounding alleys and houses.

Now alone, Goda took out his tape measure and quickly determined the distance from the spot where he had retrieved the note to the front gate, then wrote it down in his notebook. He would not be the one to write up the investigative report; he was merely doing what any detective first to arrive at the scene would do. However, as he went through these motions, he had the feeling—one that he hadn't experienced in a long while—of scrambling around in the cold depths on his own, and he was forced to recognize that a terrible incident had occurred.

The time was 11:21 P.M. Seventy-six minutes had passed since the incident was assumed to have taken place. It was too late to issue an emergency deployment.

With the note in hand, Goda went back in through the front door. He held up the crumpled paper to show the president's wife and son, who had planted themselves on the wooden ledge of the raised entranceway platform. "I found this out in the yard. I'm sorry, but please refrain from touching it."

They both blinked vacantly and then, unable to utter a word, they each looked away quickly.

"Mom, we don't know anything yet so don't worry. I'm going to call Shoko."

Mitsuaki reached for the cell phone, and Goda called out to him, "Please make sure this stays within your family."

"I know," Mitsuaki replied with irritation. Then he started to dial his sister.

The president's wife drooped her shoulders forlornly. Seeming not to know what kind of expression she should be wearing at a time like this, she put on the faintest smile and began to murmur, almost to herself, "My husband, he always says that if something were to happen to him it would cause trouble for other people, so he is rather vigilant about his own safety and yet . . . He's so concerned with everyone around him, he didn't want to alarm the neighbors, so since the beginning of the year he has refused the bodyguard that his company had hired for him. I have no idea what we should do . . . And next week is the shareholders' meeting, too. I'm sure he is out there somewhere now, worrying about the company. He'd been in such a good mood lately, what with orders for the new product coming in so well. Just this morning, as he went off to work, he was telling me that as long as the shareholders' meeting goes well, he would finally be able to take a break."

"Does your husband have any chronic illnesses?" Goda asked.

"No, not really."

"So he is in good health?"

"Yes. I wouldn't say he's particularly energetic, but he's fine."

No chronic illness. Good health. Goda wrote in his notebook.

11:30 P.M. The intercom buzzed, and when Goda stuck his head out the front door, he saw two men wearing jeans and sneakers outside the front gate. Goda stepped out and opened the gate, letting the two of them in.

Both were young police officers in their twenties; their names were Izawa and Konno. It had been barely six months since they were transferred from Community Police Affairs to CID, so for these rookie detectives, no doubt this situation made their heads spin, and both of them appeared tense. Goda intended to teach them everything from scratch, and he looked the two young men squarely in the eyes.

"Now listen. No matter the circumstances, always put the safety of the victim first. This requires strict confidentiality. Unless instructed from the top, no matter what anyone asks, play dumb and say you've got nothing, haven't heard anything."

"Yes, sir."

"Until the Mobile CI Unit gets here, you guys control traffic. Izawa, you're in charge of the corner of that T-intersection. Konno, you get the corner of the other T-intersection. Confirm the name and address of any passerby and don't let anyone through other than residents returning home. Same for cars. Be especially on the lookout for newspaper journalists and TV reporters. All right, get to it."

Goda watched the two men dart out on either side to the T-intersections about seventy meters apart, and he gently closed the gate so as not to make a sound. 11:32 P.M.

He went back inside and confirmed with the wife and son, who were still sitting by the front door, that they had not received any suspicious calls to the house. "It's getting cold, please wait in the living room," Goda told them.

Goda had barely finished his sentence when Mitsuaki cried out, "It's already been an hour and a half! Hurry up and find my father!" and buried his head in his hands.

Goda surmised that by now the perpetrators who had abducted the victim would have already fled to a neighboring prefecture, rather than staying within the city limits where the police hunt could easily reach them. What was more, it was customary for the police to wait until the victim was safely in protective custody before launching a formal investigation, which may have seemed contrary to the family's wish for a speedy implementation. The victim being who he was, Goda predicted that the heads of MPD would be even more cautious than usual going forward.

Contemplating his own lack of agency both in the present and the future, Goda's gaze dropped to his feet. As a precinct detective, he did not have the authority to move things from the right to the left. Once the investigation started, he would be lucky if he could gain access to even a nugget of information, and by this time tomorrow, he would no longer have any knowledge of the situation. These thoughts made him feel as if he were as useless as a twig.

When the intercom buzzed at 11:35 P.M., it signaled the arrival of the Mobile CI Unit at last. As soon as he heard the buzzer Goda raced outside and opened the front gate from the inside.

Four officers from the Kamata sub-unit had arrived, as well as the leader of the First Mobile CI Unit's main squad and another four officers from the Crime Scene Unit. Each of them wore wireless earpieces connected to the investigation radio; some held bulging paper bags, while others carried toolboxes as they slipped stealthily onto the property. Perhaps there had been trouble deciding how to handle the case or securing a wireless vehicle—either way, it was unclear why it had taken them half an hour to get here.

The first man through the gate looked at Goda and demanded, "Has the NTT arrived?"

"Not yet," Goda responded. As he spoke, he realized that he recognized the sergeant from the sub-unit, but the man with the fierce expression paid him no notice.

The squad leader, who walked in next, shouted instructions to the officers from the sub-unit: "Get them to sign the consent form first, then ask for a photo of the vic!" He quickly turned his attention to Goda. "Where was the note found?"

"Over there." Goda pointed with his flashlight to the spot on path. The squad leader glared at the circle of light on the paving stone, then summoned the Crime Scene Unit officers behind him, "Go to it." Two of them immediately spread out a tarp and began the task of collecting and preserving any evidence from the scene.

"And the note itself?" The squad leader stuck out his hand. Goda handed him the piece of paper.

The squad leader looked at the paper without saying a word, while behind him, the Crime Scene Unit swiftly set up another tarp inside the front gate to block the view from outside. The squad leader lifted his gaze and verified, "There's been no call from the perpetrator, correct?"

"Correct," Goda answered.

"You've spoke with the family?"

"Yes." Goda ripped about five pages out of his notebook and handed them over. The squad leader quickly scanned the notes with his flashlight.

"No chronic illness, in good health. Good," he murmured. Then, "We'll take it from here. Those two men controlling traffic outside, leave them where they are until we say so. I want everyone at the department on stand by." The squad leader spoke brusquely, as if he were loath to waste a minute, before hastening inside the front door.

One of the officers from the sub-unit called out to Goda. "Hey, this gate—how do you open it from inside?"

"Like this." Goda showed him how the inner switch worked.

"I see. If it can be opened that easily from inside, then this has gotta be their 'out.' They must have had a car . . ." the officer mumbled to himself. He called out to a fellow officer, "Omura!"

They spread open a map, and shined the beam of a flashlight on it. "First, see if anyone heard any noise or the sound of a car ignition right around 10:05. Then, check if anyone saw any suspicious vehicles—"

"Many of the streets around here dead-end in a cul-de-sac, so pay attention," Goda said and marked the map with his own ballpoint pen.

"Got it. Omura, you go right. I'll take the left. We'll circle back here in half an hour. We'll communicate via radio over 100A."

The two sub-unit officers quickly went off down their respective streets and were soon replaced by two new faces that ducked through the tarp covering the front gate. It was a lieutenant and a sergeant from the second unit of MPD's First Special Investigation Team whose names and faces Goda knew, but for the moment neither of them gave Goda even a nod in greeting.

The two men glanced over to where the Crime Scene Unit was working, then took in the entire view of the mansion before the lieutenant, whose name was Satoru Hirase, spoke up.

"Goda-san? Is that you?"

"Yes, it's me."

"Where's the squad?"

"They're here."

"Sure is cold tonight . . . was the vic wearing a coat?"

"No."

"I see—"

The proficient engine of the Special Investigation Team had taken over the situation in which the president of a major corporation had been abducted, and was only just getting revved up. After repeatedly surveying the premises of the estate, which was now a crime scene, the lieutenant and the sergeant also disappeared behind the front door. The four officers from the Crime Scene Unit were crawling around on the path, having already placed five markers. Taking a last look at it all, Goda ducked under the tarp and went out the front gate.

Mounting the bike he had left on the street, Goda looked up again at the mansion enveloped by the pitch-black shadows of the trees and let his imagination run free, just for the sake of it. *Bet there are at least three perps.* Two of them must have jumped the wall and waited by the shrubs along the path for the victim to come home, and after capturing the victim, they whisked him out the gate, where someone else had a car by the roadside that they forced him into, and then drove away. Goda was easily able to imagine the details of such a crime from beginning to end, but the profiles of those who might have actually executed it were obscured by a thick haze.

Even if the perps had closely examined the area in advance, how could they have pulled off a crime that exploited the exact gap in time when there was no policeman on patrol nearby? They could not have done so by sheer chance—how on earth could they have been confident that the patrol would not return during those few minutes that they needed? The question that had flickered in his thoughts while speaking with Officer Sawaguchi still pulsed in a corner of his mind.

But in reality, as Goda peddled away on his bicycle, he wondered where he would be and what he would be doing come tomorrow. He might be canvassing this neighborhood on foot or investigating suspicious vehicles; on the other hand, he might not even be recruited to Special Investigation headquarters, and he'd find himself back with the rank and file at the precinct, writing up cases as usual. No matter what, he had no doubt that he would be somewhere far away whenever any developments occurred.

11:42 P.M. The alley was as silent as it had been half an hour earlier. It would still be a while before the MPD held a press conference, but for the time being, it seemed as if nothing had been leaked to the public. After telling the two young officers who were controlling traffic to stay put until instructed otherwise, Goda set off toward the police box by Omori Station only a short distance away. As he traveled back through the maze of alleys, he spotted three unmarked cars of the Crime Scene Unit and the Special Investigation Team parked in the darkness.

根来史彰　Fumiaki Negoro

ON THE COPY DESK OF *Toho News*'s Metro section, Kei'ichi Tabe, the slot editor, tore off a sheet from his page-a-day calendar. His arm inscribed a large arc in the air and the ripped-out piece of paper sailed away from his hand.

Tabe had a habit of doing this when the date changed at midnight. The slot editor's desk had a conspicuously large desktop computer on it, so that Fumiaki Negoro, sitting a little distance away in the section for reserve reporters who floated wherever they were needed among the various hard news sections, could only see Tabe's arm and the flyaway paper behind the massive monitor.

The clock showed the time as one minute after midnight. It was Saturday, March 25.

Ripping off and throwing away the page from his own small daily calendar with one hand, Negoro resumed working on his unfinished draft. It was the next day's installment of a six-part series, "Waste or Resource?" and he had taken this brief moment of free time to begin writing it. The thirteenth edition of the morning paper had gone to press half an hour ago, and there was an hour and a half until the final deadline for the fourteenth edition. The crowd in the news room could best be compared to that in the lobby of a theater running a play that boasted a relatively good turnout, if not a full house. Directions to confirm or finesse articles before press time bounced from one corner of the office to another, and phone calls came in now and then from reporters in the field. However, since everyone spoke in low tones and with few words, their voices didn't travel far.

In addition to Tabe, the slot editor, there was a rim editor on duty and four overnight reporters on the Metro desk. In the Reserve section, the only one left was the chief, Negoro. Until half an hour ago, there had been at least three other reporters getting their research materials together, but after Tabe asked them to do some additional reporting for the final edition, they had gone off somewhere, leaving behind an ashtray with a mountain of cigarette butts.

During the Great Hanshin Earthquake that struck in January, the reserve reporters—eighteen in total—were for the most part allocated to the earthquake and disaster news crew, but just when they thought the confusion in the aftermath of the disaster had subsided, March brought a succession of major incidents beginning four days ago with the unprecedented crimes of a poison gas terror attack and random killings by a religious sect, followed by the bankruptcy of two credit unions within the metropolitan area. Added to this were suicides of children being bullied, a spate of gun-related crime, city expos, waste issues, urban disaster prevention, a resolution to commemorate the 50th anniversary of the end of the war—the reserve reporters were hardly at their desks long enough to warm their seats.

It was rare to have such a bustling year, and Negoro did not have to wait until spring to complete his annual transformation into "the solitary reserve," the lone reporter rooted to his desk, churning out article after article.

Always watching the clock, all year long Negoro assembled the drafts filed from all over by the other reserve reporters into a coherent whole, revising and rewriting to create feature articles to fill the Metro page and sending them off to the slot editor. In between all this he would touch up articles for his own column and pre-write advance articles on occasion. As it came down to the wire before press time he would check headlines, and in the event of an exclusive he would immediately swap around, punch up, or correct articles as per the slot editor's specs. For the most part the work felt automatic, and after twenty-three years on the job his body had grown accustomed to it, but when the clock ticked past midnight, his lumbago, the result of a car accident four years ago, would start to trouble him. To make matters worse, yesterday he had stayed up reading a book—knowing all along that he should get some sleep—and he was paying for it now, his eyes hurting a little as he looked at the computer screen.

"Hey, Yoshida, this piece on the Product Liability Act—I think the consumers come out too strong," Tabe was saying on the other side of the desktop computer. "Which do you prefer, add in some corporate voices, or shorten the opinions of the consumer group?"

With the phone in one hand, Tsutomu Yoshida, the overnight reporter covering the Ministry of International Trade and Industry, responded, "Please shorten it." The rim editor, Takano, sat in front of another desktop computer next to Tabe, and he turned to him, putting a hand over the receiver he had tucked between his ear and shoulder. "That fire in Itabashi, apparently it's arson. What do you want to do?"

"Just keep it below the fold," Tabe said brusquely. On the six-man Metro desk, Tabe was the most blunt. Judging from the tone of his voice, it seemed unlikely that there would be any last-minute prime scoops for the final edition. With this thought in the corner of his mind, Negoro continued to type up his draft.

Over on the Political desk, which was preparing for the nation-wide local elections, things seemed a bit busier, with continuous calls coming in from the Prime Minister's Official Residence and the reporters gathered at the Hirakawa kisha club. Just a moment ago, their slot editor had run over to the Layout desk across the aisle and even now an argument could be heard from that direction. "With this election as dull as it is, why not hit 'em with a headline like AOSHIMA IN THE LEAD?" followed by, "Can't you be a little more reasonable? It's the front page!"

Across from the Political desk, there were still about five or six people on Foreign, but aside from their slot editor crying out in a high-pitched voice, "Call New York!" no other sounds rose above the fray. On the other side of Foreign was the Business section where—thanks to a recent string of financial scandals, the strong yen, and slumping stock prices—reporters were coming and going even at this hour, leaving their computers connected to the internet, the screens streaming figures from markets overseas.

Further over, where the National, Culture, and Sports sections were side by side, several people still lingered, but nothing about their desktop computers or mountains of files suggested anything notable would crop up. Beyond them the photo room was partitioned off. While a few overnight photographers should have been around, they might either be taking a nap or getting some coffee, since there hadn't been any signs of them running out on assignment.

The news room floor, measuring roughly 1,300 square meters, was illuminated by the same overhead lights as during the day, yet it appeared slightly dim, and even though there were nearly a hundred people spread out everywhere, the atmosphere could be described as both lively and quiet, enveloped in a fog of ennui unique to these late hours of the night. Looking around him, Negoro noticed how each section had one or two televisions on which brightly colored images danced on the screen without any sound, and in his mind they appeared like underwater mirages of Ryugujo, the Dragon Palace Castle.

He rubbed his eyes, wondering if something was wrong with them, and just then Tabe's voice came hurtling toward the Reserve section.

"Hey, Negoro, about your series. Would you mind cutting the chart and adding five more lines to the main text to adjust? We secured an interview with a member of the credit association so I'd like to run it there."

Negoro raised a hand and replied, "Okay." He saved the draft he had been working on for tomorrow and pulled up today's draft instead. If he were to cut out the chart that detailed the recycling process, those five lines allotted him only seventy characters in which to explain it.

He tried adding a sentence—*In the process that begins with the production and output of industrial waste and ends in its permanent disposal, the technology and costs required for handling it become progressively more expensive for in-house disposal, reuse, and recycling*—and as he was counting the number of lines again, the overnight reporter covering the Ministry of Health and Welfare called out to him. "Negoro-san, telephone."

Reaching for the phone with an outside line, Negoro looked at the clock out of habit. 12:05 A.M.

The caller was the chief of CID at the Setagaya Police Department, whom Negoro had been friends with for going on fifteen years. When he was thirty, Negoro had been assigned to the MPD beat, but he had struggled. As bad as he was at finding sources, he was at least as inept at socializing. He had never gotten used to the police force, no matter how much he tried, and thus he had little incentive to try harder, but he still maintained cordial friendships outside of work with a handful of detectives he had gotten to know over time, and this guy was one of them.

"Negoro-san, I might not be able to make it to the rose show tomorrow after all," the chief said.

This formidable man, who held a fifth dan in judo, had begun growing roses in his garden at home in Komae ten years ago, and since then he had been busy creating new rose hybrids and submitting them to international competitions. Negoro, on the other hand, lived in an apartment building and had no garden, but acting on a whim to take advantage of the chance to admire at least a flower or two, he had promised to go see the rose show at the Jindai Botanical Garden tomorrow afternoon.

"Did something happen?" As Negoro asked this, he noticed that the chief was not calling from his home phone but from the police department, and he wondered if there could have been an incident.

"Seems like something happened in Sanno. You should check it out."

"Sanno, in Ota district?"

"Something's going on with the department radio."

After this brief exchange, the call ended. It took about two seconds for him to get goose bumps from the realization that—for the first time in a long while—one of his sources had leaked a story. In the past, all the hairs on his body would have stood up at once. Negoro quickly reached for the receiver of the direct line to their nook in the kisha club at the MPD.

"This is Negoro. Did anything happen in Sanno, in Ota district?"

"No." The person who picked up was Tetsuo Sugano, the chief reporter. "Everything's quiet here."

"A friend just called, he said something's going on with the police radio."

"The radio—? Anything else?"

"That's it."

"Sanno, huh. I'll ask one of the guys who's out at the evening session."

This call ended briefly too. Sugano was a shrewd reporter with years of experience on the MPD's Public Security Bureau beat. In addition to being a man of few words, he always thought of three things in the time it took a normal person to think of one, so with both younger colleagues and his contemporaries, he couldn't hold much of a conversation. In spite of this Negoro had managed to be friendly with him for quite a while, though no matter how many years they had known each other, every time he heard Sugano's voice he felt as if he were consulting a workbook that gave him all the right answers without offering any insight on how to solve the questions. Actually, Sugano was one of the heaviest drinkers on *Toho News*'s hundred-member-strong Metro section, but since he never mentioned it himself, not many people knew about it. That's the type of man he was.

As soon as Negoro replaced the receiver, Tabe, famous for his keen ears, called out from his desk, "Something up?"

"No, not yet," Negoro replied briskly, annoyed that he couldn't really focus as he returned to his draft. For the time being he printed out the article to which he had added five lines, circled the revisions in red, handed it to the overnight reporter nearby, and asked, "Can you get this to copy?" Having left the matter up to Sugano, he felt confident that things would move forward without a hitch, but at the same time his own hands were now idle. The goose bumps from only a few seconds ago had also passed, so Negoro was at a bit of a loss.

Returning to his earlier draft, he continued writing—*When it comes to thermal energy from urban waste*—and looked at the clock. 12:10 A.M. By now, the beat reporter for MPD's First Investigation Division, having been paged by Chief Sugano, would be in a hired car, rushing to Omori Police Department and Sanno Ni-chome. For a moment Negoro tried to remember how, fifteen or sixteen years ago, he used to go running around like that, but he could not immediately retrieve a single memory, and as he caught himself wondering if this were the fate of the brain cells of a third-rate reporter, his fingers had typed, *When it comes to thermal energy from urban waste, its fate is* . . . He deleted and retyped, *When it comes to thermal energy from urban waste, its current state is* . . .

◆ ◆ ◆

THE CLOCK SAID THIRTEEN MINUTES after midnight. Over at the copy desk, the direct line to the press box rang once, and the rim editor Takano grabbed the receiver. The call lasted a few seconds, and Takano turned and said something to Tabe next to him. Tabe's head, with its hairline that had receded five centimeters, rose above his desktop computer as he shouted toward the layout desk across the aisle, "The front page and the Metro page, we might have to swap out an article!"

Then Tabe cried out in a voice that resounded through the entire Metro section, "There's an unmarked police car in Sanno Ni-chome. They've also spotted vehicles from the investigation unit in the back lot of Omori Police Department." Right away, the overnight reporters looked up, asking, "Something up?"

"Don't know yet. In any case, the chief inspectors of the First Investigation Division and the Crime Scene Unit have not returned to their official residences. The police departments in each of the two areas are keeping mum. The kisha nook is waiting for the broadcast. Hey, Doi, make sure we have a residential map of the Sanno neighborhood. And keep the overnight staff in the photo section on standby."

As he spoke, Tabe's eyes darted to the large wall clock. Negoro also looked up at it. 12:16 A.M. No matter how much they pushed back, they had only an hour and a half until deadline. Whatever had happened, they wouldn't be able to write much about it.

"Negoro, could you mark down two places where we can set up near Sanno Ni-chome and Omori Police Department?"

Negoro acknowledged Tabe's directive with a raised hand. Setting aside his half-finished draft, from the files in his desk drawer he pulled out a list of the five hundred newspaper vendors in the entire metropolitan area. He had used this same list every time there had been an incident, so the pages were well worn and tattered. As he opened the list, he immediately thought of the vendor next to the post office at the intersection in Sanno Ni-chome, but it took a little while for him to call to mind the area where Omori Police Department stood.

Omori Police Department was located on the east side of Omori-machi Station on the Keihin Kyuko Line. It was where the Dai-Ichi Keihin highway branched off from Sangyo Road; at the fork in the road there was a Denny's, and adjacent to the restaurant's colorful roof was a small and inconspicuous four-story government building. On the same side of the street as the building, which could easily be overlooked if not careful, there were private apartment buildings and warehouses, as well as various small office buildings. The entrance of the police department faced the Dai-Ichi Keihin highway, and the rear exit faced Sangyo Road, and both sets of doors were shielded from view by the elevated road directly in front of them. *Yes, that's right, the entire area is like the bottom of a ravine, deprived of sunlight even during the daytime*—as all these vivid details finally came back to him, he found a suitable vendor from the list and wrote down the telephone number. It was positioned along Dai-Ichi Keihin and about three hundred meters away from the police department, but with a pair of binoculars, it would be an ideal spot to stakeout the coming and goings of investigators.

He put the list back in the drawer. Since there was no way he could concentrate now he gave up on his draft, and saved and closed the file. Then, from his drawer he took out a pencil that did not get much use these days, and started to sharpen it with a Higo no Kami pocket knife. This is what Negoro did whenever he was waiting for something. Tabe, at his desk, was talking on the direct line. "Has there been any broadcast yet? What are the other papers doing?"

Just as Negoro had started sharpening a second pencil, the phone rang for the umpteenth time, and Negoro froze, his hand still on the Higo no Kami. He checked the clock on the wall. 12:18 A.M.

Tabe picked up the receiver, his body bent forward as he stooped over the computer and his forehead shining.

"I see—got it. Let me know the details ASAP. I'm calling the Metro chief." He nodded once and straightened himself as he put down the receiver, but he hesitated before letting the next words escape from his mouth. "Kidnapping. They've got the president of Hinode Beer—!"

His voice was not all that loud, but it reached every corner of the 1,300-square meter office in a flash, and for a second or two, it seemed as if time had stopped on the whole floor.

Then, Takano the rim editor's bellow rumbled through the office. "The president of Hinode Beer has been kidnapped! Hinode's president! Kidnapped!" His shouting was drowned out by the hum of voices erupting all at once, chairs scraping the floor as the reporters got to their feet, and footsteps rushing toward Metro.

"Well, the election's a bust," the Political slot editor nearby huffed, looking up at the ceiling.

"Hinode Beer? You sure it's Hinode Beer?" yelled the Finance slot editor as he raced over.

"What do we do for space? How many columns should we keep open for now?" This from the layout editor as he came running.

"If it really is a kidnapping, I'm sure they'll force a news embargo on us—" That was the voice of the acting deputy managing editor.

A throng had formed in a matter of seconds. In its middle, Tabe rapidly launched into a short summary of the situation at hand. MPD's Public Information Division had already put a call out to the chief reporters from each newspaper, and Sugano was on his way there now. It seemed to be a given that a temporary embargo would be requested—that much they knew. Everyone turned to look at the clock at once. If the news embargo were issued, all reporting activities would be shut down. Even if talks over the details of the embargo with the publishing managers dragged on, there was a finite limit to how much time they had. Until the embargo officially would take effect, they had one or two hours, tops. In any case, gathering news was a race against time.

As if to signal the start of a hundred-meter race, the crowd that had gathered dispersed in all directions.

"Get all staff who's available back here now!" Tabe cried out. "Doi, Harada—you guys first look for anyone with a family member who works for Hinode. Negoro, I need you to work on the assignment chart. Yoshida, you get everyone from the photo section over here. And find any material we have on Hinode—everything we've got in the archives! Also get anything on the beer manufacturers' labor union. Arai-san, you're in charge of the financial side and the liquor industry!"

"Ah!" From the Business desk, Arai cried out hysterically. "Hinode has a shareholders' meeting at the end of March—"

"Then we'd better interview shareholders too! Be sure not to let on about the incident, keep the conversation on the economy and the industry and so forth."

Negoro was busy paging each reserve reporter who could be called back to the office, one by one, as he turned over a commemorative poster from the 100th anniversary of the newspaper and spread it on the Reserve desk to start creating the assignment chart.

Behind him, the rim editor Takano was on the direct line with the press box, furiously scribbling on his notepad. As soon as the call ended he read these aloud in a voice that reverberated across the floor.

"The name of the victim, Kyosuke Shiroyama. Fifty-eight years old. President of Hinode Beer. At approximately 10:05 P.M. on the twenty-third, after returning in a company car to his residence at 2-16 Sanno, he was ambushed and abducted by a person or persons who had been lying in waiting inside the front gate. In the shrubs of the front yard, a crumpled letter has been found that appears to have been left by the perp. It said, 'We have your president.' The case is being treated as abduction and unlawful confinement. As of now, 12:20 A.M., there has been no contact from the perp. The name of the president's driver is Tatsuo Yamazaki. Sixty years old. Employed by the company for twenty years. The next briefing will be at 2 A.M.— that's all that's been released to the press for now!"

Negoro picked up the receiver of the direct line.

"Yes, Sugano speaking!" he shouted. He sounded like a different man than he'd been half an hour ago.

"Do you have somewhere you want me to send the reserve reporters?" Negoro asked.

"I need you to follow up with the Hinode executives. Not one of them is returning our calls. Have them try going directly to their homes, knocking on doors."

Negoro hung up and called out to Yoshida, who had just run back from the archives. "Can you look up the names and addresses of Hinode executives?"

The clock read half past midnight. As Negoro conveyed Sugano's instructions to the reserve reporters responding to his page, he was also working on the assignment chart with Tabe. On the reverse side of the poster, first he wrote out the headings in large characters, ten centimeters square, and then added names of the reporters. Excluding the reporters on the MPD beat and those covering the District Public Prosecutor's Office and the courts, the players he had left totaled about fifty reporters.

Across the top, he had written 1) Supervisor and 2) Deputy Supervisor, followed by 3) Hard News 4) Feature Articles 5) Victim, et al. 6) Hinode Main Office 7) Hinode Executives 8) Hinode Employees 9) Hinode Affiliated Companies 10) Distributors 11) Competitors & Labor Union 12) Liquor Shops 13) National Tax Agency 14) Omori Police Department Stakeout 15) Sanno Stakeout 16) Standbys, and so on.

He put the Metro chief under "Supervisor" and the deputy chief under "Deputy Supervisor." For each team in charge of replacing stories for Hard News and Feature Articles, he would assign one slot editor from each section along with a supervising chief and three reporters. For each reporting crew and the two stakeout headquarters, he'd assign a chief and a few more reporters. The name of Yoshida, the overnight reporter who had covered the joint venture between Hinode and Limelight last year, was listed under 10) and 13), while Tabe wrote his own name under Hard News, and Negoro put himself down for Feature Articles as a supervising chief.

The overnight photographers had already raced off in the direction of the victim's residence and Hinode's main office in Shinagawa. The news room floor had become a vortex of noise—calls being made, phones ringing, footsteps coming and going, and voices flying across the room. As his Magic Marker darted around the assignment chart, Tabe was unable to contain the excitement in his voice. "Looks like we'll be spending nights here for a while," he muttered.

Once the managers and section editors gathered, they would be entrenched in meeting after meeting. Negoro would pull together the articles that would flood in during the intervals and, with one eye always on the clock, just when he thought he had a final draft, things would get switched around and he'd be rewriting articles down to the last second. While every staff member embedded at the main office—including Negoro—was transformed into human word processors, the reporters were working in the field, hunting down interviews as they launched into their dog race. Negoro was concerned about his own engine, which seemed to be taking a little longer than usual to rev up, and as he blinked his sleep-deprived eyes, the thought of the rose show floated into his mind again. He realized that he would miss the opportunity—again and for the fore-seeable future—that he had secretly hoped would bring about a small change in his life.

久保晴久　Haruhisa Kubo

EARLIER THAT EVENING, THE CHECK-IN for the regular interview session at the official residence of the chief inspector of the First Investigation Division hadn't started until 11 P.M. since the MPD was hosting a party for incoming and outgoing officials at the Hanzomon Kaikan. That night, Haruhisa Kubo, on his second year as the beat reporter for the MPD, arrived in front of the chief inspector's official residence in Himonya in Meguro district a little more than ten minutes past eleven, and was ninth on the list after reporters from various commercial broadcasting companies, NHK, Asahi, and Kyodo. Other media companies followed, arriving in groups of twos and threes, and the line of reporters quickly materialized in the alley, standing silently with their shoulders hunched, wearing headphones from their portable radios.

For the majority of those present, the night's topics of interest related to First Investigation included the whereabouts of the cult leader, who had an arrest warrant out on him on suspicion of a murder plot to unleash poisonous gas, and developments in the interrogation of senior members of the cult who had already been arrested. Since there had only been a handful of official announcements from the MPD, each organization had spent these last few days feeling out the leader of First Investigation. Kubo, curious to know what leads his competitors might have up their sleeves, approached this evening's session by gulping down his requisite nightly antacid and energy drink. In spite of this practice he never lost any weight. Even in his student days, he had had a large build, but since becoming a Metro reporter, thanks to the irregular lifestyle, he had put on another ten kilograms, and during his company medical checkup the doctor had told him that he was on the verge of fatty liver disease.

The night was terribly cold for the beginning of spring, with rain drizzling off and on. At 11:25 P.M., a complaint rose from the scrum of reporters from the commercial broadcasting companies. "He's late." It was past the expected arrival time of the official vehicle for the chief inspector, but since he was sometimes even a full half hour late, Kubo wasn't particularly concerned. No doubt the other reporters had come to the same conclusion, for no one joined in the grumbling.

But the second time someone murmured, "He's late," it was contagious, and the words were repeated over and over. It was now three minutes past midnight. Along with the mumblings of "Did something happen?" and "Something's up," another voice quipped, "His neighbor hasn't returned yet either." The official residence of the chief inspector of First Investigation stood next to that of the chief inspector of the Crime Scene Unit, and since the latter didn't drink, there was no way he would have stayed out late for an after party or some other social gathering. This fact, and that it was now past midnight and the chief inspector of First Investigation had still not returned home either, did not take more than a few seconds to sound an alarm in the minds of the dozen or so reporters huddling in the alley.

Had they located the cult members wanted by the police? Or was it another incident? The reporters exchanged dubious looks of suspicion, and after another moment, the impatient ones began disappearing from the alley without a sound. Kubo told himself that if something had happened he would hear from the kisha club and so he did not budge from his spot, yet during the couple of minutes he continued to stand there, needles of anxiety and irritation that his competitors would beat him to a story continued to prickle him. At six minutes after midnight, one of those needles suddenly sunk in deep when his pager went off.

The number that showed on the LCD belonged to the kisha club at MPD. The other newspaper reporters immediately shouted out, "Did something happen?" and "What do you know?"

"I have no idea," Kubo replied, which wasn't a lie, and he began trotting away from the alley at last. For the fifty meters he had to run to the side street off Meguro-dori where his hired car was parked, his ample belly swayed beneath his jacket, and the strained buttons of his dress shirt threatened to pop off.

When he dialed the number from the car phone, Chief Sugano answered immediately and asked in his perpetually aggressive tone, "Can you get to Sanno Ni-chome?"

It was still unclear what exactly might have happened in Sanno, but just hearing that something was going on made his heart leap before his mind could catch up.

"Head for Sanno Ni-chome, please," he told the driver, and as he quickly opened a map, he felt himself already anticipating what had yet to take shape. A new incident had occurred, and every time his point of focus shifted the illusion swelled in his heart that a new horizon might unfold before him, that he might break away and discover a place that was—at the very least—different from the one in which he found himself scrambling around now.

The car passed through the intersection in Kakinokizaka and headed toward Kanpachi, and it took about twelve or thirteen minutes to cover the distance to Sanno Ni-chome, but it wasn't until they crossed the tracks of the Tokyu Ikegami Line that the deputy chief reporter finally made first contact. "Apparently there's an unmarked police car in the backyard of Omori Police Department. Try circling around the Sanno neighborhood."

From what he said, Kubo's partner on the First Investigation beat, Yuichi Kuriyama, had scoped out the precinct already and reported back, but they still did not know the scene of the incident.

As soon as Kubo heard about the unmarked police car, his vision of a new horizon was supplanted by ambitions of an exclusive story, which lit a fire under him. Stuck in traffic at the Magome intersection, he glared first at the hands on his wristwatch, which showed seventeen minutes after midnight, then at the chain of red tail lights on the cars in front of him, and was just wondering which alley in Sanno he should go down when the second call came in.

"Get to Hinode Beer's main office in Kita-Shinagawa now! The president of Hinode has been kidnapped!" blared the voice over the phone.

It wasn't that his mind immediately reacted to the name of the company Hinode Beer and the news that its president had been kidnapped; he just automatically absorbed the instructions he was given. He was to report directly to Hinode's main office and observe the comings and goings of employees. If possible, he was to get the first comment from an employee or executive. There was no time—the news embargo would soon take effect.

If this really were a kidnapping, the upside of not being able to report whatever they uncovered was that at least they would not be scooped by a rival paper—an inappropriate sense of relief at this briefly crossed his mind in the next moment. Before he knew it, the ambition to snag an exclusive was replaced by speculation about how they would gain an advantage over their competitors once the embargo was lifted, but this too only lasted a second—as soon as Kubo had informed the driver of their new destination, he suddenly came to his senses and leaned forward in his seat. The black shadows of trees in the Sanno hills streamed past his car window. As he watched them go by, in his mind three or four question marks lined up after the intangible word—*kidnapping???*

12:35 A.M. During the third phone call he learned the simple yet implausible fact that the president of Hinode had been abducted from his own home, and when Kubo's car arrived in front of the building of Hinode's main office in Kita-Shinagawa, he found the street along Yatsuyama-dori completely empty. At first Kubo was surprised that there was no sign of any other newspaper or TV reporters and, realizing that he was first on the scene, his heart skipped a beat. He looked up at the luxurious forty-story high-rise and tried once again to imprint upon his mind that the master of this tower had been kidnapped—it remained a fuzzy reality to him.

There was only a smattering of lights on on the bottom three-quarters of the building—the rest was pitch dark. The remaining top floors were shrouded in a low-hanging mist, and the red beacons that must have been on each of the four corners of the roof flashed blurrily in the mist. When his gaze returned to the ground, he saw that the entrance to the building, which was set back twenty meters from the sidewalk, was also dark, with no signs of people there, either.

On the signpost facing the sidewalk, gleaming gold lettering and arrows pointed the way to Hinode Opera Hall, Hinode Contemporary Art Museum, and Hinode Sky Beer Restaurant, but the entrance for the general public that could be seen just beyond was shuttered, and a fence barricaded the walkway leading up to it. The entrance to the underground parking lot was on the west side, but this too was shuttered at the bottom of the slope leading down to it.

Trotting back to Yatsuyama-dori where his hired car was parked, Kubo called the kisha club and asked them to try calling Hinode's night-time number. He spoke with the overnight reporter covering Second Investigation, who told Kubo that they had already tried calling Hinode's main office as well as their Tokyo and Yokohama branch offices, and all they got was a recording that business had closed for the day. Right now, he said, they were calling Hinode's branch offices, regional offices, and sales offices one by one, but the result was all the same. Calls to the executives' homes all reached answering machines, and while surely the executives and managers were gathered together somewhere, they had no clue where. Moreover, MPD's Public Information director had called in the chief reporters from every media organization, so it was certain that they intended to request a temporary embargo.

As Kubo replaced the receiver, worried that time was running out, he saw that several hired cars from other media companies were now flanking his. The time was 12:41 A.M. There were even TV crews with video cameras in tow. Just as Kubo had done when he first arrived, the other reporters ran around the darkened building, then, once they had given up, gathered on the sidewalk. A reporter Kubo recognized from the *Yomiuri Shimbun* scurried toward Kubo's car, where he rapped on the window.

"You got here first, didn't you? Any way we can get in?" he asked, sticking his neck in as soon as Kubo had opened the car door.

"I wouldn't be here if there were. Any bright ideas?" Kubo shot back, and he heard the other reporters who had gathered behind him sigh in unison.

It was obvious that none of the other journalists had made contact with anyone at Hinode. Still, every one of them standing there in the road knew the Hinode executives must all be together somewhere, and their eyes darted around like foxes as they racked their brains trying to figure out where that might be.

"This is going to be an uphill battle . . ." someone muttered.

Fifteen meters away by the side of the road, where a van from a commercial broadcasting company was parked, one of the crew members signaled to them by making an X with his arms. The time was now 12:45 A.M. The embargo had been issued.

Kubo and the rest of the reporters looked at one another, and signaled back "okay" to the crew. Cries of "Shit" and "Damn it" erupted all around him, followed by pitiful goodbyes and "See ya"s as the group scattered to their hired cars. In Kubo's window as his car pulled away, the towering Hinode building seemed even more formidable than a few minutes earlier, as if mocking the challenges the reporters would face in the days ahead—but at the same time, the few lights visible on perhaps the thirtieth floor appeared blurry in the mist, almost weakened and cowering in such unexpected circumstances. Looking up at the skyscraper, Kubo tried to convince himself for the third time that night that the master of this castle had been kidnapped.

IT WAS 1:18 A.M. WHEN Kubo returned to MPD in Sakuradamon. In the elevator, he ran into a few other reporters who had also returned there after the embargo went into effect. In lieu of a greeting, they searched one another's faces and asked tersely, "So?" "Got anything?" "What about you?" There was no need to answer—it was clear from their expressions that none of them had managed to reach Hinode.

There were three kisha clubs on the ninth floor, and *Toho*'s press nook was located inside the Nanashakai kisha club, to which the six major national daily newspapers belonged. Even the entrance to the Nanashakai was crowded, and Kubo had to weave this way and that to slip past the tumult of people and reach his paper's nook. Every paper had assembled their chief kisha club reporters as well as all of their beat reporters. *Toho*'s nook was partitioned off from the others, and when Kubo parted the entry curtain he bumped up against an unfamiliar back right away. In the few steps it took him to make his way to his desk, calling out "Excuse me, coming through," he became nauseated from the stench of hair tonic and cigarette smoke, several times more potent than usual. The nook, which was as tiny as an eel's lair, typically accommodated at most four or five journalists working at the desks while others were out reporting or sleeping in the built-in bunk bed, so now that it was packed with all seventeen or eighteen members of their team, including the beat reporters, there was not even standing room. Amidst this melee the direct line to the news room rang incessantly, and the fax machine spat out pages that everyone scrambled for and passed from hand to hand.

In the innermost seat amongst this crowd, there was Chief Sugano, his expression immutable no matter the situation, holding the receiver for the outside line in one hand while raking a comb through his salt-and-pepper hair with the other. Whenever there was a crisis, Sugano had the indelicate habit of taking out his comb, no matter where he was.

"Apparently the Hinode executives are gathered at the Hinode Club in Kioi-cho," Kagawa, the deputy chief reporter, called out from beside Sugano. *Makes perfect sense,* Kubo thought, immediately recalling the old European-style stone mansion near the New Otani Hotel in Kioi-cho. It was a corporate guesthouse used for entertaining, and sometimes there would be luxury cars in the driveway, idling in front of the entrance tucked away from the main road.

"Did somebody go check it out?" Kubo asked, looking around him.

"No. We heard them talking about it next door," responded Yuichi Kuriyama, the reporter in charge of First Investigation, as he rapped on the partition wall with his fist. Beneath the spot where he knocked sat Kondo, another reporter on the First Investigation beat, along with Maki and Kanai, who were on the Second and Fourth Investigation beats, respectively, and were now manning the phones that were ringing off the hook. The Reserve section of the Metro desk had already created an assignment chart and launched into action, and was now relaying information—"We sent copies of all the materials from the archives" and "We sent you the articles related to Hinode that we pulled from our database"—and haranguing them for a story: "Did you get anything?" and "Any movement?"

In due time, Chief Sugano finished his phone call. "Listen, everyone." His voice carried through the entire nook, and Kubo and the rest of the reporters pricked up their ears at once. "We'll prepare two advance articles: one in the event that the president is safely rescued, and the other in the event that things take a turn for the worse. If a criminal profile or motive is not clear at the point when the president is in protective custody, the first draft will cover everything chronologically from abduction to rescue, and then let's plan on steadily spotlighting the unresolved issues, one by one. First and foremost, I want it made clear that this is a heinous crime. Your team can handle that, Kubo."

"Yes, sir."

"Maki, Kanai, and Momoi will track the movements of the extortionists and the ultranationalists. Tazawa and Ogawa will focus on any issues related to roadblocks and checkpoints, and also check whether any of the vehicles come from a car rental company. The beat reporters will work in three shifts, and take turns staking out Hinode's main office, their Tokyo branch, and the Hinode Club until the embargo is lifted. Observe the comings and goings of the executives and any unmarked cars. I'm sure Hinode will put up a formidable defense—they'll have strong corporate security and protection in place—so don't overdo it. Kagawa, you make the assignment chart for the beat reporters."

"Yes, sir."

"Once the chart is worked up I need the beat reporters to go out to their assigned posts. Everyone, make sure you look over the materials on Hinode. Finally, this case may take a while to crack, so we need all hands on deck. That's all from me."

Sugano always gave such specific instructions, and as far as Kubo knew, he had never erred in his judgment.

And Sugano, who took out his comb again, held in his arsenal a vast network of sources the likes of which Kubo could only dream about. Whenever Kubo marveled at the technique, time, and toil that must have been required for Sugano to build such a tremendous wealth of information—which awed one and all alike—a tangle of jealousy and suspicion came over him, and he was forced to question his own capabilities as a journalist.

Even now, as he repeated Sugano's speech in his mind, Kubo imagined that, ultimately, MPD's Public Security Bureau would be moving with a suspicious eye on the actions of ultranationalist groups embroiled in underground banking, and Sugano himself must have information on the bureau within his grasp. If ultranationalist groups were involved, there would be politicians on the outside, with crime syndicates and extortionists underneath. Kubo quickly ran through his own dossier of sources, but he could not come up with a single person who might provide the kernel of a story from that angle.

As Kubo thought all this through, a can of oolong tea appeared before him.

"Have some Hinode Oolong Tea," Kuriyama spoke up beside him.

Kubo pondered it for another two seconds before noticing with surprise the moon cake in his left hand. He had apparently been eating the round pastry without even realizing it—all that remained now was a crescent moon. He must have found it on his desk, but he could not remember picking it up. He had no memory of his stomach conveying hunger. Resigned to sabotaging his earlier efforts at healthy eating—he had made do with a small meal of simmered fish at lunch—he washed down the rest of the moon cake with the oolong tea and hurriedly turned on his computer. Kuriyama immediately handed him a memo from the press conference.

"Here's a rundown of the first briefing. From the chief's notes," he said.

Solicitous and with a breezy air about him, Kuriyama was thirty years old and still in his first year on the First Investigation beat. With his lustrous complexion and bright smile, he was a model of that new type of investigative reporter who proved that even the so-called "penal servitude" of the MPD track could be handled with ease with the right attitude and a certain knack. What's more, Kuriyama had a fair number of sources and wrote good articles, and even if Kubo thought that the diligence of his reporting left something to be desired, it still fell within a tolerable range. As he thanked Kuriyama for the memo, Kubo realized he was measuring himself against one of his colleagues yet again.

The subject matter of the first press conference, held at 12:15 A.M., was as follows:

Kyosuke Shiroyama (58), residing at 2-16 Sanno / 22:05: Returns home in company car. Driver Tatsuo Yamazaki (60), residing at 2-13 Zoshigaya / Yamazaki departs after watching Shiroyama go through the front gate / 22:50: Police receive 110 emergency call—husband hasn't come home / 23:16: Confirmed as incident. Victim taken hostage and abducted between front gate and front door / Note found in shrubs by path to front door. Balled up letter. White paper. Handwritten. Katakana letters: "We have your president" / Deemed abduction and unlawful confinement / Details unknown / Next briefing, 2 A.M.

"They say the CI director's hands were trembling," Kuriyama said.

"Really?"

"And a little while ago Hiroda-san from Criminal Administration was screaming his head off."

"Oh, yeah?"

Kubo could not imagine what Hiroda—a mild-mannered man who had managed to remain calm even when he learned of the poison gas terror attack the other day—might have sounded like earlier. Kubo glared at the memo again and after checking the time—1:25 A.M.—he started writing down questions in preparation for the second press conference that would take place in thirty-five minutes.

Had the president taken his usual route home? Exactly how far past the gate had the driver seen him go? Had anyone at home heard anything? Why had it taken his family forty-five minutes to call the police? How were the family members doing? What had been the president's schedule that day? What had he been wearing? What was the writing like on the note they found? Has there been any contact from the perpetrators? Had anyone seen a strange person or vehicle? What was the progress of the Crime Scene Unit? Any footprints? Evidence left behind?

A bold crime, deftly executed. Are they pros?

Kubo hunched over his laptop while his colleagues passed documents back and forth behind him and, according to their assignments on the chart Deputy Kagawa had made, the beat reporters filed out of the nook one by one. The phone kept ringing and terse retorts— "I've got nothing," "Not yet," and "What about you?"—volleyed through the air. Chief Sugano was on the phone discussing whom to deploy where once the embargo was lifted. Kubo added another line—*Has there ever been any threat, blackmail, or harassment made against Hinode in the past?*—and gazed at the can of Hinode Oolong Tea on his desk.

As his eyes again traced over the trademark seal of a golden phoenix, which he had never really looked at carefully before, the gravity of the situation sunk in at last.

合田雄一郎　Yuichiro Goda

BY HALF PAST MIDNIGHT, A total of twenty-three officers from Criminal Investigation—not counting the two standing watch at the crime scene, three from the crime scene team who had gone there for backup, as well as the chief inspector and deputy chief inspector—had assembled in the CI office at Omori Police Department. Per instructions from the MPD, they had created a large sketch of the vicinity of the crime scene and a current survey map that included the premises of the victim's home, but once that was complete they ran out of things to do. In the back lot of their building the 103 SWAT vehicle was parked, and there were at least two officers encamped inside, but in regard to what was happening at the scene and who was doing what where, there was very little information coming in over the investigation radio, and on the third floor they had very little read on the situation at the scene. The same was true for the superintendent and vice commander, and Chief Inspector Hakamada and Deputy Chief Inspector Dohi were pacing back and forth between the superintendent's office, the CI office, and the control room with rather bewildered expressions.

As of 12:40 A.M., there were no witnesses, no suspicious vehicles, no evidence left behind, and no movement or contact from the perpetrators.

Having been the first one on the scene, Goda had explained the situation to his fellow officers, but that hadn't taken more than five minutes. Next, Inspector Anzai from White Collar Crime pulled out Hinode's comprehensive asset securities report from the previous year from a forgotten corner shelf and had started reading out an overview of the company from page one but, once he got to the summary of their specialized facilities with a catalog of their twelve factories, fifteen branch offices, and research labs, he tossed aside the pamphlet and concluded, "So basically, in terms of assets, sales, operating income, and equity, there's about a three-digit difference between Hinode and your typical local business."

Someone else then picked up the pamphlet and leafed through it, and it was passed around a few hands, but before long that stopped too, and without any other idle chatter, the team was once again engulfed by silence. Every one of them looked melancholy, torn between the desire to get a little shut-eye before work tomorrow and dismay over their misfortune that a VIP had been kidnapped within their jurisdiction, of all places.

The CI office was not designed to accommodate a full turnout of their team. There weren't enough chairs, and no personal space to speak of. Aside from the chief inspector's and the deputy chief inspector's spots by the window, there were four rows of steel desks belonging to no one in particular, five desks to a row arranged close together, while along the wall were file cabinets and shelves of the same steel, and blackboards covered with various flyers and posters. When twenty-three grown men filed into the room, it was nearly as stifling and gloomy as the area around the betting windows at the racecourse. Goda found this to be an unacceptable work environment given the mountain of investigation documents they were required to produce day after day, and the only solution that he had ever come up with was to get outside as much as possible, and to use one of the unoccupied interrogation rooms to write up his case files.

On the steel desks, there were eight phones for internal use and four phones with an outside line, four computer terminals connected to the mainframe that managed all inquiries and two word processors that were dirty and discolored from use. There were also several string-bound MPD telephone directories, a worn-out copy of the White Pages, ballpoint pens and pencils, official directive paperwork and newspaper flyers with notes written on the flipside, ashtrays, and a few heavily stained tea mugs.

Goda was sitting with his back to the wall in a spot close to the door. In his shirt pocket was a detailed, minute-by-minute record of officer activity prior to the incident, which he had gotten from the police box by Omori Station before coming here, but his instinct had not yet managed to clearly work out what each emergency call or command from the department might signify. The excitement he had felt when he had first arrived on the scene had dulled, but now it circled slowly around his instinct. Was the president the target, or the company itself? Why Hinode Beer? Were there troubles within Hinode that would provoke a crime? Did they have any connections to extortionists and organized crime? When he had spoken with the Vice President Kurata on the phone, something about the man's forceful tone and the way he cautiously chose his words seemed out of balance to Goda's ear—did Hinode already know something about what had transpired tonight?

Finally, what was their motive? If the perpetrators' ultimate aim was money, why choose such a high-risk scheme as kidnapping? The end result would be the same had they abducted any other executive, so why did it have to be the president?

Technically Goda was the designated investigator at his precinct, but as the guy who had been chucked sideways from the MPD to a local department, this entire past year he had not received a single call to report to Investigation Headquarters. This time, even if he were to be pulled in because they were short-handed, the only tasks that might trickle down to him would be either canvassing the vicinity on foot or searching for evidence. Even as he contemplated all this, it was his natural tendency to keep turning the pages of the financial report pamphlet to learn more, however mechanically, about Hinode as a company.

First, he checked the important figures in the management index. The company's sales revenue for 1993 was 1.35 trillion yen. For consolidated accounts it was close to 1.6 trillion. The company's operating income was 77 billion. Net profit was about half that amount. Total assets were 1.2 trillion. Equity ratio, 47 percent. One share of their stock cost 10 yen. Number of employees, 8,200. Each and every number told the same story—they were a behemoth, "the bluest of blue-chips"—but how they could yield 1.35 trillion by peddling two-hundred-yen-or-so cans of beer—with a high liquor tax, to boot—was not something he could readily fathom. These figures were from two years ago, so now they would have swelled even more.

Next, he turned to the section on the 105-year history of the company. Even before the war, the company already had four factories, and after the war ended they steadily expanded with more factories, branch offices, and sales offices, while aggressively making headway in developing technological fields such as pharmaceuticals, biotechnology, state-of-the-art medical treatment, and data network systems—the corporation's ultimate goal of diversification gradually came into focus for Goda.

Once he had scanned their current stock condition, he saw that Toei and several other major city banks as well as life insurance companies dominated the list of their biggest shareholders, as expected, and their aggregate covered 27 percent of shares outstanding. The company's stock price had remained stable even after the economic bubble burst, and their dividend payout ratio had maintained the high rate of 25 percent.

Then he turned to their current executives. He quickly familiarized himself with the names of the thirty-five executives under the president and the multiple titles they held, such as general manager of beer division and general manager of business development. Perched at the top of the list, Kyosuke Shiroyama was described as a graduate of the faculty of law at the University of Tokyo. Judging from how, after he joined the company in 1959, he had risen to general manager of beer division after years of working as a sales manager and then a branch manager in Sendai and Osaka, he had clearly been in the sales trenches all along. The world of selling things was the furthest from what a detective knew, and as Goda stared at the name—Kyosuke Shiroyama—he allowed himself to wonder what kind of man Shiroyama was. Guessing from the appearance of his home and the impression made by his wife and son, Goda reasoned that Shiroyama must be a rather modest and conservative individual.

On the other hand, the vice president he had spoken to on the phone, Seigo Kurata, also held the title of general manager of beer division, so there was no doubt that Shiroyama and Kurata were the most closely connected among members of the board of directors. Thinking Kurata might be the one to prod, Goda briefly recalled the voice of the seemingly complicated man he heard on the line.

Moving on to the index of their various business sectors, Goda found their company organizational chart. Beneath the shareholders' meeting was the board of directors and board of company auditors; then beneath that the president and the management council. The company, with various departments such as general affairs, human resources, accounting, public relations, data network development as well as a planning office, secretarial office, and a consumer advisory office was as common as could be, with the business itself divided into beer, pharmaceutical, business development, laboratory, and the like. However, although the company was pursuing diversification, when he looked at the figures of each primary business sector, beer still counted for 96 percent of sales.

As Goda skipped over a few pages to look at performance details, a voice nearby asked, "Interesting?"

He looked up to see Osanai, an inspector from Burglary Investigation, casting a sullen gaze his way. Osanai had been on duty tonight, but when the call came in from Sanno Ni-chome, he happened to be in Omori-Minami where a robbery had taken place, so he had missed the chance to be first on the scene in Sanno Ni-chome. His look conveyed that he would not soon forget this resentment.

"I guess. The names of the beers I drink every day are all here," Goda said in response. "Hinode Lager, Hinode Supreme, Supreme Draft, Limelight Diner . . ."

"I doubt you drink beer," Osanai scoffed, and Goda ignored him after that.

It was true that the familiar brand names were listed on the page, which reported this quarter's business conditions, along with the sales performance for each product. The current situation for liquor sales—affected by last year's increase in the liquor tax, which had caused every company to raise prices across the board, the intensified discounting at mass retailers, and Limelight's full-scale entry into the market—seemed to indicate that the things were not in fact so easy for the company. Despite this, thanks to the steady performance of their two pillars—the lager and the supreme—as well as their efforts to stabilize the cost of raw materials and to streamline their distribution, Hinode's operating income for 1993 had apparently sustained a slight increase over the previous year. Incidentally, the total volume of beer sold in one year was 3.45 million kiloliters. Unable to grasp such a number quantitatively, Goda reached over to the blackboard behind him and did a bit of long division to figure out how many large bottles this could be converted to, but the number he came up with—5.45 billion—was all the more incomprehensible to him.

Goda wiped away the number with the eraser, and went back to patiently turning the pages. In the section on sales performance, there was a chart explaining their distribution channels, how the product flowed from primary wholesalers to secondary wholesalers before it got to retailers, until finally reaching drinking establishments and consumers. The words "drinking establishment" caught his eye, and as he wondered what proportion of total sales was beer sold on commercial premises, and had just started to flip around the pages when the door to the CI office opened.

Deputy Chief Inspector Katsuhiko Dohi stuck his head in the

opened doorway and fixed his saucer-like eyes on Goda nearby. Goda glanced at the time—12:50 A.M.—and with every eye in the CI office on him, set down the pamphlet and walked out into the hallway.

As soon as Goda was in the corridor Dohi demanded, "Two guys from SIT are downstairs. You were at MPD so you should recognize them. Go ask them when the brass are coming down here."

This spring, ahead of his compulsory retirement next year, Dohi would be promoted to the rank of chief inspector, having assumed that title after his time as inspector in Burglary Investigation. Stubbornly earnest, his face managed to be both complex and dull at the same time—as if all the good and bad of his generally lackluster police career were cobbled together in his expression. As long as nothing was on the blotter he would laugh and say this was his last year, he had nothing to worry about, but when push came to shove, he was a cop, always wringing his hands and trying to gauge his superiors. Even now, his demand was born of his conscientious desire to deliver even a fragment of news to the superintendent and chief inspector, who were anxious about the lack of information.

Goda answered, "Yes sir," headed downstairs, where there was no one at the back door, and after stepping outside to take a deep breath of air, he returned directly to the third floor and told Dohi, "Apparently they don't know yet."

With the addition of Dohi, the CI office was now even more claustrophobic; the majority of those inside had their arms folded and eyes closed, while a few of them had a newspaper or magazine spread open in front of them, with the earphone for the scanner in their ear, as Goda returned to his seat and resumed leafing through the pamphlet back in his seat. Tonight of all nights the police phone didn't ring even once; every now and then the siren from a patrol car or ambulance speeding along the Dai-ichi Keihin or Sangyo Road echoed as if from a faraway world.

Goda moved on to the section for the so-called cost of goods sold on the profit and loss statement, tracking his eye across the heading for each figure for the current quarter—manufacturing costs, three hundred fifty billion; liquor tax, seven hundred billion. From time to time he looked up at the clock and, listening to the sound of the rain falling on the pavement outside, thought about how it must be snowing in the countryside and the mountain regions by now, imagining the cold that the victim and the perpetrators must be feeling, wherever they were. With the passage of time, however, the visceral sensations that he had first experienced when the incident occurred were starting to wane.

At half past one in the morning, those who had been listening to the investigation radio looked up and murmured to one another, "Sounds like they got an eyewitness who saw a car . . ."

Goda, Dohi, and even those who had been dozing off pricked up their ears at once. "What's the location?"

Someone spread open the map. "Number twenty-one at the cul-de-sac. Katsuichi Sasaki, seventy-six years old . . ."

"It's here," said someone near the map.

"Circle it in red and put it up on the board!" barked Dohi, and the residential map was promptly taped to the black board.

"Time witnessed, around 10 P.M. Witness saw the car from the second floor of his home. Color was either navy or black. A van or possibly an RV. Make and model unknown, license plate unknown . . ."

That was the extent of the information from the wireless, and the twenty-four officers, who had perked up somewhat, sunk back into their seats. Since the details from the car eyewitness were unknown, this seemed unlikely to lead to a clue. Nevertheless, number twenty-one bordered number sixteen to the north, and if there had been a car lurking on the cul-de-sac just before the incident occurred, the likelihood of it being connected was about fifty-fifty. Goda considered this, his partially deflated hope suspended in midair.

At the exact same moment, he again recalled the copy of the dispatch record from the police box in his pocket and felt convinced of the need, while the officer's memory was still fresh, to calculate the precise, minute-by-minute route that the patrol car had taken before and after 10 P.M., but that thought too hung in midair.

The hands on the clock pointed to just before two in the morning. Goda turned back to the next heading on the profit and loss statement, details regarding sales costs and general administrative costs. Just as he registered the number twenty-five billion listed under advertising costs, a commercial for Hinode Lemon Sour flickered through his mind—a strange beast dancing along to a gamelan under a moonlit night.

久保晴久　Haruhisa Kubo

TWO-OH-TWO A.M. APPEARING IN THE press conference hall on the ninth floor of the Tokyo Metropolitan Police Department, the director of Criminal Investigation, Tsuyoshi Teraoka, took a small silent bow in front of the more than sixty gathered reporters from seventeen media companies, then bent his head over the notebook in his hands.

"Unfortunately, as of 2 A.M., there has been no contact from the perpetrator. The situation remains the same."

As those first words were uttered, the unspoken incredulity of the reporters pressed heavily into every corner of the hall.

"And I'd like to take this opportunity to express my gratitude for your cooperation with the media embargo," Teraoka addressed them formulaically. "Currently, we've acknowledged the incident as abduction and unlawful confinement, but we consider the victim to be in an extremely precarious situation. It goes without saying that the entire police force will do all it can to conduct a thorough investigation, and in respect to the spirit of the embargo we will strive to respond to the media in good faith, so I ask for your continued cooperation."

Director Teraoka's voice sounded as stiff and monotonous as ever, at least to the ears of those in attendance, and without looking up to meet the eyes of the reporters, he solemnly continued to recite only the words in his notebook.

"The layout of the victim's home is as you see it in the map we've distributed to each of you. The victim was captured in the location marked with an X and we believe he was taken out through the front gate. At this time, that's the extent of what we know. The front gate, marked A, has an automatic lock manufactured by the company SECOM that can be opened from the outside with a passcode and from the inside with a switch. After arriving home, the victim manually turns on the nighttime alarm system himself, therefore, at the estimated time of the incident—10:05 P.M. on the twenty-fourth—the alarm system was turned off. We've detected several footwear impressions near the shrubbery as well as in numerous spots inside the exterior wall surrounding the property, and we are currently analyzing them. As for the note retrieved from the spot marked with a circle, we are working quickly to identify any fingerprints and the type of ink used. As of 2 A.M. right now, we have not managed to find any witnesses. That's all."

As soon as the director's voice broke off, there was a barrage of questions from the assertive commercial broadcasting reporters. "Does that mean they jumped in over the wall and escaped through the gate?" "Do you have a profile of the suspect?"

Without missing a beat, the director of Public Information standing next to Teraoka replied sharply, "One question at a time, please," and the voices died down. In the momentary silence, Haruhisa Kubo, encamped in the front row, clearly registered the beads of sweat running down Director Teraoka's forehead, even though the room wasn't the least bit warm.

The questions began immediately in the usual order by the usual suspects from the Nanashakai kisha club who were also installed in the front row. Each question was short, as was its reply, exchanged at rapid-fire speed. The reporters took notes while organizing everything in their heads, forced to decide what was important and what wasn't on the spot. Kubo's hand gripping his ballpoint pen quickly turned clammy with sweat.

"First, please name the family members who were home at the time of the incident."

"The victim's wife, Reiko Shiroyama, fifty-eight years old."

"What was the wife doing last night around 10, and where was she exactly?"

"She told us she was in the living room on the first floor, reading."

"Does she usually hear the front gate close?"

"She said it depends. Sometimes she hears it, sometimes she doesn't."

"Last night, did the driver take the same route home as usual?"

"He did."

"Does the president always return home at a specific time?"

"It depends on the day, but she told us he most often returns around 10 P.M."

"You said they made the hundred-ten call at 10:50 P.M. How did the family come to the decision that they needed to make an emergency call?"

"Around 10:28 P.M., there was a call from the office to the president's home, and when the person from the company learned that he had not returned home, they contacted the driver and as a result determined that something was wrong."

"What is the name of the individual who called from the company?"

"I'm not able to disclose that information."

"How many different footwear impressions were collected from the crime scene?"

"I am not able to answer that as they are still under analysis."

"So you're saying there are several?"

"I'm not able to disclose that at this time."

"There's no way one guy can hold down a grown man and drag him off without making a sound. It has to be the work of a team, is that what you think?"

"We do not know that at this time."

"So the perp breached the wall beforehand and was waiting in the bushes, correct?"

"At this time, we are not able to confirm either way."

"Describe what the victim was wearing."

"Navy suit, black wool vest, blue and silver necktie, black shoes."

"What about a coat?"

"He wasn't wearing one."

"A briefcase?"

"An attaché case by Burberry. Brown in color."

"It's unlikely that they'd abduct a person without a car. Do you or do you not have any information about that?"

"At this time, we have not obtained accurate eyewitness information."

"So you do have some information?"

"We have not received any reports of that nature."

"The note—what else was written besides the four words, 'We have your president'?"

"Four words, that's it."

"Will the note be released?"

"We have not reached the stage to consider that."

"You said the incident is being treated as abduction and unlawful confinement, but could it possibly develop into kidnapping for ransom?"

"We are not able to comment at this time."

"What about corporate extortion?"

"At this point, we do not know anything about the perpetrators' objective."

"Before this incident, have there been any harassment or threats made against Hinode? Are there any matters that the police are aware of?"

"Not at this time, no."

"Could this be considered part of a series of corporate terrorism incidents?"

"We are not able to comment at this time."

"Is it possible that they've targeted the victim as an individual?"

"We are not able to determine that at this time."

"What's your understanding of the perpetrators' profile?"

"At this time, I cannot say."

"I think it's impossible for an amateur to pull off a crime like this—have you considered that pros, like a crime syndicate, could be involved?"

"We have not come to such a conclusion at this time."

"No way an amateur would sit and wait in the yard, a stone's throw from the front door."

"We can't know that until we ask the perpetrator."

"What's your outlook for the investigation ahead?"

"We will make every effort. That's all I can say about that."

After responding to this point, with sweat glistening on his blue-veined forehead, Teraoka put away his notebook. Without waiting for the director of Public Information to announce, "That's all for now. Next briefing at four," Teraoka walked out quickly, looking straight ahead with an even more obstinate expression than when he had first appeared in the hall. The reporters also withdrew without a word, but since there wasn't a single newsworthy item, all of them moved slowly. Whenever a significant incident occurred, invariably the press conference would be peppered with phrases such as, "We're not able to say," "We're not sure," and "We're not aware," but even the same "not" would be uttered with a subtly different nuance each time. Kubo felt that just now, in addition to appearing jittery and pained from beginning to end, Teraoka seemed abstracted as he repeated over and over that he didn't know. Four and a half hours had already passed since the current president of Hinode Beer had been abducted. If the police didn't have a clue at this point, Kubo thought—just as the Chief Reporter Sugano had predicted—it could take a while to crack this case.

合田雄一郎 Yuichiro Goda

AT THREE IN THE MORNING, the announcement came in from the chief inspector of First Investigation at MPD that, with the exception of the ten members of the Criminal Investigation Division and another two from the Crime Prevention Division who were to be absorbed into Investigation Headquarters, the rest of the department was dismissed for the time being. Since the grounds for mobilizing a large group of investigators had never materialized, MPD decided that the perpetrators were unlikely to make any moves until dawn. The other officers who had been standing by at Omori Police Department since right after the incident occurred were left with nothing but a sense of regret and fatigue from lack of sleep. Although they had been released, it wasn't as if there were any trains running at that hour to take them home, so a few of the unelected left the CI office to lie down until morning in the dojo on the fourth-floor, while others retreated elsewhere or nowhere in particular.

Remaining in the Omori CI office were four inspectors—Goda from Violent Crime, Noriaki Anzai from White Collar Crime, Takafumi Saito from Organized Crime, and Takuya Osanai from Burglary—as well as six police sergeants from these units, along with Deputy Chief Inspector Dohi acting as the self-proclaimed head of liaison and coordination, which came out to eleven men in total. Everyone but Dohi and Anzai went back to dozing while they waited for the investigation meeting, whose start time remained unknown.

Inspector Anzai, having perked up as soon as he realized he was likely to be called up to Investigation Headquarters, nudged Goda's shoulder just as the latter had buried his face in his arms on the desk. Anzai whispered, "Think we'll find out about Hinode's financial standing?"

Goda thought it was too soon for that but, detecting a whiff of expectation in Anzai's loaded question, he replied vaguely, "Who knows?"

Anzai had spent the majority of his thirty-three years of service specializing in white collar crime, transferring from one precinct to another every five or six years, but Goda had heard that he had never had the opportunity to take part in a large-scale bribery case or commercial law violation. Goda didn't know why Anzai, despite being a licensed CPA, had never been called in to work at MPD, but he could easily imagine the kind of work Anzai had toiled over for years: real estate transactions involving unlawful registration and sales contracts, fraudulent promissory notes, scams, a miscellany of complaints and charges that could hardly be distinguished from civil suits, petty election violations over the placement of flyers, and so on and so forth. Over the past year, even the cases occurring within Goda's scope of vision were mostly along the lines of complaints against door-to-door sales, counterfeit calling cards, unauthorized use of credit cards and loan shark troubles, and creditors rushing in when their debtor had skipped town. Most of these never resulted in prosecution, or were resolved with a minor punishment or a dialogue among the parties involved, so all in all his job was not very different from that of a jack-of-all-trades consultant.

Sitting beside Goda, Anzai had started flipping through the Hinode financial report, which Goda had tossed aside. "You had better get some sleep," Goda suggested.

"I doubt you'll understand," Anzai muttered and flashed him a small, crooked smile. "I've been counting money all this time, but the loot in the cases I've handled only went up to ten digits. Suddenly dangling thirteen digits in front of me, well, that's like a monkey that sees a banana—there's no chance I'm sleeping now."

As he whispered this, Anzai hung his head over the report spread open on the desk. Given his age and experience, Anzai was likely to be promoted to chief inspector soon, but he must have been anxious— if he wanted to move up to MPD with distinction, this might be his last chance. Goda could relate to this, at least.

Even Goda had been relieved to be whisked up to Investigation Headquarters. If he were honest, he had had enough of lovers' quarrels involving kitchen knives, drunken brawls, and the dead bodies of vagrants by the roadside. *I've been desperate for a big case, doesn't matter what it is*, Goda thought as he closed his eyes atop the pillow of his arms. Just then, like a reflex springing from his selfish desire, the faces of the victim's wife and son flashed through his mind. Deputy Chief Inspector Dohi, over at his desk, was on a call with a nearby 7-Eleven. "Get me thirty Makunouchi bento boxes. Make it out to the Omori Police Department, Police Affairs Division."

The investigation radio didn't make a peep. By four in the morning, the sound of rain beating down on the roof of the building and the asphalt of the highway had subsided as well, and the CI office filled with the silence of early dawn and a chill that numbed his hands and feet. Drawing up the collar of his down jacket, Goda fell into a brief but deep sleep. Just as he reached the brink of some dream, he was pulled back into consciousness by the abrupt ringing of the police phone, and his conditioned reflex was to peek at his wristwatch.

4:30 A.M. Dohi, who had answered the phone, replaced the receiver and announced, "The investigation meeting will convene at 7 A.M. The official name of the HQ is Hinode Beer President Abduction and Unlawful Confinement Special Investigation Headquarters."

After hearing as much, Goda and the others went back to sleep. Dohi set himself to the silent task of taping together four sheets of B4 copy paper and, with a calligraphy brush, inking the solemn name that had just been bestowed upon the incident. Regardless of what his countenance might suggest, Dohi had beautiful penmanship, and all the cautionary postings on the walls of the department—*Keep It Neat*, *Be Polite on the Phone*, and *Point & Check*—were his handiwork.

It was before six when Goda was awakened again, this time by the sound of cars pulling into the back lot. The officer on duty from Police Affairs came in and asked for help setting up chairs. When he went down to the main conference room on the second floor, he saw that the Communications Bureau from MPD had arrived to install equipment and add police phone lines in preparation for the investigation command headquarters. They had been told that roughly one hundred members would be coming from MPD, so all department staff helped with gathering every available folding table and chair, and once these were all crammed into the conference room, it looked like they were ready for a meeting of creditors. Outside the door to the room, Dohi's poster had already been put up.

Next, Goda and the other officers went back up to the third floor to wash their faces, shave, and eat the Makunouchi bentos from 7-Eleven. Goda had a tendency to become sleepy when full, so he threw away his bento half untouched, then started to write out the tasks he would be turning over to his subordinates in Violent Crime. The ones who would remain in his unit were a sergeant with a bad back named Hirai, along with the duo Konno and Izawa, neither of whom could write a decent case file.

Saito from Organized Crime, having scarfed down his entire bento, mumbled with a tooth pick in his mouth, "My head's getting cold." Back when he was with the Fourth Investigation Division at MPD, Saito got into a physical altercation with a member of the yakuza family Inagawa-kai and earned himself ten stitches on his now shaven head, which he rubbed as he walked all the way to the window. He raised the blinds only to cry out, "Oh, hell!" Outside, spring snow had turned everything the color of quartz.

AT 7 A.M., A PHOTOGRAPH of the victim and a large sketch of the layout of his home were posted on the blackboard at the front of the main conference room. The members who had managed to assemble there after being called in during the early morning hours included the first and second units of the First SIT as well as the fourth unit of the Second SIT from MPD's First Investigation Division. It was an impressive gathering of thirty-five SIT officers, not counting those stationed at the victim's home and in the communications vehicles. Among them were also undercover investigators who specialized in apprehending perps.

Since this matter involved a major corporation like Hinode Beer, the arrival of a few members from MPD's Second Investigation Division was to be expected, but Goda was a little surprised to see all ten members of the third unit from Fourth White Collar Crime specializing in corruption and bribery. All eight members of the first unit of Special Violence and Organized Crime Investigation specializing in commercial law violations and extortion had come from the Fourth Investigation Division. In addition, ten members from the ninth unit of Third Violent Crime Investigation from the First Investigation Division were in attendance. Since there were few faces he recognized, Goda resorted to giving them a quick bow. Then, there were another seventeen members from among the eight sub-units of the First Mobile CI Unit as well as the leader of the unit head-quarters. From the precinct, there were ten detectives from CID, including Goda, and the assistant police inspector and sergeant from the Crime Prevention Division, and six members combined from the on-scene forensics team and the precinct's crime scene team from CID. All told, Investigation Headquarters headcount totaled ninety-nine officers.

The seats at the front were helmed by Hidetsugu Kanzaki, chief inspector of First Investigation, along with other top brass, including the chief inspector of the Crime Scene Division; the respective direc-tors of First and Second SIT, Third Violent Crime, Fourth White Collar Crime, and Special Violence and Organized Crime; the deputy leader of First Mobile CI and Superintendent Tobita from Omori Police Department; while off to the side sat inspectors from various units and the leader of the unit headquarters, with Omori's very own Chief Inspector Hakamada of CID hunkered down on the far end.

"Attention!" On command, everyone rose to their feet, standing straight and still. This morning, as he strode into the room, Kanzaki had worn his usual detached expression, neither confirming nor denying that he was an absolute authority who inspired awe from every detective within the Tokyo Metropolitan Police Department. His stature and facial features, all of them average, were indistin-guishable from that of any middle-aged salaryman swaying on the commuter train, but as soon as his short greeting—"Thank you all for coming so early"—issued from his mouth, it was as if a stick ruler had been thrust into the back of each investigator in attendance. Their fingers extended tautly along the seams of their slacks, and a tremor rippled through the entire conference room.

Back when he was at MPD, Goda knew Kanzaki as chief inspector of the Crime Scene Division, but even back then he was known as "walking efficiency." From his greeting and demeanor to his inter-personal relationships and the way he commanded investigations, everything he did seemed to run with accuracy, speed, and clarity. This spring, when he was promoted to first investigation chief inspector, he made the following remarks in *Frontline*, the internal newsletter for detectives: "When we consider the anxiety of citizens and the distress of victims exposed to increasingly heinous crimes, as well as the duty that detectives and police officers must fulfill, all logic, compromises, and excuses arising from the internal organization of criminal investigation become utterly superfluous."

As Goda had read these remarks, he had pondered just what the resolve of the police force was, but when all was said and done, no doubt Kanzaki's own resolve was buttressed by a byzantine, quake-proof resilience that was essential to ascending the ranks of a bureaucratic organization. Lost in such thoughts, Goda never managed to fully extend his fingers, pressed against the casual khaki pants he had been wearing since last night.

Kanzaki opened his notebook as soon as he took the seat directly before the blackboard, and fixed his immobile gaze on the investigators.

"Regarding the incident that occurred last night on the twenty-fourth at approximately 10:05 P.M., in which the president of Hinode Beer, Kyosuke Shiroyama, age fifty-eight, was taken from the front yard of his home in Sanno Ni-chome: irrespective of the perpetrators' motive, I would like all of you to consider this an extremely serious crime that poses a definitive threat to the well-being of our country's citizenry and economic activities." Kanzaki's briefing began with this introduction. He had a tendency to speak softly, and even with the microphone his voice was nothing more than a murmur—nonetheless, every word was trenchant and sharp.

"Other than a note stating, 'We have your president,' which was left behind at the scene of the abduction, at this point the perpetrators have not made any contact whatsoever. Therefore, as of now we have no choice but to treat this as a case of abduction and unlawful confinement, whereas in time we will either receive a specific demand from the criminals, or we will hear nothing at all. In addition to preparing to the best of our abilities for both outcomes, we must dedicate ourselves to the immediate task of narrowing down suspects and criminal objectives. Furthermore, judging from the meticulous and premeditated strategy of leaving behind a single note and then breaking off all communication, and the abduction's close resemblance to the work of a professional crime group, this incident bears the hallmarks of both a violent crime and what could develop into a white collar crime, so we must avoid any assumptions or prejudgments during the course of our investigation. As for the direction of the investigation, for the time being, as we work toward a swift rescue of the victim, we will focus first on deducing the suspects. In addition to canvassing on foot, tracing their movements through legwork, identifying vehicles used in the crime, and establishing any connections to the perpetrators, the cross section of the victim's personal network will commence with a request to provide all necessary materials regarding Hinode Beer, and inquiring of those involved about every detail of the situation, so that we can quickly gather precise information to conduct our analysis. Lastly, because this is a situation in which we have reason to fear for the safety and welfare of the victim, all information related to the incident will be kept strictly confidential. Therefore all communications and reports will be made via a communications specialist in charge. That will be all from me."

Kanzaki seemed to be taking a particularly cautious stance concerning the incident. Looking at it another way, this could also mean that he did not have a specific trajectory for the investigation at this point in time, but as long as Second Investigation and Special Violence and Organized Crime had shown up at such an early stage, it was clear that the concerns of the top brass—guided by causes inscrutable to those on the fringes, like Goda—must veer toward Hinode's conflicts with extortionists.

Then, using the sketch posted on the blackboard, the director of First SIT gave a detailed explanation starting with the onset of the incident. It did not cover anything more than what Goda, as the first detective to arrive upon the scene, had seen. The director continued reading from his notebook: "At this time, we have established two lines of communication: the victim assistance hotline, and another exclusively for any threats or demands coming in from the perpetrators. Two SIT members, including policewomen, are on duty at the victim's home, working in three shifts, and there are another two officers at the relay point . . ."

As he listened, Goda stared at the communications equipment set up on the table near the blackboard. Once again, he remembered the police dispatch record tucked into his shirt pocket.

How did the perpetrators manage to carry out the abduction while evading the cops, who could have appeared at any time? The full shape of this idea—which had originally snagged his thought process at the crime scene and whose contours had still not come into full relief—flashed through his mind for the first time.

The radio, he thought.

However, this amounted to no more than a fleeting hunch, so transitory that Goda could not fully grasp it. He continued to stare at the table where the DG transmitter for the system for Investigation's first unit sat, next to another transmitter for the Victim Assistance Unit and three types of inter-unit radios, and the thought evaporated again.

The briefing had moved on to the chief inspector of Crime Scene Division. In the vicinity of the shrubs along the path leading to the victim's home and inside the exterior wall, they had collected a total of ten incomplete impressions of canvas shoes. Four left footprints, six right, two different pairs. Both measured twenty-six centimeters. The patterns of the rubber soles, while indistinct, could apparently both be verified. By some time today they would be able to determine the manufacturer of the shoes, identifying the brand name, stock number, and even the period of production, but they would still have to identify two pairs from among the millions of shoes distributed to tens of thousands of retailers across the country. A fiber fragment collected from the Japanese andesine stone of the wall was white cotton. The glove prints that came from the switch on the electronic lock by the front gate, based on the weave of the fabric, turned out to be from a cotton work glove. Like the canvas shoes, the gloves were manufactured in units of hundreds of thousands.

The note recovered at the crime scene was written on Kokuyo letter paper, and the product ID number was Hi-51. It was from a hundred-page stationery pad with a yellow cover that cost 250 yen and could probably be found in any household in Japan. There were no fingerprints, nor any other traces of microscopic evidence. The ink of the ballpoint pen was still being analyzed.

Next up, the unit headquarters leader from First Mobile CI reported on the results of questioning conducted after they arrived on the scene. In three homes near the victim's, two people had heard a car engine starting around the time when the crime was committed; another person had heard a sliding car door opening and closing. The leader read aloud the names and addresses of each witness. The person who had heard the sliding door was able to give an accurate time for when he heard the noise—10:07 P.M.—since he had been about to make phone call and happened to look at the clock.

Subsequently, there was a detailed report about a resident of number twenty-one on the cul-de-sac, to the north of the victim's home, who saw a car parked in the alley from his second-floor window at "around 10 at night." The eyewitness was a seventy-six-year-old man, and he had gone to close a small window that had been left open in his bathroom on the second floor, which was when he happened to see, over the wall and bushes that were about one meter from his home, the roof of the car parked in the alley. The car's lights were off, and since he was looking down from above, he could not see if there was anyone inside.

The color of the car was either dark blue or black. Since there were no street lamps in the alley, it was also possibly dark green. The vehicle was either a van or a long-body RV. None of the residents of the four other homes on the cul-de-sac had seen the car. A female office worker who lived next to the sole eyewitness had returned home around 10:15 P.M., but no car had been parked there at that time. Likewise, the eyewitness had not heard the sound of a car starting in the alley.

The man who saw the car lived with his wife, and by nine every night he would turn off all the lights in the house before going to bed. Three of the four homes belonged to elderly residents who never went out at night. The eyewitness's neighbor was the twenty-eight-year-old office worker who lived with her parents, and though she generally returned by eight every night, yesterday she had happened to work overtime and had come home late. If the van that was seen in the alley were indeed connected to the incident, it meant that the perpetrators had dedicated a significant amount of time to surveying the area beforehand.

Lastly, the director of First SIT read aloud from the deployment chart for all 105 officers, including the SIT members who were not present. There was the first squad of the Victim Assistance Team, stationed at the victim's home, six SIT members working in three shifts. The second squad from Crime Scene would be in charge of interviewing company employees and would include one group leader and four teams, eight members from SIT, the fourth unit of White Collar Crime from Second Investigation, and Special Violence and Organized Crime from Fourth Investigation. The third squad from Crime Scene would be in charge of questioning Hinode Beer's branch offices and sales offices, subsidiaries, affiliated companies, and distributors, and would similarly be made up of one group leader and twelve teams, twenty-four members from SIT, the fourth unit of White Collar Crime from Second Investigation, Special Violence and Organized Crime from Fourth Investigation, including the precinct's own Noriaki Anzai. The fourth Crime Scene squad, in charge of interviewing the victim's family, relatives, friends, and acquaintances, would be four teams, eight SIT members. The fifth Crime Scene squad, handling matters of extortion, would be five teams, ten members including eight members from Special Violence and Organized Crime from Fourth Investigation, the ninth unit of Violent Crime, and SIT, as well as Takafumi Saito from the precinct's CID and an inspector from Crime Prevention. Saito and the other inspector had both formerly worked in Fourth Investigation at MPD.

Then, the first squad of the Communications and Relay Team would be assigned to the victim's home, while the second squad would be assigned to the 103—each included six SIT members working in three shifts. The Search and Inquiry Squad would consist of one group leader and five teams, ten members total that included three members of the Mobile CI Unit along with five members of the ninth unit of Violent Crime and two officers from the precinct. The Evidence and Vehicle Investigation Squad would be made up of fourteen members of the Mobile CI Unit and seven officers from the precinct, including Osanai and Goda. The head of the ninth unit of Violent Crime would be squad leader. Since no evidence had yet surfaced, they would all commence with vehicle searches.

When his name was called, Goda felt a little shudder, but he consoled himself with the fact that he would be working with inanimate objects. He automatically thought, *First stolen vehicles, then rental cars*, then reminded himself, *Patience, patience, patience*, emptying his mind of all distractions. The director of First SIT had designated the Communications and Report Commanders, and Director Miyoshi of Third Violent Crime Investigation had been named as the contact person for the Evidence and Vehicle Investigation Squad. Goda had met him some five years ago, back when Miyoshi was chief of CID at Shinagawa Police Department, during a murder investigation in which an old man who liked to wander had been struck in the head with a golf club and killed. Even though both he and Dohi were self-made men who had climbed the ranks, Miyoshi gave a different impression, that of a man who took pride in being a cop, to the marrow of his bones.

Thus the first investigation meeting ended at 7:30 in the morning, and each squad broke off for their own short meetings. The majority of SIT dispersed immediately, followed quickly by the Search and Inquiry Squad and then the Crime Scene Squad, which was interviewing company employees, but the remaining three squads were faced with armfuls of documents to review, and the directors of both fourth unit of White Collar Crime from Second Investigation Division and Special Violence and Organized Crime from Fourth Investigation Division continued to give out instructions in a low voice.

Goda and his cohort gathered in a corner, away from them.

"First, we'll go down the list of stolen vehicles and rental cars," Abe, the head of the ninth unit of Violent Crime, said tersely to Director Miyoshi.

"That's fine." Miyoshi nodded, and their meeting was over within five seconds.

As they waited for a fax of the list of stolen vans and RVs from the Criminal Information Management System, they divided up the string of tasks: calling the dealerships of car rental companies, requesting yesterday's rental records from each office, addressing formal documents of inquiry related to the investigation to each dealership under the name of the superintendent of Omori Police Department, administering the superintendent's seal, and faxing them out. Since they didn't know the type of car or the license number of the vehicle connected to the crime, they had no choice but to eliminate, one by one, each and every stolen vehicle or car rented in the city, with only the color and the shape seen by a seventy-six-year-old man as clues. If this led nowhere, next they'd have to cast their net wider to neighboring prefectures, to the entire Kantō region, and then to the whole country. And if they still came up empty-handed, they'd have to go to every parking lot in the city on foot, and if that failed, they'd have to check each of the hundreds of thousands or even millions of vans registered at the District Land Transport Bureau.

The time was now 7:40 A.M. The radio connected to the victim's home and the staging points remained silent; Chief Inspector Kanzaki and the other directors looked like nothing more than figureheads on a tiered doll stand; and outside the window above Goda's head as he continued to write out his documents, the light snow was starting to accumulate.

根来史彰　Fumiaki Negoro

THE MPD'S FIFTH PRESS CONFERENCE at 8 A.M. stuck to the same script: "No contact from the perpetrators. Situation remains unchanged."

At the same time, over on *Toho News*'s Metro section, the slot editor for the evening edition, who was named Murai, had just taken his regular seat and shouted out, "Better get moving." The evening edition for Saturday, March 25, had to be put together as usual, provided no sudden developments such as the rescue of the president of Hinode Beer occurred before the final deadline at 1:30 P.M. Murai had already been in the office by three in the morning after receiving a report of the incident, but once he had skimmed through early editions of the other morning newspapers to confirm that they had not missed any scoops, he had managed to fall asleep on the sofa despite the utter chaos swirling around him. He woke up before eight, in time to hear the outcome of the MPD's press conference and, agreeing with his colleagues that there was, in fact, "Nothing we can do," he planted himself in front of his desktop computer and cracked open the notebook with takeover instructions from the slot editor before him. Next to him, the rim editor on duty echoed the words, "Nothing we can do," and took his own seat.

Once he had shifted into gear, Murai started barking out instructions even to Negoro, who sat half-asleep over in the Reserve section. "If this keeps up, we won't have much to fill pages, so make those articles on the two credit associations and the candidates in the gubernatorial election on the longer side. You can even run each candidate's self-recommendation remarks."

"Yes," Negoro replied, but instead of turning on his computer, he stood up to go to the lavatory and devoted ample time to washing and shaving his face.

A pale seamless gray filled the world outside the windows of the news room, as if they were ensconced in a cloud, and large snowflakes continued to fall on the moat of Chidori-ga-fuchi just beneath them. Several of the reporters who had been called in during the wee hours after news of the incident broke were stretched out on the row of sofas near the windows. The rest were either staked out on the frontlines in Omori and Sanno or stalking an early-morning interview subject, mindful of the news embargo.

On the other side, the editor-in-chief and managing editor,

along with the chiefs of Metro, Political, Finance, and Layout, had been locked in a meeting since around 7:30 A.M. Based upon Chief Sugano's assessment from MPD that there was unlikely to be any movement in the abduction and unlawful confinement of the president of Hinode Beer, and that the police had not yet narrowed down any suspects, they were discussing what to do with the Metro pages should the situation remain unchanged for the foreseeable future.

The Political and Finance sections had the nationwide local elections in two weeks to worry about, and if the news embargo were not lifted until right before the election, media coverage would then be dominated by news about the kidnapping, which would have a detrimental impact on voter turnout, so they were rightly concerned about the outlook of the situation. Depending on how it developed, they might have to redraw a significant portion of their election projection map, and the anticipation of election results could even have considerable effects on both exchange rates and stock prices.

Meanwhile the Metro section had a backlog of crucial incidents all requiring follow-up articles, so if the present situation were to drag on, they would run into complications with dispatching reporters. What was more, their branch manager in Hachioji, whose older brother was a human resources manager at Hinode Beer's main office, proffered the information that late last year, Hinode had distributed a strictly confidential manual detailing the company's crisis management system to the leadership at each of their branch and sales offices, which did not bode well for *Toho*'s reporting going forward.

Hinode had overhauled their online system last fall, and the company had installed a new access management and feedback system, in addition to strengthening their system surveillance. Since then the addresses and phone numbers of all executive staff above the level of manager had apparently been scrubbed from company directories and computer files. This meant that Hinode had presumably contracted with a specialized overseas insurance affiliate to install a risk management system—these were not yet widespread in Japan—and since the existence of such a contract itself would be considered a trade secret, no one outside the company would have known about it. When Negoro floated this story past Sugano, he gave his own opinion on the matter. "I've heard that Hinode's negotiations with Limelight over their merger leaked straight to the CIA, so no doubt Hinode's on their toes now."

Before going into the executive meeting, the Metro chief, Toru Maeda, had rubbed his ample belly and remarked, "This is a quandary . . ." But from where Negoro sat in the Reserve section, the elation evident on Maeda's face suggested that the situation, though still a quandary, was not entirely unwelcome.

The first words out of Maeda's mouth when he got to the office shortly after two that morning had been, "Bet this is linked to extortionists." And shortly after, a reporter covering the evening interview session at the District Public Prosecutor's Office informed them from the courthouse kisha club that some of the officers from the special investigative division of the District Public Prosecutor's Office had indeed been summoned to meet at 7 A.M., and another reporter on his morning interview prowl at the MPD kisha club—this was before 6 A.M.—confirmed that the Fourth Investigation Division in charge of corporate extortion would most likely be convened at the Special Investigation Headquarters set up at Omori Police Department. Following Maeda's speculation, at dawn the Metro section had tweaked the assignment chart and rounded up however many reporters they could find to hit up extortionists and their corporate underlings, and they had just fanned out.

If extortionists were involved then organized crime would soon follow. In certain cases even ultranationalists and politicians might be in the mix. Before the war, because of the liquor tax, Hinode Beer had a history of involvement with the political world, and though they treaded much more carefully after the war, there was no doubt that they were among the corporations inducted into the troika of politics, bureaucracy, and business established alongside the "1955 system" of the Liberal Democratic Party's decades-long dominance. There was also no doubt that, judging from their purchase record of political party fund-raising tickets, Hinode's pipeline to the current political world ran through Taiichi Sakata, who served as the Secretary-General of the LDP. There had been no particular problems as of yet between Sakata and Hinode, but the so-called "S. Memo" that emerged during the infamous Ogura Transport and Chunichi Mutual Savings Bank scandal had belonged to none other than Sakata himself. Behind the ultranationalist Zenzo Tamaru, who had maneuvered behind the scenes to bring down Chunichi, was the group known as the Okada Association, which held in its arsenal extortionists, corporate raiders, and loan sharks, and behind Okada the vast crime syndicate the Seiwakai stood in the wings. Now that the head of the corporation had been kidnapped, it would be impossible for the investigating authorities not to be gravely concerned about these mysterious connections.

Negoro returned to his seat as he ran through all this in his mind. "Go get some coffee," he said to the reporter in the Reserve section who was yawning repeatedly beside him. "But before you do—those interviews you got from the campaign offices of the gubernatorial candidates? For the piece that didn't make it in yesterday? I'm going to use some of the comments, so could you show them to me?"

"If you like, I also have what I call the Collected Off-the-Record Pomposity," the reporter said as he slid over a few pages of notes and walked away. Up until the previous night he had been part of the election reporting team.

Negoro turned on his computer and glanced at the first line of the notes. But his gaze soon drifted away, and he wasted several more minutes before starting to work. By and large, the distance he felt toward each new incident widened year after year, and the victim's suffering resonated less and less with him, but still, in his own way, Negoro could not keep himself away from the scent of the trail. He left his computer as it was and reached for the receiver of the outside line. He dialed the eight-digit number and stared into the void outside the window as he listened to the ringtone.

The call should have connected with a desk of one of the

prosecutors on the eighth floor of the joint government building of the Legal Affairs and Public Prosecutors Bureau, not so far away from *Toho*'s main office. The occupant of said desk, if Negoro's assumption was correct, was currently in charge of the fraudulent loan case involving the two credit unions, and he and his clerk should have been knee-deep in a mountain of confiscated documents, flipping through payment slips and slaving away from eight in the morning till all hours of the night. He was a guy Negoro had become friendly with three years ago, while he was the chief reporter at the courthouse kisha club, but it had been at a used bookstore in Kanda where they had gotten to know each other. He was an avid reader with a sincerity about him, yet for someone who worked in the special investigation division he was surprisingly unconcerned with ranks or factions—still in his youth, he was that rare prosecutor who did not consider himself a member of the elite.

The phone picked up after three rings. The fact that the guy who answered was at his desk now meant that he was not among the special investigation prosecutors who had been temporarily summoned onto the Hinode Beer case, but since Negoro's acquaintance with him had never been about work, he had no reason to be disappointed.

"I'm calling from Sanseido Bookstore in Kanda," Negoro identified himself with their standard code.

"I thought I'd deposited my payment last month," came the prosecutor's reply. "How're you hanging in over there? Must be busy. Did you stay overnight?"

"Yeah, pretty much. How about you?" Negoro asked.

"Seems like I won't be involved."

"Does that mean you'll still come out for some saké under the cherry blossoms? It's almost that time of year."

"Let's do that, if it ever stops snowing," the prosecutor replied affably.

"By the way, and I guess I'm not entirely without ulterior motives here, but your brother-in-law, he's at Omori Police Department now, isn't he?"

As soon as Negoro broached the subject, he thought he heard a bitter laugh on the other end of the line.

"Well that one, he's much more of a stiff than I am, so I doubt he'll be of any use to you. Though he has changed somewhat lately . . . I guess he's heading into a pretty difficult stage in his life, age-wise."

Whenever he talked about his former brother-in-law, the prosecutor allowed fragments of his emotional life to slip out from beneath the armor of his work, and the tone of his voice also turned ambiguous. As far as Negoro knew, the prosecutor's former brother-in-law, Yuichiro Goda, was the only person he ever allowed into his simple bachelor life, and he was the only person whom the prosecutor ever spoke about.

Last year, when this detective Goda had been transferred from MPD's First Investigation to a local precinct, there had been talk that he had been demoted over mismanagement of some case, but at the time Negoro recalled that the prosecutor, in a moment of confidence, admitted, "The mid-thirties are a difficult time for a man." He must have been close in age to Goda, so perhaps he had been talking about himself.

At any rate, Negoro had met Goda three years ago under some circumstance or other, and he could vividly recall the fierce look in the eyes of the shrewd detective from First Investigation, who was at the time in the throes of an investigation, with no time to care about other people. Negoro didn't know how a person like that might have changed in three years, but he remembered his impression of the raw fragility and youthfulness peeking out from the fringes of Goda's arrogant gaze. Whatever his motives were, Negoro felt a desire to meet him again.

"We don't have to talk about work, let's meet for a drink soon. I'd like to see Goda-san again. I don't know how to say this, but there was something magnetic about his eyes."

The prosecutor once again let out a private, amiable laugh, and replied gamely, "Give me a call when you have the time. I'm not sure if he'll go along, but it might do him some good to breathe in some fresh air, too. I'd love it if you could school him on the everyday world."

"Of course. I'll definitely call you."

"Talk to you soon then. Goodbye."

As he replaced the receiver, Negoro blinked away the image of the noble-faced prosecutor, whose courtesy always remained genuine. He also pushed aside the image of Detective Goda's slender face, which had seemed both haughty and delicate when he had seen it three years ago. Returning to the second line of the reporter's notes, he began gathering the comments of the gubernatorial candidates.

城山恭介

KYOSUKE SHIROYAMA

2

Kyosuke Shiroyama lost consciousness, hurtling into a void of spiritual darkness, shuddering beneath a force that pressed down on him like densely packed mud. When he came to for the briefest of moments, there was again a suffocating heaviness, now the mud was jolting up and down, he heard a groaning sound, and again he sank deeply into nowhere.

He did not know how much time had passed, but as he ever so briefly floated up yet again from the depths of the mud, all at once Shiroyama saw a dark blood-red stain before his eyes. The pool of red caught fire as it seeped into the mud, and just as it transformed into a fetid, roaring flame, an ear-splitting clatter erupted. He heard the wail of a fire bomb as it cut through the sky, and countless cries mingled with the sound of sirens, signal bells, and the bellowing of the volunteer guards.

You two over there! Who do you belong to? Where are your parents? What are you doing? Why haven't you evacuated to the shelter yet?

My sister and I, we're from the Shiroyama Clinic in Shinagawa. Our parents are at the clinic.

Shinagawa is burning! Hurry up and take shelter. Someone, take these children with you!

You two, you've lost your parents? Come with us aunties—quick, get going!

Mister, do you know the Shiroyama Clinic by the west exit of Shinagawa Station? My sister and I, our parents run the Shiroyama Clinic. Please, does anybody know the Shiroyama Clinic in Shinagawa?

Who do these two belong to? Has anyone seen their parents?

How old are you two? Eight and four? If you're from a family of doctors, then you must have had plenty to eat. I'm sorry, I don't have enough hot water for your little sister.

My sister is fine, thank you.

In his dream, Shiroyama felt a chafing thirst. His eight-year-old self stared resentfully at the bottle that a lady he did not know was giving to an infant in her arms, as he crouched next to his younger sister, who would not stop crying, and placed a hand over her mouth. Nevertheless, the eight-year-old Kyosuke did not look all that frightened, and since he was warmly bundled in a jacket of fine woolen cloth, he was in no danger of being cold, nor was he hungry either. His younger sister, Haruko, still so little, did nothing but cry, but Kyosuke had a tacit understanding of why their physician father and mother worked so tirelessly day and night tending to patients. His mother occasionally returned to their home in Sanno Ni-chome to hide special procurement cans of food and dried biscuits in the deep recesses of the kitchen cabinet with strict instructions— "Never tell the neighbors about them"—and he knew to take them out and eat them whenever he and his sister were hungry, and then to dispose of them by crushing the empty cans and burying them in a corner of the yard. He wanted to share the food with his neighborhood friends, but he also had the presence of mind to know not to because once he did, that would be the end. Other things he must have known were that enemy planes targeting the switchyard were closing in on the area around Shinagawa Station where his parents' clinic was located; that sooner or later the clinic would be burned to the ground; that his mother and father would probably die—and the face of the child who Shiroyama saw now in his dream-like trance wore grown-up expressions of those who understood such logic all too well.

As he listened to the rumbling of the fire bombs in a corner of the air-raid shelter, his eight-year-old mind continued to wonder. If their parents were to die, he and his sister would be taken into an orphanage. There they would be under the watchful eye of a terrifying custodian, their every move scrutinized, forced to sleep in a dirty bed, slapped if they cried, or beaten if they failed to respond quickly enough. He could get by without books or toys, but he could not stand being hit, so perhaps it would be better to run away and live on the streets. If it came to that, he would take the books and kimonos from his parents' home and sell them.

Shiroyama strained his ears against the exhaustive ruminations of his eight-year-old self and peered at his obstinate, peculiarly sang-froid expression, he sank yet again into the bottomless mud, thrust down by a mass of bitter confusion.

WHEN HE REGAINED CONSCIOUSNESS, AT first Shiroyama writhed against the dull pain that permeated every inch of his body, but his heart lurched as he realized that he could not move his arms or legs, the blood rippling through every vessel in his head. He had no sense of which way was forward or back, nor any means of determining that, which sent him into a panic. For a few seconds, perhaps longer, he screamed at the furious beating of his heart and the throbbing in his head. In reality he was unable to make a sound, but the howling of his every muscle and cell created a vibration and his whole body trembled.

Then, just when it seemed that silence had abruptly returned, he was besieged by an astonishing thought—*I am going to die.* Shrouded by an otherworldly chill, he remembered how, long ago, the same sensation had always engulfed him in the midst of the air raids. Deranged and confused, the thought repeated itself—*I am going to die*—and his entire body seized up, this time by a strangely cold terror and grief.

Death was something that appeared as a sudden shock, and if there was even the slightest delay in its onset, terror arrived in its stead, and with even more time to spare, a deep grief soon followed. *I see, so this is what it feels like to die.*

From a vast reservoir of sorrows—each one formless and indistinguishable—Shiroyama tried urgently to single out something recognizable before losing all hope, and he wept bitterly. The faces of his children, Mitsuaki and Shoko, from when they were young and from when they were grown up jumbled together in his mind. Meanwhile he could not even remember now what his wife of many years had looked like that morning as he left the house—the only image he could manage to reel in was a blurry face from who knew which era in his life; he was not sure if it even belonged to Reiko. In his mind, he begged his wife for forgiveness and hoped that she would be able get by with his life insurance, savings, and the property in Sanno Ni-chome. In between such thoughts fluttered the azure-blue label of Hinode Meister, the new product set to launch on April 1st, and the dancing amber-colored bubbles of their second Hinode lager, three years in the making.

Then, in his daze, Shiroyama's mind flashed on an image of the lively crowd at the launch party for the new product—he could hear the voices of the executives lined up in the conference room of the main office discussing whether they should set the interim dividend that would be announced at the shareholder meeting to six or seven yen, and he called out futilely, *I'm here! Hey, I'm right here!* Tears came to his eyes again.

Following such confusion, a fresh ache spread throughout his entire body, and the pain jolted Shiroyama fully awake. As he slowly regained his powers of judgment, at last he attempted to discern just what had happened to him. He couldn't move his mouth at all, it felt as if something like duct tape was plastered across it; he was blindfolded, and against his ears and cheeks he could feel the coarseness of a sack over his entire head. Through the sack, his face, tilted downward, was pressed up against a rough-textured material like a vinyl sheet, beneath which was a hard surface that smelled of gasoline and rattled and rumbled as it jostled up and down. At last Shiroyama was able to draw a single conclusion: he was inside a moving car.

His hands were tied behind his back, his ankles were bound too—his knees were slightly bent, but there was constant pressure against his back, knees, and the top of his head, and he could tell he was in a terribly confined space, presumably the floor of the backseat of the car. Placed over the upper half of his prone body was something fairly heavy, and after considering it for some time, Shiroyama figured it must be a cardboard box or a bag containing a quilt.

There was something resting on his ankles and knees as well, but rather than a box or a stone or some other inanimate object, it was the shoes on someone's feet. If Shiroyama tried to shift around, they pressed down on him with greater force. Someone was sitting in the backseat, and had placed his or her feet on top of Shiroyama's legs as he lay across the floor of the backseat. The only noise he could hear was the roar of the engine—indeed, he didn't hear any voices at all.

Hoping to alleviate the pain in his joints, Shiroyama moved his body a few centimeters at a time, which completely exhausted him. His mind grew duller by the minute, as if a fog had been draped over it, and a single word—*kidnapping*—floated up, then vanished, only to appear again, while another word—*death*—drifted hazily around it. He was shocked to realize that he had never even been able to fathom what was, in fact, happening to him here and now, and as he rationalized that he was only human, he succumbed again and again to a sense of utter apathy.

His thoughts grew fuzzy while his body still prickled with pain. The car suddenly pitched, which snapped his mind awake. Unable to do anything about his body's bouncing in sync with the vehicle, Shiroyama pondered futilely where the car might be going, and what time it must be. However, this did not go on for very long, because the vibration stopped, the reverberating engine cut off, and the journey came to an end.

Immediately, he sensed people moving in the front and back

seats, and heard the sound of the front and back doors opening. He was suddenly relieved of the pressure—the heavy object on top of him had been removed—and dragged out of the car. Shiroyama was hoisted from under the arms, then his body was suspended in the air before being heaved over someone's shoulder.

Cold air stung his skin, slipping past his collar and the cuffs of his sleeves. The air was still, and even as several pairs of feet trampled over the ground, the only sound was a faint squeaking. Then, he heard the low rustling of tree branches or leaves, and as he was being carried Shiroyama felt something cold fall down the nape of his neck. *Snow*, Shiroyama thought with his head upside-down. *We're in the snow-covered mountains.*

He was not carried very far. The crunching of snow underfoot soon shifted to footsteps on something solid like stone, and there was also the faint sound of a hinge. Still held aloft, Shiroyama felt his shoes being yanked off, and after being carried a few steps further, he was set down. He did not detect the grassy smell of tatami, but the texture that registered on his body was that of a tatami mat.

He sensed two or perhaps three people moving around him, and within a few minutes of being set down on the tatami floor, Shiroyama was lifted from under his arms and by his legs and placed on top of what felt like a futon, forced to lie down, then immediately covered up by blankets and quilts.

Then, for the first time during his ordeal, Shiroyama heard the voice of a man, directly above his head. "We won't hurt you. When nature calls—and only then—sit up. Other than that, stay in this position."

The voice was impersonal, and neither particularly high- nor low-pitched. It had an unnatural, perhaps intentionally slow tempo, with neither an accent nor intonation. Would they really not harm him? Would they spare his life? Shiroyama held his breath as he waited to hear the next words, but the voice said no more, and as he waited and waited his body grew stiff and numb. Then he heard the faint sound of a car engine starting somewhere in the distance, and once it receded, all sound ceased. He could tell that someone was keeping watch nearby, but no one made a noise, there was no smell of cigarette smoke or anything else.

The futon and blankets were a little damp, and smelled of mold and camphor mothballs. He didn't have the wherewithal to feel repulsed by this—his nerves were primarily absorbed with the pain in his bound wrists, and the ache in the pit of his stomach, where he must have been struck when they first took him away; for the next while, Shiroyama fought against his mind, which was refusing to think, and his senses, which threatened to fall into a torpor.

Shiroyama's mind refused to consider any matters related to the kidnapping. His family, who must be awake with worry at this very moment. His company, panic-stricken that their president had been kidnapped. The ransom, and threats that would accompany such demands. The collateral damage he had no way of imagining. The sacrifices the company would have to make to remedy the situation. All of these simply blended together.

I can't think about it now, I'm too tired tonight. Shiroyama told himself, and in the deepening warmth of the bed, he closed his eyes.

HE KNEW THAT IT WAS dawn from the clear resonance of a bird's sharp cry. It seemed freezing outside—his ears sticking out from the quilt were stiff with cold. There were still no voices or other sounds, and in his vulnerable state just after waking, as he tried to sit up he wondered if someone was keeping watch, when hands shot out from somewhere to grab him and lift him up.

"I'll untie you while you go to the bathroom, so don't lift your hands."

This voice was different from the first voice he had heard last night—this one definitely sounded younger. However, both voices spoke in a measured, deliberate tone that was almost brazenly calm.

Led by the arm, Shiroyama was taken a few steps. He sensed a door opening, and as he was pulled by the wrists his hands touched the edge of the toilet, to show him where it was. The lookout stood right behind him, not saying a word. With hands shriveled from the cold and humiliation, Shiroyama did his business. Amid the cold rising off the toilet and the stench around it, he heard his own urine trickle down softly.

Once he was back on the tatami, the same man asked, "Do you want something to drink?"

Shiroyama nodded, and from a short distance away the voice from the previous night warned, "If you make any noise, I'll kill you," then he felt a cotton work glove on his cheek as the duct tape was ripped off. Immediately the area around his mouth felt better. However, the muscles in his face had gone numb from being restrained and he had lost almost all feeling—he could barely sense the gentle, cool air, and he couldn't have made a sound if he had wanted to. His throat was dry, and the inside of his mouth was sticky from being closed the whole night long.

In the next moment, a paper carton was placed in his hand. A straw was inserted, and Shiroyama brought it to his lips and took a sip. It was oolong tea. When the first mouthful of cold liquid reached his throat, his body trembled as every nerve that had been in crisis mode all night relaxed, and tears pooled in his eyes under the cloth blindfold. He drank deeply on the second sip, and in a moment Shiroyama had emptied the two-hundred-milliliter carton. Feeling his voice return, he couldn't keep himself from mumbling, "Are you after money?" His voice was withered and hoarse, and barely audible.

"You'll find out soon enough." The reply came from that short distance away, and no other words followed. Instead, he heard a light sound as the man who seemed close by tore a thin film or cellophane, and then Shiroyama felt something else being placed in his hands.

"Breakfast," the man said.

He brought it close to his mouth and smelled seaweed—Shiroyama guessed that it was a store-bought rice ball. He wasn't hungry, and he couldn't figure out how his mind, which stubbornly refused to work, had made any decisions, but Shiroyama did as he was told and bit into the lump. The rice grains caught once, twice in his throat, but still he managed to get them down to where they needed to settle. Once he finished, he was surprised to have been able to eat it all, but right away his hands were bound behind his back again, new duct tape was placed over his mouth, he was forced to lie down again and he was covered with a quilt.

The hours of sleeping and waking, only to sleep and awake again, had begun. He drifted restlessly before dozing off, and upon waking he grew restless again. At first, he heard the hum of a small motor interspersed with the crinkling of static. He contemplated just what the noise could be, and convincing himself as he listened to it that one of the men was using an electric shaver. When the shaver noise ceased after a while, a faint jingling started up from that short distance away from where he lay—the sound seemed to belong to a Walkman. But the men made no other sound, they didn't even speak to each other.

The bird he had heard that morning had only let out that solitary cry—the world outside had returned to complete silence. He was used to hearing the low-frequency noise of cars passing by on the streets and the hum of buildings' air conditioning units, and such stillness bore down on his eardrums oppressively. There was no sign of any movement at all—not even the branches on the trees or the wind—nothing. As he continued to drift in and out of wakefulness, he grew less certain that when he had heard the cry of the bird it had been morning, and he soon lost all sense of time.

Driven by his biological needs, Shiroyama did his business every few hours, and each time the restraints on his hands were undone and then bound again, and he was given cartons of fruit-flavored milk, orange juice, or oolong tea. Other than the rice ball, he was given bean-jam buns, cream buns, canned pork and beans, matchbox-size blocks of processed cheese, bananas, and mandarin oranges.

Whenever the duct tape was taken off so that he could eat and drink, Shiroyama had the opportunity to speak up, a little at a time. Twice he asked them, "Are you after money?" and also, "How much do you want?" but neither question received a response. Nor was there a reply to his questions of "Where am I?" and "When will this end?" However, when he asked, "What day is it now, and what time?" a mechanical reply came back to him: "March twenty-fifth. 10:24 P.M." Shiroyama shivered from the joy of obtaining these sought-after, impersonal words, yet at the same time, he was dismayed to learn that a whole day had gone by, and he was dumbfounded as he suddenly recalled, in excruciating detail, the frail shoulders of his wife as she stood at the front door of his home in Sanno the previous morning, and the color of the cardigan she had worn.

What type of men were his captors? He tried to imagine them over and over, but he simply had no clue. Did they hold a grudge against the company, or against Shiroyama himself? Or was this a farsighted scheme that involved a greater design? Every time his thoughts branched out in search of an answer, they led nowhere—almost as if he had an automatic shutdown mechanism—and he became exhausted from the attempt.

Since he was given food to eat and felt no hunger, and there continued to be no threat to his wellbeing, Shiroyama acclimated mentally and physically to the humiliation, while his initial overwhelming knot of terror from the beginning splintered more specifically into anguish, bewilderment, and doubt. The hours stretched interminably into introspection and delusion, which descended upon him alongside the unbearable silence.

As he lay in the bed, whether awake or asleep, Shiroyama could not escape the feeling of being suffocated, and was forced to excavate the contents of his heart over and over again. His memories of wartime, roused for the first time in decades, were particularly troubling. What ought to have been vividly recollected fear was now a murky thicket, and he could no longer fathom the crux of it. When everyone had been starving, Shiroyama did not go hungry; he did not share in the misery experienced by children who remained in the city, too young to have been evacuated to the countryside. Instead he had hidden in a corner of the air raid shelter, his younger sister in his arms, coolly contemplating the death of his parents, and when he lived to see the end of the war, his family intact and reunited, what remained in his childhood heart was a jumble of unspeakable turmoil and remorse. Shiroyama now realized he had never told anyone about all this.

When his father had nagged him about not going to medical school, the eighteen-year-old Shiroyama told him only that he wasn't interested, without revealing the truth. As a student at the faculty of law, all of the classmates in his seminar had gone on to take the bar exam, but Shiroyama had known early on that he would not pursue a career in law either. What had that young and green twenty-two-year-old been thinking when he joined the corporate world after graduation? He felt he had no right to become a physician or a lawyer, professions that required a deep affection for humanity, but he figured he could take part in a capitalist economy, making a living by selling things and without having to answer to anyone. The fact that such arrogance had propelled him to take his first step as a member of society was a truth that no one beside himself knew.

Shiroyama was suited to corporate society, where sales were king and pursuit of profit ruled, and his life in business—thanks to the good fortune of coinciding with the period of rapid economic growth after the war, when sales volume practically grew on its own, and then continuing in an era when Hinode Lager was the first choice in beer, product appeal that led to the company's market dominance—had been smooth sailing for the most part. He had spared no effort in paying visits to loyal clients; toured retail shops, bars, and restaurants with their distributors' employees; handled everything from incidental tasks to consultations with precision; and in order to keep his pride in check he kept his attention keenly focused on the day-to-day figures—it was a time when, so long as he did all these things, his sales performance would without fail rise above that of his colleagues. His true sales skills, ingenuity, or creativity had never been called into question; he did not possess shrewdness, talent, or even so much as a striking character; and still, sales machine that he was—with no real understanding of the fundamentals of business—he had escalated through the ranks. Though confounded by the harsh reality and at the mercy of human resources and management, before he knew it he was sales manager, branch manager, manager of the beer division, and, finally, president.

To manufacture something, to sell it, to function as a company—what did all these things mean? He was well past forty before he finally began to consider the meaning of product appeal and sales acumen. It was around this time—with the second oil crisis in 1979 and the Plaza Accord of 1985 finally inflicting their tolls, and changes looming for the future of Japan's economy and society—when he had struggled to envision the prospects for the Japanese beer business, and privately he had started to lose confidence in himself. Yet the reason he could afford to lose himself in such leisurely concerns was precisely because, throughout the late seventies and early eighties, the strong economy and improving quality of civic life had sustained increasing beer sales.

It had been at that particular moment that Shiroyama had decided to reflect upon his personal misgivings, which were worthless to the company. When their share of the market had begun to slip as a result of their failure to adapt to shifts in consumer behavior and their late start in both the race for new products and the company's need for a structural shakeup, what had he done, as head of the beer division? Despite being aware of all the issues that needed to be handled, had he failed to summon the appropriate sense of crisis, being pressured by near-term sales figures and lacking the ability to propel the company forward? When this same man was then promoted to president in a personnel shuffle meant to shore up the beer division, he had sworn to himself that he would ensure shareholders' profit and employees' livelihood, now and in the future—such was his straightforward and clear sense of duty and responsibility as manager of the company. Had he not compensated for the creativity and volition he lacked with this notion of duty, he could never have taken on the role of president.

And when he considered what was necessary in order to fulfill his duty of securing the company's current and future profits, the answer had come to him easily. One solution was the radical reform of their production and distribution lines, as well as of the rigid structure endemic to a large company like Hinode; another solution was to cultivate their key products in order to strengthen their foundation. The future of the beer industry itself had plateaued, and if he hoped to bequeath Hinode's assets to the next century in which the ongoing contraction of domestic manufacturers was all but guaranteed, there was no choice but to diversify. In order to generate the capital needed to make such diversification a reality, he needed to create one more stable, lucrative product—a keystone as basic as miso or soy sauce. To bring a second Hinode lager out into the world—this had been Shiroyama's aspiration when he had taken over as president.

Those who believe there are limits to what beer can taste like should not participate in the development of the test product.

Shiroyama had spewed such histrionics three years ago January in his opening remarks at the meeting of the New Product Development Committee, which had assembled all the engineers and researchers from the beer division, as well as the executives from Product Planning. With the launch of a second Hinode lager as their goal, they quickly began narrowing down concepts based on analysis from a vast accumulation of market research. At the time, all of their competitors were focused on alleviating the bitterness of the hops; they had removed the astringency from the grain husk and improved the consistency of the carbonation, bringing out products known for their clarity and cool, crisp flavor. The results of their market research plainly showed that such light and clean "dry" beers would continue to be on trend, but the whole point of developing a second Hinode lager was to create a timeless product to be enjoyed for all time, impervious to the whims of the latest fad.

Ultimately, by taking into account Hinode's century-old penchant for the real thing—"the beer of all beers"—along with the shifting preferences of the era, they had narrowed it down to three concepts:

"Joy," for the blissful delight of drinking; "Levity," for the uplifting experience; and finally, "Serenity," for a drink that went down easy without being too heavy, too sharp, or too uncomplicated.

Next came the process of correlating these three concepts—joy, levity, and serenity—to specific flavors and aromas such as "light" and "bitter" on a chart, then conducting a series of sensory and taste tests to further substantiate the chart, and in the end a half a year was spent harnessing the vague idea of the flavor they hoped to achieve into a workable technology. At which point the trials began, but Shiroyama had ordered that the selection of the barley, the processing of the grains, the creation of the wort, the selection of the yeast, and the fermentation conditions all be reassessed from zero. The trial process—selecting the best yeast from among hundreds of varieties and fine-tuning myriad possible conditions during fermentation while checking the results of each—was akin to searching for an undiscovered one-horned beast on the immense African continent, or like reaching out and grabbing a cloud. Over the course of a year and a half, Shiroyama had visited the plant where the trials were taking place once a week, listened to each and every member of the development team, and whenever a prototype was ready he tested it with the executives from product planning and Sales, asking for their feedback.

Shiroyama's duty, as it was, had been to watch over, believe in, and entrust this difficult challenge to the thirty full-time engineers and fifteen full-time members of the product planning division, and to wait. This product eschewed the mainstream; its point was to pursue a lasting strategy in the beer business, whose long-range outlook remained uncertain, and to survive the structural shifts of Japanese society that awaited them in the future. As such, Shiroyama had concerns about how it would be received by the market. Moreover, the pursuit of a new product launch had not necessarily been the consensus of the board members. And yet, he held fast to his singular and indomitable ambition: to secure the future of Hinode—that the beer that had been consumed for the past half century would still be the beer of the next century.

Last February, when the development team came back with a sample product, saying they might have finally created a beer that came close to a unicorn, Shiroyama had assembled not only the executives but also the entire planning and sales divisions and had them participate in the tasting. At the time, everyone agreed that the beer "wasn't too heavy or too light, with a mellow body and a refreshing aftertaste," but they decided that its aroma had room for further improvement, especially if it were to live up to the concept of "levity." This time, Shiroyama lit a fire under the development team by setting a strict deadline and telling them to have a completed product by September; he also instructed Seigo Kurata, general manager of the beer division, to outline a strategy to sell fifty million cases in the first year, and set out to draft a product name as well as sales and marketing plans.

On schedule, as soon as September came around, the finished product was delivered to the executive conference room in an unlabeled brown glass bottle. After everyone had sampled the beer together, Shiroyama turned to the board members and asked, "What do you think?" A few of them nodded at first, and as soon as Sei'ichi Shirai sparked the initial comment, "It's delicious," the others followed one by one with "Such a fragrant, mild taste," and "The aroma is superb." After carefully ascertaining everyone's expression and tone of voice, Shiroyama made a call on the spot to the plant at the Kanagawa factory where the trials were taking place and consecutively thanked each and every engineer on the development team.

The entire staff of the beer division had spent the next six months immersed in preparations for the product launch. The product name had been finalized in November, but since the announcement of their new product was, after all, their biggest trade secret, they withheld the name and instead their salesmen ran around to each of their six hundred distributors across the country with a large bottle of the product sample in hand. Their reaction wasn't bad. At the annual New Year's gatherings of distributors held around the country, they had conducted tastings and laid the groundwork, publicizing the scale of their sales promotion that was planned ahead of the national launch on April 1st. Ordinarily, they would give a presentation of their new product at a distributors' conference and dive right into selling the product, but this time their strategy had been to arouse curiosity from both within and outside the company by taking such clandestine steps. As they built up the anticipation for April 1st, Shiroyama waited with bated breath for the numbers that were soon to arrive.

The beer division revised their order projections on a daily basis, and at the end of January when the orders started coming in at once, the numbers far exceeded their expectations, quickly climbing to 20 percent of their April target of six million cases. At the time, Shiroyama, alone in his office, had raised his hands in the air again and again in a solitary "Banzai!"

In preparation for the high-demand summer season, they had also decided to increase the production line for the new product in every factory by mid-February. At the same time they planned to rearrange their production lines, they also took initiatives toward their mid-term plans to both streamline and differentiate their products by discontinuing their regional products that competed with microbreweries, instead advancing their consignment production. Such steps were meant to pave the way for abandoning their multiproduct strategy, which Shiroyama had decided upon even before he took over as president. For the future, Hinode would have to transform itself into the trunk of a strong tree, trimmed of all unnecessary branches and leaves, with the Lager, Supreme, and their new product as its three main pillars. These last few days, Shiroyama had just begun to savor the feeling of taking the very first step toward the realization of his vision.

As he thought about Hinode Meister, the second lager he had dreamed about since he became president, Shiroyama's anguish briefly lessened, and a warmth filled his heart.

A Japanese beer for the 21st century. Introducing the Hinode Meister.

This was the copy that was to run across their full-page ad in the national newspapers tomorrow, Sunday the twenty-sixth. Their trademark seal of a phoenix, until now always golden, had this time been tinted azure blue to express a subtle vivacity, while the words "Hinode Meister" were rendered in a rounded, handwritten brush font that was majestic yet gentle, and colored indigo. The letters were set against an ecru background, slightly uneven, like the texture of handmade Japanese paper. The same design also adorned the canned beer.

Perhaps he would never see the product again, but the advertising campaign that had cost the sum total of five billion yen would go on, even without him. The disappearance of the president was an unforeseen internal crisis for the company, but there was nothing to stop the release of the product now. *I have done all that I could,* Shiroyama told himself over and over. *I have done all that I could for the future of the company.* But then he'd think, *And yet—*

Shiroyama could not imagine what effects an unexpected situation such as the abduction of its president would have on the operations of the company. Once the matter became known to the public, what was the extent of the damage—both tangible and intangible—that the company would suffer? What impact would it have on sales of the recently launched Hinode Meister?

*Ah, and the shareholder meeting is around the corner—*Just as this occurred to him, Shiroyama was thrown into a brief panic. No, at this very moment, the executives would surely be discussing which of the two vice presidents would take over in his place. Whether it would be Sei'ichi Shirai, manager of business development, or Seigo Kurata, manager of the beer division, who stood at the front was a significant issue within the company, but seen from a broader vantage point of the company's future, it did not seem to matter to Shiroyama. Part of him felt that Hinode's long-term course had already been set and that, no matter who assumed leadership, things would not change dramatically. On the other hand, he was hopeful and yet skeptical that if someone who possessed a more ingenious character—someone unlike him—were to take charge, he might be able to take control of the lumbering giant that was Hinode.

Shiroyama asked himself, when it came down to it, had he or had he not fulfilled his duty? With regard to his yearly responsibilities, his achievements clearly showed that he had met them, but what about the long-term obligation to stabilize and strengthen the management infrastructure of the company?

Shiroyama did not have confidence in this. He felt sure that Hinode Meister would meet their short-term goals, but who knew if it would really lay a solid foundation for the company in the coming century? Any mistakes he had made would become clear in half a year, but his success would only be evident half a century from now.

As he pondered such things, it seemed to Shiroyama that now, in this present moment, there wasn't much left of himself as an individual. Though he did not feel especially regretful, he came to the conclusion that his corporate life had been far from satisfying. And if he were asked about his development as a person, the fact was that he had never broken free from the impertinent worldview he had held at twenty-two, and even now he had still not repented for the original sin of self-doubt that he had committed at the age of eight.

It's all well and good for you to act blasé, but what are you going to do now that you've been kidnapped at your ripe old age? It seemed as if his life would be spared, but once the ransom was paid and he was released, how could he ever return to face the world again? As he quashed these reflections, which he had taken pains to collect in his mind, he came to the realization that, even if he were to survive, he would no longer have a place in society, and Shiroyama was again plunged into confusion.

SHIROYAMA WAS AWAKENED ABRUPTLY. THE quilt was torn away and he was made to sit directly on the tatami floor. The men made noises as they moved around him: the sound of the futon and blankets being shaken and patted down; the drone of a motor like that of a vacuum; footsteps back and forth on the tatami; and the sound of wastepaper being stuffed into a garbage bag. He figured that cleanup had begun.

After a while, with the vacuum still going in the background, one of the men sat back down in front of Shiroyama.

"Right now, it's 2:16 A.M. on Monday, March twenty-seventh. You'll be released soon." The man spoke slowly, as if he were reading something aloud. "I will now go over what you need to know. Listen carefully, and keep it all in mind. First, our demand is two billion. Hear that? Two billion in old, ten-thousand-yen notes. Cash."

The amount—two billion—did not immediately register. Reciting the number over and over in his mind, Shiroyama told himself that this, at last, was their ransom.

"Come up with a slush fund within one month, and wait for further instructions," the man's voice continued. "You will be released, so you take the lead in coming up with the money. You have one month to get the board to agree to it."

Shiroyama, weighed down by grave doubts, was jounced ever so slightly—both mentally and physically—by the word "released." He could not immediately grasp the motive of a captor who demands money after promising to release his hostage.

"Listen carefully. Our demand is two billion, but give the police a different story. Tell them that we demanded six hundred million, and that we will communicate the method of delivery to you later. Got it? You'll understand soon why you're telling them six hundred million instead of two billion. You're going to convince the police that first we demanded six hundred million, then we abandoned you and disappeared. It's for your own good."

The man paused as if to give Shiroyama time to reflect on this. Shiroyama was nothing if not confused after being told two billion, then six hundred million, then to lie to the police, but of one thing he was sure—that what was happening to him now was not a reckless unplanned crime. This just made the situation all the more eerie.

The man's voice droned on. "After all, you are the president, so you had better think carefully about whether to cooperate with the police investigation and destroy the company, or to pay us with the slush fund and save the company. Once we have the two billion, we promise not to make any further demands whatsoever. Our hostage is three point five million kiloliters of beer. If the money is not paid, the hostage will die. Got it? We'll be in touch before Golden Week. That's all."

The reason he had been kidnapped slowly became clear to Shiroyama. This was done in order to force the company to pay the kind of money that would have been impossible for an individual to pay. The kidnapping victim was not Shiroyama the president, but Hinode the beer itself. Shiroyama had only been detained so that he could reliably communicate their demands. These criminals were taking as their hostage beer that could be purchased anywhere, anytime, by anyone, and if their demands were not met, they intended to launch an attack on the product. As soon as he realized this, he envisioned a sinister shadow blotting out the azure phoenix of Hinode Meister, which was just about to line store shelves. His eyes and mouth were still covered, and without his being aware of it Shiroyama's teeth began to chatter, and he almost fainted in agony.

It took a while longer for Shiroyama to notice that the bonds around his ankles had been removed. His wrists were untied and then bound again with duct tape. He also felt a man's hand touch the front of his vest and his back, but Shiroyama could not tell what had been done to him. He was pulled to his feet but he could not walk right away, and he was practically carried away, his shoes put back on his feet. Then all at once there was a creaking sound, and a rush of cold outdoor air engulfed him.

Just as when he had been carried inside, snow fell from the tree branches, and he heard the sounds of footsteps crunching on ice or earth. However, this time the walk continued for a while longer. The ground was uneven, and whenever his feet caught on something and he stumbled, he was dragged up from under his arms. All around him the heavy reverberations of snow falling were overlapped by the sound of feet trampling over frozen earth, snow, and grass. He had no idea how far they had walked, but their early dawn march soon ended, and Shiroyama found himself standing on a flat road. He was then led by the arm and turned to face a particular direction, after which he heard the older man's voice.

"We'll release you here. Your attaché case is behind your heels. Take the duct tape from around your wrists and the blindfold off yourself. Once you take the blindfold off, you won't be able to see anything until your eyes adjust, but don't panic. Your vision will return after a little while. Until then, do not move from this spot. You are standing on a road. If you walk in the direction that your toes are pointing, you will find a fire station on your right. If you walk the opposite way, there are no houses. Follow the direction you're facing now. Do you understand?"

They left Shiroyama with these final words: "There is a photograph in the interior pocket of your jacket. Before you start walking, make sure you look at it. You'll have a lot to think about before you dash to the fire station."

After a brief pause, he heard the two men take off running. Their footsteps faded into the distance behind Shiroyama, until the soft echoes of a door opening and closing and an engine revving reached Shiroyama's ears.

Those noises were soon replaced by a near total silence that descended upon him like a force, and Shiroyama's knees buckled and he sank to the ground. He moved his bound wrists behind him furiously, and once he had ripped apart the duct tape, his unfettered hands slipped the ring of cloth around his eyes off his head. Unconsciously he jammed it into his pocket, along with the duct tape, without even taking the time to notice the material he now touched for the first time.

The muscles around his eyes, having been constricted for more than two days, hurt intensely, and though he was able to open them, his eyeballs had been under an abnormal amount of pressure and at first could not withstand the external stimulation. As he blinked his eyelids open and closed, his eyes and nose ran to ease the pain. In the meantime Shiroyama ripped off the duct tape covering his mouth. Touching his chin and cheeks, his frozen hands felt the coarseness of his beard, which had grown long; when his fingertips touched the deep hollows of his cheeks, he could hardly believe they belonged to his own face; and as he felt his hair, which stood on end and refused to let his fingers pass through, terror overcame him.

Once the viscous film that had covered his retina thinned out, what Shiroyama saw first was a uniform blackness. The blackness then started to mottle, until gradually parting to reveal the ground, the shadows of trees, and the sky. Covered in lingering snow, the contours along the shoulders of the road appeared a shimmering indigo, while the surface of the road where there was no snow gave off a wet, black luster. The trees hanging over either side of the road were jet black, and the sky spread above them was a faintly brighter indigo. There were no guardrails or signposts along the road, and the overlapping trees stretched on without end.

His attaché case was indeed behind his heels. He picked it up first and by the time he raised himself again on unsteady legs, Shiroyama had regained a sense of composure. Suddenly remembering, he searched the interior pocket of his jacket and produced a photograph, which he held up to the light reflecting off the snow. Initially he could not make out the standard-size snapshot, but as he continued to gaze at it his eyes adjusted to the darkness, and he was able to distinguish two small faces. Shiroyama held the photo closer and peered at the two faces, disbelieving his own eyes as he brought it even closer.

His niece, Yoshiko, and her little boy, Tetsushi, who had just turned two.

After confirming that much, Shiroyama tucked the photo back in his pocket and started walking. As his mind raced again, the incident from four and a half years ago came rushing back at him like a gust of wind, and then receded—*Oh, is that what this is all about?*

The blood was gradually pumping through his body, and he registered the cold again. His heart, instead of rupturing, diligently continued to pulse as his feet propelled him forward. Once he had walked a ways, Shiroyama stopped and took the photo out of his pocket again, then tore it into pieces with his hands. Taking care not to drop any of the shreds, he ripped it again and again into tiny fragments, then clutching them all in his palm, he ventured from the shoulder of the road into the grove of trees and, a few at a time, buried them in the grassy soil he dug up with the tip of his shoe.

Meanwhile, he carefully began to amend his previous thoughts about why he had been kidnapped. The criminals had not chosen him—the president of Hinode—because he would make their demands known most effectively. No, they'd chosen him because of his liability. They knew it would be impossible for him not to comply. Finally beginning to feel like himself again, Shiroyama understood his position all the more vividly. Now that a crime group had gotten hold of his family's scandal, taken the three and a half million kiloliters of beer—the lifeblood of his company—as hostage, and demanded two billion yen from him, how and where would he go back? After his imminent safe return, weren't the only choices left for him either to damage his company by making it pay an unwarranted sum of money, or to endanger the lives of his niece and her son?

No. What if I were to never return . . .

Shiroyama looked up at the naked tree branches jutting above his head, and as his heart suddenly began to throb unbearably fast, he asked himself, *You would die?* A part of him answered back that he had no other choice if he considered the extent of the suffering he would have to bear in the days ahead and the ruin he would bring upon others in his life, but his heart raged against the raw, unbridled terror of hanging himself. After struggling with that terrible tension for a few minutes, Shiroyama came to the conclusion that he did not have such courage in him. At the same time, another question arose, as if to serve as an excuse. *Are you willing to die for the company?*

It would be one thing if this were to cause the demise of the company and its eight thousand employees would be out in the cold, but was he really willing to die for a company to which, in reality, two billion in bribery money meant nothing? Did he truly see himself as so inseparable from the company? And if he were to kill himself and save the company from suffering the loss of two billion, would the company be grateful?

The answer to all of these questions was a definitive *No*.

After dismissing the necessity of his suicide, Shiroyama had drawn the vague conclusion that somehow he would have to make the company come up with two billion. Nothing was more important than the lives of Yoshiko and Tetsushi, of course, and even if he had dedicated thirty-six years of his life to it, the company was nothing more than a company. *Why should I end my life for them?* he went on muttering to himself.

Shiroyama then returned to the road and resumed walking. Although he had been released, this was only the beginning. The Kyosuke Shiroyama trying to convince himself of this fact was not the same Kyosuke Shiroyama as before he had been kidnapped—this was someone who was desperate to make the company pay out two billion in bribery money. And yet, that same someone was even now thinking about how best to alleviate the anxiety and turmoil of his employees as soon as possible and return the company to normal operations—that, for the time being, his duties were to make Hinode Meister a success and to strengthen the corporate foundation for the various reforms to come. Underneath such concerns, this new Shiroyama also raved with false bravado, *Why should I die for the company?* Uncertain which of these was his true self, Shiroyama's mind soon shifted to consider the mountain of actual problems he faced between now and the deadline he had been given, "before Golden Week," which began on April 29th. First of all, how would he handle the police? How would he explain it to the board? And how would he convince them to agree to two billion in illicit expenses?

While his mind had been spinning about such things, Shiroyama had forgotten to check his wristwatch and, as it were, he had no idea how far he had walked. Before he knew it, the dense shadows of the tree canopy over the road had thinned, and he saw a lonesome light in the distance. As he approached, he realized that the road he had been walking on met up with another road in a T-intersection, and on the corner to his right stood a small, concrete building. The compact fire truck parked in the garage, lit by the faint glow of dawn, appeared red as if it were blushing.

久保晴久　Haruhisa Kubo

"EVERYONE, YOUR ATTENTION, PLEASE!" THE cries of a clerk from Public Information bounced along the hallway of the ninth floor of the Tokyo Metropolitan Police Department. Her footsteps and voice drew closer to the kisha nooks of the Nanashakai, then traveled up and down the aisles in front of each paper's nook. "The CI director will hold a press conference! There will be a press conference!"

Haruhisa Kubo jumped off of his nook's sofa, where he had been sleeping, as another announcement blared from the wall speaker above his head. "All media, please assemble in the press conference hall immediately! The CI director will hold a press conference starting at 7:05 A.M.!" The ones who had been asleep on the bunk bed as well as those with their heads buried in their arms on the desk also woke with a start. From a corner of the nook, Chief Sugano murmured, "If the CI director's making an appearance, guess they found the president . . ." On the other side of the partition and in the aisles, brief speculations were exchanged. "Guess they found him," followed by "Think they've caught the guys who did it?"

"Kubo, Kuriyama, get going! The rest of you get on the phone with the news room! Kondo, you page the beat reporters on stakeout!" Sugano shouted out orders.

Kubo grabbed his notebook and was about to rush off when he saw that the junior reporter Yuichi Kuriyama—who must have been sleeping somewhere else all this time—had beaten him to his feet. "Wonder if they'll lift the embargo," Kuriyama said, eyes glimmering.

Though Kubo's body was heavy with exhaustion after all this time stuck in the kisha club without any news or developments, he still felt a reflexive tightening in his gut. This would be the twenty-ninth of the briefings that had been held every two hours since the incident occurred. The reporting battle would now commence. Had the president been found at last, without the demand for a ransom ever being delivered? Was he unharmed? Where was he found? What about the kidnappers?

The embedded newspaper and broadcast journalists, along with camera crews, flooded into the conference hall, everyone clamoring to get to the front. If the camera crews had been given the okay to shoot, then without a doubt the news was either that the president had been rescued or the situation had taken a turn for the worse. The Public Information director came striding into the hall, which was now packed with a phalanx of cameras and reporters from every media company. The director—the same character who just an hour ago had had bags under his eyes and whose voice had been full of gravel—had been resurrected. He called out at the top of his lungs, "Is everyone all set to start?" Then, instead of the director of Criminal Administration, who had taken over since the second briefing, CI Director Tsuyoshi Teraoka appeared again after a long absence. His expression remained inscrutable as always, but the tension in his shoulders was plain to see.

"We'll begin!" announced the Public Information director.

Teraoka opened with the usual "Ah, yes . . ." with which he prefaced every major announcement. His utterance was quickly obscured by the flurry of shutter clicks issuing from the cameras. The jittery heat emanating off the reporters, all gripping their pens and pencils, formed an invisible tide that surged toward the director.

"Ah, yes . . . A short time ago, at 6:28 A.M., the MPD received contact from the Yamanashi Prefectural Police Headquarters that they have taken custody of the victim in the present case, Kyosuke Shiroyama, fifty-eight years old, and we are currently confirming the details. The information we received is as follows. At 5:50 A.M. today, March twenty-seventh, at the fire station in the village of Narusawa, in the district of Minamitsuru, in Yamanashi Prefecture, known officially as the western branch office of the Kawaguchiko Fire Department, a man came in alone requesting assistance . . ."

At this point, a reporter from each broadcasting company stormed out of the hall, with the hastily scribbled name of the location in hand. The time was now 7:07 A.M. They had to immediately interrupt the on-air news broadcast with a special news bulletin.

Kubo, for his part, felt his hand that was gripping the pen turn sticky with sweat. When he heard the place names Minamitsuru and Narusawa, the first thing that came to mind was the foot of Mt. Fuji covered in deep snow, but the thought was soon replaced with surprise at the unexpected words, "a man came in alone," and he strained his ears to hear what came next.

"After receiving a call from the fire station, an employee from Fujiyoshida Police Department, part of Yamanashi Prefectural Police, arrived on the scene to confirm the individual's name and address, and once it became clear that the individual was in fact Kyosuke Shiroyama, fifty-eight years old, the president of Hinode Beer, he was taken into custody at 6:20 A.M. We've received word that Mr. Shiroyama is suffering from severe exhaustion, but that he is relatively calm, able to speak clearly, and there is no apparent injury to his person. As of 6:55 A.M., Mr. Shiroyama has been taken to Fujiyoshida Police Department. Several officers from Investigation Headquarters are already on their way to the scene, expected to arrive around eight. That is all for now."

Teraoka ended his remarks there. Even before he had read aloud the last line of his announcement, this time it was one reporter from each newspaper who stormed out of the hall. At *Toho*, Kuriyama was the one appointed this role. Whatever the circumstances, once the arena had been identified, the battle was to get their own reporter there even a minute before any of the other papers.

With sideways glances at the sea of reporters scrambling out of their seats, those remaining from each newspaper shifted promptly to questions. The PR director admonished the remaining camera crews, "Please refrain from shooting at this point!" but his cry was drowned out by the rush of reporters' voices.

"When you say Mr. Shiroyama came in alone requesting assistance, does that mean he was released by the kidnappers or did he escape?"

"We don't know yet."

"But he must have at least given an explanation to the fireman when he dashed in there, no?!"

"At this point, we don't have specific details."

"That's not a detail, it's the most crucial point!" This protest was ignored as another reporter interposed his own question.

"Where did Mr. Shiroyama say he had been during the last fifty-six hours?"

"We don't have an understanding of that at this time."

"What was Mr. Shiroyama wearing when he requested assistance?"

"A dark navy suit. Leather shoes. No necktie. Reportedly carrying a brown Burberry attaché case."

"What about what was inside the case or in his wallet? Was anything stolen?"

"We cannot confirm that."

"What were Mr. Shiroyama's first words when he dashed into the station?"

"We don't have the exact information yet. According to the report we received from the prefectural police, Mr. Shiroyama gave his name to the fireman on duty at the station and asked him to contact the police."

"And you're saying he was calm at the time?"

"We have not confirmed the assessments made by the prefectural police at this time."

"Did Mr. Shiroyama mention anything about whether the kidnappers made any demands of him?"

"At this time, we are not aware of such details."

"Was the region around Lake Kawaguchi included in your area of investigation?"

"That is related to our ongoing investigation, so we are not able to comment."

"Did Mr. Shiroyama himself say anything about the kidnappers? Appearance? Age?"

"We don't have an understanding at this time."

During this entire exchange, Director Teraoka kept his eyes downcast. Kubo sympathized with him—it was a natural reaction after suddenly learning that the victim had been rescued in another prefecture after all this time with barely any developments since the incident occurred—and yet, nothing of any import was yet clear. He couldn't write an article with this.

"Will the fact that there has been no ransom demand impact the direction of the ongoing investigation?" Kubo threw out his question.

"At this time, we have not reached such a decision." This was their brusque response.

"An abduction and unlawful confinement without a ransom makes no sense! You must be hiding something!"

"No, we are not. That's all we can say."

"When and where will you be interviewing Mr. Shiroyama about what happened?" came the angry shout from one of the reporters from a commercial broadcasting company.

"We haven't decided. First Mr. Shiroyama will receive a medical examination at the Fujiyoshida Police Department, then after determining whether he is well enough to travel to Tokyo, we will decide on the place and time."

"When will that be announced?!"

合田雄一郎　Yuichiro Goda

HALF AN HOUR EARLIER, AT 6:28 A.M., the police phone in Special Investigation headquarters had rung and the switchboard had connected them with the Yamanashi Prefectural Police, who informed them that the victim had been located and taken into custody. The seventy or so investigators who had been dozing here and there assembled in the conference room at once for a verbal briefing on the contents of the report from the prefectural police. Then, six members from Crime Scene and from Search were swiftly redirected to the on-scene investigation, along with the four members from SIT, who had been ordered to rush to the scene. Meanwhile, those from the Victim

Assistance Team busied themselves with contacting Hinode's main office and the team on standby at the scene, but there were no new orders for the Evidence Investigation Squad. Now that the victim was in protective custody, there were still a few hours before they would be able to take his formal statement, and the emergence of evidence, if any, would come later.

As the conference room began buzzing all at once, Yuichiro Goda stepped out and went to the lavatory on the third floor. The moment he heard that the victim had been found, his feet almost took off running without thinking, but the part of him that had instinctively reined himself back in had now taken control. Goda cleared his mind of all distractions as he carefully shaved with a disposable razor, and after washing his face twice with soap, he rolled his sleeves back down. He had gauchely been wearing the same shirt since Friday night, and the cuffs were a bit dirty.

As he left the lavatory, he ran into his colleague Inspector Anzai, whom he had not seen in three days and, with a bit of hesitation, Goda asked, "Find anything?" At the investigation meeting, there had been no mention whatsoever of corporate intrigue or extortion, and those on the fringes had no idea what was happening to the network surrounding Hinode. Frankly, Goda wanted to take anyone involved in investigating those areas, turn them upside down, and shake them until they gave up a clue.

"I'm looking into the National Tax Agency's audit files," Anzai whispered with a wry smile. "No doubt the MPD has a huge amount of information. Haven't hit any jackpots so far, though."

"You mean they haven't found any problematic expenditures?"

"Hinode's probably using some subsidiary or affiliate company that isn't directly tied to them, or even an overseas corporation, to deal with their accounts. If that's the case, we'll never find anything."

"I know there were a number of rumors about Hinode's ties to the Okada Association during the incident with Ogura Transport and Chunichi Mutual Bank, and also back when Mainichi Beer was exposed."

"There're no leads on Hinode. I've heard that at their company, instead of going through their general affairs division, one of the executives is the personal point of contact with Okada. Of course the whole company's in on it, but their finances check out completely, so as long as there are no internal leaks or whistle-blowers, nothing will come up."

"Is there any speculation that trouble has been brewing between Hinode and Okada?"

"Even if there were, the company would never say so. Besides, word is that this abduction and unlawful confinement case has nothing to do with that particular channel."

"It's not tied up with extortionists?"

"At the very least, they say that the twenty-five crime groups in the Kantō area as well as the seven in Kansai are in the clear. According to what I heard from Fourth Investigation, yesterday the chairman of the Seiwakai sent out a letter of inquiry to the trustees of the Kantō syndicate Hatsuka-kai to determine whether any of them are involved. Then again, that could also be a strategic move on their part."

"You don't say . . ."

"The point is nobody's got a clue so far. Don't tell anyone I told you." With that, Anzai disappeared into the bathroom. Goda had been the one who had asked, but he couldn't help but wonder if Anzai's vigilance had been dulled by dealing with run-of-the-mill white-collar crime for so many years. At a Special Investigation headquarters where confidentiality was paramount, his loose tongue could be dangerous. Goda calmly concluded then and there that it would be unwise to tap this guy for further information. Nevertheless, he was intrigued to learn that the underworld was not involved in the incident.

When he returned to the conference room, the seven o'clock news on the NHK had started, and people had formed a circle in front of the television. Goda craned his neck from the back of the crowd. On the screen, a photo of the victim appeared behind the news anchor, who was rapidly reading aloud from a script. The victim had the features of an obviously genteel upper-middle-aged man, but he also seemed to have a hard outer shell that would make it impossible to intuit his exact character at first or second glance.

"I repeat. On Friday, March twenty-fourth, around 10:05 P.M, the president of Hinode Beer, Kyosuke Shiroyama, fifty-eight years old, was abducted by an unidentified person or persons in front of his residence in Sanno Ni-chome, in the district of Ota, and just a short time ago, at 6:28 A.M., Mr. Shiroyama was taken into protective custody by the staff of Fujiyoshida Police Department of the Yamanashi Prefectural Police after he arrived alone, requesting assistance, at the fire station along the Lake Kawaguchi bypass in the village of Narusawa, in the district of Minamitsuru, in Yamanashi Prefecture. . . . We interrupt our regularly scheduled broadcast to bring you this report on the abduction and unlawful confinement of the president of Hinode Beer."

No one in front of the television uttered a single word. As the array of investigators expanded ever larger, they would have no choice but to depend on television and newspaper reports in order to gain a full picture of the incident that was not made available to each of them separately. Even Goda stared dumbfounded at the screen, as he wondered if it was too soon to show the face of the rescued victim he was desperately curious to see.

"I repeat. On Friday, March twenty-fourth, around 10:05 P.M, the president of Hinode Beer, Kyosuke Shiroyama, fifty-eight years old, was abducted by an unidentified person or persons in front of his residence in Sanno Ni-chome, in the district of Ota, and just a short time ago, after fifty-six hours, he was found unharmed and taken into protective custody in the village of Narusawa, in the district of Minamitsuru, in Yamanashi Prefecture. NHK has, until now, deferred reporting on the incident to ensure the safety of Mr. Shiroyama. Now, we go to our live coverage from outside of Hinode Beer's main office in Kita-Shinagawa, in the district of Shinagawa, and outside of Mr. Shiroyama's residence in Sanno Ni-chome, in the district of Ota . . ."

As the broadcast switched over, it showed the street in front of the forty-story Hinode Beer building. It was an ordinary building that he had seen numerous times before, but Goda's eyes were drawn to it as if noticing it for the first time. The reporter, looking intent, began speaking, while a press corps had already formed a cluster behind him. The wind seemed cold, but the sky was clear.

"Since it is still early, there's no sign of any employees coming or going just yet. Fifty-six hours ago, on Friday at 9:48 P.M., a company car with President Shiroyama inside left the entrance to the underground parking lot you can see over there, and arrived in front of his home in Sanno Ni-chome, in the district of Ota, seventeen minutes later at 10:05 P.M., where he was abducted by an unidentified person or persons . . ."

Next, the screen showed the street in front of the residence in Sanno Ni-chome, where a throng of media had already gathered. Barely a minute had elapsed since the press briefing and already lurking reporters from every media company had surrounded the front gate, where a uniformed police officer blocked the way. The trees sparkled in the early morning sunlight, worlds away from the landscape Goda had seen in the depths of the night on Friday.

"As you can see, this is a quiet residential street. At 10:05 P.M. on Friday, President Shiroyama's car stopped in front of that gate over there and . . ."

As he listened to the voice on television, once again Goda began to imagine the movements of the policeman who had patrolled the neighborhood on the night in question.

Late on Saturday night, after the investigation meeting ended, Goda had made up an excuse and snuck out of the police department, to see for himself how fast an officer on a motorcycle would have been going. He rode his own bicycle for two hours along the backstreets of the adjacent neighborhood Sanno Itchome, which wasn't all that close to Shiroyama's home. And last night, he secretly invited Senior Police Officer Sawaguchi from the police box in front of Omori Station out to dinner after his shift, treating him to sushi, and during the meal he inquired in detail about the route he took to the scene and the precise timing after he was dispatched there by the command center.

Once Goda had deduced the minute-by-minute locations of the motorcycle patrol and drawn up his own map, the results backed up his theory about how the perpetrators had abducted the victim without ever attracting the attention of the police. But how were the perpetrators able to trace the random patrol routes of the police?

The answer had to be the wireless radio. By now Goda was practically convinced that the perpetrators had ears on the department-level radio that the police listened to at all times. What's more, considering that it was impossible for an ordinary person to intercept the police radio, which further scrambled a traditional digital signal, it was clear who was listening to the radio to carry out the crime that night—a police officer on active duty.

A police officer.

The shape of the words appeared out of the haze that had permeated his mind ever since he had arrived at the crime scene. However, the solid logic of it prevented Goda's mind from proceeding further. He would have preferred to be unaware of it. In truth, Goda had already stopped thinking about it, simply and prudently shifting his brain to the allocated task before him. His ego no longer allowed him to make a disappointing mistake in a crime scene that was already disappointing enough—he wouldn't give anyone in the police force more reason to look down upon him. Besides, come April, he would turn thirty-six—what else could he do with his life if he were to quit being a detective?

Goda stepped away from the television and moved over to the corner of the conference room where the Evidence Investigation Squad had set up camp. Stacked on the table were copies of rental records submitted by various rental car companies within the metropolitan area and neighboring prefectures, and the list of stolen vehicles compiled by the Criminal Information Management System. They had finished going through the rental cars yesterday, but for the stolen vehicles they had to check each theft report one by one, and they were still in the midst of conducting further questioning with the owners of the cars for which the exact nature of the theft remained unclear. The number of stolen vehicles for which a theft report had been submitted, during the three months from January to March 24, totaled about 350.

When Goda picked up the list assigned to his team, the head of the ninth Violence unit, who was serving as their squad leader, said, "He might specify the model of car or color, so let's wait for the president's statement."

Goda agreed, so he returned the computer printouts in his hand to the table. With the victim now safe, the fact was that tracking down the vehicle no longer seemed as urgent a matter.

"They nabbed him on a Friday night and released him on Monday morning without even demanding a ransom. Gimme a break . . ." Goda heard someone say wearily.

"Bet these perps have day jobs with weekends off," quipped another. "If they have time to pull off a kidnapping over the weekend, things must be awfully slow at work," he went on, inciting laughter.

Goda, avoiding the banter his colleagues, sat down in a chair as he murmured to himself, *You're wrong. At least one of the members of the group does not have weekends off,* as his thoughts shifted back to the issue of the radio. On the night of the incident, whoever had been listening to the department-level radio and informed the abductors of the whereabouts of the police patrols in Sanno Ni-chome would most likely have been working the night shift. On March 24, the number of officers who had been on night duty at the nine police departments within the two areas including Omori Police Department could not have been more than 400. There were officers carrying department-level shortwave 101 transceivers, those on duty in the communications room, those inside patrol cars, and detectives on stakeout or on the trail who were carrying the wireless, and if an accomplice were among them, then it would be a cinch to narrow him down. *No,* Goda thought, *Crime Scene must already be investigating this very thread.*

Before disappointment could set in, Goda pushed this lead out of his mind—seems it would never see the light of day anyway—and he opened the morning paper out of boredom.

He remembered that Hinode's full-page ad had appeared yesterday in the Sunday national papers. *A Japanese beer for the 21st century. Introducing the Hinode Meister.* Even though their president had returned safely, if the incident itself were to drag on in some form or another, it could have an effect on the summertime sales war that had already launched. Goda picked up the financial report on Hinode that he had leafed through while waiting to be summoned to the CI room before dawn on Saturday, and now his eyes leisurely considered a single number—3.5 million kiloliters—which represented the company's annual sales volume of beer. *That's right, they may have released the president, but there is still the beer to bargain with,* the thought occurred to him.

Goda's mind then drifted back to several hours earlier, and he tried to recall what he had been doing before he had been called to the crime scene in Sanno Ni-chome. His efforts were in vain. Instead, realizing that Kano might have dropped by his apartment, which had been empty since Friday night, he took out his cell phone and quickly checked his answering machine at home. Sure enough, Kano had called.

"Right now, it's 10 P.M. on the twenty-sixth. I figure you won't be coming home for a while, so I checked in on the apartment. I'll lay out the money for the payment due at the end of the month. Give me a call when things settle down."

No big deal, should be home today, Goda thought as he put away his cell phone and glanced out the window. The press corps, which had been milling about since seven this morning, had become a swirl of footsteps and voices.

城山恭介　Kyosuke Shiroyama

SHIROYAMA NOW SAT IN A room inside the Fujiyoshida Police Department.

Ever since he had been taken into custody at the fire station, different people had materialized one after another, repeating a similar line of questioning—*Where did you start walking from? Was there anyone with you? Two people, you say? Men? Do you have any idea what they looked like or what their build was? Where were you with these two men? When did you realize you were alone?*—and when Shiroyama replied that he did not know, this time they spread out a map and started up again—*Is this the road you walked along? Where on the road exactly? How long were you walking?*

In the midst of the questioning, he was asked, "Would you like something to eat?" and all Shiroyama asked for was a single cup of tea. He did not feel any hunger, and the pain in his shoulders and elbows did not even seem like it was part of his own body. Once he had been moved over to the police department, he was given a simple physical checkup, and was surprised to find that there were five or six adhesive body warming patches on his body—on the abdomen of his vest, on his back, and along the waistband of his slacks—but there was no need to hide the truth about them, so he told the police that the criminals had stuck them on right before they released him. His necktie, the scraps of duct tape, and his own crumpled handkerchief, which had been used as a blindfold, also emerged from the pockets of his jacket. Those items were promptly collected by the white-glove-wearing department staff.

First Shiroyama asked if he could wash his face, and in the lavatory he did so for the first time in dozens of hours, but he was dumbstruck when he saw the change to his own reflection in the mirror. His salt and pepper hair, which was quite abundant for his age, looked much greyer than he remembered it. His eyes and cheeks were so sunken that water could have pooled there, and the wrinkles around the corners of his eyes and mouth had increased tenfold, all of which made him wonder who was this old man staring back at him. What struck him the most was how somber his eyes were. Looking into them, these eyes that did not register any sense of relief or happiness at being released from his captors, he felt a vague though deep-seated terror.

Shiroyama draped a blanket over himself and an electric heater was placed at his feet. Inside the room were three metal folding chairs and two desks, and the frosted glass on the iron-barred window prevented him from looking outside.

Shiroyama was not a criminal, but his present state of mind made him feel like one. Ever since he had stood outside the fire station, wondering what he should tell the police and how, once inside, he had stubbornly insisted, "I'm fine. Nothing's wrong with me. I can walk by myself. I'm not hurt," evading their questions of his whereabouts for the last fifty-six hours with ambiguous replies of "I don't know" and "I can't remember." Had his company received any demands from the criminals? If so, how were they handling them? How were they explaining things to the police? As long as he did not know those things, it was a given that he couldn't say anything imprudent to the police, but also the photo he had been given by the criminals upon his release suggested the possibility that the crime group could be connected to the Okada Association. Shiroyama wished he could clam himself up in a shell, but he could only obfuscate like this for a few more hours. Once a formal interview began, he would have to say something.

Shiroyama turned over and over in his mind the fact that, no matter which path he decided to take, he would end up lying to the police and to his company. He intended to conceal his family's scandal from both parties and somehow remedy the situation by bowing to the criminals' demands. He confirmed this with himself repeatedly. The trouble was, now that he had been rescued and was seated before the warmth of a heater, he had started to gravitate toward the idea that it would all be easier if he disclosed everything to the police. Each time Shiroyama reminded himself that as long as the Okada Association was involved, he could not expect anything from the police anyway, and admonished himself to stay calm and hold his ground. Shiroyama spent his brief respite in such internal conflict as he waited for the investigators from the Tokyo Metropolitan Police Department who were expected to arrive shortly.

At half past eight, four men appeared, saying they were from

MPD. Shiroyama greeted them with a bow and apologized for putting them to this trouble, but when he realized that the investigators were already scrutinizing his expression and demeanor, he felt a sudden chill and had to turn his eyes away.

The investigators confirmed his identity once more—Shiroyama repeated his legal domicile, current address, full name, age, and occupation. For his part, all Shiroyama could manage was to inquire about the wellbeing of his family. He was told that no harm had come to them.

Next, they asked him to undergo a more thorough medical examination by a physician before traveling back to Tokyo, and when he insisted that he was fine, that it wasn't necessary, they pushed back, saying, "Just in case." Even in that moment, he felt the piercing eyes of the investigators on him. Part of him wondered if such looks weren't just a hazard of their occupation, but on the other hand, Shiroyama had his own doubts and fears that the police suspected him of something, and for some time, he fell prey to speculating why this might be, growing ever more cautious.

The physician checked his eyes and the inside of his mouth, pressed a stethoscope to his chest, and took his blood pressure. After the physician announced that there were no significant problems and left, one of the investigators finally acknowledged the incident by saying, "You've been through quite an ordeal." Spoken in such a formulaic and unemotional tone, the words did not sound the least bit sympathetic.

"To get right to the point, do you have any idea who the kidnappers are?" an investigator asked.

"No," Shiroyama replied.

"You say you were blindfolded the entire time, meaning you did not see the perpetrators at all?"

"I did not."

"We will ask for more details later at Investigation Headquarters, but at this point in time, the perpetrators have not made any contact whatsoever with your family, either. However, there is no mistake that this is a premeditated crime, so whether it is financially motivated or has to do with some kind of grudge, we are currently doing our utmost to pursue an investigation of anyone with a connection to your company along those lines."

At the mention of anyone with a connection to his company, Shiroyama imagined how, in his absence, the police must have probed and pried into their business. Because of the risk management system they had installed last autumn, Hinode's firewalls were now stronger than that of other companies, which no doubt had raised the ire of the police.

"So you say you went along a path in the mountains with the perpetrators and they led you to the road. Did the perpetrators clearly state that they were releasing you before they left you and fled?"

"Yes, they did."

"Did they say why they were releasing you?"

"No."

"You couldn't see because of the blindfold, but right after the two men took off running, you heard the sound of a car starting on the road, correct? If that's the case, you could say that releasing you at dawn today was part of their plan, too."

There was no way for Shiroyama to speculate, but he was keenly aware that the police seemed to find the circumstances of his release suspicious. But then again, he assumed that such a healthy dose of skepticism from the police was a normal reaction when the victim of an extensive abduction plot returned two days later, unharmed. Besides, seeing as how he had decided to give into the criminals' demands, he had no other choice but to reply according to their instructions. And so he repeated to himself, *Yes, the criminals took off without giving a reason for releasing their hostage.* As long as he, the victim, maintained this as his testimony, the police should have no reason to dispute his words, at least for the time being.

After a long pause, the investigator started questioning him again. "By the way, did the perpetrators say why they had abducted and unlawfully confined you?"

"No."

The investigator increased his pressure. "Did they make any specific demands for money?"

The answer could be only yes or no. Shiroyama instinctively decided that it would seem unnatural for him to take his time responding, so he replied, "Yes, they did."

"How much did they ask for?"

"Six hundred million."

"Did they give instructions about how to deliver the money?"

"They said they would be in touch . . . I'm sorry, but I can't help but worry about what's happening at my company. Please let me see one of my employees so that I can confirm this hasn't affected our business. I can talk to you more after that."

Shiroyama attempted to deflect any further questioning as he scanned the thoughts racing through his mind, sparked by what he had just said. He wondered if it was really the right decision to follow the criminals' instructions and tell the police that the demand was six hundred million and that the criminals would be in touch with delivery instructions. The facts would soon be reported in the media, which would indicate to the criminals that Hinode was moving things along according to their demands. But was there any guarantee that this would indeed remedy the whole situation? Unfortunately that was nowhere to be found.

And yet, Shiroyama felt he had no other options. He had been able to console himself somewhat that for now there was no alternative other than to do as the criminals said—in order to avoid giving any worse of an impression to the police and the media, in order to assess the future moves of the criminals, and in order to buy the time he needed to formulate a plan of action for the company.

LED IN BY INVESTIGATORS SHORTLY before nine in the morning was none other than Seigo Kurata, who appeared with sunken, bloodshot eyes. He wore the same suit and tie that Shiroyama had seen him in on Friday night, and was carrying two cloth-wrapped bundles and a garment bag with a suit inside.

"We are so thankful for your assistance. I've brought over a change of clothes prepared by President Shiroyama's wife." Kurata gave a gracious bow to the investigators and then turned to Shiroyama, bowing even more deeply. "I cannot imagine the strain you've been through. I am so relieved that you are safe."

Shiroyama automatically rose from his chair and bowed in return. "As you can see I am fine. I am sorry to have caused so much concern."

With the investigators' attention focused on them, Kurata straightened up and let his eyes—besieged by both relief and anguish—rest for a fleeting, clandestine moment on Shiroyama's face. Shiroyama returned his gaze, conveying as best he could with only a look—*I understand.*

Shiroyama did not even have to imagine how Kurata felt, what went through his mind, and what his concerns were when he learned that Shiroyama had been abducted. Zenzo Tamaru, the advisor to the Okada Association, with whom Hinode had reached a settlement to sever all ties two years ago, had suddenly reappeared this year and had relentlessly hounded Hinode to purchase land meant for a mountain resort in the forests of Gunma Prefecture, and Kurata had been the one to bear the full brunt of these talks, adamantly refusing. Shiroyama had deliberated the issue repeatedly during his captivity, wondering if it were possibly related, but at the same time he denied it could be, assuming that the Okada Association, now firmly rooted in the political and business world, would hardly resort to such violent threats. However, between thinking of the photo of his niece and now seeing Kurata's expression, he struggled to maintain his composure as he began to wonder anew if this could in fact have to do with the resort property in Gunma Prefecture. For his part, Kurata still seemed to possess enough equanimity to behave discreetly before the investigators, for he now held both of Shiroyama's hands in his and uttered in an emotive voice, "You must have been so worried!

Everyone in your family is fine. Business is moving along as usual, and the orders have been coming in just fine this morning, so there's no need to worry."

"I see. Thank you, thank you so much," Shiroyama also answered in a discreet manner, but the tears that brimmed in his eyes were genuine.

"Well then, you can change now." Prompted by the investigator, Kurata began to unwrap the cloth bundle. The investigators made no motion to leave their seats, their eyes fixed upon the contents of the parcel. Kurata first handed Shiroyama a toothbrush, a razor, soap, a towel, a comb, and other sundry toiletries and said, "Perhaps you'd like to wash your face first."

One of the investigators immediately stood up and said, "The lavatory is this way." Shiroyama, it would seem, would be going in with an investigator watching over him. At this point Shiroyama finally realized that the police were trying to keep him from meeting with his employee alone.

But as soon as he entered the bathroom, Shiroyama understood why their precautions weren't so unreasonable. Inside the portable toothbrush case was a piece of paper folded to fit its exact size. Tucking the paper furtively into his left palm, Shiroyama finished brushing his teeth before moving on to shaving his beard. Then he went into one of the stalls where he unfolded the paper in his hand and saw the rows of tiny letters jotted in ballpoint pen on the thin, B5-size Japanese paper.

At the top of the note were the words, *ATTN: President Shiroyama.* It was signed by Kotani, who was their representative from the risk management company.

> *During your interview with the police, please bear the following points in mind:*
>
> *Express your willingness to cooperate fully with the investigation.*
>
> *In exchange, vehemently request that they prevent any information from leaking to the media.*

In the event we must comply with the criminals' monetary demands, regardless of their true intentions, be sure to give the impression that it is the company that is the blackmail target. Were the company to pay off a threat against an individual, it could be construed as a breach of trust.

At this point in time, when we cannot predict future developments, it is best to avoid giving detailed testimony during your first formal interview.

Please dispose of this paper once you have read it.

In the margin of the text was a message written in Kurata's handwriting: *No confirmation of O.'s involvement in the case. But chances high they will take advantage of the situation. Please take heed.* Even if the perpetrators were not connected to Okada, the results were the same. Shiroyama determined as much.

Shiroyama flushed the note along with some toilet paper, and exited the stall. Then, he washed his face, and once he had combed his seemingly greyer hair, which still stood on end, he became more or less presentable, despite looking like a different person from two and a half days earlier.

Next, Shiroyama returned to the same room and changed clothes in front of the investigators. His humiliation and patience had reached the limit, but thanks to the amount of tension he felt, by the time he had slid his arms through the sleeves of his brand-new dress shirt, Shiroyama had enough presence of mind to arrange administrative concerns in their appropriate order in his head. As he buttoned his shirt, he dictated a series of messages to Kurata.

"First, please send a fax to every branch and sales office, factory, and affiliated company apologizing for the trouble and telling them the president has returned safely, and so on. Then, before the end of the day, send a letter of apology under my name to shareholders and clients. Please have the executives and the branch and sales office managers divide amongst themselves and apologize in person at the headquarters and branch offices of our larger distributors. By the way, what is the status of the press conference we will hold as a company?"

"I wanted to see how you were doing first, but we've planned it for 10 A.M."

"Please tell them I'll be ready to hold my own press conference by the end of the day tomorrow. Make sure every division proceeds with their regular business without delay, and that they provide a report. The board meeting might have to be delayed, but I would like to hold a meeting during the day today with just the managing and executive directors working at the main office, so please set that up. And please let my secretary Ms. Nozaki know that if it gets too late she doesn't need to wait for me."

"I understand."

"And, my family—tell them I might be home a little late . . ."

"I will. Please don't worry about it."

Shiroyama put on a fresh tie and slipped on his jacket. Having cleaned up, he wasn't entirely back to himself, but he did finally feel able to take control of the vagaries of his emotions over the past three hours. The clothing Shiroyama had taken off would be seized and examined for residue, and an investigator filled out a form: "One white dress shirt, one wool vest," and so on. His briefcase was also taken away so that it could be tested for fingerprints, and then he was asked to write out his name and address and add a thumbprint to the form. He saw that under the column SUBMITTER'S PREFERENCE FOR ITEM HANDLING, someone had already written, *Please return.*

"Okay then, let's go." At this signal, the investigators escorted Shiroyama out of the room. Kurata shouted from behind Shiroyama, "There are cameras out there!" and as soon as he stepped outside the glass doors at the front entrance, the media descended on him. Television crews and newspaper reporters had surrounded the area around the covered driveway. The police department staff made an effort to hold them back, but it made no difference whatsoever from Shiroyama's point of view. For a few seconds Shiroyama stood before the sea of people surging toward him, stunned and frozen, as he looked at each and every anonymous face, male and female. At first he couldn't understand what they wanted, but when he heard Kurata murmur, "It's TV, bow to them," at last he snapped back to himself.

Shiroyama managed to bow once to the press corps, and then he climbed into the waiting car as prompted by the investigators, but just before the door closed he finally registered what some of the cries were. "How do you feel right now?" "What were you thinking about while you were being held?" "What is your opinion about Hinode Beer being targeted?"

How I feel right now, what I thought about while being held, my opinion about Hinode Beer being targeted . . . ?

Thinking that he had become confused all over again, Shiroyama buried himself in the backseat of the car and hung his head. The only thing he was sure about was that the situation in which he now found himself would not be so different if he were the culprit, and he had the vague realization that the reality he had been thrown into—the press corps before him just a part of it—was far from what he had imagined during his kidnapping.

根来史彰　Fumiaki Negoro

THE EARLY EDITION OF EVERY evening newspaper featured a full-banner headline, in huge print that leaped off the front page. *Toho News* had decided on HINODE BEER PRESIDENT FREED AFTER FIFTY-SIX HOURS, adding a vertical headline that read, LATE-NIGHT ABDUCTION AND CONFINEMENT, and running a panoramic photo of Shiroyama's residence that stretched across four columns. When the early editions came out, every paper merely reiterated the substance of the press conference verbatim, so the battle had yet to commence; nevertheless, articles and photos related to the Hinode incident were set to dominate the front page and the majority of the Metro page for the second and third editions, as well as most of the final fourth edition.

The time was now just before ten in the morning. Every television monitor on the news room floor flickered with the ongoing report from the commercial broadcasting company. Against the roaring whir of a helicopter, a shrill female reporter shouted, "The car with President Shiroyama inside has just passed the Sagamiko Interchange. In about forty minutes they will arrive at Omori Police Department, where the Investigation Headquarters is located!"

Tabe, leading the coverage as slot editor, hung up the direct line to the MPD kisha club and barked out orders. "Next press conference at twelve noon! Layout! Keep two columns open on the front page. We'll insert a document. Okamura, how are we doing with the expert comments? Negoro! I want another piece for the Metro page. What have you got?"

"A chronological history of corporate terrorism, a profile of the president, remarks about the president from other industry figures, previous arrests in incidents involving abduction and unlawful confinement, a list of lawsuits involving Hinode Beer, the commercial environment of the beer industry, Hinode's new product launch that occurred on the day of the incident, the corporate image of Hinode Beer judged by its popularity among new recruits . . ." Negoro randomly cataloged the possibilities as he leafed through the stack of drafts on his desk with his left hand. His right hand held the phone, a call with a reporter at their Hachioji branch that he had placed on hold, while one eye was still on the computer screen, where he had been taking notes.

"Let me see the drafts of that profile of the president and the remarks about him," Tabe said.

Negoro grabbed the article with his left hand and passed it to a reporter nearby, saying, "Give this to the slot," before returning to his call. "Sorry about that, please go on."

The reporter on the other end of the line continued. ". . . So, the talk of a land purchase came up in early 1940—apparently they signed a memorandum with the landowner—but in 1943 the whole thing was suddenly withdrawn, so the landowner filed a lawsuit. They later settled out of court, but I bet Hinode ended up paying them a little something. Anyway, that's the story."

The wall clock in the Metro section read 9:55 A.M. A half hour left before the deadline for the second edition.

Negoro typed up brief notes as he listened. *Lawsuit #10: Saitama prefecture. Land purchase memo for a factory, 1940. Fully withdrawn, 1943. Landowner sues, settles out of court. * Segregated buraku community. Still hard feelings?*

The reporter from Hachioji had previously worked out of the Urawa branch. He had called in after hearing about the local lawsuit from more than half a century ago by sheer chance from an acquaintance, someone from Saitama prefecture involved with the Buraku Liberation League who had seen a report about the Hinode president's abduction and unlawful confinement on television. "It's probably not a story worth digging up after all this time, but I'll keep you posted just in case," he said, and the short call from Hachioji ended there.

A legal altercation with a landowner involving a factory-site acquisition. Residents of a segregated buraku community revolting under threat of losing their tenant land. Condemnation.

Negoro took a few seconds to ruminate upon the key elements of this freshly delivered news item. The truth was, if he were to pick apart every single problem stemming from the ordinary enterprises of any company, plenty of issues would come up, and the likelihood of a connection between an incident from before the war and the present-day Hinode was small. But whether or not he understood its significance, this counted as information. Negoro's hands moved automatically as he saved the notes he had just taken in the file with the rest of the related lawsuits.

No sooner was the draft he had just passed to the slot back on his desk than Tabe yelled, "We'll go with the profile on the president. Cut it down to fifty lines!"

"Yes," Negoro raised a hand and replied, but when he looked around for the reserve reporter who had written said draft, the guy was nowhere to be found. Reluctantly, he grabbed the draft that had come back and started to make corrections himself when the television above his head blared out, "The Hinode Beer press conference seems to be starting. We'll switch over to our live coverage at Hinode's main office!"

Negoro's hand paused as he looked up. The screen showed two executives from Hinode Beer standing before several microphones and bowing so deeply that their foreheads almost touched the desk. One of them, a slim man with a tuft of gray hair at the crown of his head like a woodpecker, read from a script with eyes downcast. "I am Vice President Sei'ichi Shirai. I am grateful to the members of the media for gathering here today," he began. "On the evening of March twenty-fourth, under unexpected circumstances, Kyosuke Shiroyama, the president and CEO of our company, was abducted from outside of his home and held in confinement by unknown persons, but fortunately today we received word from the police early this morning that Shiroyama was unharmed and had been taken into protective custody in Yamanashi Prefecture. At this time, words cannot express our deepest apologies for the grave concern we have caused our shareholders, our clients and customers, and of course the public as well. To be embroiled in such a bewildering incident, as a company we feel nothing but confusion and embarrassment, but we are hoping for swift progress with the investigation and that the perpetrators will be soon be apprehended."

That the apology was addressed to their shareholders briefly caught Negoro's attention, but it was nothing new for this type of press conference. He returned to the draft, adding and pulling out quotes from other industry figures, hastily arranging the character of Kyosuke Shiroyama, president of Hinode Beer, in fifty lines. All the while, voices continued to fly around him, the murmuring tide of reporters looking for comments over the phone ebbed and flowed, and the direct line to the kisha club never stopped ringing. Once the news embargo ended, there had been a constant stream of calls, not only from the reporters at the kisha club but also from those who had fanned out to cover the areas surrounding the incident. What was more, there were related op-ed pieces to tweak before they went to print, articles that came back needing to be proofread, and finally the growing stack of drafts whose usefulness had yet to be determined, and under the mounting pressure Negoro's hands were moving incessantly. Though he was far from catching up, owing to long years of conditioning his mind managed to focus on each story as much as possible, organizing and grasping the crucial points. Was there a sure way to locate the heart of the matter, which may or may not even have existed somewhere in all this? Negoro didn't have much confidence.

"The lead on the extortionists doesn't seem to be turning up anything," muttered the junior reserve reporter sitting nearby. He held a cigarette in one hand and a paper coffee cup in the other.

Negoro brushed off the ash that had fallen right in front of him as he asked, "Says who?"

"The slot editor said so on the phone with the kisha club."

Amid the continuous ringing of the phone, someone yelled out, "I got the location! It's in Jukai, along the prefectural highway between Narusawa and Fujinomiya!"

Immediately, Tanaba began to shout, "Get a map! How far is it from the bypass? You have the location of the on-scene investigation team?"

More reports followed in quick succession. "Call from the club! The on-site team is at a resort. One of two properties located inside Jukai . . ."

"A correction from the Communications Bureau. The first character in the last name of the staff member from the fire station—they had it wrong."

"Layout! Hold off on the Metro page!" Tabe bellowed.

"Five more minutes!" came the reply from the layout desk. "Tabe-san, for Metro's headline, we're going for a horizontal, CORPORATE TERRORISM BARES ITS TEETH. Keep the front-page headline as is!"

In the midst of the hustle and bustle, the rim editor suddenly let out a sound and rushed toward the television, just as the screen switched over to an image of the president's family standing outside the front door of their home in Sanno Ni-chome. "Better get this down!" Several reporters pulled out notepads and ballpoint pens.

The young man leaning away from the onslaught of cameras and microphones looked nervous and confused, with a dash of anger mixed in. "I am Shiroyama's son. I apologize for the terrible concern this has caused . . . We have received word that our father is safe, and our family is so relieved . . ."

"Okamura! Cut two quotes and insert quotes from the son instead. Layout! Give me five more minutes for Metro. Negoro, the profile!"

On the television above his head, there was a cacophony of voices. "What word would you use to describe what your family went through during these fifty-six hours?" "There has been an uptick in attacks targeting corporate executives, but has the president ever spoken to your family about such matters?" "What were you doing when you found out that he was unharmed and had been taken into protective custody?" "A word about how your mother is doing?"

Negoro's red pencil moved mechanically back and forth over the page as he quickly counted the lines of the draft, now riddled with red marks indicating deletions, replacements, and corrections. "Give this to the slot." He handed the document to the reporter behind him, then looked back at the television screen and gazed upon the face of Shiroyama's son.

"I, uh, I don't . . ." The son had reluctantly started speaking, and for a brief second, Negoro saw his temple quiver as he glared sharply at the press corps.

"I don't want to disturb our neighbors any further, so please, if we could be excused for now . . ." With those words, just as his mouth twisted in a grimace, and perhaps to hide his expression, the son bent forward at a forty-five degree angle and bowed.

合田雄一郎　Yuichiro Goda

THE MORNING SUNLIGHT STREAMING THROUGH the train window fell across Goda's back. Having left Investigation Headquarters behind, the scent of the case quickly receded, and the only thing that lingered was an uncomfortable drowsiness.

"The president should arrive at Omori just after 10:30. I bet it'll be on TV," Goda said.

"What will?" asked the inspector from Crime Prevention who was with him.

"They'll show the face of Hinode Beer's president," Goda clarified.

"What about his face?"

"I just want to see his face in its natural state."

"Why?"

Goda was at somewhat of a loss to explain why. With each passing hour, the victim's external defenses would strengthen, he would wise up, and he would develop a new face. There were likely to be more opportunities to see Kyosuke Shiroyama at press conferences and such events, but by then he might look like a completely different person. Now, as he returned to Tokyo from Fujiyoshida, could be the last possible time to see his true face—that of a victim freshly embroiled in the incident, before the heap of emotions changed shape. The only chance to catch a glimpse of this version of his face would be when he arrived at Omori Police Department. Shiroyama's face was not material to the investigation, of course, and it wasn't even close to the level of what might have been encouraging—Goda simply wanted to see it for his own sake.

"Not everyday you get to gawk at the president of a trillion-yen company." Goda went for a noncommittal answer, and left it at that.

It was now 10:32 A.M. As soon as the train carrying Goda and his partner pulled into Tanashi Station on the Seibu Shinjuku Line, he was on his feet and running off ahead toward the south exit, in the opposite direction of the bus stop where they were going. Television screens in the train station and nearby cafes were dominated by news of the case, but since he'd been constantly on the move while he was doing legwork on stolen vehicles, it had been rather difficult to come across the desired broadcast at just the right time. Goda dashed into a private clinic not fifty meters from the station and stood before the television in the waiting room.

As he had expected, the commercial broadcast showed the press corps clustered outside the entrance of Omori Police Department. The president had not yet arrived. Goda sat down on an empty bench and jutted his neck out toward the TV, relieved that he'd still be able to get a look at his face, as long as the president came to the front door. Goda's partner walked in a moment later and took a seat next to him, the corners of his mouth twisting into a snicker. "Don't you feel sorry for yourself? Glued to the TV in a place like this?"

"I'd be sorrier if they didn't have a TV."

"You're a strange one."

His partner fell silent, and Goda stared at the screen.

The familiar scenery surrounding his police department—the elevated highway with the Dai-ichi Keihin and the string of office buildings beneath it—for Goda, this all symbolized suffocation, to put it plainly. His eyes were not necessarily focused on the press corps with their stepladders lined up in the street or on the stream of traffic along the Dai-ichi Keihin that every one of the cameras was trained upon. He had simply fallen into futile self-scrutiny, questioning his own existential purpose, as he wondered how his heart could go on beating so placidly despite this feeling of suffocation.

Except, in the depths of this suffocation, his gloom was a pool of lava, part of which was still molten, and every so often it would erupt out of nowhere. He told himself not to think about it but he couldn't help it, he tried not to expect anything and yet he still did, his legs moved on their own, his frustration mounted out of his control, until all of a sudden he was overwhelmed by strange desires, like laying eyes on the face of the victim. These impulses came over him with a fierceness he could not have imagined back when he was still at MPD, and at times he scared even himself.

After a few more minutes' wait, the press corps surrounding the entrance to the building began to swarm en masse, and the footage from the broadcast revealed the patrol car that appeared in the lead at the intersection opposite the police department, then the jet-black Toyota Crown that followed. The cameras began flashing at once. The image wobbled. A uniformed police officer obstructed half the screen, leaving visible only the roof of the car that had stopped in front of the entrance.

The car doors opened. The heads of three or four plainclothes policemen parted and a cap of silver hair appeared among them. He was taller than expected, with a small head. He shook it to the left and to the right, as if giving a little bow, and as he stepped onto the few meters of sidewalk, glimpses of his profile and torso flashed through the gaps within the crowd. Kyosuke Shiroyama was wearing a decidedly well-tailored dark gray suit with a golden brown necktie, and the collar of his brand new dress shirt was dazzlingly white. His short hair was parted on the side and appeared to have been combed. His face, visible a number of times, bore little trace of a victim who had just been released from fifty-six hours of captivity—like the rest of his appearance, it seemed to have been promptly scrubbed clean of any scent of the case. His cheeks were considerably more hollow, and his jaw more pointed, than in the photos, but Goda thought these looked different from the wounds of mind and body—like terror or exhaustion—that the victim of a crime usually suffered. Was his mind occupied with particular thoughts that made him seem either abstracted or resolute? At the very least, the physical effects of any fear experienced while he was held hostage seemed minimal.

Altogether it took no more than ten seconds for Goda to gaze upon Kyosuke Shiroyama's face and to imprint in his mind the man's meticulous appearance—which did not resemble the victim of a heinous crime—along with his expression, which could be interpreted as sincere as well as formidable. In particular, what caught Goda's eye was the steady look Shiroyama gave the surrounding horde of press and police, which reminded him of those company men who were occasionally arrested for financial crimes. At first, such men would use their triple layers of armor—corporate, civilian, and personal—to confront the judicial system. Shiroyama was in the position of a victim for the moment, but perhaps he had already predicted the eventual conflict of interests between the investigation and the company, for his face did not give the impression of someone who would be wholly dependent upon the police investigation.

With the press cameras chasing him, the police closed in around Shiroyama and they disappeared swiftly behind the doors. Goda stood up from the bench.

"So? What's your opinion now that you've eyeballed him?" his partner quizzed him.

"Looks like a tough one to crack," Goda replied.

"He's making backroom deals, that's what I see on his face," his partner remarked, but Goda's ruminations had stopped short of such a judgment, and he could neither agree nor disagree. Since he knew next to nothing about the corporate society to which a great many Japanese people belonged, upon further reflection, Goda did not feel confident that his eye could accurately appraise the expression of the president of a huge company like Hinode Beer. And now, having gone out of his way to duck into this random clinic just to glimpse the face of a victim of abduction and unlawful confinement, his only true impression was a renewed sense of suffocation at the constrains of his own life.

Goda went along with his partner back to the bus stop at the north exit of the station and waited for the bus. The subject of their inquiry this morning was a resident of the Hibarigaoka public housing complex whom they had been unable to reach. The license plate of the van for which said resident had filed a stolen vehicle report one month ago had been found affixed to a different-make van that was listed as an abandoned vehicle in Kita City two weeks earlier. While the precinct had attempted to locate the owner of the abandoned vehicle with the switched license plate, that van also disappeared without a trace. Both of those cars were white, unlike the dark-colored vehicle that had been witnessed in the alley near the scene of the crime.

"By the way, Goda-san. Did you have a secret chat with old man Anzai outside the third-floor bathroom?"

As his partner mumbled this question, Goda felt a sudden irritation at being checked up on, and he spat out, "You jealous?"

"The guys from MPD's Second Investigation were watching you two from the stairway, you know. Word is Anzai's older brother is a lawyer in Fukushima and a card-carrying member of the Japanese Communist Party," whispered his partner.

Hearing this, Goda could now understand why Inspector Anzai had to pay his dues on the lower rungs of an anti-communist organization like the police force, but the person whom Goda felt wary of was not Anzai but his own partner, who had gotten wind of this Japanese Communist Party chatter from who knows where.

Goda looked at his partner and mustered a bitter laugh. "Makes me wonder just what our organization is doing . . ."

"Ain't that the truth." His partner shrugged with an equally forced laugh and then yawned.

Goda looked away, summoning what little patience he had left as he tried to figure out who was in the wrong. By now, the select members of SIT and Second Investigation at the center of the case must be sharpening their minds to a razor focus to grasp every detail of the incident, and while those on the fringes like him and his partner stood here yawning, still others were engaged in a game of collusion that had nothing to do with to the crime itself.

久保晴久　Haruhisa Kubo

AS HE SILENCED THE BEEPING of the pager on his hip with his left hand, Haruhisa Kubo noted the time on his wristwatch first—11:51 A.M.—then looked at the number displayed on the LCD of his pager. The person was calling from a private cell phone. His colleagues on either side stole a glance his way.

Kubo hoped that the call would take no more than a minute and, setting aside his unfinished draft for the third edition, he picked up the receiver for the outside line. "Takeuchi-san? This is Kubo," he said when the call went through.

"You guys must have it rough over there, too." Takeuchi's tone was somewhat leisurely. Takeuchi was from Marunouchi Police Department, and a police beat reporter and his source were not on equal ground, which always made it a little difficult for them to be on the same wavelength. Even without bridging that gap, though, it was second nature—an unconditioned response—for the reporter to answer a call from a source.

Glaring at the clock, Kubo's irritation mounted. Restlessness crept into his voice as he responded, "Yeah, I guess," so he forced himself to sound calmer. "Thanks for calling. Where are you now?"

"Out making the rounds," Takeuchi said. "I was watching TV this morning. Kubo-san, Saturday night on the phone, you asked if there was anything worth checking out in corporate relations. A younger colleague of mine used to work in records for CID at Shinagawa Police Department up until two years ago . . ."

"Oh, that sounds promising. I can accommodate his schedule—please set it up."

"The name's Kitagawa. He's an assistant inspector now at Fukagawa Police Department. Apparently there was an incident with Hinode a few years back."

Just hearing that Hinode might have been involved in something made his voice rise with eagerness. "That's fantastic, thanks for introducing me!"

"Who knows if it'll be useful, but the earlier the better for you, right? I'll reach out to Kitagawa and call you back this afternoon. You said it's best to call after two?"

"Yes, thanks again for everything. I'll wait to hear from you."

"Fine. Later then."

At this early stage, a reporter had no right or reason to criticize the content of the information supplied by a source. That unequal ground on which they stood often meant they were focused on different things, too, but the content was best judged once it was in hand, and until then his priority was to take the call, keep alert, remember to breathe, and then pounce on any lead that came his way.

"Hey, there's Yamada. Look, that's our guy!" Kagawa, the deputy chief reporter, shouted from the desk behind Kubo. At some point the commercial broadcast's live coverage had switched over to show the press corps that had gathered along the highway in Jukai, where the search continued for the location where the victim had been held hostage. Kubo glanced briefly at the television. The screen showed a reserve reporter named Yamada standing in front of a road closure, stamping his feet, his shoulders hunched. At his feet the snow had melted to a dirty slush.

"Wonder if we'll get it in time . . ." murmured Chief Reporter Sugano as he looked askance at the television.

It had been two hours since the forty-some investigators from both the local Fujiyoshida Police Department and the Tokyo Metropolitan Police Department had begun searching the resort area that appeared to be where the victim had been held hostage. There were two such locales that could be accessed from the highway in Jukai, and both consisted of narrow roads that cut through over 800 acres of backwoods, and were dotted with vacation homes big and small. There was hardly a soul to be found there during this season but, according to reporters on the scene, the snow that had fallen three days ago had already melted—any tire tracks along with it—and the fresh snow from last night had frozen over, so the search for footwear impressions and tread marks was probably slow going. It was only a matter of time before the location would be discovered—the question was whether or not this would happen before the deadline for the final edition of the evening newspaper. For the advance article Kubo was working on, so far he had typed: *The location where the victim was held hostage has been identified as a residence in the resort area of XX, at [XX address], and the on-scene investigation is in progress,* leaving four lines for further description after the words, *The location was . . .*

The time was now 11:53 A.M. Kubo turned back to his work on the draft, which had been interrupted, and recounted the number of lines in the last paragraph.

> . . . *With the victim safely in protective custody, yet neither the objective nor motive of the perpetrators known, Investigation Headquarters increased the number of investigators to three hundred, who are dedicated to a thorough inquiry and are gathering information from eyewitnesses. In addition, Hinode Beer held a press conference at their main office at 10 A.M., during which Vice President Sei'ichi Shirai, looking visibly relieved, recounted the details of the incident, and expressed their consternation at being the target of such an unimaginable and heinous crime, as well as their acute outrage toward the perpetrators.*

This would add thirteen lines to what had appeared in the second edition. Kubo was unsure about the clause, "yet neither the objective nor the motive of the perpetrators known." Was it worded too strongly? Did it betray his personal feelings, that the explanation of the victim's release was unsatisfactory? *To hell with it,* he thought as he deleted it and rewrote the beginning of the paragraph as, *Now that President Shiroyama is reportedly safe in protective custody . . .* Then he considered the phrase, "acute outrage toward the perpetrators." He tried to recall whether the vice president who had appeared at the press conference had really sounded all that outraged and, deciding it didn't matter either way, he also scrapped the word "acute."

For the second-edition draft he had submitted an hour and a half ago, he had barely managed to insert the facts and format them into the semblance of an article, but from the looks of it he would not have anything significant to add for the third edition, and this irritated Kubo as he continued to type. Over the last two and a half days, he had been calling every single one of his dozen sources, but his contacts at Special Investigation headquarters remained even more tight-lipped than usual. Meanwhile, thanks to strict confidentiality this time, his sources who did not have any connection to headquarters received no information whatsoever regarding the investigation, and as a result no story reached Kubo from them, either.

What would be revealed in the noon press conference that would start in three minutes? The course of events from abduction to release. The victim's condition when held hostage. What the crime group had said and done. Whether or not there was a ransom demand. Any clue that could lead to the perpetrators' profile. If only he knew these things, he'd be able to fill up the third and the final evening editions, but the real problem was the next morning's edition and every one after that. As he anxiously wondered what the hell he would do tomorrow if he didn't get his hands on a lead—any lead—Kubo looked at the clock and then, leaving the blank spaces in his draft for the time being, he got up from his desk. Next to him, Kuriyama was hastily laying out a document with a timetable, leaving various parts of the main text empty, while deep in conversation with someone on an outside line; and beside Kuriyama was their junior colleague Kondo, who was constitutionally unfit for these journalistic battles that required him to hit the ground running without even thinking, looking as if he might actually burst into tears as he silently dialed a number on the phone. Kubo called out to these two as well as to Chief Sugano, "I'm going to the press conference," and he left the nook.

Kubo knew he ought to lend a helping hand to his younger colleague, but despite this inclination, he could never afford to do so. For the two years since he'd been moved to the MPD beat from the Sendai branch office—every second of every day—Kubo couldn't shake the obsessive feeling that he himself was falling one, then two steps behind his competitors. Or rather, like he was in a permanent and unmanageable state of excitement. Even during the ten or so seconds it took him to walk to the press conference hall, Kubo realized that still, after all this time, he felt buoyed with excitement, and he wallowed for a while in this mild discomfort. When he had no story, he became excited even as he felt anxious, and chasing leads was so stimulating that in the end he lost track of what he was even doing. The truth was that, night and day, his mind was consumed with chasing stories.

News of the victim's safe return would ordinarily have resulted in the disclosure of information related to the investigation that had yet to be made public, but that seemed unlikely this time. The fact that the hostage had suddenly been released after fifty-six hours of captivity led him to assume that either a ransom had been secretly paid out or there had been some kind of backroom deal, but it was next to impossible to back up such speculations. While the investigation would inevitably drag on, the beer company and the police were likely to become only more tight-lipped.

Under such circumstances, Kubo grew even more anxious that if he did not find a story—no matter how small—one of the other papers would beat him to the punch, and in his mind he ran through the interviews he had planned for the day, after filing his draft for the final edition. For now, he would wait to decide on whom to chase down, depending on the contents of the imminent press conference, and he would call a few of his sources. There would also be the call from his guy at Marunouchi Police Department after 2 P.M. If he had time after that, he would stop by the Metro desk at *Toho*'s main office—only a five-minute walk from MPD—where he might pick up a few details while making small talk, and his night entailed wining and dining his sources while fishing for leads. Then there'd be the evening interview session.

As these last thoughts occurred to him, Kubo drew to one side of the hallway, furtively taking out his wallet to check that there was about a hundred thousand yen in it. Some of his sources liked to drink at bars that did not accept credit cards. Putting his wallet back in his pocket, Kubo dashed into the press conference hall.

根来史彰　Fumiaki Negoro

"SIX HUNDRED MILLION! SIX HUNDRED million!" shouted the slot editor Kei'ichi Tabe, the phone receiver in one hand. "The perps demanded six hundred million!"

The news room floor stirred for a moment, then someone from the layout desk cried out, "Six hundred million? You sure? Then we'll go with SIX HUNDRED MILLION DEMANDED as the front-page headline!"

"Have they paid that yet, or not?" asked another.

"The perps told Hinode's president they'd be in touch, then they let him go—" Tabe shouted back.

Fumiaki Negoro looked up at the wall clock, which showed 1:15 P.M. His hand paused on the corrections he was making to the draft of an article and he promptly began rifling through the heap of articles for the Metro page before him. The nuance of many of these articles would change now that a monetary demand had become clear. Notwithstanding suspicions about backroom deals, any mention along the lines of the "perpetrators' motives remain unknown" had to be either deleted or replaced.

First, on the chronological list of incidents of corporate terrorism, "Abduction and Unlawful Confinement of Hinode Beer President" would have to be changed to "Kidnapping for Ransom." Next, he needed to check or swap out comments from experts and sources in the financial and liquor industries and Hinode's rival companies. Some statements were difficult to give the axe to, and for those he'd hand the article to one of the reserve reporters hanging around and have them call the source to reconfirm. Now, the chronology of the incident in relation to Hinode should be okay as it was; the profile on the company president as well. Also fine was the testimony from the staff member of the fire department at the foot of Mt. Fuji who told the press corps, "When he told me he was the president of Hinode Beer and asked me to alert the police, his words and expression were so clear and resolute—I could scarcely believe it. I never would have imagined that this person had been held against his will in the mountains for dozens of hours."

Even as Negoro continued revising, putting in calls to the respective reporters and making the corrections himself, follow-up items from the kisha club were zinging past his desk and the phone was ringing off the hook with calls from reporters out in the field dictating their stories. Time was running out—reporters in the Reserve and slot editor's section typed furiously as they improvised articles on their computers, phone receivers tucked between their shoulders and ears—calling to mind the scene in the Kabuki drama *Kanjincho*, when Benkei contrives to recite from what is, in fact, a blank scroll. The time was now 1:25 P.M.

"There were six adhesive body warm patches, not five. Fix it."

"His mouth was taped with duct tape. His blindfold was a hand-kerchief, the president's own!"

Amid the whirl of such cries, someone handed Negoro an item that had come in from the deputy chief reporter to check. Negoro's eyes flitted over the draft, which read: *Food supplied to the victim at the hideout included six rice balls, four pastry buns, two bananas, three mandarin oranges, two blocks of processed cheese, and two cans of pork and beans. In addition, they gave him paper cartons of oolong tea, orange juice, and fruit-flavored milk . . .*

"We have the address of the hideout!" someone shouted.

"Fuji Village, number twelve. A vacation home, single story, a bit more than five hundred thirty square feet. Owner's name is Takeji Sasamoto. The place is in shambles, hasn't been used for years. Electric, gas, water have all been turned off. A police dog detected the place by scent. Fingerprints and footwear impressions are forthcoming—"

"Matsuoka! Add what you just heard to your article. Yamane, you contact the owner. Layout, hold off on the Metro page! Negoro, I need that draft now, quick!"

"Hurry it up!" Layout replied with typical urgency.

An abandoned, snowbound vacation home with no one around, Negoro thought. For a brief moment he tried to imagine the house that served as the hideout, but his eyes were already racing after the wording "they gave him paper cartons of oolong, tea, orange juice, and fruit-flavored milk." No sooner had his hand automatically changed "they gave him" to "he was given," he passed back the draft, saying, "Give this to the slot." It wasn't until after he had handed it off that his mind finally made the connections—the six heat patches; the details about the food; the reason the victim had appeared so calm when he arrived at the fire station; why, at the Fujiyoshida Police Department, when asked if he wanted anything to eat, he had requested only a cup of hot tea—but it was too late.

Negoro glanced over at his colleagues in the Reserve section. Then, after checking the pile of paper on his desk to make sure there were no stray drafts, he went ahead and let out a deep sigh of relief from his seat. The clock on the wall read 1:32 P.M.

HAVING FILED THEIR ARTICLES, THE reporters were beginning to stretch and quietly drift away from their desks. The slot editor announced, "There'll be a five-minute meeting at one fifty-five!" Negoro sipped an oolong tea—his third of the day—from the vending machine and bit into a piece of dried sour kelp from the stash he kept in his desk drawer. He had been glued to his seat since the incident occurred, and his lower back felt heavy. He didn't have the luxury of taking a walk to clear his mind, though the younger fellows had already disappeared, using the brief window to make personal calls to their sources or take a break, leaving the Reserve section completely empty.

Negoro knew the evening edition that had just gone to press would be the last time they got away with inconsequential factoids such as orange juice and fruit-flavored milk. Starting with tomorrow's morning edition, their pages would have to zero in on the truth behind the incident. More than anything, there was the mystery of why the crime group had suddenly released their hostage while demanding six hundred million in ransom. In the meeting that was about to begin, no doubt the Metro chief would ask, "So, Negoro, what do you think?" Just how would he respond?

For now, it was certain that this crime had targeted the Hinode Beer corporation. Since Negoro was in charge of feature articles, his first task was to gather a wide range of reactions and testimonies from the main player and victim—Hinode—as well as from those connected to the organization. Follow-up stories spanning the public and private life of the individual victim, Kyosuke Shiroyama, were also crucial. Since the victim had returned unharmed, another option would be to double down on covering the peripherals of the incident—depending on how the investigation developed. For instance, he could run a three-part series about why the CEO had been targeted. The first installment would list kidnapping cases involving executives of Western companies. The second installment would cover how Japanese companies, in the context of the current economic stagnation and stalled structural development within industries, have detected and responded to various corporate risks, and so on.

But there was a limit to how many features he could run on the topic of corporations. There had to be a reason the perpetrators had chosen Hinode from among the multitudes of major companies. No doubt backroom deals had been made, but the persons in question would never admit anything, and if the police did not formally release the information, he could not write about it anyway. From his position at the helm of the Metro page, he knew they had no choice but to wait for a criminal profile on the perpetrators to become a little clearer. If nothing emerged, coverage of the impending elections would supersede articles about the incident, forcing them back to the drawing board.

He mulled over such things as he bit into another piece of kelp. Just then he saw a light on the phone blink, signaling an incoming call on the outside line, and he reached for the receiver.

"Metro," he answered. His eye caught the wall clock. 1:39 P.M.

"Is Takeshi Kikuchi-san there?" A man who sounded like he was in his sixties or seventies, his voice muffled with a thick Kansai accent.

In that instant, Negoro managed to rouse his rusty instincts as an investigative reporter, and he pressed the receiver to his ear. "May I ask who's calling?"

"Name's Toda. Wanna talk to Kikuchi-san. Go get him."

A person in whom, in various ways, very little patience remained. Either he had given up on society or had never trusted it in the first place—whichever the reason, there was a sense of arrogance, or perhaps it was despair, in the way he refused to even bother speaking in complete sentences. A life lived in defiance. Negoro's imagination spun out in a conditioned reflex. Nevertheless, he was sure that the speaker on the other end of the line was not an underworld character—distinguishable by a subtle difference in his tone.

"I'm sorry, but Takeshi Kikuchi works for the Metro section of the Osaka bureau. Perhaps I can help you instead? My name is Negoro, I work in the Metro section here."

"If Kikuchi-san's not there, then who's responsible for writing that article about the Ogura Transport and Chunichi Mutual Bank scandal? Get me that guy."

Ogura Transport. Chunichi Mutual Bank. Hearing these two names struck something of a chord with Negoro. Back in 1990, Negoro, who had been working out of the courthouse kisha club at the time, had snagged a lead from a source at the public prosecutor's that a big-shot politico and an ultranationalist were behind the uproar over the founding clan of Chunichi Mutual Bank's transferring their shares over to a third party. However, a year went by and Negoro had been unable to get any traction on the lead. In 1991 came the announcement that Toei Bank, a major city bank, was to absorb Chunichi Mutual. By that time Negoro had moved on to a different beat. When a leak from the public prosecutor finally brought to light the so-called "S. Memo" scandal—a former Minister of Finance had reportedly promised to support Toei's bailout of Chunichi Mutual Bank, with a big-time ultranationalist playing go-between—Negoro figured that a police investigation would finally excavate the crime. But in the end, the scandal concluded with a group of corporate raiders and the executives at Ogura Transport being charged with malfeasance. Negoro still carried a vivid memory of his regret at not being able to dig deeper into the story.

Negoro swiftly racked his brain, looking for an immediate response. It was unlikely that this guy Toda, calling the Metro section of *Toho News* now, would have contacted Takeshi Kikuchi back then about the scandal. Kikuchi had always worked for the Osaka bureau; even though he had been transferred to the Tokyo Metro section in the late '80s, he had returned to Osaka by 1990, and so he had never been part of the reporting team for the Ogura Transport and Chunichi Mutual Bank Scandal, which broke the following year.

So the guy on the phone and Kikuchi must have come into contact earlier, on a different case. Or perhaps, like Negoro, Kikuchi had sniffed out the story on Ogura and Chunichi early on while he was still in Tokyo and had been sleuthing around for information. But Negoro had no personal relationship with Kikuchi, thus he had no way of knowing which might be the case.

"Back then our slot editors rotated being in charge," Negoro offered a lie for the time being. "If this is about Ogura Transport and Chunichi Mutual Bank, I was also on the reporting team so I may be able to help you."

Negoro could feel the caller hesitating for a second or two on the other end. "Just so you know, I'm not leaking this for money," the man said. Following, unexpectedly, with "This is about Hinode."

"Yes?"

"I'll tell you what kind of company Hinode is. If you were on the reporting team you might have heard this already. In 1990, when Chunichi Mutual Bank was busy trying to buy back the shares that had fallen into the hands of a third party, the Chunichi president Akita went to Hinode asking for a large deposit. That was January tenth, 1990. But Hinode didn't agree to it. Remember, the date of the S. Memo was February seventeenth. After Akita secured the memo, in late February he sent a letter to the Ministry of Finance saying that Chunichi Bank could be rehabilitated. By the way, on February sixteenth—the day before the S. Memo—Terata, the president of Toei; Suzuki, the chairman of Hinode; and 'S.' from the Liberal Democratic Party met up at the Hotel Okura. The special investigation section must also know about this meeting on the sixteenth."

"I see."

Negoro had instinctively grabbed a ballpoint pen and was dashing all this down, running back through his memory to confirm to himself that there was no mention in his reporter's notebook of the meeting at the Hotel Okura back on February 16, 1990.

The gloomy voice on the phone droned on. "And here's the important part. At that meeting on the sixteenth, it was agreed that Hinode would absorb Ogura Transport and that it would guarantee part of Ogura's bad debt, which Chunichi Mutual Bank had been carrying. Point is, this was a sham negotiation, based on the prereqs that came out in the S. memo."

"Was Hinode confident about Chunichi's recovery when it joined the negotiations?"

"I've got no idea if Hinode was in on it all along. In order to save face for S. and make Chunichi's fraudulent loan to Ogura Transport look plausible, Hinode had to, as they agreed, at least appear to make an effort to bail out Ogura Transport. But in the end Hinode reneged and the ultranationalist who acted as mediator, Zenzo Tamura, ended up losing face. I'm not saying that's the reason Hinode's president was kidnapped, but that's the kind of company Hinode is. The men who threw dirt on S. by refusing to take a stake in Ogura, and those who severed ties with the Okada Association—they're all current executives at Hinode. And their boss is Kyosuke Shiroyama."

"Excuse me, but do you mind telling me how you know all this about Ogura, Chunichi, and Hinode?"

"What I'll tell you is that it all starts with Hinode. Not counting extortionists, there're at least a hundred men in this country who, hearing that Hinode's president had been kidnapped, thought it was just deserts—including me. But there's not a single national paper with the balls to rip Hinode's mask off because they're all scared of offending one of their advertisers. I called to say as much."

At which point, he hung up.

Negoro had unconsciously reached for the drawer to pull out his old reporter's notebook, but his hand stopped short and instead he picked up the notes he had jotted down. Having just risen out of his chair, he now took his seat again and looked more closely.

A single point drew his particular interest. Whenever something happened, a correlation diagram of political and business circles always surfaced, but none had ever included the name of an individual with ties to Hinode. Whether or not it was true, here was a leak connected to Hinode. However, this current incident of the president's abduction did not appear to be linked to the hard-liners and extortionists. Even if it were true that Hinode was involved with the Ogura and Chunichi scandal and that they had in fact thrown dirt on the Okada Association, it didn't seem likely that this had triggered the abduction.

If, as this Toda or whoever he was had implied, there were various facets of Hinode that were not publicly known, who were these legions of men who bore ill will toward Hinode? Despite all the efforts of the reporting team, not a single Hinode backstory had emerged that would explain the existence of some kind of grudge.

Still wondering if the whole thing could be a prank, Negoro had already reached for the outside phone line.

"Sorry to trouble you—this is Negoro from Tokyo." He announced himself when the Osaka Metro desk picked up.

"O-ho! Things must be topsy-turvy over there, with the whole Hinode thing!" Negoro recognized the boisterous voice of a slot editor he had known for years. It was the voice he had heard on the phone every day for the month following the Great Hanshin earthquake that had struck at the beginning of the year. "Hearing from you reminds me about that salted kelp from Yodoya—I never did send any to you, did I? Anyway, how can I help you?"

"Is Takeshi Kikuchi-san there?"

"What would you want with that ol' jobber? He quit a long time ago."

"Oh, did he now?"

"That guy was practically a yakuza stockbroker. He made hundreds of millions in speculative dealings during the bubble years and set up his own investment management company. What do you want Kikuchi for?"

"A call came in from someone trying to get in touch with him. Do you have his contact information?"

Apparently Kikuchi had left a business card when he resigned from the paper, and Negoro waited a few minutes before being given a number that was obviously a cell phone and the name of Kikuchi's company, GSC, Ltd. Negoro thanked the slot editor and hung up. Then, still unable to clearly recall the face of the man in question, he dialed the number he had just tracked down.

"Kikuchi-san? This is Negoro from *Toho News*. It's been a while."

"From *Toho* . . . Well, well, it *has* been a long time." The man's tactful reply did not stimulate Negoro's memory, either. In the current economic downturn the stock game must have been in shambles; Negoro could not even be sure that the number he was calling belonged to an actual company. The man's voice was calm but somber, and his tone did carry a certain hint of the underworld.

"You must have your hands full. Poison gas, the elections, and now Hinode Beer. Something I can help you with?"

"I may as well get right to it. Do you know a man by the name of Toda? Speaks in a Kansai dialect, an elderly man . . ."

"Oh, old Toda," Kikuchi replied immediately.

"So you do know him. He just called here asking for you. If it's all right, would you mind telling me what kind of character he is?"

"Is this an interview?"

"You could say that, yes."

Negoro heard a clicking sound on the other end of the line; Kikuchi must have been slowly tapping his desk with a pen or some other object. "The man is a has-been left-wing Osaka journalist, first of all. He published a small independent newsletter until about twenty years ago, but when that went bust he went freelance. He made ends meet as a day laborer in Kamagasaki, Osaka. I met Toda back in '86, when I was reporting on that corruption case in Airin district, you know, the one where an Osaka city employee was skimming off medical aid. Back at the time, an old man tried to engage me in a debate at the labor welfare center. That was Toda."

"Have you kept in touch with him since then?"

"No. Did he have anything to tell you?"

"Well, yes. Something about how there are at least a hundred men who harbor ill will toward Hinode."

"The guy's pushing eighty, there's no need to take him seriously. Whenever anything happens, he blames it on the establishment—always has. To put it bluntly, he's got ties to segregated buraku communities. Come to think of it, he used to work for Hinode before the war. That's right, now I remember—I've heard him talk about it."

Segregated buraku communities. Negoro's ballpoint pen, which had been doodling circles on his notepad, now drew a single question mark as if of its own accord. Immediately, his thoughts returned to the call he received three hours ago from a reporter working out of the Hachioji branch. The reporter had mentioned a prewar lawsuit involving the purchase of land intended for a factory. He drew another question mark.

"This Toda, where did he work for Hinode before the war?"

"Hmm . . . in Fushimi, probably. That's Hinode's Kyoto factory. Right, right—remember the general strike that took place soon after the war ended, the February first strike? Toda said that he marched for the union before and after the strike and was let go because of it. I never looked it up or anything, so I don't know if there's any truth to it."

1947. General strike of February 1st. Hinode's Kyoto factory. Labor dispute. Employee layoffs. Segregated buraku community. Negoro wrote it all down in his notes.

"Does Toda belong to any organization or group?"

"You mean like the Buraku Liberation League? I don't know about that."

"What's his full name?"

"I can find out for you. Why don't I give you a call tonight?"

"I'd appreciate that. Sorry to phone you out of the blue."

"Not at all."

Kikuchi hung up, as if loath to waste any more time. Negoro thought that, for a man who had just received an unexpected call from a former colleague, Kikuchi had been pretty brusque, displaying neither a sense of nostalgia nor awkwardness.

Negoro could only vaguely recall the face of Kikuchi, who had once roamed this same news room floor; and yet somehow he could imagine the mien of the man whose voice he had just heard on the phone. He could picture an office in one of countless buildings found all over the city, a shingle bearing an inscrutable company name outside, furnished with a desk and a telephone. Beside a messy stack of market newspapers and stock chart books, a man wearing a Rolex watch talks on the phone, sums of money in the tens and hundreds of million rolling smoothly off his tongue, his eyes dull and empty. At night, the same man lazily throws up his feet in the corner of an upscale club and tosses back whisky and water, then takes a taxi home, casually handing a ten-thousand-yen note to the driver and saying, "Keep the change." Of the various financial strata that existed in the world, the one into which Kikuchi had submerged himself might have been the most chilling. Kikuchi had rid himself of any scent of being a former newsman.

After replacing the receiver, Negoro again reflected on the strange phone call from the man named Toda. When Toda met Kikuchi nine years ago in Osaka, Kikuchi would no doubt have said he was a reporter with the Metro section of the Osaka bureau of *Toho News*— so why had Toda called the Tokyo office? If he had thought to call here because the Hinode incident had occurred in Tokyo, it was still strange for him to mention the name of a reporter from the Osaka Metro section. It made no sense to Negoro.

It also puzzled him why a day laborer from Kamagasaki knew so much about the series of events that had transpired while Chunichi Mutual Bank was busy managing its cash-flow problems. But it was not Toda, the former would-be labor activist who once worked for Hinode, who left a woolly and sour aftertaste in Negoro's mouth—it was Takeshi Kikuchi. His former colleague's transformation notwithstanding, so many things about the call that just ended disturbed Negoro. Kikuchi's voice had not brightened at the unexpected call from his former workplace nor had he shown much interest in the conversation. The way he talked about a day laborer he only met once while covering a story nine years ago was, however, oddly vivid.

Without much thought, Negoro jotted down *Takeshi Kikuchi. Some kind of corporate raider?* in his reporter's notebook. There was no way he could have dabbled in speculation on a journalist's salary, so he must have borrowed capital or been tasked with managing funds, or else he had been assisting a group of corporate raiders. Whatever the case, if one were to trace the source of his funds, one would bump up against a financial institution or shadowy connections. During the Ogura-Chunichi scandal, Negoro had spent more time than he would have liked delving around in such realms, and he knew the obvious places to look for immediate information, in addition to having a few hunches of his own.

And speaking of hunches, Negoro wondered if Kikuchi could somehow be tied to Kimihiro Arai, the representative of Takemitsu, the group of corporate raiders that had bought up shares of Ogura Transport. The parties that circulated money underground had various links with one another, so as a matter of simple probability, a potential connection was better than zero. Were such a point of contact to surface, it was also likely not Toda but Kikuchi himself who knew the backstory about what had transpired with Ogura and Chunichi Mutual Savings. It was even possible that Kikuchi had given the information to Toda for some reason.

Realizing his bad habit had taken over, Negoro put away his notebook. Since he became a reporter, he had a tendency for negative thinking, which only worsened his distrust of others. His wife, from whom he had separated ten years ago, had often wondered cynically whether his inability to believe in people meant he wasn't capable of trusting her, either, and she had been right. These days, he tried to be more receptive to what others might have to say, but now that he was willing to listen, no one was talking.

Figuring it must be time for the meeting, Negoro glanced up at the wall clock and saw the looming figure of Haruhisa Kubo, a reporter who worked out of the Tokyo Metropolitan Police Department kisha club. Kubo was always dressed in a business suit that was much too tight for his body, a backpack stuffed with a laptop, camera, and other equipment slung over his shoulder. His unsophisticated appearance made it impossible to imagine him as anything but a newsman. He would show up unexpectedly at the main office wearing an earnest expression that betrayed his obvious intention to pick up a story and would make the rounds, striking up conversations here and there before disappearing again.

"Negoro-san, how's your back feeling?" Kubo asked him with a somewhat weary smile.

Negoro beckoned him and slid him the notes he had just taken during his call with Kikuchi. "Tell me, Kubo. If such a man were to call a newspaper office saying there are at least a hundred men who bear ill will toward Hinode, what would you think?"

"Is this a tip-off?" Kubo asked, leaning forward. The look on his face said that he was thirsty for any story just then.

"It's hard to say. It seemed like there was more to the story than just that call," Negoro replied.

"Given his background, he could be connected to the BLL."

"No. What the man wanted to talk about was the Ogura-Chunichi scandal. As you know, Hinode was involved with the rehabilitation of Ogura Transport, so I wouldn't say there's no connection."

"If it's tied up in the Ogura-Chunichi scandal, then maybe he's with the Okada Association . . ."

Kubo was a sober, hard-boiled reporter, but at the same time he always seemed tormented, never at ease. Especially when he was stretched thin by a major incident, his eyes grew even more distracted. Whereas a sharp professionalism pervaded the hundred-member-strong Metro section at *Toho News*, the look in Kubo's eyes here and now revealed the neurosis typical of reporters on the police beat, who strained under their own particular yoke.

"Will you let Chief Sugano know? I'll talk to the slot editor."

"I hope something comes out of this, doesn't matter what," Kubo mumbled, admitting his true feelings. He then quickly copied Negoro's notes into his own notebook and left.

Negoro watched Kubo go, musing that the man's bulk seemed to house a rather complex mind, then he roamed over to the meeting in the reception area by the window that overlooked the Chidori-ga-fuchi moat. The cast of characters seated randomly on the sofas included Tabe, the slot editor in charge of the incident; Murai, the slot editor for the evening edition; Negoro, who was supervising the feature articles; and finally Toru Maeda, the Metro chief. Before Maeda could say a word, Negoro handed Tabe his notes about Toda. Looking them over, Tabe simply furrowed his brow before he passed the notes over to Maeda. After scanning the notes for about two seconds, Maeda passed them on to Murai in turn. None of their expressions changed much. Negoro did not disclose Hinode's entanglement with the Ogura-Chunichi scandal, deciding to keep it to himself for the time being.

"Negoro, check this out under the radar and see what you come up with. We don't need the young cubs sniffing around randomly." That was the only directive from Maeda, and no one else offered anything further. The Metro chief's reaction was reasonable, given Toda's background and the stories about discrimination that surfaced if one were to poke around anywhere in Japan.

"I wonder what the president will say when he starts talking," the chief said, turning his attention to the construction of the Metro page. Maeda was steadfast, not the kind of man to be discouraged just because his hunch about the involvement of extortionists proved to be off the mark. "My guess is we shouldn't expect anything major, but what do you think, Tabe?"

"If a victim who has returned safely is not willing to offer a statement, then that itself is a story worth writing about."

"Whatever happens, the readers of today and tomorrow want to know about the Hinode Beer incident. Even if the press conferences run dry, keep on writing about it. I don't care what. I'll make adjustments to the other pages."

The readers of today and tomorrow. This was Maeda's catch phrase, but Negoro wondered if there was any point to digging into the details of what happened today, or to dragging out yesterday's affair with repeated follow-up stories. At the very least, it was all too clear that the news type currently filling their pages—orange juice, fruit-flavored milk, and so on—failed to describe even a shadow of the crime that embroiled the trillion-yen corporation and its titan.

城山恭介 Kyosuke Shiroyama

SHIROYAMA SAT IN AN ARTIFICIAL leather armchair presumably reserved for guests. In front of him was a table, and two investigators sat on a sofa across from him. Another investigator sat in a different armchair. At a desk a slight distance away, yet another investigator was taking notes. The shades on the windows were drawn, and in the stark light of the fluorescent bulbs, it was hard to tell if it was day or night. Clearly, inside the police department, time flowed differently than in the regular world. Not only was the language spoken here not the same, but Shiroyama also repeatedly found himself thinking how the place completely cut him off from the outside, trapping him with a sense of hopelessness. The police department was designed to torment criminals, of course, but victims of crimes and even ordinary citizens were not spared from a feeling of irreparable isolation. By this time Shiroyama's joints were beginning to ache, and he crossed his legs lightly and leaned back in the chair to ease his discomfort, but the more he tried to assume a relaxed position, the more pronounced his awkwardness seemed.

Each of the three investigators conducting the interview had introduced himself as simply so-and-so from Investigation Headquarters. Shiroyama did not know their title or post, but all three spoke with precise and courteous diction and did not take their eyes off of him for even a second. When Shiroyama's eyes moved, so did theirs. Finding their gaze unbearable, Shiroyama finally resorted to avoiding looking at them altogether. And yet, he could not escape the discomfort of having three pairs of eyes boring into him.

"Are you sure you don't need anything to eat?" an investigator asked for the second time.

"Yes, I'm fine."

"Well then, we would like to confirm a few things about what you have just told us. First, when you were attacked—you said you came up the path and were struck on your left side by a blow from behind, then because you were being choked, you were unable to turn to see the assailant. You were blindfolded for the duration of your confinement, and when you were released by the side of the prefectural highway the perpetrators left you blindfolded and your wrists bound while they fled. By the time you removed the duct tape from your wrists and the blindfold, they were nowhere in sight. Accordingly, since from beginning to end you did not see the perpetrators at all, you cannot describe their faces, physique, or clothing. Nor did you see the vehicle you were transported in. Do I have all that right?"

"Yes."

"During those few times they carried or lifted you up and you came into contact with their bodies, you sensed they were of average build. And you never detected the smell of cigarettes."

"That's correct."

"After you were attacked, there were three perpetrators with you inside the car. And after you arrived at the hideout, one left while two remained. During your confinement, you were able to distinguish between the two men's voices, and though one sounded younger than the other, you felt that neither sounded older than forty. Both spoke standard Japanese with no accent, and their tone was consistently stiff, as if they were reading from a script. They never sounded rough or violent, and refrained from whispering or making careless remarks. Finally, you did not recognize any of the voices. Correct?"

"Yes."

"And yet I wonder," the investigator continued, his tone shifting unexpectedly, "you said that during your fifty hours of confinement at the hideout, while your eyes were blindfolded and your mouth was taped shut, you listened with desperation for whatever words might come from the two men. They spoke as little as possible, always sticking to the script. You must have listened to their voices for any clues, racking your brain to figure out who they could be."

"At first, yes. But I could not come up with anyone."

"Even so, didn't you try to guess what kind of men they were?"

"I tried, but I didn't have the slightest idea."

"What did you imagine, for example?"

"I can't recall specifically. I could tell that they were not the type of men who belonged to the same stratum of society as I do, but otherwise I had no idea."

"Perhaps it was someone who held a grudge against you or the company? Or maybe they were after some money?"

"Of course I thought about these and many other things, but I couldn't figure it out," Shiroyama replied, wondering if the police had to pry into every such detail.

"You said the men did not belong to the same stratum of society, but did you base that judgment solely upon the voices you heard?"

"Yes."

"Next"—the investigator mechanically flipped through his notebook—"you said that after you were taken into the hideout, you were told that they would not harm you. They provided you with a futon and a blanket, and then you fell asleep. When you came to, you were taken to the bathroom where you did your business, the restraints on your hands were untied and the duct tape over your mouth was pulled off, and you were given oolong tea and a rice ball. During that time, you did not feel that you were in any physical danger?"

"No."

Even as he replied, Shiroyama was again aware of the three pairs of eyes that seemed to be piercing right through him, and he had to ask himself if something was amiss with his response.

"You said that every time they pulled off the duct tape from your mouth so you could eat, you repeatedly asked them what they were after and at first they did not respond. But eventually, the older man mentioned that they wanted money, and when you asked how much, he told you six hundred million in cash. Shocked when you heard the amount, you wondered how the company could ever respond to such a huge demand . . . Is that an accurate description of what you said?"

"Yes."

"At that point, why did you immediately assume that they were demanding money from the company?"

"I didn't think it was feasible they would demand six hundred million from an individual."

"If that's true, when you determined that they were demanding money from the company, did you ask them why they were extorting Hinode Beer?"

That's right, Shiroyama thought. He realized that while he was held captive, that was one question he had never asked. Why had the perpetrators chosen him, the president of Hinode Beer? Why did they choose Hinode from among the myriad companies that existed? These questions had been on the tip of his tongue, but perhaps what nagged at him and prevented him from asking was the memory, somewhere in the recesses of his mind, of his niece and her family's blunder from four and a half years ago. Feeling as if he were again staring into an abyss of melancholy, Shiroyama grasped for an answer and all he managed to come up with was, "I asked but they didn't reply."

"Did you ask them just once?" the investigator swiftly followed up.

"Several times."

"Let me go back to the ransom. You told us the only thing the perpetrators ever said was that they wanted money, six hundred million in cash, and they did not offer any further details. Does that mean they didn't reply to any of your other questions?"

"That's right."

"What else did you ask them?"

"I asked them why they were doing this and . . . I told them six hundred million was too much . . ."

"And the perpetrators did not reply, right? When one of them started gathering up trash and vacuuming, another one told you that you were being released and they would be in touch about how to deliver the money. And right after that you were taken out of the hideout—Is that right? Did I get everything they said to you then accurately?"

"Yes."

"Did the perpetrators say anything else to you?"

"No."

"Did you say anything else to them?"

"No. My mouth was taped shut."

"When the one perpetrator began cleaning up and the other one told you that you were being released, and so on, did you notice any sudden changes in either their demeanor or way of speaking? Did they seem anxious or hurried at all?"

"I was blindfolded, so I don't really know."

"Were there any signs of sudden commotion?"

"No. There didn't seem to be."

"How did you feel when the perpetrators told you they would be in touch about how to deliver the money?"

"I felt a little relieved to hear that the money had not yet been delivered."

"During your confinement, did it ever occur to you that you might be the hostage in a kidnapping for ransom?"

"I did."

"Then weren't you suspicious or concerned that they were letting you go without the money being delivered?"

"No. I was just so relieved to hear that I was being released, I was in a daze."

"How do you feel now?"

As Shiroyama cast his gaze downward, three pairs of eyes drilled into his forehead. Occasionally their scrutiny transformed into suspicion. Their eyes were like daggers, and Shiroyama their target; his previous physical discomfort was now compounded by a sense of abhorrence. All the while, he found himself indulging in untimely self-reflection, remembering that for most of his life forbearance had never been his strong suit. Now that he was on thin ice, forced to stack one lie upon another, it was a wonder that a part of his mind was able to remain so coolly detached.

How did he feel, now, about the actions taken by the perpetrators? There was no room for doubt about the intention behind their cash demand. What was more, the reasons they had chosen him—the president of Hinode—as well as why they let him go and what they intended to do hereafter, were all so simple and clear that there was no choice but to accept them. Thus cornered, all that was left for him to do was to focus on figuring out how to respond, but he could not reveal any of this to the police.

"For now, I'm just thankful that I made it back in one piece. I haven't yet had the wherewithal to analyze the perpetrators' actions," Shiroyama responded.

"I see." The investigator gave a perfunctory nod, then immediately threw out a fresh feeler. "And yet if the motive for the crime is money, then it must be said that this crime group's actions are extremely peculiar. Even though they left a note claiming 'We have your president,' during the fifty-six hours of confinement they made no contact with your family or company. On the other hand, they made their demand for six hundred million clear to you. What's more, they said they would get in touch later before letting you—their hostage—go. I'm sure you understand, but in the same way that blackmail requires incriminating material, a demand for ransom cannot occur without a hostage . . ." The investigator said this much and, quite inexplicably, he looked at Shiroyama with what could have been construed as either a smirk or a wry smile.

Shiroyama, contemplating how this superficial affect was identical to the pervading mood when he entertained bureaucrats, was convinced that this procedure was indeed a waste of time, an unproductive formality in which neither party could reveal their true intentions, so he merely responded with, "I can understand."

"But again, seeing as the perpetrators told you they would be in touch, we have no choice but to assume that their demand still stands. If, going forward, this crime group actually makes a demand for cash without there being a hostage, that would mean they didn't need a hostage in the first place. And if that's the case, why did they take the risk of kidnapping you at all? I can't get my head around it." The investigator searched Shiroyama's eyes again, and Shiroyama responded with silence.

"Shiroyama-san. What I'm trying to say is that your story's inconsistent. From the way they kidnapped you and held you captive to their process of letting you go, this crime seems premeditated from start to finish. During the fifty-six hours of confinement, you never detected the third man in the group coming and going from the hideout, and there was no cell phone reception at the hideout due to interference from a magnetic field. If there was no contact from outside to the two men who were watching you, we can only assume that your release was also executed as planned. So if, having released their hostage, the perpetrators are still demanding six hundred million, well, to be honest with you, there's no way for us to grasp their true intentions—"

"The perpetrators definitely told me they would get in touch about how the money should be delivered."

"That's precisely the point. If the perpetrators are after a ransom, it's reasonable to think that they must have some kind of business with you, the one they kidnapped in order to extract that money. To speak frankly, isn't there something that you still haven't told us?"

"I believe I've told you everything I can remember."

"I hesitate to bring this up, but do you have any personal problems that you would rather not be made public? Women troubles or financial issues perhaps . . ."

"There's no reason for me personally to be extorted."

"It could be a problem within your family. Or some trouble at the company, over the course of the thirty-six years you've worked there—"

"No, nothing."

"Around the time of the election for the Lower House of the Diet in '92, an employee at your Hiroshima factory was forced to resign by the company, which cited a breach of employee regulations. It seems there was significant backlash from a certain religious organization following the dismissal."

Shiroyama was surprised anew. Trying to recall the details about an event of which he had no memory felt like extricating a sheet of memo paper from a mountain of junk, and he shook his head. He realized that former employees or others in the periphery who had learned about the incident in the media must have gone to the police, and the sheer breadth of the incident's direct and indirect influence sent a fresh chill up his spine.

"In '93, at your Nagoya branch, wasn't there a case in which the manager from the second sales division, forty years old at the time, caused an accident while driving a company car? The male victim was a member of a large crime syndicate."

"I'm aware of that case but—"

"Following the accident, the amount that the insurance company had paid out by the end of last year was around thirty million yen, including full coverage of two years' worth of medical treatment costs and compensation for temporary disability as well as three million in property damage to the victim's foreign car. Your company paid him five million in consolation funds. For a mere whiplash injury, one must admit this is an exceptionally large sum, but word has it that your company actually paid closer to ten million in compensation."

"I understand that we dealt with the aftermath of the accident appropriately after consulting with the prefectural police chief."

"According to what I confirmed with a person at your company named Ide, manager of general affairs, there were numerous instances of harassment against the company by the syndicate to which the victim belonged regarding the construction of Hinode's new factory in Nagoya—"

"In accordance with the local organized crime exclusion ordinance, we filed a cease-and-desist order signed by the precinct's superintendent. I have not been informed of any further problems."

"Well, just know that when something happens to any company, even if it's not as large a corporation as Hinode Beer, various speculations both true and untrue emerge—like ants swarming after spilled sugar. The media companies are engaged in a fierce reporting battle as well. Of course, your company's risk management is top-notch, so I'm sure there won't be any leaks from the inside."

An intimidation followed by a wisecrack. Shiroyama paid no attention to either.

"What do you think, Shiroyama-san? Didn't something else happen other than what you have told us? A threat or blackmail regarding some specific matter—"

"No, there's nothing."

"You tell us nothing comes to mind at all, but from tens of thousands of publicly traded companies, the perpetrators have chosen Hinode Beer. If this were a kidnapping where the only objective was money, it could have been any one of the thirty-five board members based at your main office, but they came after you. If we are talking purely about accessibility, your circumstances make it especially difficult. To be honest, the other executives would have been much easier marks. However, the perpetrators took the risk of kidnapping you. Therefore, it's reasonable to think—"

"I hear you, but nothing comes to mind."

"Shiroyama-san. You must give the police an accurate account of everything that happened."

"I told you everything I can remember."

"It would be a different story if a child had been kidnapped. But when a grown man comes back from a kidnapping unharmed and he cannot give us a single detail to paint a clearer picture of the perpetrators, no one, I assure you—not the police, not the public—will be satisfied. And even though you were taken from in front of your own home by force and kept in confinement for fifty-six hours, you returned alone and with nary a scratch. Besides that, the perpetrators made sure to outfit you with body warming patches when they released you so that you wouldn't freeze to death. If you don't start talking, both you and Hinode Beer could be subject to an excessive amount of scrutiny."

"What do you mean by scrutiny?"

"Maybe you made some kind of a deal with the perpetrators. Or maybe you planned and staged the whole kidnapping yourself. That kind of thing."

Immediately after Shiroyama had gone into the fire department for help, he had become acutely aware that such suspicions might arise, and by the time he was back in Tokyo, he was already surrounded by disbelieving eyes on all sides. Thinking back, it was almost eerie how the perpetrators had never laid a hand on him. But those same men—the ones who had explained their financial demands and instructed him as to how he should respond to the police's questioning—must have also obviously known beforehand what kind of public reaction would be triggered once their actions and the instructions they had given him came to light. The entire abduction, confinement, and release must have been the result of their careful calculation of the predicament in which the victim and the corporation would then find themselves. Realizing this, Shiroyama had no doubt that even sitting here now, he was still a pawn in the hands of the perpetrators. Nevertheless, he wondered what other options had really been feasible.

"I for one would like to see these criminals arrested, but I cannot tell you what did not happen."

"I see . . . Then, what do you make of this case?" One of the investigators pulled a sheet of paper from a manila envelope and handed it to him. Shiroyama's eyes beheld the words LETTER OF COMPLAINT at the top, followed by the claimant's address and the name HINODE BEER COMPANY, and finally the date NOVEMBER 13, 1990, at the end of the letter. That was enough.

When he looked up, his eyes met the watchful gazes of the investigators.

"I understand your company filed this complaint against the accused, who had sent a defamatory cassette tape addressed to your company. The complaint itself was withdrawn on November twentieth, but how did that come about?"

The question came so abruptly that Shiroyama had to pretend to look down at the letter once more. The text typed out on a word processer blurred before his eyes.

"I'm aware of this case but—"

"As president of the company, when and how did you hear about the cassette tape?"

"I wrote down the exact date in my journal. But I can't recall it now. Before work started that day, the human resources manager at the time—Tsukamoto—and the vice president with whom Tsukamoto had consulted—Shirai—came into my office. They informed me they had received such a tape and wanted to discuss how it should be handled . . . That's what I remember."

"Did you listen to the tape?"

"At the time they handed me a transcript of the tape, but there was so much text I remember not having sufficient time to read it thoroughly."

"Then who made the decision to file a complaint?"

"I think Shirai suggested it and I approved it. Tsukamoto had informed me that before they received the tape, two slanderous letters from what appeared to be the same person who had sent the tape had been delivered to the office."

"Why wasn't the matter brought before the board of directors?"

"The matter didn't call for it. Ordinarily human resources should have settled it on their own."

"But the contents of both the letters and the tape, which compelled you to file the complaint, were quite delicate."

"The contents of the tape were not what mattered. I believe we determined at that point in time that simply receiving letters written under an assumed name and a cryptic tape from an unidentified sender was a problem in and of itself."

"I heard the same from Tsukamoto-san himself, but on October tenth, 1990, wasn't there a student named Takayuki Hatano who left in the middle of an interview with your company? Following the interview, that student continued to be absent, unexcused, from his university seminar, and late on the night of the fifth day after, he was killed in an accident on the Shuto Expressway. Wasn't the person who sent two separate letters to your company followed by the tape that student's father? And the father killed himself by jumping in front of a train, late on the night of November seventeenth. Even if it was not the kind of matter to have bothered the president about, I would think it would have presented a significant issue for the reputation of the company."

As Shiroyama took in each item uttered by the investigator, he realized that the police must have already gone to speak with Hatano's family. The dead student's mother would not have forgotten that her son's girlfriend and her father had come to pay their respects after the funeral. Perhaps she had already revealed her suspicions to the police, and given them all the details. . .

"Shiroyama-san, wasn't this a case of employment discrimination?"

"Sorry. What did you say?"

"The issue that the deceased dentist was trying to bring to your company's attention was whether discrimination had been a factor in his son's employment, wasn't it?"

"Yes, it was. But as far as the company was concerned, there was no such awareness. There was no basis for it—neither then nor in the past. We would have liked to have been able to decipher where the student's father was coming from, but there was a limit to how we were able to act as a company given the way he had sent the letters and the tape."

"I just want to confirm. What is the exact reason you decided that filing a complaint was the best course of action?"

"We had been moving forward with the project to build a new factory at the time, so we had no choice but to be particularly cautious. In the end we determined it was necessary to take measures against any unfounded attempts at obstruction."

"So you are familiar with the contents of the tape, for the most part?"

"I am."

"The intention behind the tape was indeed hard to grasp. The tape seemed to convey the substance of a letter sent by a certain Seiji Oka-mura to your company's Kanagawa factory back in 1947. According to Tsukamoto-san, he was able to look up this Seiji Okamura in the stu-dent registry of the former Tohoku Imperial University and confirm that he had in fact previously been a Hinode employee. But he was unable to determine whether the letter from 1947 actually existed. Do I have that right?"

"I think that's what I heard."

"We are currently looking for employees who worked out of the Kanagawa factory or the main office at that time, but as of now we lack any conclusive evidence that the letter was ever delivered to the factory in 1947. However, hypothetically speaking, if such a letter did exist, it would clearly be considered the possession of Hinode Beer. And judging from the contents of the letter, it's highly unlikely that this would have been treated lightly within the company back then, so how did you feel about a taped reading of such a letter being sent to your company by someone from the outside?"

"My only recollection from the time is that we discussed how we were unsure of the intention of the sender."

"You didn't think the letter had been leaked from within Hinode?"

"I guess when you put it that way . . . But this was something that had happened just after the war ended, and we could not even ascer-tain the existence of such a letter."

"Going back in the conversation, did your company conduct a background check on this student, Hatano?"

"No. We don't do that at Hinode."

"How about after you received the second letter and the strange tape from the student's father? What did you do then?"

"Nothing."

After a brief pause, the investigator muttered, "That can't be." Shiroyama, unsure what the investigator meant, held his breath and waited for what he would say next. He expected to hear the name of the student's girlfriend—his niece—mentioned next, but the conversation grew even more complicated.

"Seiji Okamura is the uncle of the student's mother, isn't he?" the investigator asked.

"I heard he is a distant relation."

"That's what you heard? Then you do know that Tsukamoto-san, the human resources manager, had conducted a background check anyway?"

"I suppose you're right. It must have escaped my memory. What of—"

"The student, Takayuki Hatano; his father, the dentist Hiroyuki Hatano; and the letter's sender, Seiji Okamura—seeing that these people are all related, it wouldn't be implausible for there to be some kind of confrontation or misunderstanding, but the reality is a little more complex. Hiroyuki Hatano had not even known about Seiji Okamura until shortly before he committed suicide. On November fifth, 1990, the day before Hatano mailed the tape, he had called his estranged wife in the middle of the night and asked if she knew someone by the name of Seiji Okamura. But, as his wife told him, she didn't. That same night, Hatano also called the home of his wife's father, who happens to be the younger brother of Seiji Okamura, and asked his father-in-law about him. Hatano's father-in-law confirmed that Seiji Okamura was in fact his older brother, but that Okamura had been adopted into another family before he was born. Apparently, Hatano's father-in-law had only met Okamura a handful of times before the war, and had never spoken about him to his family either. In other words, Hiroyuki Hatano had recorded a tape of himself reading the letter written by Seiji Okamura—someone he didn't know about until that very evening—and sent it off to your company."

"That man Okamura, is he still alive?"

"He died last summer in a nursing home in Tokyo. Okamura's younger brother—the father of Hiroyuki Hatano's wife—had hired a detective agency to track down Okamura's whereabouts. He had visited him at the nursing home from time to time. Okamura had dementia."

If the father of Hatano's wife was indeed the younger brother of Okamura, then perhaps this brother had heard about the girl his grandson had intended to marry. Shiroyama pondered this as he listened to the investigator's story with astonishment.

"As to the circumstances of how the original or perhaps a photocopy of Seiji Okamura's letter, presumably sent to your company's Kanagawa factory back in 1947, found its way into Hatano's hands, we do not yet know. But the fact that it ended up with Hatano means that it must have been leaked from your company."

"That seems right."

"Of course, it's possible that the letter was forged. In any case, according to professional assessment, the style of writing in Seiji Okamura's letter seems characteristic of a man in his thirties or forties at the time and who completed high school before the war."

"And that means—"

"As we told you in the beginning, at this point it is our view that an individual with some kind of connection to Hinode is involved in the crime group that targeted Hinode Beer and its president. It's clear that this individual harbors feelings of strong hostility or antagonism toward Hinode. This is why we've also asked your General Affairs Department to submit a list of retired employees from the past twenty years."

"I understand. And—"

"At this point we don't have the evidence to make any specific accusations, but for instance, I would say that whoever leaked Seiji Okamura's letter in the first place must be on the inside at Hinode, and since it's plausible that person bore malicious intent, he or she should be considered as one of the candidates."

"I follow what you're saying."

"Of course, it's also possible that the person from whom the late Hiroyuki Hatano received the copy of the letter had machinations against Hinode. Actually, there is someone we already suspect, and

I'm sure in due time he will be pulled into the fray on a different case."

As the investigator said this, Shiroyama observed how his gaze and tone of voice again shifted slightly, and Shiroyama felt another visceral chill. He was nearing his limit, having held his breath each time in anticipation of the next revelation.

"Who is this suspect?"

"An executive at Toichi Industry, a front company associated with the crime syndicate the Seiwakai, who styles himself as a corporate extortionist. It's hard to believe he acted alone, so we suspect that he had the backing of a somewhat larger organization . . . Well, how about it, Shiroyama-san? When you decided to file a complaint against Hatano the dentist, wasn't your company also aware of such matters?"

"I'm sorry, but I have no idea what sort of matters you are referring to specifically—"

"I see . . . Well, I'll refrain from questioning you any further about the extortionist," the investigator said with an ambiguous smile. Shiroyama no longer had the energy to respond. "With that said, two people are dead because of the 1990 incident with the mysterious tape, while members of Hatano's family are still alive. You can bet that sooner or later this kind of story will be blown out of proportion, never mind what's true and what's not."

Shiroyama listened, aware that a definitive threat had finally been made. Images flashed through his mind of lurid headlines in the weekly tabloids—exaggerated stories about the student who had left in the middle of his second employee interview and his relationship with Shiroyama's niece Yoshiko.

"I'm sure you already know, but hundreds of reporters from every media outlet are out there, sniffing around in a frenzy. The more they pry the harder it becomes for us to conduct our investigation, and the damage incurred to your corporate image will be considerable. We, for our part, would like to avoid such a situation, as the only people to benefit from it are the perpetrators. To that end, the only thing for us to do is to apprehend the perpetrators as soon as possible. Do you understand?"

"I do."

"In order to do so it is imperative that you—the victim and the only person to have had direct contact with the criminal group—tell us everything."

"As I already said repeatedly, I've told you everything I can remember."

"I'll ask again. Did the perpetrators tell you anything else other than their demand for six hundred million and that they would get in touch with you later?"

"No. That was all."

"But who would ever pay a ransom when there's no hostage or blackmail bait? If tomorrow the perpetrators gave you instructions on how the cash should be delivered, would your company pay the six hundred million?"

"No, we would not."

"Then why did the crime group let you go? If they said, 'We will contact you about how to deliver the money,' common sense tells us that statement is based on the assumption that a certain negotiation would take place. How do you make sense of that?"

"I have told you everything that actually happened. It is your job to make sense of the situation."

"Then—say, if tomorrow the perpetrators demanded their ransom, how does your company intend to respond?"

"We would report it to the police."

"We would only ask you the same questions."

"And I would only be able to give you the same answers."

"I understand. The perpetrators told you they would be in touch about how to deliver the money, correct? Did they say anything more? There were no provisos about what they would do if you don't agree to their demand?"

In that moment, Shiroyama was overwhelmed by the thought of what might happen if he were to admit right then and there that the beer was being held hostage. He wondered whether the police would be satisfied with that revelation and whether it was the right thing to do. He had debated this over and over again, but each time had failed to come up with a definitive conclusion. Once they found out that the hostage was the Hinode beer, the police might beef up police patrols at Hinode and spearhead increased security measures at their factories, news of which would then spread throughout their entire company, their distributors, the rest of the industry, and the market, all but assuring a negative impact on their sales. Even so, should they dare to fortify security publicly? Still, even with heightened security, to what extent would they be able to deter the perpetrators' interference? Even if they managed to keep a close enough watch on their shipments, what about the vending machines that dotted the streets all over Japan?

Thinking this through, Shiroyama ultimately decided he was unable to entrust the police with the beer company's lifeline. It wasn't that he found the police incompetent; at this point in time, the police and the company stood on different places on the horizon, and Shiroyama simply couldn't see how the distance between them would ever shrink.

"No, nothing," Shiroyama replied.

"I see . . . You must be tired, so soon after such a long ordeal. Why don't you get some rest tonight and think it all over. We'll pay a visit to your office at 9 tomorrow morning, and I'd like for us to speak again then."

"There will be quite a number of pending tasks that require my attention in the morning, so would it be possible for you to arrive at 10?"

"If it were up to us we would begin at dawn. The media is so desperate right now, they could break a story that would cause irreparable damage to your company."

There was no question the police were implying the incident involving Takayuki Hatano and Shiroyama's niece, Yoshiko. Having quickly grasped the nature of the incident with the mysterious cassette tape from 1990, the police were now using the exact same tricks as the criminal group to pressure Shiroyama. Even with the taste of utter defeat in his mouth, Shiroyama's abject hatred of the police was reaffirmed—it was stronger than what he felt toward the criminals, who had avoided saying anything superfluous to him.

"Please make it 9:15," was Shiroyama's only response.

"Fine. 9:15 it is then. Thank you for coming in today."

"Thank you."

And so it was that, at 4:40 P.M, Shiroyama stood up from the seat he had been sitting in for nearly six hours and exited the room. He was fully aware that the expression on his face bore no resemblance to that of a victim who had been freed after a fifty-six-hour confinement, and in reality, he felt not a trace of any such profound emotion.

When he reached the front lobby, three male employees from the corporate secretariat were waiting for him. The three of them lowered their heads at once in a bow, and there outside, beyond the glass doors, was another phalanx of cameras from the press corps. As Shiroyama's eyes drifted over the green public payphone beside the entrance, he suddenly longed to hear the voices of his family, but even that thought was fleeting. The only thing left was the vortex of hatred that swirled between himself as he stood at the entrance, wearing the façade of the victim, and the public who formed a barrier outside, ready and waiting for him.

THE VEHICLE THAT CAME TO retrieve him was the same company car that he had been riding in every day until three days ago, but there were now curtains covering all the windows save for the front windshield; in addition, Tatsuo Yamazaki, who had been his driver for many years, had been replaced by another man. Shiroyama had been away for less than three days, but he was forced to acknowledge all over again that many things must have transpired at the company during his brief absence. The ride from Omori Police Department to the company's main office in Kita-Shinagawa did not even take ten minutes, and the car transported him to the underground parking lot to avoid the thronging press corps that surrounded the front of the building. Once the car entered the lot, the shutter door closed behind it, and two guards from the security company immediately appeared within the dim passageway and bowed toward the car, their expressions austere, as if to convey the gravity of the situation. Shiroyama recognized neither of them.

In the underground parking lot, about a hundred people had gathered, from the chairman and the entire board of directors, all the way down to the managers and deputy managers from every department, as well as executives of the subsidiary and affiliated companies that had offices in the building. Applause arose as soon as Shiroyama disembarked from the vehicle, followed by a swirl of voices calling out, "Welcome back!" "What a relief!" and "So glad to see you safe."

This welcoming scene seemed inappropriate for a man who had caused significant aggravation to the company by being kidnapped due to his own carelessness, much less one who was lying to the company and trying to force them to pay out a sum of two billion. Though none of them knew the truth, Shiroyama wondered—who had planned such an elaborate homecoming, who had complained about it, and who had given the okay in the end. Once his suspicions began to grow they soon engulfed him, leading to a sense of isolation.

He could not survey the entire assemblage at once, but he managed to distinguish the faces of the board members from the main office in the front row. He nodded instinctively at the remarks thrown his way, he bowed, received handshakes, and with every step he took told himself that this was all following protocol. Meanwhile, he took in several other faces: Takeo Sugihara, his coarse expression failing to contain his anxiety; Sei'ichi Shirai, whose mind seemed to have kicked into high gear dealing with the aftermath of the incident; and Seigo Kurata, his visage already stripped of any personal emotion. He saw the inscrutable faces of several board members whose real feelings he could not deduce, as well as more than a few gentle faces of those who were all smiles for the time being. And, behind all these men, Shiroyama saw his secretary Takako Nozaki, peering at him with a reserved smile.

Knowing that hers was the only earnest smile among them, Shiroyama felt a new wave of anguish as he called Ms. Nozaki over to him.

"I am so glad you are safe," Nozaki said in her usual calm manner, bowing once, before asking briskly, "What can I do for you?"

"I'm so sorry to have caused you concern. It will take me about forty minutes from now to go around each floor to greet everyone. Then, I'll see to urgent matters in my office, and there will be a board meeting at 6:30 P.M. Please make arrangements accordingly. Also, if you could have a light meal ready for me in my office by 6:10 P.M.— something simple will do."

"Of course."

Several voices urged him to rest, to delay greeting employees until tomorrow, but Shiroyama feigned a smile and responded, "No need to worry. I'm fine, as you can see," and went on ahead into the waiting elevator. With him were four men: Takeo Sugihara, whom Shiroyama had signaled to join him with the merest of glances; Keizo Suzuki, the chairman of the board; Hiroshi Sakakibara, the corporate secretary and executive director of general affairs who came into the elevator saying that he needed to speak to Shiroyama briefly about the board meeting; and finally Hajime Ide, manager of general affairs. As soon as the doors closed, Suzuki began talking first, as if he had too many things to say.

"I must apologize to you and your family. Until I received the call this morning that you were safe, I felt like I could hardly breathe. Everyone here regrets having been a little too lax about the company's security. The police seemed to find our risk management procedures cumbersome, but if you ask me they're not nearly sufficient."

Sakakibara's issue, on the other hand, had to do with the proceedings of the board meeting. "I'm sorry to bother you when you must be exhausted, but before the meeting the consultants would like to take ten minutes to report on the current situation and explain the risk management countermeasures. Then Ide will brief you on his communication with law enforcement officials. Would that be all right with you? Perhaps we should delay the meeting with the consultants until tomorrow morning?"

As he spoke, Sakakibara cautiously glanced at Shiroyama's face. *I see*, Shiroyama thought. They were bracing for him to start disclosing more sensitive matters at the board meeting tonight, rendering any discussions with the outside risk management company useless. Having grasped this, Shiroyama prepared himself anew to face the thicket of anxieties and speculations of the executives. "No, I'll talk to them today."

Ide then reported, "While you were gone, the police questioned us about various matters. I will send you a memo summarizing all their inquiries."

Sakakibara and Ide got off on the twelfth floor. "Every man shows his true colors in a time of emergency," Suzuki offered casually after the elevator doors closed again. "We installed the risk management system last year after the board reached a consensus on it, but some have started to voice their frustrations now that a crisis has hit. They say it's useless and causes more trouble than it's worth. They complain about who in this company would be held responsible for a manual that was generated by an outside source—"

"Who can blame them, now that the person who suggested the idea in the first place was the one to be kidnapped?" Shiroyama shrugged it off with a bitter laugh, though his eyes conveyed an appreciation for Suzuki's considerate words.

What Suzuki, in his position as chairman, was hinting at with his carefully chosen remarks was clear to Shiroyama: during the two and a half days of his absence, there had been some outward signs of discord on the board. And yet, the consensus of the board was in essence no more than an aggregate of the individual members' compromise and restraint and preservation of self; it would have been strange had no disagreement arisen when the members were compelled to assess the delicate situation. Shiroyama still held the title at the helm of management, and steering the company's dissension had become second nature. He did not feel particularly shocked as he listened to Suzuki's advice.

"By the way, Shiroyama-kun. It's fine for you to make the rounds of the floors but you can't possibly do it alone—"

Before Suzuki had finished speaking, Takeo Sugihara volunteered, "I'll accompany him."

Shiroyama got off the elevator with Sugihara on the twenty-ninth floor, where the beer division was based. After bowing to the chairman, who was headed up to the thirtieth floor, Shiroyama made sure the elevator doors had closed before turning to Sugihara.

As if he had been waiting for the opportunity this entire time, Sugihara bent his body in half deferentially and lamented in a low voice, "I am so sorry for what happened. There are no words to express my regret . . ." What Sugihara said made it clear to Shiroyama that he too had been called in and grilled by the police about the particulars surrounding the letter of complaint from 1990.

"Stand up! What if someone sees you?"

Shiroyama was overcome by a futile irritation. There was no need to guess the position that Sugihara must be in, with his daughter's scandal made into fodder for corporate extortion. Now that the police had seized upon it, it was only a matter of time before the media would expose it.

Yet Shiroyama wondered if this man really understood the situation— that if corporate profits were given the highest priority, Sugihara's moral responsibility as a company executive was too large a topic to address now, and that they could not afford to question it—for the safety of Sugihara's family. If Sugihara did understand, there were other ways to show his deference. Certain things needed to be done before he could give vent to his personal anguish. Conceding his failure might have been inevitable, but this was not the way for him to do so.

But at the same time Shiroyama was painfully aware of how detached he felt. He harbored no ill will toward Sugihara, the husband of his younger sister, but there was no way for him to feel familial empathy for him; all that Shiroyama could do—had ever been able to do—was to engage with him as fairly as possible. Facing him now, Shiroyama perceived Sugihara as a man whose good breeding had, once he'd hit fifty, turned into obtuseness; a man caught in a vicious cycle wherein his weak bearing generated a defensive attitude, which in turn weakened his foothold even further. There was no hope of his retaining his post as deputy manager of the beer division. As president, Shiroyama would eventually need to consider which of the board members—Sugihara among them—would be temporarily transferred to an affiliate company, and when he factored in their personal circumstances, he could hardly keep himself from berating Sugihara. He was forced to tamp down his emotions once again.

"Sugihara-san. Do you know whether the police shared the matter of the tape with all the members of the board?"

"Kurata-san was the first one called in by the police, and I heard they asked him about it. Apparently Kurata-san made a statement then that the only six people who knew about the matter of the tape were himself and Shirai-san, you and me, and the human resources manager and general affairs manager at the time."

"So the story hasn't leaked to the rest of the board members, correct?"

"I believe not."

"Sugihara-san. I will talk about this in further detail at the board meeting, but the crime group's demand is money. This has nothing to do with the tape from 1990. Right now, our only duty is to come up with a countermeasure that will not damage the company. I need you to keep the affair with your family completely separate from this."

"But the media may find out about it . . ."

"Even so, that story has nothing whatsoever to do with the company. Do you understand? There must be plenty of executive tasks that require your attention right now. Be sure not to forget that, as deputy manager, the fate of the beer division rests with you."

"I am aware of that."

"Sugihara-san. I am speaking to you as a relative—I'm on your side. I feel the same way about not wanting to involve Yoshiko-chan's family in this controversy. Well, there's no time for this now. Let's go."

Shiroyama checked his watch and began walking briskly ahead. Beginning with the beer division on the twenty-ninth floor, then continuing through another sixteen or seventeen floors in descending order, all he could do was to peer into each room and to thank everyone with a slight bow. As he moved his feet around the office, conversing and displaying his usual facial expressions, Shiroyama repeated to himself that bending to the crime group's demand was what would ultimately protect this company and its employees. Were he not to think this way, it was doubtful that he could bear up against the future accumulation of lies, deceptions, and schemes—both personal and public—as well as the inevitable complications that would arise from the discord on the board.

Shiroyama returned to his executive suite on the thirtieth floor by 5:45 P.M., as planned. His secretary Ms. Nozaki followed right in after him, just as she always did, saying, "Sorry, but could you confirm this first?" She handed him the day's itinerary, which Shiroyama examined while still standing. An itemized list of things he was to have accomplished that day—receiving guests, meetings, interviews, and scheduled visits—were all crossed out in red, and in the empty spaces next to them were corrections: canceled, postponed, will contact later, and alternate date required. Pages two and three were for tomorrow and the day after.

"For today, the only urgent matter is the Takasaki factory on-site briefing—would you like to set an alternate date or instruct only the pharmaceutical division to attend?"

He had been preoccupied for some time with attaining approval from local residents for the construction of a manufacturing plant for immunosuppressive drugs based on genetic-modification technology, so he could not delay the matter any further. "Please consult with them and reschedule the date for either this weekend or early next week," Shiroyama replied.

"Understood. As for the rest, I've already sent a proxy letter to the trade issue council and the Japan Business Federation. Vice President Shirai attended the dedication ceremony for Tomioka's new distribution facility on your behalf, but he forgot to bring with him the greetings message in your name. If we are going to send one tomorrow, I think we should revise the language a little."

"Please show me the revised letter before you send it out."

"What about the calls you've received?"

"Just see what the business is for today."

"I understand. Then, please look over the schedule for tomorrow and the day after and check off the items you would like to cancel."

Shiroyama did as Ms. Nozaki requested, still on his feet but leaning over his desk as he began to edit his calendar. First he deleted tomorrow's monthly business headquarters meeting planned for nine in the morning, and wrote in, *Executive staff, Morning assembly. 5th floor hall*. The police interview was scheduled for 9:15. He had no idea how many hours it would take, but he went ahead and canceled the rest of the morning's planned visitors and meetings. At noon there was a thirty-minute press conference for the media. He kept the rehearsal for the stockholders' meeting as it was, scheduled for 12:30 P.M. He scanned the list of places he was supposed to be in the afternoon, narrowed it down to two, and canceled the rest.

For the day after tomorrow, he canceled all his outings save for the management council for major distributors, which he decided he couldn't possibly miss; the induction of the new president of Limelight Japan; and the closing ceremony for the technical training program that was to take place at the Kanagawa factory. He looked up briefly once he had amended the itinerary. His eye caught on five magnificent white tulips, mottled with pale red tinges, which had been arranged in a vase and placed upon his desk. The petals, curling and opening ever so gently, had a porcelain luster, like a still life by Jan Brueghel or Hans Bollongier, which transfixed him despite everything. Ms. Nozaki must have bought them with money out of her pocket.

As Shiroyama handed back the itinerary, he said to her, "Those must have been expensive." A brief smile of satisfaction flashed on Ms. Nozaki's face, but she did not say more.

"By the way, is Yamazaki the driver off today?"

"The police have been interviewing him for two or three days, so someone else has taken his place for now."

"I see."

"Now shall I bring in the light meal you requested? Would you like a little something to drink? I put a Hinode Meister on ice."

Ms. Nozaki swiftly disappeared from the room and, once alone, Shiroyama turned to his desk. The items that had accumulated while he had been away were piled high, arrayed like a kiosk counter. At one end he saw the *Nikkei*, the *Nikkei Marketing Journal*, the food industry newspapers and other trade publications, along with a binder of important article clippings. One section of a national daily was folded to reveal the headlines written in bold, black letters: CONFINED FOR FIFTY-SIX HOURS, HINODE BEER PRESIDENT ABDUCTED, AND SIX HUNDRED MILLION RANSOM!

Wondering how the newspapers had covered the incident, Shiroyama could not stop from reaching for the evening paper. But then, reminding himself that this was not the time to further rattle his mind, he pulled his hand back.

Next to the newspapers was the set of business reports delivered every Monday morning and another set of monthly financial statements. Shiroyama leafed through the business reports, even though he had already received them last Friday, and reconfirmed that the numbers indicated that the cumulative order volume of their newest product had reached the targeted increase of 19 percent.

Next to these reports was a mountain of well-wishing telegrams from clients and government agencies—no doubt they had been astonished by this morning's news—as well as from concerned peers within the industry. On top of the neat pile, Ms. Nozaki had attached a list of the senders, including the addresses to which thank-you notes should be sent and those whom Shiroyama should personally call. Also clipped to the list was a draft of the thank-you note, along with samples of the font, company letterhead, and envelope to be used when printing them. Beside this was a sample of the letter of apology to be sent to their valued customers, which Shiroyama had instructed Kurata to prepare earlier that morning at the Fujiyoshida Police Department, and a separate list for those addresses. There was another list of clients to whom executives had already paid personal visits and the names of those executives. Next, also per his instructions to Kurata, was the bundle of reports from each division on the general business that had been conducted that day. Shiroyama paged through those too, and for the time being, he placed the minutes from the meeting about the arrangements for the stockholders' meeting, which had been submitted by general affairs, at the top of the pile.

Next to this was another bundle of letters, about twenty of them. And a tabulated list of internal and external calls that Ms. Nozaki had fielded today, charting the callers and their messages. She had underlined in red the names of those whom Shiroyama needed to call back at a later date. Among these names were shareholders from banks and insurance companies, and others from government agencies, financial organizations, as well as members of the Tokyo Metropolitan Assembly who had called with well wishes; also included were coded names of politicians as well as political organizations and ultranationalist groups. Although it wasn't underlined, Shiroyama singled out a name that appeared on the list without a title—Kiyoshi Iwami. They were both alumni of the law department at Tokyo University and still saw each other a few times a year at public and private functions. For a moment, as Shiroyama pondered what Iwami must have looked like that day as he put in a call from the commissioner-general's office of the National Police Agency in Sakuradamon, he almost reached for the phone, but then stopped himself. Instead, Shiroyama placed the list back on his desk.

Finally, he picked up a binder of fax messages and unfolded one. There, in a rushed hand, were the words: *I'm coming home today. Now that you're back with Mother and Brother, please get some rest—Shoko.* This message had been sent from London by his daughter, who worked as a trader for Morgan. Concerned about whether it would be all right for her to leave her post at the opening of the market on a Monday—had it been the weekend, that would have been another story—Shiroyama quickly refolded his daughter's fax.

Just then, he heard a knock and Ms. Nozaki came in, carrying a tray with his light supper. In addition to the food, there was a small bottle of Hinode Meister and a single pilsner glass on the tray. Had his secretary been one who enjoyed a sip of alcohol every so often, he would have offered her a glass, too, but after twenty years at a beer company, Ms. Nozaki still could not tolerate a single drop of beer.

"The executive chef sends his regards."

With that, Ms. Nozaki left him, and Shiroyama looked down at the tray she had set on his side desk. The meal had been prepared in the beer restaurant on the fortieth floor, and it was Shiroyama's favorite. Ordinarily the salted pork was simmered in white wine with sauerkraut and Irish Cobbler potatoes, but the chef had omitted the bones from the pork for Shiroyama. The small helping of pristine white sauerkraut with juniper berries, piping hot potato, and green beans sautéed in butter and still steaming in a Meissen dish were served in the same way, and in the same portion as always.

Shiroyama poured the cold Hinode Meister into the glass. At first he poured it somewhat quickly to get the bubbles going, then more slowly as if to let the foam rise, until the amber-colored beer was capped off with a picture-perfect, three-centimeter head, and he stared at it for a minute. Shiroyama did not necessarily dwell on the fact that the beer itself was being held for ransom, but still, instead of reaching for the glass, he began with the sauerkraut.

Just as he had taken a bite of the potato, he heard Ms. Nozaki's voice over the intercom, announcing that Shirai and Kurata were here to consult with him ahead of the stockholders' meeting. Shiroyama reasoned that meeting with two vice presidents at once would save him time, so he told her to let them through, and they appeared about two minutes later.

"Please, please—finish your meal. It's nothing formal we need to talk about," Shirai said as he strode in at his usual hurried pace. Shiroyama, nevertheless, rose from his chair, bowed his head to the two of them, and felt the need to apologize again. "I'm sorry for all the trouble I've caused."

"Nonsense. First see that you get plenty to eat. We'll just sit ourselves down," Shirai said as he brought in a chair for himself, and Kurata followed suit.

"I remember that's your favorite." Shirai remarked about Shiroyama's meal, demonstrating that he could afford to make small talk. Kurata, for this part, wore a peculiar aloof expression that was even more inscrutable than usual, as if he had tucked away the anguish that had been on display first thing that morning at the Fujiyoshida Police Department. This disturbed Shiroyama, but when he considered that he himself did not present the appearance of a victim, either, he had no choice but to accept their mutual deception.

"Shiroyama-san. Over these last three days, the executives have reacted to your abduction in many different ways, but personally I think this is a prime opportunity to shake up the board." Before Shirai could get any further, Kurata interjected, "Before that, why don't we share with him what the various reactions were?"

Kurata did not so much as change his expression, but the unexpected retort made Shiroyama pause his fork in midair. Shiroyama could not tell immediately whether the remark was sarcastic or the wayward manifestation of a personal grudge, but it was an unprecedented and uncharacteristic utterance coming from Kurata the torpedo.

A flicker of annoyance passed over Shirai's eyes. "Each person's reaction? I said fuck it and you said shit." His casual deflection quickly mended any rift between the two men. Kurata responded with a short bark of laughter, which startled Shiroyama again. Shiroyama had never heard Kurata laugh this way before, but before he could doubt his ears, the burst of sound and any accompanying facial expression had already passed.

"Shiroyama-san, I can afford to tell you this now, but we didn't expect you to return so soon. We discussed the maximum amount we could pay if we received a demand for ransom, and even how we would prepare for a company funeral, if worse came to worst. Indeed, things were said that might make you faint."

Shirai made a showcase of himself, laughing loudly. These wisecracks were laced with his trademark venom, but they were also a means of evading and assuaging the unbearable truth—as well as a calculated tactic to gauge Shiroyama's reaction before deciding how best to broach the real topic. Shiroyama offered only a bitter laugh in response and went back to eating the potato, which he had mashed with his fork.

Meanwhile, Seigo Kurata had suddenly for some reason begun to seem like a stranger to Shiroyama. Kurata's face, which after fifty-five years had not lost its good looks, was impassive. Shiroyama imagined that Kurata was either in a daze following three straight days of anxiety or perhaps had experienced some sort of recalibration. Shiroyama felt bewildered, as if the pillar of support on which he had always relied had vanished from before his eyes, and all at once, he saw a flickering image of Kurata's face from thirty years ago.

Back in 1965, Shiroyama had been appointed manager of the First Sales Division of Hinode's Yokohama branch, which was where he first met Seigo Kurata, three years his junior. Kurata was already the kind of man who didn't give a damn about the appeal of Hinode's products, which at the time already dominated the market. When a colleague remarked that Hinode's product had sold ten thousand cases, Kurata would reply that a competitor's product had sold five thousand cases and would then provide an analysis as to why it had managed to sell that many. Everything Kurata did was out of the ordinary. To increase his monthly sales figures, he upped the percentage of the rebate and worked aggressively with their distributors, and in order to further boost their products in the marketplace, he went around with employees from the distributor in order to negotiate directly with liquor stores and bars. He even worked as a salesperson in stores, and if there was product he failed to sell, he would come retrieve whatever inventory was left, put the beer back into his truck, and transport it to a regional area with a less substantial sales network. After delivering one case at a time as samples to smaller, less successful distributors, he would liquidate the rest by selling them to a discounter, and only return once his truck was completely empty.

Kurata was still in his twenties back then, but he had two small children to feed, having gotten married when he was a student. One summer day, Kurata explained that his wife was at the hospital about to deliver their third child, and he piled his other two children into the truck loaded with unsold beers from the distributor, saying, "Well, I'll be off then." He did not return for three whole days. On the fourth day he finally called and told Shiroyama that he had met with the young owner of a sake wholesaler who, despite having a liquor license, was thinking of shuttering the business after the previous owner had passed; Kurata had convinced him instead to become a distributor for Hinode. He then said that he had persuaded Hinode's Fukui branch to sign an official distributor contract, and managed to start things off by selling them the fifty cases of beer left in his truck at wholesale. Shiroyama would never forget how nonchalantly Kurata had recounted it all.

That was the kind of man Kurata was. He used whatever means necessary to make a sale, always taking responsibility for the numbers he did sell; what was more, he grasped the larger picture of the sales business to expand their network and improve figures, going beyond individual performance. Everyone took notice of Kurata and his abilities, but within Hinode's antiquated corporate environment his personnel reviews were rather low. It could have been that Kurata's service as first responder to customer complaints since early on in his career had an unfairly negative effect. Shiroyama was aware that he was the first man to capitalize on, deploy, value, rely upon, and nurture Kurata's talents.

When he was promoted he made sure to recommend Kurata as his second-in-command, and when he was transferred he pushed for Kurata to be his successor. Even as he worked to keep the peace around him, he had continued to support Kurata both publicly and privately because he believed that not valuing Kurata's business acumen would be a loss for the company. In the time since the two of them had taken on managerial positions, Kurata had never disappointed Shiroyama's expectations, and as others gradually came to accept him, the dominion of the Shiroyama and Kurata partnership took hold.

But times had changed. Kurata's corporate view was conservative, even compared to Shiroyama's—which perhaps could not be helped so long as the manufacturing industry remained as it was—but the gaps in Kurata's capacities as a manager, especially in contrast with someone like Sei'ichi Shirai, had now become all too evident. Kurata was still preoccupied with increasing sales month-to-month, while Shirai, on the other hand, had been assessing the profitability of their company based on its return on shareholders' equity, declaring stagnant growth for the future of the process industry and spearheading the charge toward diversification. Now that producing and distributing beer out of their own company factory was the direction the manufacturing industry was inevitably heading, it was apparent which of these corporate views should take the lead for the betterment of Hinode's future. Shirai was handicapped by his age—he was fifty-nine now—but he was more than capable of carrying on for a few more years.

And yet, it goes without saying that the transformation of the future would not happen without those who could increase profits in the present, and did not change the fact that the beer business would remain the foundation of their company. With his steady performance, Kurata's power was as immense as ever, and precisely what gave rise to the petty swirl of personal emotions within the other departments. Over the last five years, Shiroyama had managed to keep them sufficiently balanced, but when it came down to it there was no middle ground in any matter, and he was well aware that with every decision he made he was sowing the seeds of personal grudges. He didn't know how much those seeds had grown, but whatever dissatisfaction sprouted would obviously be directed toward Kurata, as the one in line under Shiroyama. And Shiroyama was painfully aware that when an unexpected incident such as this occurred— one that could undermine the fate of the company—those internal anxieties and concerns must have all been leveled at Kurata.

Yet even this did not account for Kurata's current behavior. Previously, Kurata would have quickly suppressed the movements of any executives who seemed restive, then would have acted as if nothing had happened; or he would allow them to rebel and use that as an excuse to quash them, again pretending as if nothing had happened; or perhaps he would feign indifference and maneuver his way through them—in any case, he would never have allowed any sign of discord to reach Shiroyama. Instead, he would have run interference on any such strife, proclaiming to Shiroyama that he should not trouble himself with these matters, that he should instead focus on managing the company. But here Kurata was tonight, suggesting that Shirai share what the executives had been saying in Shiroyama's absence.

Shiroyama could not imagine that Kurata would ever defect, but he now had to consider that Kurata's devotion—in which Shiroyama had placed his trust completely over the past thirty years, and his loyalty to the company that sustained it—might be suffering from systematic fatigue.

In particular, after everyone else had proved incompetent in the company's dealings with corporate extortionists, Kurata alone had served as liaison with the Okada Association, reluctantly but diligently. By circumventing the official channel of general affairs, this tacitly presented the arrangement as a fait accompli created by the merciless corporate logic that, should it become necessary, any legal questioning would be contained to a single executive. Shiroyama could only describe Kurata's motive for carrying such a burden on his own as single-minded devotion to the company, but even devotion had its limits, he presumed.

It wasn't hard to imagine that when they learned of their president's kidnapping, everyone in the company guessed it was at the hand of the Okada Association and had focused their criticism on Kurata, wondering what he had been doing all along. For now the only three people who knew that Okada, with whom they had severed ties two years ago with a billion-yen settlement, had reappeared this year to demand that the company purchase land in Gunma prefecture were Shiroyama, Kurata, and Shirai, but no doubt Kurata must have received the most shock upon hearing the news of the president's kidnapping. It had been readily apparent—from the expression on Kurata's face at the Fujiyoshida Police Department—that he was feeling nothing but regret for devoting so much of his life to dealing with the underworld. When push came to shove, all the company did was place blame rather than show any appreciation for Kurata's years of hard work.

There was nothing strange about a certain disenchantment toward the company taking root in Kurata's mind—even when Shiroyama had seen the photo of his niece handed over by the criminals, he had not wasted any time thinking about why he should die for the sake of the company. Nevertheless, as Shiroyama beheld this transformation in the man who had been his partner for thirty years, he experienced the fleeting sensation that the ground was giving way beneath his feet. He was filled with a sense of private defeat, one that was wholly new and unexpected to him. Since being abducted, he had spent time contemplating all manner of things, but his mind could never have fathomed such a change in Kurata. And yet, recalling the vexation evident in Kurata's profile that long-ago summer day as he drove off in his truck with his two small children, Shiroyama wondered if this unfamiliar side of Kurata had existed since then.

As Shiroyama felt the foundation that had supported him at Hinode for thirty years beginning to shift under him, his thoughts returned to the ripple effect of this incident, which could not simply be resolved with backroom deals. Shiroyama had no choice but to believe that Kurata would not betray him. As he tucked away the premonition that he might not be able to trust the man in the future, a fresh sense of isolation came over him.

Shiroyama put down his fork, picked up the glass he had left untouched, and took a sip of Hinode Meister. A third of the board members had expressed concern that development of the Meister would only hasten their lager's sinking sales. Since he had ultimately overruled them and decided to forge ahead with the new product, he reminded himself that it behooved him to drink it—no matter the circumstances. He faced the two vice presidents sitting before him.

"The chairman already went over the difficulty of the situation, so I'm prepared. I'm going to tell you two what really happened before anyone else, so please, I need to ask you to take the lead at the board meeting," Shiroyama began.

"Kurata-kun and I are both ready for that—it's why we're here now. By the way, Shiroyama-san, the evening paper said something about six hundred million . . ." Shirai said, getting straight to the heart of the matter.

"Six hundred million is incorrect. That's not the amount—the sum that the crime group demanded is two billion." Shiroyama watched both pairs of eyes grow large as the two men took in this number, then continued before he himself had a chance to hesitate. "I don't know why, but the crime group gave me the preemptive instruction to tell the police that their demand was for six hundred million."

"We were thinking six hundred million wasn't so bad, but two billion is a lot," Shirai muttered.

"I didn't tell the police this, but the reason the crime group let me go was so that I could accurately convey their demand and to take preparations to make the payment. The criminals said that their hostage is the beer. Three-and-a-half million kiloliters of it."

"Our beer . . . ?" Shirai and Kurata simultaneously cried out in shock, and they both glanced at the small bottle of Hinode Meister on Shiroyama's side desk. Shirai shrugged, as if he had no words to express how he felt. Kurata, meanwhile, frowned deeply, his furious expression much easier to read than his previous mien.

"Shiroyama-san," Shirai said. "I'll ask you point-blank: Is the criminals' demand for money directed at you personally or at Hinode Beer—which is it?"

"Hinode Beer. That is beyond a doubt."

"Did they say why they've targeted Hinode?"

"No. Aside from their demand for two billion, and that they would make contact before Golden Week, they said nothing else, nor did they answer any of my questions. They were completely unyielding. Truly."

"So, are you saying they did not mention the matter with that student named Hatano and your niece?"

"No."

"What about the land in Gunma prefecture?"

"Nothing of the sort was mentioned."

"I see . . . Kurata-kun also claims that Okada and the Seiwakai are not involved, so that means at this point, we really don't know why Hinode has been targeted."

"It appears so."

"Well then, if the beer is the hostage, then there's only one thing the board has to decide," Kurata began. "We'll prepare the necessary materials for the board members to determine whether or not we should negotiate."

"That's no good, Kurata-kun," Shirai immediately objected. "The executives have different crisis mentalities, so if you mention negotiating straightaway it will only trigger a negative reaction. Our first priority is to make sure that every member recognizes—definitively and without any misunderstanding—that the beer has been taken hostage. Shiroyama-san, if possible it would be best for you to explain this yourself. If the beer is the hostage, then obviously we must assume there will be attacks on our products."

"I agree with you. All I can do is explain the situation to the best of my ability and ask for everyone to understand."

"Even so, it'll get complicated, so as Kurata-kun suggested, we'll prepare the materials they need to examine the pros and cons of whether or not to negotiate. How does that sound?" Shirai turned to Kurata.

"We've entered the high-demand season for beer, and we also have the just-launched Meister to worry about. If there were to be an incident and we needed to recall our products, in the worst-case scenario we would need to prepare for a decrease in sales by half. I'll run up some rough estimates—it'll be quickest way for everyone to recognize the gravity of the situation."

"No, no numbers," Shirai objected again. "If we start throwing around estimates, it'll look like the damage to our product is a foregone conclusion. That'll only invite more complications. For tonight, we should limit ourselves to stating that an attack on our products is a predictable outcome."

"But if the criminals say they'll get in touch before Golden Week, there is a mountain of things that need to be prepared by then. We can't afford to delay gathering the board's consensus."

Shiroyama looked at the clock, which showed 6:20 P.M. It was about time for them to wrap this up.

"Kurata-san. Regarding preparation, I believe there are practices we can implement within the framework of risk management, rather than assuming that our products will be damaged. We should aim to gather the board's consensus under a more ambiguous context. In any case, I need for everyone to have an accurate grasp of the situation in which Hinode Beer finds itself. Only then would I like for them to outline how the corporation will respond to the circumstances predicted. I also need for them to okay the fact that I lied to the police. I'm counting on the both of you to take charge of the proceedings."

"Well, that's it then," Shirai said, slapping his knee. Beside him, Kurata said, "Shirai-san, will you convey the issue we discussed?" He bowed and excused himself.

Shiroyama watched him go, then turned back to Shirai. "What issue?"

"The incident with the mysterious tape from 1990 has been leaked to the rest of the board members . . . I won't name names but I've asked a few executives whom they heard it from, and every one of them said they received an anonymous phone call at home before they came to work this morning. Actually, I received one myself."

"What did the caller say?"

"That there had been a case of employment discrimination at Hinode in 1990. The caller had a Kansai accent . . . When I checked with the other executives, some said the caller spoke in a Kansai dialect, while others said it was standard Japanese, so I suspect there were multiple callers. As far as I could confirm, there are five executives who received a call. I've explicitly instructed them not to speak of the matter to anyone."

"Did the caller make any specific threats?"

"No, nothing like that, but the names Takayuki Hatano and Hiroyuki Hatano were mentioned. Your niece's name did not come up. In any case, since all of the calls were made to the executives at their home, it seems likely the source has some kind of connection with our company."

"What is the likelihood that Okada is behind this . . . ?"

"I can't say. Kurata said it's possible they've decided to take advantage of the kidnapping incident to jolt us into making the land sale . . . In any case, we need to lock down the board."

After Shirai left, Shiroyama looked at the clock again. 6:27 P.M. He took another sip of Hinode Meister, but the beer had already gone flat and lost all flavor.

AT HALF PAST SIX IN the evening, the eighteen faces that convened in the executive conference room included the fifteen directors from Hinode's main office—excluding those from their subsidiary and affiliated companies—as well as the manager of general affairs, the director of public relations, and finally Kotani, the representative from the risk management company. There was no one to record meeting notes nor were there any beverages, and once all of the attendees had gathered, the soundproof door was closed and locked from inside, and a hush fell over the room.

Since the autumn of last year, a whiteboard—a sight unsuited to this electronic age—had been placed inside the conference room. After the risk management system was introduced within the company, the main emphasis had been on information management, and the whiteboard was a means of substantially decreasing the volume of various documents being exchanged internally in the interest of confidentiality. Most business was conducted over electronic mail, and items that needed to be saved were managed in bulk on the company's network server. The heaps of documents that used to be distributed at internal meetings had decreased, and anything that needed to be spelled out could be jotted on the whiteboard and erased after they were finished. These same rules applied to board meetings, without exception. For essential materials, each employee's ID number would be stamped onto every page that was copied and distributed, to prevent loss or leaks.

Kotani was the one who had proposed these reforms and, after obtaining the board's approval, had gone on to create an explicit system of measures. The implementation of Kotani's system met with considerable resistance from the board, and it only came about because Kurata and Shirai together pushed hard for it—the former citing the necessity of corporate defense against extortionists and the latter citing threats from industry spies and cyber crime. Yet even now, about half of the board members still grumbled about the costs incurred.

It was true that the initial installation in the information management sector alone—designing the network security system; adding servers; digitalization of all telecommunication equipment, including phones; shuffling personnel in order to further strengthen the network; expenses for training employees for managerial positions—had cost them close to two billion yen.

Moreover, in the crime prevention sector they had needed to increase the number of security cameras in all of their branch offices and factories and infrared alarm systems for after-work hours, produce all the various risk management manuals, and equip all employee ID cards with magnetic strips. When the Great Hanshin Earthquake had struck at the beginning of this year, they had taken the opportunity to further quake-proof their water tanks and private power generation system as well as to retain a company that specialized in backing up their recovery discs, so there were these additional costs. Each of these items resulted in meetings and more complications, and Shiroyama forced them all through, urging everyone that it was impossible to put a price on safety. Now that the man who himself had insisted on such measures had been kidnapped, the air that greeted Kotani in the conference room was, to say the least, chilly from the start.

Kotani had been head of the Japan branch of a large property and casualty insurance company that was contracted by Hinode's subsidiary in the US. The insurance company had referred Kotani to Hinode's main office, and he had signed with them as a consultant. The impression he gave as a typical Harvard yuppie aside, certain aspects of his behavior and manner revealed that his sensibility was slightly different from that of an average Japanese person. Even now, in the hushed meeting room, he blew his nose—loudly and deliberately—causing the executives around him to furrow their brows in disapproval.

The only person with the wherewithal to address Kotani was Shirai. "I hear the cedar pollen is particularly bad this year."

As Kotani began his report, it became clear that he did not interpret the current situation as a lapse in the system. He emphasized craftily that now was the time when risk management's effectiveness would be proven.

It was then and there Shiroyama learned that, as per the manual created the previous fall, over the last three days a special top-secret control center had been installed and was up and running in an underground storage room beneath the opera hall. Kotani said that, starting tomorrow, the point of contact between their public relations and the press would also be directly linked to this control center, as a means to streamline their information management even further.

"The crucial point is, no matter whether it's internal or external to the company, no employees other than those assigned exclusively to the control center has anything whatsoever to do with information related to the incident," Kotani said. The preventative measures were detailed indeed; he spoke about ensuring that those involved in the police investigation enter and leave from the underground parking lot and go straight to the control center, and that all communications and instructions between the control center and the board be conducted verbally and not on paper.

Kotani had not been informed about the particulars of the situation, so he was merely generalizing, but even so, the specific measures were based on the assumptions that the company faced certain circumstances that could not be made public and that the criminals would later make a monetary demand.

In closing, Kotani said, "How you maintain your relationship with the police will become an important issue as the situation progresses. It's vital to ensure that all questioning of your employees by the investigators be channeled through the control center so that your company is always aware of the flow of information. As a basic rule, I advise you to respond prudently, with the assumption that anything you share with investigators will leak out, one way or another." Thus he ended his report, which took less than ten minutes and did not elicit a peep from the board.

After Kotani left the room and the door had been locked again, someone quipped, "We're going to let that guy negotiate with the criminals?" but no one responded and the meeting proceeded to the report by Ide, the manager of general affairs.

Ide first explained what, going forward from this morning, the response had been within and outside of the company, and emphasized that there had been no notable inquiries from their clients or industry peers that required their collective attention. Internally, during the morning division heads' meeting, Ide had arranged for all employees to be given a script on how to respond whenever a customer might bring up the incident, and the procedure was already in place by that afternoon. He also reported that one of their employees had been stopped on the street in front of their Osaka branch office that morning by a television crew from a commercial broadcasting company and he had ended up talking to them. The head of the branch immediately called the main office about this occurrence, reporting that said employee had been given a stern warning.

Next, Hiroshi Sakakibara, the corporate secretary and executive director of general affairs, read aloud the list of documents he had submitted in compliance with the police's request: first was the set of materials distributed at the current term's board meeting; organizational charts and allocation of duties for every department and division in the main office as well as every factory, branch office, store, and sales office; issues of their quarterly in-house newsletter, *Hinode*, from last year going back to 1955; the two-volume *History of Hinode Beer*, compiled to commemorate their centennial; a register of retired employees from last year going back to 1965, and the employee directory for the current year; and finally a list of all their distributors and suppliers.

There was another list of documents, those they had refused to submit to the authorities: minutes from board meetings; daily logs of executives and the president; employee performance evaluations; a list of callers to the general affairs department and records of faxes sent and received, going back to January of this year; the contents of company insurance policies and a list of insurance companies; a set of their current and past ledgers.

Next Kayama, the manager of public relations, announced that their deputy manager had been assigned to the control center. But since the various media companies were so aggressive in their pursuit, and an ambiguous response might harm the company's image, he suggested that instead it would be better to refuse all interviews. To this, Tazawa—the managing director in charge of public affairs— immediately reprimanded him, "What do you think you're saying? Consider first whether you assigned the right person to deal with the media. Then we'll discuss this. That's enough from you."

Following Tazawa's rebuke, a chorus of impatient voices rose from the group, urging that they move on from the reports and proceed to the main subject. Shirai signaled with his eyes and the two managers, Ide and Kayama, quickly left the room. Once the door was sealed off for a third time, only the fifteen board members remained in the conference room.

Shiroyama sat at the head of the oval table, flanked by Shirai and Kurata. The rest of the seating had not been arranged in any particular order, but split naturally into those who aligned with Shirai on one side and those who aligned with Kurata on the other, representing the two opposing factions, as they were. Normally before a meeting Shiroyama would survey those to his left and right, meeting each man's gaze and ascertaining his expression, but now five of the executives on Kurata's side—including Takeo Sugihara beside him—avoided looking at Shiroyama, while the rest of them were bleary and red-eyed from lack of sleep or appeared in a state of utter bafflement. He had expected this, but clearly any sense of relief about the safe return of the president of the company had already dissipated within the span of half a day.

"I have caused so much worry to you all. It is shameful to have been kidnapped from the front door of my own home, and I'd like to take this opportunity to formally apologize to you all," Shiroyama said, opening his address to the group with a few simple words of regret. Next came the task of dispelling any suspicions. "I'm concerned that speculations may be rife, both inside and outside the company. However, I say this to you as the victim of the crime itself, the identity of the criminals remains a complete mystery. And as I told the police, for the duration of the time when I was under confinement they barely said a word to me, nor did they voice any grievances toward our company or mention specific troubles. The only thing they spoke of was their demand for money."

Taking up from Shiroyama's statement, as previously arranged, Shirai began posing questions, acting as a representative of the executives on the board.

"Does that mean the criminals didn't say anything about extortion-ists?"

"Nothing whatsoever."

"In 1990, during employee entrance exams, the company received slanderous letters and a recorded tape from the father of a student who claimed his son had been discriminated against—nothing of that nature was mentioned either?"

"Nothing at all."

As a buzz arose from the executives, now it was Kurata's turn to quickly add his part. "I'll give some context for those of you who may not know what transpired. The father of the student came from a segregated buraku community, and it's true that he sent letters and a tape as described to our human resources department. The human resources manager at the time consulted and reviewed the matter with Shirai-san and myself, and we determined that the defamation was extreme enough to be reported to the police. But the student in question died in a car accident, and then his father suffered a nervous breakdown and committed suicide, so the investigation ended there. There was never any fault with our company, but I'd like all of you to be aware that such an incident did occur."

With one among their doubts and fears having thus been swiftly contained by Kurata and Shirai, for the time being no objections were raised by the members gathered around the oval table.

"Now, I'll proceed to the main issue. After careful consideration, I decided not to give an exact account to the police. The amount that the crime group has demanded is two billion."

All eyes except for those of Shirai and Kurata were riveted upon him. It was hard to tell if they were reacting to the sum itself or to the vast difference between it and the six hundred million that had been reported in the evening papers, but there was more despair than surprise conveyed in everyone's gaze.

"I told the police six hundred million. That was the sum the crim-inals instructed me to tell the police was their demand. They also told me they would make contact before Golden Week. It remains unclear why they wanted me to tell the police six hundred million while demanding two billion, but after much thought I decided to do as I was told. I based this decision upon the fact that I didn't feel as though the criminals were joking around, and because they said they were holding the beer hostage. I did not mention this to the police."

The second shockwave rippled around the oval table exactly as Shiroyama had expected. This time, the sounds didn't quite form words but rather groans and grumbles that rose to quite a cacophony.

"Does that mean if we don't bend to their demand, they'll poison our beer or something?" asked one of the executives.

"All the criminals said was that the beer is the hostage, but personally I feel it would be wise to assume a variety of possible scenarios."

"Pardon me, but is that seriously what you're saying? Has the beer really been taken hostage? Did you agree to their demand? Did you negotiate with them—?"

"I have not consented to their demand nor made any negotiations with them. My mouth was taped shut so I was unable to make any kind of response to them." Shiroyama spoke these words with a sense of disillusionment as he regarded each look of mistrust, consternation, and anxiety that was directed toward him, calmly distinguishing among them which eyes were constrained by personal feelings, which by a lack of patience, and which by the nascent urge for self-preservation. Many men, many minds—the temperaments of the board members were as varied as their number, and they each had their own timetable for negotiating tactics.

"Shiroyama-san. Isn't lying to the police the same thing as consenting to the criminals' demand? It may not be necessary to cooperate fully with the police, but it solves nothing to tell them six hundred million when it's two billion, or to conceal the hostage situation," said one of the executives, offering his harsh opinion.

"People are saying Hinode has already paid the money or that some backroom deal has been made," said another.

"That's what the police suspect us of, anyway," said another.

"The newspapers have already made up their minds," said yet another.

To all this Shiroyama replied, "I'm very aware of all this."

"Shiroyama-san. You say that you told the police what you did because the criminals said they were holding the beer hostage, but that's not entirely logical. If the beer is being held hostage, we can't possibly protect the company without support from the police," said another executive.

"I understand your point exactly, but if I were to tell the police that the beer has been taken hostage and that fact leaks to the papers, that cannot be undone. There is no option but to protect our products ourselves. We're already in the midst of the summer sales season, so it's imperative that whatever measures we take will not startle our distributors and consumers."

"Does that mean you think there is no chance the criminals will be captured—?"

"No, but the reason the police don't have any leads has nothing to do with me not accurately conveying the ransom. And so long as there is no guarantee that the criminals will be captured anytime soon, I feel it's best for us to take precautions against their threats and make the best decisions possible as we go. I don't feel that I have consented to their demands."

"Do you really believe the criminals will make contact?"

"I do believe they will—it's the sense I got from what they said."

The questioning broke off there, but murmured complaints—"I can't believe this" or "Why did it have to be Hinode?"—bubbled up before silence bore down on the room again.

"Gentlemen. Please take this opportunity to share your thoughts and opinions here frankly," Shirai prompted.

"Can we really go through with the shareholders meeting with these rumors of a backroom deal?"

"I don't think there is any need to get into details at the shareholders meeting."

"But what if they actually do poison our products? Perhaps we should consider paying the two billion—"

"No, at this stage it's too soon to come to a decision."

"If we are going to reject their demand, then we should have cooperated fully with the police from the start."

"But if there's no chance that the criminals will be arrested—"

"Whatever the case, we have to avoid allowing it to affect orders during the high-demand season," said one of the executives from the Kurata faction.

For the time being, each executive held fast to his own argument, and the dearth of ideas—an utter failure to see the big picture and make a commanding decision—was nothing out of the ordinary. As Shiroyama took in the discussion, which spun in circles like a yacht that could not set its direction, his own mind shut down any attempt to reach a decision. He was in no position to opine about the disorderly scene before him in which the executives, rather than showing any sense of crisis, instead revealed glimmers of their ulterior motives, their eyes on the next regime. Shiroyama just sat amid the board of directors, bearing the lie he had told that would force the company to unrightfully pay out two billion, and even as he did so, he was losing sense of the reality surrounding him bit by bit, until he no longer knew how he had come to be there—how he had been kidnapped; how intently he had deliberated, then wavered, and finally made a decision; the fact that he was deceiving the public and his company; the fact that he was president; and the fact that he was sitting there now.

And even though I lied, what does it matter when the lie is so small that it's nothing compared to three-and-a-half million kiloliters of beer? It may seem I did it to save my niece and her family, but what are Yoshiko and Tetsushi to me? Did I return here for the sake of my company, or for my family?

Shiroyama knew he could only answer the last question. He was not doing this for anyone's sake—he simply had not had the courage to die.

"Everyone, no doubt the president is tired tonight, so let's start wrapping things up," Kurata broke in.

"I'll conclude," Shiroyama said in response. "Everyone, I'll be brief. Right now, what is being asked of us is this: how will we get through this violent crisis, as a corporation; how will we minimize the damage; and how will we keep this incident from interfering with our operations. With these as a premise, for today I have refrained from disclosing everything to the police, to leave room to negotiate with the crime group, should worse come to worst. I ask you to accept this point. If you have any objections please raise your hand."

No one did.

"Next, as to how we should respond to the crime group's subsequent movements, I would like to monitor the progress of the investigation for about a week, then have another discussion and reach a decision. Any objections? No? Then I'll assume it's approved. Next, let's discuss whether to take this opportunity to step up our crisis management and strengthen our company's general security preparedness. I will ask Kotani and the security company as well as the point person for security from each sector to come up with proposals for the necessary measures and cost for each stage—production, distribution, and wholesale—as soon as possible. With those materials in hand, I would like us to reconvene early next week to analyze our plan. How does that sound?"

"Allow me to confirm one thing before we finish." The man who spoke was Kenji Otani, managing director of the pharmaceutical business division, one of the five executives who had refused to make eye contact with Shiroyama at the beginning of the meeting. Otani was a man who had driven the pharmaceutical division by demonstrating outstanding leadership abilities in new drug development but, it must be said, his was the kind of intellect, having never experienced setbacks or failure, that did not have the same application outside his field of research.

Otani bluntly inquired about what the rest of the executives—save for Shirai before the meeting—had been too discreet to ask.

"Shiroyama-san. Is the target of the crime group's threat truly Hinode Beer?"

"Yes," Shiroyama answered tersely. "If you have any other questions, please speak up. If not, that's all from me. Once again, I'm grateful for your continued understanding and cooperation."

Following Shiroyama's concluding remarks, Shirai reiterated, "Well then, gentlemen, please keep what was discussed here tonight confidential." By the time the group dispersed it was quarter past eight in the evening.

WHEN SHIROYAMA RETURNED TO HIS office, the plate of leftover food and beer glass had been cleared away, and there was a note that Ms. Nozaki had left for him under the light of his desk lamp. *I hope you will be able to get some rest today. Before you leave, please dial 2102 and, for caution's sake, someone from the corporate secretariat will accompany you out.*

Shiroyama sat down in his chair and stared at the light from the lamp that fell upon the documents and notes arranged on his desk. He felt out of sorts with himself, in a daze caused by his unsettled mood and an excess of futile thoughts that whirred through his mind and made his head feel like it would burst. The fact that he had been kidnapped, out of the blue, and the enormous sum of two billion demanded of him. The question of whether it was right or wrong to bend to such an unreasonable demand and hide the truth from his company and the public. The uncertainty of his own grasp of everything that had happened to lead up to this point.

He had nowhere for such thoughts to reside. Although the room he sat in was familiar, the air around him seemed to percolate with energy, and as he was struck by a sense of impending doom, without realizing it Shiroyama had reached for the phone and began dialing numbers randomly. The first call he made was to the office of the general manager of the beer division on the twenty-ninth floor.

"Kurata-san? This is Shiroyama. I am so sorry for the trouble I've caused you these last three days. Please know that I deeply appreciate all of your efforts. I apologize for not being able to take the time to sit down and talk with you today."

"No, I should be the one to apologize. I made such a careless remark when I was in your office today."

"I hope we can continue to work together going forward. I urge you not to shoulder all these burdens on your own. If there's anything going on make sure you talk to me. Please."

"You needn't worry so much about me, Shiroyama-san. I'm sure you're exhausted so please get some rest tonight."

"Well, I'll see you tomorrow then."

"I appreciate the call."

This exchange of banal pleasantries took up barely a minute of their time before Shiroyama put down the receiver. Shiroyama felt a guarded sense of hesitation in Kurata's response, just as he had sensed two hours earlier. Perhaps the man really could have had some kind of recalibration during the last three days.

Shiroyama wondered what he had been expecting anyway—from people. From society. From a corporation.

With these questions echoing in his head, Shiroyama turned to look at the nightscape outside his window and recalled that he had taken in a similar view the night he first spoke to his niece about her classmate Takayuki Hatano. The uncertainty of life that had plagued him then had now been transformed into a pitch-dark hollow that yawned at his feet. The black void was indicative of how, in the seventy-two hours spanning from Friday evening, when a large black shape surged in front of him as he approached his front door, until now, there was nothing concrete or tangible save for a single photo of a member of his family. The photograph had split his life cleanly in two, and it seemed to him that the version of himself who sat here now would have been unimaginable to him just three days ago—a gutless fool who had lost the coherence of his life. Suddenly it occurred to him that the dentist must have felt like this when he had learned of his son's death in a car accident, but that event from the fall of 1990, having already drifted to the far side of the void, caused him no real pangs of regret.

This time, the call Shiroyama placed was to an outside number.

"Yamazaki-san? It's Shiroyama."

On the other end of the line, his driver, Tatsuo Yamazaki, was unable to put his emotions into words, only muttering, "I'm sorry . . . so sorry . . ."

"So much has happened, I know, but as you can tell I have returned safely, so don't worry yourself too much. I will look forward to seeing you again, once we're through with the police questioning," Shiroyama said, taking care of one call he needed to make to someone who had been on his mind.

Next he called home. His son, Mitsuaki, answered, exclaiming, "Oh, Dad!" He then shouted, "Mom! It's Dad!" and Shiroyama heard the pitter-patter of footsteps echo through the hall.

In a tiny voice, Reiko barely managed to utter the words, "Thank goodness you're safe—to think of everything you've been through!" before she was overcome by tears and fell silent. That put Shiroyama at a loss for words himself, though finally he managed to say, "It must have been terrible for you, too. How are you? Everyone all right? I should be home around ten," sounding more agitated than he would have liked.

"Yes, we're all just fine here. I've prepared a bath for you. Shoko will arrive home tomorrow. Mitsuaki says he'll stay the night here too. Oh, and Yoshiko and her husband called and said they just want to hear your voice, so they asked for you to call once you're home."

"All right. I'll be there in a little while."

The gentle voices of his son and wife soothed his ears, but while listening to them Shiroyama had contemplated the eventual ripple effects that the incident would have on his family, and the moment he replaced the receiver, he was rattled by the sudden desire to flee to a deserted island.

Then, giving in to a temptation that had lingered in a corner of his mind for the past two and a half hours, he made another call. The recipient was a bureaucrat working in a central government ministry who shared Shiroyama's distaste for the convivial requirements of his job. Shiroyama knew from experience there was little chance he would be out drinking at this hour, and as expected he reached Kiyoshi Iwami in the commissioner-general's office of the NPA.

"Iwami-san? It's Shiroyama from Hinode."

"Ah, Shiroyama-san! I'm so relieved to hear from you. Your safe return seems to have saved our necks around here. Are you sure you're all right?"

"Thank you, I'm perfectly fine. I understand you called as soon as you heard the news and I just wanted to thank you."

"Oh, there's no need for that. Fifty-six hours and the police barely managed to do anything effective—shame on us. I can't imagine how horrible it must have been for you. I haven't left my post here since hearing about the incident, and have been getting updates on the progress of the investigation."

Iwami's way of speaking conveyed none of the typical bureaucrat's cloaking of intimidation with flattery nor the stodginess of someone in power; and yet his distinctive straightforwardness, which seemed to betray no intention or emotion whatsoever, made the listener all the more aware of the power of the police force.

In his student days Iwami had been the quintessential geek, always trudging diligently to and from the library, and after joining the NPA, he played the sycophant at alumni reunions, graciously pouring drinks for their classmates who now worked for the finance or construction ministries—but not once during those times had Shiroyama ever seen joy in Iwami's eyes. When someone said that Iwami was a rising star in Public Security and that before long he would be promoted to bureau chief, and Shiroyama had marveled how Iwami's small, flat head could accommodate such distrust in humanity, faith in state power, and savvy to navigate the bureaucracy. Last year Shiroyama had attended a private celebration for Iwami's promotion from deputy commissioner general to commissioner-general after years of service as the head of Security Bureau, and it seemed to Shiroyama, having not seen Iwami for a long time, as if the mundanity was now gone from his former bland tactfulness. "Being at the top of the police is like finishing a game of sugoroku first. Once you're done you're just waiting around collecting the paperwork submitted by others while they finish the game," the man had joked with an easygoing detachment, yet Shiroyama had the strong impression of him as a well-designed robot. Their colleagues in other government or corporate sectors seemed only more world-weary with every passing year, sinking deeper into their own turmoil, whereas the police appeared to function with increasing order and ease the higher one climbed up the ranks.

"Oh no, I'm quite grateful for all of the police's efforts. It would be selfish to ask for more," Shiroyama responded. "By the way, Iwami-san. It's my opinion that Hinode Beer is entirely the victim in this incident, but do the police see things differently?"

"Don't be absurd. Why do you ask? Have our investigators been out of line?"

"This is my first encounter with the police, so I wouldn't know what's considered out of line, but there's no point in making a statement if what I say is not accepted as is."

"That's a misunderstanding. What you tell us is recorded word for word as testimony and we ask you to take a look and ensure there are no errors before it gets an official seal. So please don't worry about that. The police are never swayed by what's reported in the media."

"I see. I do hope that is the case. Otherwise, doubt may spread throughout the corporate sector that we can't be sure how much trust to place in the police's response when we get embroiled in incidents like this."

"Shiroyama-san. If you notice anything going forward, please know that you can always come to me. I'll see to it that we don't inconvenience you any further."

"I appreciate your consideration. Thank you."

Shiroyama set down the phone and applied the last of his perseverance to come to this realization: the reason every voice he had heard in the last few minutes—including those of his family members—seemed impossibly distant was because, quite simply, this was what it meant to become the victim of a crime. In the distance between himself—the man who had been informed by the criminals that three-and-a-half million kiloliters of beer had been taken hostage—and the rest of the world, rifts were developing everywhere.

I see, so this is what it feels like to be a victim. Shiroyama went through a long and meandering thought process in order to settle upon such a trivial conclusion.

Finally, he took out a sheet of company letterhead and a fountain pen to draft the speech he would give to the assembly of executives early tomorrow morning.

Shiroyama hunched over his desk, and within about half an hour he had written a decidedly mediocre speech for the morning assembly. "We all should be aware that it is the individual employee who can protect our company, without succumbing to the violent act targeting us . . ." He reminded himself as always that the duty of a manager was not to lecture employees about a specific theory but rather to inspire them to come up with a specific theory of their own, and he put down his pen and put away the stationery. He stared at the clock that read half past nine and thought, *I'm so tired, so dead tired.*

He sat in a daze for ten or fifteen minutes, without the energy to even lift a finger, before he finally made a call to the corporate secretariat as Ms. Nozaki's note had requested. Upon arriving downstairs at the underground parking lot, he found that more people than he had expected—a driver and three male employees—were waiting for him by his car. According to one of the employees, whose face betrayed his consternation, over a hundred reporters had been staked out in front of Shiroyama's home in Sanno since early this morning. His family had not been able to step foot outside, he said, so it would be impossible for him to get out of the car without an escort.

久保晴久　Haruhisa Kubo

AT HALF PAST SEVEN TAKEUCHI, the cop from Marunouchi Police Department who was Haruhisa Kubo's source, and Kitagawa, an assistant police inspector from Fukagawa Police Department who came along with him, showed up at the small Japanese restaurant in Funabashi, ascending to a tatami room on the second floor.

"Hello." Takeuchi appeared first, sliding open the *fusuma* door and popping his head in, then bowing slightly with a sheepish grin. He called to the inspector behind him to follow. Kitagawa, taking his cue from Takeuchi, bowed his head and said hello in the same way. Kubo, who had been waiting for the two men, sat formally with his legs tucked beneath him and returned the greeting, thanking them for coming. "Pleasure's all mine," Takeuchi, who was used to these encounters, affably waved off Kubo's formality. He then urged the inspector to sit down while he himself promptly took a cross-legged seat at the head of the table. Two or three seconds of awkward silence followed as Kubo sat facing the two detectives while they wiped their hands with hot towels.

"Please, have some beer." The silence was broken by a female server who came in and filled each of their glasses. "I'll be right back with the meal." The men waited until she was gone before launching into casual pleasantries. *It's sure been cold lately. Where are you going to see the cherry blossoms this year?*

Within Kubo's realm of experience, for whatever reason, secret meetings with a source invariably started off in such a manner. And for him, this marked the beginning of a long few hours in which the thought that settled into the pit of his stomach was that he would be done for if he couldn't get ahold of a story tonight.

"A lot of things being printed, huh? Six hundred million yen. They'll contact Hinode later. And so on and so forth."

Takeuchi, whom Kubo had known for going on three years, had quickly relaxed after a glass of beer. He broached the topic in a show of thoughtful consideration.

"Well, it's the official word from the police so we have no choice but to print it accordingly. Ah, allow me," Kubo said and topped up Kitagawa's glass. Though unplanned, the beer they were drinking was Hinode Supreme. The inspector, who appeared to have never been in a situation like this, awkwardly followed Takeuchi's lead, holding out his own glass and bowing his head as he thanked Kubo.

"I'm sure people will say whatever they want, but what we released came from the victim's deposition so it's difficult to say . . ." Just as Takeuchi carefully began to muddy the waters, the server returned with their meal.

"I hear the cherry blossoms will be late this year." Kubo changed the topic.

"You, going cherry-blossom-viewing, Kubo-san?" Takeuchi laughed. "No way you have time for that."

Once the server had set out the appetizers and disappeared, Kubo urged the two men to start eating. "Go ahead, please."

"Don't mind if I do," Takeuchi said, splitting his chopsticks, and the inspector did the same. After they had picked at the sea bream sashimi for a while, Takeuchi, who knew well enough how to return the favor of the dinner, pivoted the conversation to the main topic. "So, Kubo-san, this fellow here . . ."

"Name's Kitagawa," mumbled the inspector, since he hadn't actually introduced himself to Kubo yet. The inspector had worked in records for CID at Shinagawa Police Department. He seemed about forty years of age, with reserved, contemplative eyes and a fair complexion that reddened at the cheeks. Kubo got the impression from the man's rusticity that he must have been from Sendai or one of the prefectures farther north.

"Like I told you on the phone, Kitagawa says he remembers every case that was handled by the Shinagawa Department. It seems there was an incident from the nineties involving Hinode after all. Right?"

Urged on by Takeuchi, Kitagawa responded tentatively: "It was November 1990. A case of defamation and obstruction of business. Hinode had received letters and a tape from an unknown source, and they decided to file a complaint."

"The letters and tape slandered Hinode?" Kubo asked.

"I didn't see them in person, but I heard that the sender of the letter assumed the name of the Buraku Liberation League and it went on about employment discrimination at Hinode. The tape, on the other hand, was an audio recording of a letter in its entirety that had been sent to Hinode just after the war . . . That letter also mentioned the Buraku Liberation League."

"Kubo-san, I told you on the phone, right?" Takeuchi cut in. "There's a guy I know who worked out of Shinagawa Police Department back then. While the rest of us are up to our necks with work these days, he keeps yammering on about discrimination. Turns out this is what he was talking about."

"Are you talking about Inspector Takahashi?" Kitagawa asked Takeuchi.

"No, Yamashita," responded Takeuchi.

Kitagawa began muttering to himself. "Yamashita? I thought it was Handa who was working with Takahashi back then. Oh, that's right. Yamashita took over after Handa."

Takahashi, Handa, Yamashita—after committing the names of the three detectives from Shinagawa Police Department to memory, Kubo dug a little deeper. "Kitagawa-san, how did the investigation turn out after that?"

"We figured out who the sender of the letter was, so the chief ordered us to hear what the guy had to say, just in case. I think that was around the middle of November. An inspector named Takahashi from White Collar Crime and a detective named Handa who had been transferred over from Violent Crime went out first thing in the morning. They returned that evening, and they had arranged for the sender of the letter to come to the police station the next day so they could take down his statement. But that night the sender killed himself."

"What was the name and occupation of the sender?"

"He was a dentist in Seijo. I'm sure you'll find him if you look up Hatano Dental Clinic in a Setagaya phone directory from 1990. He had lost his son in a car accident a month prior, and I heard he had a nervous breakdown, convincing himself that his son had been the victim of employment discrimination during the hiring process at Hinode. I believe Hinode eventually retracted their complaint."

"This tape you mentioned—the audio recording of a letter that was sent to Hinode after the war—whose letter was it?"

"Well, that much, I don't . . ." Kitagawa responded vaguely. Kubo saw him hesitate and pressed on, "I'm sure it appeared in the official record."

"Since the accused passed away, there was never an official record but—" Here Kitagawa paused and glanced over at Takeuchi. "Can I share this bit?"

"I told you, you can trust Kubo-san." Takeuchi reached for some amaebi with his chopsticks.

Kitagawa lowered his voice a little and continued: "After the complaint was retracted, that inspector I told you about—Takahashi—made a written record of the conversation he had with the dentist—the sender of the letter—during the one and only time they met. I filed it in the register. There's no mistake about that, since I did it with my own hands. I remembered the case when I heard about this abduction incident, so I called the Shinagawa Police Department and asked them to take a look at the book. But they told me the MPD had already come and taken it."

"Meaning Investigation Headquarters already have the 1990 case in mind?"

"I'm not sure. Maybe."

"Kitagawa-san, do you remember what was in Takahashi's written record?"

"I do but, sorry, I'd rather not say."

"Yamashita said it was something to do with discrimination," Takeuchi said, helping out.

"Yes, that's true, but what's more important is how on earth the dentist got hold of the letter sent to Hinode right after the war . . ."

"You mean there's an issue with where it came from?"

"You could say that."

"Does it have to do with burakumin?" Takeuchi probed lightly.

Kitagawa smiled wryly in return and shook his head. "It's more your métier, sir."

"Oh, really? Kubo-san, it's the corporate extortionists."

"I see . . . That would explain why Investigation Headquarters hauled off the record book so quickly." Kubo nodded, but his mind was a tangle, as if he had unwrapped a furoshiki cloth and could not figure out how to tie it back up again. Hadn't his superior Negoro also told him, just that afternoon, that an anonymous tip they received over the phone had to do with discrimination involving Hinode and a labor dispute after the war? Could this anonymous letter that had been recorded on the tape in 1990 be connected somehow?

In any case, if the dentist had received the letter from corporate extortionists and members of the BLL had nothing to do with the 1990 case, it became certain that Hinode had been under some kind of threat, that maybe extortionists had attempted to blackmail the company at the time. It was also obvious that the extortionists were underlings with ties to the Okada Association.

However, a general notion had started to take shape over the last three days that the abduction of Hinode Beer's president was not entangled with the shady underworld. If that were true, talk of the complaint case from 1990 could turn out to be a swing and a miss, but in any case, it nagged at Kubo that the shadow of discrimination seemed to flutter over a blue-chip corporation like Hinode.

Kubo pondered such things as he refilled the glasses of his two cohorts with Hinode Supreme. His own glass, on the other hand, was only half drained.

"Come to think of it, sir, since even I know about the 1990 case, there must be plenty of officers who are aware of it, too. Takahashi passed away last year, but I'm sure anyone who worked in Shingawa's CID back then knows about it . . ." Kitagawa began again.

"I bet only a handful know what really happened," Takeuchi responded, ever the superior. "Yamashita, at least—he had no idea."

"I guess you could be right. The ones who knew were Takahashi and me and . . ."

"What about that Handa you mentioned? I've never met him."

"Oh, him . . . I don't think he'd get it either, now that you mention it. He was transferred over from Violent Crime and handled the case with Takahashi in the beginning, but he was completely useless when it came to the law. Takahashi begged the chief inspector to give him another partner and that's when Yamashita took over . . ."

"You can't expect a guy from Violent Crime to know commercial law, right?"

"True, true." Kitagawa laughed.

At a lull in this exchange between colleagues, Kitagawa took the beer bottle and refilled Kubo's glass. "As we were saying, other newspapers might already be onto the 1990 story," he said dutifully. "If so, I do apologize."

"No, no—there's no need to worry about that. It's a complicated story and I'll need to back it up, so I probably wouldn't be able to write about it any time soon. That's something I ought to tell you up front," Kubo said, making excuses for himself as well.

"That's no problem. It's not my story to break, so it's up to you whether to write it or not. Aside from that, this sashimi is amazing!" Kitagawa said in the daft, cheerful way characteristic of precinct policemen, and eagerly wolfed down the locally caught sea bream. Kubo snuck a glimpse at his wristwatch, calculating the time left before his deadline for the morning edition and how long it would take to get back to the kisha club. "Well then, Takeuchi-san, Kitagawa-san. Shall we move on to the hot pot?" he said.

"Great idea. It's still the season for hot pot when it's this cold out," Kitagawa replied.

Kubo called for the server, and soon a large plate of marbled Kobe beef and a pot brimming with hot water were set up on the low table. Kubo also ordered warmed saké for Takeuchi, and another beer per Kitagawa's request. As for himself, Kubo finally emptied his glass of beer, washing down two slices of sashimi as a way to warm up his stomach for the hot pot ahead.

Now that the preparations had been made, it was time for round two. Kubo expertly slipped the ingredients into the pot, which he then offered to his guests as each item was cooked, all the while pouring more saké and beer, taking bites himself, and engaging in random, innocuous conversation. He knew the topic most likely to entice his companions was gossip inside the police force. Second most popular were tidbits and anecdotes that his sources wouldn't know about the latest incidents emblazoning the front pages. Next up, the families of present company. Kubo wove all of these together, churning the conversation, making sure to lean in and listen whenever his associates were inspired to share.

That evening, Takeuchi grumbled about the case he was working on, leaking that it was about to be taken over by the District Prosecutor due to its involvement with the investigation of two bankrupt credit unions. Kitagawa, for his part, was more reserved since this was his first time meeting Kubo, but he was relaxed enough to laugh at himself when he explained that, since being transferred from CID to Crime Prevention, he was now creating slogans for an anti-sexual harassment campaign—"*Look right, look left—be aware on the streets after dark*" and "*Threats to women are right before your eyes.*"

The secret meeting ended before ten in the evening, and after putting the two men in their respective taxis with prepaid vouchers, Kubo climbed into his own hired car, which had been waiting for him. His belly was pleasantly full after two glasses of beer, hot pot, and the zosui porridge that followed, but his mind felt foggy, and he was uncertain whether it was from calm or confusion. Should he take the bait and go after the insinuations of discrimination that seemed to have trailed Hinode Beer since right after the war? Was it worthwhile to investigate the apparent fact that corporate extortionists had pressured Hinode back in 1990? And should he reconsider the assumption that the current abduction case had no ties to such underworld dealings? He remembered what Kitagawa had said: *Other newspapers might already be onto the story.*

"Oh, the cherry blossoms have started to bloom. See over there?"

Kubo heard the driver's voice, and he glanced out the car window, but the blossoms on the trees failed to catch his attention. For now, he wanted to get a better handle on Hinode's troubles from 1990. He took out his cell phone and, without a second to waste, started calling his sources.

根来史彰 Fumiaki Negoro

WHEN TAKESHI KIKUCHI CALLED BACK as promised, the sun was just beginning to set and Fumiaki Negoro was waking up from a nap. Even though his mind was still cloudy with sleep, Negoro immediately recognized Kikuchi's distinctively gruff manner of speaking. *I'd know that voice anywhere*, he thought.

"Negoro-san? The case you mentioned," Kikuchi said. "I looked up Toda's full name. Are you ready? It's Yoshinori Toda. Born 1916 in Saitama prefecture. He's seventy-nine now." Negoro thanked him, and Kikuchi retorted, "I don't see the payoff in looking into an old geezer like him." With that nebulous and enigmatic comment, he hung up.

A newspaper reporter never used words like "payoff" when it came to leads—it seemed to Negoro that a journalist who had been active until a few years ago wouldn't utter them so casually. Even setting aside Kikuchi's intentions for the moment, Negoro's internal alarm kept flashing. His newspaperman's curiosity had been piqued.

The notes he had just taken read, *Born 1916, Saitama prefecture.* First Negoro called the Hachioji bureau and left a message to page a reporter named Yabe and have him call Negoro. Yabe had called the main office that very morning about a lawsuit that had occurred in Saitama prefecture in 1940.

Then, while he waited for Yabe to call back, Negoro went to the archives and cracked open the bound compact editions of the newspaper from the years 1946 and 1947. He flipped through the pages, written with the old Japanese characters, from the period in which there was hardly a day when the word "dispute" did not appear in the headlines. He was looking for any mention of Hinode. At the same time, he also pulled out from the stacks any books on the history of the labor movement and materials about the National Federation of

Beer Industry Workers Union. There was no record—either before or after the General Strike on February 1, 1947—of any large-scale labor-management conflicts at any of the beer companies that would have been worth reporting on in the pages of the national papers. The reality was that in those days beer companies had no time for labor disputes. Under the direction of GHQ, the Act for the Elimination of Excessive Concentration of Economic Power—or the Deconcentration Law, as it was called—was being deliberated in the Diet, and every beer company was facing an existential crisis: the establishment of said law meant that all major corporations, starting with Hinode, were poised to be split up and reorganized. Even when he finally found a mention of Hinode Beer, it was a minor, below-the-fold article from November 1947 about the unsworn witness questioning in the Lower House, during which Hinode Beer's president had stated his opinion opposing the law.

Negoro took a closer look at this tiny article. The Deconcentration Law had personal relevance to him. Negoro was born in 1950 and, as early as he could remember, his father had worked in the personnel department at Fuji Iron & Steel. In fact, his father had barely managed to transfer to Fuji Iron & Steel from Japan Iron & Steel, which had been split up into four entities three years after the Deconcentration Law was approved in December 1947. Twenty years later his father would transfer again, this time to Nippon Steel Corporation, the result of a merger between Fuji Iron & Steel and Yawata Iron & Steel, where he remained until retirement. His father was now seventy-eight and fading into dementia, but memories from the turbulent years right after the war—a bewildered clerical worker with no discernable resources and a pregnant wife, wondering if every day would be his last on the job—were indelibly etched in his mind. The baby in his wife's womb at the time was Negoro himself.

After the law was established, Hinode was of course included in the list of more than 300 firms designated by the Holding Company Liquidity Committee to be split up, but when it came down to it, due to the political climate abroad at the time—the birth of the People's Republic of China, and the deteriorating relationship between the US and the Soviet Union—the standards of application for the Deconcentration Law were significantly eased, for fear of inviting a decline in Japan's power. In the end, the number of companies that were split up was closer to a dozen. Hinode was not among them.

According to the reference materials, Hinode Beer had ridden out the postwar years, when the tumult of domestic industry and civic life was at its peak, in a state wartime-regulation-induced near-hibernation, and thus managed to avoid being split up thanks to the shifting situation in world affairs, not even shuttering any of their factories. When wartime regulation lifted and the country entered the age of free-market competition, Hinode was already riding the wave of the now-recovering industrial economy. All in all, the company had prevailed throughout its relatively fortuitous history. As Negoro contemplated Hinode's progress, it seemed to him that the company had given little to no cause for its employees to incite a labor movement—no unrest about their employment or livelihood—but that made the existence of the flag-waving, dismissed Hinode employee Yoshinori Toda all the more peculiar. Negoro concluded that he would need to do more research on him.

By the time Yabe finally responded to the page Negoro had left with the Hachioji bureau, car headlights were lining up in early evening traffic along Uchibori-dori.

"Listen, about Hinode's acquisition of the factory site in Saitama—would you mind digging up as many names as you can of land owners, tenant farmers, or any residents involved in that lawsuit?"

"You have a hunch along that line?" Yabe asked skeptically. It was a long-distance call—he was still out on assignment.

"There's this guy from a segregated buraku community in Saitama prefecture who was at Hinode's factory during the war. Back then, there was a pretty high bar to land a job at Hinode—even in one of their factories. If what I've heard is true, perhaps the guy is involved somehow. I'm sorry I don't have more for you to go on."

"What's his name?" Yabe asked, suddenly curious.

"Yoshinori Toda. Born in 1916."

◆ ◆ ◆

SHORTLY BEFORE SIX IN THE evening, Negoro passed by the table where the slot editors from each section were gathered for an editorial meeting ahead of the bulldog edition. When Tabe looked up at him, Negoro signaled with his eyes that he was stepping out, and then he left the news room. It had been almost a year since he had left the company building when the evening was so young, and he was only doing so now because his boss had ordered him to get background information on the tip-off. As the automatic doors closed behind him, he felt like a monkey released from its cage—his nostrils flared in response to the welcome air, and his steps felt light.

Negoro went to a phone booth near the building to place several calls he hadn't been able to make from his desk in the Metro section. He flipped open an old notebook and began to dial. The first four phone numbers he called resulted in a message saying that the numbers were no longer in use, but that was about what he expected.

The fifth number he called was to the third-floor editorial office of a securities industry news company, a building that stood along the bank of a sewage canal near the Tokyo Stock Exchange in Kabuto-cho. At those kinds of papers, after the markets closed at three, reporters scrambled to submit their stories for the final edition of the next morning's paper by around four, and the early edition had already shipped by five—at this hour, the editorial department would be nearly empty. However, Negoro knew that right about now there would be a man lying on the sofa in a corner of the room, a book in one hand and a can of beer and rice crackers in the other.

"It's Negoro from *Toho News*," he announced when the call connected.

"It's too early to pay your condolences," the man shot back. "Though if the share price dips below fifteen thousand yen, I'm going to jump out this window here. But it looks like it'll hold up for a while. So, I need you to sit tight a little longer about your money."

"Never mind that. Consider it your funeral offering," Negoro responded.

Five or six years ago—the end of the bubble era, shortly before the Ogura-Chunichi scandal came to light—the man had given Negoro a way into an investors' group. In those days—when times were flush— he and many of his fellow employees in the securities industry news played the market, pooling cash and walking around with million-yen wads stuffed inside their suit pockets, all the while making out as if what they were doing was well within the realm of their profession as a reporter. The man on phone was only nominally a slot editor; during the day he lurked at the service counters of local back-alley brokerage houses and the coffee shops near the stock exchange, and at night he could be found in Ginza. He was so deep into stocks that even during a half-hour meeting he was never without an earpiece in one ear and a phone within reach. Negoro had heard that, sure enough, after dancing on the edge for so long, the guy was a few hundred million in the hole and had lost his apartment. The over-the-counter stocks he had convinced Negoro to invest his bonus in back in the summer of '89, saying "this one's a sure thing," weren't worth the paper they were printed on.

"More importantly, I can't get through to Hamazaki," Negoro said.

"I hear he's in Singapore."

"What about Shinoda?"

"Last time I saw him was in Kayabacho late last year. He said he was going to start up a seminar soon, but since I haven't heard any-thing about him settling his debt underground, he must still be on the run."

"So who's left in the Ezaki group?"

"Probably just Takuji Yasui and Kazumi Koshino. A few guys might come back in later this year and start it back up, but with the market in shambles like this it's tough—"

"You're right. How would you be able to come back from this?"

"I'm only saying that the share price is about to bottom out, so this is the last chance if you were up for anything. But even if you went all in, trading is so light there's no way to make any real capital."

"I'm glad you're aware of that. You know Yasui's contact?"

"I haven't seen him lately. Why don't you poke around in Ginza or Shimbashi? What are you digging around for anyway? You're not getting into corporate raiding now, are you?"

"This has nothing to do with that. I'll talk to you later."

Negoro hung up, staring at the rush hour traffic along Uchibori-dori as he replaced the phone. As always, the voice over the phone was as muddy as the banks of the sewage canal or the back streets of Kabuto-cho. The moroseness couldn't be blamed on the bursting of the bubble and the subsequent recession; it had been the same when the service counter of every brokerage was overflowing with money.

The short call gave Negoro a rough idea of how his sources in the investors' group were doing these days. He never had any intention of asking the slot editor at a trade paper about background on Takeshi Kikuchi and his company, GSC, Ltd. Negoro didn't know how the mention of a former *Toho* reporter might be picked up as gossip. If he wanted to ask, he'd try for Yasui or Koshino.

When he left the phone booth, it was exactly six in the evening. He knew from experience it was a little too early to head to Shimbashi or Ginza, so he decided to take care of another source first. With his slightly stooped shoulders hunched forward, Negoro ambled over the Chidori-ga-fuchi moat on feet that did not carry him as swiftly as they had before his accident. The dank smell of the stagnant water rose to meet him. Now that it was dark, Kitanomaru Park was empty, and the edgy officers on patrol kept a watchful eye on Negoro, a middle-aged man tottering under the dark shadows of the trees surrounding the Imperial Palace.

Half an hour later Negoro arrived in the neighborhood of Kanda. He went up the staircase of one of the small buildings that lined the intricate back alleys of Uchi-Kanda. There was an iron door with a shingle on it, and when he opened it and stepped inside a female clerk at a steel desk looked up and gave him a friendly smile.

"Oh, you're from *Toho*—" she said. "The director isn't in right now."

"Oh, I see. Does Professor Matsuda come around here these days?"

"Yes, nearly every day. He doesn't seem to be writing much lately. He was here until just a while ago. He drank two cups of tea and told us everything that was wrong with our new titles. He said since he was out he might as well go have some soba on his way home. You know the noodle shop near the foreign language school? They've got the specials today. Oh, come on in. I'll make some tea."

"No, don't trouble yourself. I'll just take one of these press releases with me. Please tell the director I'll stop by again."

The list of new books published by the small press, which had only four employees, was a single sheet of pulp paper with typed words and phrases such as HUMAN RIGHTS, THE CONSTITUTION OF JAPAN, and DEMOCRACY. Glancing at the titles of books he had no interest in reading, he stuffed the page in his pocket. As he did so, a certain long-forgotten sense of discomfort crept over him, and Negoro felt somewhat on edge.

Various configurations without origin, logic, or necessity—such notions as the emperor, democracy, discrimination, and so on—now seemed to Negoro to have mingled with car exhaust and the racket from karaoke bars, drifting through the current era like invisible fluff. While the dazzling light from the JR train streaked by above, and further beyond in the night sky a billboard with an electronic ticker flashed with news of the volatile sixteen-thousand-yen swing in share prices on the Tokyo Stock Exchange and the ransom demand of six hundred million in the kidnapping of Hinode Beer's president, that fluff settled in drifts beneath the elevated bridges, shuffled and stirred underfoot by the passing crowds. In that moment, Negoro felt an increasingly useless irritation toward the fluff of democracy. There was no doubt that democracy still existed, but in reality, as a system it had neither progressed nor diminished—no one dared get rid of it and there were some who remained caught up in the workings of it. However, the concept no longer had any societal relevance—the word itself had lost its evocative power.

On the sliding door of the soba noodle eatery that was near the foreign language school—just as the clerk had said—there was a sign announcing the specials of the day. A counter and four, five tables inside comprised the eatery. Back when he was a newly minted reserve reporter, Negoro would stop in there frequently to meet with Kazuhiko Matsuda, a lawyer turned critic who was a regular customer, and his circle of sympathizers.

"Well, if it isn't the reserve chief!" cried out Matsuda, who was perched at the counter. He looked like a hunched-back silver-haired monkey. Two men sat beside him. Glasses of beer, edamame, and a small bowl or two were set out on the counter. The way that only the area surrounding Matsuda appeared to be cast in its own private, rather enigmatic shadow was par for the course.

"Come on now, have a seat!" Matsuda said. His manner never wavered—not today, yesterday, or ten years ago. Negoro greeted the two men with only his eyes, and they returned a small nod, looking slightly annoyed.

"Tell me, Negoro. Why won't the newspapers write about things like this?" Matsuda said, his voice rising abruptly. It wasn't so much that he wanted to display his power of influence, this was just his usual way of talking that he had acquired over his many years as a critic. Negoro listened quietly. "These two have been running around town in support of a candidate for the Tokyo Assembly election, but the candidate has decided to forgo official party recognition and instead run as an independent. And that seems to have put the balance among various supporting organizations and advocacy groups in disarray. But, as you know, we're no longer in an era when a deep-rooted mainstream association would support a single party and willingly tie their own fate to a party's political rise or fall." Matsuda, after directing this diatribe to Negoro, seated to his left, Matsuda then turned his head to the two men on his right. "When it comes down to it, what generates political realignment are changes in the electorate's social consciousness. You two are responding too late. The fact that you still place such importance on political parties is proof that you are leaning too much on your assumed ability to gather votes. Excuse me, another beer please."

On the other side of Matsuda, the two men looked troubled—as if they did not want him making careless remarks in front of a reporter—and sure enough, as soon as Matsuda stopped talking, they got up from their seats.

"Well, anyway, professor, we'll be looking forward to that article," one of the men said.

Matsuda seemed to pay them hardly any attention, instead taking the fresh bottle of beer and starting to fill his and Negoro's glasses. Negoro, for his part, felt self-conscious and mumbled an apology to the men for his intrusion.

"You guys are leaving already?" Matsuda asked, finally turning their way.

"We're rather in a hurry." The men bid them an innocuous farewell and left the eatery.

"Professor Matsuda. Which district are those men from?" Negoro asked.

"If I tell you that, you'll figure out the name of the candidate."

"Are you writing something for the party's rag?"

"I'm the kind of man who believes that human rights are inherently political, in that they are just one of many interrelated affairs mandated by law. In that way I'm fundamentally at odds with the majority of human rights organizations. Heck, the article I'm writing is about a campaign speech given by that particular politician, and I only agreed to do it because I know him personally."

"I see."

As he pretended to listen to Matsuda's patter, Negoro stared at the menu, whose offerings left much to be desired. "Say, professor. They've got seared skipjack tuna, first of the season. Shall we have some?" he asked.

"I forget what a high earner you are. Sure, you can afford to treat me once in a while," Matsuda said.

Negoro ordered the seared tuna, simmered vegetables, and tempura.

Shortly after Negoro transitioned to the reserve section from the kisha club at MPD, he was assigned to a team in charge of a special feature on the constitution that had commissioned articles from several experts in both the revisionist and protectionist factions. Negoro was assigned by draw to oversee the article by Matsuda, who was infamous back then as a staunch human rights lawyer with a sharp tongue. That had been their first encounter. Since then, however, Negoro had come to realize that political journalism—not limited to the work of Matsuda—which tended to criticize A then propose B and conclude by predicting C, lacked a certain skepticism even if it always provided a lucid, albeit haphazard, argument. In his early thirties at the time, Negoro recognized political journalism was not for him, given his inability to approach things in a straightforward manner, though he still wondered if simply having a clear-cut view meant being correct.

In addition to his work as a lawyer, Matsuda still penned miscellaneous items for various monthly and weekly journals as well as for the rags of particular parties and organizations and special interest groups. But he had long been alienated from the pages of *Toho News*, ever since running into trouble over the use of real names in reporting on a minor human rights issue. And yet Negoro still made periodic visits to the soba shop, because there were valuable resources among Matsuda's network of organizations and labor unions such as the General Association of Korean Residents and the Buraku Liberation League.

"At odds with them, professor, I guess that's one way of putting it," Negoro joked a little, and poured Hinode Lager into Matsuda's glass. That reminded him—when would Hinode Meister, whose full-page ad had run in yesterday's morning edition, go on sale?

"A critic can change his mind too, you know. We just don't admit that we've changed it. What's the use in talking to you about these things anyway?" Matsuda's shoulders shook as he laughed. "Skipjack tuna, huh . . ." Matsuda said, shifting the conversation. Negoro responded with a wry chuckle of his own.

Matsuda had said that human rights were interrelated with many things, but to Negoro, it seemed that over the last dozen years or so, the subject in and around this counter had not been the nature of these interrelationships but the very essence of concepts such as human rights themselves. Just like the bottles of beer, the glasses, the warm hand towels, or even the bits of fluff outside the eatery—talk of the constitution, democracy, and human rights had been consumed here every night as surely as the beer had flowed, but without any reflection or skepticism, without any of these things improving or disappearing.

According to several of Negoro's sources, at some point there had been a flow of money to Matsuda from the Korean peninsula, but no matter how Negoro hinted around—whether it was a function of the professor's enormous and animating ego or of the typical naïveté of intellectuals—somehow Matsuda remained oblivious to the fact that someone might have dirt on him, or that he might be involved in shadowy business.

The menu had described the tuna as "freshly caught" but perhaps it was still too early in the season, for it did not have much fat on it. Negoro poured a little more beer into Matsuda's glass, worrying that the fish was not even good enough for Matsuda, who was indifferent to gastronomy.

"By the way, Negoro. How's your health these days?"

"Well, being this busy, I don't even have time to be grateful for being alive."

"You want to switch places with an old man who has too much time on his hands?"

"Aren't you writing the article about the speech?"

"You are an irritating man."

"Come on, don't say that. Here, should I add some ginger?"

As the piping hot tempura arrived, Negoro seasoned the dipping sauce with grated daikon and ginger, and since Matsuda wouldn't pick up his chopsticks unless the food was right in front of him, Negoro pushed a plate into his hands.

"Say, professor. Have you ever heard anything from BLL about their involvement with Hinode Beer?" Negoro said, directing the conversation.

"I saw the news this morning. That has to do with discrimination?"

"No, I don't want you to misunderstand me. This is an entirely different case from the kidnapping, but I was wondering if you would dig into this for me."

On the paper wrapper from his chopsticks, Negoro wrote with his ballpoint pen, *1946–7, Labor Dispute, Hinode Kyoto Factory*, and slid it over to Matsuda, who looked at it.

"Ah, this takes me back . . ." he mumbled. "That was the era when they gave us powdered skim milk, sprinkled DDT on our heads, and led us to believe that we had been freed from all sorts of oppression. So, what do you want to know about this Kyoto factory?"

"If you could look up the names of every employee who was dismissed before or after the General Strike on February 1, 1947—whether it was for a labor dispute or any other reason."

"Does this have to do with the segregated buraku communities?"

"I think so."

"Then I'm sure there will be some materials in Kyoto. Incidentally, an acquaintance of mine in Kyoto, he loves sumo and—"

"Would you like me to get tickets for the May tournament?"

"Two tickets would be great. Doesn't seem right to ask for help for free, does it?" Matsuda said, pocketing the chopsticks wrapper.

For some time after that, Negoro listened to Matsuda unfurl his customary excoriation of major corporations, including Hinode, then he picked up the tab and left the eatery alone shortly after eight in the evening.

At the end of a meeting with a source he was always inundated with businesslike concerns—Was there anything amiss about the exchange? Had he gained any information? Was the lead credible? Could there be any leaks?—but now Negoro was stuck with the same vague irritation he had felt earlier, when he had stuffed the publisher's press release in his pocket. He was born of a generation raised under the rainbow of democracy, but now that he was reaching his mid-forties, the realization that had persisted over the years—that he had been deceived all along—had grown more urgent.

Before hailing a taxi, he stopped by a drugstore to buy an energy drink. The customer in front of him, who was about his age, had recommended this particular brand and after paying for it, Negoro paused to read the advice on the label: BAD STOMACH, OVERWORKED LIVER, POOR CIRCULATION, SHOULDER ACHES, BACK PAIN, CHRONIC FATIGUE, LACK OF ENERGY. He cracked open the bottle on the spot, thinking that if only the list had included "SLEEP DEPRIVATION" and "LOSS OF FAITH IN HUMANITY" it would have been perfect.

AT HALF PAST EIGHT, NEGORO got out of a taxi beneath the elevated train tracks of the JR Shimbashi Station. He began making the rounds of his old haunts one by one, starting in the alley behind the New Shimbashi Building. Back when times were flush, Negoro hadn't gained access to Ginza, which used to teem with high-rolling stock traders, big-time investors, and financiers; he'd barely managed to make a few connections in the Korean clubs around Akasaka. He had regaled his sources—salesmen from local brokerage houses, self-styled financial analysts, investor groups, non-bank salesman, and loan sharks—at non-descript bars in areas like Tsukiji and Shimbashi, but his pay was still not enough; he had to borrow money from a credit union to cover the drinking expenses. That hard-won network of information, however, had collapsed along with the market, and since barely anyone was left, the city might well have been empty to Negoro.

He walked around for about an hour, his feet growing heavier, and after wandering through four bars, sipping a whisky at each establishment, he passed a man in the doorway of the fifth pub.

"Hello there, it's been a while," he called out. Negoro quickly remembered the man's name—Okabe—and nodded back.

He had no idea what Okabe was doing these days—up until four years ago, at least, he had worked at the Nihombashi branch of a certain major securities company.

"Would you like to get a drink?" Negoro heard himself asking, his ulterior motive getting the better of him as he considered the prospect of going back empty-handed.

"I've got no leads for you, though." Okabe laughed bitterly. "I was on my way to get some ramen before going home, so just one quick drink at the noodle shop." He started walking toward Ginza under the elevated train tracks.

"Do you still work for the same company?" Negoro asked.

"Hanging on somehow."

"Are you still trading bonds?"

"No, I got let go from that position. I'm working with individual clients now. This month earthquake recovery stocks took a tumble, so I was just at a client's home near here, bowing my head in apology."

"I see. But I hear spot purchases are doing well for private investors?"

"Picking up deep-value shares here, OTC stocks there? This isn't stockjobbing."

"What about the big accounts?"

"They prioritize returns so it's sluggish. Even futures are only moving to hedge risk."

"What about today's incident with Hinode Beer? How'd their stock do?"

"That news first thing this morning was pretty shocking. But since the president was found safe and sound, nothing much happened today. Hinode shares are expected to rise based on their new product announcement. Once it goes to market in April, it should be a good time to buy . . . Ah, now I see. For you and the other papers it will be all Hinode, all the time. What are the chances of the criminals being arrested?"

"It won't happen any time soon."

"Is that so . . ." Okabe's expression in profile revealed a flash of the inner workings of his mind—he was trying to read the stock outlook—but it only lasted a moment.

They were now on the northern side of Shimbashi Station, under the elevated Shuto Expressway, where they arrived before a red noren shop curtain on a back street. Okabe entered through the curtain first. When Negoro met him five years ago, Okabe's title had been manager of the first sales team handling major accounts, but after his branch was indicted for illegal compensation to clients for market losses, no doubt there would have been some internal reshuffling. Most securities brokers were indistinguishable from regular salarymen, but Okabe had a bit of roguishness about him. He was the kind of guy who had always worn an Audemars Piguet watch that cost a few million yen as if it were no big deal—and as Okabe opened the sliding door of the ramen shop, Negoro recognized the same item from back then, still on his wrist.

They sat down at a table covered with a cheap vinyl cloth. Okabe ordered beers, and from his suit pocket he casually tossed a crumpled red pack of Lark cigarettes and a hundred-yen lighter on the table. His manner and his expression—not much about them had changed in five years. Whatever shifts had occurred in economic conditions or the financial market, they did not affect the substance of the people who moved money around.

"Okabe-san, how are speculative stocks these days?"

"There are some stocks that have speculative potential. But they just get dragged around through arbitrage. Which causes the spot prices to fluctuate so much, and that only makes it harder for regular investors to buy right now. Lately, anyone with funds—from top of the line to the bottom—they're all aggressively trying to make a profit margin on the Nikkei 225 or with bond futures. Of course, hedging all the while. You can't turn a profit without moving money. Say, is something going on with the market?"

"Oh, no, it's just that when I bumped into you, you reminded me of an acquaintance. He called me three or four years ago out of the blue and told me he's running a boutique investment firm, but since then I haven't been able to get in touch with him."

"We had a few guys like that at our company too, who made off with clients and went out on their own. Those were good times, in the sense that we all had our dream . . . I'm having ramen, how about you, Negoro-san?"

"I'll have the same."

"Two chashu ramen, please," Okabe called, raising his hand. Over Okabe's shoulder, Negoro saw the door slide open and two men peer into the shop. There were no other customers besides him and Okabe, and the two men cast a glance in Negoro's direction before retreating and closing the door.

With nothing to accompany their drinks, Negoro took swigs of the cold beer. He was aware of his exhaustion, but in a mild attempt to press things further he lobbed, "About that acquaintance I mentioned earlier—it seems he managed to borrow money using a client's bond as collateral."

"When you go out on your own, there's a lot to deal with. I, on the other hand, if I lose money—so long as they're minor accounts—all I do is go around, bowing my head in apology. I just tell them we'll get it back next time." Okabe snickered a little, his shoulders quavering lazily.

"Don't give me that. I know you have your own fan club over in Nihombashi."

"I told you, these days I go around apologizing to all my fans."

"Okabe-san. Have you ever heard of a company called GSC, by any chance?"

"Is that your guy's company? No, I don't know it. That wouldn't be a G.S.C. group, would it?" Okabe guffawed, and Negoro laughed awkwardly as he mumbled, "No way."

G.S.C. was one of the corporate groups composed of the Seiwakai's front organizations, and the name was rumored to be an acronym for the English words Generality, Service, and Confidence. Funds loaned by financial institutions were absorbed into an inscrutable network of

G.S.C.'s affiliation of non-banks, loan sharks, investor groups, real estate companies, and so on, circulating into obscurity. The source of the capital Kimihiro Arai had used to buy up shares of Ogura Transport came via G.S.C., and Takuji Yasui—of the former Ezaki group, the same Yasui whom Negoro had been looking for that very night— had also once been an executive at a non-bank affiliated with G.S.C. Finance. In sum, the Okada Association kept up appearances while G.S.C. kept the money flowing—parallel wheels of the machinery running this shadow economy.

Even if Okabe was only joking about a connection with Takeshi Kikuchi's company, GSC Ltd., Negoro could do no more than stammer a vague reply as Okabe took the arriving bowl of ramen in his hands, exclaiming, "Oh, looks great." He must have been pretty hungry, for he wasted no time pulling a set of disposable chopsticks from the stand on the table, splitting them apart, and digging in. He fell silent as he ate.

Negoro watched Okabe slurp his noodles, his face tilted downward, and noticed that one of his front teeth was chipped. It was none of his business, but Negoro couldn't help wondering whether it was that Okabe did not have the time or the money to fix it. And yet, considering his own appearance, Negoro knew that though his teeth were all intact, his head of greying hair resembled a hedgehog, and his suit, shoes, and watch all paled in comparison to Okabe's. Negoro ruminated that the only thing the two of them had in common as they slurped ramen together was a certain indifference.

Once Okabe's hunger had been tended to, his mind seemed to start working again, and he picked up the conversation, continuing to eat noisily.

"By the way," he said, "there's an investor group that's rumored to be affiliated with that G.S.C. They also deal in stock index futures. We're not the company that's been commissioned, but I hear orders come in every day over the phone. Their margin is fifty or sixty million yen, which makes them quite the player, as far as private investors go."

"Is that so . . . So some yakuza with capital have decided to embark upon legal alchemy to make the big money, huh?"

"As long as you're willing to take risks, it's a game that offers easy profit. Perfect for a yakuza."

Negoro looked up at the sound of the door sliding open. The same two men were in the doorway again—this time they fixed their gaze for three seconds on the interior of the shop where Negoro was sitting. The men had on duster coats, and peeking from beneath their collars were shirts in colors never worn by typical salarymen, coordinated with flashy neckties. Negoro confirmed to himself that he did not recognize their faces before looking away, and the sliding door closed again. Okabe, with his back to the door, was oblivious. Having already finished his bowl of ramen, he had set it down on the table and now had a toothpick in his mouth.

"So then, Negoro-san, what should I do about Hinode Beer's stock?" he asked.

"If I knew the answer, I'd be buying too," Negoro replied.

"But with the president released unharmed, doesn't that imply some kind of vulnerability on Hinode's part, and that there was a backroom deal with the criminals? Their share price could be affected, depending on how things develop."

As Negoro listened to Okabe's frank assessment, it suddenly occurred to him, *He's exactly right.*

While no one could predict what would happen with the case, the kidnappers at least knew precisely when and how those developments would break, and what kind of outcomes they would bring about. Were the perpetrators operating on their own and demanding a mere six hundred million, the scenario Okabe proposed was unlikely, but if a more substantial organization were behind them, and if that organization was equipped with sufficient intellect and financial resources, what would be their move? If someone could control the direction of the case, knowing specifically when Hinode's stock would plummet, they could only have one thing in mind . . .

"Say, Okabe-san. Would you mind keeping an eye on any margin trading with Hinode stock, and I'll keep you posted about any new information that comes in?"

"Really? You've got a lead on something that might make the price fluctuate?"

"I don't know about that. But there might be someone in the shadows who's short-selling, in anticipation that the price will drop."

"I knew I smelled smoke. You develop a sixth sense when you inhabit this world." Okabe grinned, revealing a satisfaction with his keen nose, but also a shrewdness, as though his mind had started churning as well.

"Please keep this between us," Negoro reminded him.

After he and Okabe left the ramen shop and he sent Okabe off with a prepaid taxi voucher, Negoro stood for a moment on the sidewalk beneath the overpass. There had been something off about the two strange men who had peered inside while they were eating ramen, and it pricked at his senses persistently. He felt as if their presence still lingered, and Negoro turned around to check the empty street behind him.

He then looked down at his own feet, knowing that they wouldn't carry him fast enough to escape anyway, and with an ambiguous resignation, he started walking toward a phone booth a mere ten steps ahead of him.

Inside the booth, first Negoro called the Metro section and informed them that he was in Shimbashi now and would be back in half an hour. Next he called the Metro section of their Osaka bureau and asked for the home telephone number of the slot editor who had worked on today's evening edition. He then punched in the number, which started with "06."

The call was answered right away and he heard the screaming laughter of children—*You're so dumb! Stupid! You dope!*—and after a female voice came on and apologized, Negoro asked for the slot editor and, while he waited for him to come on the phone, he listened to the jumble of sounds—the woman calling to her children, their fleeing footsteps, and the Nintendo Famicom in the background.

As he let that ambient noise wash over him, Negoro stared idly at the sight of the two men who had reappeared again on the street, about ten meters away from the phone booth. The men were standing on the sidewalk, their shoulders and legs twitching while they smoked cigarettes, their gazes fixed on him. They were of the same ilk as the men who had trailed him night and day four years ago, when Negoro had been chasing the story about where the shareholdings of the former Chunichi Mutual Savings Bank's founding members had been transferred. These types seemed to have trouble keeping still—they were always jiggling some part of their bodies, as if out of boredom.

"Hello? Negoro-san? I'm sorry my kids make so much noise," the slot editor from Osaka said over the phone.

"No, I'm sorry to bother you at home. I just have one thing to ask. You wouldn't happen to know the name of the stock speculator that Takeshi Kikuchi was hanging around with?"

"I think it was Yasui something or other from the former Ezaki group . . ."

"Takuji Yasui?"

"Yes, yes, that's him. Back when Yasui's faction had been dabbling with the Osaka Exchange, Kikuchi interviewed him for a story and must have gotten to know him."

The men on the sidewalk tossed away their cigarettes and turned to leave, heading off toward Ginza. As he watched them, Negoro made a snap deduction: tonight, intimidation; next time, attack.

"Negoro-san?"

"Oh, sorry. I must be getting old, lately my hearing's been going . . . Thanks so much again."

Negoro hung up the phone and, still in the booth, cautiously sorted his thoughts. Tonight, the only person who knew firsthand that Negoro was going to be in the Shimbashi neighborhood was the slot editor at the securities industry news he had called earlier. Perhaps the editor happened to mention Negoro's phone call to someone, and from there the information could have been passed along. Or maybe, as he was making the rounds at the other four bars tonight, someone had seen him and triggered an alarm. But the most important question was why the same kind of threat from four years ago was suddenly being made again tonight.

Negoro didn't think that the story he was currently pursuing was one that would have drawn attention from the underworld. The only thing he had done today that could be considered outside the scope of his reporting was contacting Takeshi Kikuchi on the phone.

Even if another reporter had taken Toda's tip-off call this morning, the whole matter would have made its way to him once Toda specified "a reporter who knew about the Ogura-Chunichi scandal." Negoro now realized he himself must have been the one Toda had intended to speak to all along.

In addition, the way Toda had contrived to mention Takeshi Kikuchi's name at the beginning of the call had prompted Negoro to look up Kikuchi's whereabouts, and then even to call him directly. Negoro could have just dismissed the phone call as odd and left it at that, but he had not done so. Could it be that his opponent had tested whether he would respond? Negoro considered how the tip-off call could have meant to goad him into action. But if so, why him? The only reason he could think of was the Ogura-Chunichi scandal mentioned in the call.

Back in the summer of '88, before the shadow of the scandal was even looming, Negoro had been waiting for an interview subject in the lobby of the former building of the Akasaka Prince Hotel when he happened to cross paths with three men who were hurrying down the side staircase. He immediately recognized one of the men as the secretary to the representative Taiichi Sakata, of the eponymous S. Memo scandal, but at the time Negoro had no reason to know who the other two were. The secretary, with whom Negoro was acquainted, had met his gaze with a frantic look, and Negoro could still vividly recall the expression on his face.

Negoro later learned that one of the two men was the managing director and a founding member of the former Chunichi Mutual Savings Bank and the other was an ultranationalist who would act as a conduit of the transferred Chunichi shares, which meant the plan to bankrupt the mutual savings was already in play at that point. Then in '91, when all the newspapers were reporting on the scandal and Negoro alone found himself the target of intimidation, he had always felt that it was the result of his chance encounter with those three at the Akasaka Prince Hotel—that they had misconstrued something about him. The Ogura-Chunichi scandal was a thing of the past, but the threat that suddenly loomed tonight suggested that, somewhere amid the chaos surrounding the kidnapping of Hinode Beer's president, the same network had sprung back into action.

And it was highly probable that Takeshi Kikuchi was connected to whatever it was. If Kikuchi was indeed working for Yasui from the former Ezaki group, as the Osaka slot editor had said, it was equivalent to Kikuchi being under the influence of the Seiwakai and G.S.C., which gave Negoro reason to believe that Kikuchi had tricked him today by getting Toda to make the tip-off call.

Negoro recalled the voice he had heard today over the phone today, that of his former colleague Kikuchi—whose features were still hazy in his memory—and he thought of the watchful eyes of the men he had seen tonight. He contemplated himself, sinking into the deep backwaters of the city at night, his mind continuing to churn as he stood alone in the phone booth.

Four years ago, Negoro had been involved in a hit-and-run right in front of his home. The car was later found—it turned out to be a stolen vehicle—but the perpetrator was never identified. Negoro always maintained his testimony to the police that a car parked on the shoulder of the road had peeled out, aiming for and crashing into him, but the police steadfastly refused to file it as anything other than a hit-and-run, stating a lack of evidence of deliberate intent. Facing pressure on various fronts during his recuperation at the hospital, Negoro ultimately chose to remain silent. Tandem to that silence was the noxiousness of the era and society that he lived in, as well as of himself—a stench that now permeated him.

Negoro mechanically reinserted his telephone card and dialed a number he had not planned to call.

"I really appreciated your call last Friday night," Negoro said. "Thanks to you, we were the first to report it."

"Who knew it would turn into such a huge deal? It's crazy," said the chief of CID at the Setagaya Police Department, who had answered at his home in Komae.

"By the way, it seems I'm being tailed again."

"Any idea who?" The chief's tone shifted immediately. "Did you see his face? Where did it happen?" he peppered Negoro with questions.

"In Shimbashi. Two guys came within ten meters of me. I didn't recognize them, so I don't know who they're working for. I think one of them might be foreign. Something odd about his hairstyle."

"Negoro-san. I'm going to send one of my men to show you some mugshots. Once we know which hooligans we're dealing with, we can start digging around. I'll give you a call at 8:30 tomorrow morning."

Negoro paused. The chief raised his voice impatiently, "Negoro-san? You there?"

He was thinking of how, after the hit-and-run four years ago, this friendly police chief had also been one of the people who told him to "just forget about it."

"Thank you, sorry to trouble you," Negoro replied generically, ending the call as once again he mulled over the powerlessness of the police force, of the victim, of the newspapers, and of this country, Japan.

He proceeded to insert his phone card again and dialed another number.

"It's the Sanseido Bookstore in Kanda," he said as soon as the call connected.

"This is the second time today. Is something the matter?" the special prosecutor asked.

"No, I just forgot to tell you this morning. I don't think I'll be able to go home for a while, so if you need to get a hold of me please call the Chidori-ga-fuchi news room. It doesn't have to be today or tomorrow, but please make time to meet with me soon. And send my regards to Goda-san. Sorry to bother you so late."

Negoro ended the call without waiting for the prosecutor's reply and exited the booth.

Now should I chase down Kikuchi? he wondered to himself afresh, but he still couldn't decide. Negoro knew that, ever since being threatened and almost run down by a car, his zeal as a Metro reporter had vanished. Instead, he had wandered into a dead-end, haunted by an apathetic cynicism about the ways of this country—beginning with its very existence as a nation down to the flavor of its instant noodles. Of course his cynicism included doubts about the quality of his writing over his twenty-three-year career as a journalist, but more than that, this skepticism stemmed from the fact that, above all, his heart was no longer moved by this society and era he lived in, overflowing as it was from every corner with stuff, noise, and greed.

Trudging with his bad foot along Sotobori-Dori in search of a taxi, Negoro continued to ponder whether to follow up on Kikuchi, but he knew he lacked his former motivation. His sentiments were predictable enough, but as he lost himself in a new train of thought, he began to feel somewhat ashamed. Did it make any difference in the end to rot from evil or to rot from hatred and cynicism? Was there any distinction between contributing to the contamination of society and the era he lived in, and spending his life abhorring such a state of affairs?

Negoro looked down at his watch and was surprised to see that it was already ten-forty. By the time he leaned into the street to hail a taxi, his attention had already turned to the deadline for the thirteenth edition of the morning paper.

久保晴久

3

Tuesday, March 28th. When the phone rang at 3:30 A.M., Haruhisa Kubo leapt up from the sofa in the press nook and reached for the receiver.

"Hello, MPD division."

"We're sending over the morning editions now. You've been scooped."

Every day before dawn, the Metro section of the Osaka bureau faxed the morning editions of all the national newspapers to the Tokyo bureau so they could check the front pages. These faxes were only ever appended with a phone call when the message was, "You've been scooped."

Scooped.

Since being assigned to the police beat two years ago, Kubo had lived in fear of this word, running around in a never-ending battle for stories. He still wasn't sure whether being scooped was a matter of bad luck or lack of skill. Not that there was any room for such thoughts in his mind—the compulsory reaction of a police beat reporter upon learning that he'd been scooped was for the blood to drain from his face as the word "failure" floated before his eyes.

Still reeling from the shock, Kubo picked up the papers the fax machine had spat out. The vertical headline on the first of the Metro pages read:

COMPANY GRUDGE? SUSPICIOUS TAPE FROM 1990. On the second faxed page, a horizontal headline: MYSTERIOUS TAPE SENT TO HINODE. On the third: TROUBLE BACK IN 1990?

Being scooped by three out of the six national papers would be enough to get him fired, depending on the substance of the articles. Kubo pored over the pages to see if his competitors had included anything more than what his sources had told him last night.

All three papers reported roughly the same story. In November 1990, Hinode Beer received a letter invoking the name of a certain organization and accusing them of employment discrimination during their hiring process. Hinode Beer also received a slanderous cassette tape from an anonymous sender, and the company filed a complaint for defamation and obstruction of business without naming a suspect. Immediately after the letter was received, said organization that had allegedly sent the first letter, responding to inquiries from Hinode's main office and the police, had denied any involvement in the matter. The cassette tape was later revealed to have been an audio recording of the text of a letter written in "June 1947" by a "former Hinode employee" and sent to "Hinode Beer's Kanagawa factory." Among other things, how the letter ended up in the hands of the person who made the recording and their motivation to record it remained a mystery. Each newspaper concluded their report in the same manner: "Investigation headquarters is aware of the situation and has been conducting questioning of relevant persons connected to the case."

Kubo perfunctorily jotted down "June 1947," "former Hinode employee," and "Kanagawa factory" in his notepad. The tip-off call that Negoro, the reserve chief, had mentioned crossed his mind, but for the time being his thoughts were swimming with more immediate suspicions. Did those three papers have a transcript of the tape? If so, where did they get it? From the police, or the family of the dentist from Setagaya? Was there a way for him to get his hands on a copy?

A call came through on the direct line from the news room. It was the overnight slot editor from the Metro section. "You let quite a bombshell slip away, didn't you? What's all this about a tape from 1990?"

Kubo cursed him under his breath and replied, "I'm busy right now," then hung up the phone.

Kuriyama, wearing only his undershirt, descended from the top bunk bed in the nook. "How are the morning pages?" he asked. Then, his eyes still bleary with sleep, he picked up the fax sheets. "Oh, shit. The other papers really went for it, huh? But the chief was the one who told us yesterday to hold this story."

"True, but I still gotta let him know," Kubo replied. He fed the same pages back into the fax machine and sent them over to Chief Sugano's home. Then he gave him a ring. Sugano would know what a pre-dawn phone call from the office signified.

"Hello. It's Kubo. Sorry to wake you, but I've just sent over the fax. We've been scooped."

"Yeah, I'm looking at them now . . ." Sugano paused for a few seconds before continuing. "My opinion hasn't changed. Don't worry about it."

"But how will we do a follow-up story?"

"We won't refer to it in the main article. We'll discuss internally what to do with it on the Metro page. I'll talk to you later."

Sugano hung up the phone with a brusqueness that showed no concern for the caller. Kubo knew that Sugano couldn't reprimand him for not reporting a story that he himself had instructed him to withhold, but the chief's peremptory tone was still frustrating for whoever was on the receiving end. No doubt Sugano had his own justifications for why they didn't need to write about this story yet, but he might have considered that this placed frontline reporters like Kubo in an uncomfortable position.

"What did the chief say?" Kuriyama asked.

"He said we don't need a follow-up on the front page."

"Even so, we can't afford not to at least try to get a transcript of the tape, right? In any case, I'm going to get a bit more sleep. Today's going to be another long day."

Kuriyama quickly returned to the bunk bed. Compelled solely by the urge to get in at least another hour of sleep, Kubo lay back down on the sofa, the alarm clock set to 5:00 A.M. in one hand.

Kubo knew he had a tendency to be cocky, but as a reporter well into his thirties, he felt he'd been doing this long enough that, if they weren't going to need a follow-up, he at least deserved to know why. Perhaps Chief Sugano, having worked in the field for far too long, no longer had the patience to explain every last thing to his subordinates. He reigned over this tiny nook with peace-keeping tactics that involved holding back his opinions and never revealing himself, skirting the main issue and simply barking out orders. With someone like that as a boss, Kubo always felt thwarted, as if he were being restrained by an unseen force, and from time to time he found himself on the verge of exploding.

As of last night Kubo had had no intention of writing the article either, but he certainly would have had there been any corroborating evidence. Regardless of whether or not there was any connection to the Hinode president's kidnapping, it was obvious that they should write about it. The possibility of discrimination during the employee hiring process and the involvement of corporate extortionists who may have attempted to take advantage of the situation was of no small social significance, and what's more, it was impossible that a letter addressed to Hinode from right after the war would surface and be transformed into a tape of its own accord. Wasn't the existence of the tape newsworthy enough? If he were chief, he would definitely order reporters to find backup and write the story. These thoughts caused another wave of defeat to loom over yet another day, and he felt a rumble in his stomach that he knew would only be satisfied by binge eating.

城山恭介 Kyosuke Shiroyama

FOR THE FIRST TIME IN many years, the Shiroyama family slept in the same room, their three sets of futon quilts laid out on the tatami floor next to one another. Though his wife and son slept soundly, barely stirring until dawn, Shiroyama lay awake in panic most of the night, seized by hallucinations that he was still captive inside the hideout. Soothed by the sight of his family at rest, he was able to fall back asleep, only for his eyes to pop open again and again as an inexorable fear weighed heavily on his chest.

When his wife, an early riser, got out of bed, he had to pretend to be asleep for a while. She deftly arranged her hair in the half-light that passed through the shoji screens and left the room without making a sound. Moments later, he heard her movements in the kitchen. Beside his pillow, there was the sound of his son's breathing as he enjoyed a deep sleep, and above his head, among the trees in the garden, the high-pitched chirp of the first sparrow of the morning. When Shiroyama smelled the moist air waft in from the gap between the closed shoji screens, a sense of impending suffocation made him want to dash outside, but he shifted his head on his pillow instead.

Even if no one raised their voice, when people gathered in large numbers their presence was palpable—the movements of the press corps staked out beyond the ground of his home had reverberated all the way to his bedside throughout the night. What's more, the home to which he had returned last night after three days was beset with the traces of countless outsiders who had been coming and going during his absence. He also learned that the police had outfitted all the house phones with recording devices that were wired to outside lines. His wife acted nonchalant, saying, "They all mean well," but as the man of the house, Shiroyama could not easily dismiss the incursion into his own domain. Last night, after convincing his wife to get some rest, he stayed up for a whisky with his son, Mitsuaki. Father and son, neither of them much for talk, conversed briefly before succumbing to the power of alcohol.

His wife had been worried that, since she couldn't go out shopping, she would be unable to prepare anything special for their daughter, who hadn't been home in quite a while, and his son relayed that he planned to pick up some things on his way home from work.

During thirty-three years of marriage, the family had established a familiar pattern, but last night—with the return of his son, who lived nearby but seldom visited, and his self-sufficient daughter, who rarely sent so much as a postcard—Shiroyama had witnessed a sudden shift that was both physical and emotional. Had the head of the household not been kidnapped, he doubted there would have been a chance for the family to reconnect this way. Recognizing this as the true, unfeigned image of the family he had worked so hard to create, Shiroyama adjusted his head once again on his pillow.

Mitsuaki, sleeping peacefully with his mouth half-open, was approaching the ripe age of thirty-two. As of the first of April, he would be director of the tax office in Ibaraki prefecture. Over the next few years, he would make his way from one regional agency to another, eventually returning to Tokyo, where he would join the Budget Bureau at the Ministry of Finance, and if all went according to plan, his promotion to budget examiner would be guaranteed.

Shoko, who was two years younger than Mitsuaki, was the same— both of his children had been capable since they were young, never causing trouble for their parents or seeking attention and indulgence, and before he knew it, they had decided on their path in life and set out on their own. Shiroyama had his share of parental opinions but his offspring were more than fully fledged before he even had the chance to express any of these, so that on the rare occasion when he did see them, it was all he could do to mutter a few questions about what kind of work they were doing now.

Conversely, there weren't many opportunities to talk to his son about his own work, and Shiroyama thought about how last night he had missed another occasion to do so for a while. Perhaps at some point he would tell his son about the various emotions that led him to act in a manner so unbecoming to his position and choose to breach his company's trust, but he could not imagine when that day would come. More importantly, he had to worry about how the course of events and his own actions might affect his son's position at the finance ministry.

Such thoughts occupied Shiroyama's mind until the hands of the alarm clock read 6:15 A.M. He then rustled the futon beside him and said, "Come on, time to wake up." Shiroyama also wanted his son to retrieve the morning paper for him.

Breakfast was a simple affair—miso soup with daikon radish and seaweed, soft-boiled egg, and simmered fish—and although it had been four days since he had sat at this table, neither the scene itself nor the way things tasted nor the tenor of his emotions were much different from before. His wife and son were both taciturn by nature and, as Shiroyama set aside the now-acquired morning paper, the topics of conversation during the meal did not venture beyond Shoko, who would be coming home to Japan for the first time in two years, and Mitsuaki, who would be leaving for his new post in Ibaraki prefecture the day after tomorrow. Apparently, due to the unforeseen circumstances, Mitsuaki hadn't had time to pack his things, and so now he said, "I guess I'll just do without them for a while."

"Don't forget to pick up the mentaiko tonight for Shoko," his wife reminded Mitsuaki. "There's a counter that sells it in the basement of the Mitsukoshi department store in Nihombashi."

From this snippet Shiroyama gleaned that the salted cod roe was his daughter's favorite, but it seemed as if this were the first time he was hearing such information.

Mitsuaki headed for the office shortly before 7:20 A.M., leaving his parents at the dining table. They sipped a second cup of green tea without much to say to each other, then Reiko, who looked as if she were in good spirits, stood to clear the dishes. Shiroyama opened the morning paper and, starting with the front page, perused just the headlines and the leads, refolding the newspaper after scarcely ten minutes. His heartbeat had quickened momentarily when he saw the headline MYSTERIOUS TAPE SENT TO HINODE on the Metro page, but he was able to subdue his anxiety by running through the relevant administrative concerns in his mind. First, he must decide how to explain the matter to people both within and outside of the company.

Next, he needed to research the effect that such an article would have on consumer awareness. Finally, he had to investigate the item in question—the letter from Seiji Okamura dated June 1947.

It had not occurred to him before but, judging from the sensitive content of the letter this Okamura had sent to the Kanagawa factory—if such a letter did in fact exist—it must have been reported to the board members at the time. Moreover, regardless of how the letter had been dealt with, if an artifact written half a century ago had found its way into the hands of someone outside the company, it behooved him to conduct a thorough investigation. He decided he would search for the board meeting minutes from back then.

"Dear, you should start to get ready. Please don't forget to take your coat, it'll be chilly all day again," his wife said, the busy clatter pausing as she emerged from the kitchen, wiping her hands on her apron. Just then, the intercom rang to announce that the company car had arrived.

合田雄一郎　Yuichiro Goda

"ALL STAFF, REPORT TO THE dojo!" As the order rang out, the investigators who had been on standby in the large meeting room rose to their feet en masse. Yuichiro Goda was among them. Passing the television, which had been left on, he was lured by the sound and glanced at the screen.

"It's Hinode's president, Shiroyama! Mr. Shiroyama is coming out the front door of his home! One day after his release, Mr. Shiroyama looks refreshed and seems much more at ease!" a reporter cried out. As three men who appeared to be Hinode employees, along with two uniformed police officers, struggled to fight off the encroaching horde of reporters in front of the gate, Kyosuke Shiroyama kept his head down and slipped out through a fifty-centimeter-wide gap. The suit he was wearing today was a deep lustrous navy blue. His necktie was an understated silver with a light-green pattern. In one hand he carried a black briefcase and a duster coat.

"Were you able to get some rest last night?" "How do you feel this morning?" The reporters thrust their microphones in Shiroyama's face.

"Yes, very well, thank you," Shiroyama responded with a slight bow of his head, his voice as aloof as his facial expression.

"The perpetrators are still at large." "Do you have anything to say to them?" "Have you seen the papers this morning?"

Facing the surging crowd of people, Shiroyama spoke clearly, "I'm sorry, everyone, would you mind backing up a little?" He forced a reserved smile. As he surveyed the scene, the camera caught Shiroyama's gaze—a strong will cloaked in politesse—and it traveled through the cathode-ray tube to meet Goda's as he watched.

His eyes are a little bloodshot. Goda imagined Shiroyama would have been too psychologically charged to sleep much the first night after his release. Last night Goda had spoken to Kano—whose job as public prosecutor consisted of judging people's appearances—and when Goda had asked what he thought of Shiroyama, Kano had responded, "He'll pay lip service but never reveal what's in his heart—the type who's convinced what he's doing is right. Similar to a politician." To Goda, however, politicians were too far removed from his line of work as a police detective. As he stared at the company man on the TV screen and before he could stop himself, Goda began to wonder what it must be like to work for a private-sector enterprise. Whenever he felt the distance between the police and private citizens loom large, Goda always asked himself what the regular working people he saw outside his window must be thinking. Since being transferred from MPD to this local precinct, he had even more chances for such random ruminations.

"Hey, let's get going. We'll be late," his partner called out, and Goda pulled himself away from the television. Investigation Headquarters had that day gone through another staff increase and turnover, and a surge of detectives from various departments and members of the Mobile CI Unit had mustered. Since the large conference room could no longer accommodate the additional officers, briefings by the chief of First Investigation would now take place in the dojo, starting this morning.

With the safe return of the victim, the weight of the investigation had shifted to legwork, canvassing neighborhoods on foot, and looking into stolen goods; now that they had assembled enough men, a full-on search operation was set to begin, but for those working on the fringes, the big picture of the investigation was still elusive. SIT and the team led by Second and Fourth Investigation tasked with researching the cross sections between and among the corporate and crime-syndicate connections had been using a separate meeting room so their progress remained private, and they did not share their findings during daily morning and evening meetings. This morning's papers had reported that a mysterious tape was sent to Hinode back in November 1990—a story that was like a bolt from the blue for Goda—but he doubted that it would have any influence on the fieldwork of those tracking the perpetrators.

The narrow entrance to the dojo created a bottleneck as the procession of officers filed up the stairs to the fourth floor. In the jammed passageway, Goda caught sight of the back of the head of a detective a few steps ahead of him and thought it looked familiar. The dense hair, like a thicket of needles, and the crown with its elongated oval shape called to mind a tawashi scrub brush. After Goda entered the dojo, the back of that head entered his view again and, just as the man's name came to mind, he turned and looked at Goda.

Goda remembered that, when they bumped into each other last year near Kamata Station, the man had mentioned he was now working out of the Kamata Police Department. Handa was his name. A police sergeant from the local precinct who had been at headquarters during the investigation of the murder of an elderly man in Shinagawa in the fall of 1990, neither his personality nor his appearance were very remarkable, and he hadn't left much of an impression at the time. They were not well enough acquainted to merit the exchange of a greeting, but since Handa had given a slight nod first, Goda returned the gesture. Then Handa's figure disappeared among the rows of officers crammed into the dojo, and Goda, swept along himself by the throng, forgot about him.

"Attention!"

The command resounded through the hall, and the two hundred or so men fell into line, their feet moving like a centipede. Standing toward the back, Goda couldn't see what was happening up front—he only realized that the top brass were assembled and Chief Inspector Kanzaki of First Investigation had entered the room when he heard the command, "All bow!"

Then Kanzaki's voice over the microphone—"Good morning"—reverberated through the wooden floorboards. This was already the fourth time Goda had heard Kanzaki's voice first thing in the morning.

"As you all know very well already, the case has taken an unexpected turn due to the victim's release by the crime group and his safe return home. But of course, their release of the victim can only be interpreted as a step toward their next criminal act. I'll reiterate: this crime is highly premeditated and unusually meticulous." The excitement in Kanzaki's voice had been growing with every announcement, so that now his inflections at the end of each word now had built up to a quiet roar. "The crime group demanding a cash payment of six hundred million upon the victim's release not only indicates the intention to execute their next crime but also that they have some kind of weakness to exploit against Hinode Beer. However, suspecting the victim—the company, that is—of hiding something would be putting the cart before the horse. This morning, some of the newspapers reported on letters and a tape being sent to Hinode in 1990, but I would like you all to ignore any coverage of this sort. The sole mission of the police is to apprehend the perpetrators and prevent their next crime before it occurs."

Kanzaki went on to say what needed to be mentioned. "It is extraordinary that now, on the fifth day after the incident occurred, there is still not a single eyewitness account. Our first priority is to gather any eyewitness reports in order to determine what vehicle and escape route was used in the crime, so I hope that everyone—especially those joining the investigation today—will put in their best efforts. That's all from me."

The briefing was over in three minutes, and after SIT and the forensics teams from Second and Fourth Investigation Divisions left, those who remained were the Search and Inquiry Squad, Evidence Investigation Squad, Vehicle Investigation Squad, and the newcomers—all told around 150 members. The men were promptly divided into new teams, an endless loop playing as Director Miyoshi of Third Violent Crime Investigation conducted roll call and each man responded to his assignment.

As of yesterday evening, Goda's Vehicle Investigation Squad had completed researching the circumstances at the time of theft of all 350 vehicles that had been reported stolen in the last three months, including having ruled out the three stolen vehicles recorded by a dozen N-system cameras within the neighborhood of Sanno and westward in the timeframe before and after the incident. They were about halfway through the task of reviewing, one by one, suspicious vehicles recorded by high-speed surveillance cameras along the Shuto and Chuo Expressways provided by the Traffic Division. Their next job was to match fingerprints from each of the various cardboard boxes filled with ticket passes collected from highway toll booths.

On the other hand, the victim had said that after regaining consciousness in the moving vehicle, he had not heard the sound of any toll booths, so they were forced to consider the possibility that the crime group had carefully chosen their escape route—passing through the city on roads selected because they would not trigger any N systems and emerging on the Lake Kawaguchiko bypass without using a highway. Thus the Vehicle Investigation Squad expanded the search area, estimating several possible routes from Sanno Ni-chome to Lake Kawaguchiko, and deciding on several intermediary points. Keeping in mind the number of traffic signals and volume of traffic and assuming that the vehicle had been going an average speed of about forty or fifty kilometers per hour, they calculated the approximate time it would have passed these points. They hoped someone had spotted a suspicious vehicle around that time and were set to begin this search today. The specific protocol was twofold: the administrative work required to enlist local police to put up road signs seeking witnesses, and dynamic on-scene investigation and legwork.

Heading toward Fuji, there were a total of six potential origin points for the route that one would eventually have to pass through: the intersection at the entrance to the Ikusabata railway station in the city of Ome; the Juriki intersection in the town of Itsukaichi; the Kawarajuku intersection in Hachioji; the intersection at the entrance to Uenohara High School on Koshu Kaido Road; the Kajino intersection on National Route 413 in the town of Fujino in Kanagawa prefecture; and finally the Higuchi intersection along Route 246 that leads to Gotemba. Driving in the direction of Fuji from any of these intersections would lead to more or less a single road, and since the volume of nighttime traffic on those roads was quite low, if anyone had seen a strange van pass through on the night of the incident, chances were high that they would remember it. This was the reasoning for putting up signs along the roads.

One by one, the names of officers were called to join the ranks of the Vehicle Investigation Squad, and from the head of the line, the squad leader—who was in charge of the ninth unit of Violent Crime—passed out maps. The one Goda's team received was a road map of the Ome Highway that included the intersection at the entrance to Ikusabata Station—the intersection was marked with an X and the estimated time of passing, "23:30 ± 15." There was another X about ten kilometers to the west at the Hikawa intersection and one more X at a fork in the road on Route 139 near the prefectural border with Yamanashi. They would be responsible for having road signs put up at these three spots, and for the related dynamic on-scene investigation and legwork.

"This is like looking for a needle in a haystack," Goda's partner, an inspector from Crime Prevention, muttered, but Goda didn't feel the need to complain. Considering the distance to Lake Kawaguchiko and the road conditions late on that snowy night of the 24th, there was a better chance that the perpetrators had driven over the Daibosatsu

Pass—a relatively easy ride from Ome Highway, compared to the other routes—and besides, it was a good season to be in Okutama in western Tokyo, with the cherry blossoms coming into bloom.

The Vehicle Investigation Squad was ultimately increased to three times its original size. Now thirty-six men strong, there were eighteen teams, twelve of which were assigned to trace the perpetrators' possible movements along these six routes; three teams were assigned to investigate the recordings from N-system and speed enforcement cameras, and the remaining three were to check the toll booth ticket passes. The meeting was adjourned after less than ten minutes. The Search and Inquiry Squad, where half of the new members had been allocated, still awaited their team assignments and instructions from the top. And the Evidence Investigation Squad, which had also received a large influx, likewise awaited instructions before commencing the task of pinpointing where the food items consumed by the victim during his confinement had been purchased. It was not by chance that Goda noticed Handa again among the latter group. Quite suddenly, Handa had turned to look over at him.

While the rest of the squad members were taking notes, heads bowed, only one man had raised his eyes and was slowly looking around, as if casing his surroundings. When his gaze met Goda's, he instantly looked away, but in that moment, Goda felt like Handa's gaze had pierced him right in the gut.

Why did he do that? Was it just his imagination? *No, he definitely looked over here.* Goda dredged up his dim memories of Handa from Investigation Headquarters at the Shinagawa Police Department in the fall of 1990. Back then, during morning and evening meetings Handa had always kept his head down—he was an unremarkable detective whom Goda had rarely seen chatting with colleagues. On the random occasions when Goda happened to see him on the platform at Aomono-yokocho Station, Handa was always reading a horseracing newspaper. He'd had one in hand last year when Goda ran into him in front of Kamata Station. *The guy must be quite the racing enthusiast . . .* That was the extent of the insight Goda could conjure about the man's character, but then he recalled another matter. In the course of a murder case in Shinagawa of an old man who liked to wander, Handa himself had strayed from his assigned but dead-end territory and was later fired from headquarters for deviating from the investigation. On the morning when that happened, Goda had passed him on the stairs at the Shinagawa Police Department, Handa had suddenly lunged for him and tried to grab him.

Goda tried to remember why Handa had done such a thing, but it was beyond him. Handa's inscrutably enraged expression hovered in the fringes of his memory until Goda finally convinced himself he was reading into things too much. And yet a visceral sense of unease remained on the surface of his skin, and his mind felt fuzzy as well. Handa's gaze, whenever it was directed at him— on the stairs five years ago, or when they bumped into each other in front of Kamata Station, or today, for that matter—felt a bit too persistent, and it triggered a deep, instinctive ache that was well outside of the ordinary.

After spending nearly half the day distracted by recollections of Handa's eyes, Goda concluded that he was the one who was going off his hinges. Five years ago, Goda had been the kind of man who barely acknowledged other people, even when the veins were popping out of their temples right in front of him, but now here he was latching onto this person's behaviors and expressions, and indulging in pointless contemplation. *Something is wrong, something about me is out of order*, he mumbled, and before even starting to wonder how long he had been feeling this way, he repeated to himself, *It's all right. You'll feel better as long as you stay focused on the investigation.*

根来史彰　Fumiaki Negoro

THE METRO SECTION OF *TOHO News* had been in an uproar all morning over the breaking story that three rival papers had scooped them on—the managing editor had come by personally to check with Toru Maeda, the Metro chief.

"Are you guys all right over here?"

"We're fine, totally fine," Maeda responded, his voice energetic as he quickly turned away and beckoned the slot editors over. "The meeting's starting!"

On one of the sofas by the windows, Tetsuo Sugano, chief of the MPD beat, had suddenly materialized, and even though he was the one at the very center of this morning's maelstrom, his face was stoic. After exchanging a few dry greetings with the others, he took out his habitual comb. Negoro took a seat toward the back. In contrast to Sugano, Negoro felt a little stifled, as if the words featured in the other papers—*June 1947, a former Hinode employee, Hinode's Kanagawa factory*—were caught squirming around in the murky depths of his mind, making it hard for him to breathe.

"Everyone here? Well then, Sugano-kun, they tell me you knew about this business with the tape from 1990. Why didn't you write about it?" Maeda demanded, unfurling his anxious tongue.

"We haven't obtained the contents of the tape or determined its connection to the abduction."

"But it has to do with Hinode. It also involves employment discrimination, plus a mysterious letter from right after the war. This is not the time to fret about its connection to the incident!"

"No, we can't write anything until we confirm the contents of the tape. That's the first point. Also this is not the kind of story that all three papers can have broken together by coincidence. In other words, their source is not the police. That would make the source of the leak a problem."

"You're saying it's risky to write about it?"

"You could say that."

"How are we going to follow up?"

"After we corroborate the facts. I'll take responsibility for the front page."

Maeda and Sugano were like oil and water. The pace of their approaches was as out of sync as the hare and the tortoise, and in their arguments, they never quite managed to find common ground. Even now, the impatient Maeda abandoned hope and shifted the brunt of his attack to Tabe, the slot editor on duty when the scoop occurred. "What should we do with the Metro page?"

Tabe contorted his face as if to say this was difficult. "We can't consider that until we first determine whether Hinode discriminated in their hiring process, perhaps by asking around the family of the deceased student. But even if were to pursue this angle, I'm not sure whether a story about discrimination could stand on its own as an article related to the incident . . ."

Tabe then turned the spotlight on Negoro. "Negoro-kun, you'll be able to back up the tip-off call from yesterday, won't you?"

"I'm getting the sense that someone had Yoshinori Toda tip us off, but I'm still not sure how what he told me relates to the incident."

"Send someone to Osaka to look for this Toda guy," Maeda interrupted.

"In due time," Negoro responded.

"So, are we in agreement that we will not aggressively pursue this story on the front page or the Metro page?" Maeda asked.

"The important thing is what moves the perpetrators will make now that they've demanded six hundred million to be delivered later." The battle-hardened Tabe finally revealed his truth. "Speaking from previous experience, the developments with regard to a cash payment are hardly ever leaked. Even if it seems rather conservative for our coverage of the incident, for now perhaps we ought to keep our eyes peeled for any movements by the police and the Hinode executives so that we don't miss the moment when the perpetrators take action. Chief Sugano, what do you think?"

"I agree that these guys, the perpetrators, will definitely make a move." As always, Sugano's response came a beat too late. "I've got my reporters staking out Hinode's main office and the homes of executives in three shifts, but could you send a few more bodies from the main troops?"

"You got it."

Maeda was quick at switching gears; he slapped his knee and the follow-up-strategy meeting was thus over in ten minutes. As Tabe and Sugano had pointed out, the perpetrators' movements were crucial now—it was obvious that they should focus all their efforts on catching the moment when the cash payment was made, which was certain to happen. Especially in cases of corporate extortions, past precedent showed that unless the police made an official announcement, the movements of the parties concerned remained shrouded in darkness one hundred percent of the time.

Negoro was one person who understood this all too well, and his thoughts turned again to the flickering shadows lurking in the darkest corners and around the far fringes of this case—the tip-off caller, the stockbroker, and the crime syndicate—he had a hunch that this time, like before, these would soon become more indistinct as they receded underground. This was just as well. He couldn't care less about any of the various subterranean tendrils that were to be found beneath every stratum of this country—yet here and now, who would take on the burden of identifying these foreign entities that kept appearing and disappearing?

Maeda had told him to search for the "Toda guy." But if Negoro pulled at that thread and Takeshi Kikuchi's name spilled out, he would need to dig more into Kikuchi's background and the movements of his company GSC, Ltd., which would in turn make it necessary to probe around the Seiwakai to the Okada Association, and on to the politicians. The automatic sequence of motions that involved inching closer to the identity of such subjects—whom he couldn't write about but nevertheless must be cognizant of—was part of a newsman's peculiar sense of mission, though as a matter of course, this job was never taken on by the frontline reporters, who were much too busy chasing after stories that would occupy the pages of the daily paper. As for today's edition, Negoro saw it as a natural conclusion that he—a side-story reporter who consistently veered off the main topics of the Metro section reporters—would have to play the martyr again. And although during the Ogura-Chunichi scandal Negoro had put out feelers in various arenas, searching high and low, he never did find any leads that tied into the main story.

Send someone to Osaka to look for this Toda guy? It was out of the question to send a reserve reporter busy on the frontline on such a wild goose chase—there was no way of knowing what lay behind it, and even if they found something, they couldn't write about it. Negoro had only two options: either join forces with a tabloid or go to Osaka himself.

Looking at his watch to confirm there was still a while before the second evening edition went to press, Negoro crossed the news room floor, went out into the hallway, and stood in front of the elevators.

"Where are you going?" Sugano called out to him.

"I was thinking about getting something cold to drink," Negoro responded.

"Then maybe I will too." Sugano mumbled, and so together they headed down to the café on the third floor.

The inside of the café was bathed in warm, springlike sunshine, so Negoro thought he had made the right choice in ordering chilled tomato juice. Sugano, after taking a sip of the juice that was brought out to him, abruptly took out a miniature bottle of vodka from his jacket pocket, poured it into the glass, and tucked the empty bottle back into his pocket.

Negoro pretended not to notice but, unable to contain his urge to laugh, he ultimately gave in.

"It's stress," Sugano explained, and chuckled himself.

For going on twenty years now, the two of them had chased stories together—one homing in on public safety and the other muckraking—and though they were neither close nor distant with each other, they were adept at measuring each other's stress level. Sugano's network in the public safety sector was rock solid—even reporters from rival papers had to admit this—but on the flip side, it meant that Sugano was so fully assimilated into this web that he could no longer move a muscle. And whereas ostensibly the two men were quite different, the invisible ties that bound Negoro were not unlike the ones that held the other man in place within the police organization. And not only were their constraints similar, they were invariably connected within the larger sphere of society.

"Fumi, what were you doing in Shimbashi yesterday?"

"How's your Bloody Mary?"

"Think the Hinode stock is going to move?"

"Depends on how the case develops. Incidentally, does the source of the tape from the nineties have anything to do with the Seiwakai?"

"Probably. I'm sure they're the ones making trouble for Hinode."

"We'd better keep a close watch on their stocks, too."

"Yeah."

Negoro refrained from mentioning Takeshi Kikuchi's name, which had been on the tip of his tongue. He was all too familiar with how sharp Sugano's ears were, and the fact that Sugano already knew he had been in Shimbashi yesterday convinced him to tighten his control valve. Negoro's thoughts shifted as he stared at the light pink rose in a bud vase in front of him, and he again regretted having missed the chance to visit the rose show. The flower barely held its spindle shape, the tips of the petals curling slightly as they were beginning to unfurl. Negoro paused for a few seconds, expected to be at least a little stirred by this, but ultimately he gave up and looked away.

"Fumi, let me know when you make a move. I'll gather as much information for you as I can."

"I'll do that."

"Looks like we won't be sleeping at home for a while."

"I'd take it easy."

Sugano tossed back his vodka-spiked tomato juice, and with a "See you later, then," he took leave of Negoro.

城山恭介　**Kyosuke Shiroyama**

THE POLICE INTERVIEW WAS SCHEDULED to begin at nine-fifteen in the morning. Shiroyama wrapped up the morning assembly for executive staff in five minutes, simply reading aloud the speech he had written the night before, and was back in his office by 9:06 A.M. He took out his reading glasses before he even sat down and there, in the company of the managers of general affairs and of human resources, who had both been waiting for him, he scanned the array of documents that he had hastily demanded be assembled ahead of the noon press conference. Dismayed, Shiroyama looked up at the two executives.

"So what you're saying is, there is no trace of Seiji Okamura's letter in our records?"

"The Kanagawa factory was searched thoroughly as a result of the police's request for documents. As for the main office, quite a lot of old paperwork was disposed of when we moved into the new building."

"I see. Since we're pressed for time, let's move on. There are no materials pertaining to Hiroyuki Hatano's recruitment exam, either?"

"Answer forms and interview materials of unsuccessful candidates are shredded and discarded at the end of each year."

"Is there nothing else to prove that no discrimination took place? What about our hiring bylaws from the nineties?"

"We do have those."

"Please bring them to me."

After the human resources manager bowed and quickly left the room, Shiroyama turned his attention to the manager of general affairs, making sure to check the clock, which read 9:10 A.M.

"Were you able to contact him?"

"Yes, but it seems he's suffering from dementia . . ." Ide replied. It had been discovered that a man named Kuwata, who back in June 1947 had held the same position as Ide—manager of general affairs—was still alive at the age of ninety-six, and Shiroyama had given instructions to contact him, but apparently they were too late. With the exception of Kuwata, all the other Hinode executives from forty-eight years ago had passed away. Shiroyama had kicked himself repeatedly for not taking care of the matter when it occurred back in 1990, but he hadn't given up yet. He needed to know who had been the last person to handle Okamura's letter in June of 1947. Once that became clear, so would the source of the leak.

"Please see if you can find someone who was relatively young at the time. There may be a chance someone still remembers what happened. How about the minutes from the board meetings back then?"

"They're on your desk."

"Have you read them? Are there any references to the letter?"

"The bigger issue is that the minutes from August are missing . . ."

"They're supposed to be there?"

"I believe so. From what we can tell from the September meeting minutes, it seems two board meetings were held in August, and we can't find the minutes from either of them."

Distracted by the fact that the clock read 9:13 A.M., Shiroyama thanked Ide for his efforts and dismissed him. He was aware of the confusion within his own mind as he glanced at the black minutes log that had been set on his desk.

The forty-eight-year-old log smelled musty and its cover was so decayed that it looked as if it might peel away with a single touch. Perhaps right after the war they had not been able to hold board meetings as frequently—this log was much thinner than the ones they used nowadays. Shiroyama noticed a trace of discoloration near the knot on the binding string that held the log book together. He did not have to wonder what the mark signified—it was clear that someone had very recently retied the forty-eight-year-old knot.

Shiroyama opened the minutes log, confirmed that the date in July was followed by the date in September, and was just reaching for the intercom when Ms. Nozaki's voice announced, "It's time." Shiroyama told her to summon Shirai at once and to ask the police to wait ten minutes.

Because Shiroyama had asked him to come "at once"—an uncharacteristically urgent emphasis—Shirai appeared within two minutes, looking distracted. "Nice day out, isn't it? I'll be leaving for Sendai now. Do you remember that cooperative industry-university project with Tohoku University? I think it's better to involve the prefecture and make them pay the infrastructure maintenance fee—"

"Shirai-san. Figure out who removed the August minutes from this log. Let me know when you find him."

Shirai was silent for a count of three, holding the minutes log that Shiroyama had passed to him in his hands. Then a mock smile appeared on his face. "So now you're going to play the tyrant?"

"Does looking for the thief make me a tyrant?"

"I'll look for your thief, but only if you let me deal with him. It's better for you to appear not to know anything."

Shiroyama felt a twinge of regret after Shirai breezed out of his office without another word. Shirai had taken pity on Shiroyama, who had burdened himself with yet another issue that could land him in trouble if anyone outside the company knew about it—not only that, Shirai had provoked in Shiroyama a sense of defeat for losing his composure, and then shrewdly displayed a sense of ease by promising to take care of the matter. During their short exchange, Shiroyama again felt his mindset relegated to that of the victim—the object. Shiroyama was highly resistant to this, but in the end he was forced to admit—with a bit of self-deprecation—that the theft of the meeting minutes and the indignity of losing his cool in front of a colleague were additional burdens befitting the man who had brought misfortune home to the company.

AWARE THAT TIME WAS SCARCE, Shiroyama was hurriedly tidying the documents on his desk when Ms. Nozaki poked her head in and said, "It's time for you to go, but Tamaru-san is on the line with an urgent call."

He must want to negotiate directly about the land purchase in Gunma. With a fresh wave of panic, Shiroyama answered the outside line. "This is Shiroyama."

"This is Tamaru. It's been a long time."

"Thank you for the telegram yesterday. I'm much obliged."

"I'm sure you have a lot to worry about. And there's no need to get into a serious discussion now."

Two years ago, after the company had managed to sever ties with the Okada Association thanks to Kurata's efforts, Shiroyama had met Zenzo Tamaru at a dinner party, for what he hoped would be the first and last time. Tamaru's outward appearance could be described as nothing more than "a man in his seventies wearing a suit," but for the entire hour Shiroyama was in his company he had been assailed by a disconcerting sensation, like a faint chill running up his spine. Later, when Kurata explained to him that an ultranationalist like Tamaru showed his mettle by a willingness to stab his opponent at any given moment, it finally seemed to make sense. Frankly, it was quite an experience for Shiroyama—a man who valued his life—to come face to face with one who did not, and to feel the chill of such decisive violence, which seemed to defy logic.

Over those drinks two years ago, Tamaru had regaled Shiroyama with the story of his success, from his roots in the coal-mining town of Chikuho to his rise as a postwar black market broker. Throughout their conversation he consistently implied how vastly different the world he belonged to was from that of Shiroyama's, which thus made him immune to fear. Ultimately, there was nothing more to Tamaru than the brutality of a snake intimidating a frog, but it was something of a discovery for Shiroyama that what underpinned the life of a long-time fixer like Tamaru was a warped lust for subjugation.

If assessing calmly, however, Shiroyama could not deny Tamaru's resourcefulness. Tamaru had apparently adopted his nationalistic tendencies under the influence of Karoku Tsuji, who had been a puppet master in prewar Japanese politics, but Tamaru said what moved him most was his realization immediately following the war that, even after the democratization of Japan, politicians and money could not be separated. Another lesson for Tamaru was the political donation scandal during the 1947 general election that ended Karoku Tsuji's career, from which Tamaru had ascertained that the prewar era when ultranationalists wielded enormous power with their mere presence was over, that the dissolution of the zaibatsu conglomerates would alter the flow of money, and moreover, that these channels would shift underground from then on.

Tamaru then made a fortune from his dealings in scrap iron, moving on to shipping and port services, and no sooner had he established the Hikari Industry Group and driven up the stock price, he sold off the entire group to raise capital for the creation of the ultranationalist organization known as the Jiyu Seiwakai, the predecessor of the present-day Seiwakai. Next, in accordance with his own theory that the money would shift underground, in 1959 he helped set up a corporate underling for the Seiwakai, persuading his right-hand man, Tomoharu Okada, to create the Okada Association while he stepped behind the scenes. That was the start of his fixer business.

There was no way to know how many bribes Tamaru had smoothed the way for since then, but Shiroyama had heard that his dealings with Hinode started in 1962 when Tamaru had volunteered to act as a pipeline between the company and politico pockets over the license for a subsidiary company in the land transportation business. Though this affiliation could be described as nondescript, the fact that a single phone call, summons, or invitation to a restaurant from Tamaru was never anything less than a tacit threat was conveyed clearly in Kurata's eyes the night Shiroyama met Tamaru. As he sat with the two of them, it was Shiroyama's first faint glimpse of the world in which Kurata had been submerged for years, and though he thought he had been keenly aware of Kurata's feelings, looking back he had serious doubts about how much he had truly understood.

At that gathering two years ago, Shiroyama did as Kurata had instructed him, courteously and simply bowing his head and thanking Tamaru several times. But Tamaru had left them with the parting words, "Consider this an uncontested divorce," implying that, even though Hinode had paid the settlement and effectively severed ties with Okada, hard feelings would continue to linger. Vividly recalling Tamaru's snake-like eyes, Shiroyama asked cautiously, "How can I help you today?"

"Oh, it's just that I saw the papers this morning. You and I are hardly strangers, so I thought I ought to say something. If there's any trouble, Tamaru can be of assistance."

"Very considerate of you, I'm much obliged."

"My hunch has never been wrong, Shiroyama-san. If your family is in trouble, it might even be necessary to forcefully snuff out the news reports while there's still time. Better to do something than to sit around worrying, you know."

"I'm not concerned about what the newspapers have been reporting since it's a completely unfounded misunderstanding."

"If you say so. Whatever the case, let me know if you need me."

That was the end of their conversation. There was no question that Tamaru had been alluding to the matter of his niece Yoshiko. *Where did he catch wind of it?* Shiroyama was already asking himself. If Tamaru had homed in on not only the trouble over the recruitment exam but also the connection to the dead student's girlfriend back in 1990, then perhaps he had heard it from the student's surviving family members?

What is Tamaru's aim? The answer to this question was clear. He must be applying pressure on the land purchase deal that had been deadlocked, but to do so without any subtlety at a time like this meant that perhaps he had another ulterior motive.

Okada has already sussed out the details with Yoshiko . . . The astonishment that had buzzed in his chest during the phone call had already galloped through him, but what remained was remorse for not having considered these consequences when he was released. Yet even if he had, would there have been any other alternative for him? Would it have compelled him to tell the police everything? He interrogated himself, but the only conclusion he reached was that at this point in time he could not go back on his words, publicly or privately. He had landed himself in a complicated position, and was only half convinced about his decision.

On the phone last night with his niece Yoshiko, there had been nothing in her voice to indicate she had any inkling that suspicions were swirling around the trouble with Takayuki Hatano from four and a half years ago—she had simply been happy that her uncle had returned home safe. Shiroyama now gave some thought to how, as he had listened to her bright voice, he had repeatedly asked himself what this young woman meant to him. He had always seemed to favor the playful and cheery Yoshiko over his own daughter, who resembled her parents with her tendency to suppress her emotions, but his fondness was not so much for Yoshiko personally—rather, he simply considered her a balm for the eyes and heart. Now that Yoshiko had her own family and was a mother herself, it was beyond consideration that he, as her uncle, could in any way shoulder the weight of her life as a grown woman. *And yet, what does that matter?* Was there any point in contradicting the statements he had already made publicly and putting Yoshiko and her family in jeopardy so that he might contend with Tamaru and Okada?

After debating these things, Shiroyama reached the decision that he would first consult with Kurata about what Tamaru had said. Then, at 9:30 A.M., fifteen minutes later than scheduled, he entered the underground storage room that had been designated as the control center, where he sat for a second interview with the police.

There, arranged on a table, were ten different bean-jam buns, five varieties of cream buns, thirty beverage products in paper cartons, and four brands of canned food. Thus began the task of identifying each of the items that Shiroyama had eaten during his confinement. It seemed to Shiroyama that the investigator was fixated on the canned pork and beans and fruit-flavored milk, but whatever reason why was unclear.

久保晴久　Haruhisa Kubo

WHEN CHIEF INSPECTOR OF FIRST Investigation Hidetsugu Kanzaki appeared at the regularly scheduled 11 A.M. press conference, his opening remarks were predictable enough. "The three papers that wrote about the matter of the 1990 tape in their morning editions ought to be ashamed of themselves. The articles in these three papers represent not only an unwarranted attack on Hinode Beer as the victim, but they could also serve to benefit the perpetrators who are threatening Hinode. It shows a lack of consideration for the individuals involved in the matter of the tape, in particular the deceased and their surviving family members, none of whom have anything to do with the incident in question. I'm sure the three papers are well aware of what they have done, so I will say no more."

But his next words came as a surprise to the various reporters present, beginning with Haruhisa Kubo.

"Having said that, I know that I cannot keep you from writing about it, so with permission from Hinode, we will now distribute a transcript of said tape from 1990 to each newspaper. Nothing has been omitted from the original tape. However, the names of individuals have been redacted to protect their privacy."

This was an unexpected initiative for the police to take. Murmurs rose within the cramped office of the chief inspector as members of the Public Information Division distributed sheaves of photocopied pages to each company. As Kubo received his own set—twenty pages on A4 paper—he saw that the first line on the top page read, *Hinode Beer Company, Kanagawa Factory, To Whom It May Concern.* This was followed by the body of the letter, which began with, *I, Seiji Okamura, am one of the forty employees who resigned from the Kanagawa factory of Hinode at the end of this past February. Today, with ever so many things on my mind . . .* The last page was dated June 1947.

Given that the perpetrators' memo declaring that they had kidnapped Hinode's president had yet to be made public, the police's largess in sharing the letter indicated that it was a meaningless document irrelevant to the main story of the incident. Yet Kubo's sensors were triggered by how quickly the police had responded. What was behind their reaction? What was their intention?

"This is for each of you to read the letter and decide for yourselves if a mysterious tape is worth all the fuss," Kanzaki went on, his tone brusque. "Now, the former Hinode employee who wrote the letter and his colleague from the segregated buraku community to whom he refers in the letter have both passed away. We have been unable to confirm that this letter in fact arrived at Hinode's Kanagawa factory in 1947. No documents related to the matter still exist on Hinode's end, nor have any former employees who might recall the matter with the letter been found."

Kubo waited for Kanzaki to finish, then immediately raised his hand. "Please tell us the reason for the disclosure of the letter today."

"Investigation Headquarters decided they would like to protect the individuals affected from further harm due to excessive coverage of the matter. As you'll see when you read the letter, it makes references to a segregated buraku community, so those included in any reporting will inevitably suffer damages both tangible and intangible. It could even potentially cause a new threat. Therefore, I hereby request that no further mention of this matter be made, as it is unrelated to the incident in question."

"The newspapers may not mention it again, but disclosing materials like this might only make the tabloids go on the offensive?" Kubo ventured.

"We don't believe there is anything of interest to the tabloids here."

Kubo sincerely doubted that was true—he suspected this may be a calculated move by Kanzaki to indirectly shake up Hinode, whose executives remained tightlipped. Or, perhaps it was a last-ditch strategy to gain some kind of advantage by leaking the letter.

While Kubo mulled this over, reporters from other papers took the opportunity to hurl their own questions.

"You say there are no problems with the investigation, but there's talk that the letter was circulated by extortionists," came the angry riposte from a reporter whose paper had splashed the headline MYS-TERY TAPE across their morning edition.

"We have not found evidence that anything like that is true," Chief Kanzaki replied evasively.

"An extortionist and a pseudo-anti-discrimination organization were shaking down Hinode, isn't that right?"

"Hinode filed a complaint in 1990 after receiving a tape from an unidentified sender that slandered the company."

"The tape from 1990 and the recent kidnapping of Hinode's

president are unrelated. That's what you've decided and that's why you've released the letter?"

"It means that this is not the police's concern."

As he listened to this futile exchange, Kubo asked himself what he should do. Even if the document was meaningless, could he simply disregard a tape from 1990 that had caused enough of a dustup to lead to a complaint? Kubo shifted his gaze to the twenty-page copy in his hand and, before long, he became absorbed by the litany of unfamiliar names and places.

The author of the letter appeared to have been born and raised on a poor farm in the Tohoku region. *I was born in 1915 in the village of Herai in Aomori prefecture. My family home was in the Tamodai district of that same village. In addition to working as tenant farmers on about an acre of land, my family kept a broodmare offered on loan by the land-owner . . .* As he read the opening passage of the confession, Kubo, who had been born in 1963, felt his head fill with questions.

城山恭介

KYOSUKE SHIROYAMA

4

Friday, April 28th. Kyosuke Shiroyama began the thirty-sixth day since the incident by answering a phone call from Seigo Kurata. "My apologies for calling so early," Kurata said. "You can expect to receive a call from Iida Shokai, regarding the contract from the other day."

These pre-determined code words notified him that the criminals had made contact. It was the best they could manage, given that the police had installed recording devices on the landline at Shiroyama's home. But the code offered no details about when, where, how, or the nature of the contact that had been received.

Over the last month, Shiroyama had never wavered in his conviction that the criminals would follow through on their word to make contact before Golden Week. The fear that some unexpected contingency would arise had been ever-present, but the board of directors had already resolved that, when the time came, they would assent to the criminals' demand, so at least he knew that there would be no internal struggle to formulate a response.

When he heard Kurata's voice, Shiroyama's heart had jumped with the thought, *At last*, but he remained calm, replying, "I understand. I'll see you later then," before replacing the receiver. There was a small ping in a corner of his mind: *the days of anticipation are over, now all I need to do is focus on our response.*

But there were still various subtleties to consider. Kurata had grown extremely cautious about the company's overall response, given that Tamaru from the Okada Association had been implicitly threatening them since right after the incident. And the criminals had waited to make contact until the initial shock of the incident had worn off and a peaceful mood had begun to settle among the executives and employees alike.

Shiroyama ate his usual breakfast. After he finished, his wife called him out to the garden, saying that the irises were in bloom, and there he saw a dozen or so of the diminutive flowers showing off their purple petals at the foot of the Himalayan cedar. During the past month, he had had no time to pay any attention to the garden—now that he noticed, it was bursting with spring flowers. These irises in the shade appeared to be the last ones to bloom.

At 7:45 A.M., punctual as ever, his driver Yamazaki pulled up in front of the house. When he suggested, "Shall we take the usual route around Oi Hankyu today?" Shiroyama replied, "That'll be fine." In fact, he made this response after much hesitation, remembering how the consultant Kotani had advised him not to alter his daily routine, just in case, to avoid attracting attention from the public and the police. Thus, despite Kurata's phone call, Shiroyama spent part of that April morning exploring the city in the company car, arriving in front of Hinode's main office at 8:20 A.M.

When the new building was constructed eight years ago, it was set back twenty meters from the road to accommodate a copse of camphor and zelkova trees, which had matured splendidly. Now at the height of spring, just before Golden Week, the vivid green of their budding leaves cast a verdant hue over the white granite pavement. Again this morning, a young man sat alone on a bench along this promenade under the new foliage. From inside the car, Shiroyama gave him a slight bow, and the man returned the gesture, rising briefly from his seat.

Apparently he was from *Toho News*. Ever since the incident, their reporters had been staking out the company building around the clock in three shifts—one reporter keeping watch by the main entrance and another on the south side, by the entrance to the underground parking lot. The news media seemed to suspect that the incident would take a turn at any moment, and Shiroyama could not help but be impressed by the tenacity of their reporting.

The public's interest in the incident had waned after the first week or so—the press corps in front of Shiroyama's home had dispersed, and Hinode's name no longer appeared on the Metro pages of the newspapers. The tabloids ran special issues for two weeks, and their subway ads had been splashed with predictable headlines—THE BIZARRE FACTS BEHIND THE HINODE PRESIDENT'S KIDNAPPING, THE UNDENIABLE TRUTH ABOUT HINODE'S BACKROOM DEALINGS, ALL THE REASONS WHY HINODE WAS TARGETED, THE LINEAGE BETWEEN HINODE AND THE UNDERWORLD—and crude, titillating attacks on Shiroyama's character—CHARMED NEPOTISM, THE LIFE OF AN ELITE. From a corporate standpoint, Hinode deemed none of these stories worth an individual response, and Shiroyama hardly gave them a second glance.

On the other hand, the investigation dragged on and on. At the beginning of April, an eyewitness account of an unidentified vehicle on Ome Highway had turned up, and an investigator had informed him that the vehicle used by the criminals to transport him was most likely a dark blue Nissan Homy with a license plate ending in "54." But the alleged vehicle had yet to be located, and it had already been ten days since Shiroyama was told that the car's license plate may have been bogus and that the police were checking out every Nissan Homy registered in the metropolitan area.

Likewise, not a single fact about the criminals themselves—appearance, age, occupation, or lifestyle—had yet to be uncovered. The police had tried locating the point of sale of the cans of pork and beans and cartons of fruit-flavored milk the kidnappers had given Shiroyama, but there were no stores that stocked all of the food items, which meant they must have been purchased separately from various stores.

The figure of the reporter disappeared from the rearview mirror as the car moved toward the front entrance, pulling up right on time at the porte-cochère. Briefcase in hand, Shiroyama got out, conscious that the reporter was no doubt observing him through the leafy shade as he called out "Good morning" to the guard outside the doors. The guard returned the greeting cheerfully. Other arriving employees greeted Shiroyama as well, and Shiroyama replied to each of them in turn.

The deputy manager of general affairs who had been assigned exclusively to the special control center must have been eagerly anticipating Shiroyama's arrival and swiftly approached him. "Kurata-san is waiting for you in the control center," he whispered and ushered Shiroyama toward the elevators.

"How did they make contact?"

"A security guard at the Kanagawa factory picked up a letter that had been thrown inside the front gate. The guard alerted the factory manager, and someone on duty immediately delivered it to us here."

The elevator stopped on the second basement level, where they passed through a steel door into a restricted area and entered the control center located beneath the opera hall stage. Seigo Kurata greeted them with only a bow, his expression tense with worry.

The letter lay open on a table. It was an ordinary sheet of B5-size letter paper. When Shiroyama looked closely, the handwritten characters, apparently drawn with a ballpoint pen using a ruler, leapt out at him.

READY TO MAKE THE PAYMENT? IF SO, TAKE OUT AN AD WITH THE WORDS, "FATHER FORGIVES KYOKO" IN THE MAY 5TH ISSUE OF NIKKAN SPORTS.   —LADY JOKER

Shiroyama had to run his eyes over the letter three or four times. Partly it took time to sink in because suddenly all the events leading up to this point seemed to have lost their sense of reality. Or the cryptic name, "Lady Joker," may have been what confused him.

"Well, then—we'll follow the manual and this will be handled by the control center. Are we all good on that?"

Shiroyama had expected easy agreement, but instead Kurata parried. "May I have a word?" He gestured with his eyes toward the door, then stood up and left the room first. Shiroyama followed after him, stunned.

The suggestion that Kurata presented, in the dark hallway beneath the stage, was completely mind-boggling: consulting the board.

"I myself went back and forth many times before reaching this conclusion. If we don't take the time now to reconfirm the board's decision, including the specifics of disbursing the money and how the paperwork will be manipulated, we'll lose control of things if and when something goes awry."

"What are you saying . . . ? If we decide to consult the board now, it's possible that the consensus we worked so hard for three weeks ago will have been for nothing."

"That's exactly right. Which is why I'm saying this to you now. If we entrust this matter entirely to the control center and only get the board's approval after the fact, it could give the wrong impression to certain individuals. Sakakibara, Otani, Yoshikawa, Shinozaki, Isaka . . ." Kurata rattled off the names of executives at the main office, then continued with more names at the level of branch and factory managers. "Yamamoto, Tsuboi, Takasaka, Moriwaki . . ."

While they had worked toward that earlier consensus, there had been various opposing viewpoints about bending to the criminals' demand. In addition, executives from certain divisions felt a sense of alarm related to the possibility of the manufacturing sector being sacrificed as pieces were being strategically positioned for impending subsidiary spinoffs. Finally, there were executives who, despite having mentally processed the numerous structural reforms that Shiroyama had forged ahead with over the last five years, still could not accept them emotionally. Shiroyama was all too familiar with the current status of the board, a complicated tangle of interests, emotions, and logic that went well beyond simple categorization into Shirai or Kurata factions and which defied a simple count of votes.

Kurata, who most feared damage to the company's beer, who had meticulously calculated the potential losses in a worst-case scenario, and who had taken such a forceful lead with the board, was now suggesting they do the exact opposite of what he had said before. Shiroyama wracked his brain futilely, trying to figure out Kurata's true intentions.

"If we just consent to the criminals' demand now, then down the line we'll have no choice but to go along with Okada's demand too. Tamaru is saying that the land deal is for four billion . . ."

"When did he mention that price?"

"In February. Since I'm not responding to him, it's possible Tamaru will attempt to negotiate directly with you. I intend to do my best to prevent that, but if he were to point out the fact that we had caved to the criminals' demand, we'd lose our negotiating edge. No matter what, we must avoid a situation where we end up shelling out six billion—Tamaru's sum plus what the criminals are demanding."

"Let's keep the issue with Tamaru separate from the criminals' demand. If we were to refuse to cooperate and there were some kind of damage to our product, the losses incurred would run into the billions—that was your prediction. What would be the point of jeopardizing the board's decision?"

"I'm not saying that we shouldn't consent to their demand. But even if we do go along in the end, it won't do to give the executives the impression that we're simply putty in the hands of the criminals. That's why I'm saying we should involve the board."

"But even if we consult with them about how to handle this letter, we're still back to a simple yes or no."

"Once we let the executives air their opinions on the issue, why don't we buy some time by telling the board that we want to exercise caution by reporting it to the police and conferring with them about what our response should be? Even the most fastidious executives would consent to that. Your position would be protected too. Please, I'd like for us to do this. I'll be responsible for directing the board."

His strong tone left no room for hesitation. Shiroyama admitted he had neither the willpower to push back nor the ability to evaluate the pros and cons in the matter. As the logic that he had mentally imposed upon the circumstances began to unravel, the sheer force of his anxiety compelled him to reply with, "I suppose so."

Perhaps Kurata had seen through this, for he cracked a slight smile. "Shiroyama-san. My opinion is entirely the same as yours. You know I would never allow for a contingency that would, for example, prevent us from shipping the orders for forty-nine million cases of beer for the months of May and June."

"I suppose not."

"The police probably want to force a move by the criminals, so I assume they'll tell us to go through the motions of complying with the criminals' demand. Which is perfectly convenient for us. Pretending to go along with what the criminals want will also enable us to negotiate a backroom deal down the line."

Ultimately they agreed to call a board meeting by the end of the day, as Kurata had suggested, and they parted ways. Once alone, however, Shiroyama sighed deeply, contemplating just how delicate the situation now was.

The bridge that Shiroyama and Kurata had to cross was blocked on one end by extortionists who called themselves "Lady Joker" and by the Okada Association on the other. For now, they were trying to move toward the extortionists while holding off Okada, but reaching their destination would require them to pass constantly through the board's indeterminate checkpoints. It would come down to whether they could deceive the executives in order to engineer a consensus. More than just a gambit to avoid being the target of a later investigation, they needed to take into consideration the delicate situation brought on by their scandal from 1990, so that in the end they would be able to keep one hand free to negotiate with the Okada Association.

Moreover, Kurata, the man laying each piece in place, was in just as delicate a position, and it was clear to Shiroyama that he was wavering between either a full-scale confrontation or a compromise with Okada. Kurata had never revealed his hand to Shiroyama in this way before, and that in itself was a vivid indication of the change in him. This revelation had struck Shiroyama a month ago, the night after he was released, and now it was certain Kurata was not entirely his former self. The fact that Shiroyama had no choice but to entrust everything to him exposed his supreme vulnerability.

SHIROYAMA HAD A BUSY SCHEDULE for the rest of the day, but he spoke with Shirai on the phone and solicited his opinion about consulting the board.

"Kurata has convinced you, hasn't he?" Shirai said.

"You're a step ahead," Shiroyama said. "My point is, I'm not sure how this will play out. And it doesn't help that you refuse to disclose the name of the thief who stole the meeting minutes."

"I expect the thief will confess to you directly. More importantly, I fully understand the thorny position Kurata is in. The truth is, most of the executives—myself included—never thought the criminals would actually make contact, and the matter with Okada makes for a problem situation, not to mention our stock . . ."

"What about our stock?"

"Kurata has been nervous about it, but I'm about to meet with someone from a brokerage house, so I'll report back later with what I learn. In any case, let's hope Kurata knows what he's doing. I'll do my best to get carte blanche from as many executives as possible too."

Following this conversation, Shiroyama inferred that Shirai had decided to leave everything up to Kurata, the better to observe what would unfold from the sidelines. That was no doubt the wisest course of action.

At seven o'clock that evening, when the impromptu board meeting convened behind closed doors in the thirtieth-floor conference room, fifteen of the twenty-eight internal board members, including Shirai, were absent but had given carte blanche, leaving thirteen members in attendance. Sugihara was nowhere in sight. Everyone other than Shiroyama and Kurata looked aloof, as if the issue did not concern them. Perhaps the name "Lady Joker" had deprived the proceedings of a sense of reality, for the mood of the room felt as if they were stuck dealing with an annoying prank.

Shiroyama began his remarks, stating that he wished to consult the board as to whether it would be right, as previously agreed, to take out an advertisement in accordance with the criminals' demand without reporting it to the police, but before he finished speaking, the board members around the oval table began to look ill at ease. Sakakibara, the corporate secretary and executive director of general affairs, raised his hand and declared, "It's been three weeks since the board agreed to that resolution, and the circumstances in which we find ourselves continue to shift. I think it's necessary to assess the situation once again."

Several voices chimed in their agreement.

Sakakibara went on, "There have been pervasive rumors over the past month that Hinode has connections to the underworld, and that the company has already made a backroom deal and paid off the criminals. We can't deny that's an understandable response. If we were to accommodate the criminals' demand, and if word ever got out about it, the damage to the Hinode brand would be immeasurable."

In terms of the market effect on their corporate image, the board had already determined that whatever harm might befall their products outweighed any advantage they would gain by refusing the criminals' demand. The projected losses amounted to over a hundred billion yen. But a month without incident had been enough to lull the group's mindset.

"My position is that we should defer to the results of the risk assessment from our previous meeting." This was Shiroyama's only response.

Taking the opportunity to lay out a far more fundamental doubt,

Otani, managing director of the pharmaceutical business division, spoke up. "What I want to know is whether this Lady Joker or whoever they are merits our gathering together like this and debating how to deal with them. A demand such as this is utterly ridiculous. It amounts to a blank check."

Shiroyama reminded him that the criminals were demanding a ransom of two billion yen, but Otani rejected this. "They only ask if we're ready to pay—they didn't specify an amount. It doesn't sit right with me."

Shiroyama had to admit that Otani was right. He loathed Lady Joker for not specifying the amount in their letter, but all he could do was reiterate that the criminals had indeed told him two billion. A hushed yet noncommittal bafflement fell over the oval table.

Over the last month, there had been whispers among the board members about the tape from 1990 that had been reported in the newspapers after the incident, particularly the details of how the student who had left in the middle of his employee interview had been intimately involved with the daughter of Takeo Sugihara, as well as the fact that they had heard board meeting minutes from 1947 had gone missing. Obviously, the cause for the board members' ambivalence—more than the strange name, "Lady Joker"—was the scandal involving his family, which clung to the circumstances surrounding the incident.

Kurata, according to plan, made a suggestion. "Well, then, in the meantime, why don't we report the letter to the police?"

The members were taken aback, but as Kurata had anticipated, ultimately the board came to the hasty conclusion that they would report it to the police and see what came about, thereby delaying their decision for the time being.

After the meeting was adjourned, Shiroyama thanked Kurata, taking the opportunity to broach the subject of their stock, which Shirai had mentioned. Shiroyama's state of mind was such that the smallest thing caused him to worry.

"Our stock price had been pretty high since the beginning of April, the parity price for convertible bonds has been going up as well, and our margin account position has been increasing about hundred thousand per week, so . . ."

"I'm aware of all that."

"Yesterday's preliminary figures showed that margin buys were over two million, so when I asked them to investigate the source I was told that purchases were coming in from various brokerages all over. It seems word on the street is that in early fall we'll be adding a chain of convenience stores into our business affiliates, but perhaps that information had come from . . ."

Kurata stopped short, as if regretting what he had been about to say, and instead sighed grimly. Shiroyama had to urge him to continue.

"This is nothing more than gossip, but the name of an investment management company operating under the umbrella of the Seiwakai has surfaced. They're among the G.S.C. group."

"Does this have to do with Okada?"

"I don't know. Two million stocks don't amount to much in the grand scheme of things, but given the times we're in, we ought to be wary of any high-risk moves."

Although Shiroyama could not fully comprehend the substance of Kurata's concerns, he was sure that only a man who had glimpsed the shadow world could have hunches like these. The thought gave rise to yet another tangible worry, piled up on top of the others.

ON THE MORNING OF SATURDAY, April 29th, while the majority of the board members were out at the Matsuo Golf Club for Hinode's Kantō regional competition, police investigators disguised as Tokyo Electric Power Company maintenance workers entered the main office, which was deserted for the holiday weekend, and retrieved the letter from "Lady Joker." Shiroyama was informed of the details of this interaction when he arrived at the office on the morning of Tuesday, May 2nd. The police had explained their plan to carry on as before without disclosing anything—including the arrival of the letter—to the public.

Two mornings later, Shiroyama received a call from the usual officer from Investigation Headquarters. He wondered why the officer sounded so stiff and formal, and then the head of MPD's First Investigation Division, Chief Inspector Kanzaki, came on the phone to request a meeting with Shiroyama in person. Shiroyama replied that he had no time to spare, but Kanzaki insisted that the matter took precedence over everything else, so that ultimately Shiroyama relented, agreeing to meet him during lunchtime.

久保晴久　Haruhisa Kubo

IT WAS BEFORE NOON, AND in the Nanashakai kisha club at MPD the *Toho* press nook was tranquil, now that the follow-up report on the arrest of the cult leader-mastermind behind the subway poison-gas terror attack a week ago had been put to bed. The front-page headline on the evening's early edition pronounced HOLIDAY REFRESH-MENT alongside a color photo of the beaches of the Boso Peninsula. Although the deadline for the third edition loomed, hardly any articles needed to be replaced, and the direct line to the news room had been pretty quiet. Kubo had taken the opportunity to begin organizing his notebooks; beside him, Kuriyama flipped through a travel magazine, attempting some armchair escapism.

Just then, a call came in on the outside line. "This is Yamane, from the post in front of Hinode's main office!"

The beat reporter's energetic voice jolted Kubo out of his reverie—he was startled by mention of Hinode, whose name he hadn't heard in a while.

"A car with the head of First Investigation just entered the underground parking lot," the reporter continued. "There was no time to stop him and talk. What should I do now?"

"Keep watch by the parking lot entrance! I'm on my way. If I don't make it there in time, do whatever you can to stop the car as it comes out of the lot. Make small talk, doesn't matter what you say—just call out to him and be sure to take note of his expression. He tends to avoid eye contact when something's up. Got it?" Kubo had already grabbed his day pack by the time he hung up the phone. "Chief, it seems the head of First Investigation's inside Hinode's main office. There may be some action on the case."

No sooner had Kubo said the words than he rushed out of the press nook, propelled by a feeling of freedom after these last few days of boredom. If he sped, it would take him half an hour to get to Kita-Shinagawa, where Hinode's office was. Kanzaki had only returned to his official residence in Himonya twice during the first few weeks of April, so there was no reason to think he had time to be making courtesy visits to Hinode. Perhaps they'd received the criminals' demand. Kubo's instinct stirred. *There is no doubt about it, the criminals have made their move*, he thought to himself.

城山恭介　Kyosuke Shiroyama

IN A PRIVATE ROOM AT the beer restaurant on the fortieth floor of the building that housed Hinode's main offices, Shiroyama welcomed Hidetsugu Kanzaki, the head of MPD's First Investigation Division. During their phone call early that morning, Shiroyama had been unable to surmise what the police business was, so he had suggested that they have lunch together, an offer that Kanzaki had readily accepted with a simple word of thanks.

Kanzaki's appearance was ordinary enough, but the overall impression he gave—the head of gray hair, clipped short, with its formidable, weather-beaten forehead and small, steadfast eyes beneath—reminded Shiroyama of a non-commissioned army officer he saw once long ago. Whenever Shiroyama encountered Kanzaki, he became even more convinced that the man was a different breed from Iwami at the National Police Agency—Kanzaki had the face of a commander of a combat unit.

The first thing Kanzaki said was, "Thank you for your cooperation in this matter." He bowed, then sat down without affectation and commented frankly, "What a wonderful view." It was not small talk; Kanzaki was in fact surveying the far vista from the window of the fortieth floor. He was not like most other officers, who were all pretense.

"By the way, sir, how are you feeling these days?" Kanzaki asked.

"I'm doing fine, thank you. Which do you prefer—meat or fish?"

"I'll have the fish."

"How about beer?"

"Thank you, but I'm afraid not, since I'm on duty."

After the waiter left, Kanzaki cut right to the chase. "The first matter I came to discuss with you today is—"

Shiroyama was impressed, wishing business could always be conducted as efficiently.

"—Investigation Headquarters would very much like to lure 'Lady Joker' into taking action so that we might be able to progress with the investigation. If the perpetrators make a move, a means of closing in on them becomes available. Therefore, on the date specified—May fifth—we would like your company to take out an ad in *Nikkan Sports*, and we will await further instructions from the perpetrators."

Now Shiroyama realized that Kanzaki's plain-spoken manner of discussing things was one-sided—he still represented authorities who had no need to ever consider the other person's perspective. Moreover, his finely-honed lack of idiosyncrasy undoubtedly functioned as a sort of intimidation.

"What will we do once we receive further instructions?"

"Presumably, the next instructions will involve how to deliver the money. We'd like you to follow those instructions. Of course, the police would have the place surrounded, so if the perpetrators were to appear, rest assured that they would not get away. MPD has never let a perpetrator escape in previous cases such as this."

"You mean you want us to act as if we are going along with the perpetrators' demand?"

"That's right."

"It's not for me to judge what is best for the investigation, so if that's what you say, we'll follow instructions. I'll have the control center issue an official response."

"By the way, you contacted us the day after receiving the letter from the perpetrators. Is there any particular reason why?"

"No, nothing in particular. The executives are all so busy that it's difficult to get them together at the same time to discuss a course of action."

The arrival of their meal interrupted conversation temporarily as Kanzaki began eating—langoustine with sauce américaine, served with butter rice. "Wow, this is incredibly delicious," he commented. Shiroyama explained that the sauce américaine, prepared by the kitchen of the beer restaurant each day by pounding and simmering a ten-kilogram Japanese spiny lobster, was among the best in Tokyo.

"I see . . . Now I understand how you immediately identified the Western food item that you were given as 'pork and beans,'" Kanzaki responded, straight-laced as ever. "Speaking of which, canned pork and beans are also distributed by the Self-Defense Forces and some municipalities, who use them as emergency food supplies."

After this digression, Kanzaki got back to the point. "Now, the second matter I wanted to discuss with you. As we try to force a move by the perpetrators, I'd very much like to provide you with a detective as escort."

"You mean a bodyguard?"

"A bodyguard equipped with a handgun and an expandable baton, yes."

"I'm not so sure about that . . . It's all so sudden."

"I bring this up because there is no room for error—for the police nor for your company."

"The company has increased the number of security guards."

"You go out and about every day, and yet you only have one driver with you. That is much too vulnerable."

"That's standard for civilians."

"I don't mean to dodge the police's accountability, but the attacks on corporate executives—including last year's incident in which the managing director of Toei Bank was shot and killed—could have been avoided if the victims had been a little more prepared. And compared to those cases, the situation involving your company is much more pressing. The perpetrators who abducted you were confident that, once they released you, they'd still get their hands on the six hundred million, so once they realize that this is no longer likely, you can expect to be in quite a lot of danger."

So the police do, in fact, suspect that the criminals have some kind of connection with me, Shiroyama surmised. "You just said that in the event that the perpetrators give instructions about how to deliver the money, we should do as we're told and you'll be able to apprehend them," he said, holding firm.

"We'll be able to catch them in the act, but we can't stop what they do behind the scenes," Kanzaki retorted.

"The point being, it's all very dangerous."

"All cases are dangerous."

"If what it takes to arrest the perpetrators would expose me to a level of danger that requires a bodyguard, then I'll need to give it some thought," Shiroyama said. His resistance was meager, and Kanzaki remained unwavering.

"This is not Hinode's problem alone. Apprehending the perpetrators concerns the law and order of this country and corporate society as a whole. I would like your company to be an example for corporations all over Japan by not yielding to unwarranted corporate terrorism. All I'm suggesting is for the police to do their utmost in this effort by providing you with a security detail."

Shiroyama knew he had no recourse other than to comply with the police. A corporation did not have the capacity to prevent or respond to unforeseeable dangers. They had no grounds for refusing the police's offer to provide a detective. The reason he himself was having trouble accepting it was simple: he was utterly baffled that neither he nor the board of directors had been able to predict that such danger and constraint of personal freedom would befall him and those around him.

"Please allow me to consider this," Shiroyama responded at last. "I'll issue my final decision through the control center."

"For our part, we intend to do our due diligence when selecting the right person for the job, so as not to interfere with your routine or that of those close to you."

"If possible, I'd like to request a detective from the local precinct rather than the MPD."

"Oh? Why is that?"

"I have a family. Any danger that involves me involves my family. I'd be grateful to work with someone who appreciates the wellbeing of the local community."

久保晴久 Haruhisa Kubo

AT THE EYE SIGNAL OF the guard—*Here he comes*—Kubo, with Furukawa and Yamane the beat reporter in tow, ran down the slope from the entrance to the underground parking lot. Waving their arms frantically, the three of them jumped in front of the official vehicle making its way up from below ground with the head of First Investigation inside. The car stopped midway up the slope and the rear window opened. Kubo called out, "Sorry to bother you! We just happened to see you."

"It's been nothing but stakeouts for you guys lately, huh, Kubo-san?" Chief Kanzaki peered out from the car window, his eyes passing over Kubo's face without making eye contact.

That's it, that's the look. Kubo pressed for more. "What brings you to Hinode?"

"I'm paying a visit on the fortieth day since the incident occurred. A situation report, if you will," Kanzaki replied.

"Who requested the meeting?"

"I did."

"Would it be worthwhile for us to follow Mr. Shiroyama?"

"I said nothing of the sort."

"Chief. The perps made a move, didn't they?"

"They did not. I was simply treated to lunch today on the fortieth floor."

"It's rare for you to take a lunch meeting, isn't it?"

"When in Rome, do as the Romans do. I must be going now."

Clearly, Kanzaki had no intention of dropping any hints today. Kubo thanked him and withdrew, but as he watched the vehicle drive out of the lot, he felt the heat of a hunch surge throughout his body for the first time in a long while. His mind filled with ideas about where to start sleuthing. Kanzaki's Investigation Headquarters operated in strict privacy with regard to all corporate matters. The officers assigned to Search and Inquiry and to Evidence Investigation had been whittled down and each had been thoroughly vetted, leaving only the most tight-lipped detectives, so that it had been quite difficult to gain any access. But if the perpetrators were to make a move, so would the SIT and the Mobile CI Unit. He might finally be able to make a breakthrough this time.

Kubo put in a call to the kisha club. Hearing that the fourth edition didn't require any replacements either, he treated Yamane and Furukawa to lunch and returned by himself to Sakuradamon shortly before two. As he got out of a taxi by the front entrance of the MPD, he saw Negoro tottering along on the pedestrian path beside Uchibori Dori, and even before Kubo had a chance to nod to him, Negoro was beckoning him over from thirty meters away.

Kubo crossed the intersection. Negoro had stopped in the middle of the trail and was leaning against the railing, smiling self-consciously. Some days, even the one-and-a-half-kilometer walk from *Toho News'* main office in Chidori-ga-fuchi to MPD here in Sakuradamon, meant as physical therapy, was too much for his legs.

"It's a nice day out today, so I thought I'd make my way over, but . . ."

"You should have called. I would have come to you."

"Weren't you already out somewhere?"

"Yes. Kanzaki, the head of First Investigation, showed up at Hinode, so I chased him down, but came up dry."

"Oh, wow . . . It's about time the perps made their move."

Negoro had always appeared nondescript, a reporter whose presence barely cast a shadow whenever he surveyed the Metro section, but every so often Kubo had noted, deep within Negoro's tapered lids, a still, lizard-like gaze of quiet observation. Those were the eyes he saw flicker just then.

"I was on my way to see Chief Sugano, but give him a message for me, Kubo-kun. First, one of the tabloids confirmed the death of that guy Yoshinori Toda. We got a call just now from the editor in chief."

"I knew it . . ."

When Investigation Headquarters released a transcript of the tape from 1990 after the incident, the Metro section wasted no time deciphering the names of every individual referenced in the letter that was said to have been written back in 1947. As of early April, aside from the author's family relations the only person still alive had been Yoshinori Toda—born in Saitama prefecture in 1916 and fired from Hinode's Kyoto factory shortly after the war. *Toho Weekly* had then followed up on Toda's whereabouts, but last week they had heard that a person who seemed to be Toda was on a list of unidentified decedents in Nishinari district of Osaka. And just today, they had confirmed that this was in fact the Toda they were looking for.

It was highly likely that this Toda and the Toda who had made the tip-off call to the Metro section after the incident were one and the same, but now there was no way of knowing for sure. When it came to those involved in what had happened in 1947, "And then there were none" seemed to apply.

"Apparently he left behind no personal effects. And would you give this to the chief?" Negoro casually handed Kubo a thick manila envelope. "I got this from a guy I know. These are Hinode stock deals from April third to the twenty-eighth, from every brokerage house. They all list purchases almost every day. There seems to be a rumor going around that Hinode is going to acquire some convenience store chain. Tell the chief."

"I've seen on the Nikkei that their margin buying has been intensifying lately . . ."

"So has their margin selling since around April twentieth. As of yesterday it's been neck and neck. The trades are small in size, but given what's going on right now, it concerns me a bit that Hinode's stock is attracting the attention of investors in this way. It feels as if they are laying the groundwork for an overcorrection, if and when something happens. I'll look for the source of the rumor, too."

Negoro said no more. He raised a hand in parting to head back the way he came, but when Kubo turned again to look before crossing the intersection, he saw Negoro standing at the edge of the pedestrian path, not having gone very far, looking out at the moat as he massaged his lower back.

合田雄一郎　Yuichiro Goda

EVENING FELL ON FRIDAY, MAY 5th, without any developments. In a corner of the main meeting room on the second floor of the Omori Police Department, there were two cardboard boxes filled with energy drinks, each one bearing a note written with a calligraphy brush: *Compliments of Chief Kanzaki, First Investigation Division* and *Compliments of Chief Inspector Hakamada*. Goda saw the lettering—the exaggerated flourishes obviously the hand of Omori's Deputy Chief Inspector Dohi—and, as he took a bottle from the box, briefly wondered how the guys up on the third floor were getting along. Last week, when he had peeked into the CI office, where they were busy with an array of matters that the public prosecutors had told them to investigate further, Dohi had grumbled, "We're busy organizing the scraps." The next day, Goda had been summoned to the third floor by Chief Inspector Hakamada, who told him, "I need your stamp on this," and handed over a formal letter of apology submitted by the two-man team of rookie detectives, Izawa and Konno. According to Hakamada, the pieces of evidence seized at the scene of an attempted robbery did not match up with the number the woeful duo had written up in their case file.

After opening and knocking back the energy drink, Goda threw the empty bottle in the trash and noticed Handa from the Kamata Police Department next to him, also reaching into the cardboard box. "Long day," Goda said.

"For you too," Handa replied. Most officers, after being out and about all day, usually found it tiresome to even open their mouth to speak, but Handa did not let his dutiful manner falter. Goda still couldn't remember what had set Handa off that day on the stairs at the Shinagawa Police Department, but lately Goda had begun to suspect that Handa's punctiliousness was a pretense. As his own frustration and dissatisfaction mounted day after day, Goda would let his feelings take rein, and had been occasionally trying to strike up conversations with Handa. Even the most inconsequential notions nagged at him once he started worrying.

The third week in April, another restructuring had come down from Investigation Headquarters, and at the end of the fourth week they were scrambled again. The teams investigating the cross-sections of corporate and crime-syndicate connections were nowhere in sight, as they had been organized under a separate heading since mid-April. That night, May fifth, the number of officers who filed into the main meeting room totaled fewer than thirty, down from the hundred who had once come and gone, and now the meeting room called to mind an art house cinema on the outskirts of town. This ragtag crew who still barely knew each other's names now waited in silence, not even engaging in small talk, for the start of the 8 P.M. meeting.

Not counting the ten members of the ninth unit of Violent Crime from MPD, the remaining men all had at least ten years of experience as detectives. The majority were seasoned but unremarkable officers—among them a group who had made lateral transfers from the MPD to precinct posts, a perpetual sergeant who might fall just short of a promotion before his retirement, as well as an old-guard assistant inspector. It might have sounded good to describe them as an elite corps, but to Goda's cynical eye, they looked more like an arbitrary assemblage of guys who were destined to live out the rest of their careers like this, forever detectives. Goda's partner, an inspector from Crime Prevention with whom he had been working for just a month, had left at the end of April, so his only colleague from Omori Police Department was Inspector Anzai from White Collar Crime, currently assigned to the cross-sections.

The contraction of the Search Squad and Evidence Investigation Squad was a direct result of the already-reduced target area of investigation. Depending on how the case developed, who knew whether one day the same meeting room might again be filled with people, and it was against just such a possibility that Goda and the rest of the Vehicle Squad kept up their shoe-leather investigation for the right vehicle.

They had looked into every one of the seventy navy-colored Nissan Homys in the Tokyo metropolitan area registered at the District Land Transport Bureau, but were unable to find either a suspicious owner or any vehicles that had gone missing on the night of the incident. They had marked about ten of those as company-owned vehicles of construction firms that had been left in private parking lots, but there were none among them that the owner had forgotten to lock on the night of the incident, and none of the owners noticed anything unusual about their cars at the start of the following week, such as signs of the locks being tampered with, or decreases in gas or increases in mileage.

However, since the owners of commercial vehicles with fifty or sixty thousand kilometers on them could not be expected to closely monitor their mileage, the squad had not ruled out the possibility that the perpetrators could have snuck a Nissan Homy out of a corporate lot for the weekend. If that were the case, it meant that the perpetrators had the skills to duplicate car keys, which added a new facet to their profile.

Speaking of the perpetrators' profile, Goda had written the following line in his notebook: *A highly skilled driver or one with professional driving experience.* On the night of the incident, a kei-car had been stranded after colliding with a guardrail on the frozen-over downhill slope of the two-lane Daibosatsu Pass, and although the driver had sought help from a Nissan Homy that came along, the other driver sped past without stopping. The skill of a driver who could navigate so many curves along an icy road at sixty kilometers an hour without chains on the tires was nothing short of extraordinary. It was also certain that someone had selected the perpetrators' getaway route taking into account rapid surveillance cameras over highways and toll booth ticket passes.

Fruit-flavored milk—a child? This related to a hunch of Goda's, the note punctuated with a question mark. As Goda had continued to ponder the combination of food items that the perpetrators had given the victim while he was in captivity—fruit-flavored milk, cream buns, matchbox-size blocks of processed cheese, mandarin oranges, and bananas. Fruit-flavored milk and cream buns were not something that the perpetrators themselves would eat; these had been popular children's snacks a decade ago. He surmised that one of the perpetrators had a child—now grown up—and that there may be a particular attachment to that child.

His notebook also included the words "wireless radio," which he had jotted down right after the incident. This idea, that someone in the crime group had been listening to the police radio, had remained in midair with nowhere to alight. All he could see was the vague image of a police officer hovering on the far side of an impossible divide—a divide that he knew was "outside his territory"—but he was sure that the man belonged to one of the two police departments, and that on the night of March 24th, he had been on active duty, carrying with him a shortwave 101 receiver.

Flipping through his notebook, Goda felt the needle of his internal compass struggle to find a compromise between a compulsion to conform to the discipline of the system and the desire to rebel against it. For now, the needle was barely holding still in a delicate balance, one that required no small effort to maintain.

Goda liked to use a fresh notebook for each case, but within a month the pages would be filled up, 99 percent of which consisted of the records of hundreds of dead-end visits, each one a variant of: 3/27, 11:15A.M., 152 Hibarigaoka Housing Complex, Tanashi City, Katsushi Ono, License plate: Tama 54RA412 x Toyota Sprinter Carib, White. Owner not home. Every word was written precisely, and every line ended with a period, pressed down with extra force. A habit he had formed over the last thirteen years as a cop, each dot was filled with a genuine desire "to behold the perp's face." This case notebook was no exception.

But, undoubtedly, he would only ever "behold the perp's face" indirectly this time. Wherever the clues—the fruit-flavored milk, the Nissan Homy—led, the tools necessary to identify Suspect A or B were on the other side of the divide, along with the ability to arrest him—someone else would have that satisfaction. He knew this was the nature of police work, but it was quite difficult to continue his dogged pursuit of a single vehicle while actively compensating for his emotional wellbeing. This itself had become his main challenge.

At 8 P.M., they were called to order, and Goda put away his notebook and stood up with the assembled investigators. When Chief Kanzaki of First Investigation, who hadn't been seen around for a while lately, came through the door with the director of SIT, the conspicuously empty meeting room became slightly agitated. The tension transformed to anticipation as all the officers craned their necks.

As expected, the chief's first announcement was that the suspects had made their move. He then took out the letter that had been tossed onto the grounds of Hinode's Kanagawa factory on Friday, April 28th. "READY TO MAKE THE PAYMENT? IF SO, TAKE OUT AN AD WITH THE WORDS, 'FATHER FORGIVES KYOKO' IN THE MAY 5TH ISSUE OF NIKKAN SPORTS. —LADY JOKER," the chief read aloud. "Now, it is still unclear whether 'Lady Joker' is the name of the crime group."

Next, after it was reported that Hinode had, as instructed in the letter, taken out an ad in that day's issue of *Nikkan Sports*, one of the investigators opened a copy of the newspaper that happened to be on hand and passed it around the room.

Goda ruminated on the enigmatic name, "Lady Joker," and in his mind's eye he saw an unstoppable procession of silhouettes—those of the still anonymous perpetrators. Feeling unreasonably excited by this name, Goda sensed that the perpetrators had also been excited to sign the letter with it. They were enjoying themselves.

They asked, "Ready to make the payment?" They're more cold-blooded than businesslike. They're fueling the victim's anxiety by withholding the exact amount of their monetary demand. They don this bizarre "Lady Joker" mask and assume a cool indifference—in no hurry to carry out their purpose, reveling in perverse pleasure. They may have made a monetary demand, but they are more fixated on the act of squeezing the money out rather than on the money itself. With antipathy toward corporate society at large, they brim with confidence that they'll be able to bring a trillion-yen corporation to its knees . . . It had been a while since such distinct intuitions had surged over Goda.

Chief Inspector Kanzaki's briefing continued. "After seeing today's ad, the suspects will most likely issue instructions about the money exchange. Our next move will be toward arresting the perpetrators, but it goes without saying that we must maintain confidentiality with the utmost care, in order not to betray the victim's trust. If word gets out to the media, the perpetrators will not make their move. Hinode is giving the police their full cooperation on the condition that there will be no leaks whatsoever to the media. Bearing this in mind, I expect you all to perform better than ever. The day when your hard work will be rewarded is near."

It was only by etching the words of the perpetrators into his mind—*Ready to make the payment?*—that Goda managed to absorb the bromides to "maintain confidentiality" and "perform better than ever."

Then, Director Miyoshi of Third Violent Crime Investigation, who was in charge of the Search Squad and the Evidence Investigation Squad, announced, "No changes to each squad's investigation directive for tomorrow," and the meeting was adjourned. Goda's instincts, sent into overdrive by the name "Lady Joker" but never finding a place to settle, dispersed into the ether.

After the top brass had left the room, the investigators got up from their seats, still without a word to each other. Goda was leaving the meeting room, thinking to himself that he would hurry home, take a bath, play a little violin, sip some whisky, and read the book he had just started, when Deputy Chief Inspector Dohi loomed before him and whispered, "Chief Inspector wants to see you. Report to Reception."

Dohi's gaze rested on Goda for a few seconds, his eyes a stew of wariness, suspicion, curiosity, and resignation. Goda glared right back, struck by a sudden urge to smash the face in front of him with a concrete block.

An obscure strain of uneasiness was infiltrating the police force. This was how the machinery worked—that uneasiness created a mood of anxiety, one that at times burst forth as hysteria or neurosis. As they locked eyes, each found in the other a convenient outlet for their unfocused anxiety and discomfort. This time it was Dohi who ultimately backed down, telling Goda to report back to him later, and returning to the third floor. Goda descended the same staircase and, one minute later, he was knocking on the door to the reception room at the back of Police Affairs on the first floor.

WHEN GODA WALKED IN, HIDETSUGU Kanzaki was standing alone in the middle of the room. After giving Goda's full frame the once-over from his elevated sightline, Kanzaki said, "You've shrunk a size since you were at MPD."

Goda, caught off guard, replied, "I've lost some muscle."

"That won't do. But I think your physique is appropriate for this purpose, meaning you won't intimidate those around you. Goda-san, this is short notice, but starting Monday the eighth, I need you to guard Mr. Shiroyama."

"Yes, sir," Goda replied automatically, though there was no need to think about what he had just agreed to do. The word "no" did not exist in the police force—"yes" was the only possible response.

"Hinode and the president himself have given their consent on the premise that we need to be prepared in the case of any danger. However, we hope to do so in a way that does not interfere with the daily operations of the corporation, so ostensibly you'll look the part of a body man."

"Yes, sir."

"You'll be on duty from the morning, when the president leaves his home, until he returns there at night. You will not enter the president's office or attend meetings, informal conversations, or entertainment gatherings—you will always stand right outside the door. You will be issued a Hinode employee badge and a pass with a photo ID. You'll use an alias. You are always to be diagonally behind Mr. Shiroyama, one meter away, and conversation is strictly prohibited. This is as per the president's request."

"Yes, sir."

"Mr. Shiroyama requested that we provide him with a detective from the local precinct, not MPD."

"Yes, sir."

Whenever Kanzaki appeared before investigators, he rarely moved his eyes or the muscles in his face—he was a wall come to life. The wall was equipped with a mouth, and though orders could be heard issuing from it, there was no way to glimpse what was on the other side. No, it was normal for those on the lower rungs of the police organization not to even imagine the workings behind the wall.

"Incidentally, your mission, first and foremost, is to protect the president. Second, to observe the president. Third, to observe what goes on inside the company," Kanzaki enumerated.

Goda listened intently, realizing that his job was to spy. As yet unable to imagine any concrete reason, he felt a wrench in his bowels, a slight spasmatic twinge. In the beat it took him to respond, Kanzaki's eyes glinted, and Goda issued a robotic "yes, sir."

"As I'm sure you're well aware, with an investigation involving corporate extortion, there tends to be a subtle difference of opinion between the corporation and the police. Even when we point out past cases, the company is always inclined to try to make a backroom deal. We must prevent that from happening at any cost. That's why you will be there observing things."

"Yes, sir."

"Being by the president's side every day from morning to night will enable you to pick up on hints that there are changes in the situation—actions by internal staff, small shifts in the schedule, impromptu gatherings, who meets with whom, the expressions of the executives, their eyes, how they speak . . . Your most important mission is to detect these things."

"Yes, sir."

"Your report will be based on Mr. Shiroyama's activities—you'll record what you see and hear in full detail, and send it by fax each night to a number designated by SIT."

"Yes, sir."

"In any case, we must prevent Hinode from making any kind of backroom deal, no matter what . . ." Kanzaki emphasized each word, watching Goda as if to gauge his reaction. "My opinion is that it will be difficult to arrest this crime group unless we catch them in the act. What do you think, Goda-san? Don't hold back. Give me your honest assessment of the perpetrators."

Goda's internal needle jumped ever so slightly as he replied, "I don't know." Until now, he had never been one to care much about self-preservation in his career, but he knew better than to be so unguarded as to disclose his personal opinion when confronting a wall beyond which lay the unknown.

"Right after the incident occurred on March twenty-fourth, and then again on the night of the twenty-sixth, you met with Officer Sawaguchi from Community Police Affairs and checked the dispatch record from the police box in front of Omori Station, did you not?"

"Yes, sir."

"Did you have any particular purpose for doing so?"

"I was only checking out why, on the night in question, there was no police motorcycle patrol nearby at the time of the incident, even though Mr. Shiroyama's home was within a high security zone."

"And what did you find?"

"It turns out there happened to be multiple calls for service on that night, which is why there were no officers on patrol nearby."

Kanzaki had been regarding Goda's face with a clinical detachment, but now he abruptly turned his back and began pacing the room.

"That point has been of great interest to me as well. However, make sure you keep the matter strictly confidential."

"Yes, sir."

"The perpetrators will definitely make a move, no matter who they are, so long as a cash-grab is their objective and provided Hinode doesn't make a backroom deal with them. There'll be no complaints if we catch them in the act."

Perhaps what he meant was that if one of their own were involved with the crime group, catching them in the act would avert any complaints from the higher-ups. But since there was no need for Goda, a mere investigator, to inquire further about or weigh in on Kanzaki's monologue, he allowed the words that slipped from his boss's lips to roll off his back.

"By the way," Kanzaki came to a halt and shifted to a strictly administrative tone. "Tomorrow, be at MPD's sixth-floor meeting room at eight in the morning. The head of First SIT will go over Hinode's organizational chart and work flow, including the names and photos of executives, and teach you the basic comportment of a body man. Wear a suit tomorrow. No sneakers."

"Yes, sir."

"Since this will be necessary, going forward, we'll provide an allowance for two summer-weight suits. The honor of the police is at stake, so I expect you to present yourself accordingly."

"Yes, sir."

"About this man Kyosuke Shiroyama, himself . . . My personal impression is that he is quite different from most so-called major business leaders. At fifty-eight years old, he's in his third term as president, so he's much younger than the average president of a listed company. Whether he keeps his work compartmentalized, or whether he's simply upfront and candid, he does not have many distinguishing characteristics. And because of this, you could say it's hard to know what he's thinking."

Goda recalled the smooth and refined face of Kyosuke Shiroyama, which he had seen a few times on television—the man looked as if he could be anything save for a politician or a yakuza—and had to admit that Shiroyama did not have an imposing managerial presence. And since Goda would be working as his body man, he was grateful for this.

"SIT will detail Shiroyama's corporate philosophy, management skills, and so on tomorrow. Also, when it comes to the incident, Mr. Shiroyama has not necessarily disclosed everything to the police. It's still not clear why the crime group went to the trouble of abducting the president only to release him unharmed. However, it's conceivable that the reason for the president's reticence is related to his personal circle. Consequently, there's a significant possibility that the crime group will try to shake down the president himself. This is what you will be on the lookout for."

"Yes, sir."

"Mr. Shiroyama's personality is incredibly fastidious and sensitive. On the other hand, he can be stubborn and strong-willed. He betrays very little emotion and lacks warmth. He is not one for socializing. His private life is decidedly simple. He's not known to indulge in amusements. Essentially, you wouldn't be incorrect to consider him an orthodox man of common sense who's had a privileged and sheltered upbringing. It doesn't matter how you do it, but you must gain Mr. Shiroyama's trust and get close to him."

Gain his trust and get close to him. Goda answered "yes, sir" before he had any sense of what those words meant. He almost felt as if he no longer cared how things turned out.

"Any questions?"

"While on this assignment, am I security personnel sent by the police, or do I assume a completely different identity unrelated to the police?"

"A completely different identity. We have to deceive the perpetrators, so there's no sense raising public notice. As for that, SIT will give you thorough instructions about your disguise. As far as I could tell from the podium, your features, build, and composure are the least conspicuous. SIT said that as long as we change the way you cut your hair a little and put glasses on you, it should be fine."

"My superiors are concerned about the fact that you called me in."

"The head of CID is aware of the situation. Anything else?"

"Nothing, sir."

"Well then, we'll go over the details tomorrow. You can take Sunday off."

As he was leaving the reception room, it did not feel real to Goda that he was being excluded from the active investigation. If word that he had checked the dispatch record at the police box had caused internal rumors that reached as far as the Head of First Investigation, that meant his instincts aligned with what the investigation was really after, which offered him a small satisfaction. Now, however, he had no cards left to play. The one thing that occupied Goda's mind was a vague anxiety about just what being a body man would entail.

Goda had no interest in mulling over his thirteen-year career as a detective. He was trained to respond automatically whenever an incident occurred, his mind churning the moment he arrived at a crime scene. As long as he was getting paid to do that, the only choice he had was to do whatever he was told. But now, feeling as though he had been shunted another step further away from both material and spiritual fulfillment, a bleak mood had latched on to his anxiety. Goda told himself once again, *Apply yourself to the job and you'll forget about it,* and *It's all in your mindset,* and tried shifting his thoughts to what he needed to do that night in preparation for tomorrow: make sure his suit was in order, polish his shoes, and so on. Since he'd be going to Hinode every day, he would need to change his shirts daily, so he figured he ought to buy some permanent-press dress shirts to make ironing easy, along with antibacterial socks, and on Sunday get his hair cut and file his nails . . .

As he considered these things, in another corner of his mind his thoughts seesawed at the realization that he was at a crossroads in his life. He knew better than anyone that he had always been a cog that did not quite mesh with the machine of the police organization, and that this time, he would need to give serious thought to whether or not he could adapt himself to the order and values of the police organization. Would he remain on the force and find a way to forge ahead somehow, or would he resign and become someone new entirely?

The option of quitting the police force failed to ring true, but the notion of such an alternative gave him room to breathe. Rather than going up to the CI room, Goda went out the back door of the police department and pedaled away on his bicycle. The darkness of the Omori neighborhood that night—past nine o'clock, the lights in the office buildings were already dimmed—looked like the sea onto which he would be setting out alone. There was nothing visible, no point for which to set his course, having just been cast away from Investigation Headquarters, but when he thought about it, this was a chance to set out toward new horizons he had been so desperate to know more about. The sea was sure to be bountiful, with unfamiliar things awaiting him—the prospect allowed him to feel a modest sense of liberation.

Goda crossed the road in front of the Denny's restaurant and had gone about a hundred meters along the Dai-Ichi Keihin highway when he noticed a man climbing out of a taxi about ten meters ahead of him. Goda braked unconsciously, stopping his bicycle by the edge of the sidewalk. It was Noriaki Anzai, his colleague whom he had not seen in nearly a month—but he wondered why Anzai had gotten out of the taxi a hundred meters away from the police department. Pre-occupied by this simple suspicion, Goda waited for him to approach before calling out, "Anzai-san."

"Oh, it's you," Anzai said as he turned toward Goda, his face barely registering surprise. Anzai's flat, fifty-year-old face was as guileless as they come, and yet tonight his greasy, exhausted complexion seemed tinged with excitement—almost like he was possessed. But a passing conversation on the street at night was not enough for Goda to be certain of this.

"I've been so busy lately. Tonight's the first chance I've had to pick up the spare umbrella I keep at the department."

"Where are you working out of these days?"

"Kabuto-cho. It's outside my beat, so it's as if I've been banished."

"Are you looking into Hinode's stock?"

"I can't even be sure myself. I just pick up whatever evidence I'm ordered to get. How about you?"

"Still on the Nissan Homy."

"This must just be what investigation is all about. It feels like guerilla warfare but I have no clue where the frontline is."

Anzai walked off with those parting words, and Goda started peddling again as well, but a moment or two later it occurred to him that someone might have put Anzai in that taxi. It could have been a journalist, a stockbroker, or a gangster. Back when he had run into Anzai in the lavatory at the department, Goda had thought to himself that sooner or later Anzai, with his loose tongue, could be an easy mark, and perhaps his premonition had come to pass.

However, for the time being Goda would not have to bear witness to his senior colleague's going off course. Nor would he need to serve as an outlet for Deputy Chief Inspector Dohi to vent his grievances, or have to put up with his colleagues like Osanai from Burglary and Saito from Organized Crime, with whom he didn't see eye to eye. He wouldn't have to look at the messy desks in the CI office. These thoughts gave him another taste of liberation.

AFTER RETURNING HOME, GODA TOOK his violin and went to the park as usual. That night, on a whim, he brought his instruction book with him and played octaves—which were challenging for him—and practiced arpeggios. His bow control left something to be desired—every so often the strings emitted a noise that sounded like a chorus of frogs—but for about an hour he was absorbed in his playing, though the whole time his mind threatened to take flight. There seemed to be something he was forgetting, something lacking, something else he ought to be thinking about, or not thinking about.

Goda found himself staring at the figures crossing the park, which made him wonder when was the last time Kano had stopped by. Had it been Tuesday, or Wednesday? Was it last week when he mentioned that he had bought a car?

Goda went back home and dialed a number—it was rare for him to initiate the call. When Yusuke Kano, at his official residence for public prosecutors, realized it was his former brother-in-law on the line, he asked, "What's the occasion?" as if slightly on guard.

"I got home a little early tonight."

"I played golf today. Set a new record. Lost half a dozen balls."

It had been a year since Kano had taken up golf, influenced by his superior at the special investigative division, but every time he mentioned it, he announced he had established a "new record," and showed no sign of giving up. These days, having made his way through the organization and with a transfer to the High Public Prosecutor's Office on the horizon, Kano was enjoying a moment of promising stability. Had Goda been in his position, he would have either applied himself a little more to practicing or left his relationship with his superior out of it from the start. But for some strange reason the sound of Kano's voice on the other end of the line made any desire to quibble over work matters vanish, instead transporting him to somewhere out of time and place.

"Did you buy a new car?"

"I decided on a Volkswagen Golf after all. I couldn't justify buying a sedan just to be able to fit a golf bag in it. Anyway, do you have any time to get together with someone?" Kano asked.

Goda remembered that Kano had previously mentioned a reporter from *Toho News*. Perhaps that was what had been nagging at him.

"I'm free Sunday afternoon," Goda replied.

"You mean the seventh? What about Investigation Headquarters?"

"They gave me a day off."

"You don't say. Well then, why don't we meet up with him in the afternoon, and then go get something good to eat that evening."

"I'd prefer to go for a drink."

"I see. All right. I'll get in touch with the guy and call you back."

After finishing this trivial conversation, there were only a few things left for Goda to do. As he listened to the sea breeze outside his door, he washed his sneakers, then downed 150 grams of whisky and fell asleep flipping through the May issue of *Nikkei Science*.

久保晴久　Haruhisa Kubo

AROUND THE SAME TIME, HARUHISA Kubo slid forward on his knees across the tatami mat. It was time to apply pressure to his source. "So."

The assistant police inspector from the first Mobile CI unit of the Kamata sub-unit, his face flushed after three cups of sake, grinned and pretended to dodge Kubo's approach. "Don't come so close," he said, laughing.

"Hey, look me in the eye," Kubo said. "I'm being serious tonight. This is for real. Hinode's perps are definitely making their move."

"If they were, our unit would be the first to know, but so far—"

"Well, they'll make a move soon. I'm sure of it. And when they do, you let me know before anyone else. All right? Please?" Kubo inched toward his source again, saké bottle in hand, and filled his cup. "I'm counting on you." Kubo felt like a snapping turtle hanging tightly to his source, knowing full well his eyes looked desperate, yet he was powerless until that crucial, unforeseeable moment. "Come on, drink up. Then let's go for karaoke!"

Kubo tipped the saké bottle even more, and the karaoke-loving assistant police inspector finally came around, saying, "Sounds like a plan."

◆ ◆ ◆

根来史彰　Fumiaki Negoro

IN THE EARLY HOURS OF Sunday, May 7th, the last day of the Golden Week holiday, Fumiaki Negoro returned to the ryokan operated by an old acquaintance near the Tsukiji Hongan-ji Temple, having submitted the morning edition of the paper at half past one in the morning. Choosing at random one of the books from a five-volume collection of Simone Weil's work—the only items he had brought from home—he slipped between the covers of the futon. When he had discovered these books during his student days, they would have filled half of his list of "the Ten Books to Bring to a Deserted Island," and still, a quarter century later, he had not hesitated to choose the same five books as companions in his hideout. The volumes included a miscellany of letters, philosophical discourse, and original work by a woman who, in the midst of the rising tide of communism that swept through 1930s Europe, had contemplated the meaning of labor, revolution, and religion. There were many things about Marxist theory that Negoro found unacceptable, but he never failed to be moved by the author's tremendous vitality, faith, passion, kindness, fragility, and vulnerability, the beauty that overflowed from every single word and every single line on the page, and, struck by the sheer magnificence of the human capacity for thought, he would be filled with joy to be alive. It did not matter which page he opened to—whether a story about a labor strike or a meditation on God—he would read a few pages as though they were a letter written directly to him and, refreshed by the author's earnest observations, he would express gratitude to a woman who had died half a century ago, close the book, and go to sleep.

When he got up, it was already past ten in the morning. Although he had intended to check out of the inn that day, he could not be bothered so instead he told the innkeeper he would stay another week, giving her the forty thousand yen in advance along with his laundry, and he left to get his hair cut.

Freshly coiffed, Negoro got on the nearly empty train on the Keihin-Tohoku line before noon, then transferred in Kamata to the Mekama line, which he took to Tamagawa-en. He strolled the two kilometers or so along the bank of the Tama River, dense with the early summer greenery. Perhaps it was from basking so abruptly in the sunlight, but he could not recall any of the articles he had submitted just half a day earlier. Even the practical inconvenience of being displaced from his home had dulled to the same level as his constant backache, and with each step, he felt as if the present moment was losing its meaning. Then he remembered how Simone Weil had warned against the human tendency to sink into insensibility. *Ah, but my dear Simone,* he murmured to himself, *there is practically no one starving in this country, and our serenity is like water warmed by the sun, the result of lives spent without ever knowing hunger.*

In a society in which no one was starving, news articles did not induce any pain. Nowadays, there were no common concerns under which people could hoist a flag, no universal idea or framework to unite all mankind. What did exist was nothing more than small groupings of people with their everyday lives, inconsequential systems, and automated motions of production and consumption. Even on the day when six thousand people perished in a single earthquake, or when five thousand people suffered injuries or death after poisonous gas was unleashed in the subway, this embankment of the Tama River had still been filled with people jogging or playing tennis. And yet if people were admonished not to allow themselves to sink into such serene insensibility, then each and every one of them would be forced to engage in a lonely mental battle against the self.

Negoro's thoughts turned to his own self. The creeps who had squeezed money out of backroom deals in the Ogura-Chunichi scandal and now those who were trying to shake down Hinode Beer were strangers who meant nothing to him so long as he had enough to eat, but—he told himself—perhaps his ongoing pursuit of them was, in some small way, a means of preventing his own descent into insensibility.

Negoro had arranged to meet up with Yusuke Kano from the special investigative department at the Tokyo District Prosecutor's Office and Kano's former brother-in-law. They were waiting for him under a leafy cherry blossom tree along the embankment. Kano, unaware of Negoro's life on the run, had considerately chosen a spot within easy walking distance from Negoro's apartment. Negoro had to admit that the shady spot, warmed by the sunlight filtering through the trees and commanding a panoramic view of the verdant riverbed, was indeed inviting.

After Kano called to say that he'd be bringing his former brother-in-law, Negoro had called Kubo at the MPD kisha club, just in case, to ask if Investigation Headquarters was taking the day off on Sunday, to which Kubo had responded—his voice sounding strained over the phone—not as far as he knew. Kubo was so certain that the perpetrators were making their move, his entire body was poised like a seismometer, at the height of desperation to grasp onto anyone somehow related to the investigation. If what Kubo said was correct, the appearance of a detective who had supposedly been at Investigation Headquarters up until yesterday now enjoying a picnic along the Tama riverbank on a Sunday afternoon did raise a flag.

The two men had gotten to their feet. Both had on crisp casual wear perfect for a day off—cotton pants and sweaters with sneakers—and each of them held a half-finished bottle of red wine.

Kano's former brother-in-law approached Negoro, speaking first. "Hello. I'm Goda. Great to see you again." Negoro had only met Goda once, briefly, three years ago, but he looked rather different from the image Negoro retained in his memory. Even Goda's polite manners and composure were like that of another person. *I see. Demoted to the local precinct and handed a little life lesson,* Negoro thought. Or did Goda's expression belie that he had equipped himself with an even tougher shell than before? *No,* Negoro scrutinized him again. Rather than a tougher exterior, Goda was now fully contained within a larger shell. *That's one way for a man to get around in the world.*

Despite this first impression, once Negoro's eyes met Goda's, he found that the nuances contained there were even more inscrutable than before, perhaps now with a bit of emptiness mixed in—a truly subtle feeling, like disillusionment or rawness. Right—in Negoro's analysis, it was the imbalance between this innocuous outer shell of Goda's and the volatile look in his eyes that created an irresistible magnetism. When that subtle gaze fixed on someone, they either felt a visceral urge to punch Goda in the face or else they were enchanted by him. It occurred to Negoro for the first time that Kano perhaps fell into this latter category.

Kano, for his part, seemed the type who maintained a certain complexity beneath his disinterested expression. He managed to reconcile the ideal attributes of a prosecutor—he was diligent when it came to interpreting and applying the law and aggressive in forging ahead without fear of losing a case—but did not seem to naïvely espouse social justice and order. Judging by the way he so coolly drew a line between himself and the factions within the special investigative department, he was possibly a genuine free spirit who had mistakenly put himself on the side of the establishment. In this sense, Kano's reputation among the reporters at the courthouse kisha club—that he never revealed much about himself, a tough nut to crack—was right on the mark.

Negoro knew well enough that once Kano began to speak about books on a personal level, he had a tendency to lose himself in a poet's reverie inconsistent with his occupation as a prosecutor, or to dish out skepticism with shades of empiricism. Though Kano worked late many nights at the government office and indeed had virtually no personal life, when glimpses of his intimate affection for his younger former brother-in-law appeared in Kano's inconsequential conversations with Negoro, the façade of public prosecutor fell away. Was Kano unconsciously driven by a possessive male instinct to assume the position of patron? Or did he have a naturally obliging disposition? Was there a secret and accumulated history between Kano and Goda? Or, perhaps it was something more even, the L-word for another man.

Negoro had no idea which of these was the truth, but he did know that none of them had anything to do with him. He looked at the two men and a wry laugh escaped his lips, realizing this had somewhat stirred what little interest he had left in humanity.

"If you'll pardon us, there's nothing to do but drink on such a fine May holiday," Kano said as he pulled the cork out of another bottle of wine and handed it to Negoro. "Here you go."

Negoro joined the two of them on the grass, drinking straight from the bottle himself. As Kano explained, the food hall in the basement of the Takashimaya department store in Futako-Tamagawa had been having a sale—all bottles, two thousand yen—so he had bought three, and then also picked up a freshly baked baguette and cheese, which he and his brother-in-law had been enjoying as lunch while they drank the wine. There was something rather provocative about the indolence and insouciance of the simple act of daytime drinking beneath the shade of a cherry tree, done right in front of the throngs of wholesome folks engaged in sports on the grounds of the riverbed. Besides, it may have been a bargain at two thousand yen a pop, but the rich, full-bodied red was certainly having an effect.

From the beginning, Negoro had been 90 percent sure that he wouldn't be grilling Kano and Goda for material, but thanks to the wine, the remaining 10 percent uncertainty went quickly by the wayside, and he gave himself over to random and inoffensive conversation instead. They began talking about financial institutions that were certain to collapse by autumn, like Tokyo's K. and Osaka's K. and H., which led to a discussion of how, in wake of the financial insecurity, the problem of dealing with bad loans would come to the fore later this year.

"It'll be the moment of truth for prosecutors," Negoro said, egging Kano on.

"So you want me to find, among all the loans that went under, the ones I can hold liable for violations of the investment law, prosecute those responsible, and send them home with suspended sentences?" Kano said, laughing evasively.

"But Kano-san, with these tens of trillions in loans, you should be able to hold accountable both the lenders, who neglected to put in the effort to recover the funds, and the borrower, who failed to make an effort to pay back the money."

"If it's a question of responsibility, then the borrower or the lender should file a lawsuit first themselves."

"It's a waste of time to file lawsuits if there is no consensus to entrust everything to market mechanisms when dealing with bad loans. Those are your words."

"Under the current circumstances, this country's financial system won't be able to go on. Neither the politicians nor the parties concerned have the ability to reform anything. That means it will go the way of natural selection, so we can just sit back and wait a while."

Kano had sidestepped Negoro again, not once referring to the focus of the special investigative department of the Tokyo District Prosecutor's Office, which was no doubt engaged in a clandestine investigation with a criminal prosecution in mind.

The conversation jumped haphazardly from the resurrection of the former political faction led by Sakata within the ruling party, with an eye toward the dissolution of the Lower House; then onto the future of the securities market, where light trading continued without any prospect of economic recovery; then back to whether there was any way to use financial records to expose how the bad loans were hidden through broker loans and debt shuffling tricks. Goda did not contribute, merely listened intently, his demeanor conveying a reasonable interest in each topic.

Kano was clearly a little concerned about Negoro's motives for suggesting, a month earlier, that they get together, and he did not miss the chance to redirect the conversation. "What are you investigating right now, Negoro-san?"

"I wouldn't call it an investigation yet, but there are signs that large sums of money are again moving around the brokerage houses in Kabuto-cho," Negoro answered.

"Does this have to do with Hinode Beer?"

"It includes them."

"Is that true, Yuichiro?" Kano asked Goda, who paused as he was gulping down wine to respond succinctly, "I doubt the police investigation would not be paying any attention to Kabuto-cho."

What anyone would have imagined at the mention of money moving around Hinode stock, more than simply the presence of corporate raiders, were networks connected to the Okada Association. Kano knew just what kind of history Hinode had and, sensing how sensitive the issue was, he put a close to the subject with the vague comment, "This is where you come in, Negoro-san."

"I guess you could say that," Negoro answered in kind.

Then, Goda asked discreetly, "If you don't mind, I'd love to hear more about what goes on in Kabuto-cho," and so they gossiped a bit more. Goda talked about how last autumn, in a case where a securities guy killed himself with a pistol in a business hotel in Omori, the young detective who had been doing legwork in the financial district collected more offers for get-rich-quick schemes than evidence. Goda let it be known that he thought undercover police work in Kabuto-cho was a tricky business. Judging by his manner of speaking, Goda did not seem to have any ulterior motives other than the desire to hear about a world that was unfamiliar to him. Though never to the point of being rude, it appeared that his mind was off somewhere else the whole time—that nuanced gaze drifted absently from Negoro's face to his former brother-in-law's, and to the grassy landscape before them.

After a while, though, Negoro noticed that Goda's stare had at some point fixed upon a lizard, around fifteen centimeters long, that had crawled up onto his sneaker. In that moment, the shadows vanished from Goda's eyes, which shone like glass beads. He snatched the lizard by its tail and tossed it lightly into a field of grass, where it disappeared. It was a simple gesture, but as Negoro watched the rigid concentration in Goda's eyes as he had watched the lizard, the only word that came to mind was *cop*.

Negoro turned back and tried to rejoin the interrupted conversation, but this time it was Kano who had an intensity at the corner of his eyes, as for a moment he gazed, as though transfixed, at the face of his former brother-in-law.

城山恭介　Kyosuke Shiroyama

MONDAY MORNING, MAY 8TH. SHORTLY after six, Shiroyama received a call from the deputy manager of general affairs, who informed him that a new letter from the criminals had been thrown inside the gate of the Kyoto factory. They were demanding six hundred million in cash. Shiroyama responded that he would come into to work at the usual time so as not to arouse the media's suspicion.

After finishing a simple breakfast with his wife, Shiroyama moved into the living room to be alone, and just as he was about to open the morning paper, he happened to notice a strange object in his front yard, on the grass just outside the window. Since the object was no more than ten meters away, he immediately saw that it was a business envelope.

Shiroyama slipped on his geta sandals and went out the front door into the yard, where he picked up the envelope, slick with morning dew. The standard-issue manila envelope, both front and back left blank, was not even sealed, and he could feel its thinness as the paper flopped in his hand. He opened the envelope where he stood and took out a single sheet of stationery that had been folded into thirds, and when he opened it the rows of characters written in the same style as in the letter delivered to the Kanagawa factory on April 28th leapt before his eyes.

The characters were in katakana, drawn with a ruler, and consisted of four lines.

WE'VE DELIVERED A LETTER TO THE KYOTO FACTORY. ALERT THE POLICE AND FOLLOW OUR INSTRUCTIONS. PREPARE THE SIX HUNDRED MILLION, BUT STORE IT ON SITE AT THE COMPANY FOR A WHILE. IF YOU DON'T WANT THE HOSTAGE TO DIE, DON'T LET THE POLICE KNOW ABOUT THIS LETTER.

—LADY JOKER

This letter delivered a blow to Shiroyama that he had not experienced when he saw the previous letter. The severe, chilling indifference of "Lady Joker," who was holding the 3.5 million kiloliters of beer hostage, seemed to penetrate the ground under his feet.

For a few seconds Shiroyama stood in the middle of the lawn holding the open letter, completely unaware of his surroundings, and it was only when he began to tuck the letter back in the envelope that he suddenly noticed the man—tall and wearing a dark navy suit—standing outside the gate about ten meters away. *He saw me,* Shiroyama thought instantly, followed by, *Who is that?* As Shiroyama stood paralyzed, the man bent his body at a precise forty-five-degree angle in a deep bow.

"Who are you?"

"My name is Goda."

"I see . . . It's still early."

"I arrived a little early. I thought I should take a look around your neighborhood. I'm sorry to disturb you."

With that, the officer on guard bowed his head robotically for a second time, then disappeared without a sound.

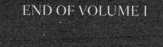

END OF VOLUME I

ABOUT THE AUTHOR

© Shinchosha Publishing Co., Ltd

KAORU TAKAMURA

KAORU TAKAMURA WAS BORN IN Osaka in 1953 and is the author of thirteen novels. Her debut, *Grab the Money and Run*, won the 1990 Japan Mystery and Suspense Grand Prize, and since then her work has been recognized with many of Japan's most prestigious awards for literary fiction as well as for crime fiction: the Naoki Prize, the Noma Literary Award, the Yomiuri Prize, the Shinran Prize, the Jiro Osagari Prize, the Mystery Writers of Japan Award, and the Japan Adventure Fiction Association Prize. *Lady Joker*, her first novel to be translated into English, received the Mainichi Arts Award and had been adapted into both a film and a television series.

MARIE IIDA

Marie Iida has served as an interpreter for the *New York Times* bestselling author Marie Kondo's Emmy-nominated Netflix documentary series, *Tidying Up with Marie Kondo*. Her nonfiction translations have appeared in *Nang, MoMA Post, Eureka* and over half a dozen monographs on contemporary Japanese artists and architects, including Yayoi Kusama, Toyo Ito, and Kenya Hara for Rizzoli New York. Marie currently writes a monthly column for Gentosha Plus about communicating in English as a native Japanese speaker.

ALLISON MARKIN POWELL

Allison Markin Powell is a literary translator, editor, and publishing consultant. She has been awarded grants from English PEN and the NEA, and the 2020 PEN America Translation Prize for *The Ten Loves of Nishino* by Hiromi Kawakami. She has translated fiction by Osamu Dazai, Kanako Nishi, and Fuminori Nakamura. She was the guest editor for the first Japan issue of Words Without Borders, and she maintains the database Japanese Literature in English.